PRAISE FOR *THE SCAR*

Named "One of the Best Science Fiction/Fantasy Books
of the Year" by *San Francisco Chronicle*, *Locus*,
Library Journal, and *Publishers Weekly*

"Astonishing . . . This is narrative simultaneously at its most commanding and most intelligent: a massive, brawling tale of maritime piracy and supernatural obsession, and a majestic orchestration of themes such as fantasy rarely sustains. . . . The wholesale remaking of the fantasy epic, already commenced by George R. R. Martin, is now in full swing. . . . *The Scar* is one of the major speculative fiction novels of 2002. . . . Miéville is now the towering giant of High Fantasy, and bids fair to remain so."
—*Locus*

"*The Scar* is a massive, sprawling, inventive Hobbesian fantasy in which Miéville once again shows his fascination with invented cities of the mind. . . . He has trawled wide and deep, and his nets have brought up as glittering, bizarre, and curious a catch as you will ever find in science fantasy. Miéville is one of those few writers helping to reinvent a form and reviving a sense of wonder you might have thought you'd lost."
—Michael Moorcock

"China Miéville is the most original voice in recent fantasy. . . . [His] world is full of intrigues and counter-intrigues in a brilliantly bizarre and captivating universe."
—*The Denver Post*

By China Miéville

KING RAT
PERDIDO STREET STATION
THE SCAR
IRON COUNCIL
LOOKING FOR JAKE
UN DUN LUN

THE
SCAR

CHINA
MIÉVILLE

BALLANTINE BOOKS • NEW YORK

The Scar is a work of fiction. Names, places, and incidents either are a product of the author's imagination or are used fictitiously.

A Del Rey® Book
Published by The Random House Publishing Group
Copyright © 2002 by China Miéville
Excerpt from *Iron Council* by China Miéville copyright © 2004 by China Miéville

Published in the United States by Del Rey Books, an imprint of The Random House Publishing Group, a division of Random House, Inc., New York, and simultaneously in Canada by Random House of Canada Limited, Toronto.

Del Rey is a registered trademark and the Del Rey colophon is a trademark of Random House, Inc.

www.delreybooks.com

ISBN 0-345-46001-4

Manufactured in the United States of America

First Edition: July 2002
First Mass Market Edition: July 2004

OPM   9   8   7   6   5   4

To Claudia, my mother

Yet the memory would not set into the setting sun, that green and frozen glance to the wide blue sea where broken hearts are wrecked out of their wounds. A blind sky bleached white the intellect of human bone, skinning the emotions from the fracture to reveal the grief underneath. And the mirror reveals me, a naked and vulnerable fact.

—Dambudzo Marechera, *Black Sunlight*

ACKNOWLEDGMENTS

With deep love and thanks to Emma Bircham, again and always.

Huge gratitude to all at Macmillan and Del Rey, especially my editors, Peter Lavery and Chris Schluep. And as ever, more thanks than I can say to Mic Cheetham.

I'm indebted to everyone who read drafts and gave me advice: my mother, Claudia Lightfoot; my sister, Jemima Miéville; Max Schaefer; Farah Mendelsohn; Mark Bould; Oliver Cheetham; Andrew Butler; Mary Sandys; Nicholas Blake; Deanna Hoak; Jonathan Strahan; Colleen Lindsay; Kathleen O'Shea; and Simon Kavanagh. This would be a much poorer book without them.

A mile below the lowest cloud, rock breaches water and the sea begins.

It has been given many names. Each inlet and bay and stream has been classified as if it were discrete. But it is one thing, where borders are absurd. It fills the spaces between stones and sand, curling around coastlines and filling trenches between the continents.

At the edges of the world the salt water is cold enough to burn. Huge slabs of frozen sea mimic the land, and break and crash and reform, crisscrossed with tunnels, the homes of frost-crabs, philosophers with shells of living ice. In the southern shallows there are forests of pipe-worms and kelp and predatory corals. Sunfish move with idiot grace. Trilobites make nests in bones and dissolving iron.

The sea throngs.

There are free-floating top-dwellers that live and die in surf without ever seeing dirt beneath them. Complex ecosystems flourish in neritic pools and flatlands, sliding on organic scree to the edge of rock shelves and dropping into a zone below light.

There are ravines. Presences something between molluscs and deities squat patiently below eight miles of water. In the lightless cold a brutality of evolution obtains. Rude creatures emit slime and phosphorescence and move with flickerings of unclear limbs. The logic of their forms derives from nightmares.

There are bottomless shafts of water. There are places where the granite and muck base of the sea falls away in vertical tunnels that plumb miles, spilling into other planes, under pressure so great that the water flows sluggish and thick. It spurts through the pores of reality, seeping back in dangerous washes, leaving fissures through which displaced forces can emerge.

In the chill middle deeps, hydrothermic vents break through the rocks and spew clouds of superheated water. Intricate creatures bask in this ambient warmth their whole short lives, never straying beyond a few feet of warm, mineral-rich water into a cold which would kill them.

The landscape below the surface is one of mountains and canyons and forests, shifting dunes, ice caverns and graveyards. The water is dense with matter. Islands float impossibly in the deeps, caught on charmed tides. Some are the size of coffins, little slivers of flint and granite that refuse to sink. Others are gnarled rocks half a mile long, suspended thousands of feet down, moving on slow, arcane streams. There are communities on these unsinking lands: there are hidden kingdoms.

There is heroism and brute warfare on the ocean floor, unnoticed by land-dwellers. There are gods and catastrophes.

Intruding vessels pass between the sea and the air. Their shadows fleck the bottom where it is high enough for light to reach. The trading ships and cogs, the whaling boats pass over the rot of other craft. Sailors' bodies fertilize the water. Scavenger fish feed on eyes and lips. There are jags in the coral architecture where masts and anchors have been reclaimed. Lost ships are mourned or forgotten, and the living floor of the sea takes them and hides them with barnacles, gives them as caves to morays and ratfish and cray outcastes; and other more savage things.

In the deepest places, where physical norms collapse under the crushing water, bodies still fall softly through the dark, days after their vessels have capsized.

They decay on their long journey down. Nothing will hit the black sand at the bottom of the world but algae-covered bones.

At the edges of the shelves of rock where cold, light water gives way to a creeping darkness, a he-cray scrambles. He sees prey, clicks and rattles deep in his throat while he slips the hood from his hunting squid and releases it.

It bolts from him, diving for the shoal of fat mackerel that boil and re-form like a cloud twenty feet above. Its foot-long tentacles open and whip closed again. The squid returns to its master, dragging a dying fish, and the school reknits behind it.

The cray slices the head and tail from the mackerel and slips the carcass into a net bag at his belt. The bloody head he gives his squid to gnaw.

The upper body of the cray, the soft, unarmored section, is sensitive to minute shifts of tide and temperature. He feels a prickling against his sallow skin as complex washes of water meet and interact. With an abrupt spasm the mackerel-cloud congeals and disappears over the crusted reef.

The cray raises his arm and calls his squid closer to him, soothes it gently. He fingers his harpoon.

He is standing on a granite ridge, where seaweed and ferns move against him, caressing his long underbelly. To his right, swells of porous stone rise above him. To the left the slope falls away fast into disphotic water. He can feel the chill emanating from below. He looks out into a steep gradation of blue. Way overhead, on the surface, there are ripples of light. Below him the rays peter swiftly out. He stands only a little way above the border of perpetual dark.

He treads carefully here, on the edge of the plateau. He often comes to hunt here, where prey are less careful, away from the lighter, warmer shallows. Sometimes big game rises curiously from the pitch, unused to his shrewd tactics and barbed spears. The cray shifts nervously in the current and stares out into the open sea. Sometimes it is not prey but predators that rise from the twilight zone.

Eddies of cold roll over him. Pebbles are dislodged around his feet and bounce slowly down the slope and out of sight. The cray braces himself on the slippery boulders.

Somewhere below him there is a soft percussion of rocks. A chill not carried by any current creeps across his skin. Stones are realigning, and a spill of thaumaturgic wash is spewing through new crevices.

Something baleful is emerging in the cold water, at the edge of the dark.

The cray hunter's squid is beginning to panic, and when he releases it again, it jets instantly up the slope, toward the light. He peers back into the murk, looking for the source of the sound.

There is an ominous vibration. As he tries to see through water stained by dust and plankton, something moves. Way below, a plug of rock bigger than a man shudders. The cray bites his lip as the great irregular stone falls suddenly free and begins a grinding descent.

The thundering of its passage reverberates long after it has become invisible.

There is a pit in the slope now, that stains the sea with darkness. It is quiet and motionless for a time, and the cray fingers his spear with anxiety, clutching at it and hefting it and feeling himself tremble.

And then, softly, something colorless and cold slips from the hole.

It confuses the eye, flitting with a grotesque organic swiftness that seems to belie intention, like gore falling from a wound. The he-cray is quite still. His fear is intense.

Another shape emerges. Again he cannot make it out: it evades him; it is like a memory or an impression; it will not be specified. It is fast and corporeal and coldly terrifying.

There is another, and then more, until a constant quick stream dribbles from the darkness. The presences shift, not quite invisible, communing and dissipating, their movements opaque.

The he-cray is still. He can hear strange, whispering discourses on the tides.

His eyes widen as he glimpses massive backbent teeth, bodies pebbled with rucks. Sinuous muscled things fluttering in the freezing water.

The he-cray starts and steps backward, his feet skittering on sloping stone, trying to quiet himself but too slow—small shattered sounds emerging from him.

With a single motion, a lazy, predatory twitch, the dark things that huddle in council below him move. The he-cray sees the darks of a score of eyes, and he knows with a sick-making fear that they are watching.

And then with a monstrous grace, they rise, and are upon him.

PART ONE

Channels

CHAPTER ONE

It is only ten miles beyond the city that the river loses its momentum, drooling into the brackish estuary that feeds Iron Bay.

The boats that make the eastward journey out of New Crobuzon enter a lower landscape. To the south there are huts and rotten little jetties, from where rural laborers fish to supplement monotonous diets. Their children wave at travelers, warily. Occasionally there is a knoll of rock or a small copse of darkwood trees, places that defy cultivation, but mostly the land is clear of stones.

From the decks, sailors can see over the fringe of hedgerow and trees and bramble to a tract of fields. This is the stubby end of the Grain Spiral, the long curl of farmland that feeds the city. Men and women can be seen among the crops, or plowing the black earth, or burning the stubble—depending on the season. Barges putter weirdly between fields, on canals hidden by banks of earth and vegetation. They go endlessly between the metropolis and the estates. They bring chymicals and fuel, stone and cement and luxuries to the country. They return to the city past acres of cultivation studded with hamlets, great houses, and mills, with sack upon sack of grain and meat.

The transport never stops. New Crobuzon is insatiable.

The north bank of the Gross Tar is wilder.

It is a long expanse of scrub and marsh. It stretches out for more than eighty miles, till the foothills and low mountains that creep at it from the west cover it completely. Ringed by the river, the mountains, and the sea, the rocky scrubland is an empty place. If there are inhabitants other than the birds, they stay out of sight.

Bellis Coldwine took her passage on an east-bound boat in the last quarter of the year, at a time of constant rain. The fields she saw were cold mud. The half-bare trees dripped. Their silhouettes looked wetly inked onto the clouds.

Later, when she thought back to that miserable time, Bellis was shaken by the detail of her memories. She could recall the formation of a flock of geese that passed over the boat, barking; the stench of sap and earth; the slate shade of the sky. She remembered searching the hedgerow with her eyes but seeing no one. Only threads of woodsmoke in the soaking air, and squat houses shuttered against weather.

The subdued movement of greenery in the wind.

She had stood on the deck enveloped in her shawl and watched and listened for children's games or anglers, or for someone tending one of the battered kitchen gardens she saw. But she heard only feral birds. The only human forms she saw were scarecrows, their rudimentary features impassive.

It had not been a long journey, but the memory of it filled her like infection. She had felt tethered by time to the city behind her, so that the minutes stretched out taut as she moved away, and slowed the farther she got, dragging out her little voyage.

And then they had snapped, and she had found herself catapulted here, now, alone and away from home.

Much later, when she was miles from everything she knew, Bellis would wake, astonished that it was not the city itself, her home for more than forty years, that she dreamed of. It was that little stretch of river, that weatherbeaten corridor of country that had surrounded her for less than half a day.

In a quiet stretch of water, a few hundred feet from the rocky shore of Iron Bay, three decrepit ships were moored. Their anchors were rooted deep in silt. The chains that attached them were scabbed with years of barnacles.

They were unseaworthy, smeared bitumen-black, with big wooden structures built precariously at the stern and bow. Their masts were stumps. Their chimneys were cold and crusted with old guano.

The ships were close together. They were ringed with buoys strung together with barbed chain, above and below the water. The three old vessels were enclosed in their own patch of sea, unmoved by any currents.

They drew the eye. They were watched.

In another ship some distance away, Bellis raised herself to her porthole and looked out at them, as she had done several times over the previous hours. She folded her arms tight below her breasts and bent forward toward the glass.

Her berth seemed quite still. The movement of the sea beneath her was slow and slight enough to be imperceptible.

The sky was flint-grey and sodden. The shoreline and the rock hills that ringed Iron Bay looked worn and very cold, patched with crabgrass and pale saline ferns.

Those wooden hulks on the water were the darkest things visible.

Bellis sat slowly back on her bunk and picked up her letter. It was written like a diary; lines or paragraphs separated by dates. As she read over what she had last written she opened a tin box of prerolled cigarillos and matches. She lit up and inhaled deeply, pulling a fountain pen from her pocket and adding several words in a terse hand before she breathed the smoke away.

Skullday 26th Rinden 1779. Aboard the *Terpsichoria*
It is nearly a week since we left the mooring in Tarmuth, and I am glad to have gone. It is an ugly, violent town.

I spent my nights in my lodgings, as advised, but my days were my own. I saw what there was to the place. It is ribbon thin, a strip of industry that juts a mile or so north and south of the estuary, split by the water. Every day, the few thousand residents are joined by huge numbers who come from the city at dawn, making their way from New Crobuzon in boat- and cartloads to work. Every night the bars and bordellos are full of foreign sailors on brief shore leave.

Most reputable ships, I am told, travel the extra miles to New Crobuzon itself, to unload in the Kelltree docks. Tarmuth docks have not worked at more than half-capacity for two hundred years. It is only tramp steamers and freebooters that unload there—their cargoes will end up in the city just the same, but they have neither the time nor the money for the extra miles and the higher duty imposed by official channels.

There are always ships. Iron Bay is full of ships—breaking off from long journeys, sheltering from the sea. Merchant boats from Gnurr Kett and Khadoh and Shankell, on their way to or from New Crobuzon, moored near enough Tarmuth for their crews to relax. Sometimes, far out in the middle of the bay, I saw seawyrms released from the bridles of chariot-ships, playing and hunting.

The economy of Tarmuth is more than prostitution and piracy. The town is full of industrial yards and sidings. It lives as it has for centuries, on the building of ships. The shoreline is punctuated with scores of shipyards, building slipways like weird forests of vertical girders. In some loom ghostly half-completed vessels. The work is ceaseless, loud, and filthy.

The streets are crisscrossed with little private railways that take timber or fuel or whatever from one side of Tarmuth to the other. Each different company has built its own line to link its various concerns, and each is jealously guarded. The town is an idiotic tangle of railways, all replicating each other's journeys.

I don't know if you know this. I don't know if you have visited this town.

The people here have an ambivalent relationship with New Crobuzon. Tarmuth could not exist a solitary day without the patronage of the capital. They know it and resent it. Their surly independence is an affectation.

I had to stay there almost three weeks. The captain of the *Terpsichoria* was shocked when I told him I would join him in Tarmuth itself, rather than sailing with him from New Crobuzon, but I insisted, as I had to. My position on this ship was conditional on a knowledge of Salkrikaltor Cray, which I falsely claimed. I had less than a month until we sailed, to make my lie a truth.

I made arrangements. I spent my days in Tarmuth in the company of one Marikkatch, an elderly he-cray who had agreed to act as my tutor. Every day I would walk to the salt canals of the cray quarter. I would sit on the low balcony that circled his room, and he would settle his armored underbody on some submerged furnishing and scratch and twitch his scrawny human chest, haranguing me from the water.

It was hard. He does not read. He is not a trained teacher. He stays in the town only because some accident or predator has maimed him, tearing off all but one leg from his left side, so that he can no longer hunt even the sluggish fish of Iron Bay. It might make a better story to claim that I had affection for him, that he is a lovable, cantankerous old gentleman, but he is a shit and a bore. I could make no complaints, however. I had no choice but to concentrate, to effect a few focus hexes, will myself into the language trance (and oh! how hard that was! I have left it so long my mind has grown fat and disgusting!) and drink in every word he gave me.

It was hurried and unsystematic—it was a mess, a bloody mess—but by the time the *Terpsichoria* tied up in the harbor I had a working understanding of his clicking tongue.

I left the embittered old bastard to his stagnant water, quit my lodgings there, and came to my cabin—this cabin from where I write.

We sailed away from Tarmuth port on the morning of Dustday, heading slowly toward the deserted southern shores of Iron Bay, twenty miles from town. In careful formation at strategic points around the edge of the bay, in quiet spots by rugged land and pine forests, I spotted ships. No one will speak of them. I know they are the ships of the New Crobuzon government. Privateers and others.

It is now Skullday.

On Chainday I was able to persuade the captain to let me disembark, and I spent the morning on the shore. Iron Bay is drab, but anything is better than the damned ship. I am beginning to doubt that it is an improvement on Tarmuth. I am driven to bedlam by the incessant, moronic slap of waves.

Two taciturn crewmen rowed me ashore, watching without pity as I stepped over the edge of the little boat and walked the last few feet through freezing surf. My boots are still stiff and salt-stained.

I sat on the pebbles and threw stones into the water. I read some of the long, bad novel I found on board. I watched the ship. It is moored close to the prisons, so that our captain can easily entertain and converse with the lieutenant-gaolers. I watched the prison-ships themselves. There was no movement from their decks, from behind their portholes. There is never any movement.

I swear, I do not know if I can do this. I miss you, and New Crobuzon.

I remember my journey.

It is hard to believe that it is only ten miles from the city to the godsforsaken sea.

There was a knocking at the door of the tiny cabin. Bellis' lips pursed, and she waved her sheaf of paper to dry it. Unhurriedly she folded it and replaced it in the chest containing her belongings. She drew her knees up a little higher and played with her pen, watching as the door opened.

A nun stood in the threshold, her arms braced at either side of the doorway.

"Miss Coldwine," she said uncertainly. "May I come in?"

"It's your cabin too, Sister," said Bellis quietly. Her pen spun over and around her thumb. It was a neurotic little trick she had perfected at university.

Sister Meriope shuffled forward a little and sat on the solitary chair. She smoothed her dark russet habit around her, fiddled with her wimple.

"It has been some days now since we became cabin-mates, Miss Coldwine," Sister Meriope began, "and I do not feel . . . as if I yet know you at all. And this is not a situation I would wish to continue. As we are to be traveling and living together for many weeks . . . some companionship, some closeness, could only make those days easier . . ." Her voice failed, and she knotted her hands.

Bellis watched her, unmoving. Despite herself, she felt a trickle of contemptuous pity. She could imagine herself as Sister Meriope must see her: Angular, harsh, and bone-thin. Pale. Lips and hair stained the cold purple of bruises. Tall and unforgiving.

You don't feel as if you know me, Sister, she thought, *because I haven't spoken twenty words to you in a week, and I don't look at you unless you speak to me, and then I stare you down.* She sighed. Meriope was crippled by her calling. Bellis could imagine her writing in her journal "Miss Coldwine is quiet, yet I know that I shall come to love her like a sister." *I am* not, thought Bellis, *getting involved with you. I will* not *become your sounding board. I will not redeem you of whatever tawdry tragedy brings you here.*

Bellis eyed Sister Meriope and did not speak.

When she had first introduced herself, Meriope had claimed

that she was traveling to the colonies to establish a church, to proselytize, for the glory of Darioch and Jabber. She had said it with a small sniff and a furtive look, idiotically unconvincing. Bellis did not know why Meriope was being sent to Nova Esperium, but it must have to do with some misfortune or disgrace, the transgression of some idiotic nunnish vow.

She glanced at Meriope's midriff, looking for swelling under those forgiving robes. That would be the most likely explanation. The Daughters of Darioch were supposed to forego sensual pleasures.

I will not serve as replacement confessor for you, thought Bellis. *I have my own bloody exile to work out.*

"Sister," she said, "I'm afraid you catch me at work. I have no time for pleasantries, I regret to say. Perhaps another time." She was irritated with herself for that last tiny concession, but it had no effect, anyway. Meriope was broken.

"The captain wishes to see you," the nun said, muffled and forlorn. "His cabin, at six o'clock." She shuffled out of the door like a bullied dog.

Bellis sighed and swore quietly. She lit another cigarillo and smoked it right through, pinching the skin above her nose hard, before pulling out her letter again.

"I will go bloody mad," she scribbled quickly, "if this damned nun does not stop fawning and leave me alone. Gods preserve me. Gods rot this damned boat."

It was dark when Bellis obeyed the captain's summons.

His cabin was his office. It was small, and pleasantly outfitted in dark wood and brass. There were a few pictures and prints on the walls, and Bellis glanced at them and knew that they were not the captain's, that they came with the ship.

Captain Myzovic gestured her to sit.

"Miss Coldwine," he said as she settled herself. "I hope your quarters are satisfactory. Your food? The crew? Good good." He looked down briefly at the papers on his desk. "I wanted to raise a couple of issues with you, Miss Coldwine," he said, and sat back.

She waited, staring at him. He was a hard-faced, handsome man in his fifties. His uniform was clean and pressed, which not all captains' were. Bellis did not know whether it would be to her advantage to meet his eyes calmly or demurely to look away.

"Miss Coldwine, we haven't spoken very much about your duties," he said quietly. "I will do you the courtesy, of course, of treating you like a lady. I must tell you I'm not used to hiring those of your sex, and had the Esperium authorities not been impressed by your records and references, I can assure you . . ." He let the sentence dissipate.

"I have no wish to make you feel uncomfortable. You're berthing in the passengers' quarters. You're eating in the passenger mess. However, as you know, you are not a paying passenger. You are an employee. You have been taken on by the agents of the Nova Esperium colony, and for the duration of this journey I am their representative. And while that makes little difference to Sister Meriope and Dr. Tearfly and the others, to you . . . it means I am your employer.

"Of course you are not crew," he continued. "I would not order you as I order them. If you prefer, I would only *request* your services. But I must insist that such requests are obeyed."

They studied each other.

"Now," he said, his tone relaxing a little, "I don't foresee any onerous demands. Most of the crew are from New Crobuzon or the Grain Spiral, and those that aren't speak perfectly good Ragamoll. It's in Salkrikaltor that I'll first need you, and we'll not be there for a good week or more, so you've plenty of time to relax, to meet the other passengers. We sail tomorrow morning, early. We'll be away by the time you're up, I shouldn't doubt."

"Tomorrow?" Bellis said. It was the first word she had spoken since entering.

The captain looked at her sharply. "Yes. Is there a problem?"

"Originally," she said without inflection, "you told me we would sail on Dustday, Captain."

"I did, Miss Coldwine, but I've changed my mind. I've finished my paperwork a deal quicker than I expected, and my brother officers are ready to transfer their inmates tonight. We sail tomorrow."

"I had hoped to return to town, to send a letter," Bellis said. She kept her voice level. "An important letter to a friend in New Crobuzon."

"Out of the question," the captain said. "It cannot be done. I'll not waste any more days here."

Bellis sat still. She was not intimidated by this man, but she had no power over him, none at all. She tried to work out what was most likely to engage his sympathy, make him acquiesce.

"Miss Coldwine," he said suddenly, and to her surprise his voice was a little gentler. "I am afraid the matter is in motion. If you wish I can give your letter to Lieutenant-Gaoler Catarrs, but I cannot in truth recommend that as entirely reliable. You'll have the opportunity to deliver your message in Salkrikaltor. Even if there are no New Crobuzon ships docking there, there is a warehouse, to which all our captains have the keys, for access to information, spare cargo, and mail. Leave your letter there. It'll be picked up by the next home-bound ship. It won't be much delayed.

"You can learn from this, Miss Coldwine," he added. "At sea, you can't waste time. Remember that: don't wait."

Bellis sat on a little longer, but there was nothing at all that she could do, so she thinned her lips and left.

She stood for a long time under Iron Bay's cold sky. The stars were invisible; the moon and its daughters, its two little satellites, were unclear. Bellis walked, tense against the chill, and climbed the short ladder to the ship's raised front, heading for the bowsprit.

Bellis held on to the iron railings and stood on the tips of her toes. She could just see out, across the lightless sea.

Behind her the sounds of the crew faded. A way off, she could see two guttering red pins of light: a torch on the bridge of a prison-ship, and its twin in the black surf.

From the crow's nest, or from somewhere in the rigging, from some indistinct spot a hundred feet or more above her, Bellis heard a strain of mouth-music. It was not like the imbecilic shanties she had heard in Tarmuth. It was slow and complex.

You will have to wait for your letter, Bellis mouthed silently across the water. *You will have to wait to hear from me. You'll have to wait a little while longer, until cray-country.*

She watched the night until the last lines of division between shore, sea, and sky were obscured. Then, cosseted by darkness, she walked slowly aft, toward the constricted doorways and stooped passages leading to her cabin, a scrap of space like a flaw in the ship's design.

(Later the ship moved uneasily, in the coldest hour, and she stirred in her bunk and she pulled the blanket up to her neck, and she realized somewhere below her dreams that the living cargo was coming aboard.)

I am tired here in the dark and I am full of pus.

My skin's taut with it, stretched till it puckers nor can I touch it without it rages. I'm infected. I hurt where I touch and I touch everywhere to make sure that I hurt that I'm not yet numb.

But still thank whatever makes these veins mine I'm full of blood. I worry my scabs and they brim I brim with it. And that's a small comfort nor mind the pain.

They come for us when the air's so still and black without not a seabird cries. They open our doors and shine lights, uncovering us. I am almost ashamed to see how we have surrendered, we've surrendered up to filth.

I can see nothing beyond their lights.

Where we lie together they beat us apart, and I wrap my arms around the spastic matter that twitches in my midriff as they begin to herd us.

We wind through tarry passages and engine chambers and I'm all cold to know what this is for. And I'm more eager, I'm quicker than some of the old ones bent double coughing and spewing and afraid to move.

And then there's a swallowing up, I'm eaten up by the cold gulped down by darkness and gods fuck me blind we are outside.

Outside.

I'm dumb with it. I'm dumb with wonder.

It has been a long time.

We huddle together, each against the next man like troglodytes like myopic trow. They're cowed by it the old ones, by the lack of walls and edges and the movement of the cold, by water and air.

I might cry gods help me. I might.

All black on black but still I can see hills and water and I can see clouds. I can see the prisons on all sides bobbing a little like fishermen's floats. Jabber take us all I can see clouds.

Bugger me I'm crooning like I soothe a baby. That's for me that coddling noise.

And then they push us on like livestock shuffling rattling chains, dripping farting muttering astonished, across the deck crippled under the weight of bodies and fetters, to a swaying rope bridge. And they hurry us along and over it, all our number, and each man pauses a moment in the middle of the low-slung passage between vessels, their thoughts visible and bright like a chymical burst.

They consider leaping.

Into the water of the bay.

But the rope walls around the bridge are high and there's barbed wire hemming us in and our poor bodies are sore and weak and each man falters, and continues, and crosses the water to a new ship.

I pause like the others in my turn. Like them I'm too afraid.

And then there's a new deck underfoot, scrubbed iron smooth and clean, vibrating from engines, and more corridors and clattering keys and after all another long unlit room where we collapse exhausted and changed over and raise ourselves slowly to see who our new neighbors are. Around me begin the hissed arguments and bickerings and fights and seductions and rapes that make up our politics. New alliances are formed. New hierarchies.

I sit apart for a while, in the shadows.

I'm still caught in that moment when I entered the night. It's like amber. I'm a grub in amber. It snares me and damn but it does it makes me beautiful.

I've a new home now. I'll live in that moment as long as I can, till the memories decay and then I'll come out, I'll come to this new place we sit in.

Somewhere pipes are banging like great hammers.

CHAPTER TWO

Outside of Iron Bay, the sea was hard. Bellis woke to its slapping assault. She quit the cabin, picking her way past Sister Meriope, who was vomiting with what Bellis did not believe was just sea-sickness.

Bellis emerged into wind, and a great cracking as sails tugged like animals at their tethers. The enormous smokestack vented a little soot, and the ship hummed with the power of the steam engine deep below.

Bellis sat on a container. *So we're off, then,* she thought nervously. *We're heading out. We're away.*

The *Terpsichoria* had seemed busy while they were moored: someone was always scrubbing something, or raising a piece of machinery, or running from one end of the ship to the other. But now that sense of activity was increased by a huge factor.

Bellis squinted out across the maindeck, not yet ready to look at the sea.

The rigging teemed. Most of the sailors were human, but here and there a spined hotchi raced along rope crawlways and onto crow's nests. On the decks men lugged containers and wound huge winches, shouting instructions in incomprehensible short-hand, threading chains onto fat flywheels. There were towering cactacae, too heavy and ungainly to climb rope but making up for that with their efforts below, with their strength, fibrous vege-table biceps bunching massively as they tugged and tied.

Officers in blue uniforms strode among them.

The wind blew across the ship, and the deck's periscopic cowls crooned like dolorous flutes.

Bellis finished her cigarillo. She stood slowly and walked to the side, her eyes lowered, till she reached the rail and she looked up and out to sea.

There was no land at all.

Oh gods, look at it all, she thought in shock.

For the first time in her life, Bellis looked out across nothing but water.

Alone beneath a colossal rearing sky, anxiety welled up in her like bile. She wanted very much to be back in the alleys of her city.

Slicks of spume spread fast around the ship, disappearing and reappearing incessantly. The water moiled in intricate marbled surges. It shifted for the ship, as it would for a whale or a canoe or a fallen leaf, a dumb accommodation that it might overturn with any sudden swell.

It was a massive moronic child. Powerful and stupid and capricious.

Bellis cast her gaze about nervously, looking for any island, any jag of coastline. At that moment, there was none.

A cloud of seabirds trailed them, plunging for carrion in the vessel's wake, spattering the deck and the foam with guano.

They sailed without stopping for two days.

Bellis felt almost stupefied with resentment that her journey was under way. She paced the corridors and decks, shut herself in her cabin. She watched blankly as the *Terpsichoria* passed rocks and tiny islands in the distance, illuminated by grey daylight or the moon.

Sailors scanned the horizon, oiling the large-bore guns. With hundreds of ill-charted islets and trading towns, with an unending number of ships supplying the insatiable commercial hole of New Crobuzon at one end, Basilisk Channel was plied by pirates.

Bellis knew that a ship this size with an ironclad hull and New Crobuzon's colors flying would almost certainly not be preyed upon. The crew's vigilance was only slightly unnerving.

The *Terpsichoria* was a merchant vessel. It was not built for passengers. There was no library, no drawing room, no games room. The passengers' mess was a halfhearted effort, its walls bare but for a few cheap lithographs.

Bellis took her meals there sitting alone, monosyllabic to any pleasantries, while the other passengers sat below the dirty windows and played cards. Bellis watched them surreptitiously and intensely.

Back in her cabin, Bellis took endless stock of what she possessed.

She had left the city in a sudden hurry. She had very few clothes, in the austere style she favored: severe and black and charcoal. She had seven books: two volumes of linguistic theory; a primer in Salkrikaltor Cray; an anthology of short fiction in various languages; a thick, empty notebook; and copies of her own two monographs, *High Kettai Grammatology* and *Codexes of the Wormseye Scrub*. She had a few pieces of jewelry in jet and garnet and platinum; a small bag of cosmetics; ink and pens.

She spent hours adding details to her letter. She described the ugliness of the open seas, the harsh rocks that poked up like traps. She wrote long, parodic descriptions of the officers and passengers, reveling in caricature. Sister Meriope; Bartol Gimgewrÿ the merchant; the cadaverous surgeon Dr. Mollificatt; Widow and Miss Cardomium, a quiet mother and daughter transformed by Bellis' pen into a scheming pair of husband hunters. Johannes Tearfly became the professorial buffoon pilloried in music halls. She invented motivations for them all, speculating on what might send them halfway across the world.

Standing at the back of the ship on the second day, by the morass of gulls and ospreys still bickering over the ship's effluent, Bellis looked for islets but saw only waves.

She felt jilted. Then, as she searched the horizon, she heard a noise.

A little way from her the naturalist, Dr. Tearfly, stood watching the birds. Bellis' face set hard. She prepared to leave as soon as he spoke to her.

When he looked down and saw her watching him coldly, he gave her an absent smile and pulled out a notebook. His attention was off her immediately. She watched as he began to sketch the gulls, paying her no mind at all.

He was in his late fifties, she guessed. His thinning hair was combed tightly back, and he wore little rectangular spectacles and a tweed waistcoat. But despite the academic uniform he did not look weak or absurdly bookish. He was tall, and he held himself well.

With quick, precise strokes, he marked out folded avian claws and the brute pugnacity of the seagulls' eyes. Bellis warmed to him very slightly.

After a while she spoke.

It made journeying easier; she admitted that to herself. Johannes Tearfly was charming. Bellis suspected he would be equally friendly to everyone on board.

They took lunch together, and she found it easy to steer him away from the other passengers, who watched them intently. Tearfly was endearingly free of intrigue. If it occurred to him that keeping the company of the rude and distant Bellis Coldwine might lead to rumors, he did not care.

Tearfly was happy to discuss his work. He enthused about the unstudied fauna of Nova Esperium. He told Bellis about his plans for publishing a monograph, on his eventual return to New Crobuzon. He was collating drawings, he told her, and helio-types and observations.

Bellis described to him a dark, mountainous island she had seen in the north, in the small hours of the previous night.

"That was North Morin," he said. "Cancir's probably off to the northwest right now. We'll be docking at Dancing Bird Island after dark."

The ship's position and progress were matters of constant conversation among the other passengers, and Tearfly looked at Bellis curiously, bewildered by her ignorance. She did not care. What was important to her was where she was fleeing from, not where she was, or where she was going.

Dancing Bird Island appeared just as the sun went down. Its volcanic rock was brick-red, and hunched into little peaks like shoulder bones. Qé Banssa clambered up the slopes of the bay. It was poor, an ugly little fishing port. The thought of setting foot in another resentful town imprisoned by maritime economics depressed Bellis.

The sailors without shore leave were sullen as their comrades and passengers disappeared down the gangplank. There were no other New Crobuzon ships at dock: nowhere for Bellis to deliver her letter. She wondered why they were stopping at this negligible port.

Apart from an arduous research trip to the Wormseye Scrub years previously, this was the furthest Bellis had ever been from New Crobuzon. She watched the small crowd at the dockside. They looked old and eager. Over the wind she heard a smattering of dialects. Most of the shouts were in Salt, the sailors' argot, a found language riveted together from the thousand vernaculars of the Basilisk Channel, Ragamoll, and Perrickish, the tongues of the Pirate and Jheshull Islands.

Bellis saw Captain Myzovic climb the steep streets toward New Crobuzon's crenellated embassy.

"Why are you staying on board?" said Johannes.

"I don't feel any great need for greasy food or trinkets," she said. "These islands depress me."

Johannes smiled slowly, as if her attitude delighted him. He shrugged and looked up at the sky. "It's going to rain," he said, as if she had returned his question, "and I have work to do aboard."

"Why are we stopping here anyway?" said Bellis.

"I suspect it's government business," said Johannes carefully. "This is the last serious outpost. Beyond this the New Crobuzon sphere of influence becomes far more . . . attenuated. There are probably all manner of things to be attended to, out here.

"Luckily," he said after a silence, "it's none of our business."

They watched the still-darkening ocean.

"Have you seen any of the prisoners?" Johannes asked suddenly.

Bellis looked at him in surprise. "No. Have you?" She felt defensive. The fact of the ship's sentient cargo discomfited her.

When it had come, Bellis' realization that she had to leave New Crobuzon had been urgent and frightening. She had made her plans in low panic. She needed to get as far away as she could, and quickly. Cobsea and Myrshock seemed too close, and she had thought feverishly of Shankell and Yoraketche, and Neovadan and Tesh. But they were all too far or too dangerous, or too alien, or too hard to reach or too frightening. There was nothing in any of them that could become her home. And Bellis had realized aghast that it was too hard for her to let go, that she was clinging to New Crobuzon, to what defined her.

And then Bellis had thought of Nova Esperium. Eager for new citizens. Asking no questions. Halfway across the world, a little blister of civilization in unknown lands. A home from home, New Crobuzon's colony. Rougher, surely, and harder and less cosseted—Nova Esperium was too young for many kindnesses— but a culture modeled on her city's own.

She realized that, with that destination, New Crobuzon would pay her passage, even as she fled it. And a channel of communication would remain open to her: regular if occasional contact with ships from home. She might then know when it was safe to return.

But the vessels that undertook the long, dangerous journey from Iron Bay across the Swollen Ocean carried with them Nova Esperium's workforce. Which meant a hold full of prisoners: peons, indentured laborers, and Remade.

It curdled the food in Bellis' stomach to think of the men and women locked below, out of the light, and so she did not think of them. She would have had nothing to do with such a voyage and such harsh traffic if she had had a choice.

Bellis looked up at Johannes, trying to gauge his thoughts.

"I must admit," he said hesitantly, "I'm surprised I've heard no sound at *all* from them. I had thought they would be let out more often than this."

Bellis said nothing. She waited for Johannes to change the subject, so that she could continue to try to forget what lay beneath them.

She could hear the bonhomie from Qé Banssa's waterfront pubs. It sounded urgent.

Under tar and steel, in the damp chambers below. Food bolted and fought over. Shit, spunk, and blood congealing. Shrieks and fistfights. And chains like stone and all around whispers.

"That's a shame, lad." The voice was rough from lack of sleep, but the sympathy was genuine. "You'll most probably get a hiding for that."

Before the bars of the prison hold, the cabin boy stood looking mournfully at shards of pottery and spilt stew. He had been spooning food into bowls for the prisoners, and his hand had slipped.

"Clay like that looks strong as iron, till you drop it." The man behind the bars was as filthy and tired as all the other prisoners. Bubbling from his chest, visible beneath a torn shirt, was a huge tumor of flesh from which emerged two long ill-smelling tentacles. They swung lifeless, deadweight blubbery encumbrances. Like most of the transportees, the man was Remade, carved by science and thaumaturgy into a new shape, in punishment for some crime.

"Reminds me of when Crawfoot went to war," said the man. "Did you ever hear that story?"

The cabin boy picked greasy meat and carrots from the floor and dropped them into a bucket. He glanced up at the man.

The prisoner shuffled back and settled against the wall.

"So one day, at the beginning of the world, Darioch looks out from his treehouse and sees an army coming toward the forest. And bugger me if it ain't the Batskin Brood come to get back their brooms. You know how Crawfoot took their brooms, don't you?"

The cabin boy was about fifteen, old for his position. He wore clothes not much cleaner than the prisoners'. He looked the man full on and grinned *yes*, he knew that story, and the sudden change in him was so marked and extraordinary it was as if he were briefly given a new body. For a moment he looked strong and cocky, and when the smile went and he returned to the slop of food and pottery, some of that sudden swagger remained.

"All right then," the prisoner continued. "So Darioch calls Crawfoot to him and shows him the Batskins on their way, and he says to him, 'This is your fuck-up, Crawfoot. You took their stuff. And it happens that Salter's away at the edge of the world, so you're going to have to do the fighting.' And Crawfoot's bitching and moaning and giving it all this . . ." The man opened and shut his fingers like a talkative mouth.

He started to continue, but the cabin boy cut him off. "I know it," he said with sudden recognition. "I heard it before."

There was a silence.

"Ah well," the man said, surprised by his own disappointment. "Ah well, I tell you what, son, I've not heard it for a while myself, so I think I'll just carry on and tell it."

The boy looked at him quizzically, as if trying to decide whether the man was mocking him. "I don't mind," he said. "Do what you want. I don't care."

The prisoner told the story, quietly, interrupted by coughing and sighs for breath. The cabin boy came and went in the darkness beyond the bars, cleaning the mess, spooning out more food. He was there at the story's end, when Crawfoot's chimney-pot-and-china-plate armor shattered, cutting him worse than if he'd worn none at all.

The boy looked at the tired man, the story finished, and grinned again.

"Ain't you going to tell me the lesson?" he said.

The man smiled weakly. "I reckon you already know it."

The boy nodded and looked up for a moment, concentrating. " 'If it's nearly right, but it isn't quite, better to have none, than make do with one,' " he recited. "I always preferred them stories without the morals," he added. He squatted down by the bars.

"Fuck but I'm with you there, lad," said the man. He paused and held out his hand through the bars. "I'm Tanner Sack."

The cabin boy hesitated a moment: not nervous, just weighing up possibilities and advantages. He took Tanner's hand.

"Ta for the story. I'm Shekel."

They continued.

Chapter Three

Bellis came out of sleep when they set sail again, though the bay was still dark. The *Terpsichoria* juddered and shivered like a cold animal, and she rolled to the porthole and watched the few lights of Qé Banssa move away.

That morning, she was not allowed onto the main deck.

"Sorry ma'am," said a sailor. He was young, and desperately uncomfortable at blocking her way. "Captain's orders: passengers not allowed onto main deck till ten."

"Why?"

He shied as if she had hit him. "Prisoners," he said, "taking a constitutional." Bellis' eyes widened fractionally. "Captain's giving them a shot of air, and then we've to clean the deck—they're awful dirty. Why'n't you have some breakfast, ma'am? This'll be done in a trice."

Out of the young man's sight she stopped and considered. She did not like the coincidence of this, so soon after her discussion with Johannes.

Bellis wanted to see the men and women they carried below. She could not tell if she was driven by prurience, or a more noble instinct.

Instead of heading abaft for the mess, she wound down side passages through dim space, past poky doors. Bass sounds traveled through the walls: human voices sounded like dogs barking. Where the corridor ended she opened the last door, onto a walk-in cupboard lined with shelves. Bellis looked behind her, but she was alone. She finished her cigarillo and entered.

Pushing aside dried-up, empty bottles, Bellis saw that an ancient window had been blocked by shelves. She cleared them of detritus and wiped ineffectually at the glass.

She started as somebody walked past the pane, outside, barely three feet away. Stooping, she squinted through the dirt, out over the ship. The enormous mizzenmast was before her, and faintly, she saw the main- and foremasts beyond it. Below her was the main deck.

The sailors were moving, climbing and cleaning and winding in their rituals.

There was a mass of others, huddled in groups, moving slowly if at all. Bellis' mouth twisted. They were mostly human and mostly men, but they defied generalization. She saw a man with a sinuous three-foot neck, a woman with a skein of spasming arms, a figure whose lower quarters were caterpillar treads, and another with metal wires jutting from his bones. The only thing they had in common were their greying clothes.

Bellis had never seen so many Remade in one place before, so many who had been altered in the punishment factories. Some were shaped for industry, while others seemed formed for no purpose other than grotesquerie, with misshapen mouths and eyes and gods-knew what.

There were a few cactacae prisoners, and other races too: a hotchi with broken spines; a tiny clutch of khepri, their scarab headbodies twitching and glinting in the washed-out sun. There were no vodyanoi, of course. On a journey like this, fresh water was too valuable to use keeping them alive.

She heard gaolers' shouts. Men and cactacae strutted among the Remade, wielding whips. In groups of two and three and ten the prisoners began to shuffle in random circles around the deck.

Some lay still, and were punished.

Bellis pulled her face away.

These were her unseen companions.

They had not seemed much invigorated by the fresh air, she reflected coldly. They had not seemed to enjoy their exercise.

Tanner Sack moved just enough to keep from being beaten. He moved his eyes in a rhythm. Down for three long steps, to keep attention from himself, then up for one, to see the sky and the water.

The ship was juddering faintly from the steam engine below, and the sails were extended. The cliffs of Dancing Bird Island moved past them fast. Tanner moved toward the port side, slowly.

He was surrounded by the men who shared his hold. The women prisoners stood in a smaller group, a little way off. They all wore the same dirty faces and cold stares as him. He did not approach them.

Tanner heard a sudden whistle, a sharp two-tone different from the scream of the gulls. He looked up, and perched on some bulky metal extrusion, scrubbing it clean, Shekel looked down at him. The boy caught his eye and gave Tanner a wink and a fast smile. Tanner smiled back, but Shekel had already looked away.

An officer and a sailor with distinctive epaulets conferred at the ship's bow, huddled over a brass engine. As Tanner strained to see what they were doing, a stick slapped across his back, not hard but with the threat of much worse. A cactacae guard was bellowing at him to keep moving, so he picked up his feet again. The alien tissue grafted to Tanner's chest twitched. The tentacles itched and shed skin like severe sunburn. He spat on them and rubbed the saliva in, as if it were unguent.

At ten o'clock precisely, Bellis swallowed her tea and went outside. The deck had been swept and scrubbed clean. There was no sign that the prisoners had ever stood upon it.

"It's odd to think," said Bellis a little later, as she and Johannes stood watching the water, "that in Nova Esperium we might be in charge of men and women who traveled with us on this very boat, and we'd never know."

"That'll never happen to you," he said. "Since when does a linguist need indentured assistants?"

"Neither does a naturalist."

"Not true at all," he said mildly. "There are crates to be taken into the bush, there are traps to be set, there are drugged and dead carcasses to lug, dangerous animals to subdue . . . It's not all watercoloring, you know. I'll show you my scars some time."

"Are you serious?"

"Yes." He was thoughtful. "I've a foot-long gash where a sardula got nasty . . . a bite from a newborn chalkydri . . ."

"A sardula? Really? Can I see?"

Johannes shook his head. "It got me . . . close to a delicate place," he said.

He did not look at her, but he did not seem prudish.

Johannes shared his cabin with Gimgewry, the failed merchant, a man crippled with the understanding of his own inadequacy, who eyed Bellis with miserable lust. Johannes was never lascivious. He seemed to think always of other things before he had a chance to notice Bellis' attractions.

It was not that she was seeking to be approached—she would spurn him quickly if he did court her. But she was used to men trying to flirt with her—usually only for a short time, until they realized that her cool demeanor was not an act they could persuade her to drop. Tearfly's company was frank and unsexual, and she found it disconcerting. She wondered briefly if he might be what her father had called an invert, but she saw no more sign that he was attracted to any of the men on board than he was to her. And then she felt vain for wondering.

There was a glimmer of something like fear in him, she thought, when an insinuation hung between them. *Perhaps,* she thought, *he's no interest in such matters. Or perhaps he's a coward.*

Shekel and Tanner traded stories.

Shekel already knew many of Crawfoot's Chronicles, but Tanner knew them all. And even those that Shekel had heard before Tanner knew variations of, and he narrated them all well. In turn Shekel told him about the officers and passengers. He was full of scorn for Gimgewry, whose frantic masturbation he had heard through the privy door. He found the vacantly avuncular Tearfly enormously dull, and he was nervous of Captain Myzovic, but blustered and told lies about him wandering the decks drunk.

He lusted after Miss Cardomium. He liked Bellis Coldwine—"Cold ain't the fucking word, though," he said, "for Miss Black-and-blue."

Tanner listened to the descriptions and insinuations, laughing and tutting where appropriate. Shekel told him the rumors and fables that the sailors told each other—about the piasa and the she-corsairs, Marichonians and the scab pirates, the things that lived below the water.

Behind Tanner stretched the long darkness of the hold.

There was a constant scavenging fight for food and fuel. It wasn't just leftover meat and bread: many prisoners were Remade with metal parts and steam engines. If their boilers went out, they were immobilized, so anything that might burn was hoarded. In the far corner of the chamber stood an old man, the pewter tripod on which he walked locked solid for days. His furnace was dead cold. He ate only when someone bothered to feed him, and no one expected him to live.

Shekel was fascinated by the brutality of that little realm. He watched the old man with avid eyes. He saw the prisoners' bruises. He glimpsed peculiar double silhouettes of men coupling in consent or rape.

He had run a gang in Raven's Gate, back in the city, and he was worried about what would happen to them now, without him. His first-ever theft, aged six, had netted him a shekel piece, and the nickname had stuck. He claimed that he could not remember any other name. He had taken this job on the ship when his gang's activities, which included the occasional burglary, had attracted too much attention from the militia.

"Another month and I'd have been in there with you, Tanner," he said. "Ain't a lot in it."

Tended by the ship's thaumaturges and wyrdshipmen, the meteoromancing engine by *Terpsichoria*'s bowsprit displaced air in front of the ship. The ship's sails bowed out to fill the vacuum; pressure billowed in from behind. They made good speed.

The machine reminded Bellis of New Crobuzon's cloudtowers. She thought of the huge engines jutting over the Tar Wedge roofscape, arcane and broken. She felt a hard longing for the streets and canals, for the *size* of the city.

And for engines. Machines. In New Crobuzon they had surrounded her. Now there was only the little meteoromancer and the mess-hall construct. The steam engine below made the whole of *Terpsichoria* a mechanism, but it was invisible. Bellis wandered the ship like a rogue cog. She missed the utilitarian chaos she had been forced to leave.

They were sailing a busy part of the sea. They passed other ships: in the two days after they left Qé Banssa, Bellis saw three. The first two were little elongated shapes at the horizon; the third was a squat caravel that came much closer. It was from Odraline, as the kites it flew from its sails announced. It pitched wildly in the choppy sea.

Bellis could see the sailors aboard it. She watched them swing in the complex rigging and scramble the triangular sails.

The *Terpsichoria* passed barren-looking islands: Cadann, Rin Lor, Eidolon Island. There were folktales concerning every one, and Johannes knew them all.

Bellis spent hours watching the sea. The water so far east was much clearer than that near Iron Bay: she could see the smudges that were huge schools of fish. The off-duty sailors sat with their legs over the side, angling with crude rods, scrimshawing bones and narwhal tusks with knives and lampblack.

Occasionally the curves of great predators like orca would breach in the distance. Once, as the sun went down, the *Terpsichoria* passed close to a little wooded knoll, a mile or two of forest that budded from the ocean. There was a clutch of smooth rocks off the shore, and Bellis' heart skidded as one of the boulders reared and a massive swan's neck uncoiled from the water. A blunt head twisted, and she watched the plesiauri paddle lazily out of the shallows and disappear.

She became briefly fascinated with submarine carnivores. Johannes took her to his cabin and rummaged among his books. She saw several titles with his name on the spine: *Sardula Anatomy; Predation in Iron Bay Rockpools; Theories of Megafauna*. When he found the monograph he was looking for, he showed her sensational depictions of ancient, blunt-headed fish thirty feet long; of goblin sharks with ragged teeth and jutting foreheads; and others.

On the evening of the second day out of Qé Banssa, *Terpsichoria* sighted the land that rimmed Salkrikaltor: a jagged grey coastline. It was past nine in the evening, but the sky, for once, was absolutely clear, and the moon and her daughters shone very bright.

Despite herself, Bellis was awed by this mountainous landscape, all channeled through by wind. Deep inland, at the limits of her vision, she could see the darkness of forest clinging to the sides of gulleys. On the coast the trees were dead, salt-blasted husks.

Johannes swore with excitement. "That's Bartoll!" he said. "A hundred miles north there's Cyrhussine Bridge, twenty-five damned miles long. I hoped we might see that, but I suppose it would have been asking for trouble."

The ship was bearing away from the island. It was cold, and Bellis flapped her thin coat impatiently.

"I'm going inside," she said, but Johannes ignored her.

He was staring back the way they had come, at Bartoll's disappearing shore.

"What's going on?" he murmured. Bellis turned back sharply. The frown was audible in his voice. "Where are we going?" Johannes gesticulated. "Look . . . we're bearing away from Bartoll." The island was now little more than an unclear fringe at the edge of the sea. "Salkrikaltor's *that* way—east. We could be sailing over the cray within a couple of hours, but we're heading south . . . We're heading *away* from the commonwealth . . ."

"Maybe they don't like ships passing overhead," Bellis said, but Johannes shook his head.

"That's the standard route," he said. "East from Bartoll gets you to Salkrikaltor City. That's how you get there. We're heading somewhere else." He drew a map in the air. "This is Bartoll and this is Gnomon Tor, and between them, in the sea . . . Salkrikaltor. Down here, where we're heading now . . . there's nothing. A line of spiky little islands. We're taking a very long way around to Salkrikaltor City. I wonder why."

By the next morning, several other passengers had noticed the unusual route. Within hours, word spread among the cloistered little corridors. Captain Myzovic addressed them in the mess. There were almost forty passengers, and all were present. Even pale, pathetic Sister Meriope and others similarly afflicted.

"There is nothing to be concerned about," the captain assured them. He was clearly angry at being summoned. Bellis looked away from him, out of the windows. *Why am I here?* she thought. *I don't care. I don't care where we're going or how we damn well get there.* But she did not convince herself, and she stayed where she was.

"But *why* have we deviated from the normal route, Captain?" someone asked.

The captain exhaled angrily. "Right," he said. "Listen. I am taking a detour around the Fins, the islands at the southern edge of Salkrikaltor. I am *not* obliged to explain this action to you. However . . ." He paused, to impress upon the passengers how privileged they were. "Under the circumstances . . . I must ask you all to observe a degree of restraint, as regards this information.

"We will be circumnavigating the Fins before reaching Salkrikaltor City, so that we might pass some of New Crobuzon's holdings. Certain maritime industries. Which are not public knowledge. Now, I could have you confined to cabins. But then you might see something from the portholes, and I'd rather not let loose the rumors that would result. So you are free to go above, to the poop-deck only. *But.* But I appeal to you as patriots and as good citizens to exercise discretion about what you see tonight. Am I clear?"

To Bellis' disgust, there was a slightly awed silence. *He's stupefying them with pomposity,* she thought, and turned away with her contempt.

The waves were broken by an occasional rock tusk, but nothing more dramatic. Most of the passengers had congregated at the back of the ship, and they gazed eagerly over the water.

Bellis kept her eyes to the horizon, irritated that she was not alone.

"Do you think we'll know when we see whatever it is?" asked a clucking woman Bellis did not know, and whom she ignored.

It grew dark and much colder, and some of the passengers retired below. The mountainous Fins dipped in and out of visibility at the horizon. Bellis sipped mulled wine for warmth. She became bored, and watched the sailors instead of the sea.

And then, at around two in the morning, with only half the passengers left on deck, something appeared in the east.

"Gods above," Johannes whispered.

For a long time it remained a forbidding, unreadable silhouette. And then, as they approached, Bellis saw that it was a huge black tower that reared from the sea. An oily light flared from its peak, a spew of dirty flame.

They were almost upon it. A little over a mile away. Bellis gasped.

It was a platform suspended above the sea. More than two hundred feet long on each side, it hung immensely, its concrete weight poised on three massive metal legs. Bellis could hear it pounding.

Waves broke against its supports. It had a skyline as intricate and twisted as a city's. Above the three leg-pillars was a cluster of seemingly random spires, and cranes moving like clawed hands; and over them all a huge minaret of girders soared and drooled fire. Thaumaturgic ripples distorted the space above the flame. In the shadows under the platform, a massive metal shaft plunged into the sea. Lights glimmered from its built-up levels.

"What in the name of Jabber is that?" Bellis breathed.

It was awesome and extraordinary. The passengers were gaping like fools.

The mountains of the southernmost Fin were a shadow in the distance. Near the base of the platform were predatory shapes: ironclad ships patrolling. Lights flashed in a complex staccato from the deck of one of them, and there was a corresponding burst from the bridge of the *Terpsichoria*.

From the deck of the fabulous structure, a klaxon sounded.

They were passing away from it now. Bellis watched it dwindle, venting flame.

Johannes remained still with astonishment.

"I have no idea," he said slowly. It took a moment for Bellis to realize he was answering her question. They kept their eyes on the enormous shape in the sea for as long as they could make it out at all.

When it was gone they walked in silence toward the corridor. And then, as they reached the door into the cabins, someone behind them shouted.

"Another!"

It was true. Miles in the distance, a second colossal platform.

Bigger than the first. It loomed on four legs of weatherbeaten concrete. This one was sparser. There was one fat, squat tower rising from each corner, and a colossal derrick at its edge. The structure growled like something alive.

Again came a lightflash challenge from the thing's defenders, and again the *Terpsichoria* responded.

There was a wind, and the sky was cold as iron. In the shallows of that bleak sea the edifice roared as the *Terpsichoria* slipped by in darkness.

Bellis and Johannes waited another hour, their hands numb, their breath coiling out of them in visible gusts, but nothing else appeared. All they could see was the water, and here and there the Fins, serrated and unlit.

Chainday 5th Arora 1779. Aboard the *Terpsichoria*

As soon as I entered the captain's office this morning, it was clear that something had angered him. He was grinding his teeth, and his expression was murderous.

"Miss Coldwine," he said, "in a few hours we will be arriving at Salkrikaltor City. The other passengers and crew will be granted a few hours' leave, but I'm afraid there'll be no such luxury for you."

His tone was neutral and dangerous. His desk was cleared of paraphernalia. This disturbed me, and I cannot explain why. Usually he is surrounded by a bulwark of detritus. Without it there was no buffer between us.

"I will be meeting with representatives of the Salkrikaltor Commonwealth, and you will translate. You have worked with trade delegations—you know the formula. You will translate *into* Salkrikaltor Cray for the representatives, and their translator will render their words into Ragamoll for me. You listen carefully to make sure of him, and he'll be listening to you. That ensures honesty on both sides. But you are *not* a participant. Do I make myself entirely clear?" He labored the point like a teacher. "You will not hear anything that passes between us. You're a conduit, and nothing more. You hear *nothing*."

I met the bastard's eye.

"Matters will be discussed of the highest security. On board a ship, Miss Coldwine, there are very few secrets. Mark me." He leaned toward me. "If you mention what is discussed to anyone—to my officers, your puking nun, or your close friend Dr. Tearfly—I will hear of it."

I am sure I do not need to tell you that I was shocked.

Thus far I have avoided confrontation with the captain, but his anger made him capricious. I will not appear weak to him. Months of bad feeling is a smaller price than to cower strategically whenever he comes close.

Besides which I was enraged.

I put frost in my voice.

"Captain, we discussed these matters when you offered me this post. My record and references are clear. It is beneath you to question me now." I was very grand. "I am not some press-ganged seventeen-year-old for you to intimidate, sir. I will do my job as contracted, and you will not impugn my professionalism."

I have no idea what had angered him, and I do not care. The gods can rot his bastard hide.

And now I sit here with the "puking nun"—although in fact she seems a little better, and has even simpered about taking a service on Shunday—and finish this letter. We are approaching Salkrikaltor, where I will have my chance to seal it and leave it, to be picked up by any New Crobuzon ship passing. It will reach you, this long farewell, only a few weeks late. Which is not so very bad. I hope it finds you well.

I hope that you miss me as I miss you. I do not know what I will do without this means to connect me with you. It will be a year or more before you hear from me again, before another ship steams or sails into the harbor at Nova Esperium, and think of me then! My hair long and braided with mud, no doubt, abjuring clothes, marked with sigils like some savage shaman! If I still remember how to write, I will write to you then, and tell you of my time, and ask what it is like in my city. And perhaps you will have written to me, and you will tell me that all is safe, and that I can come home.

The passengers debated excitedly over what they had seen the previous night. Bellis scorned them. The *Terpsichoria* passed through the Candlemaw Straits and into the calmer water of Salkrikaltor. First the lush island of Gnomon Tor loomed into view, and then, before five in the afternoon, Salkrikaltor City came over the horizon.

The sun was very low and the light was thick. The shoreline of Gnomon Tor rose green and massive a few miles north. In a horizontal forest of lengthening shadows, the towers and rooftops of Salkrikaltor City broke the waves.

They were rendered in concrete, in iron, rock and glass, and in sweeps of hardy cold-water coral. Columns spiraled with walkways, linked by spine-thin bridges. Intricate conical spires a hundred feet high, dark square keeps. A mass of contrary styles.

The outlines of the skyline were a child's exuberant sketch of a reef. Organic towers bulged like tubeworm casts. There were analogs of lace corals—high-rise dwellings that branched into scores of thin rooms—and squat many-windowed arenas like gargantuan barrel sponges. Frilled ribbons of architecture like fire coral.

The towers of the submerged city rose a hundred feet above the waves, their shapes uninterrupted. Huge doorways gaped at sea level. Green scum marks marked the height of a tide that would cover them.

There were newer buildings. Ovoid mansions carved from stone and ribbed with iron, suspended above the water on struts that jutted from the submerged roofscape. Floating platforms topped with terraces of square brick houses—like those of New Crobuzon—perched preposterously in the sea.

There were thousands of cray, and a fair number of humans, on the walkways and bridges at water level, and way above. Scores of flat-bottomed barges and boats puttered between the towers.

Oceangoing ships were docked at the town's outskirts, tied up to pillars in the sea. Cogs and junks and clippers, and here and there a steamship. The *Terpsichoria* approached.

"Look there," someone said to Bellis, and pointed downward—the water was absolutely clear. Even in the waning light Bellis could see the wide streets of Salkrikaltor's suburbs far below. They were outlined with cold-looking streetlights. The buildings stopped at least fifty feet from the surface, to ensure clearance for the ships that passed above them.

On the walkways linking the submarine spires Bellis could see yet more citizens, more cray. They scuttled and swam quickly, moving with much more facility than their compatriots above them in the air.

It was an extraordinary place. When they had docked, Bellis watched enviously as the *Terpsichoria*'s boats were lowered. Most of the crew and all the passengers lined up eagerly before the ladders. They grinned and bickered excitedly, casting their eyes toward the city.

It was dusk now. Salkrikaltor's towers were silhouettes; their lit windows reflected in the black water. There were faint sounds on the air: music, shouts, grinding machinery, waves.

"Be back aboard by two in the morning," yelled a sublieutenant. "Stick to the human quarters and whatever else you can find above water. Plenty to do there without risking your lungs."

"Miss Coldwine?"

Bellis turned to Lieutenant Commander Cumbershum.

"Please come with me, miss. The submersible's ready."

CHAPTER FOUR

Constrained within the tiny submersible, a tight tangle of copper tubing and dials, Bellis stretched to see past the obstructions of Cumbershum and Captain Myzovic, and the midshipman at the helm.

One moment the sea was lapping at the bottom of the reinforced front window; then suddenly the vessel pitched, and waves washed over the bulbous glass as the sky disappeared. The sounds of splashing and the faint wail of gulls were instantly gone. The only noise was a buzzing whine as the propeller began to spin.

Bellis was agog.

The sub tilted and moved gracefully down toward unseen rock and sand. A powerful arc light snapped on below its snub nose, opening a cone of illuminated water before them.

Near the bottom, they tilted slightly skyward. The evening light filtered faintly down, blocked by the massive black shadows of ships.

Bellis gazed over the captain's shoulder into the dark water. Her face was impassive, but her hands moved, working with awe. Fish moved in precise waves, ebbing back and forth around the ungainly metal intruder. Bellis could hear her own quick breathing unnaturally loud.

The submersible picked a careful way between the chains dangling like vines from the canopy of vessels above them. The pilot moved levers with an expert grace, and the craft curled up and over a little lip of corroded rock, and Salkrikaltor City appeared.

Bellis gasped.

Everywhere lights were suspended. Globes of cold illumination like frost moons, with no trace of the sepia of New

Crobuzon's gas lamps. The city glowed in the darkening water like a net full of ghostly lights.

The outer edges of the city were low buildings in porous stone and coral. There were other submarines moving smoothly between the towers and above the roofs. The sunken promenades beneath them climbed their way to the distant ramparts and cathedrals of the city's core, a mile or so away, seen very faintly through the sea. There at the heart of Salkrikaltor City were taller edifices that loomed all the way out of the waves. They were no less intricate below the surface. The city was convoluted and interconnected.

Everywhere there were cray. They looked up idly as the sub passed above them. They stood and haggled outside shops festooned with undulating colored cloth; they bickered in little squares of seaweed topiary; they walked along tangled backstreets. They guided carts pulled by extraordinary beasts of burden: sea snails eight feet high. Their children played games, goading caged bass and colorful blenny.

Bellis saw houses that were patched together, half-repaired. Away from the main streets, currents picked at organic rubbish moldering in coral courtyards.

Every motion seemed stretched out in the water. Cray swam over the roofs, flapping their tails in inelegant motion. They stepped off high ledges and sank slowly down, legs braced for landing.

From inside the submersible, the city seemed silent.

They flew slowly toward the monumental architecture at Salkrikaltor's center, disturbing fish and floating scraps. It was a real metropolis, Bellis reflected. It bustled and thronged. Just like New Crobuzon, but cosseted and half hidden by water.

"Housing for officials, that is," Cumbershum pointed out to her. "That's a bank. Factory over there. That's why the cray do such business with New Crobuzon: we can help them with steam technology. Very hard to get going underwater. And this is the central council of the Cray Commonwealth of Salkrikaltor."

The building was intricate. Rounded and bulbous like an impossibly huge brain coral, carved with a covering of folds. The towers jutted way up through the water and into the air. Most of its wings—all marked with coiled serpents and hieroglyph romances—had open windows and doorways in traditional Salkrikaltor style, so that small fish entered and exited unhindered.

But one section was sealed, with small portholes and thick metal doors. From its vents spewed a constant stream of bubbles.

"That's where they meet topsiders," the lieutenant said. "That's where we're heading."

"There's a human minority in Salkrikaltor City's topside," said Bellis slowly. "There are plenty of rooms above water, and the cray can take air without problems for hours at a time. Why do they make us meet them down here?"

"For the same reason we receive the Salkrikaltor ambassador in the reception rooms at Parliament, Miss Coldwine," said the captain, "no matter that it is somewhat hard and inconvenient for him. This is their city; we are mere guests. *We*—" He turned to her and waved his hand to encompass himself and Lieutenant Commander Cumbershum only. "—that is. *We* are guests." He turned slowly away.

You son of a pig, Bellis thought furiously, her face set like ice.

The pilot eased his speed down to almost nothing and maneuvered through a large, dark opening into the wing. They sailed over cray, who directed them on with sweeps of their arms, to the dead end of the concrete corridor. A huge door shut ponderously behind them.

From fat stubby pipes that lined the walls burst a massive unceasing explosion of bubbles. The sea was pushed out through valves and sluices. Slowly the water level fell. The sub settled gradually on the concrete floor and listed to one side. The water came down past the porthole and streaked and streamed it with droplets, and Bellis was staring out into air. With the sea pumped out of it, the room looked shabby.

When the pilot finally undid the screws locking them in, the hatch swung open with a merciful cool blast. The concrete floor was puddled with brine. The room itself smelled of kelp and fish. Bellis stepped from the submersible as the officers adjusted their uniforms.

Behind them stood a cray. She carried a spear—too intricate and flimsy to be anything other than ceremonial, Bellis judged—and wore a breastplate of something vivid green that was not metal. She nodded in greeting.

"Thank her for her welcome," said the captain to Bellis. "Tell her to inform the council leader that we have arrived."

Bellis breathed out and tried to relax. She composed herself and brought back to mind the vocabulary, the grammar and syntax and pronunciation and soul of Salkrikaltor Cray: everything she had learned in those intensive weeks with Marikkatch. She offered a quick, cynical, silent prayer.

Then she formed the vibrato, the cray's clicking barks, audible in air and water, and spoke.

To her intense relief, the cray nodded and responded.

"You will be announced," she said, carefully correcting Bellis' tense. *"Your pilot waits here. You come our way."*

Large, sealed portholes looked out onto a garden of garish sea plants. The walls were covered by tapestries showing famous moments of Salkrikaltor history. The floor was stone slabs—quite dry—warmed by some hidden fire. There were dark ornaments in the room—jet, black coral, black pearl.

Nodding, welcoming the humans, were three he-cray. One, much younger than his companions, stood a little back, just like Bellis.

They were pale. Compared to the cray of Tarmuth, they spent far more of their lives below the water, where the sun could not stain them. All that distinguished cray upper bodies from humans' was the little ruff of gills on the neck, but there was also something alien about their submarine pallor.

Below the waist, the crays' armored hindquarters were those of colossal rock lobsters: huge carapaces of gnarled shell and overlapping somites. Their human abdomens jutted out from above where the eyes and antennae would have been. Even in the air, an alien medium, their multitude of legs worked with intricate grace. They sounded softly as they moved, a gentle percussion of chitin.

They adorned their crustacean hindquarters with a kind of tattoo, carving designs into the shell and staining them with various extracts. The two older cray had an extraordinary array of symbols on their flanks.

One stepped forward and spoke very quickly in Salkrikaltor. There was a moment's silence.

"Welcome," said the young cray behind him, the translator. He spoke Ragamoll with a heavy accent. "We are glad you have come and speak with us."

* * *

The discussion started slowly. Council Leader King Skarakatchi and Councilman King Drood'adji made expressions of polite and ritualistic delight that were matched by Myzovic and Cumbershum. Everyone agreed that it was excellent that they had all met, and that two such great cities remained on such good terms, that trade was such a healthy way of ensuring goodwill, and so on.

The conversation shifted quickly. With impressive smoothness, Bellis found herself translating specifics. The conversation had moved on to how many apples and plums the *Terpsichoria* would leave in Salkrikaltor, and how many bottles of unguent and liquor it would receive in return.

It was not long before matters of state were discussed, information that must come from the upper echelons of New Crobuzon's parliament: details about when and if ambassadors would be replaced, about possible trade treaties with other powers, and how such arrangements would impact on relations with Salkrikaltor.

Bellis found it easy to close her ears to what she said, to pass such information straight through herself. Not out of patriotism or fealty to New Crobuzon's government—of which she felt none—but out of boredom. The secret discussions were incomprehensible, the little snippets of information that Bellis spoke underwhelming and tedious. She thought instead of the tons of water above them, intrigued that she felt no panic.

She worked automatically for some time, forgetting what she said almost immediately it was out of her mouth.

Until suddenly she heard the captain's voice change, and she discovered that she was listening.

"I have one further question, Your Excellency," said Captain Myzovic, sipping his drink. Bellis coughed and barked the Salkrikaltor sounds. "In Qé Banssa, I was ordered to check a bizarre rumor passed on by the New Crobuzon representative. It was so preposterous I was certain there had been a misunderstanding. Nevertheless, I detoured around the Fins—which is why we are late for this meeting.

"During our diversion I discovered to my . . . dismay and concern that the rumors were true. I bring this up because it concerns our good friendship with Salkrikaltor." The captain's voice was hardening. "It is to do with our concerns in Salkrikaltor waters. At the southern edge of the Fins, as the councilors know, are

the . . . vitally important investments for which we pay generous
mooring rights. I am speaking, of course, of our platforms, our
rigs."

Bellis had never heard the word *rigs* used so, and she spoke it
smoothly in Ragamoll. The crays seemed to understand. She
kept her translation automatic and smooth, but Bellis listened in
fascination to every word the captain spoke.

"We passed them after midnight. First one, then another. All
was as it should be, both for the *Manikin* and *Trashstar* rigs. But,
councilors . . ." He sat forward, put down his glass, and stared at
them predatorily. "I have a very important question. *Where is the
other one?*"

The cray officials stared at the captain. With slow, comic simul-
taneity, they looked at each other, then back at Captain Myzovic.

"We confess . . . to confusion, Captain." The translator spoke
softly for his leaders, his voice unchanging, but for the briefest
second Bellis caught his eye. Something passed between them,
some shared astonishment, some camaraderie.

What are we party to, brother? Bellis thought. She was tense,
and craved a cigarillo.

"We have no knowledge of what you speak," her opposite
number continued. "We are not concerned with the platforms, so
long as mooring rental is paid. What has happened, Captain?"

"What has *happened,*" said Captain Myzovic, his voice tight,
"is that the *Sorghum,* our deep-sea rig, our mobile platform, is
gone." He waited for Bellis to catch up with him, and then
waited some more, stretching the silence. "Along, I might add,
with her retinue of five ironclads, her officers, staff, scientists,
and geo-empath.

"The first word that the *Sorghum* was no longer at its mooring
point reached Dancing Bird Island three weeks ago. The crews
of the other rigs were asking why they had not been told of the
Sorghum's orders to relocate. No such order had been given."
The captain put down his glass and stared at the two cray. "The
Sorghum was to remain in situ for another six months at least. It
should be where we left it. Council Leader, Councilor—*what
has happened to our rig?*"

When Skarakatchi spoke, the translator mimicked his soft
tones. "We know nothing."

Captain Myzovic knotted his hands. "This happened barely a

hundred miles away, in Salkrikaltor waters, in a region your navy and hunters regularly patrol, and you know nothing?" His tone was controlled but threatening. "Councilors, that is extraordinary. You have no notion what happened? Whether she sank in a freak squall, if she was attacked and destroyed? Can you tell me that you have heard *nothing*? That something could do this to us just off your coasts, and you are quite ignorant?"

There was a long silence. The two cray leaned in and whispered to each other.

"We hear many rumors . . ." King Skarakatchi said through the translator. Drood'adji looked at them both sharply. "But we have heard nothing of this. We can offer our support and sorrow to our friends of New Crobuzon—but no information."

"I must tell you," Captain Myzovic said after a murmured consultation with Cumbershum, "that I am deeply unhappy. New Crobuzon can no longer pay mooring rights for a rig that is not there. Our rent is hereby to be cut by a third. And I will be sending word back to the city about your inability to offer assistance. This must cast in some doubt the ability of Salkrikaltor to act as custodians of our interests. My government will wish to discuss this further. New arrangements may have to be made. Thank you for your hospitality," he said, and drained his glass. "We will be staying one night in Salkrikaltor harbor. We'll head off early tomorrow morning."

"A moment, please, Captain." The council leader raised his hand. He muttered quickly to Drood'adji, who nodded and scuttled gracefully out of the room. "There is one more matter to discuss."

When Drood'adji returned, Bellis' eyes widened. Behind him walked a human man.

He was so out of place it brought her up short. She stared like a fool.

The man was a little younger than she, with an open, cheerful face. He carried a large pack and wore clean but battered clothes. He smiled disarmingly at Bellis. She frowned slightly and broke eye contact.

"Captain Myzovic?" The man spoke Ragamoll with a New Crobuzon accent. "Lieutenant Commander Cumbershum?" He shook their hands. "And I'm afraid I don't know your name, ma'am," he said, his hand outstretched.

"Miss Coldwine is our translator, sir," said the captain before Bellis could respond. "Your business is with me. Who are you?"

From his jacket the man pulled an official-looking scroll.

"That should explain everything, Captain," he said.

The captain scrutinized it carefully. After half a minute he looked up sharply, waving the scroll disdainfully.

"What, by damn, is this idiocy?" he hissed suddenly, making Bellis start. He jabbed the scroll at Cumbershum.

"I think it makes matters reasonably clear, Captain," said the man. "I have other copies, in case your anger overwhelms you. I'm afraid I'm going to have to commandeer your ship."

The captain gave a hard bark of laughter. "Oh really?" He sounded dangerously tense. "Is that right, Mr. . . ." He leaned over and read the paper in his lieutenant's hands. "Mr. Fennec? Is that *right*?"

Glancing at Cumbershum, Bellis realized that he was staring at the newcomer with astonishment and alarm. He interrupted the captain.

"Sir," he said urgently. "Might I suggest that we thank our hosts and let them return to their business?" He looked meaningfully at the cray. The translator was listening carefully.

The captain hesitated and gave a curt nod. "Please inform our hosts that their hospitality is excellent," he ordered Bellis brusquely. "Thank them for their time. We can find our own way out."

As Bellis spoke, the cray bowed gracefully. The two councilors came forward and shook hands again, to the captain's barely concealed fury. They left the way Mr. Fennec had come in.

"Miss Coldwine?" The captain indicated the door that led back to the submersible. "Wait for us outside, please. This is government business."

Bellis lingered in the corridor, silently cursing. She could hear the captain's bellicose roaring through the door. However she strained, though, she could not make out what was being said.

"Gods*damm*it," she muttered, and returned to the featureless concrete room where the submersible sat like some grotesque wallowing creature. The cray attendant waited idly, softly clucking.

The submersible pilot was picking his teeth. His breath smelled of fish.

Bellis leaned against a wall and waited.

After more than twenty minutes the captain burst through the door, followed by Cumbershum, desperately trying to placate him.

"Just don't fucking speak to me at the moment, Cumbershum, all right?" shouted the captain. Bellis stared, astonished. "Just make sure you keep *Mr. fucking Fennec* out of my sight or I will *not* be responsible for what happens, signed and sealed letter of fucking commission or not."

Behind the lieutenant, Fennec peered around the edge of the door.

Cumbershum gestured Bellis and Fennec quickly into the back of the submersible. He looked panicked. When he sat down in front of Bellis, beside the captain, she saw that he was straining away from Myzovic.

As the sea began to pour back in through the walls of the concrete room, and the sound of hidden engines made the vessel vibrate, the man in the scuffed leather coat turned to Bellis and smiled.

"Silas Fennec," he whispered, and held out his hand. Bellis paused, then took it.

"Bellis," she murmured. "Coldwine."

No one spoke on the journey to the surface. Back on the *Terpsichoria*'s deck, the captain stormed to his office.

"Mr. Cumbershum," he belted. "Bring Mr. Fennec to me."

Silas Fennec saw Bellis watching him. He jerked his head toward the captain's back and for the briefest moment rolled his eyes, then nodded in farewell and trotted off in Myzovic's wake.

Johannes was gone, off somewhere in Salkrikaltor. Bellis looked resentfully across the water at lights that picked out the towers. There were no boats by the *Terpsichoria*'s sides, and no one to row her away from the ship. Bellis brimmed with frustration. Even the mewling Sister Meriope had found the strength to leave the boat.

Bellis went to find Cumbershum. He was watching his men patch up a damaged sail.

"Miss Coldwine." He looked at her without warmth.

"Lieutenant," she said. "I wanted to know how I might place some mail in the New Crobuzon storeroom of which Captain Myzovic told me. I have something urgent to send . . ."

Her voice petered out. He was shaking his head.

"Impossible, Miss Coldwine. I can spare no one to escort you,

I don't have the key and I am *not* asking the captain for it now . . . Would you like me to go on?"

Bellis felt a sting of misery, and she held herself very still.

"Lieutenant," she said slowly, keeping her voice emotionless. "Lieutenant, the captain himself promised me that I might deposit my letter. It is extremely important."

"Miss Coldwine," he interrupted, "if it were down to me I would escort you myself, but I *cannot,* and I am afraid that is an end to the matter. But besides . . ." He looked up furtively, then whispered again. "Besides . . . please don't speak of this but . . . you'll have no need of the warehouse. I can't say any more. You'll understand in a few hours. The captain's called a meeting early tomorrow morning. He'll explain. Believe me, Miss Coldwine. You don't need to deposit your letter here. I give you my word."

What is he implying? Bellis thought, panicked and exhilarated. *What is he godsdamned implying?*

Like most of the prisoners, Tanner Sack never moved far from the space he had claimed. Near the infrequent light from above and also the food, it was sought-after. Twice someone had tried to steal it, moving in on his patch of floor when he had gone to piss or shit. Both times he had managed to persuade the intruder away without a fight.

He remained sitting, his back to the wall, at one edge of the cage, for hours at a time. Shekel never had to go looking for him.

"Oy, Sack!"

Tanner was dozing, and the clouds in his head took a long time to part.

Shekel was grinning at him from beyond the bars. "Wake up, Tanner. I want to tell you about Salkrikaltor."

"Shut up, boy," grumbled a man beside Tanner. "We're trying to sleep."

"Fuck off, Remade cunt," snapped Shekel. "D'you want any food next time I'm here, eh?"

Tanner was waving his hands in placation. "All right, lad, all right," he said, trying to wake up fully. "Tell me about whatever it is, but keep it down, eh?"

Shekel grinned. He was drunk and excited.

"Did you ever see Salkrikaltor City, Tanner?"

"No, lad. I ain't never left New Crobuzon before," Tanner said softly. He kept his voice low, hoping that Shekel would imitate him.

The boy rolled his eyes and sat back. "You take a little boat, and you row past big buildings that come plumb out of the sea. Some places they're close together like trees. And there's massive bridges way above, and sometimes . . . sometimes you see someone—human or cray—just jump. And dive, if they're a human, or tuck in all them legs otherwise, and land in the water and light out swimming, or disappear underneath.

"I was just in a bar in the Landside Quarter. There was . . ." His hands jigged in and out of tight shapes as he illustrated what he was saying. "You just step out of the boat through a big doorway, in a big room, with dancers—woman dancers." He grinned, puerile. "And next to the bar, the floor's fucking gone . . . and there's a ramp, going down for miles into the sea. All lit up underneath. And cray coming and going, up and down that walkway, into the bar or home again, in and out of the water."

Shekel kept grinning and shaking his head.

"One of our geezers gets so drunk he sets off himself." He laughed. "We had to haul him out of it, sopping. I don't know, Tanner . . . I never saw anything like it. They're scrabbling around right now, right underneath us. Right *now*. It's like a dream. The way it sits on the sea, and there's more below than above. It's like it's reflected in the water . . . but they can walk on into the reflection. I want to see it, Tanner," he said urgently. "There's suits and helmets and whatnot on the ship . . . I'd go down in a minute, you know. I'd see it the way they do . . ."

Tanner was trying to think of something to say, but he was still tired. He shook his head and tried to remember any of Crawfoot's Chronicles that told of life in the sea. Before he could speak, though, Shekel swayed to his feet.

"I better go, Tanner," he said. "Captain's put signs up everywhere. Assemble in the morning, important instructions, blah de blah. I'd best get shut-eye."

By the time Tanner remembered the story of Crawfoot and the Conch Assassins, Shekel had disappeared.

CHAPTER FIVE

When Bellis rose the next day, the *Terpsichoria* was in the middle of the open ocean.

It was growing less cold as they traveled east, and the passengers who congregated for the captain's announcement no longer wore their heaviest coats. The crew stood in the shadow of the mizzenmast, the officers by the stairway to the bridge.

The newcomer, Silas Fennec, stood alone. He saw Bellis watching him and smiled at her.

"Have you met him?" said Johannes Tearfly, behind her. He was rubbing his chin and watching Fennec with interest. "You were with the captain below, weren't you? When Mr. Fennec appeared?"

Bellis shrugged and looked away. "We didn't speak," she said.

"Do you have any idea why we've diverted?" Johannes asked. Bellis frowned to show that she did not understand. He looked at her with exasperation. "The sun," he said slowly. "It's on our left. We're heading south. We're going the wrong way."

When the captain appeared above them on the stairs, the murmurs on deck silenced. He hefted a copper funnel to his lips.

"Thank you for assembling so quickly." His raised voice echoed tinnily above them in the wind. "I have unsettling news." He put down the mouthpiece for a moment and seemed to consider what to say. When he spoke again he sounded pugnacious. "Let me say that I will brook no argument or dissent. This is not for discussion. I am responding to unforeseen circumstances, and I will not be questioned. We will not be heading to Nova Esperium. We are returning to Iron Bay."

There was a burst of shock and outrage from the passengers, and mutters of bewilderment from the crew. *He can't do this!* thought Bellis. She felt a surge of panic—but no surprise. She realized that she had been expecting this, since Cumbershum's hint. She realized, too, that somewhere inside her there was a joy at the thought of return. She battened that feeling down hard. *It won't be a homecoming for me,* she thought savagely. *I have to get away. What am I going to do?*

"Enough!" the captain shouted. "As I *said,* I do not take this decision lightly." He raised his voice over shouted protests. "Within the week we'll be back in Iron Bay, where alternative arrangements will be made for paying passengers. You may have to sail with another ship. I'm aware that this will add a month to your voyage, and I can only offer apologies."

Grim-faced and livid, he looked totally unapologetic. "Nova Esperium will have to survive a few more weeks without you. Passengers are confined to the poop deck until three o'clock. Crew remain for new orders." He put down the speaking trumpet and descended toward the deck.

For a moment he was the only thing moving. Then the stillness broke and there was a surge as several passengers strode forward, against his orders, demanding that he change his mind. The captain's barks of outrage could be heard as they reached him.

Bellis was staring at Silas Fennec. Piecing it together.

His face was immobile as he observed the agitation. He noticed Bellis watching him, held her eyes for a moment, then walked unhurriedly away.

Johannes Tearfly looked absolutely stricken. He gaped in an almost comical show of dismay.

"What's he *doing*?" he said. "What's he *talking* about? I can't wait another fortnight in the rain of Iron Bay! Godspit! And why are we heading south? He's taking the long route past the Fins again . . . What is going *on*?"

"He's looking for something," said Bellis, just loud enough for him to hear. She took his elbow and gently led him away from the crowd. "And I wouldn't waste your breath on the captain. You won't hear him admit it, but I don't think he has the slightest choice."

The captain strode from rail to rail on deck, snapping out a telescope and scouring the horizon. Officers shouted instructions to the men in the crow's nests. Bellis watched the bewilderment and rumor-mongering of the passengers.

"The man's a disgrace," she overheard, "screaming at paying passengers like that."

"I was standing outside the captain's office, and I heard some-one accuse him of wasting time—of disobeying orders," Miss Cardomium reported, bewildered. "How can that be?"

It's Fennec, thought Bellis. *He's angry because we're not go-ing directly back. Myzovic is . . . what? Looking for evidence of the* Sorghum, *on the way.*

The sea beyond the Fins was darker, more powerful, and cold—unbroken by rocks. The sky was wan. They were beyond Basilisk Channel. This was the edge of the Swollen Ocean. Bellis stared at the endless green waves with distaste. She felt ver-tiginous. She imagined three, four, five thousand miles of brine yawning away eastward, and closed her eyes. The wind butted her insistently.

Bellis realized she was thinking again about the river, the slow stretch of water that connected New Crobuzon to the sea like an umbilicus.

When Fennec reappeared, walking quickly across the poop deck, Bellis intercepted him. "Mr. Fennec," she said.

His face opened as he saw her. "Bellis Coldwine," he said. "I hope you're not too put out by the detour."

She indicated for him to follow her out of earshot of the few passengers and crew around them. She stopped in the shadow of the ship's enormous chimney.

"I'm afraid I am, Mr. Fennec," she said. "My plans are quite specific. This is a serious problem for me. I have no idea when I'll be able to find another ship that wants my services." Silas Fennec inclined his head in vague sympathy. He was clearly distracted.

Bellis spoke again. "I wonder if you'd shed light on the forced change of plans that has our captain so angry." She hesitated. "Will you tell me what is happening, please?"

Fennec raised his eyebrows. "I can't, Miss Coldwine," he said, his voice mild.

"Mr. Fennec," she muttered coldly, "you've seen the reaction of our passengers; you know how unpopular this diversion is. Don't you think I—all of us, but I most of all—deserve some ex-planation? Can't you think what would happen if I were to tell the others what I suspect—that this whole mess was instigated because of the mysterious newcomer—" Bellis spoke quickly, trying to provoke or shame him into telling her the truth, but her voice stopped short when she saw his reaction. His face changed suddenly and utterly.

His amiable, mildly sly expression went hard. He held up a finger to hush her. He looked quickly around, then spoke to her fast. He sounded sincere and very urgent.

"Miss Coldwine," he said. "I understand your anger, but you must listen to me."

She drew herself up, meeting his gaze.

"You must withdraw that threat. I won't appeal to your professional code or your bloody honor," he whispered. "Probably you're as cynical about such things as I am. But I will appeal to *you*. I have no idea what you've worked out or guessed, but let me tell you that it is *vital*—do you understand?—that I get back to New Crobuzon quickly, without interruption, without fuss." There was a long pause.

"There is . . . there is a vast amount at stake, Miss Coldwine. You cannot spread mischief. I am begging you to keep these things to yourself. I'm relying on you to be discreet."

He was not threatening her. His face and voice were stern but not aggressive. As he claimed, he was begging, not trying to intimidate her into submission. He spoke to her like a partner, a confidante.

And impressed and shocked by his fervor, she realized that she *would* keep what she had heard to herself.

He saw this decision move across her face and nodded in sharp thanks before walking away.

In her cabin, Bellis tried to work out what she was going to do. It would not be safe for her to stay long in Tarmuth. She had to join a ship as soon as possible. Her gut was heavy with hope that she might make it to Nova Esperium, but she realized with an awful foreboding that she was no longer in a position to make a choice.

She felt no shock. She simply realized, rationally and slowly, that she would have to go wherever she could. She could not delay.

Alone, away from the fug of anger and confusion that had swept over the rest of the ship, Bellis felt all her hope was dried up. She felt desiccated like old paper, as if the blustery air on the deck would burst her and blow her away.

Her partial knowledge of the captain's secrets was no comfort. She had never felt more homeless.

She cracked the seal on her letter, sighed, and began to add to its last page.

Skullday 6th Arora, 1779. Evening, she wrote. *Well, my dear, who would have thought this? A chance to add a little more.*

It comforted her. Although the arch tone she used was an affectation, it consoled her, and she did not stop writing while Sister Meriope returned and went to bed. She continued by the light of the tiny oil lamp, hinting at conspiracy and secrets, while the Swollen Ocean gnawed monotonously on the *Terpsichoria's* iron.

Confused shouting woke Bellis at seven o'clock the next morning. Still lacing up her boots, she stumbled with several other sleepy passengers out into the light. She squinted into the brightness.

Sailors pushed up against the port railings, gesticulating and shouting. Bellis followed their gazes to the horizon and realized that they were looking *up.*

A man was hanging motionless in the sky, two hundred feet above them, out over the sea.

Bellis gasped idiotically.

The man kicked his legs like a baby and stared at the boat. He seemed to stand in the air. He was strapped in a harness, dangling just below a taut balloon.

He fiddled with his belt and something, some ballast, fell away, spinning lazily into the sea. He jerked and rose forty feet. With the faint sound of a propellor he moved in an inelegant curve. He began a long, unsteady circuit of the *Terpsichoria.*

"Get back to your godsdamned stations!" The crew broke up industriously at the sound of the captain's voice. He strode out onto the main deck and peered at the slowly turning figure through his telescope. The man hovered near the top of the masts in a vaguely predatory manner.

The captain yelled up at the aviator through the funnel. "You there . . ." His voice carried well. Even the sea seemed quiet. "This is Captain Myzovic of the *Terpsichoria,* steamer in the New Crobuzon Merchant Navy. You are requested to touch down and make yourself known to me. If you do not comply I will consider it a hostile action. You have one minute to begin a descent or we will defend ourselves."

"Jabber," Johannes whispered. "Have you ever seen anything like that? He's too far out to have come from land. He's got to be scouting from some ship, out of sight over the horizon."

The man continued to circle above them, and for seconds the buzzing of his engine was the only sound.

Eventually Bellis spoke. "Pirates?" she whispered.

"Possible." Johannes shrugged. "But the freebooters out here couldn't take a ship our size, or with our guns. They go for smaller merchants, the wooden hulls. And if it's privateers . . ." He pursed his lips. "Well, if they're licensed by Figh Vadiso or wherever, then they just might have the firepower to engage us, but they'd be insane to risk war with New Crobuzon. The Pirate Wars are over, for Jabber's sake!"

"Right!" the captain shouted. "This is your last warning." Four musketeers had stationed themselves at the rail. They took aim at the airborne visitor.

Instantly the sound of his motor changed. The man jerked and began to move erratically away from the ship.

"Fire, dammit!" shouted the captain, and the muskets sounded, but the man had sped up and away and beyond their aim. For a long time he receded, sinking slowly toward the horizon. Nothing was visible in the direction the aeronaut was headed.

"His ship must be twenty miles away or more," said Johannes. "It'll take him at least an hour to reach it."

The captain was yelling at the crew, organizing them into units and arming them, stationing them around the ship's edge. They fingered their rifles nervously, staring across the slowly moving sea.

Cumbershum trotted up toward the congregated passengers and ordered them back to their cabins or to the mess. His tone was curt.

"The *Terpsichoria* is more than a match for any pirate, and that scout could easily see that," he said. "But until we're back behind the Fins, the captain insists that you remain out of the way of the crew. *Now,* please."

Bellis sat for a long while with her letter in her pocket. She smoked and drank water and tea in the half-empty mess. At first the air was tense, but after an hour fear had dissipated somewhat. She began to read.

And then there were muffled shouts and the vibration of

running feet. Bellis spilled her dregs and ran with the other passengers to the window.

Racing toward them out of the sea were a handful of dark shapes.

Squat little ironclad scouts.

"They're lunatics!" hissed Dr. Mollificatt. "There's, what, five of them? They can't take us!"

A shattering boom sounded from the deck of the *Terpsichoria,* and the sea yards in front of the leading boat exploded in a huge crater of steam and water.

"That's a warning shot," someone said. "But they're not turning."

The little craft drove on through the violent spray, hurtling suicidally toward the big iron ship. There was the sound of more running from above, more shouted orders.

"This is going to be hideous," grimaced Dr. Mollificatt, and as he spoke the *Terpsichoria* yawed violently with the grind of metal on metal.

In the hold, Tanner Sack fell violently across his neighbor. There was a massed shout of fear. As the Remade smacked into each other, scabs and infected flesh broke open. There were shrieks of pain.

Penned in the dark, the prisoners felt the ship uprooted suddenly from the sea.

"What's happening?" they screamed toward the hatches. *"What's going on? Help us!"*

They stumbled and kicked and clawed their way to the bars, crushing each other against the iron. There were more screams, and louder panic.

Tanner Sack shouted with his fellows.

No one came to them.

The ship reeled as if it had been punched. Bellis was hurled against the window. Passengers were scattering, screaming or shouting, getting to their feet with terror in their eyes, throwing spilled chairs and stools out of the way.

"What in *Jabber's name* was that?" Johannes shouted. Someone nearby was praying.

Bellis stumbled with the others out onto the deck. The little armored boats were still plowing toward the *Terpsichoria* on the port side, but looming from nowhere on the *starboard* side, where no one had been looking, tight and flush against the ship, was a massive black submersible.

It was more than a hundred feet long, striated with pipes, studded with segmented metal fins. Seawater still streamed from it, from the seams between its rivets and the ridges below its portholes.

Bellis gaped at the baleful-looking thing. Sailors and officers were shouting in confusion, running from rail to rail, trying to regroup.

Two hatches on the top of the submersible began to rise.

"You!" From the deck, Cumbershum pointed at the passengers. *"Inside, now!"*

Bellis retreated into the corridor.

Jabber help me oh dear gods *oh spit and shit,* she thought in a confused stream. She stared wildly about and heard passengers running pointlessly from place to place.

Then suddenly she remembered the little cupboard, from where she could see the deck.

Outside, beyond the thin wall, she could hear shouts and gunshots. Frantically, she cleared the shelf in front of the window and put her eyes to the dirty pane.

Bursts of smoke discolored the air. Men ran past the glass in panicked rout. Beyond them and below, across the deck, little groups of men fought in confused and ugly battle.

The invaders were mostly men and cactus-people, a few tough-looking women, and Remade. They were dressed in ostentatious and outlandish gear: long colorful coats and pantaloons, high boots, and studded belts. What distinguished them from the pirates of pantomime or cheap prints was the grime and age of their clothes, the fixed determination in their faces and the organized efficiency of their attacks.

Bellis saw everything with impossible detail. She perceived it as a series of tableaux, like heliotypes flashed up one after the other in the dark. The sound seemed disassociated from what she saw, a wiry buzz of noise at the back of her skull.

She saw the captain and Cumbershum screaming orders from the forecastle, firing their pistols and frantically reloading. Blue-clad sailors fought with inexpert desperation. A cactacae midshipman threw down his broken blade and felled one of the buccaneers with a massive punch, roared with pain as the man's comrade hacked deep into his forearm in a spray of sap. A group of terrified men attacked the pirates with muskets and bayonets, hesitated, and were caught between two Remade with massive blunderbusses. The young sailors went down screaming in a rain of ragged flesh and shrapnel.

Buzzing sedately between the masts, Bellis saw suspended figures, three or four of them, harnessed to balloons like the first scout, flying low over the fighting, firing flintlocks into the crowd.

Gore stained the deck.

There was more and more screaming. Bellis was trembling. She bit her lip. There was something unreal about the scene. The violence was grotesque and hideous, but in the wide eyes of the sailors Bellis saw bewilderment, a doubt that this could possibly be happening.

The pirates fought with heavy scimitars and squat pistols. In their multicolored clothes they looked like rabble, but they were quick and disciplined, and they fought like an army.

"Dammit!" shouted Captain Myzovic, then looked up and fired. One of the dangling balloonists jerked, and his head snapped back in an arc of blood. His hands clutched spastically at his belt, releasing ballast like heavy droppings. The corpse began to rise, swiftly, spiraling into the clouds.

The captain gesticulated frantically. "Regroup, for *fuck*'s sake," he shouted. "Take that bastard on the poop deck!"

Bellis twisted her head, but she could not quite see the captain's target. She heard him, though, close to her, giving terse orders. The invaders responded, breaking off skirmishes to form tight units, targeting officers, trying to break the line of sailors blocking their way to the bridge.

"Surrender!" shouted the voice beside her window. "Surrender and this finishes now!"

"Dispatch that bastard!" the captain shouted to his crew.

Five or six sailors ran past Bellis' window, swords and pistols drawn. There was a moment of silence, then a thud and a faint crackling.

"Oh *Jabber* . . ." The cry was hysterical, but it broke off suddenly in a retching exhalation. There was a blossoming of screams.

Two of the men stumbled back into Bellis' view, and she cried out aghast. They collapsed to the deck in great gouts of blood, and died quickly. Their clothes and bodies were savaged with an incredible number of wounds, as if they had been outnumbered by hundreds of enemies. There was not a six-inch space on any of them that was not scored with some deep gash. Their heads were shredded flesh and bone.

Bellis was transfixed. She trembled, her hands at her mouth. There was something deeply unnatural about those wounds. They seemed to shiver between states, deep rends that were suddenly insubstantial and dreamlike. But the blood that pooled below them was quite real, and the men were really dead.

The captain was staring in shock. Bellis heard a thousand overlapping whispers of air. There were two blubbering screams, and wet drumbeats as bodies fell.

The last of the sailors ran past Bellis, back the way he had come, howling in terror. A hurled flintlock smacked solidly into the back of his head. He fell to his knees.

"You godsforsaken swine!" Captain Myzovic was screaming. His voice sounded outraged and deeply afraid. *"You demon-loving bastard!"*

Paying him no attention, a grey-clad man walked slowly into Bellis' field of vision. He was not tall. He moved with studied poise, carrying his heavily muscled body as if he were a much more slender man. He wore leather armor, a dark charcoal outfit studded with pockets, belts, and holsters. It was streaked and streaked with blood. Bellis could not see his face.

He walked toward the fallen man, holding a straight sword stained completely red and dribbling thickly.

"Surrender," he said quietly to the man before him, who looked up in terror and sobbed, fumbled idiotically for his knife.

The grey-clad man spun instantly in the air, his arms and legs bent. He twirled as if he were dancing and stamped out quickly, the bottom of his foot slamming into the fallen man's face and smashing him back. The sailor sprawled, bleeding, unconscious or dead. As the man in grey landed he was instantly still. It was as if he had not moved.

"Surrender," he shouted, very loud, and the men of the *Terpsichoria* faltered.

They were losing the fight.

Bodies lay like litter, and dying men screamed for help. Most of the dead wore the blue of the New Crobuzon Merchant Navy. Every second more pirates emerged from the submersible and the armored tugs. They surrounded the *Terpsichoria*'s men, corralled them on the main deck.

"Surrender," shouted the man again, his accent unfamiliar. "Throw down your weapons and we'll end this. Raise your hands against us and we'll cull you until you hear sense."

"Gods *fuck and blast* it . . ." shouted Captain Myzovic, but the pirate commander interrupted him.

"How many of your men would you kill, Captain?" he said, projecting his voice like an actor. "Order them to drop their weapons now, and they need not feel like traitors. Otherwise you order them to die." He drew out a thick pad of felt from his pocket and began to wipe his blade. "Decide, Captain."

The deck was silent. There was only the faint sound of engines from the aeronauts.

Myzovic and Cumbershum huddled in conversation for a second, and then the captain looked out at his bewildered, frightened men and threw up his hands.

"Drop your weapons," he shouted. There was a pause before his men obeyed. Muskets and pistols and short swords smacked dully against the deck. "You have the advantage, sir," he yelled.

"Stay where you are, Captain," shouted the man in grey. "I'll come to you." He spoke quickly in Salt to the pirates standing with him in front of the window. Faintly, Bellis heard a word that sounded like "passengers," and adrenaline made her giddy.

Bellis huddled still and quiet while she heard shrieks from the corridors beyond, as the pirates led the passengers outside.

She heard Johannes Tearfly, the pitiful tears of Meriope, the frightened pomposity of Dr. Mollificatt. She heard a shot followed by a terrified scream.

From outside, Bellis could hear the terrified passengers lamenting as they were ordered onto the main deck.

The pirates were thorough. Bellis was silent, but she could hear the slamming of doors as the passages were searched. She tried desperately to wedge the door closed, but the man in the corridor shouldered it open with ease; and faced with him all grim and bloodstained, faced with his machete, she lost any heart for resistance. She dropped the bottle with which she had armed herself and let him haul her out.

The crew were lined up, almost a hundred of them, in wounded misery at one end of the deck. Their dead had been thrown over the side. The passengers were huddled together, a little way apart. Some of them, like Johannes, had bloody noses and bruises.

In the middle of the passengers, nondescript in brown and looking as subdued and miserable as all the others, was Silas Fennec. He kept his head down. He would not meet Bellis' furtive gaze.

In the center of the deck stood the *Terpsichoria*'s stinking cargo: the scores of Remade brought up from below. They were totally confused, myopic in the light, staring in confusion at the pirates.

The flamboyant invaders swung from the rigging or swept debris into the sea. They surrounded the deck and trained their guns and bows on their captives.

It had taken a long time to bring up all the terrified, bewildered Remade. When the fetid holds were checked, several dead bodies were found. They were dropped into the sea, where their metal limbs and additions took them very quickly down and out of the light.

The huge submersible still lolled fatly in the water, clamped close to the *Terpsichoria*. The two vessels bobbed in time.

The man in grey, the pirates' leader, turned slowly to face his captives. It was the first time Bellis had seen his face.

He was in his late thirties, she guessed, with cropped greying hair. Strong featured. His deep-set eyes were melancholy, his mouth set taut and sad.

Bellis stood next to Johannes, near the silent officers. The leather-clad man walked toward the captain. As he passed the passengers, he looked directly at Johannes for two or three paces, then slowly away.

"So," said Captain Myzovic, loud enough for many people to hear. "The *Terpsichoria* is yours. I take it that you intend ransom? I might as well tell you, sir, that whichever power you represent has made a grave mistake. New Crobuzon will not take kindly to this."

The pirate leader was still.

"No, Captain," he said. Now that he was not shouting over battle, his voice was soft, almost feminine. Like his face, it seemed stained by some tragedy. "Not ransom. The power I represent cares not at all about New Crobuzon, Captain." He met Myzovic's eyes and shook his head slowly and solemnly. "Not at all."

He reached behind him, without looking, and one of his men handed him a big flintlock pistol. He held it in front of him expertly, squinting at it briefly and checking the pan.

"Your men are brave, but they are not soldiers," he said, hefting the weapon. "Will you look away, Captain?"

There were seconds of silence before Bellis' stomach pitched and her legs almost buckled as she understood what he meant.

Realization hit the captain and others at the same moment. There were gasps as Myzovic's eyes widened, and his face crawled with anger and terror. The emotions crowded each other out in an ugly battle. His mouth twisted, opened, and closed.

"No I will *not* look away, sir," he shouted finally, and Bellis' breath caught at the sound of it, the hysteria and shock that broke his voice. "I will *not,* damn and fuck you, sir, you fucking *coward,* sir, you *shit . . .*"

The man in grey nodded.

"As you wish," he said. He raised the gun and shot Captain Myzovic through the eye.

There was a short crack and a burst of blood and bone as the captain spasmed backward, his ruined face snarling and stupid.

As he hit the ground there was a chorus of screams and disbelieving gasps. Beside Bellis, Johannes staggered, making guttural sounds. Bellis retched and swallowed, her breath coming very fast as she stared at the dead man twitching in a slick of gore. She bent, afraid she might vomit.

Somewhere behind her Sister Meriope stammered Darioch's Lament.

The murderer handed the gun back, received another newly primed and loaded. He turned back to the officers.

"Oh Jabber," Cumbershum crooned, his voice shaking. He stared at Myzovic's body, then looked at the pirate. "Oh dear Jabber," he whimpered, and closed his eyes. The man in grey shot him through the temple.

"Gods!" someone shouted hysterically. The officers were yelling, looking wildly around, trying to back away. The thunder of those two gunshots seemed to haunt the deck like ghost sounds.

People were screaming. Some of the officers had fallen to their knees in supplication. Bellis was hyperventilating.

The man in grey quickly scaled the ladder to the forecastle and looked out over the deck.

"The killing," he shouted through cupped hands, *"is over."*

He waited for the frightened sounds to abate.

"The killing is over," he repeated. "That's all the killing we need to do. Do you hear? It is finished."

He spread his arms as noise began to grow again, this time of bewilderment and untrusting relief.

"Listen to me," he shouted. "I have an announcement. You, in blue, you sailors of the New Crobuzon Merchant Navy. Your navy days are over. You lieutenants and sublieutenants, you must reconsider your stations. There's no room where we're going for those who venerate their New Crobuzon commissions." With desperate, panicked slyness, Bellis slid a glance at Fennec. He was gazing at his knotted hands with fierce intensity.

"You . . ." continued the man, gesturing at the men and women from the holds. "You are no longer Remade, no longer slaves. You . . ." He looked at the passengers. "Your plans for your new life must change."

He gripped the deck and swept his eyes over his mystified prisoners. Slow channels of blood reached toward them from the cadavers of the captain and his first officer.

"You must come with me," the man said, just loud enough for everyone to hear. "To a new city."

INTERLUDE I
Elsewhere

Unclear things glide and grapple rocks, pulling their way through the water.

They move in the night through sea opaque with darkness, through cultivated fields of kelp and seaweed toward the lights of cray villages that scatter the shallows. They slide silently into the kraals.

Penned seals glimpse them and taste the eddies of distorted water that spin off in their wakes, and in a panicked frenzy twist and hurl themselves against the woven walls and roofs of their cages. The intruders peer like curious goblins through the gouged window holes of huts and terrify the inhabitants, who rush out on their segmented legs wielding pitchforks and spears, fearfully jabbing.

The cray farmers are quickly overcome.

They are held, captured and held still, and questioned. Lulled by thaumaturgy, persuaded by violence, the cray mutter answers to hissed questions.

In haphazard shards of information, the sinuous hunters learn things that they need to know.

They hear about the shelled submersibles from Salkrikaltor that cruise the villages of the Basilisk Channel. Patrolling a thousand miles of water, watching the nebulous borders of the cray commonwealth's influence. Watching for intruders.

The hunters bicker and brood and caucus.

We know where he came from.

But perhaps he does not return.

There is uncertainty. To his home, or east—out?

The trail forks, and there is only one thing to do. The hunters separate into two contingents. One heads southwest for the shallow water, for Iron Bay and Tarmuth and the drooling dilute salt of the Gross Tar estuary, to watch and listen, to wait for word, to spy and hide, and seek word.

With a flutter of displaced water they are gone.

The other group, with a more uncertain task, heads away and down.

They swim low, heading for the crushing deeps.

INTERLUDE II
Bellis Coldwine

Oh. Oh where are we going?

Locked in our cabins and questioned blank-faced, as if these murderous men these pirates were census takers or bureaucrats or . . . —Name? they ask, and—Occupation? Then they want to know my—Reason for heading to Nova Esperium? and I think I will laugh in their faces.

Where are we fucking going?

They take long notes, they itemize me on their printed forms, then turn to Sister Meriope and do the same for her. They respond the same way to the linguist and the nun, with little nods and points of clarification.

Why can we keep our things? Why do they not strip the jewelry from me rape me or run me through? No weapons, they tell us, and no money and no books, but our other belongings we can keep, and they rummage through our sea chests (a halfhearted search) and take out daggers and bills and monographs and dirty my clothes but leave what else they find. They leave letters, boots, pictures, and all accumulated tat.

I argue for my books. I can't let you take them I say, let me keep them they're mine, some I wrote, and they let me keep the blank-paged notebook but the printed ones, the stories the textbooks the long novel they take from me. Effortlessly. They don't care when I show them that B. Coldwine is me. They take the Coldwines away.

And I don't know why. I cannot make sense of what they are doing.

Sister Meriope sits and prays, muttering her sacred suras, and I am surprised and pleased that she is not weeping.

We are kept inside and time to time they come to us with tea and food, not rude nor pleasant, disinterested as zookeepers. I want to get out I tell them. I rap sharp on my door and I must visit the privy I say, and peer around the door frame and the guard in my corridor bellows at me to get inside, and brings me a bucket which Sister Meriope stares at in mortification. I don't care, I was lying, I wanted to find Johannes or Fennec, I want to see what is happening elsewhere.

All over, sounds of feet and half-heard discussion in a language I almost understand.—North-north-east I hear and other side of the deck and—Ever? I couldn't tell and—where's His Guardship gone? and then I hear more that is opaque.

Through the porthole by my head I see nothing but squalls above water, darkness above and below. I smoke and smoke.

And when my cigarillos are finished I lie back and realize I'm not waiting to die, I don't believe I'll die, I am waiting for something else.

To arrive. To understand. To be at my destination.

I realize with some surprise as I watch sundown's greasepaint that I am closing my eyes and I am bone tired and godspit really? really will I? I will, I will sleep I

sleep

unquiet but long, sleeping eyes flickering with Meriope's religious whimpers, opening sometimes but still

asleep

till with a rush of panic I sit up and look out at a brightening sea.

Morning is coming. I have missed the night, hiding away in my dreaming head.

I dress carefully. I rub my long boots clean. I paint my face as always and tie back my hair.

It is half past six when a cactus man knocks at our door and brings us gruel. As we sip he tells us what will happen.—We are nearly arrived he says.—When we have tied up follow the other passengers, listen for your names and go where you are told, and you'll . . . but I lose track, I lose track, we will what? Will we understand then? Will we know then what is happening?

Where are we going?

I pack my belongings away and prepare to disembark somewhere, somewhere. I am thinking of Fennec. What is he doing and where is he, so quiet when the captain was killed (blood bursting)? He would not want it known that he has a commission, that he can command ships, reschedule ocean crossings.

(I hold him in my hands.)

Out. Into a quick bright wind. It worries at me insistently.

My eyes are like a cave-thing's. I have learnt to see in the drab brown light of my cabin and this morning startles me. My eyes are teary and I blink and blink and the sea clouds run from me above. Everywhere I can hear the soft applause of waves. I can taste salt in my air.

Around me are the others, Mollificatt and Cardomiums one and two. Murrigan and Ettenry and Cohl Gimgewry Yoreling Tearfly my Johannes glimpsing at me swiftly and with a sudden smile before swept away in a crowd, and Fennec somewhere his head down still, and all of us look made of roughcut paper in this light. We are made of baser stuff than the rest of the day. It ignores us with the arrogance of a fucking child.

I want to shout to Johannes but he's been taken away by the current of us and with my newly clear eyes I look and look.

I struggle with my sea chest, stumbling, hobbling the deck's length. I feel battered by the light and air and I look up again and see birds arcing. I struggle forward and keep them in my sights and they wheel over us, passing to starboard, and they head erratically for the horizon and I see masts in their flight path. I have been avoiding this. I have not yet looked to the side of the ship, I have not seen where we are. My destination has been skulking beyond the corner of my eye but now as I watch the gulls it leaps into view.

It is everywhere. How could I not see?

Someone is shouting names as we shuffle past, splitting us into groups and handing out instructions, complex orders but I am not listening because I am looking out over

Dear Jabber

My name is called and I am here next to Johannes again but I am not looking at him because

I am watching

mast upon mast and sail and tower and

on and more

We are here

beside this forest

Godspit Jabber and fuck
a trick a trick of perspective
a city that moves and ripples and slops endlessly side to side
  —Miss Coldwine someone says coldly but I cannot, not now I
am looking, *and I have put down my chest and I am* looking
  and someone is shaking Johannes' hand and he stares at them
bemused as they speak to him.—Dr. Tearfly, you are most wel-
come this is indeed an honor, but I am not listening because we
are here *we have arrived and* look at it all *look at it*
  Oh I'll I'll I could laugh or spew as my stomach yaws look we
are here we are here
  We are here.

PART TWO

Salt

CHAPTER SIX

There were lamps under the water. Green, grey, cold white, and amber globes of cray design, tracing the undersides of the city.

Light prickled on suspended particles. It came not only from the thousand knots of illumination but from corridors of early sunlight that angled down, picking out passages from the waves to the deep water. Fish and kree circled them and passed through them dumbly.

From below, the city was an archipelago of shadows.

It was irregular and sprawling and hugely complex. It displaced currents. Jags of keel contradicted each other in all directions. Anchor chains trailed like hair, snapped and forgotten. From its orifices billowed refuse; fecal matter and particulate, and oil eddying uneasily and rising in small slicks. A constant drool of trash fouled the water and was swallowed by it.

Below the city there were a few hundred yards of rapidly thinning light, then miles of dark water.

The underside of Armada was crisscrossed with life.

Fish eddied through its architecture. Fleeting newtlike figures moved with intellect and purpose between boltholes. There were wire mesh cages tucked into hollows and dangling from chains, crowded with fat cod and tunny. Cray dwellings like coral tumors.

Beyond the edges of the city, and below it at the far reaches of light, huge half-tame seawyrms corkscrewed and fed. Submersibles droned—rigid shadows. A dolphin made constant vigilant rounds. A moving ecology and politics were tethered to the city's calcified base.

The sea around it resonated with noise made physical: staccato clicks and the vibrations of pounding metal, the swallowed sound of watery friction as currents rubbed against each other. Barks that dissipated when they reached the air.

* * *

Among those that gripped and dangled underneath the city were scores of men and women. They fumbled in dragged-out time, clumsy beside the elegant fronds and sponges.

The water was cold, and the topsiders wore rubberized leather suits and massive helmets of copper and tempered glass, tethered to the surface by tubes of air. They hung on ladders and guy ropes, poised precariously over an unthinkable space.

Stuck tight inside their helmets, they were cut off from sound, and each of them moved ponderously alongside their fellows, quite alone. They clambered like lice across a pipe that poked into the dim sea like an inverted chimney. It was a thriving patchwork of algae and shells in extraordinary shades. Weeds and stinging filigree smothered it like ivy and dangled out and down, fingering the plankton.

There was a diver whose chest was bare, from which two long tentacles extruded, waving in the current, but also according to their own faint inclinations.

It was Tanner Sack.

Pumping its tail, the dolphin plunged up past the edges of the city, out and up toward the light. He burst through decreasing water pressure and out into the air, jackknifing, suspended in spray, fixing the city with a cunning eye.

Below again, he curled back through striae of water. Huge shapes were dimly visible some way off, unclear through water and a shimmering of thaumaturgy. Patrolled by tethered sharks, they were not to be investigated. The eye could not focus on them.

There were no divers upon them.

Bellis came out of sleep to the sound of voices.

It was weeks since she had arrived in Armada.

Every morning was the same. Waking and sitting up, waiting, looking around her little room with an incredulity, a shuddering disbelief that would not stop. It welled up even stronger than the longing with which she missed New Crobuzon.

How did I get here? The question was constant in her.

She opened her curtains, gripped her windowsill, and stood staring out over the city.

* * *

When they had arrived, on the first day, they had stood huddled with their belongings on the *Terpsichoria*'s deck, surrounded by guards, and by women and men with checklists and paperwork. The faces of the pirates were hard, made cruel by weather. Through her fear, Bellis watched carefully, and could make no sense of them. They were disparate, a mixture of ethnicities and cultures. Their skins were all different colors. Some were scarified in abstract designs; some wore batik robes. They looked as if they shared nothing except their grim demeanor.

When they stiffened suddenly into a kind of attention, Bellis knew their superiors had arrived. Two men and a woman were standing by the ship's rail. The murderer—the grey-armored leader of the raiding party—stepped up to join them. His clothes and sword were now quite clean.

The younger man and the woman stepped forward to the swordsman. When Bellis saw them she could only stare.

The man wore a dark grey suit; the woman a simple blue dress. They were tall and held themselves with immense authority. The man had a trim mustache and an easy arrogance. The woman's features were heavy and irregular, but the flesh of her mouth was sensual, the cruel cast of her eyes compelling.

What had made Bellis stare at them both with fascination and distaste, what commanded her attention, were the scars.

Curling down the outside of the woman's face, from the corner of her left eye to the corner of her mouth. Fine and uninterrupted. Another, thicker and shorter and more jagged, swept from the right side of her nose across her cheek and curled up as if to cup her eye. And others, contoured to her face. They disfigured her ocher skin with esthetic precision.

Flickering her eyes from the woman to the man, Bellis had felt something curdle inside her. *What fucking unhealthiness is this?* she had thought uneasily.

He was adorned with identical, but mirrored marks. A long curved cicatrix down the right side of his face, a shorter flourishing cut below his left eye. As if he were the woman's distorted reflection.

As Bellis watched the wounded pair, aghast, the woman spoke.

"You will have realized by now," she said in good Ragamoll, projecting her soft voice so that everyone could hear, "that Armada is not like other cities."

* * *

Is that a welcome? Bellis had thought. Was that all that the traumatized and bewildered survivors of the *Terpsichoria* were to be offered?

The woman had continued.

She told them about the city.

Sometimes she was silent, and without a pause the man would speak. They were almost like twins, finishing each other's sentences.

It had been hard to listen to what they were telling her. Bellis was agog at the feelings she saw pass between the scarred man and woman every time they glanced at each other. Above all a hunger. Bellis had felt unstuck in time: as if she were dreaming this arrival.

Later, she would realize that she had absorbed much of what had been said, that it had passed into her and been processed at some level below consciousness. It came out as she began to live in Armada, against her will.

At the time, all she had been aware of was the couple's shared intensity, and the stunned excitement that greeted the woman's final sentence.

The words had reached Bellis full seconds after they were spoken, as if her skull were some thick medium through which sound traveled sluggishly.

There was a massed gasp and a whoop and then a swell of incredulous cheering, a huge breaking wave of joy from the hundreds of exhausted Remade prisoners who stood shivering and stinking. It rose and rose, at first tentative and then rapidly delirious with triumph.

"Human, cactacae, hotchi, cray . . . *Remade,*" the woman had said. "In Armada you are all sailors and citizens. In Armada you are not distinguished. Here you are free. And equal."

There, finally, was a welcome. And the Remade accepted it with loud and tearful thanks.

Bellis had been herded away with her random companions, out into the city where the men and women of the city's trades were waiting with contracts and hard, eager looks. And as she shuffled out of the room, she looked back at the group of leaders and saw with astonishment that someone had joined them.

Johannes Tearfly was looking down, totally bewildered, at the hand that the scarred man proffered—not snubbing it, but as if he could not think what he was supposed to do with it. The elderly man who had stood with the murderer and the scarred couple stepped forward, stroking his bright white beard, and greeted Johannes loudly by name.

That was all Bellis had seen or heard before she was taken away. Off the ship, out into Armada, into her new city.

A flotilla of dwellings. A city built on old boat bones.

Everywhere battered clothes shook and dried in the constant wind. They ruffled in Armada's alleyways, by tall brickwork, steeples, masts, and chimneys and ancient rigging. Bellis looked from her window across the vista of reconfigured masts and bowsprits, a cityscape of beakheads and forecastles. Across many hundreds of ships lashed together, spread over almost a square mile of sea, and the city built on them.

Countless naval architectures: Stripped longships; scorpion galleys; luggers and brigantines; massive steamers hundreds of feet long down to canoes no larger than a man. There were alien vessels: ur-ketches, a barge carved from the ossified body of a whale. Tangled in ropes and moving wooden walkways, hundreds of vessels facing all directions rode the swells.

The city was loud. Tethered dogs, the shouts of costermongers, the drone of engines, hammers and lathes, and stones being broken. Klaxons from workshops. Laughter and shouting, all in the variant of Salt, the mongrel sailors' tongue, that was the language of Armada. And below those city sounds the throaty noise of boats. Complaining wood and the snaps of leather and rope, the percussion of ship on ship.

Armada moved constantly, its bridges swinging side to side, its towers heeling. The city shifted on the water.

The vessels had been reclaimed, from the inside out. What had once been berths and bulkheads had become houses; there were workshops in old gundecks. But the city had not been bounded by the ships' existing skins. It reshaped them. They were built up, topped with structure; styles and materials shoved together from a hundred histories and esthetics into a compound architecture.

Centuries-old pagodas tottered on the decks of ancient oar-ships, and cement monoliths rose like extra smokestacks on paddlers stolen from southern seas. The streets between the buildings were tight. They passed over the converted vessels on bridges, between mazes and plazas and what might have been mansions. Parklands crawled across clippers, above armories in deeply hidden decks. Decktop houses were cracked and strained from the boats' constant motion.

Bellis could see the awnings of Winterstraw Market: hundreds of jolly boats and flat-bottomed canal runners, none more than twenty feet long, filling the spaces between grander vessels. The little boats bumped each other constantly, tethered together with chains and crusted knotwork. The stallholders were opening up, garlanding their little shop boats with ribbons and signs and hanging up their wares. Early shoppers descended to the market from surrounding ships by steep rope bridges, stepping expertly from boat to boat.

Beside the market was a corbita smeared with ivy and climbing flowers. Low dwellings were built onto it and beautifully carved. Its masts had not been felled, but were wound with greenery that made them look like ancient trees. There was a submersible that had not dived for decades. A ridge of thin houses extended around its periscope like a dorsal fin. The two vessels were joined by rippling wooden bridges that passed above the market.

A steamship was become a residential block, its hull broken with new windows, a children's climbing frame on its deck. A boxy paddleboat housed mushroom farms. A chariot ship, its bridle polished decoratively, was covered with brick terraces that filled the curves of its naval foundations. Chains of smoke rose from its chimneys.

Buildings laced with bone, colors from greys and rusts to the flamboyant glares of heraldry: a city of esoteric shapes. Its hybridity was stark and uncharming, marred with decay and graffiti. The architecture hunkered and rose and hunkered again with the water, vaguely threatening.

There were slums and mansions in the bodies of tramp merchant ships, and built tottering across sloops. There were churches and sanatoria and deserted houses, all licked by constant damp, contoured with salt—steeped in the sounds of waves and the fresh-rot smell of the sea.

The ships were tethered together in a weave of chains and hinged girders. Every vessel was a pontoon in a web of rope bridges. Boats coiled toward each other in seawalls of embedded ships, surrounding free-floating vessels. Basilio Harbor, where Armada's navy and visitors could tie up, repair or unload, sheltered from storms.

The largest ships meandered instead around the edges of the city, beyond the tugs and steamers tethered to Armada's sides. Out in the open water were fleets of fishing boats, the city's warships, the chariot ships and whim trawlers and others. These were Armada's pirate navy, heading out across the world, coming in to dock with cargoes plundered from enemies or the sea.

And beyond all that, beyond the city sky that thronged with birds and other shapes, beyond all the vessels was the sea.

The open sea. Waves like insects in incessant motion.

Stunning and empty.

Bellis was protected by those who had caught her, she was made to understand. She was a resident of Garwater riding, ruled by the man and woman with the scars. They had promised work and a berth for all those they had taken, and it had happened quickly. Agents had met the terrified, confused new arrivals, calling out the names on their lists, checking the skills and details of the newcomers, brusquely explaining in pidgin Salt what work they offered.

It had taken Bellis some minutes to understand, and more to believe, that she was being offered work in a library.

She had signed the proffered papers. The officers and sailors from the *Terpsichoria* were being led forcibly away for "assessment" and "reeducation," and Bellis had felt in no mood to be difficult. She had scratched her name, tight with resentment. *Call this a damned contract?* she felt like shouting. *There's no choice here, and everybody knows it.* But she had signed.

The organization, the mumming of legality, confused her.

These were pirates. This was a pirate city, ruled by cruel mercantilism, existing in the pores of the world, snatching new citizens from their ships, a floating freetown for buying and selling stolen goods, where might made right. The evidence of this was everywhere: in the severity of the citizens, the weapons they wore openly, in the stocks and whipping posts she saw on the

Garhouse vessels. Armada, she thought, must be ordered by maritime discipline, the lash.

But the ship-city was not the base brutocracy that Bellis had expected. There were other logics at work. There were typed contracts, offices administrating the new arrivals. And officials of some kind: an executive, administrative caste, just as in New Crobuzon.

Alongside Armada's club law, or supporting it, or an integument around it, was bureaucratic rule. This was not a ship, but a city. She had entered another country as complex and organized as her own.

The officials had taken her to the *Chromolith,* a long-decaying paddleship, and berthed her in two little round rooms joined by a spiral staircase, built in what had been the vessel's big chimney. Somewhere far below her, in the ship's guts, was an engine that had once vented its soot through what was now her home. It had gone cold long before she was born.

The room was hers, they told her, but she must pay for it, weekly, at the Garwater Settlement Office. They had given her an advance on her wages, a handful of notes and change—"ten eyes to a flag, ten flags to a finial." The currency was rough-cut and crudely printed. The colors of the ink varied from note to note.

And then they had told her, in rudimentary Ragamoll, that she would never leave Armada, and they had left her there alone.

She had waited, but that was all. She was alone in the city, and it was a prison.

Eventually hunger had driven her down to buy greasy street-food from a vendor who jabbered at her in Salt too quick for her easily to understand. She had walked the streets, astonished that she was not accosted. She felt so alien, bowed under culture shock as crippling as migraine, surrounded by the women and men in lush, ragged dress, the street children, the cactacae and khepri, hotchi, llorgiss, massive gessin and vu-murt, and others. Cray lived below the city and walked topside in the day, sluggish on their armored legs.

The streets were narrow little ridges between the houses crammed on decks. Bellis grew used to the city's yawing, the skyline that shifted and jostled. She was surrounded by catcalls and conversations in Salt.

It was easy for her to learn: its vocabulary was obvious, stolen as it was from other languages, and its syntax was easy. She had to use it—she could not avoid buying food, asking for directions or clarification, speaking to other Armadans—and when she did her accent marked her out as a newcomer, not city-born.

For the most part those she spoke to were patient with her, even crudely good-humored, forgiving her surliness. Perhaps they expected her to relax as she made Armada her home.

She did not.

That morning, as Bellis stepped out of the *Chromolith* smoke-stack, the question *How did I get here?* broke through into her mind again.

She was out in the street in the city of ships, in the sun, en-closed in a press of her kidnappers. Men and women, tough-faced humans and other races, even a few constructs were all around her, bartering, working, jabbering in Salt. Bellis walked on through Armada, a prisoner.

She was heading for The Clockhouse Spur. This riding abutted Garwater, and was more commonly known as Booktown, or the khepri quarter.

It was a little more than a thousand feet from *Chromolith* Tow-ers to the Grand Gears Library. The walk there took her over at least six vessels.

The sky was full of craft. Gondolas swayed beneath dirigibles, ferrying passengers across the angling architecture, descending between close-quartered housing and letting down rope ladders, cruising past much larger airships that hauled goods and ma-chinery. Those were chaotic. Some were congealed from lashed-together gasbags, extruding cabins and engines randomly, like chance accretions of material. Masts were mooring posts, sprout-ing aerostats of various shapes, like plump, mutant fruit.

From *Chromolith* Bellis crossed a steep little bridge to the schooner *Jarvee,* crowded with little kiosks selling tobacco and sweets. She passed up onto the barquentine *Lynx Sejant,* its deck full of silk merchants selling offcuts from Armada's piracy. Right, past a broken llorgiss sea pillar bobbing like some ma-levolent fishing lure, and Bellis crossed Taffeta Bridge.

She was now on the *Severe,* a massive clipper, the edge of Booktown riding, where the khepri ruled. Beside carts pulled by

Armada's sickly inbred ox and horses, Bellis passed a team of three khepri guard-sisters.

There were similar trios in Kinken and Creekside, New Crobuzon's khepri ghettos. It had astonished Bellis the first time she had seen them here. The khepri in Armada, like those in New Crobuzon, must be descendants of refugees from the Mercy Ships, worshipping what was left, what they remembered, of the Bered Kai Nev pantheon. They held traditional weapons. Their lithe humanoid women's bodies were weatherbeaten, their heads like giant scarabs iridescent in the cold sun.

With so many mute khepri residents, the streets of Booktown were quieter than those of Garwater. Instead, the air was slightly spiced with residue from the chymical mists that were part of khepri communication. It was their equivalent of a boisterous hubbub.

Punctuating the alleyways and squares were khepri-spit sculptures, like those in New Crobuzon's Plaza of Statues. Figures from myth, abstract forms, sea creatures executed in the opalescent material the khepri metabolized through their headscarabs. The colors were muted, as if colorberries were less plentiful here, or of worse quality.

On an avenue on the *Compound Dust,* a khepri clockwork ship—a Mercy Ship that had fled the Ravening—Bellis slowed, fascinated by its cogs and architecture. Insects and husks blew fitfully into her path from the gusting deck-field of a farm ship aft, and the distant bleating of livestock sounded through slats in its lower decks.

Then on to the fat factory ship the *Aronnax Lab,* past metallurgy workshops and refineries, into Krome Plaza, where a great suspended platform reached out across the water onto the deck of the *Pinchermarn,* the aftmost of the vessels that made up Grand Gears Library.

"Relax . . . no one cares that you're late, you know," said Carrianne, one of the human staff, as Bellis hurried past. "You're new, you're press-ganged, so you might as well milk it." Bellis heard her laughing, but did not respond.

The corridors and converted mess halls were crammed with bookshelves and guttering oil lanterns. Scholars of all races pursed their lips, if they had them, and looked up wistfully in

Bellis' wake. The reading rooms were large and quiet. Their windows were filmed in dust and desiccated insects, and seemed to age the light falling across the communal tables and the volumes in scores of languages. Stifled coughs sounded like apologies as Bellis entered the acquisitions department. Books tottered on cabinets and trolleys and in loose towers on the floor.

She was there for hours, coding methodically. Stacking books written in scripts she could not read, recording the details of the other volumes onto cards. Filing them alphabetically—the Salt alphabet was a slightly variant form of the Ragamoll script—according to author, title, language, themes, and subjects.

A little before she was due to break for her lunch Bellis heard footsteps. It must be Shekel, she thought. He was the only person from the *Terpsichoria* she saw or spoke to. She smiled at the thought of it: herself consorting with the cabin boy. He had come swaggering in to find her, almost a fortnight previously, all adolescent nerve, excited at their capture and new situation. (Someone had told him about "a scary lofty lady in black with blue lips" working in the library, he explained to her. He grinned when he said that, and she had looked away to avoid smiling back.)

He was living by various vague means, sharing a house with a Remade man from the *Terpsichoria*. Bellis offered Shekel a brass flag to help her with reshelving, which he accepted. Since then he had come several times, done a little work, talking to her about Armada and the scattered remnants of their ship.

She learned a lot from him.

But it was not Shekel who was now approaching her in the narrow corridor, but a nervous, quizzically smiling Johannes Tearfly.

It was with some embarrassment, later, that she remembered herself rising at his arrival (*with a cry of pleasure like a gushy child, for gods' sakes*) and throwing her arms around him.

He opened to her, too, smiling with shy warmth. And after a long moment of close greeting, they disengaged and looked at each other.

This was the first chance he'd had to get out, he told her, and she demanded to know what he had been doing. He'd been sent to the library and had taken the chance to seek her out, and again she told him to tell her what he had been damn well *doing*. When

he told her that he could not, that he had to go now, she almost
stamped in frustration, but he was telling her *wait, wait,* that he
had more free time now, and that she should just *listen* a moment.

"If you're free tomorrow night," he said, "I'd like to take you
to supper. There's a place in starboard Garwater, on the *Raddletongue,* called the Unrealized Time. Do you know it?"

"I'll find it," she said.

"I could come and collect you," he began, and she cut him off.
"I'll find it."

He smiled at her, with the bemused pleasure she remembered.
If you're free indeed! she thought sardonically. *Does he really
think . . . Is it possible?* She felt suddenly uncertain, almost
afraid. *Do the others go out every night? Am I alone in exile? Are
the* Terpsichoria*'s passengers carousing every evening in their
new home?*

As she left the library that evening, Armada's close quarters and
narrow streets oppressed Bellis. But when she raised her eyes
and looked beyond the skyline, the Swollen Ocean weighed
down on her like granite, and she felt breathless. She could not
believe that the mass of water and air beyond Armada did not
drown it, disappear it in an instant. She counted her coins and
approached a skycab driver refilling his dirigible from a gas de-
pot on *Aronnax Lab.*

She swayed in the cradle as it buzzed sedately a hundred feet
above the highest deck. Bellis could see the edges of the city
bobbing randomly, moving very slowly with whatever currents
took it. There, the distant wood of the haunted quarter. The
arena. The stronghold of the Brucolac.

And in the center of Garwater riding, something extraordinary that Bellis never grew accustomed to seeing—the source of
the riding's strength. Something looming enormously over the
shipscape around it: the largest ship in the city, the largest ship
that Bellis had ever seen.

Almost nine hundred feet of black iron. Five colossal funnels
and six masts stripped of canvas, more than two hundred feet
high; and tethered way above them a huge, crippled dirigible. A
vast paddle on each side of the ship, like industrial sculptures.
The decks seemed almost bare, unbroken by the haphazard
building that misshaped other vessels. The Lovers' stronghold,

like a beached titan: the *Grand Easterly,* lolling austere amid Armada's baroque.

"I've changed my mind," Bellis said suddenly. "Don't take me to *Chromolith.*"

She directed the pilot aft-aft-star'd—the city's directions all relative to the colossal *Grand Easterly* itself. As the man gently tugged at his rudder she looked down over the crowds. Air eddied as the aeronaut picked a way through the masts and rigging that jutted up around them in the Armada sky. Around the towers Bellis saw the city birds: gulls and pigeons and parakeets. They brooded on roofs and in decktop aeries, alongside other presences.

The sun was gone, and the city sparkled. Bellis felt a gust of melancholy as she passed light-strung rigging close enough to grasp. She saw her destination, the Boulevard St. Carcheri on the steamer *Glomar's Heart,* a shabby-opulent promenade of gently colored streetlamps, knotted rustwood trees, and stucco façades. As the gondola began to descend, she kept her eyes on the shabbier, darker shape beyond the parkland.

Across four hundred feet of water glinting with impurities rose a tower of intertwined girders as high as the dirigibles, gushing with flame. A massive concrete body on legs like four splintering pillars emerging from the dirtied sea. Dark cranes moving without visible purpose.

It was a monstrous thing, awe-inspiring and ugly and foreboding. Bellis sat back in her descending aerostat and kept her eye on the *Sorghum,* New Crobuzon's stolen rig.

CHAPTER SEVEN

It rained remorselessly all the next day, hard grey drops like shards of flint.

The costermongers were quiet; very little business was done. Armada's bridges were slippery. There were accidents: the drunk or the clumsy slipping into the cold sea.

The city's monkeys sat subdued under awnings and bickered. They were pests, feral tribes that raced across the floating city, fighting, vying for scraps and territory, brachiating below bridges and careering up rigging. They were not the only animals living wild in the city, but they were the most successful scavengers. They huddled in the cold damp and groomed each other without enthusiasm.

In the dim light of Grand Gears Library, the signs requesting silence were made absurd by the percussion of rain.

The bloodhorns of Shaddler riding sounded mournfully, as they customarily did when it rained hard and the scabmettlers said that the sky was bleeding. Water beaded weirdly on the surface of the *Uroc,* Dry Fall riding's flagship. The dark and rotting fabric of the haunted quarter mildewed and glowered. People in the neighboring Thee-And-Thine riding pointed at the deserted quarter's decrepit skyline and warned, as they always did, that somewhere within, the tallow ghast was moving.

In the first hour after dusk, in the muted edifice of Barrow Hall on the *Therianthropus,* the heart of Shaddler, a bad-tempered meeting came to an end. The scabmettler guards outside could hear delegations leaving. They fingered their weapons and ran their hands over the crust of their organic armor.

There was a man among them: a few inches shy of six feet and prodigiously muscled, dressed in charcoal-colored leather, a straight sword by his side. He spoke and moved with quiet grace.

He discussed weaponry with the scabmettlers, then had them show him strokes and sweeps from *mortu crutt,* their fighting science. He let them touch the filigree of wires that wound around his right arm and down the side of his armor into the battery on his belt.

The man was comparing the Stubborn Nail strike of stamp-fighting with the *sadr* punch of *mortu crutt.* He and his sparring partner swept their arms in slow demonstration attacks, when the doors opened at the top of the stairs above them and the guards came to quick attention. The man in grey straightened slowly and walked to the corner of the entresol.

A coldly furious man descended toward them. He was tall and young-looking and built like a dancer, with freckled skin the color of pale ash. His hair seemed to belong to someone else: it was dark and long and very tightly curled, and it hung in unruly locks from his scalp like an unkempt fleece. It jounced and coiled as he descended.

As he passed the scabmettlers he gave a peremptory little bow, which they returned with more ceremony. He stood still before the man in grey. The two men eyed each other with impenetrable expressions.

"Liveman Doul," said the newcomer eventually, in a whispering voice.

"Deadman Brucolac," was the reply. Uther Doul gazed at the Brucolac's broad, handsome face.

"It seems your employers are going ahead with their idiot scheming," the Brucolac murmured, and then was silent. "I still can't believe, Uther," he said finally, "that you approve of this lunacy."

Uther Doul did not move, did not take his eyes from the other man.

The Brucolac straightened his back and gave a sneer that might have indicated contempt, or a shared confidence, or many other things. "It won't happen, you know," he said. "The city won't allow it. That's not what this city is *for*."

The Brucolac opened his mouth idly, and his great forked tongue flickered out, tasting the air and the ghosts of Uther Doul's sweat.

There were things that made very little sense to Tanner Sack.

He did not understand how he could bear the cold of the seawater. With his bulky Remade tentacles, he had to descend with his chest uncovered, and the first touch of the water had shocked him. He had almost balked, then had smeared himself with thick grease; but he had acclimatized much faster than made sense. He was still aware of the chill, but it was an abstract knowledge. It did not cripple him.

He did not understand why the brine was healing his tentacles.

Since first they had been implanted at the caprice of a New Crobuzon magister—a punishment supposedly related to his crime according to some patronizing allegorical logic that had never made any sense to him—they had hung like stinking dead limbs. He had cut at them, experimentally, and the layers of nerves implanted in them had fired and he had nearly fainted with pain. But pain was all that had lived in them, so he had wrapped them around himself like rotting pythons and tried to ignore them.

But immersed in the saltwater, they had begun to move.

Their multitude of small infections had faded, and they were now cool to the touch. After three dives, to his grinding shock, the tentacles had started to move independently of the water.

He was healing.

After a few weeks of diving, new sensations passed through them, and their sucker pads flexed gently and attached themselves on surfaces nearby. Tanner was learning to move them by choice.

In the confused first days when the captives had first arrived, Tanner had wandered through the ridings and listened bewildered as merchants and foremen offered him work in a language he was learning very quickly to understand.

When he verified that he was an engineer, the liaison officer for the Garwater Dock Authority had eyed him greedily, and had asked him in child's Salt and pantomime hand gestures whether he would learn to be a diver. It was easier to train an engineer to dive than to teach a diver the skills that Tanner had accumulated.

It was hard work learning to breathe the air pumped down from above without panicking in the hot little helmet, how to move without overcompensating and sending himself spinning. But he had learned to luxuriate in the slowed-down time, the eddying clarity of water seen through glass.

He did similar work now to that he had always done—patching and repairing, rebuilding, fumbling with tools by great engines—only now, well below the stevedores and the cranes, it was performed in the crush of water, watched by fishes and eels, buffeted by currents born miles away.

"I told you that Coldarse is working in the library, didn't I?"

"You did, lad," Tanner said. He and Shekel were eating below an awning at the docks while the deluge continued around them.

Shekel had arrived at the docks with a little group of raggedy-arsed youngsters between twelve and sixteen years old. All the others, from what Tanner could tell, were city-born; and that they had let a press-ganged join them, one who still struggled to express himself in Salt, was evidence of Shekel's adaptability.

They had left Shekel alone to share his food with Tanner.

"I like that library," he said. "I like going there, and not just because of the ice woman, neither."

"There's a lot worse you could do than settle into some reading, lad," said Tanner. "We've finished Crawfoot's Chronicles; you could find some other stories. You could read them to me, for a change. How're your letters?"

"I can make them out," said Shekel vaguely.

"Well, there you go then. You go and have a word with Miss Coldy, and get her to recommend some reading for you."

They ate silently for a while, watching a group of the Armada cray come up from their hivewreck below.

"What's it like under there?" Shekel said at last.

"Cold," said Tanner. "And dark. Dark but . . . luminous. Massive. You're just surrounded by massiveness. There are shapes you can only just see, huge dark shapes. Subs and whatnot—and sometimes you think you see others. Can't make them out properly, and they're guarded, so's you can't get too close.

"I've watched cray under their wrecks. Seawyrms that saddle up sometimes to the chariot ships. The menfish, like newts, from Bask riding. Can't hardly see them, the way they move. Bastard John, the dolphin. He's the Lovers' security chief below, and a colder, more vicious sod you could not imagine.

"And then there's a few . . . Remade." His voice eddied into silence.

"It's weird, isn't it?" said Shekel, watching Tanner closely. "I can't get used to . . ." He said nothing more.

Neither could get used to it. A place where the Remade were equal. Where a Remade might be a foreman or a manager instead of the lowest laborer.

Shekel saw Tanner rub his tentacles. "How are they?" he asked, and Tanner grinned and concentrated, and one of the rubbery things contracted a little and began to drag itself like a moribund snake toward Shekel's bread. The boy clapped appreciatively.

At the edge of the jetty where the cray were surfacing, a tall cactus-man stood, his bare chest pocked with fibrous vegetable scars. A massive rivebow was strapped across his back.

"D'you know him?" said Tanner. "His name's Hedrigall."

"That don't sound like a cactacae name," said Shekel, and Tanner shook his head.

"He's no New Crobuzon cactus," he explained, "nor even a Shankell one. He's a press-ganged, like us. Came to the city more than twenty years ago. He's from Dreer Samher. Near enough two thousand miles from New Crobuzon.

"I tell you what, Shekel, he's got some stories. You don't need books to get tales off him.

"He was a trader-pirate before he got captured and joined the city here, and he's seen just about all the things that live in the sea. He can cut your hair with that rivebow; he's that good a shot. He's seen keragorae and mosquito-men and unplaced, and whatever else you like. And gods, he knows how to tell you about 'em. In Dreer Samher, they've fablers who tell stories for a calling. Hed was one. He can make his voice hypnagogic if he wants, keep you totally drunk on it. All while he tells you stories."

The cactus-man was standing very still, letting the rain pelt his skin.

"And now he's an aeronaut," Tanner said. "He's been piloting *Grand Easterly*'s airships—scouts and warflots—for years. He's one of the Lovers' most important men, and a fine bloke he is. He spends most of his time now up in the *Arrogance*."

Tanner and Shekel looked behind them, and up. More than a thousand feet above the deck of the *Grand Easterly* the *Arrogance* was tethered. It was a big, crippled aerostat, with twisted tail fins and an engine that had not moved in years. Attached by hundreds of yards of tar-stiffened rope, winched to the great ship below it, it served as the city's crow's nest.

"He likes it up there, Hedrigall," said Tanner. "Told me he just wants things quiet, these days."

"Tanner," said Shekel slowly, "what do you reckon to the Lovers? I mean, you work for them: you've heard them talk; you know what they're like. What d'you think of them? Why d'you do what they say?"

Tanner knew, as he spoke, that Shekel would not fully understand him. But it was such an important question that he turned and looked very carefully at the boy he shared his rooms with (on the port end of an old iron hulk). The boy who had been his jailer and his audience and his friend and was becoming something different, something like family.

"I was going to be a slave in the colonies, Shekel," he said quietly. "The Lovers of *Grand Easterly* took me in and gave me a job that pays money and told me they didn't give a cup of piss that I was Remade. The Lovers gave me my life, Shekel, and a city and a home. I tell you that *whatever* they fucking want to do is *alfuckingright* by me. New Crobuzon can kiss my arse, lad. I'm an Armada man, a Garwater man. I'm learning my Salt. I'm loyal."

Shekel stared at him. Tanner was a slow-talking, quiet man, and Shekel had never seen that intensity from him before.

He was very impressed.

It continued raining. All across Armada, the passengers from the *Terpsichoria* who had been let out tried to live.

On gaudy yawls and barquentines, they were arguing, buying and selling and stealing, learning Salt, some weeping, poring over maps of the city, calculating the distance from New Crobuzon or Nova Esperium. They mourned their old lives, staring at heliotypes of friends and lovers at home.

In a reeducation jail between Garwater and Shaddler were scores of sailors from the *Terpsichoria*. Some were shouting at their guard-counselors, who were trying to soothe them, all the time gauging whether this man or that could overcome his ties, whether his link to New Crobuzon would attenuate, whether he could be won over to Armada.

And if not, deciding what was to be done with them.

Bellis arrived at the Unrealized Time with her makeup and hair rain-battered. She stood bedraggled in the doorway while a waiter greeted her, and she stared at him, astonished at this treatment. *As if he were a* real *waiter,* she found herself thinking, *in a real restaurant in a real city.*

The *Raddletongue* was a big and ancient vessel. It was so crusted with buildings, so recrafted and interfered with, that it was impossible to tell what kind of ship it had once been. It had been part of the Armada for centuries. The ship's forecastle was covered with ruins: old temples in white stone, much of their substance scattered and pounded to dust. The remnants were smothered in ivy, and nettles that did not keep the city's children away.

There were strange shapes in the *Raddletongue*'s streets, lumps of obscure sea-salvaged stuff left in corners as if forgotten.

The restaurant was small and warm and half-full, paneled in darkwood. Its windows looked out over a fringe of ketches and canoes to Urchinspine Docks, Armada's second harbor.

Bellis saw with a stab of emotion that from the restaurant's ceiling hung little strings of paper lanterns. The last place she had seen that had been in the Clock and Cockerel, in Salacus Fields in New Crobuzon.

She had to shake her head to clear it of a biting melancholy. At a table in the corner, Johannes was getting to his feet, waving to her.

They sat quietly for a while. Johannes seemed shy, and Bellis found herself resentful that it had been so long since she had heard from him, and suspecting that she was not being fair she retreated into silence.

Bellis saw with amazement that the red wine on the table was a vintage Galaggi, a House Predicus 1768. She looked up at Johannes with eyes wide. With her mouth set shut she looked disapproving.

"I thought we might celebrate," he said. "I mean, at seeing each other again."

The wine was excellent.

"Why've they just left me . . . us . . . to get on with it? Or to rot?" Bellis demanded. She picked at her concoction of fish and bitter ship-grown leaves. "I'd have thought . . . I'd have thought it ill-advised to pluck a few hundred people from their lives, then let them loose in . . . this . . ."

"They've not done that," Johannes said. "How many of the other *Terpsichoria* passengers have you seen? How many of the crew? Don't you remember the interviews, the questions, when we first arrived? They were tests," he said gently. "They were es-timating who was safe, and who not. If they think you're too troublesome, or too . . . tied to New Crobuzon . . ." His voice pe-tered away.

"Then what?" demanded Bellis. "Like the captain . . . ?"

"No no no," said Johannes quickly. "I think that they . . . work on you. Try to persuade you. I mean, you know about press-ganging. There are plenty of sailors in the New Crobuzon navy who were doing nothing more nautical than carousing in a tav-ern the night they were 'recruited.' It doesn't stop most of them working as sailors once they're taken."

"For a while," said Bellis.

"Yes. I'm not saying it's exactly the same. That's the big dif-ference: once you join Armada you don't . . . leave."

"I've been told that a thousand times," Bellis said slowly. "But what about Armada's fleet? What about the cray underneath? You think they can't get away? Anyway, if that were true, if people never did have a chance to leave, no one but the city-born would be prepared to live here."

"Obviously," Johannes said. "The city's freebooters are on sail for months, maybe years at a time till they make their way back to Armada. And they'll dock at other ports during those journeys, and I'm sure some of their crew must have disappeared. There must be ex-Armadans scattered here and there.

"But the fact is, those crews are chosen: partly for their loyalty, and partly for the fact that if they do run, it won't matter. They're almost all city-born, for a start: it's a rare press-ganged who's given a letter of pass. The likes of you and me, we couldn't hope to get on a vessel like that. Armada *is* where most of us press-ganged'll see things out.

"But dammit, think who gets taken, Bellis. Some sailors, sure, some 'rival' pirates, a few merchants. But the ships the Armadans encounter—you think they all get taken? Most of the press ganged vessels are . . . well, ships like the *Terpsichoria*. *Slavers*. Or colony ships full of transported Remade. Or jail ships. Or ships carrying prisoners of war.

"Most of the Remade on the *Terpsichoria* realized long ago that they'd never be going home. Twenty years, my eye—it's a life sentence, and a death sentence, and they know it. And here they are now, with work and money and *respect* . . . Is it any wonder they accept it? As far as I know there are only seven Remade from the *Terpsichoria* being treated for rejection, and two of those already suffer dementia."

And how the fuck, wondered Bellis, *how in the name of Jabber do you know that?*

"What about the likes of you and me?" Johannes continued. "All of us . . . we already knew we'd be away from home—away from New Crobuzon—for five years at the very, very least, and probably more. Look at the motley group we were. I'd say very few of the other passengers had unbreakable ties with the city. People arriving here are unsettled, sure; and surprised, confused, alarmed. But not destroyed. Isn't it a 'new life' that they promise Nova Esperium colonists? Wasn't that what most of us sought?"

Most, perhaps, thought Bellis. *But not all. And if it's satisfaction with this place they look for before they let us live free here, then* gods know—*I know*—*they can make mistakes of judgment.*

"I doubt," Johannes said quietly, "they're so naïve as to just leave us to roam unchecked. I'd be surprised if they didn't keep careful note of us. I suspect we don't go unwatched. But what could we do, anyway? This is a *city,* not a dinghy we can commandeer or scuttle.

"It's only the crew who'd represent any kind of real problem. Many have families waiting for them. Those are the ones who'd likely refuse to accept that this is their new home."

Only the crew? thought Bellis, a bad taste in her throat.

"So what happens to them? Like the captain?" she said in a dead voice. "Like Cumbershum?"

Johannes flinched. "I . . . I've been told it's . . . it's only the captains and first officers of any ships encountered . . . That they simply have too much to lose, that they're particularly tied to their home port . . ."

There was something fawning and apologetic in his face. With a waxing alienation, Bellis realized that she was alone.

She had come here tonight thinking that she might be able to talk to Johannes about New Crobuzon, that he would share her unhappiness, that she could touch the bloodied part of her mind and talk about the people and streets she missed so hard.

Perhaps that they might broach the subject that had burrowed through her thoughts for weeks: escape.

But Johannes was acclimatizing. He spoke in a carefully neutral register, as if what he said was just reportage. But he was trying to come to terms with the city's rulers. He had found something in Armada that made him prepared to consider it home.

What did they do to achieve this? she thought. *What is he doing?*

"Who else have you heard about?" she said after a cold silence.

"Mollificatt, I'm very sorry to say, was one of those who succumbed when we first arrived," he said, looking genuinely sad. The mongrel and changing population of Armada made it a carrier of countless diseases. The city-born were hardy, but every batch of press-ganged was afflicted with fevers and murrains on its first arrival, and several of their number inevitably died. "I've heard rumors that our newcomer, Mr. Fennec, is working somewhere in Garwater, or Thee-And-Thine riding. Sister Meriope . . ."

he said suddenly, his eyes widening. He shook his head. "Sister Meriope is . . . She is being held for her own safety. She threatens herself with violence constantly. Bellis," he whispered, *"she is with child."*

Bellis rolled her eyes.

I can't listen to this, thought Bellis, saying just enough to be in the conversation. She felt alone. *Tawdry secrets and clichés. What next?* she thought with contempt as Johannes rambled on through the passenger list and the officers of the *Terpsichoria. Some trusty sailor actually a woman disguised to go to sea? Love and buggery among the ranks?*

There was something pathetic about Johannes that night, and she had never thought so before.

"How do you know all this, Johannes?" said Bellis carefully, at last. "Where've you been? What are you actually doing?"

Johannes cleared his throat and stared into his glass for a long time.

"Bellis . . ." he said. Around him, the soft clatter of the restaurant seemed very loud. "Bellis . . . can I tell you in confidence?" Johannes sighed, then looked up at her.

"I'm working for the Lovers," he said. "And I don't mean I work in Garwater riding. I work *directly* for them. They have a team of researchers, working on a quite . . ." He shook his head and began to smile with delight. "A quite *extraordinary* project. An extraordinary opportunity. And they invited me to join them—because of my previous work.

"Their team had read some of my research, and they decided that I'd be . . . that they wanted me to work with them." He was overjoyed, she realized. He was like a child, almost exactly like a child.

"There are thaumaturges, oceanologers, marine biologists. That man—the man who defeated the *Terpsichoria,* Uther Doul—he's part of the team. He's central, in fact. He's a philosopher. There are different projects all being pursued. Projects on cryptogeography and probability theory, as well as . . . as the investigation I'm working on. The man in charge of that is fascinating. He was with the Lovers when we arrived: a tall old man with a beard."

"I remember him," said Bellis. "He welcomed you."

A look somewhere between contrition and excitement overtook Johannes.

"He did," he said. "That's Tintinnabulum. A hunter, an outsider, employed by the city. He lives on the *Castor* with seven other men, where Garwater meets Shaddler and Booktown. A small ship with a belfry . . .

"We're doing such *fascinating* work," he said suddenly, and seeing his pure pleasure Bellis could see how Armada had won him. "The equipment's old and unreliable—the analytical engines are ancient—but the work's so much more radical. I've months of research to catch up on—I'm learning Salt. This work . . . it means reading the most varied things."

He grinned at her with incredulous pride. "For my project, there are certain key texts. One of them's mine. Can you believe that? Isn't that extraordinary? They're from all over the world. From New Crobuzon, Khadoh. And there are mystery books that we can't find. They're in Ragamoll and Salt and moonscript . . . One of the most important's said to be in High Kettai. We've made a list of them from references in the books we *do* have. Gods know how they've got such a fantastic library here, Bellis. Half these books I could never find at home—"

"They stole it, Johannes," she said, and silenced him. "That's how they've got it. Every damned volume in Grand Gears Library is stolen. From ships, from the towns they plunder on the coast. From people like me, Johannes. My books that *I* wrote that have been stolen from me. That's where they get their books."

Something cold was settling in Bellis' gut.

"Tell me," she began, and stopped. She drank some wine, breathed deep, and started again. "Tell me, Johannes, that is somewhat remarkable, isn't it? That out of an entire ocean—an *entire fucking ocean*—that out of that whole empty sea they should pluck the one ship that was carrying their intellectual hero . . ."

And again she saw in his eye that uncomfortable cocktail of apology and elation.

"Yes," he said carefully. "That's the thing, Bellis. That's what I wanted to talk to you about."

She suddenly knew what he was going to say, a certainty that nauseated and repelled her, but she liked him still, she really did, and she so wanted to be wrong that she did not stand to go; she waited to be corrected, knowing that she would not be.

"It wasn't coincidence, Bellis," she heard him saying. "It wasn't. They have an agent in Salkrikaltor. They receive colonial passenger lists. They knew we were coming. They knew I was coming."

The paper lanterns swung as the door opened and closed. There was pretty laughter from a nearby table. The smell of stuffed meat cosseted them.

"That was why they took our ship. They came for me," said Johannes softly, and Bellis closed her eyes, defeated.

"Oh, Johannes," she said unsteadily.

"Bellis," he said, alarmed, reaching out, but she cut him off with a curt gesture. *What, do you think I'm going to cry?* she thought furiously.

"Johannes, let me tell you there is a world of difference between a five-year, a ten-year sentence—and *life*." She could not look at him. "It may be that for you, for Meriope, for the Cardomiums, for I don't know who else, Nova Esperium meant a new life. *Not for me.*

"Not for me. For me it was an escape, a necessary and a *temporary* escape. I was born in Chnum, Johannes. Educated in Mafaton. Was proposed to in Brock Marsh. Broke up in Salacus Fields. New Crobuzon is my home; it will always be my home."

Johannes looked at her with mounting unease.

"I have no interest in the colonies. In Nova fucking Esperium. *None.* I don't want to live with a group of venal inadequates, failed spivs, disgraced nuns, bureaucrats too incompetent or weak to make it back home, resentful terrified natives . . . Godspit, Johannes, I've no interest in the *sea*. Freezing, sickening, filthy, repetitive, stinking . . .

"I've no interest in this city. I do not want to live in a *curio*, Johannes. This is a sideshow! This is something to scare the children! 'The Floating Pirate City'! I don't want it! I don't want to live in this great bobbing parasite, like some fucking pondskater sucking its victims dry. This isn't a city, Johannes; it's a parochial little village less than a mile wide, and I do not want it.

"I was always going to return to New Crobuzon. I would never wish to see out my days outside it. It's dirty and cruel and difficult and dangerous—particularly for me, particularly now—but it's my home. Nowhere else in the world has the culture, the industry, the population, the thaumaturgy, the languages, the art, the books, the politics, the history . . . New Crobuzon," she said slowly, "is the greatest city in Bas-Lag."

And coming from her, from someone without any illusions about New Crobuzon's brutality, or squalor, or repression, the declamation was far more powerful than if it came from any Parliamentarian.

"And you're telling me," she said finally, "that I've been exiled from my city—for *life*—because of *you*?"

Johannes was looking at her, stricken.

"Bellis," he said slowly, "I don't know what to say. I can only say that . . . that I'm sorry. This wasn't my choice. The Lovers knew I was on the passenger list, and . . . That's not the only reason. They need more guns, so they might have taken her anyway, but . . ."

His voice broke off. "But probably not. Mostly they came for me. But Bellis, please!" He leaned toward her urgently. "It wasn't my choice. I didn't make this happen. I had no idea."

"But you've made your peace with it, Johannes," said Bellis. She stood at last. "You've made peace. You're lucky you've found something that makes you happy here, Johannes. I understand that it wasn't your choice, but I hope *you'll* understand that I can't just sit here as if nothing is wrong, making jolly conversation, when it's down to you that I'm without a home.

"And don't call them the fucking *Lovers,* like it's a title, like those two perverts are a celestial constellation or something. Look at you all agog at them. They're like us; they have names. You could have said no, Johannes. You could have refused."

As she turned to go, he said her name. She had never heard him use such a tone, stony and fierce. It shocked her.

He looked up at her, his hands clenched on the table. "Bellis," he said, in the same voice. "I'm sorry—I'm truly sorry—that you feel kidnapped. I had no idea. But what is it you object to? Living in a parasitic city? I doubt that. New Crobuzon may be more subtle than Armada day to day, but try telling those in the ruins of Suroch that New Crobuzon's not a pirate.

"Culture? Science? Art? Bellis, do you even understand where you *are*? This city is the sum of *hundreds* of cultures. Every maritime nation has lost vessels to war, press-ganging, desertion. And they are *here*. They're what built Armada. This city is the sum of history's lost ships. There are vagabonds and pariahs and their descendants in this place from cultures that New Crobuzon has never so much as heard of. Do you realize that? Do you understand what that means? Their renegades meet here and overlap like scales, and make something new. Armada's been plowing the Swollen Ocean for damn near ever, picking up outcasts and escapees from *everywhere*. Godspit, Bellis, do you know a bloody *thing*?

"History? There've been legends and rumors about this place among all the seafaring nations for centuries; did you know that? Do you know any sailors' tales? The oldest vessel here is more than *a thousand years old*. The ships may change, but the city traces its history back to the Flesh-Eater Wars, at least, and some say back to the godsdamned Ghosthead Empire . . . A village? Nobody knows the population of Armada, but it's hundreds of thousands at least. Count all the layers and layers of decks; there are probably as many miles of street here as in New Crobuzon.

"No, you see Bellis, I don't believe you. I don't think you have any reason for not wanting to live here, any objective reasons for preferring New Crobuzon. I think you simply miss your home. Don't misunderstand me. You don't have to offer any explanations. It's understandable you'd love New Crobuzon. But all you're actually saying is '*I* don't like it here; *I* want to go home.' "

For the first time, he looked at her with something akin to dislike.

"And if it comes to weighing up your desire to return against the desires, for example, of the several hundred *Terpsichoria* Remade who are now allowed to live as something more than animals, then I'm afraid I find your need less than pressing."

Bellis kept her eyes on him. "If anyone were by chance to tell the authorities," she said coolly, "that I might be a suitable case for incarceration and reeducation, then I swear to you I would end myself."

The threat was ridiculous and quite untrue, and she was sure he knew that, but it was as close as she could come to begging him. She knew he had it in his power to cause her serious trouble.

He was a collaborator.

She turned and left him—out into the drizzle that still enveloped Armada. There was so much that she had wanted to say to him, to ask. She had wanted to talk to him about the *Sorghum* rig, that massive flaming enigma now in a little cove of ships. She wanted to know why the Lovers had stolen it, and what it could do, and what they planned for it. Where are its crews? she wanted to ask. Where is the geo-empath whom no one has seen? And she was sure Johannes knew these things. But there was no way she would speak to him now.

She could not shake his words from her ears. She hoped fervently that her own still troubled him.

CHAPTER EIGHT

When Bellis looked out of her window the next morning, she saw, over the roofs and chimneys, that the city was moving.

At some time in the night, the hundreds of tugboats that milled constantly around Armada like bees around a hive had harnessed the city. With thick chains they had attached themselves in great numbers to the city's rim. They spread outward from the city, with their chains taut.

Bellis had become used to the city's inconsistencies. The sun would rise to the left of her smokestack house one day, to the right the next, as Armada had spun slowly during the night. The sun's antics were disorienting. Without land visible, there was nothing except the stars by which to gauge position, and Bellis had always found stargazing tedious: she was not someone who could instantly recognize the Tricorn or the Baby or the other constellations. The night sky meant nothing to her.

Today the sun rose almost directly in front of her window. The ships that strained at their chains and tugged at Armada's mass cut across her field of vision, and she calculated after a moment that they were heading south.

She was awed by that prodigious effort. The city easily dwarfed the proliferation of ships that were pulling at it. It was hard to estimate Armada's motion, but looking at the water coursing between ships, and the slap of breakers against the edges of the city, Bellis suspected that their passage was cripplingly slow.

Where are we going? she wondered, helplessly.

Bellis felt curiously shamed. It was weeks since she had arrived on Armada, and she realized that she had not wondered about the city's motion, about its passage across the sea or its itinerary, or how its fleet, out engaged in their piracy, found their way back to a home that moved. She remembered with a sudden shudder Johannes' attack on her the previous night.

Some of what he had said was true.

So was much of what she herself had said, of course, and she was still angry with him. She did not want to live on Armada, and the thought of seeing out her days on this mesh of moldering tubs made her mouth curl with anger so strong it was like panic. But still.

But still, it was true that she had locked herself off in her unhappiness. She was ignorant of her situation, ignorant of Armada's history and politics, and she realized that this was dangerous. She did not understand the city's economies; she did not know where the ships came from that sailed into the Basilio and Urchinspine harbors. She did not know where the city had been or where it was going.

She began to open her mind as she stood in her nightgown, watching the sun pour across the bows of the slowly moving city. She felt her curiosity unfurl.

The Lovers, she thought with distaste. *Let's start there. Godspit, the Lovers. What in the name of Jabber are they?*

Shekel took coffee with her on an upper deck of the library.

He was an excited boy. He told her that he was doing something with one person, and something else with another, and that he had had a fight with a third, and that a fourth lived in Dry Fall riding, and she withered beside his casual knowledge of the city. She felt disgraced again, for her ignorance, and she listened carefully to his ramblings.

Shekel told Bellis about Hedrigall the cactacae aeronaut. He told her about the cactus-man's notorious past as a pirate-merchant for Dreer Samher, and described to her the journeys Hedrigall had made to the monstrous island south of Gnurr Kett, to trade with the mosquito-men.

In turn, Bellis asked him about the ridings, the haunted quarter, the city's route, the *Sorghum* rig, Tintinnabulum. She turned up her questions like cards.

"Yeah," he said slowly. "I know Tinnabol. Him and his mates. Strange coves. Makler, Metzger, Promus, Tinnabol. There's one called Argentarius, who's mad, who no one ever sees. I can't remember the others. Inside the *Castor*'s all over trophies. Gruesome. Sea trophies. Every wall. Stuffed hammerheads and orca, things with claws and tentacles. Skulls. And harpoons. And helios of the crew standing on the corpses of things I hope I never see.

"They're hunters. They ain't been in the city so long. They're not press-ganged, exactly. There's loads of stories, rumors about what they're doing, why they're here. It's like they're waiting for something."

Bellis could not understand how Shekel knew so much about Tintinnabulum until he grinned and continued.

"Tintinnabulum's got a . . . an assistant," he said. "Her name's Angevine. She's an interesting lady." He grinned again, and Bellis turned away, embarrassed by his fumbling enthusiasm.

There were printing presses in Armada, and authors and editors and translators, and new books and Salt translations of classic texts were brought out. But paper was scarce: print runs were minuscule, and the books were expensive. The ridings of the city relied on Booktown's Grand Gears Library, and paid premiums to ensure their borrowing rights.

The books came mostly from Garwater riding's piracies. For an unknown number of centuries this most powerful riding in Armada had donated all the books it commandeered to The Clockhouse Spur. No matter who ran Booktown, these donations had ensured its loyalty. Other ridings copied the practice, though perhaps without such stern supervision. They might let their press-ganged keep this or that volume, or would trade some of the rarest volumes they snatched. Not Garwater, which treated book hoarding as a serious crime.

Sometimes Garwater ships would prowl the coastal settlements of Bas-Lag committing wordstorms, and the pirates would rampage from house to house, seizing every book and manuscript they found. All for Booktown, the Clockhouse Spur.

The delivery of all this plunder was ongoing, so Bellis and her colleagues kept busy.

The khepri newcomers in their Mercy Ships, randomly intercepted by Armada, had taken over the Booktown riding in a gentle coup more than a century before. They had been wise enough to realize that despite traditional khepri lack of interest in written texts—their compound eyes made reading somewhat difficult—the riding relied on its library. They had continued its stewardship.

Bellis could not estimate the number of books: there were so many tiny old holds in the ships of the library, so many converted chimneys and bulkheads, stripped cabins, annexes, all stuffed with texts. Many were ancient, countless thousands of them long undisturbed. Armada had been stealing books for many centuries.

The catalogs were only partial. In recent centuries a bureaucracy had arisen whose function was to list the library's contents, but during some reigns they were more careful than others. Mistakes were always made. A few acquisitions were shelved almost randomly, insufficiently checked. Errors slipped into systems and begot other errors. There were decades' worth of volumes hidden in the library, in plain view yet invisible. Rumors and legends were rife about their powerful, lost, hidden, or forbidden contents.

When she had first gone into the dark corridors, Bellis had run her fingers along the miles of shelves as she walked. She had pulled a book out at random and, opening it, had stopped short to see the handwritten name in fading ink on the top of the first page. She had tugged out another volume and there was another name, written in calligraphy and ink only a little more recent. The third book was unadorned, but the fourth, again, was marked as the property of another long-dead owner.

Bellis had stood still and read the names again and again, and felt suddenly claustrophobic. She was encased in stolen books, buried in them as if in dirt. The thought of the countless hundreds of thousands of names that surrounded her, vainly scrawled in top right-hand corners—the weight of all that ignored ink, the endless proclamations that *this is mine this is mine,* every one of them snubbed simply and imperiously—took Bellis' breath from her chest. The ease with which those little commands were broken.

She felt as if all around her, morose ghosts were milling, unable to accept that the volumes were no longer theirs.

That day, as she sorted through new arrivals, Bellis found one of her own books.

She sat for a long time on the floor with her legs splayed, propped up against the shelves, staring at the copy of *Codexes of the Wormseye Scrub*. She felt the familiar fraying spine and the slightly embossed "B. Coldwine." It was her own copy: she recognized its wear. She gazed at it guardedly, as if it were a test she might fail.

The cart did not contain her other work, *High Kettai Grammatology*, but she did find the Salkrikaltor Cray textbook she had brought to the *Terpsichoria*.

Our stuff's finally coming through, she thought.

It affected her like a blow.

This was mine, she thought. *This was taken.*

What else was from her ship? Was this Doctor Mollificatt's copy of *Future Tenses*? she wondered. Widow Cardomium's *Orthography and Hieroglyphs*?

She could not be still. She stood and walked, tense, wandering vague and stricken through the library. She passed into the open air and over the bridges that linked the library's vessels, carrying her book clutched to her, above the water and then back into the darkness by the bookshelves.

"Bellis?"

She looked up, confused. Carrianne stood before her, her mouth twisted slightly in what might be amusement or concern. She looked terribly pale, but she spoke with her usual strong voice.

The book dangled from Bellis' hands. Her breathing slowed, and she smoothed the crisis from her face, arranging it carefully once more, wondering what to say. Carrianne took her arm and tugged her away.

"Bellis," she said again, and though she wore an arch smirk there was genuine kindness in her voice. "It's high time you and I made a little effort to get to know each other. Have you eaten lunch?"

Carrianne dragged her gently through the corridors of the *Dancing Wight*, on up a half-covered walkway to the *Pinchermarn*. *This is not like me,* Bellis thought as she followed, *to let myself be tugged along in someone's wake. This is not like me at all.* But she was in a kind of daze, and she gave in to Carrianne's insistent pulling.

At the exit, Bellis realized with a gust of surprise that she was still carrying her copy of *Codexes of the Wormseye Scrub.* She had been clutching it so tight her hands looked bloodless.

Her heart sped up as she realized that under Carrianne's protection, she could walk straight past the guard, could hold the book close, out of sight, could leave the library with her contraband.

But the closer she got to the door, the more she hesitated, the less she understood her motives, the more she was suddenly terrified of capture, until with a sudden long sigh she deposited the monograph in the carrel beside the desk. Carrianne watched her inscrutably. In the light beyond the door, Bellis looked back at her deserted volume and felt a surge of something, some tremulous emotion.

Whether it was triumph or defeat she could not tell.

The *Psire* was the largest ship in the Clockhouse Spur, a big steamer of archaic design refitted for industry and cheap housing. Stubby concrete blocks loomed on its rear deck, all fouled with birdlime. Strings of washing linked windows where humans and khepris leaned out and talked. Bellis descended a rope ladder behind Carrianne, toward the sea, through the smell of salt and damp to a galley in the *Psire*'s shadow.

Below the galley's deck was the restaurant, full of noisy lunchtime diners. The waiters were khepri and human, and even a couple of rusted constructs. They strode the narrow walkway between two rows of benches, depositing bowls of gruel and plates of black bread, salads, and cheeses.

Carrianne ordered for them, then turned to Bellis with a look of sincere concern.

"So," she said. "What's happening with you?"

Bellis looked up at her, and for a dreadful second she thought she would cry. The feeling went quickly, and she set her face. She looked away from Carrianne, at the other human customers, the khepri and cactacae. A couple of tables from her were two llorgiss, their trifurcated bodies seeming to face every way at once. Behind her was some glistening amphibious thing from Bask riding, some species she could not even begin to recognize.

She felt the restaurant move as the waves lapped at it.

"I know what I'm seeing, you know," said Carrianne. "I was press-ganged, too."

Bellis looked up sharply. "When?" she said.

"Nearly twenty years ago," said Carrianne, looking through the windows at Basilio Harbor and the industrious tugs beyond, still hauling the city. She said something slowly and deliberately in a language Bellis almost recognized. The analytical part of her linguist's brain began to collate, to catalog the distinctive staccato fricatives, but Carrianne forestalled her.

"It's something we used to say, in the old country, to people feeling unhappy. Something stupid and trite like, 'It could be worse.' Literally it means 'You still have eyes and your spectacles aren't yet broken.' " She leaned in and smiled. "But I won't be hurt if you don't take any comfort from it. I'm further from my first home than you are, Crobuzoner. More than two thousand miles further. I'm from the Firewater Straits."

She laughed at Bellis' raised eyebrow, the incredulous look.

"From an island called Geshen, controlled by the Witchocracy." She tasted her dwarf Armadan chicken. "The Witchocracy, more ponderously known as Shud zar Myrion zar Koni." She waved her hands mock-mysteriously. "City of Ratjinn, Hive of the Jet Sorrow—and suchlike. I know what you New Crobuzoners say about it. Very little of which is true."

"How were you taken?" said Bellis.

"Twice," said Carrianne. "I was stolen and stolen again. We were sailing our whim-trawler for Kohnid in Gnurr Kett. That's a long, hard journey. I was seventeen. I won the lottery to be figurehead and concubine. I spent the daylight strapped to the bowsprit, scattering orchid petals in front of the ship, spent the night reading the men's cards and in their beds. That was dull, but I enjoyed the days. Dangling there, singing, sleeping, watching the sea.

"But a Dreer Samher war cog intercepted us. The Samheri were jealous of their trade with Kohnid. They had a monopoly—do they still?" she added suddenly, and Bellis could only shake her head uncertainly, *I don't know.*

"Well, they strapped our captain to my place below the bowsprit and scuttled the ship. Most of the men and women they put on lifeboats with a few provisions, and pointed in the direction of the coast. It was a long way away, and I doubt they made it.

"Some of us they kept aboard. There was no ill treatment beyond cuffs and rudeness. I tortured myself stupid wondering what they'd do to me, but then came the second interception. Dry Fall riding needed ships, and sent poachers out. Armada was far south of here then, so Dreer Samher boats were perfect prey."

"And . . . and how did you . . . ? Did you find it hard," said Bellis, "when you came here?"

Carrianne looked at her for a while.

"Some of the cactacae," she said, "never adjusted. They refused, or tried to escape, or attacked their guards. I suppose they were killed. Me and my companions . . . ?" She shrugged. "We'd been rescued, so it was very different.

"But, yes, it was hard, and I was miserable, and I missed my brother, and all of that. But, you see, I made a choice. I chose to live, to survive.

"After a time some of my shipmates moved out of Dry Fall. One lives in Shaddler, another in Thee-And-Thine. But mostly we stayed in the riding that took us in." She ate for a little while, then looked up again. "It can be done, you know. You *will* make this place your home."

She meant it reassuringly. She was being kind. But to Bellis it sounded like a threat.

Carrianne was talking to her about the ridings.

"Garwater you know," Carrianne said, her voice deadpan. "The Lovers. The scarred Lovers. Fucked-up bastards. The Clockhouse Spur you know."

The intellectuals' quarter, thought Bellis, *like Brock Marsh in New Crobuzon.*

"Shaddler's the scabmettlers'. Bask. Thee-And-Thine." Carrianne was counting off the ridings on her fingers. "Jhour. Curhouse, The Democratic Council. That brave redoubt. And Dry Fall," she concluded. "Where I live."

"Why did you leave New Crobuzon, Bellis?" she said unexpectedly. "You don't seem to me the colonist type."

Bellis looked down. "I *had* to leave," she said. "Trouble."

"With the law?"

"Something happened . . ." She sighed. "I did nothing, nothing at all." She could not keep the bitterness out of her voice. "A few months ago there was a sickness in the city. And . . . there

were rumors that someone I knew was involved. The militia
were working their way through everyone he'd known, everyone
he'd had involvement with. It was obvious they'd come for me,
eventually. I never wanted to leave." She spoke carefully. "It was
no choice."

The lunch, the company, even the small talk Bellis normally despised, had all calmed her. As they rose to leave, she asked Carrianne if she was feeling well.

"I noticed in the library . . ." she said. "I hope you don't mind
me saying, but I was thinking you look rather pale."

Carrianne smiled archly. "That's the first time you've asked
after me, Bellis," she said. "You want to watch that. I might start
thinking you give a brass eye about me." The amiable taunt
stung. "I'm fine. It's just that I was taxed last night."

Bellis waited, sifting through the information she had already
assimilated, to see if Carrianne's statement would make sudden
sense. It did not.

"I don't understand," she said, exhausted by incomprehension.

"Bellis, I live in Dry Fall riding," said Carrianne. "Sometimes
we're taxed, understand? Bellis, you know our ruler's the Brucolac, don't you? You've heard about him?"

"I've heard *of* him . . ."

"The Brucolac. He's oupyr. Loango. Katalkana." With each
esoteric word, Carrianne held Bellis' eyes and saw that she was
not understood. "Haemophage, Bellis. Ab-dead.

"Vampir."

Surrounded as she had been for weeks by a cloud of rumors and
hints like insistent midges, Bellis had learned at least a little
about most of the ridings. All the weird little femto-states clamped
together in unhealthy congregation, resenting each other and
maneuvering for position.

But somehow the most important, the most striking or unbelievable or appalling things, she had missed. At the end of the
day, she thought of that moment when she had been made to see
how ignorant she was: when Carrianne had explained her pallor
and Bellis had realized how far from home she was.

She was pleased that she had done little more than blanch at
Carrianne's explanation. Something had hardened in her when
she heard the word *vampir*—the same word in Ragamoll and

Salt. Carrianne had, at that moment, taught her that there was nowhere further for her to go. She could be no further from her home.

In Armada they talked a language she could understand. She recognized the ships, even altered and rebuilt as they were. They had money and government. The differences of calendar and terminology she could learn. The found and scavenged architecture was bizarre but comprehensible. But this was a city where vampir did not need to hide and predate furtively, but could walk in the nights openly, and could rule.

Bellis realized then that all her cultural markers were obsolete. She was sick of her ignorance.

At the Sciences card catalog Bellis' fingers fluttered through the entries, speeding through the alphabet until she found Johannes Tearfly's name. There was more than one copy of several of his books.

If the Lovers who run my life wanted to get hold of you so badly, Johannes, she thought to herself as she scribbled the classmarks of his works, *then I'm going to get inside their minds. Let's see what they're so excited about.*

One of the books was on loan, but copies of the others were available. As an employee of the library, Bellis had borrowing rights.

It was very cold as she made her way home past the crowds, under jabbering Armada monkeys in the rigging, over the swaying walkways and decks and raised streets of the city, over the waves that slopped between vessels. The sky was raucous with catcalls. In her bag, Bellis carried *Predation in Iron Bay Rockpools; Sardula Anatomy; Essays on Beasts; Theories of Megafauna;* and *Transplane Life as a Problem for the Naturalist*—all by Johannes Tearfly.

She sat up late curled close to her stove, while freezing clouds diffused the moonlight outside. She read by lamplight, skipping from book to book.

At one in the morning she looked out over the dark shipscape. The halo of boats that ringed the city still dragged it onward.

She thought of all the Armadan boats at sea, the agents of its piracy, taxing the ships and communities they passed. Ranging for months across thousands of miles, until, laden down with booty, and even as their city moved, they made their way back by arcane methods.

The city's nauscopists watched the sky, and knew from its minute variations when vessels were approaching, so the tugs could haul Armada away and out of sight. Sometimes the evasion failed, and foreign ships were intercepted, welcomed in to trade, or hunted down. By secret science, the authorities always knew when incoming vessels were Armada's own, and welcomed them home.

Even so late there were still sounds of industry from some quarters, cutting through the beat of waves and animals' night calls. Between the layers of rope and wood that overlaid her view like scratches on a heliotype, Bellis could see to the little bay of boats at the aft end of Armada, where the rig *Sorghum* wallowed. For weeks, fire and thaumaturgic wash had billowed up from the tip of its stack. Every night the stars had been effaced around it in a drab, dun light.

No more. The clouds above the *Sorghum* were dark. The flame was out.

For the first time since she had arrived in Armada, Bellis dug through her belongings and brought out her neglected letter. She faltered as she sat there by the stove, the paper folded in front of her, a fountain pen poised. And then, irritated with her own hesitation, she began to write.

Even as Armada made its slow way south toward warmer waters, for a few days the weather turned hard cold. Winds blew frost in from the north. The trees and ivy, the slim gardens that adorned the decks of boats, became brittle and blackened.

Just before the chill hit, Bellis saw whales off the city's port edge, playing with apparent pleasure. After a few minutes they came suddenly much closer to Armada, slammed the water with their huge tails, and were gone. The cold came quickly after that.

There was no winter in the city, no summer or spring, no seasons at all; there was only weather. For Armada it was a function not of time, but place. While New Crobuzon hunkered under snowstorms at the end of the year, Armadans might be basking in the Hearth Sea; or they might be bunked below while crews in thick coats tugged them slowly to anchor in the Muted Ocean, at temperatures that would have made New Crobuzon seem mild.

Armada tramped the oceans of Bas-Lag in patterns dictated by piracy, trade, agriculture, security, and other more opaque dynamics, and took what weather came.

The city's irregular climate was hard on plant life. The flora of Armada survived by thaumaturgy, luck and chance, as well as stock. Centuries of husbandry had produced strains that grew fast and hardy, and could thrive in a wide range of temperatures. There were irregular crops throughout the year.

Farmlands were draped across decks and under artificial lights. There were mushroom plantations in dank old holds, and loud, stinking berths full of generations of wiry inbred animals. Fields of kelp and edible bladderwracks grew on rafts suspended below the city, alongside mesh-cages full of crustaceans and food-fish.

As days passed, Salt came to Tanner more easily, and he began to spend more time with his workmates. They would carouse in the pubs and gambling halls on the aft edge of Basilio Harbor. Shekel came too, sometimes, happy in the company of the men, but more often he took himself off, alone, to the *Castor.*

Tanner knew that he went to see the woman Angevine, whom Tanner had not met, a servant or bodyguard for Captain Tintin-nabulum. Shekel had told him about her, in faltering adolescent terms, and Tanner had started off amused and indulgent. Nostalgic for himself at that age.

Shekel spent more and more time with the strange studious hunters who lived on the *Castor.* Once, Tanner came looking for him.

Belowdecks, Tanner had passed into a clean, dark corridor of cabins, each with a name stamped upon it: MODIST, he had read, and FABER, and ARGENTARIUS. The berths of Tintinnabulum's companions.

Shekel was in the mess, with Angevine.

Tanner had been shocked.

Angevine was in her thirties, he estimated, and she was Remade.

Shekel had not told him that.

Just below her thighs, Angevine's legs ended. She jutted like some strange figurehead from the front of a little steam-driven cart, a heavy contraption with caterpillar treads, filled with coke and wood.

She could not be city-born, Tanner had realized. That kind of Remaking was too harsh, too capricious and inefficient and cruel to have been effected for anything other than punishment.

He thought well of her for putting up with the lad's bothering.

Then he saw how intensely she spoke to Shekel, how she leaned in to him (at a bizarre angle, anchored by the heavy vehicle below her), how she held his eyes. And Tanner had stopped, shocked again.

Tanner left Shekel to his Angevine. He did not ask what was happening. Shekel, forced into a sudden new conjuncture of feelings, behaved like a hybrid of child and man, now boastful and preening, now subdued and caught up with intense emotions. In what little information he gave out, Tanner learned that Angevine had been press-ganged ten years ago. Like the *Terpsichoria,* her ship had been stolen on its way to Nova Esperium. She, too, was from New Crobuzon.

When Shekel came home to the little rooms on the portmost edge of an old factory ship, Tanner was jealous, and then contrite. He determined to keep ahold of Shekel as best as he could, but to let him go as he needed.

Tanner tried to fill a vacuum by making friends. He spent more time with his workmates. There was a strong camaraderie among the dockworkers. He took part in their lewd jokes and games.

They opened to him, brought him in by telling tales.

As a newcomer he was an excuse for them to trot out stories and rumors they had all heard a mass of times before. One of them would mention dead seas, or boiltides, or the moray king, and would turn to Tanner. *You've probably not heard of the dead seas, Tanner,* he or she would say. *Let me tell you . . .*

Tanner Sack heard the weirdest stories of the Bas-Lag seas, and the legends of the pirate city and Garwater itself. He heard of the monstrous storms that Armada had survived; the reason for the scars on the Lovers' faces; how Uther Doul had cracked the possibility code and found his puissant sword.

He joined in celebrations for this or that happy occurrence—a marriage, a birth, luck at cards. And somber things too. When a dockside accident took off half a cactus-woman's hand with a jag of glass, Tanner gave what eyes and flags he could spare to the whip-round. Another time, the riding was plunged into depression by the news that a Garwater ship, the *Magda's Threat,* had gone down near the Firewater Straits. Tanner shared the loss, and his sadness was not feigned.

But although he liked his workmates, and the taverns and convivials were a pleasant way of spending evenings—and one that improved his Salt in great gouts—there was a constant odd ambience of half-acknowledged secrecy. He could not make sense of it.

There were certain mysteries that the work of the underwater engineers threw up. What manner of things were those shadows he sometimes glimpsed, behind the tightly tethered guard sharks, unclear through what must be adumbrating glamours? What were the purposes of the repairs that he and his colleagues daily carried out? What was it that the *Sorghum,* the stolen rig that they tended carefully, sucked up from the base of the sea, thousands of feet below? Tanner had followed its fat, segmented pipe down with his eyes many times, growing giddy as it dwindled.

What was the nature of this project that was hinted at in nods and cryptic remarks? The plan that underpinned all their efforts? That no one would talk openly about, but that many seemed to know a little of, and a few pretended by omission, or hint, to understand?

Something big and important lay behind Garwater's industry, and Tanner Sack did not yet know what it was. He suspected that none of his fellows did, either, but still he felt excluded from some community: one based on lies, cant, and bullshit.

Stories occasionally reached him about the other *Terpsichoria* passengers or crew or prisoners.

Shekel had told him about Coldwine in the library. The man Johannes Tearfly he had seen himself, visiting the docks with a secretive group, all notepads and murmured discussion. A part of Tanner had thought tartly that it didn't take long for ranks to reestablish themselves, that while he worked his arse off below, the gentleman watched and ticked his little charts and fumbled with his waistcoat.

Hedrigall, the impassive cactus-man who piloted the *Arrogance,* told Tanner about a man called Fench, also from the *Terpsichoria,* who was visiting the docks quite often (*Do you know him?* Hedrigall had asked, and Tanner had shaken his head: it was too dull to explain that he had known no one above the decks). Fench was a good man, Hedrigall said, whom you could talk to, who seemed already to know everyone on the ship, who spoke on knowledgeable terms about people like King Friedrich and the Brucolac.

There was a distracted air to Hedrigall when he talked about these things, which reminded Tanner of Tintinnabulum. Hedrigall was one of those who always seemed to know something about something that he would not discuss. It would have felt to Tanner a breach of their embryonic friendship to ask him outright.

Tanner took to walking the city at night.

He would wander, surrounded by the sounds of water and ships, the sea smell in him. Under the moon and her glowing daughters, diffused through faint cloud, Tanner walked steadily around the edge of the bay containing the now-silent *Sorghum*. He trod past a cray dwelling: a suspended, half-sunk clipper, its prow and bows jutting like an iceberg. He walked up the covered bridge to the rear of the enormous *Grand Easterly,* his head down as he passed the few other insomniacs and night workers.

By rope bridge to the starboard side of Garwater. An illuminated dirigible skidded slowly overhead, and a klaxon sounded nearby while a steamhammer pounded (*some late shift*), and the sound for a moment was so reminiscent of New Crobuzon that he felt a strong, nameless emotion.

Tanner lost himself in a maze of old ships and bricks.

In the water below he thought he saw fleeting and random patches of light: the anxiety of bioluminescent plankton. The city's snarls seemed to be answered sometimes, miles away, by something big and very distant and alive.

He wound in the direction of Curhouse and Urchinspine Harbor. Below him was surf, to either side decaying brickwork damp with mildew and salt-stained. High walls and windows, many broken, and alleyways between main streets, winding between old bulkheads and cowls. Rubbish on deserted dhows. Balustrades and taffrails buffeted in the cold wind by the ragged remnants of posters; politics and entertainment advertised in garish colors rendered from squid and shellfish and stolen ink.

Cats padded past him.

The city shifted and corrected, and the tireless fleet of steamships beyond Armada's bounds plowed on, chains outstretched, hauling their home.

Tanner stood in the quiet, looking up at old towers, the silhouettes of slates, chimneys, factory roofs, and trees. Across a little stretch of water, broken by a hamlet of houseboats, lights glimmered in the cabins of boats from shores about which Tanner Sack knew nothing. Others were watching the night.

(—*Have you fucked before? she said, and Shekel could not help but remember things he did not much want to. The Remade women in the dark stinking of* Terpsichoria *who took his fumbling prick inside them for more portions of bread. Those whom the sailors held down whether they would or not (all the men catcalled him to join them) and whom twice he had lain on (once only pretending to finish before slinking away discomforted by her shrieks and) once entering for true and spending inside her, tightly struggling and crying as she was. And before them girls in the back alleys of Smog Bend, and boys (like him) showing their privates, their transactions something between barter and sex and bullying and play. Shekel opened his mouth to answer and the truths struggled, and she saw and interrupted him (it was a mercy she did him) and said—No not for games or money and not when you took it or gave it by force but when you fucked one who wanted you and who you wanted like real people like equals. And of course when she said that of course the answer was no, and he gave it, grateful to her for making this his first time (an undeserved gift that he took humble and eager).*

He watched her take off her blouse and his breath came very short at the sight of all that woman's flesh and at the eagerness in her own eyes. He felt the radiant heat of her boiler (which she could never let die she told him, which ate and ate fuel incessantly, old and broken and unreasonably greedy) and saw the dark pewter of her harness where it met the pasty flesh of her upper thighs like a tide. His own clothes were off him in easy layers and he stood shivering and thin and scrawny, prick bobbing erect and adolescent, heart and passion filling him so that it was hard to swallow.

She was Remade she was (Remade scum), he knew it, he saw it, and still he felt incessantly what was inside him, and he felt a great scab of habit and prejudice split from him, part from his skin where his homeland had inscribed him deep.

Heal me, *he thought, not understanding what he thought, hoping for a reconfiguration. There was a caustic pain as he peeled off a clot of old life and exposed himself open and unsure to her, to new air. Breathing fast again. His feelings welled out*

*and bled together (their festering ceased) and they began to re-
solve, to heal in a new form, to scar.*

*—My Remade girl, he said wondering, and she forgave him
that, instantly, because she knew he would not think it again.*

*It was not easy, with the stubs of her legs pinioned in metal, in
a tight V, parted only slightly, with only two inches of the inside
of her thighs below her cunt in flesh. She could not open to him
or lie back, and it was not easy.*

But they persevered, and succeeded.)

CHAPTER NINE

Shekel came to Bellis and asked her to teach him to read.

He knew the shapes of the Ragamoll alphabet, he told her, and
had a tentative sense of which sound each letter made, but they
remained esoteric. He had never tried to link them and make
them words.

Shekel seemed subdued, as if his thoughts were outside the
corridors of the library boats. He was slower than usual to smile.
He did not talk about Tanner Sack, or about Angevine, whose
name had peppered his conversations recently. He wanted only
to know if Bellis would help him read.

She spent more than two hours, after her shift, going through
the alphabet with him. He knew the names of the letters, but his
sense of them was abstract. Bellis had him write his name, and
he did, scratchy and inexpert, pausing halfway into the second
letter and skipping ahead to the fourth, then going back and filling in lost spaces.

He knew his written name, but only as strokes of a pen.

Bellis told him that the letters were instructions, orders, usually to make the sound that started their own name. She wrote
her own first name, separating each letter from its neighbors
by an inch or more. Then she had him obey the orders they
gave him.

She waited while he faltered through the *buh* and *eh* and *luh luh ih suh*. Then she brought the letters closer together and had him obey them—still slowly—again. And once more.

Finally she closed the characters up into a word and told him to repeat his exercise quickly, to do what the letters told him ("Look at them, so close together") in one quick run.

Buh eh luh luh ih suh.

(Confused by the double lingua-alveolar, as she had expected.)

He tried once more, and halfway through he stopped and began to smile at the word. He gave her a look so full of delight that it brought her up short. He said her name.

After she had showed him the rudiments of punctuation she had an idea. She walked with him through ships' bowels, past sections on science and humanities where scholars read hunkered beside oil lamps and little windows, then out between buildings in the drooling rain, over the bridge to the *Corrosive Memory*. It was a galleon at the outer edge of Grand Gears Library. It contained children's books.

There were very few readers on the children's deck. The shelves that surrounded them bristled with garish colors. Bellis ran her fingers along their spines as she walked, and Shekel gazed at them with a deep curiosity. They stopped at the very back of the ship, studded with portholes and listing quite sharply away from them, covered by an incline of books.

"Look," Bellis said. "Can you see?" She indicated the brass label. "Rag. A. Moll. Ragamoll. These are books in our language. Most of them'll come from New Crobuzon."

She plucked a couple and opened them. She froze for a fraction of a second, too quickly for Shekel to notice. Handwritten names peered up at her from the inside front pages, but these were scrawled in crayon, in infants' hands.

Bellis turned the pages quickly. The first book was for the very young, large and carefully hand-colored, full of pictures in the simplistic Ars Facilis style that had been in vogue sixty years previously. It was the story of an egg that went to battle against a man made of spoons, and won, to become mayor of the world.

The second was for older children. It was a history of New Crobuzon. Bellis stopped short, seeing the etched pictures of the Ribs and the Spike and Perdido Street Station. She skim-read quickly, curling her face in amused contempt at the grotesquely misleading history. The accounts of the Money Circle and the Week of Dust and, most shamefully, the Pirate Wars all suggested, in childish and disingenuous language, that New Crobuzon was a stronghold of liberty that thrived despite almost insuperable and unfair odds.

Shekel was watching her, fascinated.

"Try this one," she said, and held out to him *The Courageous Egg*. He took it reverentially. "It's for young children," she said. "Don't get worried about the story; it's much too silly for you. It means nothing. But I want to know if you can work out what's happening, if you can understand what goes on, by working through the words like I showed you. Follow the letters' orders, say the words. There are bound to be some in there that you can't understand. When you come to them, write them down, and bring the list to me."

Shekel looked up at her sharply. "Write them down?" he said.

She saw inside him. He still related to the words as if they were outside entities: subtle teases that he was finally beginning to understand, just a little. But he had not yet conceived of being able to encode them into his own secrets. He had not realized that by learning to read he had learned to write.

Bellis found a pencil and a half-used piece of paper in her pocket and handed them to him.

"Just copy the words that you don't understand, the letters in order exactly like they are in the book. Bring them to me," she said.

He eyed her, and another of those beatific smiles shot across him.

"Tomorrow," she went on, "I want you to come to me at five o'clock, and I'm going to ask you questions about the story in the book. I'm going to have you read pieces to me." Shekel stared at her as he took the book, nodded briskly, as if they'd reached some business arrangement in Dog Fenn.

Shekel's demeanor changed when they left the galleon. He held himself cocky again, and swaggered a little as he walked, and even began to talk to Bellis about his dockside gang. But he gripped *The Courageous Egg* tight. Bellis checked it out on her own ticket, an act of trust that she performed without thinking and that touched him deeply.

*   *   *

It was cold again that night, and Bellis sat close to her stove.

Cooking and eating were growing to irritate her with their relentless necessity. She performed them joylessly and as quickly as possible, then sat with Tearfly's books and continued to work through them, making notes. At nine she stopped and brought out her letter.

She wrote.

> Blueday 27th of Dust 1779 (although that means nothing here. Here it is 4th Sepredi of Hawkbill Quarto, 6/317),
> *Chromolith* Smokestack.

I will not stop looking for clues. At first, when I read Johannes' books, I opened them at random and skimmed through at random, and pieced together what I could in snippets, waiting for inspiration. But I have realized that I will not make headway thus.

Johannes' work, he has told me, is one of the driving forces behind this city. The nature of the scheme of which he is part, which he would not describe but which was important enough for Armada to risk an act of gross piracy against the greatest power in Bas-Lag, must be hidden somewhere in the pages of his books. It was, after all, one of those books that made him irresistible to the Lovers. But I cannot even work out which of his works is the "required reading" he described for this secret project.

So I am reading them carefully, taking each in turn; starting with the preface and working through to the index. Gleaning information. Trying to feel what designs might be in these works.

Of course, I am not a scientist. I have never read books like these before. A great deal of what is in them is opaque to me.

"The *acetabulum* is a depression on the outer side of the os innominatum just where the ilium and ischium fuse."

I read such sentences like poesy: ilium, ischium, os innominatum, ecto-cuneiform and cnemial crest, platelets and thrombin, keloid, cicatrix.

The book that I like least so far is *Sardula Anatomy*. Johannes was gored once by a young sardula, and it must have been at the time that he researched this book. I can imagine the creature pacing back and forth in a cell, subjected to soporific vapors, and lashing out as it feels itself slipping away.

And then dead, and transfered into a cold book that peels away Johannes' passion along with the sardula's skin. A drab list of bones and veins and sinews.

My favorite of the books comes as a surprise. It is neither *Theories of MegaFauna* nor *Transplane Life,* volumes as much philosophy as zoology, which I therefore expected to feel closer to than the others. I found their abstruse ponderings intriguing but vague.

No, the volume that I read most closely, that I felt I understood, that kept me quite entranced, was *Predation in Iron Bay Rockpools.*

Such an intricate concatenation of narratives. Chains of savagery and metamorphosis. I can see it all. Devil crabs and ragworms. The oyster drill gnawing a murderous peephole in its prey's armor. The stretched-out slow-time ripping open of a scallop by a famished starfish. A beadlet anemone devouring a young goby with an implosive burst.

It is a vivid little seascape Johannes has conjured for me, of shell-dust and sea urchins and merciless tides.

But it tells me nothing about the city's plans. Whatever Armada's rulers have in mind, I will have to look deeper to find. I will keep reading these books. They are the only clues I have. And I will not thus seek to understand Armada so that I can learn to live happily in my rusting chimney. I will understand *where we are going,* and *why,* so that I might leave.

There was a sudden knocking on Bellis' door. She looked up, alarmed. It was nearly eleven o'clock.

She stood slowly and descended the tight spiral staircase in the center of her circular room. Johannes was the only person in Armada who knew where she lived, and she had not spoken to him since their altercation in the restaurant.

Bellis padded slowly toward the door, waited, and the sharp rapping came again. Was he here to apologize? To rage at her again? Did she even want to see him, to reopen the door to that friendship?

She was still angry with him, she realized, and still somewhat ashamed.

There was a third bout of knocking, and Bellis stepped forward, her face set, ready to hear him out and see him off. When she pulled open the door she stopped short, her mouth hanging with astonishment, her curt admonition whispered away from her with her breath.

Standing on her threshold, huddled against the cold and looking up at her warily, was Silas Fennec.

They sat in silence for a little while, drinking the wine Fennec had brought.

"You've done well, Miss Coldwine," he said eventually, looking appreciatively around the battered metal cylinder that was her room. "A lot of us newcomers are in much less attractive places." She raised one eyebrow at him, but he nodded again. "I promise you it's true. Have you not seen?"

Of course she had not.

"Where are you living?" she asked.

"Near Thee-And-Thine riding," he said, "in the base of a clipper. No windows." He shrugged. "Are these yours?" He pointed to the books on her bed.

"No," she said, and tidied them quickly away. "They only let me keep my notebook. Even books I'd damn well *written,* they took away."

"Same for me," he said. "All I've got left is my journal. It's the log of years of traveling. I'd have been heartbroken to lose it." He smiled.

"What do they have you doing?" Bellis asked, and Fennec shrugged again.

"I managed to avoid all that," he said. "I'm doing what I want to do. You work in the library, don't you?"

"How?" she said sharply. "How did you keep them off your back? How do you manage to live?"

He watched her for a while without answering.

"I got three or four offers—like you, I imagine. I told the first that I'd accepted the second, the second that I'd said yes to the third, and so on. They don't care. As for how I live, well . . . It's easier than you think to make yourself indispensable, Miss Coldwine. Providing services, offering whatever it is people will pay for. Information mostly . . ." His voice petered out.

Bellis was bewildered by his candor, suggesting conspiracies and underworlds around her.

"You know . . ." he said suddenly, "I'm grateful to you, Miss Coldwine. Sincerely grateful."

Bellis waited.

"You were there in Salkrikaltor City, Miss Coldwine. You saw the conversation between the late Captain Myzovic and myself. You must have wondered what exactly was on that letter that had the captain so unhappy, that turned you back, but you remained quiet. I'm sure you realized that things could have become . . . very hard for me when we were hijacked by Armada, but you said nothing. And I'm grateful.

"You did say nothing?" he added with an anxiety he could not quite hide. "As I say, I'm very grateful."

"When we last spoke, on the *Terpsichoria*," Bellis said, "you told me it was vital you get back to New Crobuzon immediately. Well, what now?"

He shook his head uncomfortably.

"Hyperbole and . . . and bullshit," he said. He glanced up, but she showed no disapproval of his language. "I get into habits of exaggeration." He waved his hand to dispel the issue. There was an uncomfortable pause.

"So you can express yourself in Salt?" Bellis asked. "For this work you do, presumably you have to, Mr. Fennec."

"I have had many years to perfect Salt," he said in the language, swift and expert, with an unfeigned smile, and continued in Ragamoll. "And . . . Well, I'm not going by that name here. If you'd indulge me, I'm known here as Simon Fench."

"So where did you learn Salt, Mr. Fench?" she said. "You mentioned your travels . . ."

"Dammit." He looked amused and embarrassed. "You make the name sound like a hex. You can call me what you like, Miss Coldwine, in these rooms, but outside, I beg your indulgence. Rin Lor. I learnt Salt in Rin Lor, and the outer edge of the Pirate Islands."

"What were you doing there?"

"The same thing," he said, "that I do everywhere. I buy and I sell. I trade."

"I'm thirty-eight years old," he said after they had drunk some more and Bellis had fussed with the stove. "I've been a trader since before I was twenty. I'm a New Crobuzon man, don't get me wrong. Born and brought up in the shadow of the Ribs. But I doubt I've spent five hundred days in that city in the last twenty years."

"What do you trade?"

"Whatever." He shrugged. "Furs, wine, engines, livestock, books, labor. Whatever. Liquor for pelts in the tundra north of Jangsach, pelts for secrets in Hinter, secrets and artworks for labor and spices in High Cromlech . . ."

His voice drifted away as Bellis caught his eye.

"No one knows where High Cromlech is," she said, but he shook his head.

"Some of us do," he said quietly. "Now, I mean. Some of us do now. Oh it's a damn hard journey, granted. From New Crobuzon you can't go north through the ruins of Suroch, and south adds hundreds of miles through Vadaunk or the cacotopic stain. So it's Penitent's Pass to Wormseye Scrub, round Gibbing Water, skirt Kar Torrer Kingdom and over Cold Claw Sound . . ." His voice faded and Bellis hung on, eager to hear where next.

"And there are the Shatterjacks," he said softly. "And High Cromlech."

He took a long drink of wine.

"They're nervous of outsiders. Live ones. But gods know we were a sorry-looking bunch. We'd been on the road for months, lost fourteen men. We went by dirigible, barge, llama, and pterabird, and miles and miles on foot. I lived there for months. I brought back a lot of . . . amazing things to New Crobuzon. I've seen things even stranger than this city, I tell you."

Bellis could say nothing. She was wrestling with what he said. Some of the places he mentioned were virtually mythological. The idea that he might have visited them—lived in them, for Jabber's sake—was extraordinary, but she did not think he was lying.

"Most people who try to get there die," he said in a matter-of-fact tone. "But if you can do it, if you can get to the Cold Claws, especially the far shores . . . well, you're made. You've access to the Shatterjack Mines, the grasslands north of Hinter, Yanni Seckilli Island in the Cold Claw Sea—and they're eager for business, I tell you. I spent forty days there, and the only real trade they have is with the savages from the north, who turn up in coracles once a year, carrying stuff like biltong. Of which there's only so much you can eat." He grinned. "But their main problem is that The Gengris cuts them off from the south, doesn't let outsiders pass that way. Anyone who can get past that from the south, they treat like a lost brother.

"If you make it, you have access to all manner of information, places, goods, and services that no one else has. That's why I've . . . an arrangement with Parliament. That's why that pass, giving me powers to commandeer vessels, in certain circumstances; giving me certain rights. I'm in a position to provide information to the city that they can't get from anywhere else."

He was a spy.

"When Seemly crossed the Swollen Ocean and found Bered Kai Nev six and a half centuries ago," he said, "what do you think he carried in his holds? The *Fervent Mantis* was a big ship, Bellis . . ." He paused—she had not invited him to use her first name. But she made no sign of disapproval, and he continued. "It carried booze and silk and swords and gold. Seemly was look-ing to trade. That's what unlocked the eastern continent. All the explorers you've heard of—Seemly, Donleon, Brubenn, probably Libintos and bloody Jabber, too—they were traders." He spoke with childish gusto.

"It's people like me who bring back the maps and the informa-tion. We can offer insights like no one else. We can trade them with the government—that's my commission. There's no such thing as exploration or science—there's only trade. It was *mer-chants* who traveled to Suroch, who brought back the maps Dag-man Beyn used in the Pirate Wars."

He saw Bellis' expression and registered that this particular story did not cast him and his fellows in the best light.

"Bad example," he muttered, and Bellis could not help but laugh at his contrition.

"I won't live here," Bellis said. It was near two in the morning, and she was watching the stars through the window. They dragged with excruciating slowness across the pane as Armada was tugged gradually around.

"I don't like it here. I resent being kidnapped. I can under-stand why some of the other press-ganged from *Terpsichoria* don't mind . . ." She said that as a grudging sop to the guilt that Johannes had inculcated in her, and she knew uncomfortably that it was grossly insufficient, that it denigrated the freedom that had been granted to the *Terpsichoria*'s human cargo. "But I will not live out my life here. I'm going home to New Crobuzon."

She spoke with a hard certainty she did not quite feel.

"Not me," he said. "I mean, I like coming back, and living it up after some trip or other—dinners in Chnum, that sort of thing—but I couldn't *live* there. Though I understand why you'd like it. I've seen a lot of cities, and never anything to compare. But whenever I've been there more than a couple of weeks, I start to feel claustrophobic. Hemmed in by the dirt and the begging and the people . . . and the cant they spout in Parliament.

"Even when I'm uptown, you know? BilSantum Plaza or Flag Hill or Chnum—still I feel like I'm trapped in Dog Fenn or Badside. I just can't ignore them. I have to get out. And as for the bastards that run the place . . ."

Bellis was interested in his unabashed disloyalty. He was in the pay of the damn New Crobuzon government, after all, and even through the slight fog of wine, Bellis was coldly conscious that it was they, his bosses, who had caused her to flee.

But Fennec showed no commitment to them at all. He badmouthed the Crobuzoner authorities with bohemian good humor.

"They're snakes," he went on. "Rudgutter and all the others, I wouldn't trust them as far as I could piss them. Dammit, I'll take their money. If they want to pay me to tell them things I'd be happy to tell them anyway, am I going to say no? But they're no friends of mine. I can't sit easy in their city."

"So is all this . . ." Bellis spoke carefully, trying to gauge him. "Is this not a hardship, then, being here? If you've no great love for New Crobuzon—"

"No." He interrupted her with a hard manner quite unlike the amiable arrogance he had so far displayed. "That is not what I said. I'm a New Crobuzon man, Bellis. I want somewhere to come home to . . . even if I leave it again. I'm not rootless; I'm not some vague wanderer. I'm a businessman, a merchant, with a base and a house in East Gidd and friends and contacts, and New Crobuzon is always where I return to. Here . . . I'm a prisoner.

"This isn't the kind of exploring that I have in mind. I'm *damned* if I'm staying here."

And hearing that, Bellis opened another bottle of wine and poured him some more.

"What were you doing in Salkrikaltor?" she asked. "More *business*?"

Fennec shook his head. "I got picked up," he said. "Salkrikaltor patrols sometimes deploy hundreds of miles away from the city, checking the kraals. One of their craft picked me up in the outskirts of the Basilisk Channel. I was heading south in a crippled ammonite-sub, leaking and very slow. The cray in the shallows east of the Sols told them about this dubious-looking tub limping round the edge of their village." He shrugged. "I was damn well livid to get picked up, but I think they did me a favor. I doubt I'd have made it home. By the time I met any cray who could understand me, we were all the way out in Salkrikaltor City."

"Where'd you come from?" said Bellis. "Jhesshul Islands?"

Fennec shook his head and observed her, without speaking, for several seconds.

"Nothing like that," he said. "I crossed over from the other side of the mountains. I was in the Cold Claw Sea. In The Gengris."

Bellis looked up sharply, ready to laugh or sniff dismissively, but she saw Fennec's face. He nodded slowly.

"The Gengris," he said again, and she looked away, astonished.

More than a thousand miles west of New Crobuzon was a huge lake, four hundred miles across—Cold Claw Loch. From its northern tip jutted Cold Claw Sound, a corridor of freshwater a hundred miles wide and eight hundred long. At its northern end the sound expanded massively and suddenly, stretching back eastward almost the width of the continent, narrowing like a talon, became the jaggedly curving Cold Claw Sea.

These were the Cold Claws, a conjoined body of water too vast to be anything but an ocean. A massive, freshwater, inland sea ringed by mountains and scrubland and swamps and the few hardy, remote civilizations that Fennec claimed to know.

At its easternmost edge, Cold Claw Sea was separated from the saltwater of the Swollen Ocean by a tiny strip of land: a ribbon of mountainous rock less than thirty miles wide. The sea's sharp southernmost tip—the point of the talon—was almost directly north of New Crobuzon, more than seven hundred miles away. But the few travelers who made the journey from the city always bore a little west, to reach the waters of Cold Claw Sea two hundred miles or so away from its southern vertex. Because lodged like an impurity in the sea's jag was an extraordinary, dangerous place, something between an island, a half-sunk city, and a myth. An amphibious badland about which the civilized world knew next to nothing, except that it existed and that it was dangerous.

That place was called The Gengris.

It was said to be the home of the grindylow, aquatic demons or monsters or degenerate crossbred men and women, depending on which story one believed. It was said to be haunted.

The grindylow, or The Gengris (the distinction between race and place was unclear), controlled the south of the Cold Claw Sea with unbreakable power and a cruel, capricious isolationism. Their waters were lethal and uncharted.

And here was Fennec claiming—what?—to have lived there?

"It isn't true that there are no outsiders there," he was saying, and Bellis quieted her mind enough to listen. "There are even a few native human, born and bred in The Gengris . . ." His mouth twisted. "And *bred* is the word, though I'm not sure *human* is, anymore. It suits them fine that everyone thinks it's . . . like a little piece of hell there in the water, that it's beyond any kind of pale. But, shit, they deal with traders like everyone else. There're a few vodyanoi, a couple of humans . . . and others.

"I was there for more than half a year. Oh, it's dangerous like nowhere else I've been, don't get me wrong. You know if you trade in The Gengris that the rules . . . are very different. That you'll never learn, never understand them. I'd been there six weeks when my best friend there, a vodyanoi from Jangsach who'd been there for seven years, trading back and forth . . . he was taken away. I never found out what happened to him, or why," Fennec said flatly. "It might be that he insulted one of the grindylow gods, or it might have been that the catgut he supplied wasn't thick enough."

"So why did you do it?"

"Because, if you could last," he snapped, suddenly excited, "it was so worth it. There was no reason to grindylow trades, no point bartering or trying to second-guess. They ask me for a bushel of salt and glass beads in equal parts—fine. No questions, no queries; I'll provide it. Mixed fruit? It's there for them. Cod, sawdust, resin, fungus, I don't care. Because, by Jabber, when they paid, when they were happy . . .

"It was worth it."

"But you left."

"I left." Fennec sighed. He got up and rummaged around in her cupboard. She did not scold him for it.

"I was there for months, buying, selling, exploring The Gengris and its environs—diving, you understand—and keeping my journal." He spoke with his back to her, fussing with the kettle. "Then I got word that I'd . . . that I'd transgressed. That the

grindylow were angry with me, and that my life was over unless
I could get out, fast."

"What had you done?" said Bellis slowly.

"I have no idea," he snapped. "No idea at all. Maybe the ball
bearings I provided were the wrong kind of metal, or the moon
was in the wrong house, or some grindylow magus had died and
they blamed me. I don't know. All I knew was that I had to leave.

"I left a few things that gave them a false trail. See . . . I'd come
to know the southern jag of Cold Claw Sea pretty well. They like
to keep it secret, but I could find my way around it better than
any outsider's supposed to. There are tunnels. Fissures in the
ridge that cuts off Cold Claw Sea from the Swollen Ocean.
Through those burrows, out to the coast."

He paused and looked out into the sky. It was nearly five
o'clock. "I was trying to head south once I got into the ocean,
but I got dragged out into the edges of the channel. Which is
where the cray found me."

"And you waited for a New Crobuzon ship to take you home,"
Bellis said. He nodded. "Ours was going in the wrong direction,
so you decided to commandeer it . . . with the powers vested in
your little letter."

He was lying, or leaving out some important part of the truth.
That was trivially obvious, but Bellis did not comment. If he
wanted to fill out his story he would do so. She would not pes-
ter him.

As she sat back in her chair, her half-drunk tea beside her on
the uneven floor, she felt a sudden gush of tiredness, so that all of
a sudden she could barely speak. She saw the first sickly light of
dawn and knew it was too late to go to bed.

Fennec watched her. He saw her slump with exhaustion. He
was more awake than she. He made himself another cup of tea as
she let fits of dozing lap at her like little waves. She flirted with
dreams.

Fennec began to tell her stories about his time in High
Cromlech.

He told her the smells of the city, flint dust and rot and ozone,
myrrh and embalming spices. He told her about the pervading
quiet, and the duels, and the high-caste men with lips sewn shut.
He described the descent of the Bonestrasse, great houses looming to either side on ornate catafalques, the Shatterjacks visible

at the thoroughfare's end, spilling out for miles. He talked on for nearly an hour.

Bellis sat with her eyes open, starting now and then as she remembered that she was awake. And as Fennec's stories lurched east, across one and a half thousand miles, and he began to tell her about the malachite chapels of The Gengris, she was conscious that there was a growing crop of shouts and clattering from below, that Armada was waking beneath them, and she stood and smoothed her hair and clothes, and told him that he had to leave.

"Bellis," he said from the stairs. Before, when he had used her first name, it had been in the spurious closeness of nighttime. Hearing him call her Bellis like that, with the sun up and people awake around them, was different. But she said nothing, and that gave him permission to continue.

"Bellis, thank you again. For . . . protecting me. When you said nothing about the letter." She watched him tight-faced, and was silent. "I'll see you again, soon. I hope that'll be all right."

And again she said nothing, conscious of the distance daylight had brought between them, and of the many things he was not telling her. But, still, she did not mind if he came again. It had been a long time since she had conversed as she had that night.

CHAPTER TEN

There were very few clouds that morning. The sky was hard and empty.

Tanner Sack was not going to the docks. He walked afore, through the industrial hulks that surrounded his home. He took a route toward the little tangle of dockside vessels punctuated with pubs and scored with alleys. He had his sea legs, his hips shifting unconsciously with each tilt of the pavements.

He was surrounded by bricks and tarred beams. The sounds of

the factory ships and the rig *Sorghum* ebbed behind him, losing
him in the twists of the city. His tentacles swung, and moved very
gently. They were wrapped in soothing brine-soaked bandages.

Last night, for the third time in succession, Shekel had not
come home.

He was with Angevine again.

Tanner thought about Shekel and the woman, still a little
shamed by his own jealousy. Jealous of Shekel or of Angevine—
it was a knot of resentment too tangled for him to untie. He tried
not to feel deserted, which he knew was not fair. He determined
that he would look out for the boy no matter what, would keep a
home for him for whenever he came back, would let him go with
as much grace as Tanner could muster.

He was just sad that it had come so fast.

Tanner could see the masts of *Grand Easterly* dominating the
skyline to star'd. Aerostats sailed like submersibles through the
city's rigging. He descended to Winterstraw Market and made
his way over its little vessels accosted by vendors and jostled by
early shoppers.

The water was very close to him here, just below his feet. It
slopped all around him in the grooves between the boats that
made up the bazaar, awash with rubbish. The smell and sound of
it were strong.

He closed his eyes momentarily and imagined himself hover-
ing in the cool saltwater. Descending, feeling the pressure increase as the sea cosseted him. His tentacles grasping at passing
fish. Making sense of the mysteries of the city's underside: the
obscure dark shapes in the distance, the gardens of pulp and
rockweed and algae.

Tanner felt his resolve waxing, and he walked more quickly.

In The Clockhouse Spur riding he almost became lost in the
unfamiliar environs. He referred carefully to his hand-scrawled
map. Tanner made his way along winding walkways stretched
out over low boats, and across ornately reconfigured caravels, to
the *Duneroller,* a fat old gunship. An unstable-looking tower tottered at the ship's rear, tethered by guy ropes to the rigging.

This was a quiet quarter. Even the water coursing between
these boats seemed subdued. This was a neighborhood of back-
alley thaumaturges and apothecaries, the scientists of Booktown.

In the office at the top of the tower, Tanner looked out from the imperfectly cut window. He could see across the restless ship-scape to the horizon that pitched gently, swung up and down in the window frame as the *Duneroller* listed with the sea.

There was no word in Salt for Remaking. Serious augmentation or change was not common. Major work—to ameliorate the effects of the New Crobuzon punishment factories or, rarely, for some more proactive purpose—relied on a handful of practitioners. Self-taught biothaumaturges, specialist doctors, and chirurgeons and—rumor held—a few exiles from New Crobuzon whose expertise had been gleaned years before in the punitive service of the state.

For these serious changes, the word was taken from the Ragamoll. It was that Ragamoll word that filled Tanner's mouth.

He brought his eyes back to the man behind the desk, patiently waiting.

"I need you to help me," Tanner said, faltering. "I want to be Remade."

Tanner had thought about it for a long time.

His coming to terms with the sea felt like a long, drawn-out birth. Every day he spent more time below, and the water felt better against him. His new limbs had adapted completely, were as strong and almost as prehensile as his arms and hands.

He had seen with envy how Bastard John the dolphin policed his watch, passing through the brine with unique motion (as he swept in to punish some slacking worker with a brutal butting); and had watched as cray from their half-sunk ships (suspended at the point of being lost, pickled in time) or the unclear menfish from Bask riding launched themselves into the water, uncontained by harnessing or chains.

When he left the sea, Tanner felt his tentacles hang heavy and uncomfortable. But when he was below, in his harness, his leather and brass, he felt tethered and constrained. He wanted to swim free, across and up into the light and even, yes, even down, into the cold and silent darkness.

There was only one thing he could do. He had considered asking the docks to subsidize him, as they surely would, gaining an infinitely more efficient worker to do their bidding. But as the days went on and his resolution grew, he had dispensed with that plan, and had begun to hoard his eyes and flags.

That morning, with Shekel away and the clear sky blowing

salt air into him, he realized, suddenly, that this was truly and completely what he wanted to do. And with a great happiness he understood that it was not because he was ashamed that he would not ask for money, nor because he was proud, but only because the process and the decision were, completely and uniquely and without confusion, his own.

When he was not with Angevine (times that stayed in his head like dreams), Shekel was in the library, moving through the towers of children's books.

He had made his way through *The Courageous Egg.* The first time it had taken him hours. He had gone back over it again and again, picking up his pace as much as he could, copying the words that he couldn't at first read and making the sounds slowly out loud, in order, until meaning wrestled its way through the separated shapes.

It was hard and unnatural at first, but the process began to come more easily. He reread the book constantly, more and more quickly, not interested by the story, but ravenous for the unprecedented sensation of meaning coming up at him from the page, from behind the letters like an escapee. It almost made him queasy, almost made him feel like spewing, it was so intense and unnerving. He turned the technique to other words.

He was surrounded by them: signs visible on the commercial street beyond the windows, signs throughout the library and across the city and on brass plaques in his hometown, in New Crobuzon, a silent clamor, and he knew that there was no way he would ever be deaf to all those words again.

Shekel finished *The Courageous Egg* and was full of rage.

How come I wasn't told? he thought, searing. *What fucker was it kept this from me?*

When Shekel came looking for Bellis in her little office off the Reading Room, his manner surprised her.

She was very tired from Fennec's visit the night before, but she made a little effort and focused on Shekel, asked him about his reading. To her own surprise, she found the fervor with which he answered her moving.

"How's Angevine?" she asked, and Shekel tried to speak but could not. Bellis eyed him.

She had expected adolescent bragging and hyperbole, but

Shekel was visibly crippled by emotions he had not learned to feel. She felt an unexpected gust of affection for him.

"I'm a bit worried about Tanner," he said slowly. "He's my best mate, and I think he's feeling a bit . . . deserted. I don't want to piss him off, you know? He's my best mate." And he began to tell her about his friend Tanner Sack and, in doing so, let her know, shyly, about how things stood with him and Angevine.

She smiled inwardly at that—an adult tactic, and he had performed it well.

He told her about their home on the factory ship. He told her about the big shapes that Tanner had half-seen under the water. He began to recite the words on boxes and books that lay around the room. He said them out loud and scribbled them on sheafs of paper, breaking them into syllables, treating each word with equal, analytical disinterest, participle or verb or noun or proper name.

As they strained to move a box of botanical pamphlets, the door to the office opened and an elderly man entered with a Re-made woman. Shekel started, and moved toward the newcomers.

"Ange—" he started, but the woman (rolling forward on a stuttering pewter contraption where her legs should be) shook her head swiftly and folded her arms. The white-haired man waited for Angevine and Shekel's wordless interaction to conclude. As Bellis watched him warily she realized that he was the one who had welcomed Johannes on board. Tintinnabulum.

He was brawny and held himself tall despite his age. His ancient bearded face, framed with stringy white hair to below his shoulders, looked transplanted onto a younger body. He turned his eyes to Bellis.

"Shekel," said Bellis quietly, "would you mind leaving for a few moments?" But Tintinnabulum interrupted her.

"There's no need for that," he said. His voice seemed very distant: dignified and melancholy. He switched to good, accented Ragamoll. "You're a New Crobuzoner, aren't you?" She did not respond, and he nodded gently as if she had. "I'm speaking to all the librarians—particularly those like you, cataloging new acquisitions."

What do you know about me? Bellis thought carefully. *What has Johannes told you? Or does he protect me, despite our argument?*

"I have here . . ." Tintinnabulum held out a sheet of paper. "I have here a list of authors whose books we're most interested in tracing. These are writers of great use to us in our work. We're requesting your help. We have some works by some of these writers, and we're eager to find whatever else we can. Others are said to have written specific volumes for which we're searching. About others we know only rumors. You'll find three of them have works in the catalog—those books we already know about, but we're interested in any others.

"It might be that one or other of these names surfaces in the next batch of books that arrives. Or it may be that the library has stocked their work for centuries, and they're lost on the shelves. We've searched the relevant sections carefully—biology, philosophy, thaumaturgy, oceanology—and have found nothing. But we could have made mistakes. We would like you to keep a watch for us, on every new book you take in, on forgotten ones you find behind shelves, any time you catalog unlisted volumes. Two of these, those that aren't from New Crobuzon, are old."

Bellis took the list and looked at it, expecting it to be very long. But, typed very neatly, in the dead center of the sheet, there were only four names. None of them meant anything to her.

"Those are the core of our list," Tintinnabulum said. "There are others—there's a much longer version that will be posted at the desks—but those four are the ones we'd ask you to commit to memory, to search for . . . assiduously."

Marcus Halprin. That was a New Crobuzon name. Angevine was motioning at Shekel surreptitiously as she and Tintinnabulum moved slowly toward the door.

Uhl-Hagd-Shajjer (*transliteration*), Bellis read, and beside it the original: a set of cursive pictograms she recognized as the lunar calligraphy of Khadoh.

Beneath that was the third name, *A. M. Fetchpaw*—New Crobuzon again.

"Halprin and Fetchpaw are relatively recent writers," said Tintinnabulum from the doorway. "The other two are older, we think—probably a century or so. We'll leave you to your work, Miss Coldwine. If you should find anything that we want, anything by any of these writers not listed in the catalogs, please come to my vessel. It's by the for'ard tip of Garwater, the *Castor.* I can assure you that anyone able to help us will be rewarded."

What do you know about me? thought Bellis anxiously as the door closed.

She sighed and looked at the paper again. Shekel looked over her shoulder and began, hesitantly, to say the names on the paper out loud.

Krüach Aum, Bellis read finally, ignoring Shekel's slow progress through the syllables. *How exotic,* she thought sardonically, looking at the script, an archaic variant of Ragamoll. *Johannes mentioned you. That's a Kettai name.*

Halprin and Fetchpaw each had books listed in the catalogs. Fetchpaw's were volumes one and two of *Against Benchamburg: A Radical Theory of Water.* Halprin's were *Maritime Ecologies* and *The Biophysics of Brine.*

Uhl-Hagd-Shajjer had a large number of works listed, Khadohi books apparently averaging little more than forty pages each. Bellis was familiar enough with the moon-writing alphabet to make out how the titles sounded, but she had no idea what they meant.

Of Krüach Aum there was nothing.

Bellis watched Shekel teaching himself to read, rifling through the sheets on which he had written difficult words, scribbling additions to them as he said their sounds, copying words from the papers around him, from files, from the list of names that Tintinnabulum had left her. It was as if the boy had once known how to read, and was now remembering.

At five o'clock he sat with her and went through *The Courageous Egg.* Shekel answered her questions about the egg's adventures with a care that skirted the comic. She pronounced the words he did not know, syllable by slow syllable, guiding him through the confusions of silent or irregular letters. He told her he already had another book ready for her, that he had read in the library itself that day.

That night, for the first time, Bellis wrote in her letter about Silas Fennec. She mocked his pseudonym, but admitted that his company, his cocky edge, had been a relief after days of being alone. She continued to work her way through Johannes' *Essays on Beasts.* She wondered whether Fennec would come by again, and when he did not, she went to bed in an irritated burst of boredom.

She dreamed, not for the first time, of the river journey to Iron Bay.

* * *

Tanner dreamed of being Remade.

He found himself back in the punishment factory in New Crobuzon, where his extra limbs had been grafted to him in searing, drugged minutes of pain and humiliation. Once again the air clamored with industrial noises and screams, and he lay strapped to damp, stained wood, but this time the man bending over him was not a masked biothaumaturge, but the Armadan chirurgeon.

Just as he had in the waking day, the chirurgeon showed him charts of his body, with red markings where work would be done, emendations marked out like corrections on a schoolchild's copybook.

"Will it hurt me?" Tanner asked, and the punishment factory faded and sleep faded, but the question remained. *Will it hurt?* he thought as he lay in his newly lonely room.

But when he had gone once more below the water, his longing overcame him again, and he realized that he was less afraid of the pain than of hankering like this forever.

Angevine told Shekel—sternly—how to treat her when she was working.

"Can't try and talk to me like that, boy," she told him. "I been working with Tintinnabulum for years. Garwater pays me to look after him, ever since they brought him in. He's trained me well, and I owe him loyalty. You don't mess with me when I'm working. D'you understand?"

She spoke to him in Salt now, most of the time, forcing him to learn (she was hard on him, she wanted to bring him into her city without delay). As she turned to go, Shekel stopped her and told her, haltingly, that he did not think he could come to her cabin that night, that he felt he should spend a night with Tanner, who must be feeling a bit low, he said.

"Good of you to think of him," she said. So many ways he was growing, so fast. Loyalty and lust and love weren't enough for her. It was these frequent glimmerings of the man underneath the childhood he was shucking that swept Angevine with true passion for him, that stained her vague parental warmth with something more hard and base and breathless.

"Give him an evening," she said. "Come by mine tomorrow, lover."

She gave him that last word carefully. He was learning to take such presents with grace.

* * *

Shekel spent hours alone in the library, in the shelfscape of wood and vellum, gently rotting leather and paperdust. He kept to the Ragamoll section, surrounded by books that he pulled carefully down and opened around him, text and pictures like flowers on the floor. He slowly took in stories about ducks and poor boys who became kings, and battles against the trow, and the history of New Crobuzon.

He kept notes of every troublesome word whose sounds tried to evade him: *Curious, saber, tough, Jhesshul, Krüach.* He practiced them constantly.

As he wandered the shelves he kept his books with him, reshelving them at the end of the day not by the classmarks he did not understand, but by invented mnemonics that told him this one belonged between the big red and the small blue spines, and this one at the end, beside the volume with the picture of an airship.

There was one terrible panicked moment. He picked a book from the wall, and the shapes inside, all the letters, were friends to him; but as he settled before them and began to mouth and mutter them, waiting for them to sound as words in his head, they were all gibberish. He grew frantic very quickly, fearing that he had lost what it was he had gained.

But then he realized that he had taken a book from a shelf just to one side of the Ragamoll section; that it shared the alphabet that was now his, but pieced it together into a different language. Shekel was dumbstruck at the realization that these glyphs he had conquered could do the same job for so many peoples who could not understand each other at all. He grinned as he thought about it. He was glad to share.

He opened more foreign volumes, making or trying to make the noises that the letters spelled and laughing at how strange they sounded. He looked carefully at the pictures and cross-referenced them again. Tentatively he concluded that in this language, this particular clutch of letters meant *boat,* and this other set *moon*.

Shekel moved off slowly, making his way further from the Ragamoll section, picking up random works and gaping at their impenetrable stories, moving down the long corridors of children's books until he reached new shelving and opened a book

whose script was like nothing he knew. He laughed, delighted at
its strange curves.

He moved off further and found yet another alphabet. And a
little way off there was another.

For hours he found intrigue and astonishment by exploring the non-Ragamoll shelves. He found in those meaningless
words and illegible alphabets not only an awe at the world, but
the remnants of the fetishism to which he had been subjected before, when all books had existed for him as these did now, only
as mute objects with mass and dimension and color, but without
content.

Though it was not quite the same. It was not the same to see
these alien pages and know that they would have meaning to
some foreign child, as *The Courageous Egg* and *The History of
New Crobuzon* and *The Wasp in a Wig* now surrendered meaning
to him.

He gazed at the books in Base and High Kettai and Sunglari
and Lubbock and Khadohi with a kind of fascinated nostalgia for
his own illiteracy, without for a fraction of a moment missing it.

CHAPTER ELEVEN

Silas was waiting for Bellis as she emerged from the *Pinchermarn,* the sun low over the sea. She saw him leaning back
against a railing and watching for her.

He smiled when he saw her.

They ate together, and talked, gently fencing around one another. Bellis could not tell if it was him she was glad to see, or
whether she had simply had enough of loneliness, but either way
she welcomed his company.

He had a suggestion. It was the fourth Bookdi of Hawkbill.
That was a scabmettler blood-day, and in Thee-And-Thine riding there was a major fight festival. Several of the best fighters

from Shaddler riding were coming, to show their skills. Had she ever seen *mortu crutt,* or stampfighting?

Bellis took convincing. In New Crobuzon she had never visited Cadnebar's glad circus, or any of its lesser imitators. The idea of watching such combat repelled her somewhat, and bored her more. Silas was insistent. Studying him, she realized that his desire to see these fights was not motivated by sadism or voyeurism; she did not know what did drive it, but it was less base than that. Or differently base, perhaps.

She also knew that he was eager for her to come with him.

To get to Thee-And-Thine, they passed over Shaddler riding, the scabmettler home. Their aircab moved sedately past a spindly tower of girders at the rear of the great iron *Therianthropus,* and on, star'd.

This was to be Bellis' first time in Thee-And-Thine. *It's about time,* she told herself with shame. She was committed to understanding the city, but her resolution risked waning and becoming a nebulous depression again.

The fighting ground was a little way fore of Thee-And-Thine's flagship, a big clipper with sails sliced into decorative patterns, in the thick of the merchant riding's backstreets. The arena was a ring of small vessels with benches laid in gradients on their decks, facing into the circle of sea. Opulent gondolas hung from dirigibles around the edges of the arena. These were the private boxes of the rich.

Tethered in the middle was the stage itself; it was a wooden platform, its edges studded with brass gas lamps to light it and barrels to keep it afloat. That was the fighting ground: a circle of refitted ships and balloons around a piece of driftwood.

With a flourish of money and a brief word, Silas freed up two seats in the front row. He talked continuously in a low voice that outlined the politics and personalities around them.

"That's the vizier of Thee-And-Thine," he would explain, "come to make up the money he lost at the start of the quarto." "The woman over there with the veil never shows her face. She's said to be on the Curhouse council." His eyes moved constantly over the crowd.

Vendors sold food and spiced wine, and bookmakers shouted odds. The festival was unpretentious and profane, like most of what went on in Thee-And-Thine.

The crowd was not all human.

"Where are the scabmettlers?" Bellis said, and Silas began to point, seemingly randomly, around the arena. Bellis struggled to see what he saw: he was indicating humans, she thought, but their skin was blanched grey, and they looked squat and strong. Scarification marked their faces.

Bloodhorns sounded, and by chymical trickery the lights of the stage burst suddenly red. The crowd brayed enthusiastically. Two seats along from her, Bellis saw a woman whose physiognomy marked her as scabmettler. She did not cheer or shout, but sat still through the vulgar enthusiasm. Bellis could see other scabmettlers reacting similarly, waiting stolidly for the holy-day battles.

At least the general bloodlust was honest, she thought, contemptuous. There were enough scabmettler bookies to show that this was an industry, whatever the Shaddler elders might pretend.

Bellis realized wryly that she was tense to see what would happen. Excited.

When the first three fighters were ferried over to the arena, the crowd fell silent. The scabmettler men stepped onto the platform, naked except for loincloths, and stood in a triangle back-to-back in the center.

They were poised, all of them well muscled, their grey skin pallid in the gas jets.

One of the men seemed to be facing her directly. He must have been blinded by the lights, but still she entertained the fancy that it was a private performance for her.

The fighters kneeled and washed themselves, each from a bowl of steaming infusion the color of green tea. Bellis saw leaves and buds in it.

Then she started. From their bowls each man had pulled out a knife. They held them still and dripping. They were recurved, the cutting edge curling like a hook or a talon. Skinning knives. Something with which to score, to pare off flesh.

"Is that what they fight with?" she turned to Silas to ask, but the sudden mass gasp from the crowd pulled her attention back to the stage. Her own cry came an instant later.

The scabmettlers were carving furrows in their own flesh.

The fighter right before Bellis was tracing the outlines of his muscles in wicked strokes. He hooked the knife under the skin of his shoulder, then curled around with surgical precision, drawing a red line that linked deltoid and biceps.

The blood seemed to hesitate for a second, then to blossom, an eructation of it, bursting out from the fissure like boiling water, pouring out of him in great gouts, as if the pressure in his veins was immeasurably greater than in Bellis'. It raced across the man's skin in a macabre slick, and he turned his arm expertly this way and that, channeling his own blood according to some design Bellis could not see. She watched, waiting for a cascade of gore to foul the stage, which *did not happen,* and her breath stopped in her throat as she saw that the blood was setting.

It poured in great oozing washes from the man's wounds, the substance of the blood crawling over itself to reach higher, and she saw that the edges of the wound were crusted with embankments of clotting blood, vast accretions of the stuff, the red turning swiftly brown and blue and black, and freezing in crystalline jags that jutted inches from his skin.

The blood that ran down his arm was setting also, expanding at an impossible rate and changing color like vivid mold. Shards of scab matter frosted into place like salt or ice.

He dipped his knife again in the green liquid and continued to cut, as did his fellows behind him. He grimaced against the pain. Where he sliced the blood exploded, and coursed along the runnels in his anatomy, and set hard in an abstract armor.

"The liquid's an infusion that slows coagulation. It allows them to shape the armor," Silas whispered to Bellis. "Each warrior perfects his own pattern of cuts. That's part of their skill. Quick-moving men cut themselves and direct the blood so as to leave their joints free, and they pare off excess armor. Slow, powerful ones coat themselves in scab until they're as clumsy and heavily armored as constructs."

Bellis did not want to speak.

The men's grisly, careful preparations took time. Each of them sliced in turn at his face and chest and belly and thighs, and grew a unique integument of dried blood: hardened cuirasses and greaves and vambraces and helmets with irregular edges and coloration; random extrusions like lava flows, organic and mineral at once.

The laborious act of cutting turned Bellis' stomach. The sight of that armor so carefully cultivated in pain astounded her.

* * *

After that cruel and beautiful preparation, the fight itself was as dull and unpleasant as Bellis had thought it would be.

The three scabmettlers circled each other, each wielding two fat scimitars. Encumbered by their bizarre armor, they looked like animals in outlandish plumage. But the armor was harder than wax-boiled leather, deflecting strokes from the weighted swords. After a long, sweaty battering, a clot of the stuff fell free from the forearm of one fighter, and the quickest man slashed out at him.

But scabmettler blood provided another defense. As the man's flesh parted, his blood gushed out and over his enemy's blade. Unthinned by anticoagulant, it set almost instantly as it met the air, in an ugly, unsculpted knot that grasped the scimitar's metal like solder. The wounded man bellowed and spun, ripping the sword out of his opponent's hand. It juddered absurdly in his wound.

The third man stepped in and cut his throat.

He moved with speed, at such an angle that although his blade was spattered with quick-setting gore, it was not trapped by the glacier of blood that bloomed and froze in the ragged hole.

Bellis was holding her breath with shock, but the defeated man did not die. He fell to his knees in obvious pain, but the rime of scab had immediately sealed his wound, saving him.

"You see how hard it is for them to die in that arena?" murmured Silas. "If you want to kill a scabmettler, use a club or a bludgeon, not a blade." He looked briefly around him and then spoke intensely and quietly, his voice muffled by the spectators. "You've got to try to *learn* things, Bellis. You want to defeat Armada, don't you? You want out? So you have to know where you are. Are you accumulating knowledge? Godspit, trust me, Bellis; this is what I do. Now you know how not to try to kill a scabmettler, right?"

She stared at him, eyes widening in astonishment, but his brutal logic made sense. He committed to nothing and collated everything. She imagined him doing the same thing in High Cromlech and The Gengris and Yoraketche, hoarding money and information and ideas and contacts, all of it raw material, all of it potentially a weapon or a commodity.

He was, she realized uneasily, more serious, far more serious, than she. He was preparing and planning all the time.

"You have to know," he said. "And there's more to come. There are some people you need to know."

There were other scabmettler fights, all with their oddly stunted savagery: varieties of scab armor, different styles of combat all executed with the stylized movements and ostentation of *mortu crutt*.

And there were other contests, between humans and cactacae and all the nonaquatic races of the city—displays of stampfighting.

Combatants used the bottom of their clenched fists, as if they were banging a tabletop—a blow called a hammerpunch. They did not kick with the front of the foot but stamped with the base. They swept and pulled and tripped and slammed, moving with quick and jerky sinuosity.

Bellis watched minutes and minutes of broken noses, bruises, blackouts. The bouts blurred into one. She tried to see possibilities in everything, tried to hoard what she saw, as she sensed Silas was doing.

Little waves lapped over the edges of the stage, and she wondered when this display would end.

Bellis heard a rhythmic, pounding sound in the crowd.

At first it was a murmur, a repeated murmur that beat below the susurrus of the spectators like a heartbeat. But it gathered strength, and became louder and more insistent, and people began to look around and to smile, and to join their voices to it with increasing excitement.

"Yes . . ." said Silas, stretching out the word with a hard delight. "Finally. This is what I wanted to see."

At first Bellis heard the sound like it was drums, spoken drums. Then suddenly as an exclamation—*Oh, Oh, Oh*—repeated in perfect time, accompanied by banging arms and kicking feet.

It was only when the frenzy spread to her own boat that she realized it was a word.

"Doul." It came from all around her. *"Doul, Doul, Doul."*

A name.

"What are they saying?" she hissed to Silas.

"They're calling for someone," he said, his eyes scanning the surrounds. "They want a display. They're demanding a fight from Uther Doul."

He gave her a quick, cold smile.

"You'll recognize him," he said. "You'll know him when you see him."

And then the percussion of the name broke down into cheers and applause, an ecstatic wave of it that grew and grew as one of the little dirigibles tethered to the rigging cast off and drew slowly closer to the stage. Its crest was a steamer against a red moon, the sigil of Garwater. The gondola below it was polished wood.

"It's the Lovers' carriage," Silas said. "They're giving up their lieutenant for a moment, another 'spontaneous' display. I knew he couldn't resist."

Sixty feet above the arena, a rope spilled down from the airborne craft. The shrieks from the spectators were extraordinary. With great speed and skill, a man leaped from the vessel and slipped, hand over hand, to the blood-spattered fighting ground.

He stood, shoeless and bare-chested, wearing only a pair of leather britches. With his arms relaxed by his sides he rotated slowly to take in the crowd (frenzied now that he had touched down to fight). And as he turned his face swept slowly past Bellis', and she gripped the rail in front of her, her breath catching momentarily, recognizing the crop-haired man, the man in grey, the murderer who had taken *Terpsichoria*.

By some goading, a clutch of men were blandished into fighting him.

Doul—the sad-faced butcher of Captain Myzovic—did not move, did not stretch or bounce or pull his muscles this way or that. He merely stood waiting.

Four opponents stood ill at ease on the edge of the arena. They were buoyed on the audience's enthusiasm, shouts and raging washing over them as they shifted and murmured tactics to each other.

Doul's face was set absolutely blank. When his rivals fanned out opposite him, he dropped slowly into stampfighting stance, his arms slightly raised, his knees bent, looking quite relaxed.

In the first brutal, astonishing seconds, Bellis did not even breathe. One hand to her mouth, her lips pursed shut. Then she emitted little gasps of astonishment with the rest of the crowd.

Uther Doul did not seem to live in the same time as anyone else. He seemed like some visitor to a world much more gross and sluggish than his own. Despite the bulk of his body, he moved with such speed that even gravity seemed to operate more quickly for him.

There was nothing sparc to his movements. As he shifted from stamp to hammerpunch to block, his limbs slipped from one poise, one state, to the next by the most utterly seamless and pared-down routes, like machines.

Doul slapped open-handed, and one man went down; he stepped sideways and, poised on one leg, kicked twice to another's solar plexus, then used the raised leg to block the attack of the third. He spun and shoved without flourish, with brutal precision, dispatching his rivals at his ease.

He took the last one with a throw, scooping his arm from the air and hugging it tight to him, pulling the man after his trapped limb. Doul seemed to roll through the air, preparing his body as he fell, landing astride the other's back, pinioning his arm and immobilizing him.

There was a long silence, and then a rapture burst from the crowd like blood from a scabmettler, a tide of applause and cheers.

Bellis watched, and went cold, and held her breath again.

The fallen men raised themselves, or were dragged off, and Uther Doul stood, breathing heavily but rhythmically, his arms held very slightly out, the ridges of his muscles running with sweat and other men's blood.

"The Lovers' guard," said Silas amid the audience's frenzy. "Uther Doul. Scholar, refugee, soldier. Expert in probability theory, in Ghosthead history, and in fighting. The Lovers' guard, their second, their assassin and strong-arm and champion. That's what you had to see, Bellis. That is what's trying to stop us leaving."

They left and walked the winding nightlit pathways of Thee-And-Thine toward Shaddler, and Garwater and the *Chromolith*.

Neither spoke.

At the end of Doul's fight, Bellis had seen something that had brought her up short and made her afraid. As he had turned, his hands clawed, his chest taut and heaving, she had seen his face.

It was stretched tight, every muscle straining, into a glare of feral savagery unlike anything she had ever seen on a human being.

Then a second later, with his bout won, he had turned to

acknowledge the crowd and had looked once more like a contemplative priest.

Bellis could imagine some fatuous warrior code, some mysticism that abstracted the violence of combat and allowed one to fight like a holy man. And equally she could imagine tapping into savagery, letting atavistic viciousness take over in a berserker fugue. But Doul's combination stunned her.

She thought of it later, as she lay in her bed, listening to light rain. He had readied and recovered himself like a monk, fought like a machine, and seemed to feel it like a predatory beast. That tension frightened her, much more than the combat skills he had shown. Those could be learned.

Bellis helped Shekel through books that grew more complex by the hour. When they separated she left him exploring the children's section again, and went back to the rooms where Silas waited for her.

They drank tea and talked about New Crobuzon. He seemed sadder, quieter than usual. She asked him why, and he would only shake his head. There was something tentative about him. For the first time since meeting him, Bellis felt something like pity or concern for him. He wanted to tell or ask her something, and she waited.

She told him what Johannes had said to her. She showed him the naturalist's books and explained how she was trying to piece together Armada's secret from those volumes, without ever knowing which were important, or what within them might be clues.

At half-past eleven, after an extended silence, Silas turned to her. "Why did you leave New Crobuzon, Bellis?" he asked.

She opened her mouth, and all her usual evasions came to her throat, but she remained silent.

"You love New Crobuzon," he continued. "Or . . . is that the best way to put it? You _need_ New Crobuzon. You can't let it go, so it doesn't make sense. Why would you leave?"

Bellis sighed, but the question did not go away.

"When were you last in New Crobuzon?" she said.

"More than two years ago," he calculated. "Why?"

"Did word reach you, when you were in The Gengris . . . Did you ever hear of the Midsummer Nightmare? The Dream Curse? Sleeping Sickness? Nocturne Syndrome?"

He was flicking his hand vaguely, trying to catch the memory. "I heard something from a merchant, a few months back . . ."

"It was about six months ago," she said. "Tathis, Sinn . . . Summer. Something happened. Something went wrong with . . . with the nights." She shook her head vaguely. Silas was listening without scepticism. "I still have no idea what it was—it's important you know that.

"Two things happened. Nightmares. That was the first thing. People were having nightmares. And I mean *everybody* was having nightmares. It was as if we'd all . . . breathed bad air, or something."

The words were inadequate. She remembered the exhaustion and the misery, the weeks of dreading sleep. The dreams that woke her screaming and weeping hysterically.

"The other thing. There was a . . . a disease, or something. People were being afflicted all over the place. All races. It did something . . . It killed the mind, so there was nothing left but the body. People would be found in the morning, in the streets or in bed or whatever, alive, but . . . mindless."

"And the two were linked?"

She glanced at him and nodded, then shook her head. "I don't know. Nobody knows, but it seems so. And one day it all stopped, all of a sudden. People had been talking about martial law, about the militia coming out openly onto the streets . . . It was a crisis. I'm telling you it was *horrendous*. It arrived for no reason. It ruined our sleep and stole hundreds of peoples' minds away—they were never cured—and then suddenly it went. For no reason."

She went on eventually. "After it quieted, there were rumors . . . There were a thousand rumors about what had happened. Daemons, Torque, biological experiments gone wrong, a new strain of vampirism . . . ? No one knew. But there were certain names that came up again and again. And then in early Octuary, people I knew began to disappear.

"At first I just heard some story about some friend of a friend whom no one could find. Then, a little while later, there was another, and another. I wasn't yet worrying. No one was. But they never reappeared. And they got closer to me. The first person to go I barely knew. The second I'd seen at a party some months before. The third was someone I worked with at the university, and drank with now and then. And the rumors about the Midsummer

Nightmare, the names began to get whispered a bit louder, and I heard them again and again, until . . . until one name came out loudest. One person was being blamed; a person who linked everyone who was disappearing to me.

"His name was der Grimnebulin. He's a scientist and a . . . a renegade, I suppose. There was money on his head—you know how the militia puts the word out, all hints and pass-it-ons, so no one knew how much or for what. But it was understood that he was gone, and that the government was keen to find him.

"And they were coming for the people who knew him: colleagues, acquaintances, friends, lovers." She held Silas' gaze bleakly. "We'd been lovers. Godspit, four, five years ago. We'd not even spoken for probably two. He'd taken up with a khepri, I heard." She shrugged. "Whatever he'd done, the Mayor's boys were trying to find him. And I could see it was soon my turn to disappear.

"I was paranoid, but I was right to be. I was avoiding going to work, I was avoiding the people I knew, and I realized I was waiting to be taken. The militia," she spoke with sudden zeal, "were fucking *predatory* in those months.

"We'd been close, Isaac and me. We'd lived together. I knew the militia would want me. And maybe they did let some of the people they questioned go, but I never heard from any of them again. And whatever questions they wanted to ask, I had no answers. Gods knew what they'd have done to me."

It had been a forlorn, miserable time. Never one with many close friends, those that she had she had been too afraid to seek, in case of incriminating them, or in case they had been bought. She remembered her frantic preparations, her furtive deals and dubious sanctuaries. New Crobuzon had been a dreadful place then, she remembered. Oppressive and coldly tyrannical.

"So I made plans. I realized . . . I realized that I had to leave. I had no money and no contacts in Myrshock or Shankell; I had no time to organize. But the government pays you to go to Nova Esperium." Silas began to nod slowly. Bellis jerked her head in a desultory laughing motion. "So one branch of government was hunting me, while another was processing my application to leave and discussing pay. That's the advantage of bureaucracy. But I didn't have long to play games like that with them, so I took passage on the first ship I could. I learnt Salkrikaltor Cray to do it.

"Two years? Three?" She shrugged. "I didn't know how long it would be till I'd be safe. Ships come from home at least annually to Nova Esperium. My contract was five years, but I've broken contracts before. I thought I'd stay until they forgot, till some other public enemy or crisis or whatever took over their attention. Until I got word that it was safe to go back—there are people who know where . . . where I was going." She had been about to say *where I am.* "And so . . ." she concluded.

They looked at each other for a long time.

"So that's why I ran away."

Bellis thought of the people she had left, the few people she had trusted, and was suddenly and briefly overwhelmed by how much she missed them.

These were strange circumstances. She was a fugitive, eager, desperate to return to the place she had fled. Well, she thought, in all plans, circumstances intervene. She smiled with cold humor. *I tried to leave the city for a year or two, and circumstances intervened—some things happened—and instead I find myself trapped for the rest of my life as a librarian in an itinerant pirate city.*

Silas was subdued. He seemed moved by what she had told him, and she studied him and knew that he was thinking over his own story. Neither of them were self-pitying. But they had come to be here through no fault or design of their own, and they did not wish to stay.

There were minutes more silence within the room. Outside, of course, the subdued puttering from the hundreds of engines that dragged them south continued. And the glottals of waves continued; and the other sounds—city noise, night noise.

When Silas rose to leave, Bellis came with him to the door, sticking quite close by him, though she did not touch or look at him. He paused at her entrance and met her eyes, melancholy. There was a long second, and then they bent in to each other, his arms on the door, hers unmoving by her sides, committing to nothing.

They kissed, and only their lips and tongues moved. They were carefully poised, so as not to breathe, or to encroach too far on the other with touches or sound, but finding a connection nonetheless, warily and with relief.

When their long and deep kiss broke, Silas risked moving his lips gently as they parted, finding her again with a little succession of mouth-to-mouth touches; and she allowed him that, even though that first moment was passed and these tiny codas took place in real time.

Bellis breathed slowly and looked at him steadily, and he at her, for just as long as they would have done anyway, and he opened the door and walked out into the cool, speaking his *goodnight* quietly, not hearing her echo.

CHAPTER TWELVE

The next day was New Year's Eve.

Not, of course, to the Armadans, for whom it was a day marked only by a sudden increase in warmth, making it merely autumnal. They could not ignore the fact that it was the solstice, the shortest day of the year: but they did not treat that as of much importance. Beyond a few cheerful remarks about the nights drawing in, the day went unremarked.

But Bellis was sure that, among the New Crobuzon pressganged, she was not alone in keeping track of the days back home. She speculated that there would be subdued parties speckled across the ridings that night. Quiet, so as not to stand out, or to alert the yeomanry or the proctors, or whatever authority there was in a particular riding, that some among the cramped terraces and galleys of Armada were loyal to alternative calendars.

It was a kind of hypocrisy, she vaguely acknowledged: New Year's Eve had never meant anything to her before.

For the Armadans, it was Horndi, the beginning of another nine-day week, and a day that Bellis had free. She met Silas on the bare deck of the *Grand Easterly*.

He took her to the star'd-aft edge of Garwater, to Croom Park. He had been surprised that she had not visited it before, and as they entered it and passed deep into its byways, she could understand why.

The bulk of the park was a long strip, more than a hundred feet wide and almost six hundred long, on the huge body of an ancient steamer whose nameplate had long been effaced by nature. The greenery spread across broad, swaying bridges to two old schooners lined up back-to-back, almost parallel to the great ship. Fore of the steamer, it extended onto a hunkered little sloop with long-dead guns, part of the fabric of Curhouse riding, sharing the park between the two boroughs.

Bellis and Silas wandered tangled pathways, passing the granite statue of Croom, the pirate hero from Armada's past. Bellis was overwhelmed.

Unknown centuries before, the architects of Croom Park had set to covering the fabric of the war-shattered steamer with mulch and loam. Eddying on ocean currents, there was no ground for Armadans to till or fertilize and, like their books and money, they had had to steal it. Even that, even their earth, their mud, was plundered over years, dragged in great trenches from coastal farms and forests, torn from bewildered peasants' plots and taken back across the waves to the city.

They had let the ruined steamer rust and rot, and had filled its holed carcass with the soil they had stolen, starting in the fore-peak and engine rooms and the lowest coal bunkers (deposits of coke still unused, packed once again in seams below tons of dirt), piling the earth around the moldering propeller shaft. They filled some of the big furnaces and left others half empty, encased them, metal air bubbles in the striae of marl and chalk.

The landscapers moved up to decks of cabins and staterooms. Where walls and ceilings had escaped injury, they perforated them raggedly, rupturing the integrity of the little rooms and opening passageways for roots and moles and worms. Then they filled the scraps of space with earth.

The ship was low in the water, kept buoyant by judicious air pockets and by its tethering neighbors.

Above the water, in the open air, layers of peat and dirt spread out and reclaimed the main deck. The raised bridge, the aftercastle and observation decks and lounges, became steep knolls skinned in topsoil. Abrupt little hills, they burst in tight curves of earth from the surrounding plateau.

The unknown designers had performed similar transformations on the three smaller wooden boats close by. That had been much easier than working on iron.

And then there was the planting, and the parkland had bloomed.

There were copses of trees across the steamer's body, old and densely spaced, tiny conspiratorial forests. Saplings, and many midsize trees a century or two old. But there were also some massive specimens, ancient and huge, that must have been uprooted full-grown from wooded shorelines and replanted scores of years ago, to grow old aboard. Grass was everywhere underfoot, and cow parsley and nettles. There were cultivated flowerbeds on the Curhouse gunboat, but on the steamer's corpse the woods and meadows of Croom Park were wild.

Not all the plants were familiar to Bellis. In its slow journeys around Bas-Lag, Armada had visited places unknown to New Crobuzon's scientists, and it had plundered those exotic ecosystems. On the smaller ships were little glades of head-high fungus, that shifted and hissed as walkers passed through them. There was a tower covered in vivid red, thorned creepers that stank like rotting roses. The long forecastle of the star'd-most ship was out of bounds, and Silas told Bellis that beyond the intricately woven fence of briars, the flora was dangerous: pitcher plants of odd and unquantified power, wake trees like predatory weeping willows.

But on the old steamer itself, the landscape and the foliage were more familiar. One of its raised deck-hills was paved inside with moss and turf and made into sunken gardens. Lit and kept alive by bright gaslight and what little day came through dirt-caked portholes, plants of different themes filled each of the cabins. There was a tiny tundra garden of rocks and purple scrub; a desert full of succulents; woodland flowers and meadowland—all adjoining, all linked by a dim corridor knee-high in grass. In its sepia light, under warpaint of verdigris and climbing plants, plaques pointing to the mess and the heads and boiler rooms could still be read. They were crossed by paths well-worn by woodlice and ladybirds.

A little way from its entrance—a door in the hill—out in the air, Bellis and Silas walked slowly in the damp shade.

They had visited each of the four ships of the park. There were only a few other people in the green environs with them. On the aft-most of the vessels Bellis had stopped, shocked, and pointed across the gardens and the reclaimed rails of the deck, out over a hundred feet of ocean to the city's edge. Tethered there, she had seen the *Terpsichoria*. The chains and ropes that bound it were

clean. New bridges connected it to the rest of the city. An architectural skeleton of wood loomed from its main deck: a building
site, foundations.

This was how Armada grew for its populace, swallowing up
prey and reconfiguring them, rendering them into its own material like mindless plankton.

Bellis felt nothing for the *Terpsichoria,* had only contempt for
those who felt affection for boats. But seeing her last link to New
Crobuzon brazenly and effortlessly assimilated depressed her.

The trees around them were evergreen and deciduous in an
unruly mix. Silas and Bellis walked through pines and the black
claws of leafless oaks and ash. Old masts soared over the canopy
like the most ancient trees in the forest, barked in rust, dangling
ragged foliage of long-frayed wire rigging. Bellis and Silas
walked in their shadows, and in the shadows of the wood, past
grassy undulations broken by little windows and doors, where
cabins had been effaced by earth. Worms and burrowing animals
moved behind the cracked glass.

The steamer's ivy-caked chimneys disappeared behind them
as they moved into the heart of the wood, out of sight of the surrounding ships. They traced spiraling paths that wound back on
themselves arcanely, seeming to multiply the space of the park.
Blistered cowls broke from the ground, choked with brambles;
roots and vines entrapped the capstans and coiled intricately
through the guardrails of moss-cushioned ladders leading into
blank hillsides.

In the shade of a cargo derrick become some obscure skeleton, Bellis and Silas sat in the wintery landscape and drank
wine. As Silas rummaged in his little bag for a corkscrew, Bellis
saw his bulging notebook inside. She picked it up and looked at
him questioningly, and when he nodded his permission she
opened it.

There were lists of words: the jottings of someone trying to
learn a foreign language.

"Most of that stuff's from The Gengris," he said.

She turned slowly through the pages of nouns and verbs, and
came to a little section like a diary, with dated entries written in
a shorthand code she could make little of, words pared down
to two or three letters, punctuation dispensed with. She saw
commodity prices, and scribbled descriptions of the grindylow themselves: unpleasant little pencil sketches of figures with

prodigious eyes and teeth and obscure limbs, flat eel-tails. There were heliotypes attached to the pages, executed furtively, it seemed, in dim light; unclear sepia tints, discolored and water-stained, the monstrosity of the figures they depicted exaggerated by blisters and impurities in the paper.

There were hand-drawn maps of The Gengris, covered in arrows and annotations, and other maps of the surrounding water of the Cold Claw Sea, the topography of submerged hills and valleys and grindylow fortresses picked out in different colors for different rocks, granite and quartz and limestone, carefully corrected over several pages. There were suggestive sketches of machinery, of defensive engines.

Silas leaned over her as she read, pointing out features.

"That's a gorge just south of the city," he said, "that leads right up to the rocks separating off the sea. That tower there"—some irregular smudge—"was the skin library, and those were the salp vats."

Beyond those pages were scrawled diagrams of gashes and tunnels and clawed machines, and mechanisms like locks and sluices.

"What are these?" she said, and Silas glanced over, and laughed when he saw what she was looking at.

"Oh, the embryos of big ideas—that sort of thing," he said, and smiled at her.

They sat with their backs to an overgrown stump, or perhaps the earth-smothered anatomy of a binnacle. Bellis put Silas' book away. Still not quite at ease, she leaned in and kissed him.

He responded gently, and an aggression came to her, and she pushed herself into him more firmly. She drew away for a moment, her face set, and looked at him staring back at her with pleasure and uncertainty. She tried to parse him, to understand the grammar of his actions and reactions, and she could not.

But frustrated as she was by that, she felt intimately how his antagonisms mirrored hers. His despite and hers—at Armada, at this absurd existence—had become conjoined. And it was an extraordinary relief and release to share even something as cold as that.

She held his face and kissed him hard. He responded eagerly. When his arm came slowly around her waist, and his fingers crooked and combed her hair, she broke from him and took hold of his hand. She pulled him after her, back through the winding ways of the park, portward, to her home.

In Bellis' room, Silas watched silently as she undressed.

She draped her skirt, shirt, jacket, and bloomers over the back of her chair and stood stripped bare in the fading light of her window, letting down her scraped-up hair. Silas stirred. His clothes were scattered like seed. He smiled at her again, and she sighed and smiled too, finally, deprecatingly, for what seemed the first time in months. With that smile came an unexpected little stab of shyness, and with the smile it quickly left again.

They were not children; they were not new to this. They did not fumble or panic. She walked to him and straddled him with practiced grace and desire. And when she did, pushing against his cock, when he wrestled his hands out from where she had pinioned them, he knew how to move her.

Passionate; loveless but not joyless; expert; eager. It made her smile again, and gasp and come in a great gout of relief and pleasure. When she lay back in the narrow bed, having taught him how she liked to fuck and learned his own predilections, she glanced up at him (his eyes closed, sweating). She checked herself and verified that she was still lonely, still as numb to this place as ever. She would have been astounded to find it any other way.

But still, but still. Even so. She smiled again. She felt better.

For three days, Tanner lay in the surgery, strapped to the wooden table, feeling the tower and the ship move slowly and slightly beneath him.

Three days. He moved only inches at a time, wriggling against the restraints, shifting slightly to the left or right.

Most of the time he swam in glutinous aether dreams.

The chirurgeon was kindly, and kept him drugged as much as was possible without damaging him, so Tanner meandered in and out of twilight consciousness. He muttered to himself, and to the chirurgeon, who fed him and wiped him like a baby. He would sit with Tanner in his spare minutes or hours, and talk to him, pretending that his absurd and frightening responses made sense. Tanner spat out words or was silent, or wept and giggled: drugged; feverish; sluggish; cold; soundly sleeping.

Tanner had blanched when the chirurgeon had told him how it would have to be. To be shackled again, to be strapped down while his body was rebuilt. The narcotic- and agony-raddled memories of the punishment factory had assaulted him.

But the chirurgeon had gently explained that some of the procedures were fundamental; some would involve the reconfiguration of his insides from the tiniest building blocks up. He could not move while the atoms and particles of his blood and lungs and brain found their ways along new pathways and met in alternative combinations. He must be still and patient.

Tanner acquiesced, as he had known he would.

On the first day, as Tanner lay deep in chymical and thaumaturgic sleep, the chirurgeon opened him.

He scored deep gashes in the sides of Tanner's neck, then lifted off the skin and outer tissue, gently wiping away the blood that coursed from the raw flesh. With the exposed flaps oozing, the chirurgeon turned his attention to Tanner's mouth. He reached inside with a kind of iron chisel and slid it into the pulp of the throat, twisting as he pushed, carving tunnels in the flesh.

Constantly vigilant that Tanner was not choking on the blood that ran into his mouth and throat, the chirurgeon created new passageways in his body. Runnels linked the back of Tanner's mouth to the openings in his neck. Where the new orifices opened behind and below his teeth, the chirurgeon ringed them with muscle, pushing it into place with a clayflesh hex, stimulating it with little crackles of elyctricity.

He stoked the fire that drove his bulky analytical engine, and fed it program cards, gathering data. Finally, he wheeled into place alongside the gurney a tank containing a sedated cod, and linked the motionless fish to Tanner's body by a cryptic and unwieldy construction of valves, gutta-percha tubes, and wires.

Homeomorphic chymicals sluiced dilute in brine across the cod's gills, and then through the ragged wounds that would be Tanner's. Wires linked the two of them. The chirurgeon muttered hexes as he operated the juddering apparatus—he was rusty with bio-thaumaturgy, but methodical and careful—and kneaded Tanner's bleeding neck. Water began to drool through the holes and over the opened-up skin.

For most of the night, the scene was replayed, the surgery swaying gently with the water below. The chirurgeon slept a little, periodically checking Tanner's progress, and that of the slowly dying cod suspended in a matrix of thaumaturgic strands that dragged out its demise. He applied pressure when it was needed, changed the settings of finely calibrated gauges, added chymicals to the sluicing water.

In those hours, Tanner dreamed of choking (while he opened and closed his eyes, unknowing).

When the sun came up, the chirurgeon uncoupled Tanner and the fish from his machinery (the cod dying instantly, its body shrunken and wrinkled). He closed up the flaps of skin in Tanner's neck, slimy with gelatinous gore. He smoothed them down, his fingers tingling with puissance as the gashes sealed.

Without Tanner waking—still drugged as he was, there was no danger of that—the chirurgeon placed a mask over Tanner's mouth, sealed his nose with his fingers, and began to pump brine gently into him. For several seconds there was no reaction. Then Tanner coughed and gagged violently, spattering water. The chirurgeon stood poised, ready to release Tanner's nose.

And then Tanner calmed. All without waking, his epiglottis flexed and his windpipe constricted, keeping the saltwater from entering his lungs. The chirurgeon smiled as water began to seep from Tanner's new gills.

It came sluggishly at first, bringing with it blood and dirt and scab matter. And then the water ran clean and the gills began to flex, regulating it, and it pulsed across the floor in measured draughts.

Tanner Sack was breathing water.

He woke later, too vague to understand what had happened, but infected by the chirurgeon's enthusiasm. His throat hurt terribly, so he slept again.

That was by far the hardest thing done.

The chirurgeon peeled back Tanner's eyelids and bound to him clear nictitating membranes taken and modified from a caiman bred in one of the city's farms. He injected Tanner with particulate life-forms that thrived in him harmlessly and interacted with his body, making his sweat a touch more oleaginous, to warm him and slide him through water. He grafted in a little ridge of muscle at the base of Tanner's nostrils, and little nubs of cartilage, so that he could flex them closed.

Finally, the chirurgeon performed by far the easiest, if the most visible, alteration. Between Tanner's fingers and his thumb, he stretched a membrane, a web of rubbery skin that he pinched into position, tethering it in Tanner's epidermis. He removed Tanner's toes and replaced them with the fingers from a cadaver, sewing and sealing them onto Tanner's foot until he looked simian; then he changed the resemblance from ape to frog as he stretched more webbing between those once-more living digits.

He bathed Tanner, washed him in seawater. Kept him clean and cool, and watched his tentacles writhe in his sleep.

And on the fourth day Tanner woke, properly and completely. Untied, free to move, his mind empty of chymicals.

He sat up, slowly.

His body hurt; it raged in fact. It assaulted him in waves that beat with his heart. His neck, his feet, his eyes, dammit. He saw his new toes and looked away for a moment, a memory of the old horror of the punishment factory come back for a second, till he battened it down and looked again (*More pus,* he thought, with a shade of humor).

He clenched his new hands. He blinked slowly and saw something translucent slip across his vision before his eyelid came down. He breathed deep into water-bruised lungs and coughed, and it hurt, as the chirurgeon had warned it would.

Tanner, despite the pain and the weakness and the hunger and nervousness, began to smile.

The chirurgeon came in as Tanner grinned and grinned, and grunted to himself, and rubbed himself gently.

"Mr. Sack," he said, and Tanner turned to him and held out his shaking arms as if to grab him, trying to shake his hand. Tanner's tentacles flexed as well, trying to reach out in echo through the too-thin air. The chirurgeon smiled.

"Congratulations, Mr. Sack," he said. "The procedures were successful. You are now amphibian."

And at that—they couldn't help themselves and didn't try— both he and Tanner Sack laughed uproariously, even though it hurt Tanner's chest, and even though the chirurgeon wasn't certain what was funny.

When he got home, after hauling himself gingerly through the valleys of Booktown and Garwater, he found Shekel waiting in rooms that had never been so clean.

"Ah now, lad," he said, shy of him. "That's great what you've done, ain't it?"

Shekel tried to grab him in welcome, but Tanner was too sore and held him back good-naturedly. They talked quietly into the evening. Tanner asked carefully after Angevine. Shekel told Tanner that his reading was improving, and that nothing much had happened, but that it was warmer now, could Tanner feel it?

He could. They crawled south at an almost geologically slow pace, but the tugs and steamers had been dragging them continuously for two weeks now. They were perhaps five hundred miles south of where they had been—they had traveled so far, with a motion so slow it was unnoticed—and the winter was waning as they approached the band of temperate sea and air.

Tanner showed Shekel the additions, the changes to his body, and Shekel winced at their oddness and inflammations, but was fascinated. Tanner told him all the things the chirurgeon had explained.

"You'll be tender, Mr. Sack," he had said. "And even when you're well, I want to warn you: some of the cuts I've made, some of the wounds, they may heal hard. They might scar. In that case, I want you not to be downhearted or disappointed. Scars are not injuries, Tanner Sack. A scar is a healing. After injury, a scar is what makes you whole."

"A fortnight, lad," Tanner said, "before I'm back at work, he reckons. If I practice and all."

But Tanner had an advantage the doctor had not considered: he had never learned to swim. He did not have to adjust a flailing, inefficient, slapping paddle into the sinuous motion of a sea dweller.

He sat by the dockside while his workmates greeted him. They were surprised, solicitous, and friendly. Bastard John the dolphin broke surface nearby, glaring at Tanner with his liquid, piggy eyes and emitting what were doubtless insults in his imbecilic cetacean chittering. But Tanner was not cowed that morning. He received his colleagues like a king, thanking them for their concern.

At the border of Garwater and Jhour ridings, there was a space in the fabric of the city, between vessels: a patch of sea that might have housed a modest ship formed a swimming area. Only

a very few of the Armadan pirates could swim, and in such temperatures, few would try. There were only a handful of humans
swimming in that patch of open sea, brave or masochistic.

Under the water, slowly, nervous of his new buoyancy and
freedom, over hours that day and the next and next, Tanner
spread his arms and hands, opening out the webs of skin and
capturing the water, pushing himself forward in inexpert bursts.
He kicked out in something like a breaststroke, those still-sore
toes flexing, painful and powerful. The little presences he could
not see or feel beneath his skin pulsed infinitesimal glands and
lubricated his sweat.

He opened his eyes and learned to close only his inner eyelids—
an extraordinary sensation. He learned to see in the water, unconstrained by any unwieldy helmet, any iron and brass and
glass. Not peering through a porthole, but looking out freely, pe-
ripheral vision and all.

Slowest and most frightening of all, alone—who could possibly teach him?—Tanner learned to breathe.

The first inrush of water into his mouth closed his windpipe
reflexively, and his tongue clamped back and his throat tightened and blocked the route to his stomach, and the seawater
scored its way through his tender new pathways, opening him
up. He tasted salt so totally it became quickly insensible. He felt
rills of water pass through him, through his neck, his gills, and
Godspit and shit and all he thought, because he felt no need to
breathe.

He had filled his lungs before descending, out of habit, but
aerated he was too buoyant. Slowly, in a kind of luxuriant panic,
he exhaled through his nose and let his air disappear above him.

And felt nothing. No dizziness or pain or fear. Oxygen still
reached his blood, and his heart kept pumping.

Above him, the pasty little bodies of his fellow citizens floundered across the surface of the water, tethered to the air they
breathed. Tanner spun beneath them, clumsy still but learning,
corkscrewing, looking above and below—up into the light and
bodies and the massive sprawling interlocking shape of the city,
down into the boundless blue dark.

CHAPTER THIRTEEN

Silas and Bellis spent two nights together.

During the days, Bellis shelved, helped Shekel to read and told him about Croom Park, sometimes ate with Carrianne. Then she returned to Silas. They talked some, but he left her quite ignorant of how he passed his hours. She had a sense that he was full of secret ideas. They fucked several times.

After the second night, Silas disappeared. Bellis was glad. She had been neglecting Johannes' books, and she now returned to their unfamiliar science.

Silas was gone for three days.

Bellis explored.

She ventured finally into the farthest parts of the city. She saw the burn temples of Bask riding, and its triptych statues spread across the fabric of several boats. In Thee-And-Thine (which was not as rough or as frightening as she had been led to believe, was little more than an exaggerated, pugnacious marketplace) she saw the Armada asylum, a massive edifice that loomed from a steamer, cruelly placed, it seemed to Bellis, right next to the haunted quarter.

There was a little outcropping of Garwater boats like a buffer between Curhouse and Bask, separated off from the main body of their riding by some historical caprice. There, Bellis found the Lyceum, its workshops and classrooms staggering precipitously down the sides of a ship, layered like a mountainside town.

Armada had all the institutions of any city on land, devoted to learning and politics and religion, only perhaps in a harder form. And if the city's scholars were tougher than their landside equivalents, and looked more like rogues and pirates than doctors, it did not invalidate their expertise. There were different constabularies in each riding, from the uniformed proctors of Bask to

Garwater's loosely defined yeomanry who were marked out only by their sashes—a badge as much of loyalty as office. Each riding's law was different. There was a species of court and disputation in Curhouse, while the lax, violent, piratical discipline of Garwater was doled out with the whip.

Armada was a profane and secular city, and its unkempt churches were treated as irreverently as its bakers. There were temples to the deified Croom; to the moon and her daughters, to thank them for the tides; to sea gods.

If she ever became lost, Bellis needed only to find her way out from backstreets or alleys, look up through all the aerostats moored to masts, and find the *Arrogance,* looming stately over the glowering *Grand Easterly.* It was her beacon, and by it she steered her way home.

In the midst of the city there were rafts—wooden floats extending scores of yards to each side. Houses perched ludicrously on them. There were needle-thin submarines bobbing tethered between barquentines, and chariot ships filled with hotchi burrows. Tumbledown buildings smothered decks or perched precarious across the backs of tens of tiny vessels in the cheap neighborhoods. There were playhouses and prisons and deserted hulks.

When she raised her eyes to the horizon, Bellis could see disturbances out to sea: churning water, wakes without obvious cause. Wind- and weather-born, usually, but sometimes she might glimpse a pod of porpoises, or a plesiaur or seawyrm neck, or the back of something big and fast that she could not identify. The life beyond the city, and all around it.

Bellis watched the city's fishing boats return in the evenings. Sometimes pirate ships would appear and be welcomed back into the harbors of Basilio or Urchinspine, the motors of Armada's economy finding their way, uncannily, home.

Armada was full of figureheads. They poked up in unlikely places, ornate and ignored like the carved door knockers on New Crobuzon houses. At the end of a terrace, walking between rows of close brick dwellings, Bellis might come face-to-face with a splendid corroded woman, her breastplate moldering, her painted gaze flaked and vague. Hanging in the air like a spirit, below the bowsprit of her ship, which jutted across its neighbor's deck and pointed into the alley.

They were all around. Otters, drakows, fish, warriors, and

women. Above all women. Bellis hated the blank-eyed, curva-
ceous figures, wobbling up and down moronically with the swell,
haunting the city like banal ghosts.

In her room, she finished *Essays on Beasts* and remained un-
comprehending of Armada's secret project.

She wondered where Silas was, and what he was doing. She
was not upset or angry at his absence, but she was curious and a
little frustrated. He was, after all, the closest thing she had to
an ally.

He returned on the evening of the fifth of Lunuary.

Bellis let him enter. She did not touch him, nor he her.

He was tired and subdued. His hair was mussed, his clothes
dusty. He sat back in a chair and covered his eyes with his hands,
murmuring something inaudible, some greeting. Bellis made
him tea. She waited for him to speak, and when after a while he
did not, she returned to her book and her cigarillo.

She had made several more pages of notes before he spoke.

"Bellis. Bellis." He rubbed his eyes and looked up at her. "I
have to tell you something. I have to tell you the truth. I've kept
things from you."

She nodded, turning to face him. His eyes were closed.

"Let's . . . take stock," he said slowly. "The city's heading
south. The *Sorghum* . . . Do you know what the *Sorghum*'s for?
The *Sorghum,* and the other rigs that I gather the *Terpsichoria*
took you past, suck fuel from under the sea."

He spread his hands wide, indicating massiveness. "There are
fields of oil and rockmilk and mercus under the earth, Bellis.
You've seen the screwbores they use to plumb for the stuff on
land. Well, geo-empaths and the like have found vast deposits
under the rock, lying under the sea.

"There's oil under southern Salkrikaltor. That's why the *Manikin* and the *Trashstar* and *Sorghum* have been perched out there
for more than three decades. The supports of the *Manikin* and
Trashstar go down four hundred feet and sit on the bottom. But
the *Sorghum* . . . The *Sorghum*'s different." He spoke with a morbid relish. "Someone in Armada knew what they were doing, I
tell you. The *Sorghum* sits on two iron hulls—submersibles. The
Sorghum's not tethered. The *Sorghum*'s a deepwater rig. The
Sorghum can travel.

"You can just keep adding sections to its drill shaft, and it can

go down Jabber fucking knows how far. Miles down. You can't
find oil and so on everywhere. That's why we were stationary for
so long. Armada was sitting over a field of something or other
the *Sorghum* could get at, and we couldn't move off until it had
stored up for wherever it's going."

How do you know all this? thought Bellis. *What's this truth
you have to tell me?*

"I don't think it's just oil," Silas continued. "I've been watching the flame over the rig, Bellis. I think they've been drawing up
rockmilk."

Rockmilk. *Lactus saxi.* Viscous and heavy as magma, but
bone cold. And dense with thaumaturgons, the charged particles. Worth several times its considerable weight in gold, or dia-
monds, or oil or blood.

"Ships don't use fucking rockmilk to fire their engines," Silas
said. "Whatever they've stockpiled for, it's not just to keep their
vessels trim. Look at what's happening. We're heading south, to
deeper, warmer seas. I'll bet you a finial we're skirting close to
ridges beneath, where there are deposits, a route that lets the
Sorghum drill. And when we get wherever we're going, your
friend Johannes and his new employers are going to use . . .
what, several *tons* of rockmilk and Jabber knows how much oil
to do . . . something. By which time . . ." He paused, and held her
gaze. "By which time it'll be too late."

Tell me, Bellis thought, and Silas was nodding as if he had
heard her.

"When we met on the *Terpsichoria,* I was in something of a
state, I remember. I told you I had to return to New Crobuzon
immediately. You reminded me of that yourself, recently. And I
told you that I'd been lying. But I wasn't. What I said on *Terpsichoria* was true: I have to return. Dammit, you probably realized
all this."

Bellis said nothing.

"I didn't know how to . . . I didn't know if I could trust you, if
you'd care," he continued. "I'm sorry I wasn't honest with you,
but I didn't know how far I could go. But dammit, Bellis, I trust
you now. And I need your help.

"It's true, what I told you, that sometimes the grindylow turn
against some poor sod for no reason anyone can figure. That people
disappear at their whim. The grindylows' whim, the deeplings. But

it's not true, what I said then, about that happening to me. I know exactly why the grindylow wanted to kill me.

"If they chose, the grindylow could swim upriver to the top of the Bezheks, where all the rivers join together, and they could cross into the Canker. Be swept downriver on the other side of the mountains, all the way to New Crobuzon.

"Others could cross into the ocean through the tunnels, come at the city by sea. They're euryhalinic, the grindylow, happy in freshwater or brine. They could make their way to Iron Bay. To the Gross Tar, and New Crobuzon. All it would take for the grindylow to get to the city is determination. And I know they have that."

Bellis had never seen Silas so tense.

"When I was there, there were rumors. Some big plan was in the offing. One of my clients, a magus, a kind of thug-priest, its name came up again and again. I started to keep my eyes and ears open. That's why they want to kill me. I found something out.

"The grindylow don't do secrecy; they don't do policing as we do. There was evidence in front of me for weeks, but it took me a long time to recognize it. Mosaics, blueprints, librettos, and such like. Took me a long time to understand."

"Tell me what you found," said Bellis.

"Plans," he said. "Plans for an invasion."

"It would be like nothing you can imagine," he said. "Gods know our history's littered with betrayal and fucking blood, but . . . 'Stail, Bellis . . . You've never seen The Gengris." There was a desperation in his voice that Bellis had never heard before. "You've never seen the limb-farms. The workshops, the fucking bile workshops. You've never heard the *music*.

"If the grindylow take New Crobuzon, they wouldn't enslave us, or kill us, or even eat us all. They wouldn't do anything so . . . comprehensible."

"But why?" said Bellis, finally. "What do they want? Do you think they can do it?"

"I don't godsdamned know. No one knows a thing about them. I suspect the New Crobuzon government has more plans about what to do if fucking *Tesh* invades than if the grindylow do. We've never had any reason to be scared of them. But they have their own . . . methods, their own sciences and thaumaturgies. Yes," he said. "I think they have a chance.

"They want New Crobuzon for the same reason every other state or savage on Ragamoll does. It's the richest, the biggest, the most powerful. Our industries, our resources, our militia—look at everything we have. But unlike Shankell or Dreer Samher or Neovadan or Yoraketche, The Gengris . . . The Gengris has a chance.

"They can come with surprise . . . Poison the water, come into the sewers. Every godsdamn crevice and crack and water tank in the city would be a fucking encampment. They can storm us with weapons we'd never understand, in an endless guerrilla war.

"I've seen what the grindylow can do, Bellis." Silas sounded exhausted. "I've seen it, and I'm scared."

From outside came the far-off sound of monkeys squabbling sleepily.

"That's why you left," said Bellis in the quiet that followed.

"That's why I left. I couldn't believe what I'd found out. But I dithered . . . I fucking farted time away." His anger welled up suddenly. "And when I realized that there was no fucking mistake, that this wasn't a confusion, that they really did intend to unleash some godsforsaken unthinkable apocalypse on my hometown . . . then I left. I stole the sub, and left."

"Do they know that . . . you know?" she asked.

He shook his head. "I don't think so," he said. "I took some stuff with me, so that it looks like I stole and ran."

Bellis could see that he was tight with tension. She could remember some of the heliotypes she had seen in his notebook. Her heart lurched, and slow alarm crept through her with her blood, like a sickness. Bellis struggled to grasp what he was telling her. It was too big for her; it made no sense. She could not contain it. New Crobuzon . . . How could it be threatened?

"Do you know how long?" she whispered.

"They have to wait till Chet to harvest their weapons," he said. "So maybe six months. We have to find out what Armada's planning to do, because we have to know where we're going, with this fucking rockmilk and all. Because we . . . we have to get a message back to New Crobuzon."

"Why," Bellis breathed, "didn't you tell me before?"

Silas laughed hollowly. "I didn't know who on this place to trust. I was trying to get away from here myself, trying to find some way home. It took me a long time to believe that . . . that

there wasn't any. I thought I could just take the message to New
Crobuzon myself. What if you didn't believe me? Or what if you
were a spy? What if you told our new fucking rulers—"

"Well, what about that?" Bellis interrupted. "Isn't it worth
thinking about? Maybe they'd help us get a message . . ."

Silas stared at her with nasty incredulity.

"Are you mad?" he said. "You think they'd help us? They
don't give spit what happens to New Crobuzon. They'd most
likely welcome its fucking destruction—one less competitor nation on the sea. You think they'd let us ride to the rescue? You
think they'd care? The bastards would probably do everything
they could to *hold us back,* to let the grindylow do their worst.
And, besides, you've seen how they treat . . . Crobuzoner officials and agents. They'd search my notes, my papers, and it
would come out that I have a commission. That I work for New
Crobuzon. Jabber Almighty, Bellis, you saw what they did to the
captain. What do you think they'd do to me?"

There was a long silence at that.

"I needed . . . I need someone to work with me. We have no
friends in this city. We have no allies. And thousands of miles
away, our home's in danger, and we can't trust anyone to help us.
So it's up to us to get a message back."

After he said that there was a pause that became a silence. It
dragged out, longer and longer, and became terrible because
they both knew it should be filled. They should be coming up
with plans.

And both of them tried. Bellis opened her mouth several
times, but words dried in her throat.

We'll hijack one of their boats, she wanted to say but could
not; the idiocy of it choked her. *We'll sneak out just the two of us
in a dinghy; we'll get through the guard boats and row and sail
for home.* She tried to say that, tried to think it without scorn, and
almost moaned. *We'll steal an airship. All we need are guns and
gas, and coal and water for the engine, and food and drink for a
two-thousand-mile journey, and a map, a chart of where in the
godsforsaken fucking middle of the fucking entire Swollen
Ocean we* are, *for Jabber's sake . . .*

Nothing, there was nothing, she could say nothing; she could
think nothing.

She sat and tried to speak, tried to think of ways she could save
New Crobuzon, her city which she treasured with a ferocious,

unromantic love, and which lay under the most baleful threat.
And the moments passed and passed, and Chet and the summer
and the grindylow harvest kept coming closer, and she could say
nothing.

Bellis imagined bodies like puffy eels, eyes and slablike recurved teeth heading under cold water toward her home.

"Oh dear gods, dear Jabber . . ." she heard herself say. She met
Silas' troubled eyes. "Dear gods, what are we going to *do*?"

CHAPTER FOURTEEN

Slow like some vast, bloated creature, Armada passed into warmer
water.

The citizens and the yeomanry put aside their heavier clothes.
The press-ganged from the *Terpsichoria* were disoriented. The
idea that seasons could be escaped, could be outrun physically,
was profoundly unsettling.

The seasons were only points of view—matters of perspective. When it was winter in New Crobuzon, it was summer in
Bered Kai Nev (so they said), though they shared the days and
nights that grew long and short in antiphase. Dawn was dawn all
across the world. In the eastern continent, summer days were
short.

The birds of Armada's microclimate increased in number. The
small, inbred community of finches and sparrows and pigeons
that clung to the city's skyline wherever it moved were joined by
transients: migrators that crossed the Swollen Ocean, following
the year's heat. A few were waylaid from their gigantic flocks by
Armada, coming down to rest and drink, and staying.

They circled confused over the wheeled spires of Curhouse,
where the Democratic Council met in session after emergency
session, fiercely and ineffectually debating Armada's direction.
They agreed that the Lovers' secret plans could not be good

for the city, that they must do something, bickering miserably as their impotence became more and more clear.

Garwater had always been the most powerful riding, and now Garwater had the *Sorghum,* and the Democratic Council of Curhouse could do nothing at all.

(Nevertheless, Curhouse opened tentative communications with the Brucolac.)

The hardest thing for Tanner was not gill-breathing, not moving his arms and legs like a frog or vodyanoi, but staring into the face of the colossal gradient of dark water below him. Attempting to look it full-on and not be cowed.

When he had worn his diving suit, he had been an intruder. He had challenged the sea, and he had worn armor. Clinging to the rungs and the guy ropes, hanging on for life, he had known that the endless space below him that stretched out like a maw was exactly that: a mouth the size of the world, straining to swallow him.

Now he swam free, descending toward darkness that no longer seemed to hunger for him. Tanner swam lower and lower. At first he seemed close enough to reach up and stroke the toes of the swimmers above him. It gave him a voyeuristic pleasure to see their frantic, paddling little bodies above him. But when he turned his face to the sunless water below him his stomach pitched at its implacable hugeness, and he turned quickly and made back for the light.

Each day he descended further.

He slipped below the level of Armada's keels and rudders and descending pipeways. The long sentinels of weed that fringed them, that delimited the city's lowest points, reached out for him, but he slipped past them like a thief. He stared at the deep.

Tanner passed through a rain of baitfish that nibbled at the city's scraps, and then he was down in clear water, and there was nothing of Armada around him. He was below the city, all the way below it.

He hung still in the water. It was not difficult.

The pressure coddled him, tightly as if in swaddling.

The ships of Armada sprawled almost a mile across the sea, occluding his light. Above him, Bastard John fussed around below the docks like a hornet. In the twilight water around him Tanner saw a thick suspension of particles, life upon tiny life.

And beyond the plankton and krill he faintly saw Armada's sea-wyrms and its submersibles, a handful of dark shadows around the city's base.

He struggled to overcome his vertigo; he made it something else. No less awe, but less fear. He took what was like fear in him, and made it humility.

I'm damn small, he thought, hanging like a mote of dust in still air, *in a sea that's damn big. But that's alright. I can do that.*

With Angevine he was shy and a little resentful, but he worked hard for Shekel's sake.

She came to eat with them. Tanner tried to chat with her, but she was withdrawn and hard. For some time they sat and chewed their kelp bread without any sounds. After half an hour, Angevine motioned to Shekel, and he, well-practiced, stood behind her and scooped pieces of coke from the container behind her back into her boiler.

Angevine met Tanner's gaze without embarrassment.

"Keeping your engines stoked?" he said eventually.

"They aren't the most efficient," she replied slowly (in Salt, spurning the Ragamoll that he had used, though it was her native tongue).

Tanner nodded. He remembered the old man in the hold of the *Terpsichoria*. It took a while for him to say more. Tanner was shy of this stern Remade woman.

"What model is your engine?" he said eventually, in Salt. She stared at him in consternation, and he realized with astonishment that she was ignorant of the mechanics of her own Remade body.

"It's probably an old pre-exchange model," he continued slowly. "With only one set of pistons and no recombination box. They were never any good." He stopped there for a while. *Go on,* he thought. *She might say yes, and the lad'd like it.* "If you fancy, I could take a look. Worked with engines all my life. I could . . . I could even . . ." He hesitated at a verb that sounded somehow obscene, discussing a person. "I could even refit you."

He wandered away from the table, ostensibly for more stew, to avoid listening to Shekel's embarrassing monologue: gratitude to Tanner and cajoling of the unconvinced Angevine combined. Over the chorus of *go on Ange best mate Tanner you're my best mate,* Tanner saw that Angevine was unsettled. She was not used to offers like this, unless they meant incurring debts.

It ain't for you, Tanner thought fervently, wishing he could tell her. *It's for the boy.*

He moved further away while she and Shekel whispered to each other. He turned his back on them politely, stripped to his longjohns, and slipped into a tin bath full of brine. It soothed him. He soaked with the same sense of luxury that he once would have had for a hot bath, and he hoped that Angevine would understand his motivations.

She was nobody's fool. After a short time she said with dignity something like *thanks then, Tanner, that might be good.* She said yes, and Tanner found to his mild surprise that he was glad.

Shekel was still excited by the clamor of silent sounds reading had given him, but with familiarity came control. He no longer found himself stopping midway along a corridor and gasping as the word *bulkhead* or *heads* shouted itself to him from some ship's sign.

For the first week or so, graffiti had been an intoxication. He had stood in front of walls and ships' sides and let his eyes crawl across the morass of messages scratched or scrawled or painted on the city's flanks. Such a diversity of styles: the same letters could be written tens of different ways but always say the same thing. Shekel never stopped enjoying that fact.

Most of what was written was rude or political or scatological. *Dry Fall Fuck Off,* he read. Names in scores. Somebody loves somebody, repeated again and again. Accusations, sexual and otherwise. *Barsum* or *Peter* or *Oliver is a Cunt* or a *Whore* or a *Queer* or whatever else it might be. The writing gave each declaration a different voice.

In the library, his ransacking of the shelves had become less furious, less drunken in its haste and exhilaration, but he still picked books out and laid them down in great numbers, and read them slowly and wrote down words he did not understand.

Sometimes he opened books and found words that had defeated him the first time he had seen them, and that he had then written down and learned. It delighted him. He felt like a fox that had tracked them. That was how it was with *thorough,* and *climber,* and *khepri.* When he encountered them for the second time, they surrendered to him, and he read them without pause.

In the shelves of foreign volumes, Shekel found release. He was fascinated by their cryptic alphabets and orthographies, their strange pictures for foreign children. He came and rummaged among them when he needed quiet in his head. He could be assured that they would be silent.

Until the day that he picked one up and turned it in his hands, and it spoke to him.

At twilight, something idled out of the deep sea and came toward Armada.

It approached the last day-shift of engineers below the water. They were coming slowly up, clambering hand over hand up the ladders and pitted surfaces of the undercity, wheezing into their helmets, not looking down, not seeing what was coming.

Tanner Sack was sitting with Hedrigall on the edge of the Basilio docks. They dangled their legs like children over the side of a little cog, watching the cranes shift cargo.

Hedrigall was hinting at something. He spoke to Tanner obliquely. He hedged and implied, and Tanner understood that this was about the secret project, the unspoken thing that so many of his workmates shared. Without a scrap of that knowledge, Tanner could not make sense of what Hedrigall was saying. He could tell only that his friend was unhappy, and fearful of something.

A little way away they could see the corps of engineers emerge streaming from the water, climbing the ladders to rafts and weatherbeaten steamers where juddering engines and colleagues and constructs pumped air for them.

The water in that little corner of the harbor began abruptly to bubble as if at a boil. Tanner touched Hedrigall's forearm to quiet him, and stood, craning his neck.

There was a commotion at the water's edge. Several workers rushed over and began to haul in the divers. More men surfaced, breaking the water in little bursts and scrabbling desperately at their helmets and at the ladders, fighting to get into the air. A furrow in the water swelled and broke the surface as Bastard John breached. He thrashed his tail wildly until it looked as if he stood unsteadily on the surface of the sea, and chattered like a monkey.

One man, hanging from a ladder, hunched out of the green water, finally threw off his helmet, and shrieked for help.

"Bonefish!" he screamed. "There are men down there!"

All around them people looked out of windows in alarm, left their work, and ran to the water, leaning out over the little trawlers bobbing in the middle of the harbor, pointing into the water and shouting to those on the docksides.

Tanner's heart froze as billows of red coiled to the surface.

"Your knife!" he shouted to Hedrigall. "Give me your fucking knife!" He threw off his shirt and ran, without hesitating.

He leaped, his tentacles unwrapping from him, Hedrigall bellowing something unheard behind him. Then his long, webbed toes broke the surface, and with a burst of cold, he was in the water, and then under it.

Tanner blinked frantically, sliding his inner eyelid into place and peering down. In the middle distance, obscured by the sea, the shadows of submersibles prowled clumsily under the city.

He could see the last of the men clambering desperately toward the light, appallingly slow and clumsy in their suits. He saw places where great patches of blood discolored the water. A chunk of cartilage was drifting down through a haze of flesh, where one of Armada's guard sharks had been torn apart.

Tanner kicked down, swimming fast. Some way off, at the base of a huge sunken pipe, sixty or more feet down, he saw a man clinging, immobilized by fear. And under him in the shadowy water, flickering this way and that like a flame, was a dark body.

Tanner balked, appalled. The thing was massive.

Above him, he heard the flattened reports of bodies hitting the water. Armed men were descending, lowered from cranes, standing in harnesses, bristling with harpoons and spears, but they moved slowly, edging down by inches, at the mercy of the engines above them.

Bastard John streaked past Tanner, startling him, and from hidden corners of the city's underside, Tanner saw the silent menfish of Bask riding slip through the water toward the predator below.

Emboldened, he kicked and plunged down again.

His mind rushed. He knew that attacks by big predators occurred sometimes—red sharks, wolffish, hooksquid, and others smashing into the fish cages and attacking the workers—but he had never experienced one. He had never seen a dinichthys, a bonefish.

He hefted Hedrigall's knife.

With sudden disgust Tanner realized that he was passing through a cloud of blood-fouled water, and he could taste it in his mouth and across his gills. His stomach lurched as he saw, sinking slowly beside him, the ragged remnants of a diving suit with indistinct shreds waving within it.

And then he reached the bottom of the pipe, a few bodies' lengths from the bleeding, motionless diver, and the creature beneath rose up to meet him.

He heard the pounding of water and felt an onrush of pressure, and looked down and screamed silently into the brine.

A great blunt-faced fish was rushing up toward him. Its head was encased in skull-armor, smooth and round like a cannon-ball, split by massive jaws in which Tanner saw not teeth, but two razor-ridges of bone chewing at the water, scraps of flesh fluttering from them. Its body was long and tapered, without contours or a fanning tail; its dorsal fin was low and streamlined, merging with its tailbone like some fat-bodied eel.

It was more than thirty feet long. It came at him, its mouth big enough to bite him in half without effort, its tiny little eyes stupid and malevolent behind their protective ridge.

Tanner howled with idiot bravery, brandishing his little knife.

Bastard John streaked across Tanner's view, coming up behind the dinichthys, and butted it hard in the eye. The huge predator swerved with frightening speed and grace and snapped at the dolphin. The slabs of bone in its mouth crunched together and grated.

It veered violently and shot after Bastard John. With rushes of displaced water, little ivory lances streaked past as the newt-people fired their strange weapons at the dinichthys. It ignored them and bore down on the dolphin.

Tanner kicked violently away, his legs spasming as he raced toward the clinging diver. As he swam he looked around him and saw, to his horror, that the massive bone-plated fish had gone deep, despite Bastard John's attempts to goad it, and was doubling back from below, heading straight for Tanner.

With a last kick, Tanner touched the rough metal of the pipe and scrabbled for the diver. Tanner stared at the dinichthys, his heart hammering as the monstrous thing powered toward him. The suckers of his tentacles anchored him to the shaft. He waved the knife in his right hand, praying for Bastard John or the newt-men or the armed divers to reach him. With his left he reached out for the trapped man.

His fumbling hand reached into something warm and soft, something that gave to his fingers in a horrifying way, and Tanner snatched his hand back. He glanced up for a second at the man beside him.

He looked into a faceplate full of water, and a wide-eyed white face, eyes protuberant, mouth distended and still. The leather in the center of the suit had been gouged away, and the man's stomach was torn from him. Entrails waved in the water like anemones.

Tanner moaned and snapped away, sensing the dinichthys below him, kicking out fearfully, slashing ineffectually at nothing as with a sudden vicious tide the ridges and scales swept past him, tons of muscle flexing, the sound of bone on bone jarring through the water. The pipe shuddered as the corpse was snatched from it. The snub-skulled hunter zigzagged away through the inverted forest of Armada's keels, the dead man dangling in its jaws.

Bastard John and the Bask menfish followed it, unable to match its effortless pace. In shock, Tanner kicked toward them pointlessly, the memory of the monstrous fish's presence slowing him and making him cold. He was vaguely aware that he should surface, should keep himself warm and drink sweetened tea, that he felt sick and very frightened.

The dinichthys was heading down now, into the realms of crushing pressures its pursuers could not hope to survive. Tanner watched it go, moving slowly, trying not to breathe in any dissipating blood. He was alone now.

He dragged himself through water like tar, up past unfamiliar undersides, disoriented and lost. He could still see the dead man's face and slick bowels. And as he found his bearings, as he twisted and saw the mobile ships in Basilio docks and the sprinkled crumblike boats of Winterstraw Market, he looked up and saw in the cold lancing shadow of the boat above him one of the huge, vague shapes that dangled from the city's undersides, that was obscured by charms and carefully guarded, that he was forbidden to see. He saw that it was linked to others, and he drifted higher, unchallenged now the shark that had guarded it was dead, and the shape was clearer, and suddenly he was close, he was only a few yards from it, and he had penetrated the murk and the obfuscatory hexes, and he could see it clearly now, and he knew what it was.

The next day, Bellis was treated to lurid descriptions of the monster's attack from several of her colleagues.

"Gods and fuck above," said Carrianne to her, appalled. "Can you imagine? Sliced in pieces by that bastard?" Her descriptions became more grotesque and unpleasant.

Bellis did not give Carrianne her attention. She was thinking about what Silas had told her. She approached it as she did most things—coolly, trying to grasp it intellectually. She searched for books on The Gengris and the grindylow, but found very little that was not children's myths or absurd speculation. She found it hard—impossibly hard, almost—to grasp the scale of danger to New Crobuzon. All the years of her life the city had squatted around her, massive and variegated and permanent. The idea that it could be threatened was almost inconceivable.

But, then, the grindylow were inconceivable, too.

Bellis found herself truly alarmed by Silas' descriptions and his obvious fear. With a kind of morbid extravagance, Bellis had tried to imagine New Crobuzon after an invasion. Ruined and broken. It started as a game, a sort of dare, where she filled her mind with horrifying images. But then they flickered through her unstoppably, as if projected by a magic lantern, and they appalled her.

She saw the rivers congealed with bodies, and shimmering as grindylow passed beneath. She saw petal-ash spewing from the burnt-out Fuchsia House; shattered rubble in Gargoyle Park; the Glasshouse cracked open like an egg and stacked with cactus corpses. She imagined Perdido Street Station itself in collapse, its train lines twisted and splayed, its façade torn off, forcing its intricate architectural byways into the light.

Bellis imagined the ancient, massive Ribs that arced over the city snapped, their curves interrupted in a cascade of bone-dust.

It chilled her. But there was nothing she could do. No one here, no one in power in this city, could possibly care. She and Silas were alone, and until they understood what was happening in Armada, until they knew where they were going, Bellis could not think of any way she could get away.

*   *   *

Bellis heard the door open and looked up from her piles of books. Shekel stood at the threshold, holding something in his hands. She was about to greet him, but paused at the sight of his face.

He wore an expression of great seriousness and uncertainty, as if not sure whether he had done something wrong.

"I've got something to show you," he said slowly. "You know I write down all the words I can't work out at first. And then when I find them again in other books, I know them. Well . . ." He looked at the book he was holding. "Well, I found one of them yesterday. And the book's not in Ragamoll, and the word's not a . . . not a verb or a noun or whatever." He stressed the technical words she had taught him: not with pride, but to make a point.

He handed the little book to her. "It's a name."

Bellis examined it. Sunk into the cover and picked out in stained metal leaf was the author's name.

Krüach Aum.

The work that Tintinnabulum was looking for, one central to the Lovers' project. Shekel had found it.

He had picked it off the children's shelves. As Bellis sat and flicked through its pages, she saw that it was no wonder it had been misshelved. It was full of pictures in a primitive style: executed in thick, simple lines with childish perspective, so that proportions were unclear, and a man might be nearly the size of a tower next to him. Each recto page was text, each verso a picture, so that the whole short book had the feel of an illustrated fable.

Whoever had shelved it had obviously looked at it briefly without understanding it, and put it, without examination, with other picture books—children's books. It had not been recorded. It had lain undisturbed for years.

Shekel was talking to Bellis, but she did not hear him clearly: *don't know what to do,* he was saying awkwardly, *thought you could help, the one Tintinnabulum was looking for, did the best thing.* Adrenaline and tremulous excitement were filling her as she studied the volume. There was no title. She turned to the first page, and her heartbeat quickened in her throat as she realized that she had been right about Aum's name. The book was in High Kettai.

It was the arcane, classical language of Gnurr Kett, the island nation thousands of miles south of New Crobuzon, at the edge of the Swollen Ocean, where the warm water became the Black Sandbar Sea. It was a strange, very difficult tongue that used the Ragamoll script but derived from quite another root. Base Kettai, the everyday language, was much easier, but the relationship between the two was attenuated and ancient. Fluency in one gave only the slightest understanding of the other. High Kettai, even in Gnurr Kett itself, was the preserve of the cantors and a few intellectuals.

Bellis had studied it. Fascinated by its structures of embedded verbs, it was High Kettai that Bellis had made the subject of her first book. It was fifteen years since she had published *High Kettai Grammatology,* but even rusty as she was, looking at the opening chapter of the book, the meaning came slowly to her.

"I would lie if I told you that I write this without pride," Bellis read silently, and looked up, trying to calm herself, almost afraid to go on.

She turned the pages rapidly, looking at the pictures. A man in a tower by the sea. The man on the shore, the skeletons of great engines littering the sand. The man making calculations by the sun, and by the shadows of strange trees. She turned to the fourth picture and caught her breath. A rill of goosebumps came and went over her.

In the fourth picture, the man stood again on the shore—his blank, stylized eyes the only features on his face, rendered by the artist as placid as a cow's—and above the sea, swarming toward an approaching boat, was a cloud of dark figures. The picture was vague, but Bellis could see thin arms and legs dangling, and a blur of wings.

It made her uneasy.

She scanned, trying to remember the language. There was something very odd about this book. It felt very different from all the other High Kettai works Bellis had seen. Something incongruous was in the tone, quite at odds with the poetry that characterized the old Gnurr Kett canon.

"He would have sought help from outsiders," she hesitantly made out, *"but all others shun our island, fearful of our hungry women."*

Bellis looked up. *Jabber knows,* she thought, *what I've got my hands on.*

She thought quickly, trying to work out what she should do.

Her hands still turned the pages like a construct's, and she looked down to see that, midway through the volume, the man was at sea in a little boat. He and his vessel were drawn very small. He was lowering a chain and a massive recurved hook into the sea.

Deep below, in the midst of the spirals that signified the water, were concentric circles, dwarfing his yacht.

The picture held her attention.

She stared at it, and something deep within her moved. She held her breath. And with a wash of realization the picture reconfigured itself like a child's optical illusion. She saw what it was—she knew what she was looking at—and her stomach pitched so hard that she felt she was falling.

She knew what Garwater's secret project was. She knew where they were heading. She knew what Johannes was doing.

Shekel was still talking. He had moved on to the dinichthys attack.

"Tanner was down there," she heard him say with pride. "Tanner went to help 'em, only he couldn't get there in time. But I'll tell you a funny thing. You remember a while ago I told you there's things under the city, shapes he couldn't make out? And he weren't allowed to see? Well, after the bonefish swims off yesterday, poor old Tanner comes up right underneath one, doesn't he? He gets to see it clearly—he knows what's under there, now. So guess what it was . . ."

He paused theatrically for Bellis to guess. She still stared at the picture.

"A bridle," she said, almost inaudible. Shekel's expression changed to confusion. Suddenly she spoke loudly. "A giant bridle, a bit, reins, a harness bigger than a building.

"Chains, Shekel, the size of boats," she said. He stared at her and nodded in bewilderment as she concluded. "Tanner saw chains."

She still did not take her gaze from the picture she held: a little man in a little ship on a sea of frozen waves that overlapped in perfect sequence like fish scales, and below them deeps rendered in crosshatched and tightly spiraled ink, and at the bottom, easily eclipsing the vessel above, a circle in a circle in a circle, vast no matter how vague the perspective, unthinkably big, with darkness at the center. Looking up, looking up at the fisherman hunting his prey.

Sclera, iris, and pupil.

An eye.

INTERLUDE III

Elsewhere

There are intruders in Salkrikaltor. They sit quiet, their eyes taking in the city and the cray, measured and inexorable like plugholes.

They have left a trail of missing farmers and submarine adventurers and wanderers and minor bureaucrats. They have extracted information with coddling tones and thaumaturgy and torture.

The intruders watch with eyes like oil.

They have explored. They have seen the temples and the shark pits and the galleries and arcades, and the cray slums, the architecture of the shallows. As light fails and Salkrikaltor's globes glow, traffic increases. Young cray dandies fight and posture on the spiraling walkways above (their actions are reflected in the hidden watchers' eyes).

Hours pass. The streets empty out. The globes dim a little in the hours before dawn.

And there is silence. And dark. And cold.

And the intruders move.

They pass through empty streets, cloaked in darkness.

The intruders move like ribbons of waste, as if they are nothing, as if they are tugged by random ebbs and tides. They trace anemone-scarred backstreets.

Nothing living is in the trench-streets except night fishes, the snails, the crabs that freeze with fear as the intruders approach. They pass beggars in the atomies of buildings. Through a rip in a warehouse poised on the brink of being dust. Out over the lowest level of a water-beaten roofscape like coral, insinuating themselves into shadows that seem too small for them. Quick as morays.

A name was whispered to them in a coil of blood, a clue that they have accepted, and stalked and found.

They rise and look down on the roofscape through the sea.

* * *

He sleeps there, his legs folded below him, his torso rocking faintly in the current, his eyes closed—the he-cray they have hunted. The intruders hunker low. They stroke him and touch him and make sounds from within their throats, and his eyes open slowly and he spasms violently in the bonds in which they have spread-eagled him (*as quietly and gently as nannies, not to wake him*), and his mouth strains so wide that it looks as if it will split and bleed. He would be screaming and screaming in cray vibrato if they had not fit him with a collar of bone that skewers painlessly into certain nerves in his neck and back and cuts off his sound.

Little gouts of blood float up from the cray's throat. The intruders watch him curiously. When finally his frenzy exhausts him, a captor moves with alien grace and speaks.

—*you know something* it says.—*we need to know it too.*

They begin their work, whispering questions as they touch and touch the cray translator with unthinkable expertise, and he snaps back his head and screams again.

Again, without a sound.

The intruders continue.

And later.

The wormcast floor of the ocean plunges out of sight and the water opens endlessly and the dark figures (far from home) sit motionless suspended in the dark, and ponder.

The trail has exploded.

Little filigrees of rumor twist away from them, recurve, and tease. The southern ship has disappeared. From the rock edges of the continent, where land rises to separate fresh- from saltwater, they have tracked to the Basilisk Channel, to the up-pointing fingers of Salkrikaltor City, to the ship puttering between the sea and New Crobuzon the river-straddler. But that ship has disappeared, leaving lies and stories eddying behind it.

Mouths from the deep. Ghost pirates. Torque. Hidden storms. The floating city.

Again and again the floating city.

The hunters investigate the rigs that loom from Salkrikaltor's southern waters: supports like outsize trees, like pachyderms' legs, crumbling concrete shafts in the seabed, mud oozing up around them as if around toes.

Drills worry at the soft rock, sucking at its juices. The rigs feed in shallows like swamp things.

Men in shells of leather and air descend on chains to tend to the mumbling giants, and the hunters spirit them away with predatory ease. They take away the masks, and the men scrabble futilely and emit their lives in bubbling howls of air. Their captors keep them alive with hexes, with mouth-kisses of oxygen, with massage to slow their hearts, and in caves under the light water the men beg for mercy and, at their captors' insistence, tell them all manner of stories.

Stories, above all, of the floating city that snatched the *Terpsichoria* away.

Night falls, and the shadows shed by day are smothered.

The unclear figures have all the water of the world to search. The Oceans: the Rime; the Boxash; the Vassilly and Tarribor and Teuchor; the Muted and Swollen. And the Gentleman's Sea and the Spiral Sea and the Clock and Hidden and others; and all the straits and sounds and channels. And the bays, and the bights.

How can they search it all? How can they start?

They ask the sea.

They strike out for the deep waters.

—*where is the floating city?* they ask.

The king of the goblin sharks does not know or care. The corokanth will not tell. The hunters ask elsewhere.—*where is the floating city?*

They find monkish intelligences masquerading as cod and congers that claim ignorance and swim away for more contemplation. The hunters ask the salinae, the brine elementals, but cannot make sense of the liquid shrieks of information with which they are answered.

Rising with the sun and breaching, the hunters bob in waves and think again.

They ask the whales.

—*where is the floating city?* they ask the great stupid krill-swillers, the grey and the humpback and the blue. They straddle them like mountaineers and manipulate the pleasure centers of their heavy brains. They bribe them, funneling tons of plankton in a panicked soup into the whale's gurning grins.

The hunters make the question a demand.

—*find the floating city,* they say carefully, in concepts simple enough for the whales to understand.

Which they do. The huge animals ponder, their synapses so sluggish the hunters grow impatient (but they know they must wait). Finally, after minutes when the only noise is a sluicing as the whales jaw the water, with a concerted thunder of flukes they break their silence.

They moan across thousands of miles; echo-locating; sounding; sending friendly, stupid messages to each other; doing what they have been told: Looking for Armada.

PART THREE

The Compass Factory

CHAPTER FIFTEEN

"They're raising an avanc."

Silas' face fluttered with astonishment, with denial, with a gamut of incredulities.

"That can't be," he said quietly, shaking his head.

Bellis' mouth twisted. "Because avancs are legends?" she offered harshly. "Extinct? Stories for children?" She pursed her lips and shook Krüach Aum's book. "Whoever shelved this, twenty years ago, thought that they were children's stories, Silas. I can read High Kettai." Her voice was urgent. "This is not a children's book."

The day was waning, and the muttering of the city continued outside. Bellis looked through the window at the light dying in sheets of spectacular colors. She handed Silas the book and spoke again.

"I've been doing little else for two days. I've been haunting the library like a damned eidolon, reading Aum's book." Silas was turning the pages one by one, carefully, his eyes scanning the text as if he could understand it, which Bellis knew he could not.

"It's in High Kettai," she said, "but it's not from Gnurr Kett, and it's not old. Krüach Aum is anophelii."

Silas looked up, aghast. There was a very long silence.

"Believe me," said Bellis. She felt, and sounded, drained. "I know how it sounds. I've spent the last two days trying to find out everything I can.

"I thought they were dead, too, but they're only dying, Silas. They've been dying for more than two thousand years. When the Malarial Queendom collapsed they were eradicated in Shoteka, in Rohagi, in most of the Shards. But they managed to survive . . . They've clung on to a little hold on some shithole of a rock south of Gnurr Kett. And believe it or not, even after the Queendom, there are people who trade with them." She nodded grimly.

"They have some arrangement with Dreer Samher or Gnurr Kett or both, or something. I can't work it out.

"And they write books, it seems." She pointed at the volume. "Gods only knows why it's in High Kettai. Maybe that's what they speak now—they'd be the only people in the world who do. I don't know, Godsdammit, Silas. Maybe it's all crap," she snapped with sudden irritation. "Maybe that damn thing's a forgery or a lie or, yes, a children's story. But I've been told by Tintinnabulum to look for anything by Krüach Aum, so do you think the subject matter of this damn book is just coincidence?"

"What does it say?" he asked.

Bellis took the book from him and slowly translated the first lines.

" 'I would lie if I told you that I write this without pride. I am full of it like food, because I have . . . found a story to tell, of what had not been done since the Ghosthead Empire and was achieved once more, a thousand years ago. One of our ancestors, after our queens collapsed and we came here to hide . . . With . . . devices and thaumaturgy . . . he went out over the water . . . to a dark place . . . and he sent hexes into the mouth of the water and after twenty-one days of heat and thirst and hunger he . . . drew out a great and mysterious thing.' " She looked up at Silas and concluded, " 'The mountain-that-swims, the godwhale, the greatest beast ever to visit our world, the avanc.' "

She closed the book softly.

"He called up an avanc, Silas."

"What happened?" he said. "You've read it, what *happened*?"

Bellis sighed. "It doesn't say how or where, but Aum found a bunch of old manuscripts, an old story. And he's put them together and made sense of them, and retold them. The story of an anophelius, who's never named. Centuries ago. There are ten pages about his preparations. The man fasts; he researches; he stares out to sea a lot; he gathers the things he needs: barrels, liquor, old machines that have been moldering on the beach. He goes out to sea. Alone. Trying to keep control of a yacht way too big for one man, but no one would come with him. He's looking for a particular place, some kind of . . . deep, deep shaft, a hole in the ocean's floor. That's where he's hunting. That's where he casts. That's where he wants the avanc to . . . come through, from where they normally live.

"Then we get twenty very dull pages about the privations of

the sea. Hungry, thirsty, tired, wet, hot . . . That sort of thing. He knows he's in the right place. He's sure his hook is . . . extending into somewhere else. Bleeding through the world. But he can't attract the avanc. There's no worm that big.

"Then on the third day, when he's totally exhausted, and his ship's being moved around by weird currents, the sky darkens. There's an elyctric storm coming. And he decides it's not enough to be in the right place—he needs power to snare the thing. He's being pounded by hail and rain, and the sea's going berserk. The boat's plowing through huge waves, banging like it's going to shatter."

Silas was listening to her with eyes wide, and Bellis had a sudden ridiculous image of herself as a teacher telling the children a story.

"As the middle of the storm gets nearer and nearer, he yanks a load of wire to the top of the mainmast, coiling it round the rigging, and links it up to some kind of generator. Then . . ."

Bellis sighed. "I couldn't really follow what happened then. He does some thaumaturgy or other. I think he was trying to conjure fulmen, elyctric elementals, or sacrifice them or something, but it's not clear. Well . . ." She shrugged. "Whether he succeeds or not, whether it's an elemental answering him or just the result of winding copper wire up a hundred-foot mast in the middle of a thunderstorm, lightning strikes the conductor."

She held open the relevant illustration: the boat in silhouette, outlined in white, with a rather squat, geometrically rendered lightning bolt stuck like a saw into the top of the mast.

"There's a massive burst of energy through the engines. The thaumaturgic controls he's rigged up to try to bait and control the avanc suddenly spasm with supercharged puissance, then burn out instantly. And his boat lurches, and the cranes and winches tethering his hook bend suddenly, and there's a rushing from underneath.

"He hooked an avanc, says Aum. And it rose."

Bellis fell quiet. She turned the pages and read Aum's words to herself.

The ocean vibrated with a scream five miles down, and the water rose and shuddered and was unsteady as it was displaced, vastly, and the waves died as the tides were supplanted by a great onrush from below and the water tossed the boat like a mote, and the horizon disappeared as the avanc surfaced.

That was all. No description of the creature. The verso page that should have held an illustration was left blank.

"He sees it," she said quietly. "When he sees the size of it he realizes that he'd only snagged it with his hooks and hexes. He'd thought he'd reel it in like an angler . . . Impossible. The avanc breaks the chains, effortlessly. And then it sinks again, and the sea's empty. And he's all alone, and he has to get himself all the way home."

Bellis could picture it, and it moved her. She imagined the broken figure, sodden with brine and in the middle of a still-terrible storm, crawling to his feet, stumbling across the deck of his ill-prepared ship. Setting dying motors in motion, limping back across the sea hungry and exhausted, and above all alone.

"Do you think it's the truth?" said Silas.

Bellis opened the book to its last section and held it out for him to see. The pages were crammed with strange-looking mathematic notations.

"The last twenty pages are taken up with equations, thaumaturgic notes, references to his colleagues. Aum calls it a data appendix. It's almost impossible to translate. I don't understand it—it's high theory, crypto-algebra and the like. But it's incredibly carefully done. If it's a fake it's needlessly complex. What he's done . . . Aum has checked the details—of the dates, the techniques, the thaumaturgies, and the science . . . He's worked out how it was done. These last pages . . . They're an exposition, a scientific treatise, explaining how you'd go about it. How you'd raise an avanc.

"Silas, this book was written and printed in the last Kettai Vullfinch Year. That was twenty-three years ago. Which incidentally means that Tintinnabulum and his cohorts have it wrong—he thought Aum was writing in the last century. It was printed in Kohnid in Gnurr Kett, part of the imprint Shivering Wisdom. There aren't too many Kettai works in this library, as you'd expect. And of those there are, the vast bulk are in Base Kettai. But there are a few High Kettai, and I've looked at them all. Shivering Wisdom publish in High Kettai: philosophy and science and ancient texts, gnostic mechonomy and the like.

"Shivering Wisdom obviously think this is on the level, Silas. If it's a fraud, it's taken in a scientific publishing house—as well, dammit, as the best fucking minds on Armada.

"What else are the Lovers' scientists reading, Silas? My friend Johannes' book *Theories of MegaFauna*. Another of his, about transplane life. Radical theories about the nature of water, books on maritime ecology. And they're going crazy to find this little book here, probably because Tintinnabulum and his hunters have seen a few references to it, and they can't damn well find it. Jabber's sake, what do you think that's all about?

"Silas, I've read this thing." She made him meet her eyes. "This is for real. This is a book on how to raise an avanc. And how to control it. The anophelius Aum writes about . . . the avanc broke loose from him easy." She leaned forward.

"But he was one man. Armada's a city. He scavenged steam engines: Armada has whole industrial *districts*. There are giant chains under the city—did you know that? What do you think they plan on doing with them? And Armada has the *Sorghum*." She let that sink in and saw his eyes change fractionally. "This city has hundreds of gallons of fucking rockmilk, Silas, and the means to get hundreds more. Jabber knows what thaumaturgy they can fuel with that shit.

"The Lovers think they can succeed where Aum's man failed," she said simply. "They're heading for the sinkhole, to call up an avanc. They're going to harness it to the city. And they're going to control it."

"Who else knows about the book?" said Silas, and Bellis shook her head.

"No one knows," she said. "Only the boy, Shekel. He has no idea what it is, what it means."

You did the right thing bringing this to me, Bellis had said. *I'll see what this is all about and pass it right on to Tintinnabulum as soon as I've seen if it's of any use.*

She remembered Shekel's disquiet, his fear. He visited Tintinnabulum's *Castor* often, to be with Angevine. Bellis knew, with a quick stab of pity, that he had not taken the book there directly himself because he was afraid that he had made a mistake. His reading was still inexpert, and faced with something of such apparent importance, his confidence had left him. He had stared at the combination of letters spelling *Krüach,* and had looked at the

name he had copied from Tintinnabulum's paper, and had seen
that they were the same, but still, but still.

But still he was not quite sure. He did not want to make a fool
of himself, or waste people's time. He had taken it to Bellis, his
friend and teacher, to check, to make sure. And ruthlessly, she
had taken it from him, knowing that it gave her power.

The Lovers were bringing them south to a fissure in the seabed
from where the avanc might rise. They had collected what was
necessary—the scientist they needed, a rig to fuel the hexes—and
now they were heading toward their quarry, their experts working in tight and ceaseless concert to complete their calculations,
to solve the enigma of the summoning, even as they traveled.

And immediately Silas and Bellis saw this, as soon as they
realized that they had achieved their aim, that they knew the
Lovers' plan, that they could work out where the city was heading, they began to talk frantically about how they could use that
knowledge to escape.

What are we doing? thought Bellis in the silence. *Another night
we're sitting in my stupid little round chimney room, saying* oh
gods oh gods *to ourselves and each other, because we've picked
off one layer of mystery and underneath is yet more shit, yet
more trouble, that we can do nothing about.* She felt like moaning with exhaustion. *I don't want to wonder what I'm going to do
anymore,* she thought. *I want to just do something.*

She drummed her fingers across the book's script. A script
that she and few others could read.

Looking at that arcane language, a vague, unpleasant suspi-
cion ached in her. She felt as she had that night in the restaurant,
when Johannes had told her that the Lovers used his books.

The constant grinding of the flotilla of tugs and others that
dragged the city had become background noise. But, unnoticed
and forgotten, they continued. There was not a moment of night
or day that Armada did not inch south. The effort was prodigious
and the pace glacial, slower than a human could crawl.

But days passed at that torturous rate, and the city did move.
People shed coats and woolen trousers. The days were still short,
but without fuss or proclamation, Armada had passed into a tem-

perate zone of the sea. And it continued to move toward warmer water.

Armada's plants—crops of wheat and barley, decktop grasslands, weed regiments reclaiming old stone and metal—felt the change. Scavenging constantly for heat, they drew sustenance from the random change of season and began rapidly to grow, to bud. The smells of the parklands became richer; the green began to be broken by hardy little flowers.

Every day there were more birds overhead. The pirate ships sailed over new and colorful fish in the warm waters. In Armada's multitude of little temples, services welcomed the latest of the city's irregular, contingent springs.

Tanner had seen the chains, and having done so, it did not take him very long to realize what was planned for the city.

Of course he could not know the details. But he remembered what he had seen, even through the shock and cold that had been settling on him as he rose through the water. He had come up below one of the forbidden ships and at the heart of an obscuring glamour, the scale of what he observed had at first confused him, but then it had resolved itself and he had realized it was a chain link, fifty feet long.

The *Grand Easterly* stretched out overhead like an ominous cloud. The metal was riveted to its underside with ancient bolts bigger than a man. Through the centuries of growth that encased the ship's hull, Tanner realized that another link connected to the first, flush against the steamer's hull. Beyond that, the weed growth and the charmed water had obscured his vision.

There were great chains below the city. And, knowing that, it did not take him very long to guess what was planned. With an almost rueful surprise, Tanner Sack realized that he now knew the secret that had seemed always to hover at the edge of conversation in the docks. The source of unease and winks and shared glances, the unspoken project that shaped all their efforts.

We're going to raise something from the sea, he thought calmly. *Some beastie? Are we going to tether some sea serpents or kraken or Jabber knows what and . . . what then? Could it pull Armada? Like a seawyrm does a chariot ship?*

That makes sense enough, he thought, awed by the scale of the thing, whatever it was, but not afraid nor disapproving.

Why hide that from the likes of me? he thought. *Ain't it as if I'm loyal?*

It took Tanner days to recover from the dinichthys attack. His sleep was poor; he broke into fearful sweats. He remembered the feeling of the burst man's bowels in his hand, and although he had seen and held the dead before, there was a quality of terror to that corpse's eyes that distressed him days later. He could not shake the memory of the bonefish plunging at him, as implacable as a geological event.

His workmates treated him with respect. "You tried, Tanner, man," they said to him.

After two days, Tanner went back to the pool between Garwater and Jhour, to swim and soothe his cracking skin. He watched the men and women in the water; there were a few more of them in these hospitable temperatures. Other pirate-citizens watched from the side, marveling at the esoteric skill of swimming.

Tanner saw the spinning drops of water shed by inexpert paddling and up-flung arms, saw the fractured surface of the water, and he found himself twitching uneasily as swimmers ducked below, out of sight, into the deep water. He could not see them, could not see what was below them. He moved forward, made to jump, and felt his stomach pitch.

He was afraid.

Too late now, he told himself with an edge of hysteria. *It's too late now, man! You're Remade for this! You live in the damn water, and you ain't never going back.*

He was doubly frightened: of the sea and of his own fear that threatened to landlock him, turn him into a freakshow, gilled and webbed but airbound, skin peeling and gills drying painfully, tentacles rotting, too scared to swim. So he forced himself in, and the brine soothed him and brought him some peace.

It was terribly hard, opening his eyes and forcing his gaze down into diffuse, sunlit blue below him, knowing that he would likely never see rock beneath the water again, but only that stretching deep where predators flicked their tails and eddied out of sight.

It was appallingly hard, but he swam, and felt better for it.

At Shekel's insistence, Angevine let Tanner rummage in her metal innards. She was still uncomfortable about it. For him to operate, they had had to put out her boiler, immobilizing her. It was the first time for years she had allowed that to happen. She lived in fear of her fires going cold.

He tinkered as he would with any engine, tapping at pipes and wielding his wrench with gusto, till he glanced up and saw how bloodless her knuckles were as she clenched Shekel's hand.

The last time anyone had put their hands in her like this, Tanner realized, was when she was Remade. He was gentler with her then.

As he had expected, she was powered by an old, inefficient engine. It needed replacing, and with a curt warning to Angevine, and to the sound of her horrified yells, he began to dismantle it.

Eventually she calmed down (too late to back out anyway, he explained somewhat ruthlessly: she'd never move again if he left her like this). And when, after several hours, he had finished, and he rolled out from under her, sweating and oil-covered, and began to light the fuel in her reconfigured boiler, it was clear she could feel the difference immediately.

They were both tired and embarrassed. When the pressure built in her engine, and Angevine began to move, to feel the new reserves of power he had given her, to check on her fire and realize how much longer the coke was lasting, she recognized how much he had done for her. But Tanner was no more comfortable being thanked than she was in thanking him, and there was little more than overlapping mutterings on each side.

Later, Tanner settled in his tub of seawater and thought about what he had done. She shouldn't have to scrabble continually for scraps of fuel anymore. Her mind was freed up: no more thinking all the time about the boiler, no more rousing herself in the small hours to feed her fires.

He grinned.

When first he had stood up, Tanner had noticed a newly gouged mark on her chassis, from the edge of his spanner or screwdriver. He had scratched a wound in the stained iron. Angevine always made an effort to keep her metal parts clean, so the mark Tanner had made stood out. He had shifted uneasily.

When Angevine had seen it, her mouth and face had stiffened with anger. But as the minutes went on, and she swayed with the sense of steam, her expression had changed. And as she had left, while Shekel waited for her in the doorway, Angevine had rolled to Tanner and spoken to him quietly.

"Never mind about the scratch, eh?" she had said. "You've

done a great job, Tanner. And that mark . . . Well, it's part of re-building, eh? Part of the new." She had smiled at him quickly and had left without looking back.

"Oh, you're welcome, for Jabber's sake," murmured Tanner out loud at the memory, pleased and embarrassed. He sat back in his bath. "For the lad, really. It's for the lad's sake."

There were only ten ships of any size in the haunted quarter of Armada, tucked away at the city's fore-port corner, bordering Dry Fall and King Friedrich's Thee-And-Thine.

The subjects of Friedrich's violent mercantile rule for the most part ignored the eerie ships next to their riding, concentrating on their bazaars and glad' circuses and moneylenders. In Dry Fall, however, the baleful influence of the haunted quarter crept over the little fringe of sea and stained the Brucolac's riding. Where Dry Fall neighbored the deserted ships, its own vessels were subdued and unpleasant.

Perhaps it was the presence of the Brucolac and his cadre of vampir lieutenants in Dry Fall itself that sharpened the inhabitants' senses to the dead and ab-dead. Perhaps that was why unlike those in Thee-And-Thine, the citizens of Dry Fall riding could not forget the presence of the fearful haunted quarter beside them.

Uncanny noises emanated from it: mutterings that carried on the wind; the faint grind of motors; things grating against other things. Some claimed that the sounds were illusory, the product of wind and the bizarre architecture of the ancient ships. Very few believed that. Sometimes a foolhardy group—invariably the recently press-ganged—would enter the hulks, to emerge some hours later closed-mouthed and pale and refusing to speak. And on occasion, of course, they did not return.

Attempts to sever the ten ships from the fabric of the city, to scuttle them and scour the haunted quarter from Armada's map, were reputed to have been tried and to have failed in alarming ways. Most citizens were superstitious about that quiet place: frightened as they were of it, they would have argued strongly against any attempts to remove it.

Birds would not settle in the haunted ships. Their skyline of old masts and mast stumps, their moldering bituminous carcasses and ragged sails were stark and deserted.

The border of Dry Fall and the haunted quarter was where one went to be undisturbed.

Two men stood in the night's cool drizzle. They were alone on the deck of a clipper.

In front of them, thirty feet away, was a long, slim vessel, some ancient galley that creaked in Armada's incessant wind and motion, empty and unlit. The bridges that linked it to the clipper were rotting and blocked with chains. It was the foremost ship of the haunted quarter.

From way behind the men rose the noises of the city center, the irregular shopping arcades that wound across the bodies of several vessels, the playhouses and dance halls. The clipper it-self was silent. A row of tent houses on its deck was mostly unin-habited. Those few who lived there had realized who stood on the clipper's deck, and were staying very carefully out of sight.

"I'm bewildered," said the Brucolac quietly, not looking at his companion. His quiet, hoarse voice was only just audible. Wind and rain pushed his shaggy hair back from his face as he looked out past the galley at the black sea. "Explain it to me." He turned and raised his eyebrows, in a look of mild consternation, at Uther Doul.

With no bodyguards, no yeomanry or bystanders to see this interaction, the glowering tension that characterized the two men's public confrontations was absent. Their body language was only a little cautious, like people meeting for the first time.

"It's not like I don't know you, Uther," the Brucolac said. "It's not like we haven't stood together. I trust you, sincerely. I trust your instincts. I know how you think. And we both know it's just a matter of . . . of fucking chance that you're their man . . . rather than mine." There was regret in his voice, a small note of regret.

The Brucolac stared at Uther Doul with his pale eyes. His long, forked tongue tasted the air, and he spoke again.

"Tell me, man. Tell me what's happening. Moon's Tits, you can't support this idiotic idea. Are you feeling guilty? Is that it? That it was you who gave them the notion? That they'd never have thought of this if it weren't for what you told them?" He leaned in a little as he spoke.

"It's not the power, Uther. You know that. I don't give a sailor's toss who runs Armada. Dry Fall's all I want. Garwater's always been the strongest, and that's fine by me. And it's not the fucking avanc, either. Shit, if I thought that would work, I'd be with you.

I'm not one of those Curhouse arseholes jabbering on about what's 'against nature,' and 'tampering with deadly forces' and crap like that. Shit, Uther, if I thought doing deals with *daemons* would strengthen the city, don't you think I'd do it?"

Uther Doul glanced at him, and for the first time his face moved, twitching in contained amusement.

"You're ab-dead, Brucolac," he said in his singer's voice. "You know there are plenty who think you've already done deals with the Hellkin."

The Brucolac ignored him and continued. "I'm against this because we both know this won't stop with the avanc." His voice was cold. Doul looked away. The night was without stars or horizon: the sea and sky bled ink into each other. "And it's not going to take long for others to clock that. Shaddler might do whatever it's told till the fucking sea boils, but do you think Jhour and Booktown will stick with the Lovers when they realize what the plan really is? Uther, you're heading for mutiny."

"Deadman . . ." began Doul, and paused heavily. Doul was the only man in the city who used the foreign honorific. It came from his homeland. "Deadman Brucolac. I'm the Lovers' man. You know it, and you know why. And maybe it could have been another way, but it isn't. I'm a soldier, Brucolac. A good soldier. If I didn't think they could do it—if I didn't think it would work—then I wouldn't support it."

"Bullshit." The Brucolac's voice came hard and throaty. "Gods fuck and damn it, Uther, that . . . is a lie. Do you remember, do you even remember how I found out what they want to do with the avanc?"

"Spies," said Doul levelly, meeting his eyes again.

The Brucolac was dismissive. "Spies could only ever get insinuations and hints. Don't lie to yourself. I know because *you* told me."

Doul's eyes went quite cold and sharp.

"That is slander and I will not have you repeat it—" he said, but the Brucolac broke him off with laughter.

"Look at yourself," he urged, incredulous. "Who do you think you're talking to? Stop being so fucking pompous. You know what I mean. Of course you didn't *volunteer* the information, or even damn well admit it. But shit, Uther, I came to you and confronted you with what I'd worked out, and you . . . Well, you're too professional to give away anything that could come back to bite you, but if you'd wanted to mislead me or leave me thinking I was wrong you could have.

"You didn't. And I'm grateful. And fair enough, if you want to play this stupid game where you'll not admit what we both know to be the case, and you won't confirm my suspicions but you damn well won't deny them either, then that's . . . that's fine. Just keep on being silent.

"The facts remain, Uther." The Brucolac absently picked splinters of wood from the guardrail and let them drift down into the dark. "The fact remains that you let me know. And you know the other riding leaders won't trust me if I tell them. You've given me something I have to carry alone. And I think that's because you know it's a stupid, dangerous plan, and you don't know what to do with that knowledge, and you wanted an ally."

Doul smiled. "Are you so arrogant?" he said lightly. "Are you that sure of yourself, that you can turn any conversation, any miscommunication, round?"

"Remember the razor golems?" said the Brucolac suddenly, and Uther Doul fell silent. "The steamwind plain?" the Brucolac continued. "Remember that place? The things we *saw*? This city owes us, Uther. We were the ones who saved it, whether they'll admit it, whether they *know* it or not. Where were the damn Lovers then? That was you . . . and me."

The call of gulls. The sound of wind between the boats, the creaking of the haunted quarter.

"I learnt things then, Uther." The Brucolac spoke quietly. "I learnt how to read you. I know you."

"Godsdammit!" Uther Doul faced him. "How dare you play old soldiers with me? I am not on your side, Brucolac! I do not agree with you! Can you understand that? We have history, it's true, and Khyriad knows I'll not willingly turn on you, Deadman, but . . . that is all. I'm a lieutenant, and you were never my captain. I came here tonight as you asked, out of courtesy to you. Nothing more."

The Brucolac held his hand to his mouth and eyed Doul. His long tongue flickered over his fingers. When he lowered his hand, he looked sad.

"The Scar does not exist," he said. There was silence.

"The Scar does not exist," he repeated, "and if by some chance the astrolonomers are wrong, and it does, then we'll not find it. And if by some fucking miracle we do find it, then you know—you, Uther, of all people know—that it'll mean our deaths."

He pointed briefly at the sword scabbarded on Doul's left side. He moved his finger, indicating his companion's right sleeve, ridged with branching wires like veins.

"You know that, Uther," the Brucolac said. "You know the forces that would spill from something like that. You know we couldn't possibly face them. You know that better than anyone, whatever those fools think they've learnt from you. It would mean the end of us all."

Uther Doul looked down at his sword.

"Not our deaths," he said, and smiled unexpectedly and beautifully. "Nothing so straightforward."

The Brucolac shook his head.

"You're the bravest man I've known, Doul, in more ways than I can count." His tone was wistful, regretful. "Which is why it bewilders me to face this side of you. This base, pusillanimous, cowardly, recreant, craven aspect." Doul did not move or react, and the Brucolac did not sound as if he was taunting. "Have you convinced yourself that the bravest thing is to do your duty, come what may, Uther?"

He shook his head, his gaze incredulous. "Are you a masochist, Uther Doul? Is that it? Does it make you hard to debase yourself like this? Do you find yourself erect when those cut-up cunts give you orders you know to be idiocy? Do you come, do you touch yourself when you obey them regardless? Well good godspit, your cock must be raw from tugging by now, because these are the most lunatic orders you have ever tried to obey, and you know that.

"And I will not allow you to carry them out."

Doul watched, motionless, as the Brucolac turned his back and strode away.

The vampir wrapped shadow around himself as he walked, vanishing quickly into a fog of glamour, his footsteps muting as he disappeared. There was a rustling sound in the air, and way above the deck the old rigging thrummed briefly as something brushed it and was gone.

Doul followed the noises up through the air with his eyes. Only when everything around him was still did he turn back to the sea and the haunted quarter, his hand resting on the pommel of his sword.

CHAPTER SIXTEEN

With atlases and explorers' monographs, Bellis and Silas drew maps of Gnurr Kett and the Cymek and Iron Bay. They tried to trace a route home.

The anophelii island was unmarked, but interpreting the stories of the cactacae merchants, they worked it out to be some scores of miles from the southern tip of Gnurr Kett, a thousand miles or so from the island's civilized northern shores. And from that northern edge it was almost another two thousand to New Crobuzon.

Bellis knew how uncommon it was to see Kettai ships at harbor in the city's Kelltree docks. She foraged in works of political economy and traced the routes of commodities from Dreer Samher to Gnurr Kett, to Shankell, to the Mandrake Islands and Perrick Nigh and Myrshock, and eventually, perhaps, by some tortuous route or other, to New Crobuzon.

"From the mosquito island we'll be almost as far from the city as if we'd made it to the damn colonies," said Bellis bitterly. "Thousands of miles of unknown waters and mapless places and rumors and crap in between. Right at the wrong end of a long, long trading chain."

All their free moments were spent like this, hunched together in Bellis' cylindrical room, ignoring the sounds and the daylight or lamplight outside, she smoking furiously, cursing at Armada's unpleasant ship-grown tobacco, both of them scribbling note after note, hunting through old books. Trying to make something from the knowledge they'd stolen. Trying to work out an escape.

They had hunted hard for the city's secret. Now that they had it, the slowly dawning understanding that still, even so, even with that knowledge they might not make it home, appalled them.

If we can just work out where we'll be . . . Bellis would think, and a queasy understanding would grow in her that it was not as if the whole damn city would dock, or would trundle past Kohnid or some other port in plain view. And if it did, she would still have to fight her own way from the city to the shore, to the docks, to a ship, across the water again, home. And there was no way at all that she could make that happen.

Get me to the shore, she thought. *If I could get to the shore, maybe I could persuade someone to help me, or I could steal a boat, or I could stow away, or . . . something . . .*

But she could not get to the shore. And even if she could, all those ideas might come to nothing, and she knew it.

"Shekel came to see me today," she said. "It's been near enough a week since he gave me the book, Silas. He asked me what it was, whether it was what Tintinnabulum was looking for. I told him I'd know for certain soon.

"It won't be long," she said ominously. "It won't be long till he overcomes his shyness and tells someone. He's friends with some loyal dockhand who works for the Lovers. He's *fucking* Tintinnabulum's servant, for Jabber's sake.

"We have to move, Silas. We have to make a decision. We have to decide what we're going to do. When he tells his friends that he found the book by Krüach Aum, the yeomanry'll be here in minutes. And then not only will they have the book, but they'll know we were keeping it from them. And gods know I don't want to see the inside of an Armadan jail."

It was impossible to judge how much exactly the Lovers knew about raising the avanc. They must know something—the location of the sinkholes, the scale of the engines and thaumaturgy necessary, perhaps some parts of the science required. But they were particularly seeking the volume by Krüach Aum.

The only description of a successful attempt to call and capture an avanc, Bellis thought. *They know whereabouts in the world to go, but I'm betting there's a load they don't know. They must think they can piece it together, and probably they can, in time. But I just bet this would make things a damn sight easier.*

And she wrestled with stupid ideas, like demanding her freedom in exchange for the book, knowing miserably that that would never work. Hope was slipping away from her, and that made her cold.

In a kind of desperate carelessness, she talked with Carrianne about escape. Couching all her questions and ideas in an idiotically unconvincing *what if*? register, she asked Carrianne whether she had ever wanted to leave the city.

Carrianne grinned with friendly cruelty. "Never crossed my mind," she said.

They were in a pub in Dry Fall, and Carrianne looked around ostentatiously before turning back to Bellis and speaking more quietly. "Of course. But what had I got to go back to, Bellis? Why would I risk something like that? Some press-ganged try it every few years, you know. Off in a little boat, or what have you. They're always, always stopped."

Only the ones you hear about, thought Bellis.

"What happens to them?" she said.

Carrianne looked down at her drink for a while, then back up at Bellis with another hard smile.

"It's just about the one thing that every ruler in Armada agrees on," she said, "the Lovers, the Brucolac, King Friedrich and Braginod and the Council and all. Armada can't afford to be found. Of course there are sailors that know we're out here somewhere, and there are communities like Dreer Samher that we can trade with. But to be found out by some big power—like New Crobuzon? That would want us off the seas? People trying to escape are stopped, Bellis. Not caught, you understand. Stopped."

Carrianne slapped Bellis on the back.

"Godsdammit, don't look so appalled!" she said heartily. "You can't really tell me you're surprised. You know what would happen if they got home and let out the wrong sort of information, and your lot got hold of Armada? Just ask any of the Remade who made it out of the New Crobuzon slave ships, see how loyal they feel about the Crobuzoner navy. Ask some of those who've been to Nova Esperium and seen what happened to the natives. Or some of the sailors who've come up against New Crobuzon freebooters waving their damn letters of marque. You think *we're* pirates, Bellis? Drink up and shut up!"

* * *

That night for the first time, Bellis wondered aloud what she and Silas might do if they could not return home. She raised the possibility as a spur.

But a kind of calm horror descended on her as she realized that her own escape was not the only consideration. _What if we can't escape?_ she thought coolly. _Is that the end of it? Is that the last word?_

Silas was watching her, his face bleak and tired. Looking at him, Bellis saw the spires and markets and brick rookeries of her home city with sudden, stark clarity. She remembered her friends. She thought again about New Crobuzon. In spring, stinking of sap; at the close of the year, cold and intricate; at the festival of Jabber's Morning, lit up, strung with gimgews and lanterns, jostled by singing crowds, the trains decked out in pious livery. At midnight on any day of the year, in the lamplight.

At war, at bloody war with The Gengris.

"We have to get a message to them," she said quietly. "That's the most important thing. Whether or not we can get back, we have to warn them."

With that, she let go of what she could not achieve. And miserable as it made her, something inside her became less frantic. The schemes that she tentatively suggested now were more grounded, more systematic, more likely to succeed.

Bellis realized that Hedrigall was key.

There were many stories about the big cactus-man, the Samheri fabler and aeronaut. A cloud of rumors, truth and lies. And among the things that Shekel had breathlessly told her, one had stuck hard in Bellis' memory: Hedrigall had been to the island of the mosquito-people.

It could be true. He had been a trader-pirate from Dreer Samher, who were the only group known regularly to deal with the anophelii. Sap, not blood, ran in them: they were undrinkable. They could barter without fear.

And he might remember things.

The day was overcast and warm, and Bellis sweated from the moment she left her rooms for work. Even scrawny as she was, by the end of the day she felt laden down with excess flesh. The smoke from her cigarillos seemed to cosset her head like a stinking hat, and even Armada's unending winds didn't dust her clean.

Silas was waiting for her outside her rooms.

"It's true," he said, grimly elated. "Hedrigall's been there. He remembers it. I know how the Dreer Samher traders operate."

Their maps could become more accurate, their knowledge of the island less tenuous.

"He's loyal, is Hedrigall," Silas said, "so I've got to be careful. Agree or disagree with what he's told to do, he's a Garwater man. But I can get information out of him. It's my job."

Even with what they learned from Hedrigall, they were armed with nothing more than a sheaf of unconnected facts. They shuffled and reshuffled them, dropped them like spillikins and watched how they fell. And, having stripped herself of that unrealistic desperation for her own freedom, Bellis began to see order in the facts' patterns.

Until they had a plan.

It was so loose, so nebulous, it was hard to admit that it was all they had.

They sat back in silent unease. Bellis heard the recurring muttering of the waves, watched the smoke from her cigarillo unravel in front of the window, obscuring the night sky. The conjuncture disgusted her suddenly: it seemed to have trapped her. Her life was reduced to a succession of nights and smoking and scratching for ideas. But now something had changed.

It might be the last night that she needed to do this.

"I hate this," said Silas eventually. "I fucking *hate* it, that I can't . . . But can you do it? There's a lot falling on you."

"I have to," she replied. "You don't know High Kettai. Is there any other way you could convince them to take you?"

Silas grit his teeth and shook his head.

"But what about you?" he said. "Your friend Johannes knows you're not exactly a model Armadan citizen, doesn't he?"

"I can convince him," Bellis said. "There aren't going to be too many Kettai readers in Armada. But you're right; he's the only real barrier." She was silent for some time, eventually continuing thoughtfully. "I don't think he's mentioned me to them. If he'd wanted to make life hard, if he suspected me of being . . . dangerous, I'd know it by now. I think he has a sense of . . . of honor, or something, that stops him talking about me."

That's not what it is, she thought even as she spoke. *You know why he hasn't reported you for dissidence.*

*Like it or not, however you left it, whatever you think of him,
he counts you a friend.*

"When they read this," said Silas, "and they realize that Krüach Aum's not from Kohnid, and that he may still be alive, they'll
probably fall over themselves to find him. But . . . what if they
don't?

"We have to get them to that island, Bellis. If we can't do that,
we have nothing. It's no small thing we want them to do. You
know where we're trying to head them. You know what's there.
You can leave me to do the rest—I can put together what we
need. I have the seal, so I can get the messages written. I can do
all that. But dammit, that's all I can do." He was bitter. "And if
we can't get them to the fucking island, we have nothing at all."

He picked up Krüach Aum's book and turned the pages slowly.
When he reached the data appendix, he held it up to Bellis.

"You've translated this, haven't you?" he said.

"What I can."

"They're not expecting ever to see this book, but they think
they can maybe raise the avanc anyway. If we give them this—"
He waggled it, and the pages flapped like wings. "—maybe it's
all they'll need. Maybe they'll just look through these pages, and
do whatever decoding they have to do to make sense of it, using
you, using all the other translators and scientists in the Lyceum
and in the *Grand Easterly* . . . Maybe everything they'd need to
raise the avanc is right here. We might just be handing them the
last piece they need."

He was right. If Aum's claims were true, all the data he had
used, all the information, all the configurations were there in
those pages.

"But without this book," Silas continued, "we have nothing.
Nothing to sell *you* to them, nothing to entice them to the island.
They'll just head off as they were planning, and work on whatever they've got, and maybe raise the avanc anyway. If they
had nothing, they'd make do. But if we give them a *part* of what
they want, they'll have to have it all. We have to turn this from a
gift . . . into bait."

And after a moment, Bellis understood. She pursed her lips
and nodded quickly. "Yes," she said. "Give it to me."

She leafed through to the data appendix and paused, wondering how to start.

Eventually she shrugged and simply tore out a clutch of pages.

After that initial, oddly euphoric moment, she was more careful. She had to make it look right. She thought about other damaged volumes she had seen, picturing the misfortunes that could befall books. Water and fire? Mold? Those were impossible to mimic well.

Trauma, then.

She placed the appendix open, flat, on a strategic nail on her floor, trod on it, and kicked it hard. The nail hooked into the equations and footnotes and yanked them away, to lie in a crumpled pile.

It was perfect. There were three pages at the start of the appendix, where terms were discussed and defined, and then the paper was torn out by its roots. Only the ragged fringes remained, little wedges of half-eradicated words. It looked like the result of a random, stupid accident.

They burned the appendix, whispering like reprobate children.

It did not take long for all the pages to vent as smoke and particles out over Armada, where the wind took and dissipated them.

Tomorrow we make our move, thought Bellis. *Tomorrow we start.*

The wind was from the south. The fingers of smoke from Armada's chimneys pointed back the way they had come.

Standing on the deck of the *Shadeskinner* and looking out, with her back to the city, Bellis could pretend that she was on a normal ship.

The clipper was part of Garwater's suburbs: the people there lived below in preexisting cabins. No houses were built on its decks. The *Shadeskinner* was bronze-trimmed wood, and rope and old canvas. It was without any taverns or cafés or whorehouses, and very few people lingered on its deck. Bellis stared at the ocean, just like a passenger on a clipper at sea.

She stood alone for a long time.

The sea glimmered under the gaslights.

Finally, at a little past nine in the evening, she heard hurried footsteps.

Johannes Tearfly stood before her, the expression on his face unreadable. She nodded at him, slowly, and said his name.

"Bellis, I'm so sorry I'm late," he said. "Your message . . . It was short notice and I couldn't rearrange everything. I got here as quickly as I could."

Is that right? thought Bellis coldly. *Or are you almost an hour late to punish me?*

But she realized that his voice sounded sincerely contrite: that his smile was uncertain, but not cold.

They walked the deck aimlessly, meandering toward the narrowing front, then turning back again. They talked awkwardly, the memory of their argument heavy on them.

"How goes the research, Johannes?" Bellis said eventually. "Are we nearly . . . wherever we're going?"

"Bellis . . ." He shucked his shoulders in irritation. "I thought perhaps you might have . . . Dammit, if you've called me here just to—"

She cut him off with her hands. There was a long silence and Bellis closed her eyes. When she opened them, her face and voice had softened.

"I'm sorry," she said. "I'm sorry. The fact is, Johannes, that what you said to me hurt. Because I know you're right." His face was guarded as she forced the words out. "Don't misunderstand me," she said quickly. "This place'll never be my home. I was taken here by piracy, Johannes: I was stolen.

"But . . . but, you were right that . . . that I'd cut myself off. I knew nothing about the city, and I felt ashamed of that." He started to interrupt, but she would not let him. "And more than anything, I saw the . . . the chance of it all." Her voice grew impassioned. She spoke what sounded like uncomfortable truths. "I've seen things here, I've learnt things . . . New Crobuzon's still my home, but you're right that there is nothing that binds me to it but chance. I've given up on going home, Johannes," she said (and instantly her stomach clenched because it was so nearly true), "and it's made me realize that there are things here worth doing."

Something seemed to be shifting in him; some expression was burgeoning on Johannes' face. Bellis suspected that it was delight, and quickly she interrupted it.

"Don't expect me to fall in love with this damned place, alright? But . . . but for most of the people on the *Terpsichoria,* for the Remade, this press-ganging is the best thing that could have happened. And as for the rest of us . . . well, it's fair that we

should live with that. You helped me see that, Johannes. And I
wanted to say thank you."

Bellis' face was impassive, the words tasting like curdled milk
in her mouth (even though she realized they were not entirely
lies).

There had been a time when Bellis had considered telling Johannes the truth about the threat to New Crobuzon. But she was
still stunned by the speed with which he had allied himself to Armada and Garwater. It was clear that he had very little love for
the city of his birth. But still, she thought, he would not (*surely*)
be neutral in the case of The Gengris. He must have friends,
family in New Crobuzon. He could not be indifferent to that
threat. Surely?

But what if he did not believe her? If he did not, if he thought
this was a convoluted attempt to escape, if he brought her and
her claims to the attention of the Lovers, who would not give two
shits about the fate of New Crobuzon, then she would have frit-
tered away her only chance to get a message back to the city.

Why should the rulers of Armada care what one far-off nation
did to another? Perhaps they would even welcome the grindylow
plans. New Crobuzon's was a strong navy. Bellis had no idea
how deep Johannes' new allegiance extended. She could not risk
telling him the truth.

She waited carefully on the *Shadeskinner*'s deck, sensing Johannes' guarded pleasure.

"Do you think you can do it?" she said eventually.

He frowned. "Do what?"

"Do you think you can raise the avanc?"

He was stunned. She watched the thoughts race across him. Incredulity and anger and fear. She saw him consider lying for a
tiny moment, *I don't know what you're talking about,* but that
temptation ebbed, taking all the other emotions with it.

He was composed again in seconds.

"I suppose I shouldn't really be surprised," he said quietly.
"It's absurd to think you can keep something like that secret." He
drummed his fingers on the rail. "To be honest, it's a constant
amazement to me how few people seem to know. It's as if those
who don't are conspiring with those who do. How did you know?
No amount of care or thaumaturgy can keep plans this big secret,

I suppose. They'll have to come clean soon: too many people know already."

"Why are you doing it?" Bellis said.

"Because of what it'll do for the city," he said. "That's why the Lovers are doing it." He kicked the rail contemptuously and jerked a thumb at the steamboats and tugs way to starboard, massed at the end of their chains, hauling southward. "Look at how this bloody thing moves. A mile an hour? Two with a strong wind? It's absurd. And this kind of effort is so fuel-intensive it's damn rare for them. Most of the time this place just bobs around, circling the ocean. But think how all that can change if they can snare this thing. They'll be able to travel wherever they want. Think about the *power*. They'll rule the fucking seas.

"It was tried once before." He looked away, rubbing his chin. "They think. There's evidence under the city. Chains. Hidden by hexes centuries old. The Lovers . . . they're not like any rulers this place has ever had. Especially her. And something changed when Uther Doul came to be their guard, more than a decade back. Since then they've pursued this. They got messages to Tinnabol and his crew, the best hunters there are. Not just quick with a harpoon; they're scientists: marine biologists, coordinators. They've been in charge of the avanc hunt for years. There's nothing they don't know about trapping. If anyone had tried to do this before, they'd have heard stories about it.

"Of course on their own they could never catch an avanc. But they have more information on them now than anyone in the world. Can you imagine what it would mean to a hunter, to succeed in this? So that's why the Lovers are doing it, and that's why Tintinnabulum's crew are doing it." He caught Bellis' eye, and a smile broke on him.

"And me?" he said. "I'm doing it, Bellis, because it's an *avanc*!"

His enthusiasm was as sudden, irritating, and infectious as a child's. His passion for his work was quite sincere.

"I have to be honest," she said carefully. "I would not have believed that I'd say or think this, but . . . but I *understand*." She looked at him levelly. "To tell the truth, it's part of what mellowed me about this place. When I first found out what was happening, what the plan was with the avanc, I was so overwhelmed that it just frightened me." She shook her head and groped for words.

"But that changed. It's the most . . . It's the most extraordinary project, Johannes. And I realized that I want it to succeed."

Bellis was aware that she was doing this well.

"I care, Johannes. I never thought I'd give a stiver for anything that happened in this place, but the scale of this plan, the hubris . . . And the thought that I might help . . ." Johannes watched her with cautious pleasure. "Because of how I found out the truth. That's why I asked you to come here, Johannes. I have something for you."

She reached into her bag and handed him the book.

Poor Johannes was suffering so many shocks tonight, Bellis thought vaguely, wave after wave of them: the shock of her contacting him, of seeing her, of her apparent change of mind about the city, of the fact that she knew about the avanc, and now this.

She was silent through his breathless incredulity and gasps and choked joy.

Finally he looked up at her.

"Where did you get this?" He could hardly speak.

She told him about Shekel and his fervor for the children's section. She reached out gently to the book in his hands and turned the pages back.

"Look at the illustrations," she said. "You can see how it got misshelved. I doubt there's many people aboard who can read High Kettai. It was this that got under my skin. *This.*" She stopped at the picture of the massive eye under the boat. Even now as she dissembled, even having seen the simple picture scores of times, still she felt a little rill of astonishment as she looked at it.

"It wasn't just the pictures that told me what was going on, Johannes." From her bag she pulled a mass of paper, covered with her tight handwriting. "I *do* read High Kettai, Johannes," she said. "I wrote a damn book about it." And again, something about that fact sat ill inside her. She ignored it and waved the manuscript at him.

"I've translated Aum."

And here was yet another shock for Johannes, who reacted with the same noises and fervor as before.

That's the last one, Bellis thought, calculating. She watched him dancing with delight on the empty deck. *That's the end of them.* When he had finished his stupid little jig, she began to steer him in the direction of the city, toward the pubs. *Let's sit and ponder this,* she thought coolly. *Let's get drunk together, eh? Look at you, so overjoyed that I'm back on your side. So thrilled to have your friend back. Let's work out what's to be done, you and me.*

Let's help you come up with my plan.

CHAPTER SEVENTEEN

In these warm waters, the night-lights and the sound of the waves against the city's flanks were softer, as if the sea was aerated and the light diffuse: brine and illumination became less starkly elemental. Armada nestled in the long, balmy darkness of what was now, unquestionably, a summer.

At night, in pub gardens that abutted Armada's parklands, its plots, its meadowland left fallow on forecastles and main decks, cicadas sang over the wave noise and the puttering tug motors. Bees and hornets and flies had appeared. They clustered at Bellis' windows, butting themselves to death.

Armadans were not people of the cold, or of the heat, or of New Crobuzon's temperate climate. Elsewhere Bellis might apply climatic stereotypes (the stolid cold-dweller, the emotive southerner), but in Armada she could not. On that nomadic city, such factors were irregular, they defied generalization. All that could be said was that for that summer, at that conjuncture of date and place, the city softened.

The streets were full for longer, and the patchwork phonemes of Salt conversations were everywhere. It was looking to be a loud season.

In a hall in the *Castor,* Tintinnabulum's ship, a meeting was taking place.

It was not a big room. It strained to contain everyone within it. They sat in uncomfortable formality on stiff chairs around a battered table. Tintinnabulum and his companions, Johannes and his colleagues, biomathematicians and thaumaturges and others, mostly human but not all so.

And the Lovers. Behind them, Uther Doul stood by the door, his arms folded.

Johannes, faltering and excited, had been speaking for some time. At the climax of his story, he paused ostentatiously and slapped Krüach Aum's book onto the table. And after the pause, at the crescendo of the first wave of gasps, he followed it with Bellis' translation.

"You can see now," he said with a trembling voice, "why I called this extraordinary meeting."

The Lover picked up the two documents and carefully compared them. Johannes watched her in silence. Her mouth curled in concentration, and the scars on her face coiled to contain her expression. On the right side of her chin, he noticed the puckered flesh and scab of a new wound. He looked briefly at her lover beside her and saw a matching wound below his mouth, on the left.

Johannes felt the unease he always did at the sight. No matter how often he saw the Lovers, their proximity brought on a nervousness in him that did not fade. They had an extraordinary presence.

Perhaps it's authority, Johannes thought. *Perhaps that's what authority is.*

"Who here speaks Kettai?" the Lover said.

Opposite her, a llorgiss raised an arm.

"Turgan," she acknowledged.

"I know some," it said in its breathy tones, "mostly Base, a little High. But this woman is much more proficient than me. I have looked at the manuscripts, and much of the original was beyond me."

"Don't forget," said Johannes, raising his hand, "Coldwine's *High Kettai Grammatology* is a standard reference book. There aren't that many textbooks for High Kettai . . ." He shook his head. "Weird, difficult language. But of those that there are, Coldwine's is one of the best. If she weren't on board, if Turgan or someone else had to translate this, they'd probably spend most of their time referring to her damn book anyway."

His hands were jerking in aggressive, choppy movements.

"She's translated into Ragamoll, obviously," he said, "but it's easy enough to render that into Salt. But, look, the translation is not the most exciting thing here. Maybe I've not been clear . . . *Aum's not Kettai*. We couldn't visit a Kettai scientist, obviously. Kohnid's way off our route, and Armada wouldn't be safe in those seas . . . but Krüach Aum's not from Kohnid. *He's anophelii*. Their island's a thousand miles south. And there's every chance he's alive.

It brought them up short.

Johannes nodded slowly. "What we have here," he continued, "is invaluable. We have a description of the process, the effects, we have confirmation of the area involved—all those things. But unfortunately Aum's footnotes and calculations are missing— as I said, the text is badly damaged. So what we have is merely the . . . the lay description. The science is missing.

"We're heading for a sinkhole some way off the southern coast of Gnurr Kett. Now, I've checked with a couple of cactacae ex of Dreer Samher, who used to deal with the anophelii: where we're going, we'll only be a couple of hundred miles from the anophelii island." He paused, aware that he was speaking too quickly in his excitement.

"Obviously," he went on, more slowly, "we could continue as previously planned. In which case we know *roughly* where we're going; we know more or less the kind of power involved in the summoning; we have some idea of the thaumaturgy involved . . . And we could risk it.

"But we *could* go to the island. A landing party. Tintinnabulum, some of our scientists, one or other or both of you." He looked at the Lovers.

"We'd need Bellis to translate," he went on. "The cactacae who've been there can't help us: when they traded it was all hand signs and head shaking, apparently, but obviously some of the anophelii speak High Kettai. We'd need guards—and engineers, because we're going to have to start thinking about containment for the avanc. And . . . we find Aum."

He sat back, aware that it was not one iota as simple as he had presented it, but still he felt excited.

"In the very worst case," he said, "Aum's dead. In which case we've lost nothing. Perhaps there'll be others there, who remember him, who can help us."

"That's not the worst case," said Uther Doul. The atmosphere shifted: all whispering stopped, and everyone in the room faced him—except the Lovers, who listened gravely without turning.

"You're talking," Doul continued softly, in his singer's voice, "as if this is just a place, like other places. It's not. You have no idea what you're saying. Do you understand what you've discovered? What Aum's race means? This is the island of the mosquito-people. The worst case is that the anophelii women come upon us on the beach and suck us dry, leaving our husks to rot. The worst case is that we are all instantly butchered."

There was a silence.

"Not me," someone said. Johannes gave a half smile. It was Breyatt, a cactacae mathematician. Johannes tried to catch his eye. *Well scored,* he thought.

The Lovers were nodding.

"Your point is taken, Uther," said the Lover. He stroked his small mustache. "But let's not . . . exaggerate. There are ways around the problem, as this gentleman points out . . ."

"This gentleman is cactus," said Doul. "For those of us with blood the problem remains."

"Nevertheless—" The Lover spoke with authority. "—I think it would be foolish to suggest that there's no way this can be done. That's not how we proceed. We start by working out what's to our advantage, what is the best plan . . . Then we work our way around problems. If it seems that our best chance of success lies on this island, then that's where we'll go."

Doul did not move. He looked impassive. There was nothing in his demeanor to suggest that he had been overruled.

"Godsdammit!" Johannes barked in frustration, and everyone turned to him. He was shocked at his own outburst, but he continued without losing momentum. "Of course there are problems and difficulties," he said passionately, "of course it'll take organization, it'll take work and effort and . . . and maybe we'll need protecting, and we can bring cactacae fighters with us, or constructs, or I don't damn well know what . . . But what's going on here? Are you all in the same room as me?"

He picked up Aum's book and held it reverentially like a sacred sutra.

"We have the *book*. We have a translator. This is the testimony of one who *knows how to raise an avanc*. This changes everything . . . Does it *matter* where he lives? So his home is inhospitable." He stared at the Lovers. "Is there anywhere we wouldn't go for this? Surely we can't even *consider* not going."

* * *

When they broke up, the Lovers spoke noncommittally. But everything was different now, and Johannes knew he was not alone in knowing that.

"It may be time to announce our intentions," the Lover said as they gathered their notes.

The room was full of people trained into a culture of secrecy. Her suggestion shocked them. But, Johannes realized, it made sense.

"We knew we'd have to be open about this some time," she continued. Her lover nodded.

There were scientists from Jhour and Shaddler and The Clockhouse Spur taking part in the attempt to raise the avanc, and the rulers of those ridings had been consulted out of courtesy. But the inner circle was all Garwater: those who once had not been, the Lovers had, in a breach of tradition, persuaded to defect. Information about the project was tightly circumscribed.

But a plan of such magnitude could not be hidden forever.

"We have the *Sorghum*," said the Lover, "so we decide where we all go. But what will the rest of the city think while they sit stranded in some patch of sea waiting for our landing party to return? What are they going to think when we reach the sinkhole, raise the damned avanc? Their rulers won't talk: our allies take our lead, and our enemies don't want this in the open. They're afraid of which way their people will turn.

"Perhaps," she concluded slowly, "it's time to bring the citizens to our side. Enthuse them . . ."

She looked at her partner. As always, they seemed to be communicating silently.

"We need lists," the Lover said, "of everyone who should go to the island. We must look at new arrivals—there may be expertise we've missed. And we need security details for all candidates. And we have to represent all ridings." He smiled, his scars tracing the contours of his face, and picked up Bellis' translation.

When Johannes reached the door, the Lovers called his name.

"Come with us," said the Lover, and Johannes' stomach yawed uneasily.

Oh Jabber, he thought. *What now? I've had enough of your company.*

"Come and talk to us," the Lover continued, and waited while his partner finished for him.

"We want to talk to you about this woman, Coldwine," she said.

Past midnight, Bellis was woken by a repeated banging on her door. She looked up, thinking it must be Silas, until she saw him lying motionless and awake beside her.

It was Johannes. She tugged her hair out of her face and blinked at him on her doorstep.

"I think they're going to go ahead," he said. Bellis gasped.

"Listen, Bellis. They were . . . well, intrigued by you. What they've heard has suggested that . . . well, that you're not their material. Nothing bad, you know?" He was eager to mollify her. "Nothing, you know, dangerous . . . but not exactly sympathetic. Like a lot of press-ganged: best left aboard at all costs. It's normally years before incomers get letters of pass."

Was that all it was? thought Bellis slowly. The misery and loneliness, the aching for New Crobuzon that made her feel something had been torn from her—was it just an everyday symptom, shared by a thousand like her? Was it so banal?

"But . . . well I told them all the things you'd said to me," Johannes said, and smiled. "And I can't promise anything, but . . . I think you'd be the best person, and I told them that."

Silas seemed to be sleeping when she returned to bed, but something in the shallowness of his breath told her he was not. She leaned over him as if about to kiss him hard, her lips found his ear, and she whispered, "It's working."

They came for her the next morning.

It was after Silas had left, heading for Armada's underworld to perform his opaque, illegal activities. To the work that kept him under the city's skin, that made him too dangerous even to attempt passage to the anophelii island.

Two of the Garwater yeomanry, pistols slung easy in their belts, steered Bellis to an aerostat cab. It was not far from *Chromolith* to the *Grand Easterly*. The mass of the enormous steamer stretched out above the city. Its six colossal masts, its chimneys, its bare decks unadorned by houses or towers.

The sky was full of aerostats: Scores of little cabs studding the air like bees around a hive; outlandish vessels built for freight, transporting heavy goods between the ridings; the peculiar little single-rider balloons with their pendulous occupants. A little way out were warflots, elliptical flying guns. And above them all the massive, crippled *Arrogance*.

They wound over the skyscape of Armada, lower than Bellis was used to, rising and sinking with the topography of roofs and rigging. Warrens of brick like New Crobuzon slums passed below. Built on the cramped space of deck tops, they looked precarious: their outer walls too close to the water, the alleyways that riddled them impossibly thin.

Beyond the haze above the *Gigue,* whose fore was an industrial district of foundries and chymical plants, the *Grand Easterly* was approaching.

Bellis was uncertain. She had never been inside the *Grand Easterly* before.

Its architecture was austere: darkwood panels, lithographs and heliotypes, stained glass. A little age-blistered, but well kept, its innards were a tangle of passageways and staterooms. Bellis was left to wait in a small chamber. The door was locked on her.

She went to the iron-fringed window and looked down over Armada's random ships. In the distance she could see the green of Croom Park, spread like disease across the bodies of several ships. The room she was in was higher by far than any of the surrounding vessels, the side of the ship falling away below. At eye level she saw dirigibles and a mass of thin masts.

"This is a New Crobuzon ship, you know."

Even as she turned, Bellis recognized the voice. It was the scarred man, the Lover, standing in the doorway, alone.

Bellis was shocked. She had known that there would be interrogation, investigation, but she had not expected this: to be questioned by *him. I translated the book,* she thought. *I get special treatment.*

The Lover closed the door behind him.

"It was built more than two and a half centuries ago, at the end of the Full Years," he continued. He spoke to her in Ragamoll, with only a slight accent. He sat, indicated to her to do the same. "In fact, it's been claimed that the *Grand Easterly*'s building itself brought the Full Years to an end. Obviously," he said, deadpan, "that is ridiculous. But it's a useful symbolic coincidence. Decline was setting in at the end of the 1400s, and what more potent symbol of the failure of science than this ship? In a scramble to prove that New Crobuzon was still in its golden age, they come up with this thing.

"It's a very poor design, you know. Trying to combine the paddle power of those stupid huge wheels, on her flanks, with a screw propeller." He shook his head, not taking his eyes from Bellis. "You can't power something of this size with paddles. So they just loomed there like tumors, ruining the ship's line, acting as brakes. Which meant the screw didn't work very well, either, and you couldn't sail it. Isn't it ironic?

"But there's one thing that they did right. They set out to build the biggest vessel ever seen. They had to launch the thing sideways, in the estuary by Iron Bay. And for a few years it limped around. Awesome but . . . ungainly. They tried to use it during the Second Pirate Wars, but it lumbered like a massively armed rhinoceros while the Suroch and Jheshull ships danced around it.

"Then, they'll tell you, it sank. Of course, it didn't. We took it.

"They were wonderful years for Armada, the Pirate Wars. All that carnage; ships disappearing every day; missing cargos; sailors and soldiers fed up with fighting and dying, eager to escape. We stole ships and technology and people. We grew and grew.

"We took the *Grand Easterly* because we could. That was when Garwater took control, which it has never lost. This ship is our heart. Our factory, our palace. It was a dreadful steamer, but it is a superlative fortress. That was the last . . . great age for Armada."

There was silence for a long time.

"Until now," he said, and smiled at her. And the interrogation began.

When it was all finished, and she emerged mole-eyed into the afternoon, she found it hard to recall his questions exactly.

He had asked her a great deal about the translation. Had she found it hard? Was there anything that had not made sense? Could she also speak High Kettai, or merely read it? And on and on.

There had been questions designed to gauge her state of mind, her relationship to the city. She had spoken carefully: it was a tentative line between the truth and lies. She did not try to hide all of her distrust, her distaste at what had been done to her, her resentment. But she battened it down, somewhat: contained it, made it safe.

She tried not to seem to try.

There was no one to meet her outside, of course, and that gladdened her, obscurely. She crossed the steep bridges that descended from the *Grand Easterly* to the lower ships beside it.

She made her way home through some of the most intricate byways and alleys. Passing under brick arches that dripped with Armada's constant salt damp; by groups of children playing variants of the shove-stiver and catch-as-can she remembered from the streets at home, as if there were a deep grammar of street games shared across the world; beside small cafés in the shadow of raised forecastles, where their parents played their own games, backgammon and chatarang.

Gulls arced and shat. The backstreets pitched and shifted with the surface of the sea.

Bellis relished her solitude. She knew that if Silas had been with her, the sense of complicity would have been cloying.

They had not had sex for a long time. It had only ever happened twice.

After those times, they had shared her bed and thrown off their clothes in front of each other without shyness or hesitation. But neither, it seemed, was moved to fuck. It was as if having used sex to connect and open to each other, the channel was in place and the act was superfluous.

It was not that she had no desires. The last two or three nights they had been together, she had waited for him to sleep, then masturbated quietly. She often kept her thoughts from him, sharing only what they needed to make their plans.

Bellis was not inordinately fond of Silas, she realized with mild surprise.

She was grateful to him; she found him interesting and impressive, though not so charming as he thought himself. They held something between them: extraordinary secrets, plans that could not be allowed to fail. They were comrades in this. She did not mind him sharing her bed; she might even tup him again, she thought with an inadvertent smirk. But they were not close.

Given what they had shared, this seemed a little bizarre, but she acknowledged it.

The next morning, before six, when the sky was still dark, men and women gathered in a fleet of dirigibles on the deck of the *Grand Easterly*. Between them they hauled bundles of raggedly printed leaflets. They lugged them into the aerostat carriages, argued over routes, and consulted maps. They divided Armada into quadrants.

The daylight was filling up the city as they lifted off sedately.

Costermongers, factory workers, yeomanry, and a thousand others looked up from the brick and wood warrens around the *Grand Easterly:* from Winterstraw Market's intricate concatenation of vessels, from towers in Booktown and Jhour and Thee-And-Thine, peering over the city's rigging. They saw the first wave of dirigibles lift off and spread out over the city's chambers, out across the ridings. And at strategic points in the airflow, tacking against the wind, the aerostats began to shed paper.

Like confetti, like the blossom already straining to grow on Armada's hardy trees, the leaflets coiled out and down in great billows. The air sounded with them—a susurrus of paper sliding against paper—and with the gulls and city sparrows that cut away from them in confusion. Armadans looked up, shielding their eyes against the rising sun, and saw the scudding clouds and clear warm blue, and descending below them the snips of paper skittering through the air.

Some fell into chimneys. Hundreds more touched the water. They funneled into the trenches between vessels and settled on the sea. They bobbed on the waves, becoming saturated, their ink spreading to become unreadable, nibbled by fishes, till the brine clogged their fibers and they sank. Below the surface there was a snow of disintegrating paper. But many thousands landed on the decks of Armada's ships.

Again and again the dirigibles circled the city's airspace, passing over each of the ridings, finding pathways between the tallest towers and masts, scattering their leaflets. Curious and delighted, people picked them out of the air. In a city where paper was expensive, this extravagance was extraordinary.

Word spread fast. When Bellis descended to the deck of the *Chromolith,* onto a layer of leaflets rustling like dead skin, all around her there were arguments. People stood in the doorways of their shops and houses, shouting to each other or muttering or laughing, waving the leaflets in inky hands.

Bellis looked up and saw one of the last of the aerostats to port, moving away from her out over Jhour, another fluttering cloud descending behind it. She picked up one of the papers gusting at her feet.

Armadan citizens, she read, *after long and careful study, some-thing can be achieved that would have astounded our grand-parents. A new day is soon to dawn. We are to change our city's movements forever.*

She scanned the page quickly, racing through the propagan-dist explanation, and her eyes moved slower over the key word, picked out in bold.

Avanc . . .

Bellis felt a thrill of confused emotion. *I did this,* she thought with weird pride. *I set this in motion.*

"It is choice work," said Tintinnabulum thoughtfully.

He was hunkered down in front of Angevine, thrusting his face and hands into the engines in her metal underparts. She leaned her flesh body back, impassive and patient.

For some days, Tintinnabulum had been conscious of a change in his servant, a difference in the clattering of her engines. She moved more quickly and exactly, turning in tight arcs and stop-ping without a wheezing slowdown. She found it easier to nego-tiate Armada's swaying bridges. An edge of anxiety in her was gone—her constant scavenging, her scrabbling for discarded coal and wood, had stopped.

"What has happened to your engines, Angevine?" he had asked her. And smiling with immense, shy pleasure, she had shown him.

He rummaged in her tubework, burning his hands stoically on her boiler, examining her reconfigured metal viscera.

Tintinnabulum knew that Armadan science was a mongrel. It was as piratical as the city's economy and politics, the product of theft and chance—as various and inconsistent. The engineers and thaumaturges learned their skills on equipment that was rot-ted and out of date, and on stolen artifacts of such sophisticated design that they were mostly incomprehensible. It was a patch-work of technologies.

"This man," he murmured, up to his elbow in Angevine's mo-tor, fingering a three-way switch at the back of her chassis, "this man may be just a jobbing engineer, but . . . this is the choicest work. Not many aboard Armada could make this. Why did he do it?" he asked her.

She could only respond vaguely to that.

"Is he trustworthy?" Tintinnabulum said.

Tintinnabulum and his crew were not Armadan-born, but

their commitment to Garwater was unquestionable. Stories were told about how they had joined Armada—the Lovers had tracked them by esoteric means, persuaded them to work in the city for unknown wages. For them, the ropes and chains linking the fabric of Garwater had been parted. The riding had opened itself, let Tintinnabulum enter and embed himself in the very heart of the city, which had resealed behind him.

That morning, Angevine too had picked up one of the slew of leaflets that suddenly clogged up Armada's alleys, and had learned the purpose of the Garwater project. It had excited her, but had not, she realized, come as a particular surprise. She had been present on the edge of official discussions for a long time, had seen the literature left lying on Tintinnabulum's desk, had caught glimpses of scribbled diagrams and half-finished calculations. As soon as she discovered what it was that Garwater was attempting, she felt that she had always known. After all, did she not work for Tintinnabulum? And what was he but a hunter?

His room was full of evidence. Books—the only ones that she knew of outside the library—etchings, carved tusks, broken harpoons. Bones and horns and hides. In the years she had worked for him, Tintinnabulum and his crew of seven had lent their expertise to Garwater. Horned sharks and whales and ceti, bonefish, shellarc—he had snared and harpooned and caught them all, for food, for protection, for sport.

Sometimes, when the eight were meeting, Angevine would put her ear flat against the wood and press hard, but she could only ever hear the occasional snatch of sound. Enough to learn tantalizing things.

The ship's madman, Argentarius, whom no one ever saw, she would hear railing and screaming to them, telling them he was afraid. Some prey of theirs had done this to him long ago, Angevine came to understand. It had galvanized his comrades. They were stamping their authority on the deep sea, thumbing their noses at that terrible realm.

When she had heard them speak of hunting, it was the largest game that enthused them: the leviathan and lahamu, the cuttlegod.

Why not the avanc?

None of it was any surprise, really, Angevine thought.

"Is he trustworthy?" Tintinnabulum repeated.

"He is," Angevine said. "He's a good man. He's grateful for being spared the colonies; he's angry with New Crobuzon. He's had himself Remade, the better to dive, the better to work in the docks—he's a sea creature now. He's loyal as any Garwater born, I'd say."

Tintinnabulum raised himself and shut Angevine's boiler. His mouth pursed thoughtfully. On his desk he found a long, hand-written list of names.

"What's he called?" he said.

He nodded, leaned over, and carefully added *Tanner Sack*.

CHAPTER EIGHTEEN

Rumor and word of mouth were even stronger forces in Armada than in New Crobuzon, but Armada was not without a more organized media than that. There were criers, most yelling the semiofficial line of one or other of the ridings. A few news sheets and periodicals were available, printed on dreadful-quality, ink-saturated sheets that were constantly recycled.

Most were irregular, available when writers and printers could be bothered or find the resources. Many were free; most were thin: one or two folded sheets crammed with print.

Armada's halls were full of plays and music, coarse and very popular, so the publications were full of reviews. Some contained titillation and scandal mongering, but to Bellis they were depressingly parochial. Disputes about allocation of seized goods, or over which riding was responsible for which haul, were generally the most provocative and controversial topics they carried. And those were just the news sheets she could make sense of.

In the hybrid culture of Armada, as many different traditions of journal were represented as existed in the world of Bas-Lag, alongside unique forms born on the pirate city. *More Often Than Not* was a weekly that reported only on the city's deaths, in verse. *Juhangirr's Concern,* published in Thee-And-Thine riding, was wordless, telling what stories it considered important (according to criteria quite opaque to Bellis) in sequences of crude pictures.

Occasionally, Bellis would read *The Flag* or *Council's Call,* both published out of Curhouse. *The Flag* was probably the best news-gathering organ in the city. *Council's Call* was a political publication, carrying arguments between proponents of the various ridings' governmental systems: Curhouse's democracy, Jhour's solar queendom, the "absolutist benevolence" of Garwater, the Brucolac's protectorate, and so on.

Both the publications, for all their vaunted toleration of dissent, were more or less loyal to Curhouse's Democratic Council. It was therefore no great surprise to Bellis, who had started to understand the tussles of Armadan politics, when *The Flag* and *Council's Call* began to raise doubts about conjuring the avanc.

They were circumspect at first.

"The Summoning would be a triumph of science," read the editorial in *The Flag,* "but there are questions. More motive power for the city can only be good, but what will be the cost?"

It was not long before their objections became more strident.

But with Armada still in the swell of thrill from Garwater's extraordinary declaration, voices of caution and outright rejection were a small minority. In the pubs—even those of Curhouse and Dry Fall—there was massive excitement. The scale of the undertaking, the promised capturing of an *avanc,* for gods' sakes, was giddying.

Still, through a few journals, through pamphlets and posters, sceptics voiced their ignored opposition.

Recruitment began.

A special meeting was convened at the Basilio docks. Tanner Sack rubbed his tentacles and waited. Eventually the yeoman-sergeant stepped forward.

"I've a list here," he shouted, "of engineers and others who've been requested for special duty by the Lovers." The whispers and murmurs swelled briefly, then subsided. No one was in any doubt as to what the special duty was.

As each name was read out, there was audible excitement from its bearer and those nearby. Those named came as no surprise to Tanner. He recognized the best of his colleagues: the fastest workers, the most skillful engineers who had most recently been in contact with cutting-edge technology. Several were relatively recently press-ganged—a disproportion came from New

Crobuzon, and more than a handful were Remade from the *Terp-sichoria* itself.

He only realized that he himself had been called as he felt his back pounded by some enthusiastic mate. A tension that he had not known was built up inside him broke, and he relaxed. He realized that he had been waiting for this. He deserved this.

There were others already assembled at the *Grand Easterly,* workers from the industrial districts, from foundries and laboratories. There were interviews. Metallurgists were separated from engineers and from chymical workers. They were quizzed, their expertise judged. Persuasion was used, but not coercion. At the first (unclear) mention of the anophelii, the first hint of the nature of the island, several men and women refused to be part of the project. Tanner was troubled. *But there's no way you'll say no to this,* he admitted to himself, *come what may.*

After dark, when the tests and questions were completed, Tanner and the others were taken to one of the *Grand Easterly*'s staterooms. The chamber was huge and exquisite, picked out in brass and black wood. There were about thirty people left. *We've been whittled down,* Tanner thought.

What noises there were died immediately when the Lovers entered. As on that very first day, they were flanked by Tintinnabulum and Uther Doul.

What will you tell me this time? thought Tanner slowly. *More wonders? More changes?*

When the Lovers spoke, they told the full story of the island, and their plans, and everyone in the room was committed.

Tanner leaned back against a wall and listened. He tried to cultivate scepticism—the plans were so absurd, there were so many ways they could fail!—but he found that he could not. He listened, his heart rate increasing, as the Lovers and Tintinnabulum told him and his new companions how they would go to the home of the mosquito people, how they would search for a scientist who might not still be alive, and consult and build machines for containing the most extraordinary creature ever to swim in Bas-Lag's seas.

Elsewhere, the hidden side of the campaign against the Summoning was convening.

At the heart of Dry Fall riding was the *Uroc.* It was a huge old vessel, fat and glowering, five hundred feet long and more than a hundred wide at the middle of its main deck. Its dimensions, silhouette, and specifications were unique. No one in Armada was certain how old it was, or from where it originally came.

There were rumors, in fact, that the *Uroc* was as counterfeit as a pinchbeck ring. It was not a clipper or a barque or a chariot ship or any other known design, after all: nothing of its peculiar shape could ever have sailed, was the claim. The *Uroc* had been built in Armada, said the cynics, already hemmed in by its surroundings. It was not a found and reappropriated vessel, they said: it was nothing more than wood and iron mimicking a stilled ship.

Some knew better. There were still a very few in Armada who remembered the *Uroc*'s arrival.

They included the Brucolac, who had been sailing it, alone, at the time.

Every night, when the sun set, he would rouse himself. Safe from daylight's rays he would climb the *Uroc*'s baroque masttowers. He would reach out from the slit windows and caress the tines and scales that draped from the irregular crossbars. With fingertips of suprahuman sensitivity, he could feel the little pulses of power below those slats of thin metal and ceramic and wood, like blood through capillaries. He knew that the *Uroc* could still sail, if need be.

It had been built before his ab-death or his first birth. It had been constructed thousands of miles away, somewhere that no one alive in Armada had ever seen. It had been generations since the floating city had visited that place, and the Brucolac hoped passionately that it would never return.

The *Uroc* was a moonship. It tacked and sailed on gusts of lunar light.

Weird decks jutted like land formations on the vessel's body. The intricate segments of its multilayered bridge, the chasm that was constructed in the center of its body, the twisted architecture of its portholes and chambers marked it out. Spires broke its wide body, some doubling as masts, some tapering randomly into nothing. Like the *Grand Easterly*, the *Uroc* was not built upon at all, despite the crowded brick rookeries on the vessels to either side. But where the *Grand Easterly* was kept pristine as a matter of policy, no one had ever suggested building on the moonship. Its topography would not allow it.

By day it looked bleached and sickly. It was not pleasant to see. But as the light failed its surface would shimmer with a subtle nacre, as if it were haunted by ghost-colors. It became awesome then. That was when the Brucolac would walk its decks.

Sometimes he held meetings in its unsettling chambers. He would summon his ab-dead lieutenants to discuss riding business like the goretax, Dry Fall's tithing. *It is what makes us unique,* he would tell them. *It is what gives us our strength and makes our citizens loyal.*

That night, while Tanner Sack and the others inducted into Garwater's scheme slept, or reflected on what they would have to do, the Brucolac welcomed visitors aboard the *Uroc*: a delegation from the Curhouse Council, naïve enough to believe that they traveled and met in secret (the Brucolac had no such illusions: he picked one set of footsteps out of the palimpsest he could hear on the surrounding boats, and idly attributed them to a Garwater spy).

The Curhouse councilors were nervous in the moonship. They followed the Brucolac in a huddle, trying not to show discomfort as they scurried after him. Conscious of his guests' requirements for light, the Brucolac had lit torches in the corridors. He had chosen not to use gaslights, taking a small malicious pleasure in the ostentation, and in the knowledge that the shadows the torches cast would flutter as unpredictable and predatory as bats in the ship's narrow passages.

The circular meeting room was set in the ship's broadest mast-tower, looking out over the deck fifty feet up. It was opulent and unwelcoming, inlaid with jet and pewter and finely worked lead. There were no candles or flames here, but an icy light picked out the interior with scientific clarity: moon- and starlight were gathered on the ship's masts, amplified, and sent through mirrored shafts like veins to bleed out into the chamber. The strange illumination stripped the scene of any color.

"Gentlemen, ladies," said the Brucolac in his guttural whisper. He smiled and pulled back his mass of hair; tasted the air with his long, serpentine tongue; and indicated that his guests should sit around the darkwood table. He watched them find places—human, hotchi, llorgiss, and others all watching him warily.

"We have been outmaneuvered," the Brucolac continued. "I suggest we consider our response."

* * *

Dry Fall seemed much like Garwater. The decks of a hundred skiffs and barges and hulks were lit up against the darkness, and bustled with the sound of pubs and playhouses.

But looming silently over them all was the *Uroc*'s distorted silhouette. It watched over the convivials of Dry Fall without comment or censure or enthusiasm, and they responded, glancing at it now and then with a kind of wary, uneasy pride. They had more freedom and more say than those who lived in Garwater, they reminded themselves; more protection than Thee-And-Thine; more autonomy than Shaddler.

The Dry Fallers knew that many citizens of other ridings regarded the goretax as a price too high, but that was squeamish stupidity. It was the recently press-ganged who were most vociferous about that, Dry Fallers pointed out—superstitious outsiders who had not yet learned Armadan ways.

There were no floggings in Dry Fall, the inhabitants reminded such newcomers. Their goods and entertainments were subsidized for all those who carried a Dry Fall seal. For matters of importance, the Brucolac held meetings where everyone could have a say. He protected them. There was nothing like the anarchic, violent rule that existed elsewhere in the city. Dry Fall was safe, civilized, its streets well maintained. The goretax was a reasonable trade.

They were protective of their riding, and insecure. The *Uroc* was their talisman, and no matter how raucous and chaotic the evening, they would glance occasionally at its skyline as if for reassurance.

That night, like every night, the mast-towers of the *Uroc* blossomed with the unearthly luminescence known as saint's fire. It afflicted all ships at some time—during an elyctric storm, or when the air was desiccated—but for the moonship it was as certain and regular as tides.

Night birds, bats, and moths flocked to it and danced in its glare. They battered and snapped at each other, and some descended to be waylaid by the other, smaller lights emitted by windows. In the Brucolac's meeting room, the Curhouse councilors looked up, made nervous by the constant drumming of little wings on the glass.

The meeting was not going well.

The Brucolac was struggling. He sincerely needed to engage

with the councilors, and he tried to work with them, to propose
strategies, to review possibilities. But he found it hard to rein in
his ability to intimidate. It was at the heart of his power and his
strategy. He was not Armadan born: the Brucolac had seen
scores of cities and nations, in life and in ab-death, and something had been made clear to him: if the quick did not exist in
fear, then the vampir would.

They might style themselves merciless night hunters, of
course, where they hunkered and hid their identities in cities,
emerging at night to feed, but they slept and fed in fear. The
quick would not tolerate their presence—discovery meant true
death. That had become unacceptable to him. When he had
brought haemophagy to Armada two centuries back, he had come
to a city free of the reflexive, murderous horror for his kind—
a place he could live openly.

But the Brucolac had always understood the payoff. He did
not fear the quick, so they must fear him. Which he had always
found easy to ensure.

And now, when he was sick of intrigue, when he hungered for
complicity, when he needed help and this mixed bag of bureaucrats was all he had, the dynamic of terror was too strong to overcome. The Curhouse Council were too afraid to work with him.
With every look, every lick of his teeth, every exhalation and
slow clenching of his fists, he reminded them of what he was.

Perhaps it meant nothing, he reflected savagely. What help
could they be? He could not tell them about the Scar. They
would ask him how he knew, and he could say nothing; then
they would not believe him. Or he could try to explain about
Doul, in which case they would see him as a traitor, swapping secrets with the Garwater right-hand man. And still they would almost certainly not believe him.

Uther, he thought slowly, *you are a clever, manipulative
swine.*

Sitting in this room surrounded by his supposed allies, all he
could think was how much closer he felt to Doul, how much he
and Doul shared. He could not shake the sensation—which made
no sense at all—that the two of them were working together.

The Brucolac sat and listened to the pontifications and bad
reasoning of the councilors, who were terrified of change, concerned for the balance of power. He endured preposterous and
meaningless abstractions quite divorced from the real nature of

the problem. There were arguments over the precise nature of the Lovers' transgression. There were suggestions that they might appeal to the bureaucrats of Garwater below their rulers' noses—fleshless and unworkable ideas, without systematicity.

At one point, someone around the table mentioned the name Simon Fench. No one knew who he was, but his name was mentioned more and more frequently among that minority opposed to the Summoning. The Brucolac waited, eager to hear some concrete suggestion. But the debate degenerated again, quickly, into wasted air. He waited and waited, but nothing valid was said.

He could feel the passage of the sun below the world. A little more than an hour before dawn, he gave up trying to contain himself.

"Gods and fuck," he growled in his graveyard whisper. The councilors were silent instantly, and aghast. He stood and spread out his arms. "I have been listening to you for hours," he hissed, "spewing your trite horseshit. Platitudes and desperation. You are *ineffectual.*" He made the word sound like a soul-blasting curse. "You are failures. You are pointless. Get out of my boat."

There was a moment's silence before the mass of councilors began to scramble to their feet, trying and failing to retain at least a part of their dignity. One of them—Vordakine, one of the better ones, a woman for whom the Brucolac retained a scrap or two of respect—opened her mouth to remonstrate with him. Her face was white, but she stood her ground.

The Brucolac curved his arms above his head like wings and opened his mouth, unrolling his tongue and letting his poisoned fangs snap down, his hands crooked and feral.

Vordakine's mouth swiftly closed, and she followed her colleagues to the door, anger and fear on her face.

When they had all left, and he was alone, the Brucolac sank back into his chair. *Run home, you little fuck bloodbags,* he thought. He gave a sudden bone-cold grin, thinking of his absurd pantomime at the end. *Moon's tits,* he thought wryly, *they probably think I can change into a bat.*

Recalling their terror, he suddenly remembered the only other place he had ever lived openly as ab-dead, and he shuddered. The exception to his rule, the only place where the payoff of fear between quick and vampir did not apply.

Thank the bloodlords, the shriven, the gods of salt and fire, I will never have to go back there again. To that place where he was free—forced to be free—of all pretense, all illusion. Where the true nature of the quick, the dead, and the ab-dead was laid bare.

Uther Doul's homeland. In the mountains. He remembered the cold mountains, the merciless flint skree, more forgiving by far than Doul's fucking city.

CHAPTER NINETEEN

In the great workshops of Jhour riding, an extraordinary commission had arrived.

One of the mainstays of Jhour's economy was airship building. For rigid, semi-, and nonrigid dirigibles, for aeroflots and engines, the Jhour factories were the guarantors of quality.

The *Arrogance* was the biggest craft in the Armadan sky. It had been captured decades back, crippled in the aftermath of some obscure battle, and had been retained as a folly and a watchtower. The city's mobile aerostats were half its length, the greatest of them only a little more than two hundred feet, buzzing sedately around the city, bearing inappropriate names like *Barracuda*. The aerostatic engineers were constrained by space—nowhere in Armada was there room for the vast hangars in which huge craft like the largest of the New Crobuzon airships—the explorers and Myrshock shuttles, seven hundred feet of metal and leather—could be made. And, in any case, Armada had no need for any such craft.

Until now, it seemed.

The morning after the leaflets had fallen, the entire workforce of Jhour's *Custody* Aeroworks—stitchers, engineers, designers, metallurgists, and countless others—were summoned by an incredulous-looking foreman. All around the plant in the reshaped steamer, the skeletal frames of dirigibles lay untended as he told the workers falteringly of their commission.

They had two weeks.

* * *

Silas was right, Bellis thought. There was no chance he could have unobtrusively smuggled himself onto the island trip. Even she, cut off as she was from the city's scandal and intrigue, was hearing about Simon Fench with increasing regularity.

Of course it was still vague whisperings. Carrianne had mentioned something about someone who had doubts about the Summoning, who had read a pamphlet put out by someone known as Fink or Fitch or Fench. Shekel told Bellis that he thought the Summoning was an excellent idea but that he'd heard that someone called Fench said that the Lovers were heading for trouble.

Bellis was still amazed at Silas' ability to insinuate himself under the city's skin. Was he not at risk? she wondered. Weren't the Lovers searching for him?

She smiled to think of Shekel. She had not been able to continue with his lessons for some time now, but when he had recently visited her he had taken a few quick, proud minutes to show her that her help was no longer necessary.

He had come to ask her what was in Krüach Aum's book. Shekel was not stupid. It was clear to him that what he had given her must be related to the sudden tumultuous events of the last week—the cascade of leaflets, the extraordinary plan, Tanner's bizarre new commission.

"You were right," she had told him. "It took me a while to translate the book, but when I realized what it was—the account of an experiment—"

"They raised an avanc," Shekel had interrupted her, and she had nodded.

"When I realized what the book was," she went on, "I made sure that Tintinnabulum and the Lovers saw it. It was something that they needed, part of their plan . . ."

"The book *I* found," Shekel had said and begun to grin incredulously.

In the *Custody* Aeroworks, a massive framework of wires and curving girders was taking shape.

At one corner of the enormous room there was a heavy cloud of buff-colored leather. A hundred men and women sat around its edges, thick finger-long needles in each hand, stitching ambidextrously. There were vats of chymicals and resin and gutta-percha to seal the enormous gasbags. Wood frames and metal incandescent from forges were beginning to take the outlines of control and observation gondolas.

The *Custody* workshop, big as it was, could not contain this commission in its final form. Instead, all the finished components were to be lifted onto the bare deck of the *Grand Easterly,* where the bags would be inserted, the sections of skeleton riveted together, and the leather covering stitched into place.

The *Grand Easterly* was the only ship in Armada big enough for that.

It was Chainday the twentieth, or the seventh Skydi of Hawkbill—Bellis no longer cared which. She had not seen Silas for four days.

The air was warm and thick with birdsong. Bellis felt claustrophobic in her rooms, but when she left to walk the streets the feeling did not ebb. The houses and flanks of ships seemed to sweat in the sea-heat. Bellis had not changed her opinion of the sea: its size and monotony affronted her. But that morning she suddenly and urgently needed to get out from under the city's eaves.

She was reproachful with herself for the hours she had waited for Silas. She had no idea what had happened to him, but the sense that she was alone, that he might not be coming back, had hardened her quickly. She realized how vulnerable she had become, and she reerected a wall around herself, like bone. *Sitting and waiting like a fucking child,* she thought furiously.

The yeomanry came for her every day, took her to the Lover and Tintinnabulum and the *Castor*'s hunters, and to committees whose roles in the Summoning she did not understand. Her translation was scrutinized and picked apart: she had to face a man who read High Kettai, though not so well as she. He had demanded intricate details: Why had she chosen this tense, this part of speech? why had she rendered this word in this way? His manner was combative, and she took a small pleasure in undermining him.

"And on this page here," he had snapped in one typical exchange, "why render the word *morghol* 'willing.' It means the opposite!"

"Because of voice and tense," she had responded without apparent emotion. "The entire clause is in the ironic-continuous."

She had almost added *It's common to mistake it for the pluper-fect,* but had contained herself.

Bellis had no idea what all this grilling meant. She felt as if she were being siphoned dry. She had been cautiously proud of her act. She was enthusiastic about the project and the island, then reined herself quickly in, as if a tussle was going on within her between an unfurling desire and a sulky, curmudgeonly, press-ganged response.

But no one had yet told her she would come with them to the island, the crux of her whole plan. She wondered if something had gone wrong. And, anyway, Silas had disappeared. Perhaps it was time, she told herself coolly, for a new plan. If it did not work out, if they left her behind for another translator, then she would tell them the truth, she decided. She would beg mercy for New Crobuzon, would tell them about the grindylow attack so that they would know and might send the message for her.

But with an unpleasant fear she remembered Uther Doul's words just before he shot Captain Myzovic. *The power I repre-sent cares not at all about New Crobuzon,* he had said. *Not at all.*

She crossed the Whiskey Bridge from the *Badmark,* a barge at the outer edge of Garwater, to the broad clipper *Darioch's Concern.*

The streets of Shaddler seemed bleaker to her than Garwater, more pared down. Façades were simpler, where they existed at all. Wood was scrubbed and cut into spare, repeating patterns. Pomp's Way was a market street abutting both Garwater and The Clockhouse Spur, and the pavement was full of carts and animals and visiting shoppers—khepri, human, and others—jostling with the scabmettlers who made up half of Shaddler.

Bellis could recognize the scabmettlers now even without their armor, from their distinctive, heavy physiognomy and ashen complexions. She passed a temple, its bloodhorns silent, its guards adorned with clot-plate. Beyond it was a herbarium, with sheafs of dried astringents smelling strong in the warmth.

There were sacks of the distinctive yellow blodfrey that boiled up into the anticoagulant tea. She could see men and women drinking it from a cauldron. It was taken to ward off allclot attacks: the scabmettlers were prone to sudden and total setting of the blood in their veins, which killed them quickly and painfully, transforming sufferers into twisted statues.

Bellis was standing between wheel ruts in front of a warehouse, and she ducked out of the way of the beast tugging a wagon toward her, some crossbred pygmy horse, onto a swaying bridge leading to a quieter part of town. Poised between two vessels, Bellis looked across the water. She could see the stubby bulk of a chariot ship, the curves of a cog, a fat paddleboat. And beyond them there were more. Each vessel embedded in a web of bridges, suspended by gently belling walkways.

There was a constant traffic of people on them. Bellis felt alone.

The Sculpture Garden took up the front of a two-hundred-foot corvette. Its guns were long gone; its cowls and masts had been crushed.

.   A little plaza of cafés and pubs passed seamlessly into the garden, like a beach into the sea. Bellis felt her footing change as she passed from the wood and gravel paths to the garden's soft earth.

It was only a fraction the size of Croom Park, a patch of young trees and well-tended grass interspersed with decades' worth of sculpture in various styles and materials. There were curlicued wrought-iron benches under the trees and the artwork. And at the edge of the park, over a little low railing, was the sea.

Bellis' breath caught on seeing it. She could not help herself.

Men and women sat at tables covered with liqueurs and teas, or walked the garden. They looked bright and garish in the sun. Watching them wander calmly and sip their drinks, Bellis almost shook her head to remember that these were pirates: grizzled, scarred, armed, living off plunder. They were all of them pirates.

She looked up at her favored sculptures as she passed them: *The Threatening Rossignol; Doll and Teeth.*

Bellis sat and looked past *The Proposal,* a slab of featureless jade like a tombstone, over the wooden wall, out to sea—at the steamers and tugboats doggedly dragging the city. She could see two gunboats, an armed airship above them, prowling protectively at the edge of Armada's waters.

A pirate brig was sailing north, around the edge of the city and away. She watched it set out on its month-long, or two- or three-or four-month hunting voyage. According to the will of its captain? According to some grand scheme handed down by the ridings' rulers?

At the other edge of the sea, miles off, Bellis caught sight of a steamer heading in toward the city. Clearly an Armadan ship, or perhaps some favored trader. Had it not been, it would not have got so close. It might have come from a thousand miles away, she thought. When it had set sail, Armada might have been in another sea. And yet when its job was done— its thieving, its robbery—it sailed unerringly for home. That was one of Armada's enduring mysteries.

There was a burst of birdsong behind her. She had no idea, nor did she care, what breed it was that sang, but she listened with ignorant pleasure. And then, as if announced by the avian fanfare, Silas walked slowly into view.

She started and began to rise, but he did not slow as he passed close to her.

"Sit," he said curtly, and stood by the guardrail, leaning out over the edge of the ship. She froze and waited.

He stood, without looking at her, some distance away. They stayed like that for a long time.

"They've been watching your rooms," he said at last. "That's why I've not been coming. That's why I've stayed away."

"They're tracking me?" said Bellis, hating how ineffectual she sounded.

"This is my business, Bellis," Silas said. "I know how it's done. Interviews can only tell them so much. They need to check up on you. You shouldn't be surprised."

"And . . . they're watching *now*?"

Silas shrugged fractionally.

"I don't think so." He slowly turned. "I don't think so, but I can't be sure." His mouth was hardly moving as he spoke. "They've been outside your house for four days. They were with you at least to the outskirts of Shaddler. I think they lost interest there, but I don't want to risk it.

"If they connect us, if they realize that their translator consorts with Simon Fench . . . then we're fucked."

"Silas." Bellis spoke with cold resignation. "I'm not their translator. I've not been asked to go with them. I think they must have someone else—"

"Tomorrow," he said. "They're going to ask you tomorrow."

"Is that right?" Bellis said calmly. Her insides, though, were shuddering, with excitement or foreboding or something. She controlled herself and did not ask him *What are you talking about?* or *How do you know?*

"Tomorrow," he repeated. "Believe me."

She did. And she felt almost sick suddenly, watching him penetrate layers of intrigue without apparent effort. His tentacles of influence and information were sunk so deep, he was like some parasite living off information, siphoning it from beneath the city's skin. Bellis looked at him with wary respect.

"They'll come for you tomorrow," he went on. "You'll be in the landing party. The plan's as we discussed it. They're allowing two weeks on the island, so you'll have a fortnight to get the information to a Dreer Samher vessel. You'll have everything you need to get them to go to New Crobuzon. I'll get it to you."

"Do you really think you can persuade them?" said Bellis. "They don't often sail north of Shankell—New Crobuzon's about a thousand miles out of their way."

"Jabber, Bellis . . ." Silas' voice remained hushed. "No, I can't persuade them. I'll not be there. *You* have to persuade them."

Bellis clucked her tongue, irritated with him, but said nothing.

"I'll bring what you need," he said. "A letter in Salt and Ragamoll. Seals, advice, papers, and proof. Enough to convince the cactus traders to go north for us. And enough to let the New Crobuzon government know what's happening. Enough to protect them."

The park shifted with the waves. The sculptures creaked as they corrected. Neither Bellis nor Silas spoke. For a while there was only the sound of water and birds.

They'll know we're alive, thought Bellis. *At least, they'll know he's alive.*

She stopped that thought, quickly. "We can get word to them," she said decisively.

"You'll have to find a way," said Silas. "Do you realize what's at stake here?"

Don't treat me like a fucking imbecile, she thought furiously, but he caught her eye for a second and seemed quite unabashed.

"Do you realize," he repeated, "what you'll have to do? There'll be guards, Armadan guards. You'll have to get past them. You'll have to get past the anophelii, for Jabber's sake. Can you do this?"

"I will make it happen," said Bellis coldly, and he nodded

slowly. He started to speak again, and for the briefest moment
seemed unsure of what to say. "I'll not . . . have a chance to see
you," he said slowly. "I'd better stay away."

"Of course," said Bellis. "We can't risk anything now."

His face betrayed an unhappiness, something unfulfilled. Bellis pursed her lips.

"I'm sorry for that, and for . . ." he said. He shrugged and
looked away from her. "When you return, and it's all done, perhaps then we can . . ." His voice petered out.

Bellis felt a flicker of slight surprise at his sadness. She felt
nothing. She was not even disappointed. They had sought and
found something in each other, and they had business together
(an absurdly understated formulation for their project), but that
was all. She bore him no ill feelings. She even felt a residue of
affection and gratitude to him, like a film of grease. But no more
than that. She was surprised by his faltering tone, his regret and
apology and hints of deeper feelings.

Bellis discovered, with unfolding interest, that she was not
quite convinced by him. She did not believe his insinuations.
She could not tell whether he believed them himself, but she
knew, suddenly, that she did not.

She found that calming. She sat still, after he was gone, with her
hands folded, her pale face immobile and lapped by the wind.

They came and told her that her language skills were requested,
that she was to travel on a scientific expedition.

On the *Grand Easterly,* in one of the low clusters of rooms a
scant story or two above the deck, Bellis looked out over the surrounding ships of Garwater and at the *Grand Easterly*'s bowsprit
above them. The ship's funnels were clean; its masts jutted two,
three hundred feet into the sky, as bare as dead trees, their shafts
embedded below in striae of dining rooms and mezzanines.

Stretched out across the deck, like a broken fossil, were laid
the innards of a huge airship. Curves of metal like barrel straps
or ribs; propellers and their engines; massive detumescent gasbags. They stretched for hundreds of feet along the side of the
Grand Easterly, skirting the bases of the masts. Gangs of engineers riveted them in place, constructing the enormous thing in
segments. The noises and the glow from hot metal reached Bellis through the windows.

The Lovers arrived, and the briefing sessions began.

* * *

At night Bellis found herself affected by insomnia. She stopped
trying to sleep and tentatively began to write her letter again.

She felt as if everything was occurring at one remove from
her. Each day she was escorted to the *Grand Easterly*. Perhaps
thirty-five men and women gathered daily in that room. They
were of various races. Some were Remade. One or two, Bellis
was sure, came from the *Terpsichoria*. She recognized Shekel's
companion Tanner Sack, and saw that he recognized her.

Quite suddenly it had become hot. The city had passed, at its
groaning rate, into a new stretch of the world's sea. The air was
dry, and it was as warm every day as the rarest moment of a New
Crobuzon summer. Bellis did not relish it. She would stare into
a new, hard sky and feel herself waning in its influence. She
sweated, and smoked less, and wore thinner clothes.

People walked stripped to the waist, and the sky was full of
arcing summer birds. The water around the city was clear, and
big schools of colorful fish were close to the surface. The byways of Garwater began to smell.

The briefings were given by Hedrigall and others like him—
press-ganged cactacae, once pirate-traders from Dreer Samher.
Hedrigall was a brilliant orator, his fabler training making his
descriptions and explanations sound like wildly exciting stories.
It was a dangerous trait.

He told Bellis and her new companions about the island of the
anophelii. And, hearing the stories, Bellis began to wonder if she
had taken on a task she could not complete.

Tintinnabulum came sometimes to the meetings. Always one
or both of the Lovers was present. And sometimes, to Bellis' unease, Uther Doul lounged beside the gathering, leaning against a
wall, his hand to his sword.

She could not stop watching him.

Outside, the aerostat took shape like some enormous vague-
edged whale. Bellis saw ladders being laid internally. Flimsy-
seeming cabins were constructed. Tar- and sap-coated leather
was hauled into position.

It had been a mass of parts, and then a cut-up body, and then a
work in progress, and now it was becoming a vast airship. It
lolled on the deck. It was like some insect just emerged from

chrysalis: still too weak to fly, but now clearly become what it would be.

Bellis sat alone in her bed, in the hot nights, sweating and smoking, terribly afraid of what she had to do but almost trembling with excitement. She would rise, sometimes, and walk, just to hear her feet slapping on the metal floor, relishing the fact that she was the only thing in her room making a sound.

CHAPTER TWENTY

Short, uncomfortably hot days and interminable sweaty nights. Daylight lasted longer as the weeks progressed, but still early every evening the light had gone and the stretched-out, sticky summer night drained the city of strength.

There were half-hearted fights at the junctions of ridings. Bravos from Garwater out drinking might end up in the same bar as a group of Dry Fallers. At first there would be nothing but a few surly murmurs: the Garwater lads might mutter about leech lovers or daemon's bum-boys. The Dry Fall mob would make a loud joke or two about perverts at the helm, and laugh too much at bad puns about cutting.

A few drinks or sniffs or puffs later and the punches would be thrown, but somehow the antagonists' energies rarely seemed entirely in the fray. They did what they expected of themselves— little more than that.

By midnight the streets were clearing out, and by two or three they were mostly empty.

The drone from the surrounding ships never dimmed. There were factories and workshops in various industrial districts, perched stinking and smoke-bawling on the arse-ends of old ships, which did not stop. The nightwatch moved through the city's shadows, each riding's in its own colors.

Armada was not like New Crobuzon. Here there was not a whole alternative economy of rubbish and squalor and survival:

the basements of empty buildings did not harbor a mass of beggars and homeless. There were no dumps to plunder: the city's rubbish was stripped of everything that could be reused, and the remainder was jettisoned into the sea with the city's corpses, spoor dissolving as it sank.

There were slums draped across the sloops and frigates, found housing moldering in the brine air and heat, sweating matter onto their inhabitants. The cactacae laborers of Jhour stood, sleeping, tight-packed in cheap flophouses. But the New Crobuzon press-ganged could see the difference. Poverty here was less likely to kill. Fights were more likely to be fueled by booze than desperation. A roof was likely to be found, even if it drizzled plaster. There were no vagrants huddled in angles of architecture to watch late-night walkers.

So in the dead hours, as a man made his way toward the *Grand Easterly,* he was unseen.

He walked without hurry along Garwater's less salubrious byways. Needle Street and Blodmead Street and the Wattlandaub Maze on the *Surge Instigant;* the *Cable's Weft,* a barquentine decaying into fungus-mottled camouflage; and on to the submersible *Plengant.* He picked his way past the trapdoors cut into its top, stayed in shadow close to the blistering periscope tower.

Behind him, its tower unlit among the spires and masts, he could see the derrick of the *Sorghum.*

The flat flank of the *Grand Easterly* swept up beside the *Plengant* like the side of a canyon. From deep within it, behind its metal skin, there were the vibrations of unceasing industry. There were trees on the surface of the submersible, gripping the iron with roots like knotted toes. The man walked in their shadow and heard the quick skin-sounds of bats above him.

There were thirty or forty feet of sea between the submarine and the cliff face of the steamship. The man saw the lights and shadows of late-night dirigibles in the sky, weak shifting rays spilling over the *Grand Easterly's* guardrail from the torches of the yeomanry patrolling the deck.

Opposite him was the enormous sweeping curve of the *Grand Easterly's* starboard sponson, the cover to the paddlewheel. From the bottom of its bell-shaped covering, the slats of a great wheel within emerged like ankles from a skirt.

The man emerged from the shade of the sickly trees. He removed his shoes, tying them to his belt. When no one came, and there were no sounds, he walked to the curving edge of the *Plengant* and slid suddenly into the cool water, with only a faint sound. It was only a short swim to the flank of the *Grand Easterly,* and into the shadows below the sponson.

Where, brine-soaked and dogged, the man hauled himself up the slats of the sixty-foot paddle, into the darkness. He was as quiet as he could be in the echoes. He climbed to the side of the wheel's huge crankshaft and to a service hatchway, long forgotten, that he had known was there.

It took minutes of effort to break the scab of age, but the man finally managed to open it, to make his way along the crawl space into an enormous, silent engine room abandoned a long time ago to the dust.

He crept past the thirty-ton cylinders and huge, ignored engines. The chamber was a maze of walkways and monolithic pistons, thickets of gears and flywheels as tangled as a forest.

Neither dust nor light stirred. It was as if time had been bled dry and given up. The man picked the lock of the door, then stood motionless, holding the handle. He remembered the layout of the ship. He knew where he was heading—past the guards.

It was in the nature of the man's profession that he knew a few hexes: passes to send dogs to sleep; words that made him sticky to shadows; hedge-magic and trickery. But he doubted very much that it would protect him here.

With a sigh, the man reached for the cloth-wrapped package tied to his belt. He felt a gust of foreboding.

And a trembling excitement.

As he unwrapped the heavy thing, he reflected nervously that if he really understood how to use it, the stiff lock of the service hatch and the unpleasant night swim could probably have been dispelled like breath. He was still a fumbling ignorant.

He picked the last of the stiff cloth away and held up a carving.

It was larger than his fist, cut out of a slick stone that looked black or grey or green. It was ugly. It curled around itself like a fetus, etched with lines and coils that suggested fins or tentacles or folds of skin. The work was expert but unpleasant, seemingly designed to make the eye recoil. The statue watched the man with its one open eye, a perfect black half-sphere above a round mouth ringed in little teeth like a lamprey's. It gaped at him with a darkness in its throat.

Twisting down the little figurine's back, curving tightly back and forth in layers, sandwiching its folds together, was a flap of thin, dark skin. A sliver of tissue. A fin.

It was embedded into the fabric of the stone. The man ran his finger along its length. His face wrinkled in distaste, but he knew what he had to do.

He placed his lips close to the statue's head and began to whisper in a hissing language. The sibilants echoed faintly in the big room, threading through the still machinery.

The man recited puissant doggerel to the statue and caressed it in prescribed patterns. His fingers began to numb as something leached from him.

Finally, he swallowed and turned the statue so that its face regarded him. He brought it close, hesitated, and turning his head slightly in a ghastly parody of passion, he began to kiss its mouth.

He opened his own lips and pushed his tongue into the statue's craw. He felt the cold thorns of its teeth, and he probed further. The figurine's mouth was cavernous, and the man's tongue seemed to reach into the center of the little piece. It was very cold to his mouth. He had to steel himself not to gag on its taste, musty and salt and piscine.

And as the man wriggled his tongue in the stone throat, something kissed him back.

He had expected it—hoped for it, relied on it. But still it came with a jolt of nausea and shock. A little flickering something tonguing his own tongue. Cold and wet and unpleasantly organic, as if a fat maggot lurked at the statue's core.

The taste intensified. The man felt his gorge rise and his stomach spasm, but he kept his bile down. The statue lapped at him with stupid lasciviousness, and he steeled himself to its affections. He had asked a boon of it, and it graced him with a kiss.

He felt saliva flow from him and, abominably, back into him from the statue. His tongue numbed at its slippery touch, and the coldness faded back toward his teeth. Seconds passed, and he could hardly feel his mouth. The man felt tingling like a drug pass through his body, from the back of his throat down.

The statue stopped kissing him; the little tongue was withdrawn.

He pulled his own tongue out too fast and tore it on the obsidian teeth. He did not feel that, did not realize until he saw the blood drip onto his hand.

Carefully he rewrapped the statue, then stood and waited for its kiss to course through him. The man's perception trembled, rippled. He smiled unsteadily and opened the door.

He could see musty oil portraits and heliotypes retreating in perspective on either side. He could sense a patrol of yeomen with dogs approaching him.

He grinned. He raised his arms, reached out and up, and pitched slowly forward, falling as if his knees had been shot out. He could taste his own blood, and the saltfish-rot of the statue. His tongue was filling his mouth, and he never hit the ground.

He moved in a new way.

He saw with the statue's sight, which it had bestowed on him with a kiss, and he slipped and oozed through spaces as the statue dreamed of moving. He questioned the angles of the corridor, reconfigured them.

The man did not walk and did not swim. He inveigled his way through crevices in possible spaces and passed, without effort and sometimes with, along channels he could now see. When he saw two yeomen and their mastiffs approaching, his way was clear.

He was not invisible, nor did he pass into another plane. Instead he moved to the wall and watched its texture, looked at its scale anew, saw the dust motes close up so that they filled his view; then he slithered behind them, hidden away, and the patrol passed away without noticing him.

At the end of the corridor was a right turn. The man squinted at the corner after the patrol had disappeared, and he managed with a little effort to use it to head left instead.

He passed like that through the *Grand Easterly,* remembering the maps he had seen. When patrols came he turned the architecture against them by a variety of means and slipped quickly past them. Where he was trapped behind them at the wrong end of a long passage, he might pass them by looking askance and stretching out his arm, gripping hold of the far wall and pulling himself quickly around its corner. He turned so that doors were below him, plummeting, with gravity, the length of corridors for speed.

Giddy, queasy with a kind of motion sickness brought on by his new movements, the man went quickly and inexorably aft, toward the rear and bottom of the ship.

Toward the compass factory.

* * *

Its security was tight. Guards with flintlocks surrounded it. The man had to squeeze carefully and slowly through layers of slant and perspective to reach the door. He hid in front of the guards, too big and close for them to see, out of focus and looming, and he bent over them and peered into the keyhole, at the intricate gears that dwarfed him.

He conquered them and was inside.

The room was deserted. Desks and benches were laid out in rows. There were machines, their drive belts and motors still.

At some places were copper and brass housings like large fob watches. At others were slivers of glass and equipment to grind them. There were intricately carved hands, chains and engraving needles, tightly wound springs. And hundreds of thousands of gears. Ranging in size from small to minuscule, like atom-sized relations of the wheels in the engine room. They were scattered everywhere, like grooved coins or fish scales or dust.

It was an artisanal factory. Each station was worked by an expert, a craftsperson of exquisite skill, passing his or her part-finished work to the next. The intruder knew how specialized each job was, what rare minerals had to be incorporated, the precision of the thaumaturgy necessary. Each of the finished articles was worth many times its weight in gold.

And there they were, in a locked cabinet like a jeweler's, behind a desk at the back of the long room. The compasses themselves.

It took several minutes of careful effort for the man to open the case. The statue's gifts were still strong in him, and he adapted well to his new perception; but still, it took a long time.

Each of the pieces was different. His hand trembling, he drew out one of the smallest: a simple, stark model, its edges picked out in polished wood. He clicked it open. Its bone face was marked with several concentric dials, some numbered, some etched with obscure sigils. Spinning loosely around the center was a single black hand.

On the compass's back was a production number. The man noted it carefully and began the most important part of this mission. He searched for all records of this compass's existence: in the book of records behind the display cabinet, on the list made by the metalworker who had finished the casing, in parts lists of incorrect and replacement fittings.

The man was thorough, and after half an hour he had found

every mention. He laid them out in front of him and checked whether the timing worked.

The piece had been completed a year and a half ago, and it had not yet been assigned to any ship. The man smiled cautiously.

He found pens and ink, and examined the main record book more closely. Forgery was easy to him. He began to add, very carefully, to his compass's details. In the column "Assigned To," the man added a date, a year ago (rapidly calculating the Armadan quartos), and the name *Magda's Threat.*

If anyone should, for any reason, look for information on compass model CTM4E, they would now find it. They would discover that it had been installed a year previously on the poor *Magda's Threat,* a ship that had gone down months ago, with all hands and cargo, without a trace, in waters a thousand miles away.

When he had replaced everything, the man had just one task left.

He opened the compass, brooding on the intricacies of its metaclockwork entrails, stolen and adapted from a khepri design centuries before. On the tiny shaving of stone he knew was embedded at its core, bound in with homeotropic thaumaturgy. Its hand swung vaguely on its axis.

With ten quick twists the man wound it up.

He held it to his ear and heard its faint, almost inaudible ticking. He watched its face. Its dials spasmed and snapped into new positions.

The hand spun wildly, then set hard, pointing afore, back toward the center of the *Grand Easterly.*

It was not a conventional compass, of course. The hand was not pointing north.

This hand was pointing to a chunk of rock that was hemmed in by thaumaturgy, encased in glass, bolted under iron, depending on which rumor one believed. It had fallen from the sky, it was from the heart of the sun, it was from hell.

For the years until its clockwork ran down, the compass would point precisely toward the city's lodestone, the godrock buried somewhere in the core of the *Grand Easterly.*

The man wrapped the compass very tight in oiled cloth and then in leather, and buttoned it into his pocket.

It must be almost dawn. The man was exhausted. He was finding it hard to see the room and its angles and planes, its walls and materials and dimensionality, other than as he usually did. He sighed, and his heart sank. He was losing the statue's powers, but he had yet to get out of there.

And so, moistening his lips, flexing his tongue, surrounded by armed officers who would kill him for even knowing about the factory, the man began to unwrap his statue again.

INTERLUDE IV
Elsewhere

On keep on.
   The water is like sweat and our whales do not like it.
   Nonetheless.
   South.
   The trail is clear.

Into temperate and then into warm seas.

The submarine rockscape was dramatic here, jags and clefts in the world's crust. Atolls and reefs rose from the deep water in a melee of vivid colors. The water was fertilized by rotting palm leaves and lotuses and the corpses of unique creatures: amphibious things that swam in mud, and fish that breathed air, and aquatic bats.

On every island there were scores of ecological niches, and for each unique opportunity there was a beast. Sometimes there were two or more, fighting for ascendancy.

The hunters made their way into shallows, into salt lagoons and caves, and ate what they found there.

The whales moaned and mewled and begged to return to the cold waters, and their masters ignored them or punished them, and told them again what it was they were looking for.

The hunters remarked upon the water temperature, and the new quality of light, and the crystalline colors of the fish that surrounded them, but they did not complain. It would have been unthinkable for them to care, with their quarry still loose.

South, they commanded, and even when their whales began to die, one by one, their colossal bodies falling prey to alien warmwater viruses and collapsing, their skins peeling off grey and rotten, their bodies bloating with gas and bobbing stinking and pustulant to the surface to be torn to pieces by carrion birds till their bones and the remnants of their flesh slid down into darkening water, their masters did not hesitate.

South, they said, and followed the trail into tropical seas.

PART FOUR

Blood

CHAPTER TWENTY-ONE

Shunday 29th Lunuary 1780—or the Eighth Bookdi of
Hawkbill Quarto 6/317, as you please. On the *Trident*.

Another addition to this letter. It has been some time since I
have written. I would apologize if it made any sense. I feel as
if I should, somehow—absurdly. As if you read while I write,
and fret during the delays. Of course, when you finally get this
letter, a day's silence or a week's or a year's will be the same—
a line left clear, a row of stars. My months will be collapsed.
But I am confused by time.

I am digressing—making little sense. Forgive me.

I am excited, and somewhat afraid.

I sit on the privy and write this. I am beside a window, and the
morning sun is streaming in on me. I am thousands of feet
above the sea.

It was awesome at first; I will admit that. It was desperately
beautiful. After a time, the monotony of wrinkled water and
sky and occasional cloud is numbing.

The sea here is quite empty. I must be able to see sixty, sev-
enty, ninety miles to the horizon, and there is not a sail, not a
skiff or fishing boat. The water color shifts between green,
blue, and grey according to I don't know what beneath the
surface.

Our motion through the air is almost undetectable. We can
feel the vibrations, of course, from the steam engines aft, the
big propellers, but there is no sense of acceleration, of passage or direction.

This *Trident* is an astonishing vessel. Garwater is pouring
effort and money into this journey. That is clear.

* * *

It must have been a sight, when the *Trident* lifted off from the deck of the *Grand Easterly*. It had spent long enough jutting over the ocean, lifted on a framework to keep it clear of the deck's little capstans and bulkheads. I don't doubt that there were bets taken on whether we would smash into the sea or into the fabric of the city.

But we lifted clear. It was late afternoon, and there was a darkness at the edge of the sky. I can imagine the *Trident* hanging there like gods know what, as big as most of the ships of the city, new and scrubbed clean.

We have brought with us the most bizarre thing. Hanging between our engines is a pen full of sheep and pigs.

The animals have food and water for our two-day journey. They must be able to see the gulf of air through the slats in their floor. I thought they might panic, but they can only stare down at the clouds below their hooves, with blank lack of interest. They are too stupid to fear. Vertigo is too complex for them.

I sit here in this little cubby, the lavatory, between the livestock and the control car where the captain and his crew steer us. A corridor from the main chamber.

I have come here to write, several times, since we lifted off.

The others spend their times sitting, whispering or playing cards. I suppose some are in their berths, tucked in the deck above me, below the gasbags. Perhaps they are being talked once more through what is expected of them. Perhaps they are practicing.

My own role is simple, and has been made very clear. After all these weeks and all these thousands of miles, I am back to being told that I am a conduit, that I will merely pass information and language through me, that I do not hear what is spoken.

I can do that. And until then, I have nothing to do but write.

Where possible, cactus-people have been chosen for this mission. At least five of those aboard have actually been to the anophelii island before, years ago. Hedrigall, of course, and others I do not know.

This raises issues of desertion: it is rare for any Armadan press-ganged to come into contact with their old compatriots again, but there must be Samheri on the island. My business here relies on such a meeting. All the cactacae on this mission, I understand, have reasons not to wish to return to their first home. They are like Johannes, or Hedrigall, or Shekel's friend Tanner—loyal to their adopted country.

Hedrigall, though, makes me wonder. He knows Silas—or at least he knows one Simon Fench.

I of all people know that the Garwater authorities can misjudge who is to be trusted.

Dreer Samher is pragmatic. At sea, a meeting of Samheri ships and those of Perrick Nigh or the Mandrake Islands might mean battle, but relations with Armada are courteous, for safety's sake. And besides, they will be at dock. Port-peace operates there as law-merchant does on the land, and it is a strong code, adhered to and administered by those subordinated to it.

Tanner Sack is on the airship, and I can tell that he knows who I am. He watches me with what might be distaste, or shyness, or almost any other emotion. Tintinnabulum is aboard, and several of his crew. Johannes is not—I am relieved at that.

The scientists who are here are a strange mixture. The press-ganged look mostly as I expect scholars to. The Armadans look like pirates. I am told that this one is a mathematician, this one a biologist, this one an oceanologer: they all look like pirates, scarred and pugnacious in ragged regalia.

There are the guards: cactus and scabmettler. I have seen inside their armory, and there are rivebows and flintlocks and polearms. They have brought black powder with them, and what look to me like war engines. In case the anophelii do not cooperate, I think we have brought plenty to persuade them.

In charge of all the guards is Uther Doul. And giving him his orders is one-half of Garwater's ruling pair, alone, the Lover.

Doul stalks from room to room. He talks to Hedrigall more than to anyone else, I think. He seems disquieted. I do my best not to meet his eye.

He intrigues me: his presence, his anomolous voice. He wears the grey leather that is his uniform, much-scarred and pocked, but immaculately clean. The right arm of the tunic is interwoven with wires that extend down to his belt. He wears his sword on his left hip, and he bristles with pistols.

He stares aggressively from windows, then stalks back, usually to wherever the Lover is standing.

The Lover's scarred face revolts me somewhat. I've known—I have been with—those who found release in pain, who made it part of sex; and though I find the prediliction slightly absurd, it does not trouble or disturb me at all. That is not what I find wrong with the Lovers. I have a sense that their cutting is somehow almost contingent. What makes me queasy is something deeper that inheres between them.

I try to avoid the Lover's eye, but I find myself pruriently drawn by her marks. It is as if they have been carved into some mesmeric pattern. But peering at them surreptitiously from behind my fingers, I see nothing romantic or secret or revelatory, nothing but the evidence of old wounds. Nothing but scars.

*   *   *   *   *   *   *

Later, same day.

Silas delivered what was needed, at the last possible minute. As if for theatrics.

I have to admire his methods.

Ever since our terse conversation in the Sculpture Garden I had been wondering how he would give me the materials for our message. *My rooms are guarded, I am watched, what am I to do?*

On the morning of the twenty-sixth of Lunuary, I woke to find a packet from him on the floor of my room.

It was an ostentatious piece of prestidigitation. I could not help laughing when I looked up and saw a patch of iron on my ceiling, freshly bolted over a six-inch hole.

Silas had climbed to the top of *Chromolith* Smokestacks, onto the roof of thin metal that booms like an orchestral drum under the rain, and he had cut a hole in it. Dropping the package inside, he had conscientiously bolted a new roof piece into position. All without the slightest sound: neither awakening me, nor alerting those who must have been watching.

When he performs tricks like that, under duress, to protect

himself, it is easy to imagine him at his job for the government. I suppose I am lucky to have him on my side, and so is New Crobuzon.

I was pleased not to see him. I feel very distant from him now. I bear him no ill will: I took from him something that I needed, and I hope that I gave it back to him; but that really must be the end of the matter. We are coincidental comrades, is all.

Inside the little leather bag, Silas had put several items.

He had written a letter to me, explaining everything. I read it carefully before examining the bag's other contents.

There were other letters. He had written to the pirate captain we hope to find: two copies of the same letter, in Ragamoll and Salt. *To Whomever Agrees to Courier This Missive to New Crobuzon,* it begins.

It is formal and to the point. It promises the reader that he will receive a commission on safe, sealed delivery to its destination. That by the power vested in Procurator Fennec (license number such-and-such) by Mayor Bentham Rudgutter and the office of mayor in perpetuity, it is declared that the bearers of this letter are to be treated as honored guests of New Crobuzon, their ship is to be refitted to their specifications, they are to receive an honorarium of three thousand guineas. And most important of all, they are to be granted a special tax-free letter of marque from the New Crobuzon government, exempting the vessel, for a year, from prosecution or attack under New Crobuzon's self-declared maritime law for any reason other than the immediate self-defense of a New Crobuzon ship.

The money is very enticing, but it is the promised exemption with which we hope to sway our cactacae. Silas is offering them the status of recognized pirate *without tariffs.* They can pillage what they like, never paying a stiver, and the New Crobuzon navy will not molest them—will indeed protect them—for the duration of the contract.

It is a powerful incentive.

At the bottom of the letters, Silas has signed his name, and across some just-visible passwords has imprinted in wax the seal of the New Crobuzon Parliament.

I did not know he had such a seal. It is strange to see it here, so far from home. It is astonishingly fine work: the stylized wall, the chair and paraphernalia of office, and below in tiny figures a number, identifying him. The seal is an extraordinarily powerful symbol.

What is more, he has given it to me.

But I am digressing. I will come to the ring.

The other letter is much longer. It spreads over four sides, in an intricate, condensed hand. I have read it carefully, and it has chilled me.

It is to Mayor Rudgutter, and it is an outline of the grindylow invasion plan.

Much of it is opaque to me. Silas has written in a terse shorthand that approaches code—there are abbreviations I do not recognize and references to things of which I have never heard—but there is no mistaking its meaning.

Status Seven, I read at the top of the sheet, *Code: Arrowhead,* and though I do not understand them the words chill me.

Silas has been sparing me details, I realize (the most dubious favor one can do). He knows the plans of the invasion well, has laid them out in cold, precise terms. He warns of units and squadrons in specific numbers, carrying obscure ordnance described in one letter or syllable, no less disturbing for that.

Demi-regiment Ivory Magi/Groac'h to advance south along Canker equipped with E.Y.D. and P-T capacity, Third Moon Quarter, I read, and the scale of what faces us terrifies me. Our previous eagerness to escape, the effort we poured into focusing on that, appalls me now, it is so petty and so small.

There is enough information here to defend the city. Silas has discharged his duty.

Again, at the bottom of that letter is the city's seal, vindicating it, making it, for all its soulless, banal language, horribly real.

With the letters is a box.

It is a jewelry box; simple, solid, and very heavy darkwood. And within, nestling on its plumply cushioned lining, is a necklace and a ring.

The ring is for me. Its large silver-and-jade face is carved with an inverted imprint—it is the seal. It is crafted with breathtaking artistry. Within its circuit Silas has placed a nugget of red sealing wax.

This is mine. When I have shown our captain the letters and the necklace, I will close them within the cushioned box and lock it, seal it within the leather pouch, and touch the hot wax with this ring, which I will keep. That way the captain will know what is inside, that we are not betraying him, but that he cannot tamper with the contents if the recipients are to believe and reward him.

(As I think through this chain of events I could become dispirited, I must confess. It seems so tenuous. I am sighing as I write this. I will think on this no longer.)

The necklace is to cross the sea. In distinction to the ring, it is a crude, simple piece, designed without any esthetics at all. A thin, plain iron chain. At its end, an ugly little flap of metal that is adorned only with a serial number, a stamped symbol (two owls under a crescent moon), and three words: *Silas Fennec Procurator.*

It is my identification, Silas tells me in his letter. *It is the ultimate proof that the letters are genuine. That I am lost to New Crobuzon, and that this is my valedictory.*

* * * * * * *

Later still. The sky is darkening.

I am disturbed.

Uther Doul has spoken to me.

I was on the deck of berths above the gondola, coming out of the heads. I was vaguely amused by the thought of all our amassed stools and piss cascading from the sky.

A little way down the corridor I heard a shuffling sound and saw light from a doorway. I peered in.

The Lover was changing. I caught my breath.

Her back was as crosshatched with scars as her face. Most looked old, the scored skin greying and pale. One or two, though, were livid. The marks spread down her back and over her buttocks. She was like a marked animal.

I could not but gasp.

The Lover turned at the sound, unhurried. I saw her bosom and sternum, as wounded as her back. She watched me, pulling a shirt on. Her face, with all its intricate cuts, was impassive.

I stammered some apology and turned abruptly and walked toward the stairs. But with horror I saw Uther Doul emerge from the same room and eye me, his hand on his fucking sword.

This letter I write was burning in my pocket. I was carrying enough evidence to have myself and Silas executed for crimes against Garwater—which would doom New Crobuzon in the process. I was very afraid.

Pretending I had not seen Doul, I descended to the main gondola and took a post by the window, frantically watching the cirrus. I hoped that Doul would leave me be.

It was no good. He came to me.

I felt him standing by my table, and I waited a long time for him to go, to leave without speaking, his intimidation successfully completed, but he did not. Eventually, against my will, it seemed, I turned my head and looked at him.

He watched me silently for a while. I grew more and more anxious, though I held my face still. Then he spoke. I had forgotten how beautiful his voice is.

"They are called freggios," he said.

"The scars: they're called freggios." He indicated the seat opposite me and inclined his head. "May I sit?"

What could I say to that? Could I say *No, I wish to be alone,* to the Lovers' right-hand man, their guard and assassin, the most dangerous man on Armada? I pressed my lips together and shrugged politely: *It is no concern of mine where you sit, sir.*

He clasped his hands on the table. He spoke (exquisitely), and I did not interrupt him or walk away or discourage him with apparent lack of interest. Partly, of course, I was afraid for my life and safety—my heart was beating very fast.

But it was also his oration: he speaks like one reading from a book, every sentence carefully formed, written by a poet. I have never heard anything like it. He held my gaze and seemed not to blink.

I was fascinated by what he told me.

"They are both press-ganged," he said. "The Lovers." I must have gaped. "Twenty-five, thirty years ago.

"He came first. He was a fisherman. A water peasant from the north end of the Shards. Spent all his life on one or other of those little rocks, casting his nets and lines, gutting and cleaning and filleting and flensing. Ignorant and dull." He watched me with eyes a darker grey than his armor.

"One day he rowed too far out and the wind took him. A Garwater scout found him and stole his cargo and debated whether or not to kill him, terrified, skinny little fisherboy. In the end they took him back to the city."

His fingers shifted, and he began gently to massage his own hands.

"People are made and broken and remade by their circumstances," he said. "Within three years the boy ruled Garwater." He smiled.

"Less than three quartos after that, one of our ironclads intercepts a vessel—a gaudy recurved sloop—on its way from Perrick Nigh to Myrshock. One of Figh Vadiso's noble families, it appears: A husband and wife and daughter, with their retainers, relocating to the mainland. Their cargo was stripped. The passengers were of no interest to anyone, and I've no idea what happened to them. They may have been killed; I don't know. What is known is that when the servants were inducted and welcomed as citizens, there was one maid who caught the new ruler's eye."

He looked out into the sky.

"There are some who were there, on board the *Grand Easterly,* at that meeting," he said quietly. "They say she stood tall and smiled crooked at the ruler—not like one trying to ingratiate herself, or one terrified, but as if she liked what she saw.

"Women don't have it well in the northern Shards," he said. "Each island has its own customs and laws, and some of them are unpleasant." He clasped his hands. "There are places where they sew women shut," he said, and watched me. I met his eye: I do not intimidate. "Or cut them, excise what they were born with. Or keep them chained in houses to serve the men. The isle our boss was born to was not so harsh as that, but it . . . exaggerated certain traits that you might recognize from other cultures. From New Crobuzon, for example. A certain sacralization of the woman. A contempt masked as adoration. You understand, I'm sure. You published your books as by B. Coldwine. I'm sure you understand."

That shook me; I admit it. That he knew this much about

me, that he understood my reasons for that harmless little piece of obfuscation.

"On the boss's island, the men go to sea and leave their wives and lovers on the land, and no amount of custom or tradition can chain legs closed. A man who loves a woman with a fierce enough passion—or says he does, or thinks he does—aches when he leaves her. He knows intimately how strong, how powerful her charms are. He himself succumbed to them, after all. So he must lessen them.

"On the boss's island, a man who loves strongly enough will *cut* his woman's *face*. . ." We watched each other, unmoving. "He'll mark her, to make her his, inscribe his property, notch it like wood. Spoil her just enough that no other will want her.

"Those scars are freggios.

"Love, or lust, or something, some combination, overtook the boss. He courted the newcomer and quickly claimed her, with the masculine assertiveness he had been trained into. And by all accounts she welcomed his attentions and returned them, and she was his concubine. Until the day he decided she was his entirely, and with a kind of clumsy bravado, he drew his knife after coitus and cut her face." Doul paused, then smiled with sudden and sincere pleasure.

"She was still; she let him do it . . . And then she took the knife and cut him back."

"It was the making of them both," he said softly.

"You can see the disingenuity. He was a remarkable boy to have risen so high so fast, but he was still a peasant playing peasant games. I don't doubt he *believed* it when he told her that it was for love that he cut her, that he did not trust other men to resist her, but whether he did or not, it was a lie. He was marking territory, like a pissing dog. Telling others where his holdings began. And yet she cut him back."

Doul was smiling at me again. "That was not expected. Property does not mark its owner. She did not fight him; while he marked her, she took him at his word. The blood, the split skin, the tissue and pain, the clot and the scar were for *love,* so they were hers to give as well as receive.

"Pretending that freggios were what he claimed they were, she changed them, and made them much more. Changing them, she changed him, too. Scarred his culture as well as his face. They found solace and strength in each other, then. They found an intensity and a connection in those wounds, wounds made suddenly pure.

"I do not know how he reacted, that first time. But that night she stopped being his courtesan and became his equal. They lost their names that night and became the Lovers. And we had two rulers on Garwater—two who ruled with more single-minded purpose than one ever had. And everything is open to them. She taught him that night how to remake rules, how always to go further. She made him like her. She was hungry for transformations.

"She remains so. I know that better than many: the eagerness with which she greeted me and my work, when I first came." He spoke very softly, thoughtfully. "She takes the scraps of knowledge newcomers bring and makes them . . . remakes them with a drive and zeal that's impossible to resist. However much you may want to.

"They reaffirm their purpose every day, those two. There are new freggios all the time. Their bodies and faces have become maps of their love. It's a geography that changes, that becomes more manifest, as the years move. One for one, every time: marks of respect and equality."

I said nothing—I had said nothing for many minutes—but Doul's monologue had come to an end, and he waited for me to respond.

"Were you not there, then?" I asked finally.

"I came later," he said.

"Press-ganged?" I said, astonished, but he shook his head again.

"I came of my own will," he said. "I sought Armada out, a little more than ten years ago."

"Why," I said slowly, "are you telling me this?"

He shrugged a very little. "It's important," he said. "It's important you understand. I saw you—you're afraid of the scars. You should know what it is that you see. Who rules us, their motivation and passion. Drive. Intensity. It is the scars," he said, "that give Garwater its strength."

He nodded and left me then, abruptly. I waited for several minutes, but he did not reappear.

I am deeply perturbed. I do not understand what happened,

why he spoke to me. Was he sent by the Lover? Did she instruct him to tell me her history, or was he operating on his own agenda?

Does he believe everything he told me?

The scars give Garwater its strength, he tells me, and I am left wondering if he is blind to another possibility. Has he not noticed, I wonder? Is it coincidence that the three most powerful people in Garwater, hence in Armada and hence on the seas, are outlanders? That they were not born within Armada's confines? That they grew to cognition and agency unconstrained by the limits of what is, what remains, and cannot but be a mess of old boats, a little town—even if the most extraordinary one in the history of Bas-Lag—and that they can therefore see a world beyond its petty robberies and claustrophobic pride?

They are not beholden to Armada's dynamics. What are their priorities?

I want to know the Lovers' names.

Except when he fights (I remember that, and it terrifies me), Uther Doul's face is almost motionless. It is compelling and a little tragic, and it is nigh impossible to tell what he thinks or believes. Whatever he says to me, I have seen the Lover's scars, and they are ugly and unpleasant. And the fact that they bespeak some sordid ritual, some game for the emotionally arrested to play, does not change that.

They are ugly and unpleasant.

CHAPTER TWENTY-TWO

Thirty-six hours after the aerostat had risen over Armada and headed away to the southwest, land began to appear beneath them.

Bellis had slept little. She was not tired, however, and rose before five on the second morning to watch the dawn from the stateroom.

When she entered, there were others already awake and watching: several of the crewmen, Tintinnabulum and his companions, and Uther Doul. Her heart sank a little at the sight of him. She found his manner—even more reserved and measured than her own—troubling, and she did not understand his interest in her.

He noticed her and wordlessly indicated the windows.

In the sunless predawn light, rocks were breaking the water below. It was hard to judge the size or distance of the land formations. A scatter-pattern of stones like whales' backs, none more than a mile across, few larger than Armada itself. Bellis could see no birds or animals—nothing but bleak brown rock and the green of scrubland.

"We'll reach the island within the hour," someone said.

The airship hummed with vague industry, with preparations that Bellis did not care to understand. She returned to her berth and packed quickly, then sat in the stateroom in her black clothes, her thick carpetbag at her feet. Deep within it, nestled in the folds of her spare skirts, was the little leather pouch and its contents that Silas Fennec had given her, along with the letter she was writing.

The crew were walking quickly back and forth, barking incomprehensible orders to each other. Those of them who were not working congregated by the windows.

The airship had descended considerably. They were only a thousand feet or so above the water, and the face of the sea had grown more intricate. Its wrinkles had resolved themselves into wave shapes and foam and currents, and the darknesses and colors of reefs and weed forests—and was that a wreck?—below.

The island was ahead of them. Bellis shivered to see it, laid out so stark in the hot sea. It stretched perhaps thirty miles long and twenty across. It was jagged with dust-colored peaks and little mountains.

"Sunshit, I didn't think I'd have to see this place again!" said Hedrigall in Sunglari-accented Salt. He pointed at the island's farthest shore. "There's more than a hundred and fifty miles between it and Gnurr Kett," he continued. "They're not strong in the air, the anophelii. Couldn't last more than sixty miles. That's why the Kettai let them live, and trade with them through the likes of me and my old comrades, knowing they'll never make the mainland. That—" He jerked a thick green thumb. "—is a *ghetto*."

The dirigibles were slanting, skirting the coastline. Bellis watched the island intently. There was nothing to see, no life apart from plants. With a sudden chill, Bellis realized that the skies were empty. There were no birds. Every other island they had passed had been a mass of shifting feathered bodies, the rocks that edged it smeared with guano. The gulls had surrounded every landmass in a little gusting corona, swooping to take fish from the warm seas, squabbling on thermals.

The air above the anophelii island's volcanic cliffs was as dead as bone.

The aerostat passed over silent ocher hills. The inlands were hidden by a ridge of rock, a spine that ran parallel to the coast. There was a long silence broken only by the engines and the wind, and when someone finally did speak—shouting "Look!"— the sound seemed intrusive and defensive.

It was Tanner Sack, pointing at a little crabgrass meadow nestling in rocks, sheltered from the waves. The green was broken by a little clutch of moving white specks.

"Sheep," said Hedrigall after a moment. "We're nearing the bay. There must have been a delivery recently. There'll be a few herds of them left for a while longer."

The shape and nature of the coastline was changing. The stone spines and jags were giving way to lower, less antagonistic geography. There were short beaches of black shale; slopes of hard earth and ferns; low, bleached trees. Once or twice, Bellis saw farmyard animals, wandering feral: pigs, sheep, goats, cattle. Just a very few of them, here and there.

Inland a mile or two, there were ribbons of grey water, sluggish rivers oozing from the hills, intersecting and crisscrossing the island. The waters slowed over plateaus of flat land and burst their banks, diffusing and becoming pools and swampland, feeding white mango trees, vines, greenery as thick and cloying as vomit. In the distance, on the other edge of the island, Bellis saw stark shapes that she thought were ruins.

Below her there was motion.

She tried to track whatever it was, but it was too fast, too erratic. She was left with nothing more than an impression fleeting across her eye. Something had skated through the air, emerging from some dark hole in the rocks and entering another.

"What do they trade?" said Tanner Sack, without looking away from the landscape. "The sheep and pigs and whatnot get left here: your lot bring them and other stuff in from Dreer Samher, for the Kettai. What's in it for them? What do the anophelii trade?"

Hedrigall stood back from the window and gave a curt laugh. "Books and intelligence, Tanner, man," he said. "And flotsam and jetsam, driftwood, bits and pieces they find on the beach."

There was more motion in the air below the dirigible, but Bellis simply could not focus on whatever it was that moved. She bit her lip, frustrated and nervous. She knew she was not imagining things. There was really only one thing the shapes could be. She was perturbed that no one else had mentioned them. *Don't they see?* she thought. *Why does no one say anything? Why don't I?*

The dirigible slowed, moving against a faint wind.

Surmounting a ridge of rockland, it was buffeted. There was an explosion of breath and whispers, incredulous excitement. Below them, in the shadows of hills patched barren and lush in random patterns, was a rocky bay. Anchored in the bay were three ships.

"We're here," Hedrigall whispered. "Those are Dreer Samher vessels. That's Machinery Beach."

The ships were galleons, ornately picked out in gold, surrounded, enclosed by cosseting rocks that jutted into the sea and curled around the natural harbor. Bellis realized she was holding her breath.

The sand and shale of the inlet's beach was a dark red, dirty like old blood. It was broken by weirdly shaped boulders the size of torsos and houses. Bellis' eyes skittered over the dark surface, and she saw trails, pathways scored in the matter of the shoreline. Beyond the boundary of stringy boscage that edged the beach, the trails became more defined. They entered rocky elevations that rose slowly from the earth to overlook the sea. The air was broken by heat waves where the sun baked the stone, and trees like olives and dwarf jungle species specked the slopes.

Bellis followed the trails winding up the scorched hillsides until (her breath stopping again) her eyes came to rest on a scattering of light-bleached houses, dwellings that extruded from the rocks like organic growth—the anophelii township.

There was no wind in the bay. There was a tiny grouping of clouds like paint dots around the sun, but heat blasted through them and reverberated around the enclosed rock walls.

There were no sounds of life. The tedious repetition of the sea seemed to underline the silence rather than break it. The dirigible hung quietly, its engines powered down. The Samheri boats creaked and shifted nearby. They were empty. No one had come to greet the airship.

Scabmettler guards in their bloodclot armor kept watch with cactacae as the passengers descended. Bellis touched land, crouching beside the rope ladder, and ran her fingers through the sand. Her breathing was quick and very loud in her head.

At first she was conscious of nothing but the novelty of being on ground that did not sway. She remembered her land-legs delightedly, only realizing at that moment that she had forgotten them. Then she became aware of her surroundings again, and felt the beach beneath her closely, and for the first time registered its strangeness.

She remembered the naïve woodcuts in Aum's book. The stylized monochrome of the man in profile on the beach, broken mechanisms around him.

Machinery Beach, she thought, and looked out across the dirty-red sand and scree.

Some way off were the shapes she had taken to be boulders—huge things the size of rooms, breaking up the shoreline. They were engines. Squat and enormous and coated with rust and verdigris, long-forgotten appliances for unknown purposes, their pistons seized by age and salt.

There were smaller rocks, too, and Bellis saw that these were shards of the larger machines, bolts and pipework junctions; or finer, more intricate, and complete pieces; gauges and glasswork and compact steam-power engines. The pebbles were gears, cogs, flywheels, bolts, and screws.

Bellis looked down at her cupped hands. They were full of thousands of minuscule ratchets and gear wheels and ossified springs, like the innards of inconceivably tiny clocks. Each particle of wreckage a grain like sand, hard and sun-warmed, smaller than a crumb. Bellis let them sift from her hands, and her fingers were stained the dark blood color of the shoreline—painted with rust.

The beach was an imitation, a found sculpture mimicking nature in the materials of the junkyard. Every atom from some shattered machine.

When does this age from? How old is this? What happened here? thought Bellis. She was too numb to feel any but the most tired awe. *What disaster, what violence?* She imagined the seafloor around the bay—a reclaimed reef of decaying industry, the contents of a city's factories allowed to collapse, pounded by waves and sun, oxidizing, bleeding with rust, breaking into their constituent parts and then into smaller shards, thrown back by the water onto the island's edge, evolving into this freakish shore.

She picked up another handful of machine-sand, let it dissipate. She could smell the metal.

This is the flotsam Hedrigall meant, she realized. *This is a graveyard of dead devices. There must be millions of secrets moldering here into rust-dust. They must sift through it, and scrub it clean, and offer the most promising bits for trade—two or three pieces picked randomly from a thousand-piece puzzle. Opaque and impenetrable, but if you could put it together, if you could make sense of it, what might you have?*

She stumbled away from the rope ladder, listening to the crunch of ancient engines underfoot.

As the last of the passengers descended, the guards kept careful watch on the horizon, muttering. A little way from Bellis, the pen of livestock had been winched to the ground. It stank like a farmyard, and its inhabitants sounded noisily and stupidly into the still air.

"Close together and listen to me," said the Lover harshly, and she was surrounded. The engineers and scientists had been scattering, dumbly running their fingers through the metal shale. A few, like Tanner Sack, had gone to the sea. (He had submerged briefly, with a sigh of pleasure.) For a moment, there was no sound except little breakers foaming on the rust shore.

"Now listen, if you want to live," the Lover went on. People shifted, uneasy. "It's a mile or two to the village, up those rocks overlooking this place." They gazed up at them; the hillside looked empty. "Keep together. Take the weapon issued to you, but don't use it unless you're in immediate danger of your life. There are too many of us here, and too many untrained, and we don't want to start shooting each other in panic. We'll be flanked by cactacae and scabmettler guards, and they know how to use what they're carrying, so hold fire wherever possible.

"The anophelii are fast," she said. "Famined, and dangerous. You remember the briefings, I hope, so you know what we face. The menfolk are somewhere in that village, and we have to find them. A little way over there are the swamplands, and the waters. Where the women live. And if they hear or smell us, they'll come. So move quickly. Is everybody ready?"

She indicated with her arms, and cactacae guards corralled them. They unlocked the animal pen, still attached like an anchor to the *Trident* by its chains. Bellis raised her eyebrow on seeing that the pigs and sheep wore collars and strained against leashes. The muscular cactacae held them in check.

"Then let's go."

It was a nightmarish journey from Machinery Beach to the hillside township. When it was done, and she thought back on it, days or weeks later, Bellis found it impossible to distinguish events into any coherent stream. There was no sense of time in her memories, nothing but snippets of images pieced into something like a dream.

There is the heat, which clots the air around her and stops up her pores and her eyes and ears, and the rich smell of rot and sap; insects in relentless profusion, stinging and licking. Bellis has been given a flintlock, and (*she remembered*) holds it away from herself as if it stinks.

She is herded, shuffling with the other passengers—the solitary hotchi's spines bristling and relaxing in nervous alternation, the khepri headlegs squirming—surrounded by those whose physiognomy makes them safe: the cactacae and the scabmettlers, who drag the livestock after them. The one group is bloodless, the other full of blood so sensitive it protects them. They carry guns and rivebows. Uther Doul is the only human guard. He holds weapons in each hand, and Bellis would swear that whenever she looks at him they have changed: knife and knife; gun and knife; gun and gun.

Looking out over the vine-smothered rocks and into clearings, down inland, over slopes of dense foliage and pools that look as thick as snot. Hearing sounds. Bursts of motion in the leaves, at first; nothing more offensive. But then the start of a horrible keening, impossible to pinpoint, as if the air itself is in pain.

The proliferation of that sound, all around them.

Bellis and her neighbors bump into each other, clumsy with terror and exhaustion and the wet heat, trying to watch all sides at once, and seeing the first signs of movement, shapes zigzagging through the trees like buffeted dust motes, always getting closer, an unstable mix of random motion and malign intent.

And then the first of the she-anophelii breaks the cover of the trees, running.

Like a woman bent double and then bent again against the grain of her bones, crooked and knotted into a stance subtly wrong. Her neck twisted too far and hard, her long bony shoulders thrown back, her flesh worm-white and her huge eyes open very wide, utterly emaciated, her breasts empty skin rags, her arms outstretched like twists of wire. Her legs judder insanely fast as she runs until she falls forward but does not hit the ground, continues toward them, just above the earth, her arms and legs dangling ungainly and predatory, as (*Gods and Jabber and fuck*) wings open on her back and take her weight, giant mosquito wings, nacreous paddles shudder into motion with that sudden vibrato whine, moving so fast they cannot be seen, and the terrible woman seems borne toward them below a patch of unclear air.

What happened next came back to Bellis again and again in memories and dreams.

Gazing hungrily, the mosquito-woman stretches her mouth open, spewing slaver, lips peeled back from toothless gums. She retches, and with a shocking motion a jag snaps from her mouth. A spit-wet proboscis, jutting a foot from her lips.

It extrudes from her in an organic movement, something like vomiting, but unmistakably and unsettlingly sexual. It seems to come from nowhere: her throat and head do not look long enough to contain it. She veers toward them on screaming wings, and from the undergrowth come others.

Memories were blurry. Bellis remained sure of the heat, and of what she had seen, but the immediacy of the images shocked her whenever she thought back. The landing party almost breaks up in sudden terror, and random shots are fired in dangerous, chaotic directions (Doul barking angrily *hold fire*).

Bellis sees the first of the flitting mosquito-women skirting the cactacae, uninterested in them. They fly instead for the scab-mettler guards, alighting on them (the muscular men moving only slightly under the weight of the fatless winged women), stabbing mindlessly at them with their lancelike mouthparts, unable to penetrate the scabs that armor them. Bellis hears the snap of cut leashes as the terrified pigs and sheep scatter in a trail of shit and dust.

There are ten or twelve of the mosquito-women now (*so many so quickly*), and as the livestock bolt they turn instantly to that easier prey. They rise on those thin wings, their heads hunkered, their hips and limbs loose beneath them, dangling in the air like puppets suspended from their elongated shoulderblades, their dark proboscises still wet and extended; and they descend on the petrified animals. They overtake them easily, descending with their half-random motion to block their paths and intercept them, their arms outstretched, their fingers wide, tugging hold of hair and skin. Bellis watches (*she remembered moving backward inexpertly, constantly, stumbling over the feet of those around her but staying upright through force of horror*), aghast and hypnotized, as the first of the she-anophelii moves in to feed.

The woman-thing straddles a huge sow, pulling herself out of the air and wrapping her limbs around it as if it is a loved toy. Her head draws back, and the long mouth-jag extends a few inches extra, as smooth as a crossbow quarrel. Then the mosquito-woman jerks her face forward, her stretched-open mouth twisting, and she slams the proboscis into the body of the animal.

The pig screams and screams. Bellis still watches (*her legs taking her away from that sight, but her eyes staying desperately fixed on it*). The pig's legs give way in sudden shock as its skin is punctured, as six, ten, twelve inches of chitin ease through the resistance of skin and muscle and infiltrate the deepest parts of its bloodstream. The mosquito-woman straddles the collapsed animal and pushes her mouth into it, and grinds her proboscis deep, and tenses her body (every muscle and tendon and vein visible through the shrunken skin) and begins to suck.

For a few seconds, the pig continues to scream. And then its voice gives out.

It is thinning.

Bellis can see it shrink.

Its skin shifts uneasily and begins to wrinkle. The tiniest trickles of blood ooze out from the imperfect seal where the anophelii mouthparts puncture it. Bellis watches in disbelief, but it is not her imagination—the pig is *shrinking*. Its legs kick with spastic terror, and then with the judder of dying nerves as its extremities are drained. Its fat shanks are compressing as its in-

nards shrivel, drying. Its skin is well creased now, in tides and
ridges all over its diminishing body. The color is leaving it.

And as the blood and health disappear from the sow, they enter the mosquito-woman.

Her belly swells. She attached herself to the pig a husk, gaunt
and malnourished. As the pig lessens, she grows, becoming fat-
ter at an astonishing rate, color flooding her from her distending
stomach outward. She moves oily on the dying animal, growing
sluggish and replete.

Bellis watches with sick fascination as the pints of pig blood
pass fast through that bony fletch, rushing from one body into
another.

The pig is dead now, its rucked skin sinking into new valleys
between its drained muscles and its bones. The anophelius is fat
and pinking. Her arms and legs have nearly doubled in girth, and
the skin is now stretched around them. The swelling is mostly
concentrated on her bosoms and belly and arse, which are obese
now, but not soft like human fat. They look tumorous: taut, gore-
swelled, and pendulous growths.

All around the clearing, the same is happening to the other
animals. Some are adorned with one woman, some with two. All
are shriveling, as if sun-dried and desiccated, and all the anophelii are growing gross and tight with blood.

It has taken that first mosquito-woman a minute and a half
to suck the last of the liquid from the pig (*Bellis could never
shake the memories of that sight, or of the little sounds of the
woman-thing's satisfaction*).

The anophelius rolls from the animal's shrunken carcass, sleepy-
eyed, drooling a little blood as her proboscis retracts. She with-
draws, leaving the pig a sack of tubes and bone.

The hot air around Bellis is thick now with the stink of spew
as her companions lose control of themselves at the sight of the
anophelii feeding. Bellis does not vomit, but her mouth twists
violently and she feels herself raising her pistol in what does not
feel like anger or fear, but disgust.

But she does not fire. (*And what would have happened if
someone untrained as she had pulled the trigger? Bellis wondered much later, looking back.*) The danger seems to have
passed. The Armadans are moving on up the hill, past that little
clearing and the smells of dung and hot blood, past more rocks

and pestilential water, toward the township they had seen from the air.

The sequence of events became less blurred, less mashed together by heat and fear and disbelief. But then, at that point, at that moment, as Bellis retreated from that hot carnage of pig and sheep blood and drained offal, the repulsive frenzy of the anophelii repast and then (*worse*) their bloated torpor, a mosquito-woman looked up from the sheep she had arrived at too late to drain and saw their retreat. She hunched her shoulders and flew dangling toward them, her mouth agape and her proboscis dripping, her stomach only a little swelled by her sisters' leftovers, eager for fresh meat, angling past the cactacae and scabmettler guards and bearing down on the terrified humans, her wings awail.

Bellis felt herself jerked by fear back toward that confused trash of disjointed images, and she saw Uther Doul step forward calmly into the mosquito-woman's path, raise his hands (*carrying two guns now*) and wait until she was nearly upon him, till her mouthparts jutted at his face and he fired.

Heat and noise and black lead exploded from his weapons and burst the mosquito-woman's stomach and face.

Even half-empty as she was, the woman's gut split audibly, in a great gout of blood. She collapsed from the air, her shattered face runnelling in the dirt, her proboscis still extended, a greasy red slick soaking rapidly into the earth. Her body came to rest in front of Doul.

Bellis was back in linear time. She felt stunned, but remote from what she saw. Some yards away, the gorged anophelii did not notice their fallen sister. As the landing party turned on the steep path and headed into the foothills, the mosquito-women were beginning to haul their newly heavy bodies away from the now-bloodless carnage they left to rot. Swollen as grapes, they hung below their malevolently piping wings and flew slowly back toward their jungle.

CHAPTER TWENTY-THREE

They waited, silent: the Lover, Doul, Tintinnabulum, Hedrigall, and Bellis. And standing before their visitors, their faces cocked in what looked like polite confusion, were two anophelii.

Bellis was astonished by the two mosquito-men. She had expected something dramatic, skin discolored by chitin, stiff little wings like their women's.

They looked like nothing more or less than small men, bent a little by age. Their ocher robes were discolored with dust and the stains of plants. The older man was balding, and the arms protruding from his sleeves were extraordinarily thin. They had no lips, no jawbones, no teeth. Their mouths were sphincters, tight little rings of muscle that looked exactly like anuses. The skin on all sides simply slid in toward that hole.

"Bellis," said the Lover, her voice hard, "try again."

They had entered the town to the stares and astonishment of the mosquito-men.

Disheveled and sweating and dust-blind, the Armadan landing party had stumbled the last yards up the hill into the sudden shade of houses cut and built into the sides of the gorge that split the rock. There was little apparent plan to the township: little square dwellings sprawled up on the main slopes, in the sun, and swept as if spilt down the steep edges of the fissure itself, linked by chiseled steps and pathways. The chimneys of submerged chambers poked like mushrooms from the earth around them.

The town was punctuated with engines reclaimed from Machinery Beach, each piece scrubbed clean of rust, in hundreds of obscure shapes. Some moved; some were still. Those in the sunlight glinted. None was powered by the noisy steam pistons of New Crobuzon and Armada; there was no oily smoke in the air.

These were heliotropic engines, Bellis supposed, their paddles and blades whirring in the hard sunlight, their cracked glass housings sucking it up, sending arcane energies down the wires that linked random houses. The longer wires were knotted together, from whatever short lengths had been salvaged.

On their flat roofs, on the sides of the hills, in the shade of the narrow cleft itself, and from the canopies of the gnarled trees around the township, from doorways and windows, the mosquito-men turned to stare. There was no sound at all, no whoops or shouts or gasps. Nothing but the astonished gaze of all those eyes.

Once, Bellis (with a horrible spasm of fear) thought she saw the drifting, meandering flight of a she-anophelius over some of the higher-up buildings. But the males nearby turned and began to throw stones at the figure, driving it away before it had spotted the Armadans or entered any of the houses.

They reached a kind of square, ringed by the same dirt-colored houses and the skeletal sun-engines, where the crevice widened and admitted light from the baked blue sky. At the far end, Bellis saw a split in the rocks and a jutting cliff, a precipitous path down to the sea. And here, finally, someone came to meet them: a little delegation of nervous anophelii males, bowing and ushering them forward, into a great hall in the stone of the hills.

In an inner room, lit by immensely long bored shafts full of light, by mirrors that refracted the day and recycled it in the mountain, two anophelii had come to stand before them, bowing politely, and Bellis (remembering that day in Salkrikaltor City, different language but the same job), had come forward and greeted them in her clearest High Kettai.

The anophelii had stood still, their expressions quizzical, not understanding a word.

Bellis tried again to make sense in the stilted eloquence of High Kettai. The anophelii looked at each other and emitted hissing noises like farts.

Seeing their mouth-sphincters twitch and dilate, Bellis realized the truth, and she wrote, rather than spoke, the High Kettai words.

I am named Bellis, she wrote. *We have come very, very far to speak to your people. Do you understand me?*

When she handed the paper to the anophelii, their eyes opened wide and they looked at each other and crooned enthusiastically. The older man took Bellis' pen.

I am Mauril Crahn, he wrote. *It is scores of years since we have had visitors such as you.* He looked up at her, his eyes crinkling. *Welcome to our home.*

The anophelii hooting tongue had no written form. For them High Kettai *was* written language, but they had never heard it spoken. They could express themselves perfectly in elegant script, but they had no idea how it would sound. The very concept of High Kettai "sounding" was alien to them.

Over scores or hundreds of years, a symbiosis had built up between the Samheri sailors and the Gnurr Kett authorities in Kohnid. The Samheri cactacae came to the island with livestock and a few trade goods, and took their cut as middlemen. Kohnid bought from them whatever the anophelii gave.

Between them, they controlled the flow of information to the mosquito-people. They had carefully ensured that no language other than High Kettai reached the island's shores, and that none of the anophelii ever left it.

The terrible memories of the Malarial Queendom abided. Kohnid was playing a game, keeping the brilliant anophelii as pet thinkers; giving them nothing that might make them powerful, or let them escape—Kohnid would not risk unleashing the she-anophelii on the world again—but just enough to think with. The Kettai would not allow anophelii access to any information outside of its control: the centuries-long maintenance of High Kettai as the island's written language ensured that. And that way, anophelii science and philosophy were in the hands of the Kohnid elite, who were almost alone in being able to read it.

The jigsaw pieces of ancient technology that the anophelii possessed, the works of their philosophers must be quite astonishing, thought Bellis, to allow this convoluted system to continue. Each Samheri journey from Kohnid to the island would bring with it a few carefully chosen books, and sometimes commissions. *Given these conditions,* some Kohnid theorist might demand, *and remembering the paradox laid out in your previous essay, what is the answer to the following problem?* And handwritten anophelii works, under chosen Kettai names, made the return journey, in response to such questions, or to problems posed by the anophelii themselves, to be printed by Kohnid publishers—without payment. Sometimes they were doubtless

claimed by some Kettai scholar as his or her own work, all adding
to the prestige of the High Kettai canon.

The mosquito-people had been reduced to captive scholars.

The island's ruins housed old texts, in the High Kettai language the anophelii could read, or in long-dead codes they carefully broke. And with the slow accretion of the books from
Kohnid, and the written records of their ancestors, the anophelii
also pursued their own investigations. Sometimes such a result-
ing work was sent overseas to the island's masters in Kohnid. It
might even be published.

That was what had happened to Krüach Aum's book.

Two thousand years ago, the mosquito-people had ruled the
southern lands in a short-lived nightmare of blood and plague
and monstrous thirst. Bellis did not know how much the anophelii men knew of their own history, but they had no illusions about
the nature of their own womenfolk.

How many did you kill? wrote Crahn. *How many of the
women?*

And when, after a hesitation, Bellis wrote *One,* he nodded and
responded, *That is not so many.*

The township was without rank. Crahn was not a ruler. But he
was eager to help, and to tell the guests everything they might
want to know. The anophelii responded to the Armadans with a
courteous, measured fascination, a contemplative, almost abstract
reaction. In their phlegmatic response, Bellis detected an alien
psychology.

Bellis wrote the Lover's and Tintinnabulum's questions as
quickly as she could. They had not yet broached the most important subject, the very reason they were on this island, when they
heard a ruckus from the other room where their companions
waited. Loud voices in Sunglari, and responses in shouted Salt.

The Dreer Samher trader-pirates stationed on the island had
returned to their ships and had discovered the newcomers. A
gaudily adorned cactus-man strode into the little room followed
by two of his erstwhile compatriots, now Armadan cactacae, angrily remonstrating with him in Sunglari.

"Sunshit!" he yelled in accented Salt. "Who the fuck are
you?" He held a massive cutlass in one hand, hefting it angrily.
"This island is Kohnid territory, and it's forbidden to come here.
We're their agents here, and we're authorized to protect their

fucking holdings. Tell me why I shouldn't have you fucking killed here and now."

"Ma'am," said one of the Armadan cactacae, waving his hand wearily in introduction. "This is Nurjhitt Sengka, captain of the *Tetneghi Dustheart*."

"Captain," said the Lover, stepping forward, Uther Doul moving behind her like her shadow. "It's good to meet you. We must talk."

Sengka was not a freebooter, but an official Dreer Samher pirate. The Samheri's regular stationing on the island was monotonous and easy and dull: nothing happened, nobody came, nobody went. Every month, or two, or six, a new Samheri mission would arrive from Kohnid or Dreer Samher with a cargo full of livestock for the she-anophelii, and perhaps some random collection of commodities for the men. The newcomers would relieve their bored compatriots, letting them go off with whatever brilliant essays and reclaimed scientific refuse they had gathered to trade.

Whoever was stationed on the island spent their time bickering and fighting and betting amongst themselves, ignoring the mosquito-women, visiting the men only to take what they needed by way of food or machinery. And officially, they were there to police the flow of information into the island, the linguistic purity that gave Kohnid its stranglehold—and to stand in the way of any anophelii escape.

The idea was ridiculous; no one ever came to the island. Very few sailors knew of it. There were occasional very rare cases of lost vessels arriving on the shore, but their ignorant crews generally suffered rapid death at the hands of the island's women.

And no anophelii ever left.

Formally, therefore, the Armadan newcomers' presence on the island was not forbidden under the agreement between Dreer Samher and Kohnid. Only High Kettai was being used, after all, and nothing had been brought in to trade. But the presence of strangers who could converse with the natives was unprecedented.

Sengka looked wildly around. When he realized that these bizarre intruders came from the mysterious boat city of Armada, his eyes widened. But they were courteous and seemed keen to explain themselves. And although he cast angry glances at the cactus-people who had once been his countrymen, and hissed insults at them, called them traitors and pretended disdain for the Lover, he did listen, and he let himself be led back to the large room where the Armadan party waited.

And while the Lover and the cactus guards and Uther Doul moved away, Tintinnabulum came to Bellis' side. He gathered his long, white hair in a ponytail, blocking her from the view of the others with his powerful shoulders and arms.

"Don't stop now," he murmured. "Get to the point."

Crahn, she wrote.

For a brief moment, she felt slightly hysterical with the absurdity of this. If she set foot outside, she knew, she risked instant and unpleasant death. Those ravenous mosquito-women would find her before very long, a sack of blood like her; they'd smell her out and siphon every drop out of her, drain her as easily as turning a spigot.

Yet within these sheltering walls, only an hour since she had seen the carnage on the path, a dead anophelius burst on the heat-split skin and bones of the drained animals, she was asking polite questions of an attentive host in a long-dead language. She shook her head.

We are looking for one of your people, she wrote. *We need to speak to him. This is greatly important. Do you know one named Krüach Aum?*

Aum, he responded, no slower or quicker than before, without a shred more or less interest, *who fishes for old books in ruins. All of us know Aum.*

I can bring him to you.

CHAPTER TWENTY-FOUR

Tanner Sack missed the sea.

His skin was blistering in the heat, and his tentacles felt sore.

He had waited for most of a day as the Lover and Tintinnabulum and Bellis Coldwine and the others conversed with the silent anophelii men. He and his companions had muttered to each other, had chewed their biltong and tried without success to ask for fresher food from their curious, reserved hosts.

"Stupid arse-faced pricks," Tanner heard from some hungry men.

The Armadans were traumatized by the starving ferocity of the she-anophelii. They were conscious that their hosts' mates lurked in the air just beyond the walls, that the placid silence of the township outside was misleading—that they were trapped.

Some of Tanner's companions made nervous jokes about the she-anophelii. "Women," they said, and laughed shakily about females of all species being bloodsuckers, and so on.

Tanner tried, for the sake of conviviality, but he could not bring himself to laugh at their idiocies.

There were two camps in the big, austere chamber. On one side were the Armadans, and on the other the Dreer Samher cactacae. They watched each other warily. Captain Sengka was engaged in fierce Sunglari discussion with Hedrigall and two other Armadan cactus-people, and his crew watched and listened uncertainly. When, finally, Sengka and his crew stormed out, the Armadans relaxed. Hedrigall walked slowly to the wall and sat beside Tanner.

"Well, he don't like me much," he said, and grinned wearily. "Kept calling me a traitor." He rolled his eyes. "But he's not going to do anything stupid. He's scared of Armada. I told him we'd be gone quickly, and that we'd brought nothing and we'd take nothing, but I also implied that if he cut up rough, he'd be declaring war. There ain't going to be any trouble."

After a time, Hedrigall noticed how Tanner was endlessly stroking his skin, how he licked his fingers and soothed it down. He left the big chamber, and Tanner was deeply touched when the cactus-man came back, fifteen minutes later, carrying three fat leather waterskins full of brine. Tanner drooled them over himself and sluiced the water through his gills.

Anophelii men came in and watched the Armadans. They nodded to each other, and hooted and whistled. Tanner watched the herbivorous men eat, forcing handfuls of garish flowers into their tight mouth orifices and sucking, with the same force, he supposed, with which their women drained living meat. Then they would eject the spent petals with a little burst of air, crushed and tissue-thin, drained of nectar and juices, colorless.

* * *

The Armadan crew were left to thirst and sweat for hours as the Lover and Tintinnabulum made plans. Eventually, Hedrigall and several other cactacae left the chamber, led by an anophelius.

The light that came through the shafts in the rock began to ebb away. Dusk came fast. Through the little rock slits, and in reflections in mirrors, Tanner could see that the sky was violet.

They were barracked uncomfortably wherever they sat and lay. The anophelii scattered reeds thickly around the room. The night was hot. Tanner removed his stinking shirt and folded it for a pillow. He doused himself in more brine and saw that, around the room, the other Armadans were also attempting what limited ablutions they could.

He had never been so tired. He felt as if every spark of energy had been sucked from him and replaced with the night heat. He rested his head on a makeshift pillow, damp with his own sweat, and even on that hard floor, that thin and ineffectual layer of vegetation (the smell of pollen and plant dust strong), he was very quickly asleep.

When he woke he thought it was only minutes later, but he saw the daylight and groaned miserably. His head ached, and he drank desperately from the jugs of water left them.

As the Armadans woke, the Lover and Doul and Coldwine stepped from the little side room, accompanied by the cactacae who had set out the previous night. They looked tired and dusty, but they were smiling. A very old anophelius was with them, dressed in the same robes as all his fellows, and with the same expression of calm interest.

The Lover faced the assembled Armadans. "This," she said, "is Krüach Aum."

Krüach Aum stood beside her, bowing, his old eyes taking in the crowd.

"I know that many of you have been bemused by this trip," the Lover said. "We've told you that there was something on this island that we need, that's vital to the raising of the avanc. Well, this—" She indicated Aum. "—is what we need. Krüach Aum knows how to raise an avanc." She waited for that to sink in.

"We've come here to learn from him. There are many processes involved. The problems of containment and control demand that we use engineering as sophisticated as our thaumaturgy and oceanology. Miss Coldwine will be translating for us. It's a time-consuming process, so patience will be required.

"We're hoping to be off this rock within a week or two. But that means working hard, and quickly." She was silent for a moment. Her stern voice broke, and she gave an unexpected grin. "Congratulations to all of you. To all of us. This is a great, great day for Armada."

And though most of those gathered had no real idea what was going on, her words had the intended effect, and Tanner joined in with the cheer.

The cactacae crew set up camp around the township. They found empty rooms safe from the she-anophelii, to house the Armadans in smaller groups and greater comfort.

The anophelii were as passionlessly curious as ever, keen to talk, keen to be involved. It was quickly clear that Aum had a dubious reputation: he lived and worked alone. But with the newcomers on the island, all the township's best thinkers wanted to help. The weapons hidden on the *Trident* could not have been less needed. And out of politeness, the Lover allowed them all to join the consultations, though it was only Aum she listened to, and she told Bellis to précis all other contributions.

For the first five hours of the day, Aum sat in discussion with the Armadan scientists. They pored over his book and showed him the damaged appendix, and although, to their astonishment, he had no copies of the work himself, he was able to remember. With the help of an abacus and some of the cryptic engines scattered around, he began to fill in the missing information.

After eating—the cactacae had gathered for their crewmates enough edible plants and fish to supplement the dried rations—the engineers and builders studied with Krüach Aum. In the morning Tanner and his colleagues argued about strain thresholds and engine capacities, drew up rough blueprints, and came up with lists of questions that they put to Aum, shyly, in the afternoon.

The Lover and Tintinnabulum sat in on all sessions, beside Bellis Coldwine. She must be exhausted, Tanner thought with pity. Her writing hand was cramped and covered in ink, but she never complained or asked for a break. She only passed the questions and answers through herself endlessly, scrawling on innumerable reams of paper, translating Aum's written replies into Salt.

* * *

At the end of each day came a short, fearful time as the humans, hotchi, and khepri ran in small groups to wherever they had been lodged. None had to spend more than thirty seconds in the open air, but still they were watched over by rivebow-wielding cactacae and male anophelii protecting their guests from their deadly females with sticks and rocks and klaxons.

There was another engineer already quartered in Tanner's chambers, a woman in the further room. Tanner lay awake for a while.

"There's another one to come," said a cactus voice from outside his window, making them start. "Don't bolt the door."

Tanner blew out his candle and slept. But when, much later, Bellis Coldwine was escorted through the vestibule by a cactus guard, and crept in and bolted the door and stumbled, more exhausted than she had ever been before, through Tanner's dark room into the one beyond, he woke and saw her.

Even in such a hot and strange a place as this, amid all the blood and the threat of violence, even so far from home, routine was powerful.

It took a day, no more, before the Armadans had their routine. The cactacae guards foraged and fished and escorted their fellow crew members, and hauled the Armadans' rubbish, as the anophelii did, to the gorge at the rear of the village, onto the rock shelf and then into the sea.

Every morning Aum and his constantly shifting anophelii hangers-on debated and lectured Armada's scientists, and every afternoon the same with the engineers. It was draining: intensely hot, ceaseless work. Bellis became semiconscious. She became a writing syntactical machine, existing only to parse and translate and scribble questions and read out answers.

For the most part, the meaning she imparted was opaque to her. On rare occasions she had to refer to the glossary in her own High Kettai monograph. She kept it hidden from the anophelii. She did not want to be responsible for them learning another language, breaking out of their prison.

There was no systematicity or coherence to the island's library. Most of the works available were the most abstract theory. The authorities in Kohnid and Dreer Samher kept from their subjects any works they deemed dangerous. There was almost nothing that related the anophelii to the world outside. To find those, the anophelii had to search the ruins of their ancestors' habitations on the other side of the island.

And sometimes they found fables, like the story of the man who raised the avanc.

Stories were self-generating. Little references in abstruse philosophical texts, footnotes, vague folk memories. The mosquito-people had their own etiolated legends.

Bellis did not see a raging curiosity about the world as she had expected. The anophelii seemed intrigued only by the most abstract of questions. But there appeared a glimmer of a more fierce, more earthed interest from Krüach Aum himself.

There are currents in the water, he wrote, *that we can measure, that cannot be born in our seas.*

Aum had started at the highest conceptual level and had proved to himself the reality of the avanc, The Armadan scientists sat spellbound as Bellis falteringly translated his story. From three or four scrawled equations to a page of logical propositions, mining what works of biology, oceanology, dimensional philosophy he could find. A hypothesis. Testing his results, checking the details of the story of the first summoning.

The scientists gasped and nodded excitedly at the equations and notations she copied into Salt.

And after eating, Bellis gathered her strength again and sat with the engineers.

Tanner Sack was one of the first to speak. "What manner of beast is it?" he said. "What'll we need to bind it?"

Many of the engineers were press-ganged, and several were Remade. She was surrounded by criminals, Bellis realized, most from New Crobuzon. They spoke Salt with Dog Fenn and Badside accents, peppered with slum slang she had not heard for months, which made her blink with surprise. Their expertise was as arcane to her as the scientists'. They asked about the strength of steel and iron and various alloys, and the honeycomb structure of the chains below New Crobuzon, and the power of the avanc. Soon matters turned to steam engines and gas turbines, and rockmilk, and the gearwork of a harness, and bits and bridles the size of ships.

She knew it would be to her advantage to make sense of it all, but it was beyond her and she stopped trying.

* * *

That night, as one of the men was taken to his room, a she-anophelii came close to him, screaming gibberish, her hands extended, and a cactus guard shot her dead with his rivebow.

Bellis heard the thwacking report and watched through the window slits. The he-anophelii crooned with their sphincter mouths, and knelt beside her body, and felt her. Her mouth hung open, and her proboscis lolled like a massive stiff tongue. She had fed recently. Her still-plump body was cut almost in half by the rivebow's massive, spinning chakri, and enormous gouts of blood were soaking into the earth and pooling in dusty slicks.

The males shook their heads. A he-anophelius beside her plucked at Bellis' arms and wrote something on her pad.

Not necessary. She did not want to feed.

And then he explained to her, and Bellis' head swam with the monstrousness of it.

Bellis was hungry to be alone. She had spent every minute of the day with others, and it exhausted her. So when the day's tasks had ended, and the scientists were talking together, trying to agree on a direction for the next day's research, she slipped briefly into the smaller side room, thinking it empty. It was not.

She made an apologetic noise and turned away, but Uther Doul spoke quickly.

"Please don't leave," he said.

She turned back, grasping the bag she carried, painfully aware of the weight of the box Silas had given her at the bottom of it. She stood by the doorway, waiting, her face immobile.

Doul had been training. He stood in the room's center, relaxed, holding his sword. It was a straight blade, thin and edged on both sides, something over two feet long. It was not big or ornate or impressive, or carved with puissant signs.

The blade was white. It moved suddenly, flickered like water, soundless and impossible to follow, in a sudden murderous formation. And then it was sheathed, too fast for her to see.

"I'm done here, Miss Coldwine," he said. "The room is yours." But he did not leave.

Bellis nodded thank-you and sat, waiting.

"Let's hope that unfortunate killing won't sour our relations with the mosquito-men," he said.

"It won't," said Bellis. "They hold no grudges when their

womenfolk die. They remember enough to know it's necessary."
He knows this, she thought suddenly, incredulous. *He's making
conversation with me again.*

But even suspicious as she was, the details she had been told
were so ghastly and fascinating that she wanted to share them;
she wanted to make someone else know them.

"They don't know much history, the anophelii, but they know
that the cactacae—the sapwalkers—aren't the only people
across the sea. They know about us, the bloodwalkers, and they
know why usually none of us visit. They've forgotten the details
of the Malarial Queendom, but they have a sense that their
womenfolk . . . did wrong . . . centuries ago." She paused to let
that understatement sink in. "They treat them without . . . affection or distaste."

It was a melancholy pragmatism. They bore their women
no ill will. They coupled with them eagerly enough once in the
year, but they ignored them where possible and killed them if
necessary.

"She wasn't trying to feed, you know," Bellis went on. She
kept her voice neutral. "She was full. They're . . . they're intelligent. It's not that they're mindless. It's the hunger, he told me. It
takes a long, long time for them to starve. They can spend a year
without feeding, screaming ravenous for all those weeks: it's all
they can think about. But when they've fed, when they're full—
really sated—there's a day or two, maybe a week, when the
hunger abates. And that's the time they try to talk.

"He described them coming up from the swamplands, landing
in the square and shrieking at the men, trying to make words.
But they could never learn language, you see. They were always
too hungry. They know what they are."

Bellis caught Uther Doul's eye. She was aware, suddenly, that
he respected her. "They *know.* Once in a while they can stop
themselves, when their bellies are full and their minds clear for
a few days or hours, and they know what it is they do, how they
live. They're as intelligent as you or me, but they grow up too
distracted by starvation to speak, and then once every few months,
for a handful of days, they can concentrate, they try to learn.

"But they don't have the males' mouthparts, obviously, so
they can't make the same sounds. It's only the most inexperi-
enced, the youngest, who try to mimic the anophelii men. With

their proboscises retracted, their mouths are much more like ours." She saw that he understood.

"Their voices sound like ours," she went on softly. "They've never heard language they could mimic before. Full as she was, without language but conscious that she was without it, it must have made her quite giddy to hear us all conversing, in sounds that she herself could make. That's why she came for that man. She was trying to talk to him."

"It's a strange sword," she said a little later.

He hesitated for a tiny moment (the first time, Bellis realized, she had ever seen him uncertain) then drew it with his right hand, held it out for her to see.

Three little buds of metal seemed embedded in the heel of his right hand, connected to the veinlike mass of wires under his sleeve, running down his side to a little pack on his belt. The handle of the sword was padded in leather or skin, but a patch was bare metal, which the nodes in his flesh touched when he held the sword.

The blade was not, as Bellis had supposed, stained metal.

"May I touch it?"

Doul nodded. She tapped the flat of the blade with a finger-nail. It sounded dull and unresonant.

"It's ceramic," he said. "More like china than iron."

The edges of the sword did not have the matte sheen of a sharpened blade. They were the same featureless white as the flat (a white stained fractionally yellow, like teeth or ivory).

"It'll cut deeper than bone," Doul said quietly in that melodious voice. "This is not a ceramic you've seen or used before. It won't bend or give—it has no flex—but nor is it brittle. And it's strong."

"How strong?"

Uther looked at her, and she felt his respect again. Something inside her responded.

"Diamond," he said. He sheathed his blade (with another exquisite, instantaneous motion).

"Where does it come from?" she said, but he did not answer her. "Is it from the same place as you?" She was surprised by her own persistence and . . . what? Bravery?

She did not feel as if she was being brave. Instead, she felt as if

she and Uther Doul understood each other. He turned to her
from the doorway and inclined his head in farewell.

"No," he said. "It would be . . . hard to be less accurate." For
the first time, she saw a smile take him, very quickly.

"Good night," he said.

Bellis took the solitary moments she had craved, steeped herself in her own company. She breathed deeply. And finally, she
allowed herself to wonder about Uther Doul. She wondered why
he was speaking to her, tolerating her company, respecting her, it
seemed.

She could not read him, but she realized that she felt a faint
connection to him, something woven out of shared cynicism, de-
tachment, strength, understanding, and —yes—attraction. She
did not know when or why she had stopped fearing him. She had
no idea what he was doing.

CHAPTER TWENTY-FIVE

Two days became three, and four, and then a week had passed,
every day in the inexact light of that little room. Bellis felt as if
her eyes were atrophying, only able to see the earth shades inside
the mountain, surrounded by halfhearted, edgeless shadows.

In the night, she would make the same short run across the
open air (looking up eagerly to see naked light and colors, even
the scorched colors of that sky). The mosquito whine of the
women came at her sometimes, to her abject terror, and sometimes it did not. But always she huddled in the shelter of the cactus warrior or scabmettler who protected her.

Sometimes she could hear the scuffling and muttering of the
she-anophelii outside the long window shafts. The mosquito-
women were appalling, and strong, and their hunger was a force
of almost elemental power. They would kill any bloodwalkers
who landed, might drain an entire ship in a day and then lie

bloated on the beach. For all that, there was something indelibly pathetic about the women of this ghetto island.

Bellis did not know what chain of circumstances had allowed the Malarial Queendom to exist, but they were unthinkable to her. It was impossible to imagine these shrieking creatures on other shores, their petty terrorism despoiling half a continent.

The food was as monotonous as the setting. Bellis' tongue was quite numb to the fish-and-grass taste, and she chewed stolidly on whatever rust-nourished sealife the cactacae caught in the bay, whatever edible weed they uprooted.

The Samheri officers tolerated them uneasily, but did not trust them. Captain Sengka continued to curse the cactus Armadans in rapid Sunglari as turncoats and renegades.

With each morning's fevered calculations, the scientists became more and more excited. The stacks of their notes and calculations grew massive. The ember that distinguished Krüach Aum from his compatriots—which Bellis thought of as true curiosity—waxed.

Bellis struggled but did not fail. She was translating now without even trying to understand what she said, just passing on what was said as if she were an analytical engine breaking down and reconstituting formulae. She knew that to the men and women hunched over the table, debating with Aum, she was more or less invisible.

She focused on voices as if they were music: the measured sonority of Tintinnabulum, the staccato excitement of Faber, the seesawing oboe tones of the bio-philosopher whose name Bellis could never remember.

Aum was tireless. Bellis felt faintly dismayed by exhaustion when she sat with Tanner Sack and the other engineers in the afternoon, but Aum continued without apparent difficulty, shifting his attention from the conceptual problems and philosophy of the avancs to practical issues of bait, and control, and capture of something the size of an island. And when the failing light and general fatigue forced the day's work to end, it was never Aum who suggested it.

Bellis could not fail to realize that research problems were being overcome, one by one. It had not taken long for Aum to rewrite his data appendix, and then for the Armadans to point out errors and miscalculations, holes in his research. The excitement of the scientists was palpable; they were almost drunk on it. It was a problem—a project—of unthinkable scale, and yet one by one, the problems, the objections and obstacles, were being overcome.

They were teetering on the edge of something extraordinary. The fact of its possibility was utterly giddying.

Bellis did not fraternize with the Armadans, but she could not spend her days without speaking to them. "There you go. Get that down you," one might say, handing her a bowl of dull stew, and to refuse a word of thanks would have been a quite unnecessary violence.

Occasionally in the evenings—amid the Armadans' dice and singsongs, which entranced the sough-voiced anophelii—she found herself on the edge of conversations.

The only one she knew by name was Tanner Sack. The fact that she had traveled above him on the *Terpsichoria,* free while he had been incarcerated, had poisoned any chance of trust between them, she supposed, though she had the sense that he was an open man. He was one of those who would make a little attempt to include her when he spoke. Bellis now came closer than she had ever been to Armadan society. She was allowed to listen to stories.

Most were about secrets. She heard about the chains that dangled below Armada: ancient, hidden for tens of decades; years' worth of work, and many ships' worth of metal. "Long before the Lovers made up their minds what to do with them," the teller of one story said, "this was tried before."

Uther Doul was prey to the storytellers, too.

"He comes from the land of the dead," someone said once, conspiratorially. "Old Doul was born more'n three thousand years ago. It was him started the Contumancy. He was born a slave in the Ghosthead Empire, and he stole that sword, Mightblade, and fought free, and destroyed the empire. He died. But a warrior like him, greatest fighter there's ever been, he's the only man was able to fight his way out of the shadeworld, back to the living."

Those listening made good-humored, derisory noises. They did not believe it, of course, but then they did not know what to believe about Uther Doul.

Doul himself spent his days quietly. The main person whose company he sought, the only one who came anything close to a friend, seemed to be Hedrigall. The cactus aeronaut and the human warrior often talked quietly at the edge of the room. They muttered in quick undertones, as if they were ashamed of friendship.

There was only one other person with whom Uther Doul was prepared to spend time, and to whom he talked, and that was Bellis.

It had not taken her long to realize that the apparently chance meetings, the brief pleasantries, were not coincidental. In an elliptical and tentative way, he was trying to make friends with her.

Bellis could not make sense of him, and she did not try to second-guess him. She trusted herself to cope. Though a sense of danger always remained, part of her enjoyed the encounters—the formal air, the slightest sense of flirtation. It was hardly coquetry. She did not compromise her dignity with simpering suggestiveness. But she was drawn to him, and she scolded herself for that.

Bellis thought of Silas. Not with any sense of guilt or betrayal—the idea of that made her pout in disdain. But she remembered the time he had taken her to the glad' fight, specifically to see Uther Doul. *That's what's trying to stop us leaving,* he had told her, and she could not afford to forget it. *Why,* she asked herself, *would you risk spending time with Doul?*

Deep in her bag, she felt the weight of the box Silas had given her. She was acutely aware that she had a job to do on this island (*one she must plan soon*). It placed her very directly against Doul.

Bellis realized why she let their conversations continue. It was rare that she felt herself in the company of someone with as much or more control over his own reactions to the world, and its reception of them, as she had. Uther Doul was one. That was why they respected each other. To speak simply, without smiling, to someone else with the same manner; to know that of her would have intimidated most people but did not fluster him, and that the same was true the other way round: that was rare, and a pleasure.

Bellis felt that they should be looking out over a city, at night. They should be on a balcony. They should be wandering through backstreets, their hands in their pockets.

Instead they were in a small room that jutted off the central hall. They stood near one of the window slits, and Bellis was desperately sick of the colors of rock. She stared at the little patch of night-lit black hungrily.

"Do you understand it all?" Bellis asked.

Doul moved his head ambiguously. "Enough," he said slowly, "to know that they're close. I have very different expertise. My research will come after this. Your job will change soon. You'll be asked to start teaching him Salt."

Bellis blinked, and Doul nodded.

"It's a breach of Samheri and Kohnid laws, but we're not bringing new knowledge to the island. Aum will come with us."

Of course, thought Bellis.

"So . . ." Doul continued. "So we return." His wonderful voice was low. "With our prize. It's a monumental project, what we're attempting. Armada's been stationed at a seam of oil and rock-milk since we left. Drilling, storing what's needed for the invocation. We'll make for the sinkholes. And then we use our fuel and our bait and the shackles we'll build, and so on, and we . . . hook ourselves an avanc." It sounded so bathetic. There was a long silence after that.

"And then," said Doul very softly, "our work begins."

Bellis did not speak.

I knew you were playing games with me, she thought coolly. *What work begins?*

It did not surprise her. It was no great shock to realize that the avanc was only the start of the Lovers' project, that there was more going on, that there was some grand scheme behind all this effort, an agenda to which virtually no one—certainly not she— was party.

Except that now, in one way, she was.

She did not understand why Doul was telling her. His motives were impenetrable. All Bellis knew was that she was being used. She did not even resent it, she realized—she would expect no less.

The following morning, the sun came up on the body of one of the human engineers. His skeleton was constricted by his newly tight skin: his arms were curled tight around his chest, and his hands were claws; his spine was arced as if with great age.

In the cavity below his ribs, his skin clung to the rubbery piping of his drained intestines. His eyes were half-shriveled like drying fruit, baking in the sun. The gums in his open mouth were almost as white as his teeth.

Surrounded by crooning mosquito-men, Hedrigall turned him over (*the body rocking on its curved spine like a wooden horse*) and found the fat hole between his ribs where the she-anophelius had punctured him.

The Armadans had become complacent. The death dismayed them.

"Stupid fucker," Bellis heard Tanner Sack mutter. "What was he fucking doing?" She watched him turn from the window. He did not want to see Hedrigall bending down and with a gruff tenderness picking up the pathetic remains, cradling the skin-and-bone man and walking out of the village, to bury him.

But even that tragedy could not dampen the agitation in the air. Even in that shock and grief, Bellis could feel an excitement among the scientists. Even those who had known the engineer felt their sadness vie with a very different feeling.

"Look at this!" hissed Théobal, a pirate and a theoretical oceanologer. He waved a thick document, pages sewn together at one end. "We've damn well got it! This is the math we need, the thaumaturgy, the biology."

Bellis looked at the papers with a vague astonishment. *All of that came through me,* she thought.

When Aum entered, they had Bellis write, *We need you to help us. Will you leave this place and learn our language and help us call this avanc from the sea? Will you come with us?*

And though it was almost impossible to read that sphinctermouthed face, Bellis was sure that she saw fear and joy in Aum's eyes.

He said yes, of course.

The news passed quickly around the village, and the heanophelii came in great numbers to croon with Aum and hiss their feelings. Their happiness? Bellis wondered. Their jealousy? Grief?

Some of them looked at the Armadan party with something akin to hunger, she thought. Their abstraction from the world was tenuous, and could be broken, as Aum appeared to have broken his.

"We leave in two days," said the Lover, and there was a rush of blood from Bellis' chest so quick it hurt her. She had completely neglected her commission. New Crobuzon relied on her. She felt despondency take her and begin to pull her down. *This will not happen,* she thought quickly. *It is not too late.*

The crew were delighted at the thought of leaving, of escaping this cloying air and those voracious women. Bellis, however, was desperate for more time, for a few more days. She thought again of that dried-up corpse, but not for very long. She was terrified of despairing.

That night as the scabmettlers and cactacae escorted their vulnerable comrades to their beds, she sat alone, massaging her hand, breathing deep, trying fearfully to work out some plan, some way to get to the Dreer Samher ship. For brief moments she considered deserting. Demanding Captain Sengka's mercy and staying on board. Or stowing away. Anything to see New Crobuzon again. But she knew she could not. As soon as she was missed, the Lover would order the Dreer Samher ships searched, and the Samheri would not refuse them. And then she would be caught, and her package would be undelivered, and New Crobuzon would be in terrible danger.

And besides, she cautiously let herself remember, she still had no way of reaching the Samheri ship.

Bellis heard a faint sound from one of the adjoining rooms. She came closer to the closed door.

It was the Lover's voice. She could not hear the words, but the firm, hard voice was unmistakable. She sounded as if she was singing gently, like a mother to her child. Hushed and very intense, there was something in those sounds that made Bellis shiver and close her eyes. She was listening to a concentration of emotion that almost made her head swim.

Bellis leaned against the wall and heard emotions that were not hers. She could not tell if they affirmed love, or the most draining kind of obsession. But still she waited, her eyes on the door, parasitic like the mosquito-women, steeping herself in stolen feelings.

And after some minutes, when the sounds were done and Bellis had moved away, the Lover emerged. Her heavy features were calm. She saw Bellis watching her, and met her eyes without shame or pugnacity. Blood was leaking sluggish as molasses from a new wound in the Lover's face, a long split in the skin from the right corner of her lip, under her chin and down toward the hollow of her neck.

The Lover had stanched most of the blood, and only a few fat drops welled up like sweat, broke, and ran, marking her skin.

The women watched each other for seconds. Bellis felt as if they shared no language. The gulf between them giddied her.

Chapter Twenty-six

That night Bellis roused herself many hours after everyone had gone to sleep.

She removed the sweat-damp sheet that covered her and stood. The air was still warm, even in these dark hours. She picked up Silas' package from below her pillow, pulled aside the curtain, and walked slow and quiet through the room where Tanner lay wrapped in shadows on his pallet. When she reached the wooden door she leaned her head against it and felt its grain on her skin.

Bellis was afraid.

She peered very carefully through the window and saw a cactus-man guard wandering through the deserted square, from doorway to doorway, checking them idly, moving on. He was some way from her, and she thought she could open the door and run without him seeing or hearing her.

And then?

Bellis could see nothing in the sky. There was no threatening whine, no voracious insectile woman with claw-hands and jutting mouth, hungry for her blood. She put her hand on the bolt and waited—waited to hear or see one of the she-anophelii, for confirmation, so that she could avoid her (*easier to hide if you know where it is*), and she thought about that leather-and-bone sack she had seen that morning, which had once been a man. She froze, her hand like wire on the door.

"What you doing?"

The words came in a hard whisper from behind her. Bellis spun, her hands gripping her shift. Tanner had sat up and was staring at her from within his dark alcove.

She moved a little, and he stood. She saw the odd encumbrances of tentacles spill from his midriff. He faced her, his stance tense and suspicious. He looked as if he was about to attack her. And yet he whispered, and something in that reassured her.

"I'm sorry," she said quietly. He stood in the entranceway to hear her, and his face was as hard and untrusting as she had ever seen it. "I didn't mean to wake you," she whispered. "I just . . . I had to . . ." And her inventiveness fled her: she did not know what she would say she had had to do. Her words dried up.

"What are you doing?" he said. Slow and angry and curious, he spoke to her in Ragamoll.

"I'm sorry," she said again, and shook her head. "I felt . . ." She held her breath and looked at him again, her eyes steady.

"Can't open that bolt," he said.

He was looking at the package in her hands, and with an effort, Bellis did not try to hide it or move her fingers nervously, but kept it in plain view as if it was nothing important.

"What is it, call of nature? Was that what it was? You'll have to use the pot, lady. You can't be shamed of things like that here. You saw what happened to William."

She straightened then and nodded, keeping her face immobile, and walked back to where her bed lay. "Sleep better, won't you," said Tanner Sack behind her, and settled himself slowly. At the curtain between the rooms, Bellis turned briefly to look at him. He sat up, obviously waiting and listening, and setting her teeth she pulled the curtain to.

For a few moments there was silence. Then Tanner heard the sound of a tiny little spray, a few grudging drops, and he grinned humorlessly into his sheet. A few feet from him, separated by the curtain, Bellis stood up from the chamberpot, her face set and furious.

Through her humiliated anger, she grasped at something. Began to shape a hope, an idea.

The next day was the Armadans' last full day on the island.

The scientists put together their reams of paper and their sketches, talking and laughing like children. Even the taciturn Tintinnabulum and his companions seemed buoyed up. All around Bellis schedules and plans were taking shape, and it seemed like the avanc was caught in all but fact.

The Lover flitted into the discussions and out again, a heavy smile on her, her new cut red and shining. Only Uther Doul was impassive—Uther Doul and Bellis herself. Their eyes met, across the room. Motionless, the only still points in the bustling hall, they shared a moment of some superior feeling akin to scorn.

All day, the anophelii came and went, their sedate, monkish manner shaken. They were very sorry to see the newcomers go, realizing they were soon to be bereft of the sudden influx of theories and impressions that they had brought.

Bellis watched Krüach Aum and saw how like a child the old anophelius was. He watched his new companions packing what bags and clothes and books they had brought, and he tried to copy them, though he had nothing. He left the hall and returned a little while later with a bundle of rags and edges of scrap paper that he collected and tied together at the top in a crude imitation of a traveling sack. It made Bellis shiver to watch.

Deep in her own bag, Bellis could feel Silas' package: the letters, the necklace, the box, the wax, the ring. *Tonight,* she told herself, and felt panic. *Tonight, come what may.*

For the rest of the short day she tracked the sun's passage. In the late afternoon, when the light had become thick and slow and every shape bled shadows, dread overtook her. Because she realized that there was no way she could cross past the swamps and the territories of the murderous mosquito-women.

Bellis looked up in alarm as the door was thrown open.

Captain Sengka stepped forward into the room, flanked by two of his crew.

The three cactacae stood at the entrance, their arms crossed. They were big men, even for their race. Their vegetable muscles bunched around their sashes and loincloths. Light gleamed on their jewelry and on their weapons.

Sengka pointed his massive finger at Krüach Aum. "This anophelius," he announced, "is going nowhere."

No one moved. After several still seconds, the Lover stepped forward.

Sengka spoke before she could. "What did you think, Captain?" he said, disgusted. "Captain? Is that what I should fucking call you, woman? What did you think? I've turned a blind sunfucked eye on your presence here, which I did not have to do. I've put up with your communication with the natives, which is a

breach of security risking a new fucking Malarial Age . . ." The
Lover shook her head impatiently at this hyperbole, but Sengka
continued. "I've waited patiently for you to get the fuck off this
island, and what? You think you can smuggle one of these creatures off-land without my knowledge? You think I'd let you go?

"Your vessels will be searched," he said decisively. "Any contraband lifted from Machinery Beach, any anophelii books or
treatises, any heliotypes of the island will be confiscated." He indicated Aum again and shook his head incredulously. "Have you
read history, woman? You want to take an anophelius *out*?"

Krüach Aum watched the altercation with wide eyes.

"Captain Sengka," said the Lover. Bellis had never seen her
more alive with presence, more magnificent. "No one would
ever criticize your concern for safety, or your commitment to
your commission. But you know as well as I that the male anophelius is a harmless herbivore. We have no intention of bringing out any but this one."

"I will not have it!" Sengka shouted. "Sunshit, this system is
absolute, and it's absolute because we can learn the lessons of
history. No anophelii are to leave this island. That is a condition
of their being allowed to live. There are no exceptions."

"I'm tiring of this, Captain." Bellis could not but admire the
Lover's calm, cold and hard as iron. "Krüach Aum is leaving
with us. We have no wish to antagonize Dreer Samher, but we
are taking this anophelius." She turned her back on him and began to walk away.

"My men on Machinery Beach," he said, and she paused, then
turned back to him. He drew a huge pistol and held it loose, dangling down. The Armadans were quite still. "Trained cactacae
fighters," Sengka said. "Defy me and you will not leave this island alive." So slowly that the motion did not seem threatening,
he raised his gun and pointed it at the Lover. "This anophelius . . .
Aum, you said . . . he is coming with me."

The guards all around the room were poised on the edge of
motion. Their hands fluttered over their swords and bows and
pistols. Scabmettlers in cracked armor and huge cactacae, their
eyes moved quickly from Sengka to the Lover and back again.

The Lover did not look at any of them. Instead, Bellis saw her
catch the eye of Uther Doul.

Doul walked forward, placing himself between the Lover and
the gun.

"Captain Sengka," he said in that beautiful voice. He stood still, the pistol now trained on his head, looking up at the cactus-man, more than a foot taller and vastly more massive than he. He stared into the barrel of the gun as he spoke, as if it were Sengka's eye. "It falls to me to bid you good-bye."

The captain looked down and seemed momentarily uncertain. He drew back his free hand then, his biceps knotting enormously under his skin, his meaty fist tensed and ready to swing, bristling with thorns. He was moving slowly, obviously hoping not to hit Doul, but to intimidate him into submission.

Doul reached out with both his hands, as if supplicating. He paused, and there was a sudden snapping motion of such speed that Bellis—who had expected it, who had known that something of the sort would happen—could not possibly follow it. Sengka was reeling back, shocked, holding his throat where Doul had jabbed him with stiff fingers (not hard but like a warning, finding a space between those vicious spines and taking the breath from him). Doul held the gun now, still pointing toward his own skull, trapped between his flat palms like something granted him in prayer. He kept his eyes on Sengka and whispered to him, words that Bellis could not hear.

(*Bellis' heart is slamming. Doul's actions shatter her. Whether an attack is brutal or muted, the motion itself, its preternatural speed and perfection, makes it seem like an assault on the order of things, as if time and gravity can no more withstand Uther Doul than flesh.*)

The two cactacae standing behind Sengka stepped forward, sluggish and outraged. They reached to their belts, drawing weapons, and the gun held in Doul's frozen applause flickered and faced them, and flickered again and was clenched in his outstretched right hand, pointed directly first at one and then (*instantaneously*) the other sailor.

(*There is no movement. The three cactacae are appalled at this velocity and control that border on thaumaturgy.*)

Doul shifted again, the gun leaving his fingers and spinning out of reach. His white sword was in his hand. There were two reports, and Sengka's crew members yelled in pain, in quick succession, their hands snapping away from their weapons, now clutched in front of them, wrists split.

The sword's tip was at Sengka's throat now, and the cactus-man stared at Doul with fear and hatred.

"I hit your men with the flat of my blade, Captain," said Doul. "Don't make me show you the edge."

Sengka and his men backed away, retreating out of his range, through the door and into the last of the daylight. Doul waited by the entrance, his sword extended into the open air.

All around the room a sound was building, a rhythmic muttering, a triumphant, awed bark. Bellis remembered it. She had heard it before.

"Doul!" the men and women of Armada chanted. "Doul! Doul! Doul!"

As they had at the glad' circus, as if he were a deity, as if he could grant them wishes, as if they were chanting in church. Their adorations were not loud, but they were fervent and grimly joyous, and ceaseless, and in perfect time. They enraged Sengka, who heard in them a taunt.

He glared back at Doul, framed in the doorway.

"Look at you," he shouted furiously. "You coward, you pig-man, you fucking *cheat*! What demon did you let fuck you in return for those skills, pig-man? You won't leave this fucking place."

He was silent then, suddenly, his voice collapsing, as Uther Doul stepped out of the room, into what the cactacae had thought of as the safety of the open air. The Armadans gasped, but most of them kept chanting.

Bellis was at the door immediately, ready to slam it against any she-anophelii. She saw Doul stalking without hesitation toward Nurjhitt Sengka, his blade held poised. She could hear him speaking.

"I know you're angry, Captain," he said softly. "Control yourself, though. There's no danger in Aum coming with us, and you know that. It'll be his last contact with this island. You came to forbid it because you felt your authority leaching from you. That was a miscalculation, but so far only two of your men have seen this."

The three cactacae were ranged a little way around him, their eyes meeting and parting again, wondering if they could rush him. Bellis was shoved aside suddenly as Hedrigall and several other Armadan cactacae and scabmettlers came to stand outside. They did not approach the stand-off.

"You will not stop us leaving, Captain," Doul went on. "You don't want to risk war with Armada. And besides, you know as well as I that it's not my crew or even my boss you want to punish, it's me. And that . . . ," he finished softly, "will not happen."

Bellis heard the sound, then: the high drone of anophelii women approaching. She gasped, and heard others gasp, too. Sengka and his men began to look up shiftily, as if trying to avoid being seen.

Uther Doul's eyes did not move from Captain Sengka's face. A scudding shape cut across the sky, and Bellis pinched her mouth closed. The chant of "Doul!" had dwindled, but it continued almost subliminally. No one yelled out to him that he was in danger. They all knew that if they had heard the anophelii, *he* certainly had.

As the sound of their wings approached, Doul moved closer to the captain, suddenly, till he was staring very close into Sengka's eyes.

"Do we understand each other, Captain?" he said, and Sengka bellowed and tried to grab Doul and crush him in a thorned bear hug. But Doul's hands flickered in Sengka's face then swung down to block his arm, and then Doul was standing a few feet back, and the cactus-man was doubled up and cursing as sap dripped from his smashed nose. Sengka's crewmen watched with a kind of appalled indecision.

Doul turned his back to them then, and raised his sword to meet the first of the mosquito-women who came for him. Bellis stopped breathing. The she-anophelius was suddenly visible, plummeting through screaming air, a starved shape. The jag erupted from her mouth. She skirted over the earth, irregular and very fast, her arms outstretched, slavering and starving.

For long moments she was the only thing that moved.

Uther Doul was still, waiting for her, his sword held vertically on his right. And then suddenly, when the anophelius was so close that Bellis thought she could smell her, so that her proboscis seemed to be touching Doul's flesh, his arm was suddenly stretched across his body, the sword still vertical and immobile but on the other side of him, and the mosquito-woman's head and left forearm were tumbling free and bloody across the dry earth as her body crashed to the ground beyond him. Thick, sluggish gore streaked Doul's blade, and the corpse and the dust.

Doul had moved again, and was turning, leaping up, reaching with his hands as if he were plucking a fruit, spitting the second she-anophelius (*which Bellis had not even seen*) as she flew over his head, and then twisting, pulling her out of the air on the end of his blade and flicking her to the ground, where she lay screaming and drooling and still trying to reach him.

He dispatched her quickly, to Bellis' appalled relief.

And then the sky was quiet, and Doul had turned again to Sengka and was wiping his blade.

"This is the last you'll hear of me, or any of us, Captain Sengka," he assured the cactus-man, who stared at him with more fear than hatred now, and whose eyes took in the bloody corpses of those two mosquito-women, each stronger than a man. "Go now. This can end here."

Then again the hateful sound of the she-anophelii, and Bellis almost cried out at the thought of more carnage. The humming grew closer, and Sengka's eyes grew wide. He stood for a moment longer, looking quickly around him for the ravenous she-anophelii, a part of him still hoping that they might kill Doul, but knowing that they would not.

Doul did not move, no matter that the sound grew closer.

"Sun*shit*!" Sengka shouted, and turned away, defeated, waving his hands to bring his men with him. They walked quickly away.

Bellis knew that they wanted to get away before any more of the she-anophelii attacked and were killed. Not because they cared for the terrible woman-things, but because the sight of Doul's mastery was appalling to them.

Uther Doul waited until the three cactus-people had disappeared. Only then did he turn, calmly, resheathing his sword, and walk back to the room.

The sound of wings was very close by that time, but mercifully, they were a little too slow, and they did not reach him. Bellis heard the screaming wings dissipate as the mosquito-women scattered.

Doul reentered the room, and the shout of his name went up again, proud and insistent like a battle cry. And he acknowledged it this time, bowed his head and raised his arms to the height of his shoulders, his palms outstretched. He stood immobile, lowering his eyes, as if adrift on the sound.

And it was night again, the last night, and Bellis was in her room, on her bed of dusty straw, Silas' package in her hands.

* * *

Tanner Sack did not sleep. He was too wired from the excitement of the day, the fights. He was caught up in astonishment at what he now knew, what he had learned from Krüach Aum. Only tiny fragments of a much larger theory, but his new knowledge, the scale of the commission expected of him, was dizzying. Too dizzying to let him sleep.

And, besides, he was waiting for something.

It came between one and two in the morning. The curtain to the women's room was drawn back, very gently, and Bellis Coldwine crept across the room.

Tanner twisted his mouth in a hard smile. He had no idea what it was that she had been doing the previous night, but it was obvious that pissing had not been on her mind. He gave a half smile, half wince as he thought of his little cruelty, forcing her into such a performance. He had felt somewhat guilty afterward, though the thought of the prim, tight Miss Coldwine squeezing out a few drops for his benefit had kept him grinning all the next day.

He had known then that her business, whatever it was, was unfinished, and that she would come back.

Tanner watched her. She did not know he was awake. He could see her standing by the door in her white underdress, peering through the window. She was holding something. It would be that leather packet she had tried not to draw his attention to the previous night.

He felt curiosity about her actions, and a spark of cruelty, some redirected revenge for his mistreatment on the *Terpsichoria* settling on Bellis. Those feelings had stopped him from informing Doul or the Lover of her actions.

Bellis stood and looked, then hunkered down and rummaged silently in her package, and stood and looked again and bent and stood and so on. Her hand hovered ineffectually around the bolt.

Tanner Sack stood and walked soundlessly toward her; she was too engrossed with her indecision to notice him. He stood a few feet behind her, watching her, irritated and amused by her irresolution, until he had had enough and he spoke.

"Got to go again, have you?" he whispered sardonically, and Bellis spun around to face him, and he saw with shock and shame that she was crying.

His mean little smile disappeared instantly.

Tears were pouring from Bellis Coldwine's eyes, but she did

not utter a sob. She was breathing hard, and each deep breath shook and threatened to break, but she was quite silent. Her expression was fierce and controlled, her eyes intense and bloodshot. She looked like something cornered.

Furiously, she wiped her eyes and nose.

Tanner tried to speak, but her glare shook him, and it was only with an effort that he could utter words. "Now, there, now," he whispered. "I didn't mean anything by that . . ."

"*What* . . . do you *want*?" she whispered.

Chastened but not cowed, Tanner looked down at the package in her hands.

"What's the matter with you, then?" he said. "What's that? Trying to stow away, are you? Hoping the Samheri'll take you home?" As he spoke he felt his anger growing again, until he had to struggle to control it. "Want to tell Mayor Rudgutter how badly you was treated on the pirate ship, is that it, miss? Let them know about Armada so's they can try to hunt us down, and gather me and the likes of me and put us back in the fucking shit below the decks? Slaves for the colonies?"

Bellis was staring at him in a dignified, tearful rage. There was a long pause, and below the skin of her still, set face, Tanner saw her make a resolution.

"*Read it,*" she hissed suddenly. She slapped a long letter into his hands and slumped against the door.

" 'Status seven'?" he muttered. "What the fuck is a Code Arrowhead?" Bellis said nothing. She had stopped crying. She stared at him, sullen as a child (*but now there is something in the back of her eyes, some hope*).

Tanner continued, hacking his way through the thickets of code and finding trails of sense, places where meaning became suddenly and shockingly clear.

" 'Arrival of kissing magi'?" he whispered incredulously. " 'Canker to be clotted by wormtroopers'? 'Algae-bombs'? What the fuck is this? This is about some fucking invasion! What the fuck *is this*?" Bellis watched him.

"This," she echoed him remorselessly, "is about some fucking invasion."

She kept him in a cruel silence for several seconds and then told him.

* * *

He leaned back, gripping the paper, staring sightlessly at its seal, running his fingers through the chain on Silas' tag.

"You're right about me, you know," said Bellis. They whispered, to keep the woman in the other room from waking. Bellis' voice sounded dead. "You are right," she repeated. "Armada is not my place. I can see you. You think, 'I wouldn't trust that uptown bitch.' "

Tanner shook his head, trying to disagree, but she would not let him.

"You're right. I'm not trustworthy. I want to go home, Tanner Sack. And if I could open a door and walk through and be in Brock Marsh, or Salacus Fields, or Mafaton or Ludmead or anywhere in New Crobuzon, then by *Jabber* I would walk through it."

Tanner almost winced at her intensity.

"But I can't," she went on. "And yes, there was a time when I imagined rescue. I imagined the navy sailing in to whisk me home. But there are two things in the way of that.

"I want to go home, Sack. But . . ." She hesitated and slumped a little. "But there were others on the *Terpsichoria* without that urge. And I know what it would mean . . . for you, and for the others . . . for all the Crobuzoner Remade . . . to be . . . 'rescued.' " She turned her eyes to him in an unflinching stare. "And you can believe me or not, as you like, but that's not something I want. I have no illusions about New Crobuzon, about the transportation. You know nothing about my circumstances, Tanner Sack. You don't know anything about what forced me onto that fucking loathsome ship.

"No matter how I want to return home," she said, "I know that what's best for me isn't so for you, and I'd not willingly be party to that. And that's true," she said suddenly, as if in surprise, as if to herself. "I lost that argument. I concede. That is true."

She hesitated, then looked up at him.

"And even if you think I'm full of nothing but lies, Mr. Sack, there's always the second factor: *There is nothing I can do.* I can't stow away with the Samheri; I can't give directions to the New Crobuzon navy. I'm stuck with Armada. I'm damn well *stuck* with it."

"So who's Silas Fennec?" he said. "And what is this?" He waved the letter.

"Fennec is a Crobuzoner agent, no less marooned than me.

Only with information," she said coldly. "Information about a fucking invasion."

"You want it to fall?" she demanded. "Godspit, I understand you've no love for the place. Why in Jabber's name should you have? But do you really want New Crobuzon to *fall*?" Her voice was suddenly very hard. "Have you no friends left there? No family? There's nothing left in the whole fucking city you'd preserve? You wouldn't mind it falling to The Gengris?"

A little to the south of Wynion Street, in Pelorus Fields, was a tiny market. It appeared in a mews behind a warehouse on Shundays and Dustdays. It was too small to have a name.

It was a shoe market. Secondhand, new, stolen, imperfect, and perfect. Clogs, slippers, boots, and others.

For some years it had been Tanner's favorite place in New Crobuzon. Not that he bought any more shoes than anyone else, but he enjoyed walking the short length of the mews, past the tables of leather and canvas, listening to the shouts of the vendors.

There were several small cafés on that little street, and he had known the proprietors and the regulars well. When he had no work and a little money, he might spend hours in the ivy-covered Boland's Coffees, arguing and idling with Boland and Yvan Curlough and Sluchnedsher the vodyanoi, taking pity on mad Spiral Jacobs and buying him a drink.

Tanner had spent many days there, in a haze of smoke and tea and coffee, watching the shoes and the hours ebb away through Boland's imperfect windows. He could live without those days, for Jabber's sake. It wasn't as if they were a drug. It wasn't as if he lay awake missing them at night.

But they were what he thought of, instantly, when Bellis asked him if he cared whether the city fell.

Of course the thought of New Crobuzon and all those people he knew (whom he had not thought of for some time), and all the places he had been, all broken and destroyed and drowned by the grindylow (figures who existed only in a nightmare, shadow form in his head), of course that appalled him. Of course he would not wish for that.

But the immediacy of his own reaction astonished him. There was nothing intellectual, nothing thought out about it. He looked through the window into that sweltering hot island night and remembered looking through those other windows, of thick and mottled glass, onto the shoe market.

"Why didn't you tell the Lovers? Whyn't you think they'd help try to get a message to the city?"

Bellis shucked her shoulders in a false, silent laugh.

"Do you really think," she said slowly, "that they would care? Do you think they'd put themselves out? Send a boat, maybe? Pay for a message? You think they'd risk uncovering themselves? You think they'd go to all that effort, just to save a city that would destroy them if it had the slightest chance?"

"You're wrong," he said, uncertain. "There's enough Crobuzoners among the press-ganged who'd care."

"Nobody *knows*," she hissed. "Only Fennec and I know, and if we spread the word, they'll discredit us, write us off as troublemakers, dump us at sea, burn the message. Godsdammit, what if you're wrong?" She stared at him until he shifted in her gaze. "You think they'll care? You think they won't let New Crobuzon drown? If we told them and you were wrong, it would be over—our only chance gone. Do you see what's at stake? You want to risk it? Really?"

With a hollowness in his throat, Tanner realized that what she said made sense.

"And that is why I'm sitting here crying like a cretin," she spat. "Because getting this message, and this proof, and this bribe to the Samheri is the only chance we have to save New Crobuzon. Do you see? To *save* it. And I've been standing here, frozen, because I can't think of a way to get to the beach. Because I'm terrified of those woman-things out there. I do *not* want to die, and dawn is coming, and I can't go out there, and I have to. And it's more than a mile to the beach." She looked at him carefully, and then away. "I don't know what to do."

They could hear the cactacae guard walking through the moonlit township, from house to house. Tanner and Bellis sat facing each other, leaning against the walls, their eyes fixed.

Tanner looked again at the letter he held. There was the seal. He held out his hands, and Bellis gave him the rest of her little bundle. She kept her face composed. He read the letter to the Samheri pirates. The reward was generous, he thought, but hardly excessive if it meant saving New Crobuzon.

Saving it, keeping it safe from harm.

He went through each letter again, line by line. Armada was not mentioned.

He looked at the necklace with its little tag, its name and symbol. There was nothing to link this to Armada. Nothing to tell the Crobuzoner government where to find him. Bellis watched him from her silence. She knew what he was. He could sense the hope in her. He picked up the big ring, examined its intricate inverted seal, troughs for peaks and vice versa. He felt hypnotized by it. It meant more than one thing to him, like New Crobuzon.

The quiet went on while he turned the package over and over in his hands, ran his fingers over the nub of sealing wax, and the ring, and the long letter with its dreadful warning.

There was his Remaking to remember, but that was not all. There were places and people. There was more than one side to New Crobuzon.

Tanner Sack was loyal to Garwater, and he felt the passion of that loyalty inside him, beside a sad affection for New Crobuzon— a kind of melancholic regretful fondness. For the shoe market, and for other things. The two emotions flickered inside him and circled each other like fish.

He thought of his old city all blasted, destroyed.

"It's true," he whispered slowly. "It's a mile or more to Machinery Beach, down the hill past the swamps and all that, where the women live."

He jerked his head, suddenly indicating the other end of the township, the cleft in the rocks with the waves like oil below.

"But it's only a few yards from here to the sea."

INTERLUDE V

Tanner Sack

It don't take much.

Keep my eyes on the window (Bellis Coldwine herself crouched and waiting hiding behind me. Nervous I reckon that I'm playing her but still she's alight with hope). Waiting till the guard wanders off around a corner, away from the plaza and out of sight.

—Don't you move, I tell her, and she shakes her head most fervent.—Don't you move an inch from here (I'm putting it off now, scared as I am). Don't you shift a muscle till you hear me knocking.

She's to open the bolt. She's to watch to make sure no anophelii push their way in while that door's unlocked. She's to wait as long as it takes till I come back.

And then I'm nodding, that leather bag of hers fastened and folded tight and rubbed with wax to keep the water out, held by my gut as if I clutch a wound, and she's pulled that door to and I'm out, in the starlight, in the air, in the hot night, with the mosquito-women all around me.

Tanner Sack does not hesitate. He bolts toward the chasm that splits the rear of the village like its anus, from where the rubbish is thrown into the sea.

He runs with his head down, blind and quite terrified, hurtling toward the crack in the rock. His nerves scream and his body arcs as each part of him fights to be nearest to the water.

He is sure he can hear the sound of the mosquito wings.

It is only five seconds that he is out under the sky listening to the wind and the night insects until his feet touch the flat rock that perches like a balcony over the sea. The air is still, and the darkness cossets him more tightly as he plunges into the shadow-stained gap in the mountain. For a moment his feet skitter as he hesitates and considers a more laborious and careful de-

scent by the thin path that winds in tight, back and forth, down
the stone, but it is too late: his legs have taken him on and out, as
if he hears the whine of a she-anophelius, and he has left the rock
and is falling.

There is nothing but air beneath him, more than fifty feet of
air, and then the slickly moving water that glints like iron. He has
seen the movement of the sea in the chasm below. And he is a sea
creature now, and he can read the shapes of the currents. He
knows the water beneath is deep, and so it proves to be.

He pulls himself up tight, and the surf opens to him with a
plunging sound and smashes the air from his lungs, and he opens
his mouth with the shock of it and breathes the water across his
poor, desiccated gills as the sea seals itself above him again, taking him into its body. It makes him welcome, little microbe that
he is.

There is a blissful time, when he drifts unmoving in the dark
water. The space around him is giddying, the safety of it. No
mosquito-women come here (*he thinks then of other predators,
and is for a moment a little less secure*).

Tanner feels the weight of the package in its greased pouch.
He holds it against his belly and kicks out with his webbed toes.
It has been so long since he has swum. He feels as if his skin is
blossoming in the water, his pores opening like flowers.

The black is not absolute. As his pupils dilate, he can make
out varying shades of darkness: submerged crags, the detritus of
the village, the split into the open sea, and the unremitting pitch
of the deep. He swims through the hole in the cliff and feels the
flow of the water change. Above him the waves chew the shore
like something senile and toothless.

His bearings, his directions, are clear. Little presences glide
past him, little night fishes. Tanner is reaching out around him
with his tentacles, swimming low until they feel the edges of
rock and he begins to swim around the coil of coast. His tentacles are braver than he. He pushes them inquisitive as an octopus
into holes in the stone from which he would snatch away his
hands. They are the most aquatic part of him, those appendages,
and he accepts their lead.

Tanner swims around the edges of the anophelii island. He
feels anemones and urchins and realizes with sudden sadness
that this is the first time he has swum close enough to the seabed
to sense its life, and it is almost certainly the last, and it is too

dark to see. He can only imagine the gnarls of sand and stone over which he swims, the spurs of rock and dead wood that must look furry with weed, the rich colors that light would reveal.

Minutes of urgent swimming pass. This coastal sea tastes different from the open ocean around Armada. These waters are a thicker stew. The taste of tiny life and death suffuses him.

And then very suddenly the taste of rust.

Machinery Beach thinks Tanner. He has swum around a convolution in the island's outline, into the bay. His suckers caress new things: decomposing iron, engines scabbed by the sea. The water above this bed of iron is awash with metal salts and tastes to him of blood.

At the moon-glittering surface above him are three big shapes, the Samheri ships, occluding what little light there is. Their stubby chains taut in the water, their anchors at rest amid the bones of much older metal artifacts.

Tanner angles up, rising, feeling the water expand. He raises his hands, still clutching the package. The shade of the biggest ship is directly in his path.

The cactacae from Dreer Samher bluster at the sight of him, mimicking anger, threatening him with upraised fists and spined forearms, but they are dissembling. They are puzzled by this bedraggled Remade man who has scaled their chains to stand dripping on their deck, looking nervously at the sky, waiting for the sailors to take him below.

"Let me talk to the captain, lads," he says to them in Salt again and again, fearful but determined. And after their threats do not deter him, they bring him into the ship's candlelit darkness.

They lead him past the treasury, where the spoils of their trade and their battles are stored. The kitchen where the smell of rotting vegetation and stew is strong. They take him through corridors of cages where angry chimpanzees scream and rattle their bars. The cactacae are too heavy and their thick digits too imprecise to scuttle the rigging. The primates are trained from birth to obey whistled and shouted commands, capable of unfurling and tying and hanging sails like experts, without ever knowing what it is they do.

The bored apes are hidden here from the hunger of the mosquito-women.

Sengka sits quietly in his cabin, making Tanner Sack stand

drying his face and hands nervously with a rag. With his huge green arms resting on his desk, his hands clasped, Sengka looks unnervingly like a human bureaucrat. The same suspicious patience.

He is a politician. He knows as soon as he sees Tanner's unlikely figure that something illicit is occurring, something beyond the purview of the Armadan authorities. In case it is something that he alone can take advantage of, he dismisses the guards. They leave with sulky looks, curiosity not assuaged.

There are some seconds of silence.

"So tell me," says Sengka, eventually. He does not bother with preamble, and Tanner Sack (skin drooling brine on the matting, hands clutching his package, feeling fearful and guilty, full of treachery that he does not want to commit) respects that.

Inside the wax-treated leather and the box, the contents remain dry.

He hands over the shorter letter, the promise to the bearer, without a word.

Sengka reads slowly, very carefully, time and again. Tanner waits.

When he finally looks up, Sengka's face gives away nothing, (*but he sets the letter very carefully to one side*).

"What," he says, "would you like me to deliver?"

Again without words, Tanner pulls out the heavy box and shows it. He removes the ring and the wax and turns the open container toward Sengka, showing him the letter and the necklace within.

The captain examines the rough necklace, pursing his lips as if unimpressed. His hand hovers over the longer letter.

"I'd carry nothing I wasn't allowed to read," he says. "It might say 'Disregard the other letter.' I'm sure you understand that. I'd only let you seal it after I've seen what's within."

Tanner nods.

It takes Captain Sengka a very long time to scan that dense, coded letter from Silas to his city. He is not reading it—he cannot; his Ragamoll is not good enough. He is looking for words that concern him: *cactus, Dreer Samher, pirate.* There are none. There seems to be no double cross here. When he is done, he looks up quizzically.

"What does it mean?" he says. Tanner shrugs quickly.

"I don't know, Captain," he says, "truly. Makes little more

sense to me than you. All I know is that's information that New Crobuzon needs."

Sengka nods to him sympathetically, considering his options. Turn the man away and do nothing. Kill him now (*easily done*) and take his seal. Deliver the package; don't deliver it. Hand the man over to the Armadan woman, the leader he is so obviously betraying, though how and for what Sengka cannot make out. But Nurjhitt Sengka is intrigued by this situation, and by this bold little intruder. He bears him no ill will. And he cannot make out for whom the man works, which aegis protects him.

Captain Sengka is unwilling to risk war with Armada, and even less with New Crobuzon. *There is nothing in the letter to compromise us,* he thinks, and cannot, though he tries, see a reason not to act as courier.

At the worst the letter is not honored, after he has gone a very long way out of his usual trading paths. But will that be a catastrophe? He will be in the richest city in the world, and he is a trader as well as a pirate. It would not be a good outcome, he thinks, and it is not an easy journey or a short one, but perhaps it is worth it? For the possibility?

The possibility that the letter (*with the city's seal, with the authority of its procurator*) will be honored.

They stand together to complete this secret deal. Tanner seals the long letter with the ring. He nestles Silas Fennec's necklace (*And who is he?* the question comes again) into the cushioned box and covers it with both letters, folded. He locks the box, and then drools more of the wax all over its seam. He pushes his old city's ring into it as it dries, and when he pulls it away he is faced by the city's heraldic seal in miniature, in greasy bas-relief.

He ties the fastened box back in its drab leather bag, and Sengka takes it from him and locks it in his sea chest.

The two watch each other a while.

"I'll not go on about what I'll do if I find you've betrayed me," says Sengka. It is an absurd threat: each man knows that he will never see the other again.

Tanner dips his head.

"My captain," he says slowly, "she can't know." It hurts him to say that, and he must remind himself fervently of the letter's contents, of the reason for secrecy. He keeps his eyes level, meets

Captain Sengka's gaze, gives away nothing. The captain does not torment him with conspiratorial winks or smiles, but only nods.

"You're sure?" says Sengka.

Tanner Sack nods. He is looking around nervously, on the prow of the ship, fearful for the telltale mosquito sounds. The captain is fascinated anew by Tanner's refusal to accept food or wine or money. He is intrigued by this man's impenetrable mission.

"Thank you, Captain," says Tanner, and shakes the cactus-man's thorn-plucked hand.

Watching Tanner as he leaps from the guardrail, Captain Sengka leans forward, half smiling, oddly warm to the fierce little human who has visited him. He stays on deck for some time, watching the ripples that Tanner leaves behind. And when they have been assimilated by the waves, he looks up into the night, untroubled by the sounds of the she-anophelii who will do no more than circle him, sniffing eagerly, failing to smell blood.

He thinks about what he will say to his officers, the new orders he will give in the morning, when the Armadans are gone. He wonders wryly how they will react. They will be aghast. Intrigued.

Tanner Sack is swimming doggedly back to the split in the cliffs. He anticipates the terrifying climb up that staggered path, practicing the movement of kicking out from the rock should the mosquito-women come, hurtling back into the sea.

He is unhappy. It does not help to think that he had to do it.

He wishes suddenly that the sea would do what poets and painters promise of it: that it would wash everything away so that he could start again, that it would make everything new. The water sluices through him as if he were hollow, and he closes his eyes as he moves, and imagines it cleansing him from the inside.

Tanner's fist is clenched around the ugly seal ring. He wishes his memories would wash out of him, but they are tenacious as his innards.

He stops suddenly in the middle of the sea, suspended fifty feet below the surface, hanging like a condemned man in the black water. *This is my home,* he tells himself, but takes no comfort from it. Tanner feels a rage in him, a rage that he controls, sadness as much as anger, and loneliness. He thinks of Shekel and Angevine (as he has done scores of times).

He reaches out deliberately and opens his hand, and the heavy Crobuzoner ring pitches instantly away.

It is so black, the sense of his own pale skin is more memory than sight. He can only imagine the ring falling from his palm. Plunging. Falling for a long time. Coming to rest at last in a snarl of rock or lost engine parts. Threading perhaps by chance onto some frond of weed, some finger of coral—a mindless, contingent affectation.

And then, and then. Ground down by the endless motion of the water. Not swallowed as he tries to imagine, not lost forever. Reconstituted. Until one day, years or centuries from now, it will resurface, thrown up by submarine upheavals. Diminished perhaps by the implacable currents. And even if the gnawing of brine has been absolute, if the ring is dissipated, its atoms will rise to the light and add to Machinery Beach.

The sea forgets nothing, forgives nothing, whatever we're told, thinks Tanner.

He should swim on, and he will soon; he'll return and clamber up dripping into the mosquito township. Tentacles flailing like fly whisks, he will scuttle back to the door where Bellis will admit him (*he knows she'll be waiting*). And the job will be done and the city (*the old city, his first city*) safe, perhaps. But for now he can't move.

Tanner is thinking of all the things he has still to see. All the things he has been told are out there in the water. The ghost ships, the melted ships, the basalt islands. The plains of ossified waves where the water is grey and solid, where the sea has died. Places where the water is boiling. The gessin homelands. Steamstorms. The Scar. He is thinking about the ring below him, hidden in the weeds.

It's all still there, he thinks.

There is no redemption in the sea.

INTERLUDE VI
Elsewhere

The whales are dead. Without these vast, stupid guides, the going is harder.

Brother, have we lost the trail?

There are many possibilities.

Once again they are just a cabal of dark bodies above the base of the sea. They slide through blood-warm water.

Around them, the salinae are anxious. Miles off, thousands of feet below the waves, something is shaking the crust of the world.

Can you taste it?

Amid the millions of mineral particles that eddy in the sea are some in unusual strengths: splintered flint (shards and dust), little gobs of oil, and the intense, unearthly residue of rockmilk.

What are they doing?

What are they doing?

The taste of the sea here is reminiscent. This is drool that the hunters can taste; this is the world's spittle. It dribbles (*they remember*) from ragged mouths cut by the platforms that suck up what they find, where beside concrete plinths men in inefficient swaddlings of leather and glass gaze wide, and are easily stolen and questioned and killed.

The floating city is drilling.

The currents here are labyrinthine, a morass of competing flows that dissipate the impurities in convoluted chains, taste-trails that make little sense, little pockets of different dirts.

They are hard to follow.

The whales are dead.

And what of others? Dolphins (*willful*) or manatee (*slow and too stupid*) or?

There are none suitable; we are alone.

There are others, of course, who might be called from the deep sea, but they are not trackers. Their work is very different.

Alone, but still the hunters can hunt. With a patience that is implacable (that does not sit well with this hot, quick place), they continue searching, teasing through the skeins of flavor and pollution and rumor, finding the path and taking it.

They are much closer to their quarry than they were before.

Even so, this warm water is hard, and sticky and prickling, and disorienting. The hunters circle, chasing ghost spoor and lies and illusions. They cannot quite, cannot quite find the trail.

PART FIVE

Storms

Chapter Twenty-seven

He speaks to me again.

Uther Doul has decided that we will be—what? Friends? Companions? Discussants?

Since we left the island, the crew have been bustling, and the rest of us have sat quiet and watched and waited. I have been numb. Ever since Tanner Sack returned last night—wet and salt-stained and terrified by his short time under the open sky—I have been unable to settle. I shift in my seat and think about that precious letter, that ugly tin necklace—a priceless proof—and the long journey that awaits them. Tanner Sack has told me that Sengka agreed to ferry them. It is a long way, an arduous journey. I hope he does not change his mind. I pray that Silas has offered enticement enough.

Tanner Sack and I avoid each other's eyes. We shift past each other in the *Trident*'s luxurious gondola, and we are stiff with guilt. I do not know him or he me: that is our consensus.

I have spent my hours watching Krüach Aum.

It is affecting to see him. It is moving.

He is shaking with fascination and excitement. His eyes are stretched wide, and his puckered sphincter-mouth is dilating and contracting with his breath. He moves—not quite running, but if it is a walk it is an undignified and frantic one—from window to window, staring at the engines that power the vessel, going to the pilot's control booth at the front, to the privies, to the berths, and up into the great cathedral of the balloon itself, filled with the gasbags.

Aum can communicate with no one but me, and I expected him to hanker for my services. But, no, I have nothing to do.

He is content to watch. I need only sit here and watch him, trotting past me this way and that like a child.

He has spent his lifetime on that rock. He is gorging on what is around him now.

Doul approached me. As before (that first time) he sat opposite me, his arms gently crossed, his eyes impassive. He spoke in his lovely voice.

This time I felt congested with terror—as if he had seen what I did with Tanner Sack—but I could face him with the calm he would expect.

I remain convinced that we understand each other, Doul and I. That this is what underlies the connection I feel, and I have used this conviction. He sees me (I am sure) struggling to control the fear I feel in seeing him, and he respects me for not giving in to nervousness at facing the legendary Uther Doul . . .

Of course my nervousness is that he will discover that I am a traitor. But that does not occur to him.

We watched Aum, without words, for a long time. Eventually, Doul spoke. (I am never the one to break silence.)

"Now that we have him," he said, "I can't see anything that could stop the invocation. Armada will soon enter a new period."

"What of the ridings that are unhappy about this?" I asked.

"Certainly there are some who have concerns," he said, "but imagine it. Currently the city crawls. With the avanc at our control . . . harnessed to a beast like that, there's nothing we couldn't do. We could cross the world in a tiny fraction of the time it takes us now." He paused and moved his eyes briefly. "We could go to places currently denied us," he said, his voice lowering.

There it was again: a hint at some motive undisclosed.

Silas and I have only learnt half the story. There is more to this project than the conjuring of the avanc. Having thought myself to have uncovered Armada's secrets, I dislike this sudden sense of ignorance. I dislike it strongly.

"To the lands of the dead, maybe?" I said slowly. "To the shadeworld and back?"

I spoke as if idly, citing the rumors I had heard about him.

To bait him into correcting me. I want to know the truth about the project, and I want to know the truth about him.

Doul astonished me then. I had expected perhaps some elliptical hint, some vague suggestions as to his origin. He gave me much more than that.

It must be part of his own project, the creation of some kind of link between us (I cannot yet work out what kind) but for whatever reason, he gave me much more.

"It's a chain of whispers," he said. He leaned in and spoke quietly, ensuring that our conversation was private.

"When they tell you that I came from the world of the dead, you're at the end of a chain of whispers. Each link has an imperfect join with those around it, and meaning leaches out between them."

If these were not his exact words they are like them. He speaks like this, in monologues that sound scripted. My silence was not begrudging—it was an audience's.

"At my end of the chain is the truth," he continued. He took my hand suddenly and shockingly and placed my two fingers on the slow pulse in his wrist. "I was born in your lifetime. More than three millennia after the Contumancy—do they still credit me with that? There's no coming back from the world of the dead." *Beat beat beat* went the pulse, languid like some cold-blooded lizard.

I know these stories are for children, I thought. *I know you're no revenant. And you know I know that. Do you just want me touching you?*

"Not the world of the dead," he continued. "But it's true that I come from a place where the dead walk. I was born and raised in High Cromlech."

It was all I could do not to cry out. As it was, I am sure my eyes must have spasmed wide.

Ask me six months ago and I would not have been certain that High Cromlech existed. I knew it only as a vague half-imagined place of zombie factories and the aristocratic dead. A place where the ghouls are hungry.

Then Silas tells me that he has been, that he has lived there—and I believe him. But still, his descriptions are more dreamlike than exact. Only the most nebulous and austere visions.

And now I know a second person who is familiar with that place? And not a traveler this time, but a native?

I realized that I was pressing the artery in Doul's pulse hard. Gently he disengaged from my fingers.

"It's a misconception," he said, "to think that High Cromlech is all thanati. The quick are there, too." (I am listening intently to him now, trying to detect his accent.) "We are a minority, it's true. And of those born every year, many are farm-bred, kept in cages till they're of strength, when they can be snuffed and recast as zombies. Others are raised by the aristocracy until they come of age, and are slain and welcomed to dead society. But . . ."

His voice petered out, and he became introspective for a moment. "But then there's Liveside. The ghetto. That's where the true quick live. My mother was prosperous. We lived at the better end.

"There are jobs that only the living can do. Some are manual, too dangerous to risk giving to zombies—they're expensive to animate, but one can always breed more of the quick." His voice was deadpan. "And for those lucky enough, for the cream—the livemen and livewives, the quick gentry—there are the taboo jobs that the thanati won't touch, at which a quick can make a decent living.

"My mother made enough that she chose to put herself down, so that she could have herself embalmed and revivified by the necrurgeon. Not high caste, but she became thanati. Everyone knew when Livewife Doul became Deadwife Doul. But I was not there. I had left."

I do not know why he told me all this.

"I grew up," he said, "surrounded by the dead. It's not true that they are all silent, but many are, and none are loud. Where I grew up, we used to run, the boys and girls of Liveside, pugnacious through the streets past the mindless zombies and a few desperate vampir, and the thanati proper, the gentry, the liches with sewn-shut mouths, with beautiful clothes and skin like preserved leather. More than anything I remember the quiet.

"I wasn't treated badly. My mother was respected, and I was a good boy. We were treated with nothing more overtly unpleasant than a kind of sympathetic sneer. I became involved with cults and criminals and heresies. But not deep, and not for long. There are two things that the quick are more adept at than the thanati. One is noise. The other is speed. I turned my back on the first, but not the second."

After it became clear that his pause had become a silence, I spoke.

"Where did you learn to fight?" I said.

"I was a child when I left High Cromlech," he said. "I didn't think so at the time, but I was. Slipping onto the funicular railway—out, away."

He would not tell me anything more than that. Between that time and his arrival at Armada there must have been more than a decade. He would not tell me what happened then. But that, it is obvious, is when he learnt his unfathomable skills.

Doul was quieting, and I felt his willingness to talk ebb away. I did not want that. After weeks of isolation, I wanted to keep him talking. I made a clumsy attempt, something like a witticism. I must have sounded arch and flippant.

"And when you left, you fought the Ghosthead Empire and won—what do they call it?—the Mighty Blade'?" I indicated his plain ceramic sword.

His face was quite impassive for a moment, and then a sudden beautiful smile illuminated him for a second. He looks like a boy when he smiles.

"That's another chain of meaning," he said, "half of which has been lost. The Ghosthead are long gone, but there are remnants of the Empire all over Bas-Lag. And it is true that my sword is a Ghosthead artifact."

I struggled through the meanings that he might be implying. *My sword is an application of Ghosthead techniques,* I thought, and then, *My sword is based on Ghosthead designs,* but I realized to look at him that he meant exactly what he said.

I must have looked shocked. He nodded briskly.

"My sword is over three thousand years old," he said.

It is impossible. I have seen it. It is a plain, slightly weathered, and age-stained piece of clayware. If it is fifty years old I would be astonished.

"And the name . . ." He gave me another of those smiles. "Another misunderstanding. I found this sword after a very long search, after mastering a dead science. The men call it *Might*blade. Not mighty." He spoke slowly. "It might; it might not. *Might* not meaning potency, but *potentiality*. It is a bastardization of its true name. There was a time there were many weapons like this," he said. "Now, it is, I think, the only one left.

"It is a Possible Sword."

Even on the return journey, the scientists were making plans. They did not underestimate what they had yet to do. There was harder work ahead of them.

The *Trident* was not traveling in the opposite direction to the one by which it had come: Armada had moved and, by those arcane means Bellis did not understand, they were heading inexorably for it.

The dirigible began to speed up, gusted by grey clouds and bullets of rain. Bellis peered from the stateroom windows, out over the turmoil of the sea and the dark air at the edge of the sky.

A storm was coming.

They outpaced the worst of the bad weather. Within its own borders the storm was violent, but it did not move fast. It was tearing itself apart from the inside. The *Trident* ran at its edges, pelted by a periphery of rain, racing its shadow.

When she saw the broken mass of Armada breach the horizon and sprawl across the water below her, Bellis marveled at its scale. It looked like spillage, a slick of ruined and refitted boats, untidy across the waves, shapeless, its edges random and unchanging. The fringe of tugs and steamers that had hauled it for thousands of miles had been untethered while the city was still, and they puttered around it in great numbers, ferrying goods. Bellis thought again of the vast quantities of fuel that they must consume. It was no wonder that the pirate ships of Armada were voracious.

On seeing it, Bellis felt a great wash of emotion that she could not identify at all.

At the city's outside edge, she saw the *Terpsichoria*. And with its spire flaming, its effluent warping the air, Bellis could see the complex outlines of the *Sorghum* rig. There was a bustle of vessels in the sea around its legs. It was drilling again, sucking oil and rockmilk out of the pressurized veins in which they had flowed for centuries. Armada had come to where there was a seam. The *Sorghum* was storing fuel for the almighty thaumaturgy to come.

They came in over Garwater's aft-star'd, picking their way carefully over masts. Below them a mass of shapes followed the *Trident* curiously, tracking it in its shadow: aerocabs and single balloonists, odd ungainly looking airships.

The *Trident* docked at the *Grand Easterly*, at the same height as the crippled *Arrogance*. Bellis could see people staring from surrounding ships and little aircraft, but the *Grand Easterly* was sealed off. Its deck was almost empty. A small contingent of yeomanry was waiting for them, and at their head, his face alight, was the Lover.

Bellis saw a new cut on his face, a healing scab. It started at the left corner of his lips and curled below his chin. It was the mirror image of the one that Bellis had heard the Lover inflicting on herself.

When the Lovers saw each other, there was a long moment of silence, and then they crossed the distance and held each other. They gripped and tugged at each other. Their touches were passionate and intense, and went on for a minute or more. They did not look like caresses: the Lovers looked as if they were fighting in slowed-down time. The sight of them disturbed Bellis immeasurably.

Eventually they broke. Bellis was close enough to hear them hissing to each other. The Lover was slapping her man, clawing him across his neck and face, harder and harder. When she touched his new cut, her hands were suddenly as gentle as if he were a baby.

"Just as we said," the Lover whispered, touching her own wound, "at the moment we agreed. Did you feel me? Did you? I swear I felt you, I fucking felt you—every inch, every drop of blood."

The paneled room was filled with old oil portraits of engineers and politicians Bellis did not recognize—New Crobuzoners left to molder meaningless on the walls of their stolen craft. Around a huge horseshoe table sat the Armadan Senate; and gathered before them were Tintinnabulum, the leaders of the *Trident*'s scientific and engineering parties, and Krüach Aum. Beside the stunned-looking anophelius sat Bellis.

The Armadan Senate had not met for eight years. But the ridings' rulers had been waiting for the return of the *Trident* to put this defining moment in Armadan history to the vote. Due process would be seen to be done.

Each riding in Armada had one Senate vote. Some ridings were represented by one person, some by a small gang. Bellis ran her eyes slowly along the long table, taking in all of the rulers. They were not hard to identify.

Braginod, the cactus queen of Jhour, with her advisors.

Booktown was represented by a triumvirate of khepri who leaned in together and conversed in motions and chymical spray translated by their human servant. Their names were unknown: they were figureheads from the changing cabal that ran the riding.

Almost at the far end of the table was a monk-robed man: the Bask contingent. Beside him sat an unkempt man of sixty or so. Bellis recognized him from posters—he was trader-king Friedrich of Thee-And-Thine. Beside him was another man, his face grey and scarred: the general of Shaddler.

The largest assembly by far was from the Curhouse. A sizable portion of the entire Democratic Council seemed to have attended—men and women of a gaggle of races, squeezed into a tight little circle abutting the main table like a cog on a gear. They whispered constantly among themselves and watched the Garwater representatives with visible hostility.

There they were, on the far right of the table: the Lovers. Watching, not speaking. Sitting beside each other quietly, their faces mirror images of violence.

And opposite them, his eyes on them with a far more careful, a far more intelligent gaze than the defensive animosity of the Curhouse Councilors, was a pale man Bellis had never seen, dressed in dark and simple clothes. His nose was broad and his lips very full. His coiled hair was all that was unruly about him. His eyes were extraordinary. Dark and intensely clear. Mesmeric.

With a little shiver, Bellis realized that he was the leader of Dry Fall riding, the greatest rival to the Lovers. He was the reason that the meeting took place after sundown. He was the vampir—the Brucolac.

* * *

It was obvious that this meeting was a formality and that the positions of the protagonists had already been decided over a long time. The arguments and discussions were stilted, the unspoken allegiances and enmities all half visible. Bellis spoke when she was addressed, offering her brief opinion on some matter of language.

There were five ridings in favor of the Lovers' schemes. Booktown seemed genuinely enthused by the Garwater plan; Jhour and Shaddler were in its pay and would do whatever was asked of them. Friedrich of Thee-And-Thine sold his vote to the Lovers, unashamedly, knowing that they could outpay any other riding.

Only Bask and Curhouse, who acted together, and the Brucolac of Dry Fall, who stood alone, opposed the Lovers. It was five to three. The plan could go ahead immediately.

"We weren't informed," said Vordakine of the Curhouse Council, a hard-faced woman who excoriated the Lovers for their dishonesty. She was trying desperately to sway Friedrich, or the khepri of Booktown. "We weren't told of Garwater's intentions when its raiders returned towing the Crobuzoner rig *Sorghum.* At that time the talk was all of increased energy and power, elyctric generation and cheap oil. Rockmilk was never mentioned then. And now it appears that all that cheap power had already been allocated to this avanc project. Who's to say what they have in mind when the avanc is secured?"

For the first time, the Brucolac sat up. He kept his eyes on the Lovers' party—specifically, Bellis realized, on Doul.

"Well that *is* the rub," he said unexpectedly. His voice was harsh and sounded torn from his throat. "That is the question." His long, forked tongue flickered. Bellis opened her eyes wide. "What is in mind? What could one do with an avanc? Where could one go?"

Trader-king Friedrich shifted and spat. Vordakine appealed to him, reminding him of commitments and past favors about which Bellis knew nothing. He looked away. She could not change his mind. Friedrich glanced at the Lovers, and they smiled at him, and nodded simultaneously.

We will buy you, they said with that motion, *and if Curhouse and Bask or anyone else wishes to oppose us, we will simply offer more than them. Name your price.*

Across the room, those opposed to the avanc's invocation looked old and tired.

The rig, the book, Krüach Aum himself—the Lovers' plans were always, Bellis realized, bound to go ahead.

In the night outside the windows, the storm was still visible miles away, blooming briefly with lightning. Surrounded by representatives of powers she was only just beginning to understand, translating for a man of a race she had thought long-dead, Bellis felt bleak and alone.

She was one of the last to leave the room. As she reached the door, Bellis looked up at Uther Doul, who was blocking it, and realized that he was not looking at her at all. He was gazing across the room, his eyes and mouth as still as glass, meeting the eyes of the Brucolac.

The Lovers had gone. All the other representatives had gone. Only Uther Doul and the vampir were left, and between them Bellis.

She was desperate to leave, but Doul's feet were planted as if he were about to fight. She could not push past him, and she was afraid to speak. The Brucolac stood with his unkempt hair wild and his moist lips parted, that ghastly snake tongue fluttering in the air. Bellis was trapped, motionless, between them. They ignored her completely.

"Still content, Uther?" the Brucolac said. His voice never rose above an unpleasant whisper.

Uther Doul did not respond. The Brucolac coldly mummed laughter.

"Don't think this is ended, Uther," he said. "We both knew the outcome of this charade. This is not where things are decided."

"Deadman Brucolac," said Doul, "your concerns about this project have been noted. Noted, and disregarded. Now if you will excuse me, I have to escort Krüach Aum and his translator to their quarters." Doul did not take his eyes from the vampir's pale face.

"Did you *notice,* Uther," said the Brucolac urbanely, "that the other little squabblers have finally realized that something is up?" He walked slowly toward Uther Doul. Bellis was frozen. She wanted very badly to leave this room now. For years she had wrapped herself in layers of focus and cold control. There were few emotions she could not master in herself.

It appalled her to realize that the Brucolac was terrifying her. It was as if his voice modulated exactly with her fear.

The room was dark, the gaslights out and the few candles guttering. She could see nothing but his tall figure, moving as easy as a dancer (*as easy as Uther Doul*), approaching.

Doul was silent. He did not move.

"You heard Vordakine ask what was to happen next. I told you she was the best of them. They're finally working it out, Uther," the Brucolac whispered. "When will you tell them, Uther? When do they get to hear the plan?

"Do you *really think*," he continued with sudden still ferocity, "that you could face me? Do you think you can defeat me? Do you think your project can continue without my consent? Do you *know* . . . what I *am*?"

He spoke rapidly then in a language of coughing swallows, as if the dialect itself resented every sound it allowed to escape.

The speech of High Cromlech.

Whatever he said, it opened Uther Doul's eyes wide for several moments. Then he, too, advanced.

"Oh yes, Brucolac," Doul said. His voice was as hard and edged as flint. He gazed over Bellis as if she were not there, straight at the vampir. "I know exactly what you are. I, more than anyone, know exactly what you are."

The men stood a few paces apart, unmoving, with Bellis between them like a reluctant referee.

"I give you the courtesy of the gentry's title, *Deadman*," hissed Doul. "But you're no more gentry than me. You're ab-dead, not thanati. You forget yourself, Brucolac. You forget there's another place where your kind are given leave to live openly. Where your refugees flee. You forget that where the dead rule and protect the quick, there's nothing to fear from you. You forget that there are vampir in High Cromlech." He pointed at the Brucolac.

"They live beyond the quick ghetto. In hovels. In the shantytown." He smiled. "And every night, after the sun's descended, they can crawl safely out from their shacks and shuffle into the town. Stick figures in rags, leaning against the walls. Exhausted and starving, hands outstretched. Begging." His voice was soft and vicious. "Begging for the quick to take pity on them. And every so often one of us will acquiesce, and out of pity and contempt, embarrassed by our soft philanthropy, we'll stand in the eaves of a building and offer up our wrists. And you and your kind will open them, all frantic with hunger and fawning with gratitude, and take a few eager swigs, till we decide you've had enough and take back our hands while you weep and beg for more, and maybe spew because you've gone without a hit so long your stomach can't handle what it craves, and we leave you lying in the dirt, blissed by your little fix.

"In High Cromlech we know exactly what you are, Brucolac." He smiled again.

"Junkies. That some of us indulge and some of us hate and all of us, quick and dead, pity.

"So do not," he spat suddenly, "try to intimidate me. Because, yes, Brucolac, I know *exactly* what you are."

No one said any more. The two men faced each other, immobile. Only the Brucolac's tongue moved, tasting the air.

And then he was gone.

Bellis blinked and looked around her at a trail of displaced air, where dust motes roiled and languidly followed the Brucolac's sudden fleeting passage. She held her head. *What has he done to me?* she thought. *How does he do that? Hypnosis? Godsdammit, he's quicker than Doul . . .*

Uther Doul was looking at her, she sluggishly realized, as her heart slowed and her breathing became normal.

"Come with me," he said to her, his voice as bland and featureless as if nothing had happened, as if she had not witnessed anything. "You must help Krüach Aum."

As she left the room, trying not to stumble, trembling as she was, Bellis thought about what the Brucolac had said.

Where are we going? she wondered as she followed Uther Doul. *What is the plan?*

CHAPTER TWENTY-EIGHT

After long prevarication, the storm hit.

The tightly coiled mass of air unwound. The night was hot. The rain blasted Armada. Ropes and rigging arced and snapped against the flanks of the ships and buildings. There was thunder and lightning.

This was the first real squall that the city had faced in a long time, but the inhabitants responded with practiced expertise. Airships were quickly grounded, waiting out the weather in yards and under tarpaulins. The *Trident,* tethered to the *Grand Easterly* and too big to be covered, could only bob and shift uneasily in the gusts, its massive shadow rolling over the ships and houses below it.

Across the city, all except the very strongest bridges and tethers were unhitched at one end, in case the sea pulled the boats apart fast or far enough to snap their bonds. Traveling across Armada during a storm was impossible.

Channeled into canals between the vessels, Armada's waters jerked and pitched violently but could not form waves. There were no such constraints on the sea that smashed against the city's outer vessels. The boats that made the mouths of the Basilio and Urchinspine harbors were drawn together, enclosing and protecting the raiding or trading vessels—Armadan and guest—within. Beyond the city's bounds, the fleet of fighters and tugs and pirates moved far enough away to avoid being driven into their home port's walls.

Only those who patrolled the city's undersides—the submersibles, the menfish, the seawyrms, and Bastard John the dolphin—were more or less untroubled. They sat below the surface and weathered the storm.

After peering from a window in the corridor of the *Grand Easterly,* Uther Doul looked back at Bellis.

"There's a worse one than this to come," he said. At first Bellis had no idea what he was telling her. Then she remembered the story in Krüach Aum's book: the summoning of the avanc, powered by lightning elementals.

We're going to call up a hell of a storm, aren't we? she thought.

Bellis set to teaching Aum an understanding of Salt, as instructed. It troubled her. She was conscious that this was a breach of the fundamental rules of anophelii containment, as maintained by Kohnid and Dreer Samher. And however venal their reasons for policing them, those rules were a protective response to one of the most notorious empires in Bas-Lag's history. She had to remind herself that Aum was male, and old, and very far from being a threat to anyone.

Aum approached the task with the rigor and logic of a mathematician. Bellis discovered, uneasily, that he had already worked out a surprising amount of vocabulary from the Armadans' short visit (and she wondered whether they had infected the island with language).

For New Crobuzoners, or Jhesshul or Mandrake Islanders or Shankellites or Perrickish, Salt was an easy language to learn. Krüach Aum, though, knew none of its components. There were no cognates at all—vocabulary or grammar—with High Kettai. Nonetheless, he broke Salt down, made careful lists of declensions and conjugations and grammar. His method was very different from Bellis', without intuition, without the training of the language trance to make his mind receptive; but still, he made quick progress.

Bellis looked forward eagerly to the time that she would be redundant; when she would not have to sit endlessly scribbling notes in a scientific register she did not understand. She had been released from her job in the library. Now her mornings were taken up with teaching Aum, and her afternoons with translating between Aum and the scientific committee of Garwater. She enjoyed none of it.

During the day she ate with Aum, and during the evenings she sometimes accompanied him throughout the city, with a guard of Garwater yeomanry. *What else,* she thought, *can I do?* She escorted him to Croom Park, to the colorful thoroughfares and shopping streets of Garwater and Jhour and Curhouse. She took him to Grand Gears Library.

While she stood and spoke in a low voice to Carrianne, who seemed sincerely delighted to see her again, Krüach Aum wandered from shelf to shelf. When she came to tell him that they must go, he turned to her and she was truly alarmed at his expression—a reverence and joy and agony like religious ecstasy. She pointed out the High Kettai books to him, and he reeled, as if drunk at the sight of all that knowledge in his grasp.

She felt a constant low-level unease at spending her days in the presence of the Garwater authorities: the Lovers, Tintinnabulum and his crew, Uther Doul.

How did it come to this? she wondered.

Bellis had been cut off from the city since the first moment, and she had assiduously kept that wound raw and bloodied. She defined herself by it.

This is not my home, she had said to herself again and again, endless repetitions. And when the chance had come to make some connection with her true home, she had taken it with all its risk. She had not renounced her claim to New Crobuzon. She had discovered a terrible threat to her city, and had (at great risk, with careful planning) worked out a way to save it.

And somehow in that very action, in the very act of reaching out to New Crobuzon across the sea, she had tied herself closely in to Armada, and to its rulers.

How did it come to this?

It made her laugh humorlessly. She had done what was best for her true home, and as a result she spent her days working for the governors of her prison, helping them gain the power to take her anywhere they wanted.

How did it come to this?

And where is Silas?

Every day, Tanner thought about what he had done on the anophelii island.

It was not something he felt comfortable considering. He was not sure what his emotions were. He probed the memory of what he had done, as if it were a wound, and discovered a reserve of pride inside him. *I saved New Crobuzon,* he thought, not quite believing it.

Tanner thought carefully about the few people he had left

behind there. The drinking partners, the friends and girlfriends: *Zara and Pietr and Fezhenechs and Dolly-Ann* . . . He thought of them with a sort of abstracted fondness, as if they were characters in a book of whom he had grown affectionate.

Do they think of me? he thought. *Do they miss me?*

He had left them behind. He had been so long in that stinking prison in Iron Bay, and in that drab place in the *Terpsichoria,* and then his life had been so suddenly and extraordinarily renewed, that New Crobuzon had attenuated as a memory in him.

But still there was a wellspring of feeling for it, a recognition that the city had shaped him. He would not have seen it destroyed. He could not think of the men and women he had known there, murdered. So—it bewildered him to consider it—he had given them a valedictory gift that they would never know they had received. New Crobuzon had been saved. He had saved it.

The awareness of that gnawed at him. It troubled him and made him sheepishly proud. It was such a huge thing he had done, something to change the tide of history. He imagined the city preparing for war, never knowing who had saved it. It was such a big thing, and here he was remembering it with a little arch of his eyebrows, not sure how much mind to pay it, as if it were a detail.

It wasn't a betrayal of Armada, not really. No one was hurt; it was just a little thing to them—a quick night's absence. He had taken a few hours to slip away and save New Crobuzon. And he was glad of it. It made him happy to think of what he'd done. Despite the magisters and the punishment factories.

He had saved it. Now tell it good-bye.

The avanc was a rare visitor to the seas of Bas-Lag. The intricacies of transplanar life were abstruse and uncertain. Neither Tanner Sack nor any of his colleagues knew whether the creature that breached in Bas-Lag was a partial or a total manifestation, a confusion of scale (some protozöon, some plankton from a huge brine dimension), a pseudoorganism spontaneously generated in the vents between worlds. No one knew.

All they knew was what Bellis Coldwine told them, as she read the intricate scribbles of Krüach Aum.

The anophelius was clearly stunned by his new environment, but it did not affect his ability to focus, to provide answers to their questions. Every day Aum gave his new workmates enough information for their purposes.

He drew designs for them, designs for the harness (bigger than a battleship), the bit, and the reins. Even though the engineers did not understand exactly what of the avanc would go where, what flesh exactly would be trapped by what clasp, they took Aum's word that the mechanisms would work.

The science, the plans, were moving at a stunning pace. The engineers and scientists had to remind themselves of how far they had come, how fast, and how they continued to move. It was obvious to all of them that without Aum they could not have succeeded, despite what they might once have thought. It was only working with him that they came to see how much they needed him.

They incorporated engines burning in sealed containers at the yoke's joints, triple-exchange boilers and complex pulley systems to regulate movement, all suspended in the freezing darkness of the deep sea, at the end of the miles of colossal chain links suspended below the city.

And what if they went wrong? Garwater's ancient bathypelagi-crafts would have to be refitted.

There was an extraordinary amount to be done.

Tanner almost rubbed his hands with happiness.

Armada had taken only a morning to recover after the storm: clearing broken slates and wood away from decks; reattaching bridges; counting and mourning the few missing or drowned, those who had been trapped outside during the deluge.

And when that was done, Garwater turned, with more of the incredible speed, to manufacturing what it needed for its historic project.

There were five of the ancient, hidden chains under Armada. Tanner Sack and the teams traced them, plotted their end points. All industrial capacity in Garwater, and what little there was in Booktown and Shaddler and Thee-And-Thine, was turned over to the direct control of Tintinnabulum and the project committee. The work of building began.

Several recently press-ganged metal ships were designated scrap. Piece by piece, they were taken apart. Thousands of men and women swarmed over them: the regular dock work was relegated to skeleton crews, and huge day rates were offered to the city's casual workers. The iron exoskeletons of warships, the girders and innards of steamers, the enormous tempered metal masts, were stripped. The vessels were peeled and disembow-eled, and all the tons of metal were shipped by barge and air-lifted by convoys of dirigibles to the factories.

The avanc's harness would sport girders and screws still marked with the scars of previous service. In foundries, iron too ruined to be reshaped was melted down.

Armada was not a city with a grand tradition of thaumaturgy. But there were competent metallo-thaumaturgists among the pi-rates, and gangs of them entered the factories. They worked closely with the engineers, mixing arcane compounds in great vats to strengthen and lighten and bind the metal. At last, some of Garwater's stores of rockmilk were used. The liquid was brought in vials, vastly heavy and dense. When it was unstoppered it gave off disorienting vapors like spice and oil. It moiled behind the glass, a cold mother-of-pearl.

The metallo-thaumaturges would add measured drops of it as they mouthed incantations and passed their hands over the melt-ing metal in puissant currents, charging it and sealing it.

And after rolling out the metal and hammering and more ar-cane procedures, the components of the avanc's bridle began to be dragged by submersibles into place below the city. An army of divers worked on them with chymical welders that sputtered colorfully in the water, and wielded hammers and wrenches with water-slowed motions.

It was an incredible, sudden industry.

The chains were anchored in the bases of five ships. The *Psire* of Booktown; Jhour's *Saskital;* the big steamer *Tailor's Moan,* the capital ship of Bask; the *Wordhoard* in the haunted riding; and Garwater's *Grand Easterly.* From the keels and sloping flanks of each of these old, massive ships curved an arc of iron the size of some great church doorway, bolted on and veiled thaumaturgi-cally. And from each of those stretched links the size of boats.

The guard sharks were let free. It seemed impossible that the chains had ever been hidden. The rumors spread—about what had been done before and what might happen now. It was said that Bask riding had tried to sever the chain below their vessel, to scupper Garwater's plans, but that it had been too strong, too massive, too protected by puissant charms.

In a big, windowless chamber at the bottom of the *Grand Easterly,* a new engine was being built. The redundant boilers and their tangle of head-height pipes were stripped away, like clearing a rusty forest. When the ghosts of engines were gone, two great stamped-flat discs of iron were visible, embedded in the floor. Waist-high and many yards around, encrusted with age and grease. They were the ends of the chain attached to the ship, pushed through its hull, then hammered and flattened to attach them tight, centuries ago. The first time this had been tried.

Someone planned this before, Tanner Sack thought. He was stunned by the hours of work, the thaumaturgy that had been tried, the industry, the planning, the effort that had been made, generations ago, and then deliberately forgotten.

Between these two chain stubs, Tanner Sack and his colleagues began to build an extraordinary engine. They worked to specifications calculated over long hours by Krüach Aum.

Tanner examined the plans carefully. The motor they constructed did not work to any rules that he understood. It would be huge: it would fill the room with pounding hammers and ratchets, powered by some source that he did not fathom.

He worked from the base of what would be the piston-pounding boilers, upward. He started with the stumps of giant chain, drilling into them and embedding them with molten alloys, into which he plunged wrist-thick wires in rubber and tar. They passed through transformers the size of his leg, ribbed columns of white clay, and on to thickets of cables and insulators and difference engines.

This was the pacific engine, by which complex energies would be transmitted along the *Grand Easterly* chain, into that great bridle and whatever it contained, miles below the surface. A goad. Bait and whip.

The sea was clear. Divers thronged the huge underwater construction site. Components were lowered from the cranes of factory ships. The massive harness was taking shape at the end of the huge chains, still tethered scant scores of feet below the surface, its scale troubling to the eye, its outlines exotic and unfathomable, surrounded by the vividly colored fish of this sea, and by submarines and cray craftsmen and suited workers and Tanner Sack all moving with the slow fluidity of the submerged.

Sometimes there was a vibration through the water. The legs

of the rig *Sorghum* disappeared into the cylindrical iron floats that supported it below the surface like suspended ships. The shaft of its drill plunged straight down, dim through the tons and tons of water, disappearing, to puncture the seafloor like a mosquito and feed.

CHAPTER TWENTY-NINE

Silas came to Bellis three days after she returned.

She had been expecting his visit—waiting with one eye on the door every evening—but still he managed to surprise her.

Bellis had had supper with Carrianne. She liked her ex-colleague sincerely, finding her perceptive and humorous. But still, as she made an effort to smile, Bellis' sense of loneliness was unabated. *Is it a surprise?* she asked herself ruthlessly. *You court it; you milk it; you make it.*

She remembered how things had been in New Crobuzon and admitted to herself that they were not so different. At least here her isolation had a reason; it was a fuel that she burned.

Carrianne had demanded detailed descriptions of the anophelii island, and the weather, and the behavior of the mosquito-people themselves. There was melancholy in her manner—however reconciled Carrianne was to her life aboard, it had been many years since she had set foot on solid land, and Bellis' stories could only make her feel nostalgia.

Bellis had found the recent trip hard to talk about. She remembered it as if at a great distance, as a monotony of frightened boredom interspersed with grander emotions. There were some things, of course, that she could not discuss. She was deliberately vague about the anophelii, about the Samheri pirates, and most of all about Krüach Aum.

After the altercation she had witnessed between the Brucolac and Uther Doul, Bellis had become fascinated by Dry Fall's ruler. Carrianne told her what she wanted to know, about the political structure of the riding, the cadre of vampir lieutenants under the Brucolac, and the riding's goretax.

"That's when you usually get to meet him," Carrianne said. She tried to be matter-of-fact, but Bellis could hear the awe in her voice. "Not always—often it's taken by some lieutenant—but sometimes. They cut you, here or here or here." She indicated her thigh and breast and wrist. "They paint it with an anticoagulant, and vacuum it into a belljar."

"How much do they take?" said Bellis, aghast.

"Two pints. The Brucolac is the only one who drinks his fill. The rest of the cadre are restricted—they dilute it. The more they drink, the stronger they grow—that's the word. And even though the Brucolac chooses his lieutenants carefully, it's possible that one or another might get power-hungry.

"If they took it traditionally, straight from the vein, they might not be able to control themselves—and they don't want to kill. And even if they did break away, there's the contagion. In the spit. So everyone they drink directly from and leave alive, they risk turning into a competitor."

Bellis left Carrianne at the borders of Dry Fall—"I could not possibly be safer than here," Carrianne said, smiling—and walked home.

She could have taken a cab; the winds were not strong, and she heard shouts from above as the aeronauts touted for custom. Two days previously, when her day's work with Aum was finished, she had been wordlessly handed a packet of flags and finials that represented a good deal more than her weekly wage at the library.

I've been given a raise, she thought dryly, *now that I work for Garwater.*

The consciousness of her hidden centrality to all that had happened, the awareness that without her, Armada would not be where it was, doing what it was doing, oppressed her, even though her reasons had been clear and good at every stage.

She walked home not to save money but to experience Armada again. Locked in a room full of incomprehensible conversations all day, she felt herself losing contact with the city around her. *And any city,* she told herself, *is better than none.*

The walk took her through Shaddler's cool, quiet streets and into Garwater via the *Tolpandy.* Past the quiet bickerings of the monkeys that nested in building sites and rooftops, and deserted

berths and the canopy of rigging; past the city's cats (glancing at
her, predatory) and its rare dogs and the masses of rats and the
nightwalkers; around hen coops; lifeboats and steam launches
rusted into position and remade as flower beds; homes cut into
the sides of gun batteries, pigeons cooing from the bore of a
twelve-inch gun; under wooden huts built onto foretops and
yards which met masts like tree houses; through the light of gas
and phlogistic cells and oil lamps; and through darkness tinted
in various colors, squeezing along the corridors of damp brick
that covered Armada's vessels like a fur of mold. Back to her
rooms in the *Chromolith* Smokestacks, where Silas Fennec was
sitting, waiting for her.

She was shocked by his unclear figure sitting in the dark. She
hissed at him, and turned away until her heart had slowed.
    He studied her. His eyes were big and calm.
    "How did you get in?" she said. He waved the question away
like an insect.
    "You know your apartment's still watched," he said. "I can't
exactly come knocking."
    Bellis walked over to him. He was motionless except for his
face and eyes, tracking her progress. She came close—she came
within his space—and leaned toward him slowly, examining him
like some scientific specimen. She was ostentatious about it: she
inspected him coolly and intrusively. It might have been designed to intimidate, to put him off his ease.
    As she bent over him, as if cataloging his aspects, he caught
her eye, and for the first time in some weeks, he smiled at her eagerly and openly. She remembered the reasons that she had had
for kissing him, and fucking him. Not just loneliness or isolation, though they were paramount. But there were other factors,
more centered in him. And although as she stood there she felt
not the slightest urge to touch him, although she felt only a ghost
of the affection that had once motivated her, she did not regret
what had happened.
    We both needed it, she thought. *And it helped; it really did.*
    She patted the back of his head as she turned away. He ac-
cepted that with good grace.
    "So . . ." he said.
    "It's done," she said. He raised his eyebrows.
    "As simple as that?"

"Of course not as simple as that. What do you damn well think? But it's done."

He nodded slowly. When he spoke his tone was neutral, as if they discussed some academic project. "How did you manage it?"

How did we? Bellis thought in the silence. *Did we? I have no evidence, no proof of anything.*

"I couldn't do it on my own," she began slowly, and then she sat upright, shocked by Silas' look of stricken anger.

"You *what*?" he cried. "You fucking *what*?" He was on his feet. "What did you do, you stupid godsdamned *cunt* . . . ?"

"*Sit . . . down . . .*" Bellis was standing now, pointing at him, her fingers shaking with rage. "How dare you?"

"Bellis . . . what did you do?"

She glared at him. "I don't know," she said coldly, "how *you* might have managed to cross a swamp crawling with six-foot mosquitos, Silas. I don't know how *you* would have managed that. We were a mile or more from the Samheri ships—oh, they were there, don't fret about that. Now maybe *you* are a cactus-man or a fucking scabmettler or something, but I'm blood, and they would have killed me."

Silas remained quiet.

"So . . ." Bellis' voice was measured now. "I found a man who *could* travel to the ships, without danger, without being detected. A Crobuzoner, prepared to do the whole deal on the hush, just to stop his first home being devastated."

"Did you show him the stuff?" said Silas.

"Of course I did. You think he'd swim off blithely at midnight taking only my word as to what he was carrying?"

"Swim? It was Tanner fucking Sack, wasn't it? Do you think, if you'd looked long and hard"—his voice was strained—"you could have found someone *more* loyal to Garwater?"

"But he *did* it," said Bellis. "He wasn't going to do anything without proof. I showed him the letters, and *yes*, Silas, he's loyal to Garwater. He's no intention of ever going back. But, dammit, you think he doesn't have friends left behind? You think he relishes the idea of the grindylow taking New Crobuzon? Godspit!

"For the sake of the people he left. For the sake of memories. Whatever. He took the box, the seal, the letters, and I told him what to do. It was a last good-bye to his fucking city. From him as much as from me and you."

Silas was nodding slowly, acknowledging that perhaps she had had no choice.

"You gave him the stuff?" he said.

"Yes. But it all went ahead, no problems. Silas . . . we *owe* Tanner Sack."

"But does he know . . ." said Silas hesitantly, "who I am?"

"Of course not." He relaxed visibly at her words. "Do you think I'm stupid? I remember what was done to the captain. I'd not have you killed, Silas," she said. Her voice was soft but not warm. It was a statement of fact, not of closeness.

After some moments of reflection, Silas seemed to finish his deliberations.

"I suppose it was the only choice," he said, and Bellis nodded curtly.

You ungracious fuck, she thought, furious. *You weren't there. . .*

"And you say the Samheri have the package? Sealed and ready to deliver?" He was grinning furiously. "We've done it," he said. "We've done it."

"That was more the reaction I was expecting," Bellis said unpleasantly. "Yes, we have." They looked at each other for a long time. "When do you think they'll reach New Crobuzon?"

"I don't know," said Silas. "Maybe it won't work. Maybe it will, and we'll hear nothing. We'll save the city, and hear nothing about it, ever. I may see out my days on this fucking tub, desperately scheming to get off. But godsdammit, isn't it something to know what we've done?" He spoke fervently. "Even without response, even without thanks, isn't it something to know that we've saved them?"

And yes, thought Bellis Coldwine, *it was something. It was certainly something.* She felt a wave of loneliness breaking over her. Was it worse? she wondered. Could it be worse? To never know? To send that message across the world, through so many hazards, through such danger, for it to disappear without a sound? To never know?

Gods, she thought, bereft and stunned. *Is that the last of it? Is that the end?*

"What happens now?" he said. "With me and you?"

Bellis shrugged. "What did you want?" Her voice was more tired than scornful.

"I know it's hard," he said gently. "I know it's more complicated than we'd thought. I don't expect anything from you. But

Bellis . . . there are things we share, things between us—and I don't think that's the only reason we spent time together. I would like us to be friends. Can you really afford not to have me? To have *no one* who knows? How you really feel? Where you want to be?"

She was not quite sure of him, but it was as he said: they shared things that no one else did. Could she afford to lose him? There might be years ahead of her in this city (*she shudders to think it*). Could she afford to have no one to whom she could speak the truth?

When he stood to go, he held out his hand, his palm open and up, expectantly.

"Where's the New Crobuzon seal?" he said.

Bellis had been afraid of this. "I don't have it," she said.

He did not get angry this time, just closed his hand with a soft clap and raised his eyes to ask her what had happened.

"It was Tanner," she said, ready for him to fly at her. "He dropped it in the sea."

"It's a ring, Bellis," Silas said quietly. "It sits safe on your finger. You don't lose it. He hasn't lost it. He's kept it, gods know why. Souvenir from home? Something to blackmail you with? Gods know." He shook his head and sighed, and she was furious with his manner, which said *I am disappointed in you.*

"I'd better leave, Bellis," he said. "Carefully—you're watched, remember. So don't be surprised if I come and go by . . . unconventional means. Would you excuse me a moment?"

He descended the spiral stairs. Bellis heard the sound of his feet dissipating on the metal, ringing hollow like thin tin on tin. She turned at the weird sound, but he had gone. She could still hear the slightest ring of his feet on her staircase, descending, reaching the bottom step, but there was nothing to be seen. He was invisible or gone.

Bellis' eyes widened very slightly, but even in his absence she begrudged Silas any awe.

He comes and goes like a rat or a bat, now, she thought. *Keeping out of sight. Been learning thaumaturgy, has he? Got some facility, a little puissance?*

But she was unnerved and somewhat intimidated. His departure suggested a charm of exceptional subtlety and strength. *I didn't know you had that in you, Silas,* she thought. She realized again how little she knew of him. Their conversation was like an elaborate game. Despite his words, despite the fact that she knew they shared secrets, she felt alone.

And she did not think that Tanner Sack had kept the New Crobuzon seal, though she could not say why.

Bellis felt as if she were waiting.

The man stands waiting with wind gusting him on the staircase that spirals the height of her absurd chimney-pot apartment, and he knows that the eyes that might watch her door cannot see him at all.

In his hand is the statue, its filigree of fin folded like layers of cake pastry, its round betoothed remora mouth pouting upward, and his tongue is still cold where he has kissed it. He is much quicker now; he finds it much easier to accept the cold stone's flickering little tonguing, and he can direct the energies their passionless coupling unleashes far more adroitly.

He stands at angles to the night at a place the statue shows him and where its kiss allows him to stand, at a place or a kind of place where the beams of lights intersect and he is unnoticed, as doors and walls and windows do not notice him so long as he is the brine-stinking statue's lover.

The kissing is never a pleasure. But the power that he has, that enters him with the stone thing's spit, is a wonder.

He steps out into the night, unseen and emboldened, with arcane energies in him, to look for his ring.

CHAPTER THIRTY

Armada lolled in the sun. It was getting hotter.

The frantic work continued, and below the water, the shape of the avanc's harness grew slowly more solid. It was ghosted, its outlines in girders and wooden supports, like an abstract for some implausible building. As the days went on it grew a little more substantial, its intricate spines and gears more like something real. It grew through the extraordinary efforts of the crews. The city was on something like a war footing, every iota of industry and effort commandeered. People understood that they were careering at breakneck speed into a new epoch.

The scale of the harness always staggered Tanner Sack. It loomed below the ecology of scavenger fish that never left the city's underside, larger by a long, long way than any ship. It dwarfed the *Grand Easterly,* which bobbed above it like a bath toy. And the bridle was to be completed within weeks.

The work was constant. During the dark hours, the sputtering illumination of chymical flares and welding torches attracted night fish. They surrounded the chains and gangs of divers, schools of them staring big-eyed, agog at the lights.

There were moving parts, and joints, and rubberized gasbags cannibalized from old dirigibles. There were sealed motors. But essentially it was just a vast halter, its links and segments stretching more than a quarter of a mile long.

Ship after ship was gutted, stripped from the inside, scuttled, and melted down. The fleet of warships and traders that surrounded the city and its ports was thinned, for the sake of this project. A frontier of smoke plumes enveloped the sacrificed vessels while heat torches took them apart.

As Shekel made his way along the aft of Garwater one evening, to Bellis' house, he looked out toward the horizon and saw a half-gone ship at the edge of the city. It was the *Terpsichoria:* its outlines crumbled and broken; its bridge, most of its superstructure, and its deck gone; its metal viscera taken to the factories. The sight brought him up short. He had no affection for the vessel; he was not dismayed—but astonished, for reasons he could not articulate.

He stared down at the water that turned below him. It was hard to believe that it was happening, that such colossal efforts were taking place, link after link slotted together in a vast series under the fabric of the city.

There were several languages active in Bellis' life. She felt exhilarated to relearn her disciplines: the nameless technique she had perfected for segmenting her mind, keeping her internal dictionaries distinct; the language trance she had last used in Tarmuth.

Aum made quick progress with Salt. Her pupil was talented.

During the afternoon's discussions with Tintinnabulum and the other scientists, every so often—to Bellis' pleasure—Aum would intercept some question before she had translated it and written it down. He would even write down some of his own answers, in basic Salt.

It must be extraordinary for him, Bellis thought. Salt was the first language he was conscious of having both spoken and written dimensions. It was unthinkable to him to *hear* High Kettai— it had been a meaningless concept. To hear Salt questions and to write the answers in the same language must be an astonishing mental leap, but he dealt with it with aplomb.

Bellis did not warm to Krüach Aum. She found his constant wide-eyed curiosity draining, and she felt no strong sense of personality beneath it. He was a brilliant, boring man whose culture had made him like a precocious child. She was cheered by the speed with which he learned Armada's language; she suspected that she would be mostly redundant soon.

High Kettai and Salt surrounded her every day.

Her own head was the preserve of Ragamoll. She had never been one of those linguists who thought in the language she was using at the time. Silas was the only person to whom she spoke in her first language, in the rare times that she saw him.

There was a day when a fourth language entered her life, briefly. Quiesy—more popularly known as Deadish. The language of High Cromlech.

She still did not really understand Uther Doul's reasons for talking to her about his home tongue. After one of her sessions with Aum, he had asked her if she enjoyed learning new languages, and she told him truthfully that she did.

"Would you be interested to hear a bit of Quiesy?" he said. "I don't often get to speak my own tongue."

Dumbfounded, Bellis had agreed. That evening she had gone with him to his quarters aboard the *Grand Easterly*.

The sounds of Quiesy were formed in the back of the throat, softly barked, the noises swallowed, and interspersed with precisely timed silences as important as the sounds. It was, Doul warned her, a language of strange subtleties. Many of the thanati gentry had sewn-shut mouths, he reminded her, and others had voiceboxes too rotted to work. There were modes of Quiesy spoken with hands and eyes, as well as written forms.

Bellis was fascinated by the gentle language, and was held by Uther Doul's performance. In his quiet, controlled way he was enthusiastic as he recited several passages of what sounded like poetry. Bellis realized that she was not there to learn the language, but to appreciate it as an audience.

There was still a foreboding in her at being in Doul's company, alongside other emotions. Alongside excitement.

He wordlessly handed her a glass of wine. She recognized this as an invitation to stay. She sat and sipped and waited, looking around his room. She had expected some hidden stronghold, but he lived in a berth like thousands of others. It was sparse: there were a desk and two chairs, a shuttered window, a chest, one small black-and-white etching on the wall. Below the window was a weapons rack, full of familiar and arcane armaments; and in the corner of the room a complex musical instrument, with strings and keys, like a harp-accordion hybrid.

When probably a minute had passed, and Uther Doul had said nothing, Bellis spoke.

"I was . . . very interested to hear the story of your youth," she said. "I admit that I hadn't previously been sure of High Cromlech's existence—until I met you. However, apart from the whispers about the land of the dead and defeating the Ghosthead Empire, I've lost your trail of rumors." She was not practiced at the kind of hard humor for which she was trying, but he moved his eyebrows to signify a pretense at amusement. "I'd be very pleased if you wanted to tell me more about what happened after you left High Cromlech. I doubt I've ever met anyone so traveled. Have you ever . . . ?" She paused, suddenly anxious, and he replied to her.

"No. I've never visited New Crobuzon," he said. He seemed to be fretting, in his poised, silent way.

"You aren't sure you believe what I told you about my sword, are you?" he said suddenly. "I don't blame you. It isn't nearly old enough, you were thinking. What do you know about the Ghosthead Empire, Miss Coldwine?"

"Little," she admitted.

"Of course, though, you know that they were in no way human—or khepri, vodyanoi, strider, or what have you. These were not xenian in the sense we usually mean it. Whatever prints and descriptions you may have seen are fallacious. The question *What did they look like?* has no straightforward answer. This

weapon—" He indicated his belt. "—is so obviously shaped for
human hands, you might have thought my claims about its
provenance a lie."

Bellis had had no thoughts at all about the shape of the Possible Sword, as Uther Doul must have known.

"You're not seeing the sword," he went on softly. "Only one
aspect of it. It's contextual—as was so very much for the Ghosthead. I take it you've read some of their Imperial Canon? Even
as translations of translations of translations, even with all the
additions and omissions and commentary that implies, there are
some extraordinary things there. Especially the Covertiana." He
sipped his wine.

"Some purport to be passages from the earliest days of the arrival of the Ghosthead in Bas-Lag, before the Empire began." He
blinked at Bellis. "Certainly," he said as if she had disputed him.
"*Arrival.* The Ghosthead were not native to this world."

Bellis knew the myths.

"There is one passage . . . ," Doul mused (and Bellis realized
with consternation how his wonderful voice was lulling her).
" 'The Verses of the Day.' Perhaps you know them? 'Redoubt-
able, tail flicking, swimming over a plain of worlds, past orbs,
lights in the night's blindness.'

"That describes the Ghostheads' journey from . . . their place
to Bas-Lag. In the belly of a metal fish swimming through a dark
sea of stars. But what's most interesting is the description of
their home, where they came from. It has been confused with
hell."

Uther Doul sat on his crib, and did not speak for some time.

Is this why I'm here? thought Bellis suddenly. *Is this what he
wants to tell me?* He was like a boy, wanting her there but quite
uncertain what to do.

"It describes the morning coming with 'ferrous cataracts and
a wall of fire,' " he said eventually. "The entire eastern sky was
ablaze with light and heat enough to blind anyone looking up
even from the bottom of a sea, to ignite the air, burn the mountains, liquefy metal. Far, far hotter than the heart of any foundry.
Morning broke, and the world burned.

"Within minutes the wall of heat had risen and curved above
them, directly overhead, blotting out the sky and burning every
atom of gas in the air. And then, as the minutes went on, the fire
shrank, until its edges became visible, and it was a disc. And the

heat began to ebb away a little, though the oceans were still molten iron.

"The fire in the sky receded, moving west, as the day passed. By midmorning, the disc had shrunk further, and it was the sun, nearly at the far horizon. By noon it was much smaller, and the land was very cold.

"The sun shrank and traveled west in a long, drawn-out dusk, and the Ghosthead homeworld became icier than the Rime Ocean. By nightfall, the sky was already dark, and the sun was no more than a moving star.

"And it was *cold*—colder than anything we could imagine. The world was enveloped in layers of ice and frost—the very gases, the very aether piled up in bergs and walls, chilled more solid than stone."

He gave Bellis a faint smile.

"That was the Ghosthead homeland. Imagine what kind of creatures might live, might survive in such a place; how hungry they might be for rest. That's why they left."

She said nothing.

"Do you know what I mean," Doul said, "by the belief in the Broken Country?"

Bellis furrowed her brow, then suddenly nodded. "In New Crobuzon we call it . . ." She thought for the translation. "The Fractured Land Hypothesis. I once had a friend who was a scientist. He was always talking about things like this."

"The Broken Country, across an impossible sea," said Doul. "I spent a long time, in youth, studying myths and cosmogony. Fractured Land, Ghosthead Country, the Verses of the Day.

"The Ghosthead came here from the universe's eastern rim. They passed the rock globes that circulate in the sky—another, more evanescent kind of world than ours on the infinite plateau—and came here, to a land so mild it must have seemed like balm: an endless, gentle midmorning. And its rules were not theirs. Its nature was *debatable*.

"There are some who say that when they landed, the force of it was enough to unleash the chaos of Torque, up from the vent. That's fable. But their arrival was violent enough to smash open the world—reality itself. The Fractured Land is real, and was their doing. You break something . . . what's inside spills out.

"When I left my first home, I spent years studying that breakage. Searching for techniques and instruments to make sense of it, control it. And, when I came here, the Lovers saw things in what I'd learnt that I hadn't imagined.

"Think of the Ghostheads' power, their science, their thaumaturgy. Imagine what they could do, what they *did* do, to our world. You see the scale of the cataclysm of their arrival. Not just physically—ontologically. When they landed, they fractured the world's rules as well as its surface. Is it a surprise that we whisper the name of the Ghosthead Empire in fear?"

And yet, thought Bellis, reeling with the heretic philosophy, *and yet it was we who put paid to the Ghosthead. Through the Contumancy, and then the Sloughing Off. Weak as we are.*

"They say you led the Contumancy," she said.

"I lead *nothing,*" said Doul sharply, surprising her, "not anymore. I'm a soldier, not a leader. High Cromlech . . . it's a caste world. You grew up in a mercantile city, so you take it for granted. You can have no idea of the *liberation* of selling your services, doing what your employer tells you. I am *not* a leader."

Uther Doul walked with her through the *Grand Easterly*'s corridors.

When he stopped at one of the numerous intersections, she thought for a sudden second that he would kiss her, and her eyes widened. But that was not his intention.

He put his finger to his lips. "I want you to learn something," he whispered, "about the Lovers."

"What are their names?" Bellis said in tired anger. "I'm sick of the . . . the mystery, and I don't believe you can't remember."

"I can," said Uther Doul. "Of course I can remember. But what they were once called is not at all the point. They're the Lovers now. You'd better learn that."

Doul led her into the lower decks. He took her away from sound, away from the patrols. *What is this?* thought Bellis, excited and unnerved. They were now in dark, very quiet portions of the ship. There were no windows; they were below the waterline, in a long-deserted place.

Finally Doul ducked below a snarl of pipes and ushered her into a tiny chamber. It was not a room, just a little found space. All the surfaces were dusty, and the paint was peeling.

Doul gently put his finger in front of her lips.

Bellis was aware that meekly following Doul, *fraternizing* with him, was not sensible behavior from one who had been deeply involved in counter-Garwater activities. *What am I doing here?* she thought.

Uther Doul was pointing up at the ceiling, only an inch or so above her head. He cocked an ear expressively. It took some seconds before Bellis heard anything, and when she did, she was not at first sure what it was.

Voices. Muffled by layers of air and metal. Half-familiar. Bellis turned her head up. She could almost make out words now. This was an accidental little listening post. By quirk of architecture and materials, the sounds from the room above issued (by pipes, hollow walls?) through the ceiling.

Voices from the room above.

The Lovers' room.

She started in astonishment. It was the Lovers that she could hear.

Cautious and slow, as if they might somehow see her, Bellis craned her neck and listened.

Words fluttering across registers, uttered with quick breaths. Mewing, pleading, delighting. Gasps of sexual closeness and pain and other intense emotions. And words coming through the metal.

. . . love . . . soon . . . fuck . . . yes and . . . cut . . . now . . . love . . . cut . . . yes, yes . . .

Yes.

The words were thick. Bellis recoiled from them—physically, literally, stepping away from the weak spot in the metal. The words, the sounds, were crooned quickly, so steeped in passion and need that they had to be bitten out or they would become a wordless shriek.

cut yes love cut

Two streams of words, male and female, overlapping and interweaving and inextricable—their rhythms inextricable.

Dear Jabber! thought Bellis. Uther Doul watched her, expressionless.

Cut and cut and love and cut! she thought, and went for the door, appalled. She thought of what they were doing, in their room, a few feet away.

Doul led her away from that terrible little cubbyhole. They ascended through layers of metal toward the night air. Doul still did not speak.

What are you doing? she thought, staring at his back. *Why show me that?*

There had been nothing prurient in his demeanor. She did not understand. Stiff, eloquent, and formal in his own room, uncovering extraordinary stories and theories to keep himself talking, he had become, in these corridors, a truculent child with a secret hideaway. And with something like the wordless, inarticulate pride she would expect from such a child, he had led her to his private den and shown her its secret. And she could not fathom why.

She shuddered at the memory of those breathy exclamations, the Lovers' twisted declarations of passion. Of love, she supposed. She thought of their scars, the cutting. The blood and split skin, the fervor. She felt as if she would sick up. But it was not the violence, not the knives they used or what they did, that horrified her. It was not that at all. Peccadillos did not disturb her at all—those, she could understand.

This had become something else. It was the emotion itself, the intense, giddying, slick, and sick-making ardor she had heard in their voices that appalled her. They were trying to cut through the membrane between them and bleed one into the other. Rupturing their integrity for something way beyond sex.

That violent, moaning thing that they thought was love, she thought was something akin to *masturbation,* and it disgusted her.

Bellis was left aghast by it. Nauseated and threatened and aghast.

CHAPTER THIRTY-ONE

During the days, Shekel was free.

Like most of the young bravos who hung out around the Basilio docks, he made his living as he had in New Crobuzon—running errands, delivering messages and goods, keeping his eyes and ears open, for whatever handful of change his momentary employer chose to give him. His Salt was game and comprehensible, if not fluent.

A little more than half of his evenings he spent with Angevine. She berthed in Tintinnabulum's *Castor*, below its belfry. She often returned very late at night, since Tintinnabulum spent long hours in the meetings with his colleagues, and with Krüach Aum and Bellis and the Lovers, and Angevine fetched books or materials for him, from the library or from his hidden laboratory at the back of his ship. She would return tired, and Shekel would soothe her with supper and inexpert massages.

Angevine did not speak much about the avanc project, but Shekel could easily sense her tension and excitement.

Other evenings he spent at what he still thought of as his own home, which he shared with Tanner Sack.

Tanner was not always there—like Angevine, the project was keeping him at work long and difficult hours. But when he was present, he spoke more about what he was doing. He described to Shekel the extraordinary look of the bridle, stretching out in the clear water, the schools of bright tropical fish circulating through its links, which were scaling already with the plants and tenacious shellfish; picked out at night with cold lights. All the hours of work, of welding and testing and suggesting, acting as designer, foreman, and builder, left Tanner exhausted and very happy.

Shekel kept the rooms clean and warm. When he was not cooking for Angevine, he cooked for Tanner.

He was troubled.

Two nights previously, on Luddi, Shekel had woken suddenly a little after midnight, in his old rooms on the factory ship. He had sat up and stayed quiet and unmoving.

He had looked around the room, in the pale half-shadow shed by lights and stars outside: at the table and chairs, the bucket, the plates and pans, at Tanner's empty bed (*working late again*). Even swaddled in shadows, there was nowhere for anyone to hide, and Shekel could see that he was alone.

And yet he had felt as if he was not.

Shekel lit a candle. There were no unusual sounds or lights or shadows, but he kept thinking that he had just a moment before heard or seen something—again and again, as if his memories were outpacing him, reminding him of something that had not yet happened.

He went back to sleep eventually, and woke the next morning with only a vague sense of the foreboding he had felt. But the next night, the same sense of intrusion came with dusk, long before he had gone to bed. He stood—with a concentrated, silly stillness—looking about him vaguely. Had those clothes been moved? That book? Those plates?

Shekel's attention switched rapidly from one object, one drawer or collection or pile of things, to the next, his eyes moving across them, exactly as if he were watching someone move through the room, touching or rummaging in each place in turn. He grew angry and afraid at once.

He wanted to flee, but loyalty to Tanner kept him in those rooms. It made him light the lamps and sing loudly, and cook expansively and quickly until Tanner returned—mercifully, before the late evening, when the sounds outside faded away.

To Shekel's relief and surprise, when he broached the subject of his strange intuitions, Tanner reacted with interest and seriousness.

He looked around the little room and muttered carefully. "It's a peculiar time, lad." Exhausted as he was, he raised himself and followed the route that Shekel described around the room. He picked up the items he passed, carefully checking them. He hummed and rubbed his chin.

"I can't see a sign of nothing, Shekel," he admitted. His eyes did not relax. "It's a peculiar time. There's all manner of types trying all manner of things at the moment—there's lies and rumors, and Jabber knows what. Thus far, those who've problems with Garwater and the project ain't spoken of it too loud—that'll come later, I shouldn't doubt. But maybe there's some who're trying other ways of undermining things. It ain't as if I'm a bigwig in this, Shekel, lad, but I'm known to have gone to the island, and I'm known to be helping build the bridle. It might be someone's made their way in here to try to . . . I don't know . . . undermine things. To look for something to strengthen their side. As if I'm stupid enough to keep any plans here.

"People are tense. Things are moving too quick. It's like it ain't in anyone's control." He looked around him once more, then caught Shekel's eye.

"I'm tempted to say let 'em come. If you're right, then so long as they take nothing and leave us alone, then fuck 'em. I ain't scared." He grinned with bravado, and Shekel smiled back.

"All the same," Shekel said quietly. "All the same."

When he spoke to Angevine about his experience the next day, she echoed Tanner Sack almost exactly.

"Might be there's something in it," she said slowly. "It's a strange time, you know. People are excited, and some are scared. I doubt that unseen intruders'll be the strangest thing we have to face over the next weeks, lover. With the factories working overtime for the bridle, people are grumbling. There's no time or engineers to fix up machines elsewhere, no engine parts or metalwork being built. 'With all the power from that rig,' people are saying, 'when'll we see it put to *our* use? How much does the damn avanc need, anyway?'"

"Well, it needs a lot, Shekel. A damn lot, now and always." She met his eye and took his hand. "And the rumblings that you can hear now—in Bask and Curhouse and Dry Fall, most especially, but all over— are bound to grow. When people get to understand that there's other things more important to put the oil and rockmilk to than all their schemes."

She spoke absently, recalling conversations that she had overheard between Tintinnabulum and others, and Shekel could do little more than nod.

"They're appearing already, the troublemakers," she mused. "Vordakine in Curhouse, Sallow in Bask. The mysterious Simon Fench. Pamphlets, graffiti, whispers. And good people have their doubts, too. I heard that Hedrigall, who's loyal to his wooden bones, even *knows* this Fench, drinks with him sometimes. People'll get fired up if the avanc is called—something so wonderful as that, it'll excite them. But that won't be the end, Shekel, believe me."

In the blazing heat of Armada's accidental, equatorial summer, Croom Park blossomed.

When last Bellis had visited it, it had been all-over green: wet, and lush, and sap-stinking. Now the green was overlaid with spring and summer colors: a mulch of hurried blossom underfoot, and here and there still frosting the tips of trees. The first bright summer flowers vied with vivid weeds, dogwood, and daffodils. The woods rustled with small life.

Bellis came to the park not with Silas, but with Johannes Tearfly, and she was wryly amused that she felt as if she were being somehow unfaithful.

She walked her favorite route, along what had once been a corridor between ship's cabins and was now an ivy-smothered canyon. The walls were studded with passion flowers, broken windows just visible beneath a mesh of roots. Where the old cabin-hills sank into the grassy surface and the pathway opened out into the sun, there was a fringe of pungent honeysuckle purring with bees.

This is a good moment, thought Bellis carefully as she walked, Johannes shy and wondering behind her. *But you'll have to spoil it in a moment, Johannes—you'll have to speak.*

And after some more minutes of flowers and grass, when the only sound was the vibrato of warm insects, he did.

They talked for a long time about the work below the city.

"I've been down in a submersible a couple of times," Johannes told her. "It's extraordinary, Bellis. The speed with which they're constructing it—it's truly amazing."

"Well, I've seen the rate they've decommissioned the *Terpsichoria,* among others," she said. "I can just imagine."

Johannes was wary of her, still, but he was eager to feel the connection they had once had. She could feel him reaching to her, explaining away to himself any curtness she might display.

"You've not told me much about the island," he said.

Bellis sighed. "It was hard," she said. "I don't relish discussing it." But she gave him a little more than that: told him of the excruciating heat, the constant fear, the burning curiosity of the he-anophelii and the murderous hunger of their mates.

He tried to gauge her. She wondered whether he thought he was shrewd and subtle.

"They took Aum away, yesterday," she continued, and he turned to her, startled. "I've been teaching him Salt for a couple of weeks, that's all. He learns at a rate that frightens me. He takes notes on everything I say—he's already amassed enough for a textbook. But, still, I didn't think he was capable of conversing without my help—not yet. But yesterday afternoon, when we'd concluded with Tintinnabulum and the engineers' committee, they took him away and told me I wasn't needed for a while.

"Perhaps their opinion of his Salt is higher than mine. Or perhaps one of their other High Kettai experts has practiced enough to come in useful." This she said with a superior sneer, and Johannes laughed briefly. "They've been telling me for some time that I'm to bring him to fluency in Salt at the very earliest possible time; that he'll be needed for projects that don't concern me. They're trying to get rid of me."

She turned to Johannes and held his gaze. They were alone in a clearing, ringed by trees and briars, stunted spring roses.

"My usefulness is ending, and I'm delighted, because I'm so godsdamned tired. But Aum's is only just starting, it appears. And it wasn't any of the usual group who took him away. It was Uther Doul, and it was men and women I'd never seen. I don't know what that's all about. Seems to me that calling the avanc is not the end of it."

Johannes turned away from her and fingered the flowers.

"Only now realizing that, Bellis?" he said quietly. "Of course you're right. There's more to come. Given the scale of what we're attempting with the avanc, it's difficult to imagine, but it seems that perhaps that's just a . . . *prelude* to whatever's really going on. And what that is, I don't know. It's been decided it should not involve me.

"You know," he said, "it was just luck, really, that I ever got my commission here."

Luck? thought Bellis, incredulous.

"Of those in the know," he continued, "who'd seen the old chains, there've been some arguing for *decades* that Armada should try to call the avanc. But the Lovers ignored them, had no interest in it for years—that's what I heard.

"It changed when Uther Doul came to the city, came to work for them. I don't know what he did or said to them, but all of a sudden the avanc project was revived. Something he told them meant those old plans got dusted off, for the first time since those chains were built—and no one knows how long ago that was, or what happened.

"And after all that, it's just over for me. They've moved on to other things."

Jealous, realized Bellis. *Spurned, deserted, and pissed off.* Johannes' work—and Johannes himself—was invaluable to conjure up the avanc, but whatever came after that did not require him.

Gently, subtly, Bellis probed his wound. Moment by moment, interspersing her investigation with meaningless minutiae.

In his anger, Johannes was willing to talk seriously about the doubts that had been raised over the Lovers' plans.

They strolled through the wooded boat, past reclaimed funnels and bulkheads, while Bellis fed Johannes' resentment in a coy and sly interrogation, learning things piece by piece.

Once she started listening, Bellis heard the same names, the same rumors, everywhere. The veneer of loyalty that had been painted over Armada was thin. Anxieties and controversies were now as clearly traceable through it as woodgrain through varnish.

She was startled to realize that it was not only the worthies of Bask and Curhouse who were linked to such dissident voices. Some of Garwater's longest-loyal servants were doubters, linked to the renegades.

The Lovers' consensus, she realized, was not stable. And, as she half expected, the name that recurred most often, that came up again and again as a focus for this discontent, was Simon Fench.

Bellis began to search for him.

She asked all the people she knew about Simon Fench. Carrianne shrugged, but said she would keep her ears open. Johannes looked askance and said nothing. Shekel, at one of their infrequent meetings, nodded. "Ange mentioned him," he said. Feigning faint interest, Bellis asked Shekel to find out more.

Her query was tossed around on street corners, among the youths who hung over ship railings, firing catapults at the city's monkeys, or sat in pubs, playing dice and arm wrestling. Each had their own friends, their own contacts, men and women who might slip them coins and food and favors in exchange for whatever trivial services the boys and girls might perform. Bellis' question passed through them, through the drinking halls of Garwater and Shaddler and Booktown and Thee-And-Thine.

In New Crobuzon, what was not regulated was illicit. In Armada, things were different. It was, after all, a pirate city. What did not directly threaten the city did not concern its authorities. Bellis' message, like other secrets, did not have to strive to be covert, as it might back home to avoid the militia. Instead, it sped through this wrangling city with ease and speed, leaving a little trail for those who knew how to look.

* * *

"You wanted me."

Silas was standing by Bellis' bed. She had not yet undressed.
She was sitting with her knees up, reading a book by gaslight. A
moment before, she had been alone.

More thaumaturgy, Silas? she thought.

It was the evening of the tenth Scabdi of Hawkbill, the last day
of the quarto—a festival. The streets were loud; people were
drunk, shouting and laughing. The ships and streets were draped
with colored bunting. The air was full of fireworks and confetti
(and still the work went on below the water).

"I do," she said.

"You want to be careful. You don't want to advertise yourself
as dealing with dissidents."

Bellis laughed. "Jabber and fuck, Silas. You should see the list
of your—or Mr. Fench's—supposed friends. They include bigger fish than me, by far. Is it true you drink with Hedrigall?" He
did not reply. "So I don't think anyone's going to care about me."

They eyed each other quietly. *How many times have we done
this?* Bellis thought hopelessly. *Communed secretively—over
tea, in my room, at night, to discuss what we do and don't
know . . . ?*

"They're planning something," she said, and her own conspiratorial tone almost reduced her to bitter laughter. "The
avanc's not the end of it. Aum's learning Salt in double-quick
time, and they've taken him off to some new secret project. Even
some of the scientists involved are feeling cut out. There's a
core—Tintinnabulum, the Lovers, Aum—and this time Uther
Doul's part of it. They're planning something."

Silas nodded. It was obvious that he already knew.

"So?" Bellis demanded. "What is it?"

"I don't know," he said, and she could not tell if she believed him.

"If we can work out what they've planned," she said, "we
might still be able to . . . to get out of here."

"Sincerely," he said slowly, "I can't work out what their plan
is. If I find out, I'll tell you. Of course."

They studied each other.

"I gather Uther Doul's courting you," he continued. He was
not trying to be unpleasant, but his smirk was irritating.

"I don't know *what* he's doing," Bellis said curtly. "Sometimes I think that's exactly it—he's courting me—but if so, by gods he's out of practice. Sometimes I think he has other motives, but I can't make sense of them."

Again silence. Outside, a cat began to wail.

"Tell me, Silas," Bellis said. "This is your world. Is there any kind of serious opposition to their project? *Serious,* I mean? And if there is, could we use it to get out of here? Can it help us?"

What exactly might I have in mind? she wondered. *We've sent a message to our home port. We've saved it, for Jabber's sake. There's nothing else to be done. There are no factions to win over. There's no one we might persuade to take us home.*

Whatever Silas claimed about trying to escape, the way he submerged into Armada's hinterland, ducked out of sight, became Simon Fench, suspended himself in a web of deals and rumors and favors and threats—these were survival tactics. Silas was adjusting.

There was nothing for Bellis to do. No schemes she could engage in, no secret plans.

She still dreamed of that river between New Crobuzon and Iron Bay.

No, she thought fiercely, uncompromisingly. *Whatever the truth, whatever the case, however hopeless the cause—I do not give up on escape.*

It had taken her quite some effort to reach this coldly burning pitch of anger, of desire for escape, and to relinquish it now would be unbearable.

And so she kept that *No* loud in the back of her head, undiluted by doubt.

She woke the next day and leaned from her window into the warm wind, watching the exhausted, hungover crews clear the detritus of last night's party from the streets and decks. They swept up huge piles of dust and colored paper, costumes and disguises from the masque parties, the debris of drug-taking.

The bilious flames had stopped rolling from the top of the *Sorghum's* derrick. The rig had gone cold, its harvest of oil and rockmilk siphoned up and stored. Over the ships' roofscape, the steamers, the tugs, the squat industrial vessels were moving back toward the city, like iron filings toward a magnet. Bellis watched their crews attach them again to the edge of Armada.

When all the servant ships had attached themselves to the city, they bore off to the southeast, venting black smoke, their gears grinding, devouring huge quantities of stolen coal and anything else that might burn. With appalling slowness, Armada began to move.

Below, in the clear water, the divers continued working. The stripping down of ship after ship continued, their substances delivered to the industrial works. An endless train of dirigibles passed between the vessels' corpses and the forges.

The sea moved in faint currents around the massive bridle hidden below the waves. Armada's pace was almost imperceptible: only a mile or two every hour.

But it did not slacken. It was ceaseless. Bellis knew that when it reached the place it sought, when the chains were lowered, when the thaumaturgy was attempted, everything would change. And she heard herself again, *No,* refusing to acquiesce, refusing to make her home here.

As her days passed, she was needed less and less. Her translation sessions with the engineers were fewer, as the bridle's crews worked their endless hours and problems of design were reached, one by one, and solved. Bellis felt herself slipping from the core of things.

Except for Doul. He still spoke to her, still gave her wine in his cabin. There was still something shadowy between them, but Bellis could not make it out. And Doul's conversations were as cryptic as ever, and she took no comfort in them. Once, twice more, he took her again to that little room, the sound box below the Lovers' chamber. Why she went with him she could not say. It was always at night, always a secret. She heard their gasping declarations, their mews of pain and desire. The emotion still appalled and nauseated her, like something rotting in her stomach.

The second time she had heard them hiss with whatever passed for pleasure in their minds, and the next day, when she entered the meeting room with Aum, the Lovers stared at her with fresh wounds, blood crusting on their foreheads, scored deep in mirror images across their faces.

And Bellis had faltered. She could not bear the thought that she was at the mercy of people hooked on the emotion she had heard.

No.

Even as the weather grew hotter still, day after day till a week and then two had passed, and the bridle was nearly done, and Silas had not come to her, and Doul still made no sense; even as she slipped from the center of power, and her relief that she need not see the Lovers every day was effaced by the fear of her own growing ineffectuality; even as she lost the last semblance of power she had had; even as it became clear that she was trapped, the voice inside Bellis hardened and was absolutely clear.

No.

CHAPTER THIRTY-TWO

Armada found the place it was looking for.

The city was near the southern border between the Swollen Ocean and the Black Sandbar Sea. Bellis was stunned when she heard that. *Have we really come so fucking far?* she had thought.

They lay absolutely still in the water. By arcane techniques like echo-catching and sensory projection, Armada had found its way to the center of a deadeye. These existed randomly across the oceans—patches of water a few miles across, where there were no currents or winds. Without motive power, things floating on the surface of deadeyes would bob up and down with waves, but would not move an inch in any compass direction.

They were signs of sinkholes.

In this region, the ocean was between three and four miles deep. But below the deadeye the seafloor fell away in a steep cone, into a circular hole that stretched down below the reach of any geo-empath.

The sinkhole was a mile and a half wide, and bottomless.

It stretched so deep that Bas-Lag's dimension could not possibly contain the water's gravity and density, and reality was unstable in the shaft's lower reaches. The sinkhole was a duct between realms. Where the avancs breached.

* * *

There was not a time when Krüach Aum and his new subordinates declared their researches over—there was no sudden announcement, no claim that the last problems had been solved. Bellis could not say exactly when she knew that Armada was ready.

Doul did not tell her. The knowledge soaked into her, and into all the other citizens. In rumor and guesswork, in triumphant speculation and then in triumph, the word spread. *They've succeeded. They know how to do it. They're waiting.*

Bellis wanted not to believe it. The awareness that the scientists had perfected the techniques they needed took her so gently that there was no sudden shock, just a slowly waxing foreboding. *How?* she thought, again and again. She considered the scale of what was to be attempted, and the question overwhelmed her. *How can they do it?*

She considered everything that had to be done, all the knowledge that they had had to amass, the machines to be built, the puissance to channel. It seemed impossible. *Is it down to me?* she wondered incredulously. *Without Aum, without his book, could this be done?*

With every hour, Bellis could feel the tension, the anxiety and excitement, increasing all around her.

Days after they reached the deadeye, finally, the announcement was made that everyone had been expecting. Posters and criers warned people to be ready, that the research was over, that an attempt was to be made.

As momentous, as extraordinary, as it was, it surprised no one. And after such long official silence, even to Bellis, that final confirmation was almost a relief.

Tanner Sack found the bridle and the now-visible chains a great pleasure to his eye. He had been born and raised in New Crobuzon, where mountains picked out the western sky and the architecture was complex and encompassing. There were times, he would admit, when the endless open skies of Armada, the unbroken water below, troubled him.

He found a comfort in the submerged harness. It gave him something big and real to stare at, breaking the monotonous deeps.

Tanner hung in the still waters of the deadeye.

There were a very few figures in the water—Tanner, Bastard John, the menfish—watching from below.

Everything had been prepared.

It was almost midday. The city was as still as if it were before dawn.

On neighboring ships, Bellis could see people watching from their roofs, or peering from behind railings or from the city's parks. But there were not many. There was almost no noise. There were no dirigibles in the sky.

"Half the city's indoors," she hissed to Uther Doul. He had found her on the deck of the *Grand Easterly,* gathered with the few Armadans who, like Bellis, felt compelled to watch the attempt from the flagship itself.

They're frightened, she thought, staring over the empty streets on vessels below. *They've realized what's at stake here. Like shipwrecked sailors in a jolly boat tethering themselves to a whale.* She almost laughed. *And they're afraid of the storm.*

The citizens of Armada dreaded severe storms. The city could not avoid or ride the weather's tempers, and the worst winds could tear vessel from vessel, throw them together no matter how strong their buffers. Armada's history was punctuated with the stories of terrible and deadly squalls.

Never before had anyone *deliberately* called one down.

To puncture the membrane between realities, even at a weak point, to entice the avanc into this plane, a burst of colossal energy was required. Something like that required not just an elyctric storm, but a living one. An orgy, a frenzy of fulmen, lightning elementals.

And given that living storms were—thankfully—almost as rare as Torque rifts, Garwater would have to create one.

The *Grand Easterly*'s six masts, particularly its towering main mast, were swathed with copper wiring, insulated with rubber, that stretched down and disappeared into the ship itself, passing down corridors and stairs, carefully guarded by the yeomanry, winding through the vessel until it slotted into the esoteric new engine running on rockmilk at the *Grand Easterly*'s base, ready to send extraordinary charges into the stub ends of the colossal chain, down through the metal into the bridle and the deep sea.

Somewhere, scholars and pirate-thaumaturges from Booktown and Shaddler and Garwater were gathered: meteoromancers and elementalists with weird engines, furnaces, unguents, and offerings. Perhaps a sacrifice. Bellis could imagine their frantic work gauging aetherial currents, stoking and conjuring.

For a long time there was only whispering and the faint noises of gulls and the waves. Everyone who stood in the bleak heat strained to hear something that they had not heard before, but they had no idea what they were waiting for. When it finally came it was a sound so monolithic that they felt it, deep below, resonating through the ships.

Bellis heard Uther Doul exhale, then he whispered "Now," his voice thick with emotion she did not recognize.

The deck of the *Grand Easterly* moved suddenly below their feet, with a cracking percussion.

Armada vibrated violently.

"The bridle, the chains," Doul said quietly. "They're being lowered. Into the hole."

Bellis gripped the rail.

Below the water Tanner gasped, water rushing over his gills, as the vast pulleys turned and the restraining bolts on the harness were burst with explosive charges. In carefully choreographed sequence, displacing great tides of brine, the metal ring more than a quarter of a mile across, studded with cruel hooks and collars, began to descend.

It slid in stages through the water, reaching the limit of its freedom as each section of boat-long links ended. And then another charge would detonate, and huge gears would turn, and a few more hundred feet of metal would sink.

As each length of chain reached its end, the city above moved, and reconfigured a little, its dimensions shifting under the strain. The chains were so huge, they operated at a geographic scale, each weighty tug a seismic trauma. But Armada was buoyed by careful design and gas and thaumaturgy, and though the sudden jolts shook it as if in a high storm, and strained at those few wickerwork-and-rope bridges that were not uncoupled, and snapped them, they could not capsize the city.

"Jabber and *fuck*," Bellis shouted. "We have to get below!"

Doul held her, gripped her hard and kept her feet flat.

"I'll not miss this," he said, "and I don't think you should, either."

The city bucked appallingly; then, suddenly.

* * *

The bridle's descent began to speed up. Tanner Sack realized he was shouting soundlessly, airlessly, his jaw biting out silent profanities at the sight. He was hypnotized by the scale of what he saw, the rapid disappearance of the huge harness into the absolutely dark sea. Seconds and minutes passed. The city stabilized a little and there was only the continuing unfolding of the great tethered chains, five lines of links descending into the hidden deeps.

Colonies of barnacles and limpets had scabbed the chains over generations, and as the links ripped free of the ships' undersides, they sent clouds of dying shellfish into the abyss.

After many minutes had passed, Armada was almost still again, undulating very slightly with the last reverberations of the chain. Birds shunted mindlessly back and forth overhead. The huge weight of the metal settled. There was a tense expectancy.

And everyone held their breath, and nothing happened.

The bridle now dangled below miles of chain. The city above moved on the swell, peacefully.

Armadans were braced and waiting. But the water of the deadeye remained peaceful, and the sky clear. Slowly, more and more people began to emerge onto the decks. They were nervous and hesitant at first, still waiting for an occurrence the parameters of which they could not imagine. But nothing happened.

Bellis did not know precisely what manner of crisis had overtaken the scientists and thaumaturgists. The promised storm did not appear. The rockmilk engines did not move.

It was no surprise, she reflected. The techniques were unique, unproven and experimental. It was no surprise that they did not work straight away.

Still, the anticlimax was overwhelming. Within two hours the city was as it had been. The unnatural hush abated.

Disappointed pirates bickered and told jokes about the failure. No one from Garwater, no scientist or bureaucrat, made any announcement about what had happened. Armada sat in the gentle water and the heat, and the hours of official silence became half a day, and continued.

Bellis could not find Doul, who had gone to find out what had happened. She spent her evening alone. She should have been delighted at Armada's failure, but a ruefulness infected even her. A curiosity.

Two days passed.

In the deadeye's still water, some of the city's effluent congealed around the city, and lolling in the sun, Armada began to smell. Once, Bellis and Carrianne walked in Croom Park, but the odor and the raucous cries of too-hot animals, feral and in farm-ships, made the atmosphere unpleasant. It was not refreshing to be out of doors. Bellis confined herself and her smoking to her room.

Apart from that brief meeting with Carrianne, she spent the hours alone. Doul did not reappear. Bellis fidgeted in the heat and smoked and waited, watching the city return to its raucous routine with willful speed. It infuriated her. *How can you all pretend that nothing's going on?* she thought, watching the vendors in Winterstraw Market. *As if this is just a place like any other, as if this is a normal time?*

There was still no word as Krüach Aum, his assistants, and the crews of engineers and hunters, all unseen, worked over their calculations again, took measurements, tinkered with their engines, as Bellis was sure they must be doing.

Two days passed.

Tanner lay under the city, floating motionless, facing down. It was as if he stood at the entrance to a dark pentangular tunnel edged with chains. In line with his head, each arm and each leg, the five great fetters soared downward, converging with perspective and disappearing into the dark.

He was exhausted. The frantic repairs since the first attempt had robbed him of sleep. He had been yelled at by overseers livid from failure.

The enormous chain corridor stretched out below him was more than four miles long. Hanging absolutely motionless in the darkness at its end was the bridle, bigger than any ship. It dangled into the pit below, investigated, perhaps, by the oarfish and huge-mouthed eels that frequented that depth.

Sitting and reading beside her window, Bellis became slowly aware of an odd stillness: a silence and a shift in the quality of the light. A neurotic pause, as if the air and the bleaching sun were waiting. She knew with a shock of amazed fear what was happening.

At last, she thought. *Gods help me, they've done it.*

From her front step, high up on the *Chromolith* chimney, she looked out over Armada's gently bobbing vessels, at the *Grand Easterly*'s masts. She stared into the crowded city. There had been no warning that another attempt was to be made: there were people everywhere. They were standing still in the markets and streets, peering up, trying to work out what they had sensed.

The sky began to change.

"Dear Jabber," whispered Bellis. "Oh my gods."

In the middle of the sun-bleached blue stretched out over Armada, a darkness unfolded. Thousands of feet above them, the clear sky spasmed for an instant and shat out of nothingness a tiny smear of cloud, a mote, an atom of impurity that unfurled like a flower, like a trick box—a conjuror's prop that opened again and again, multiplying itself with its own substance.

It spread quickly like squid ink, uncoiling, staining the sky, spreading in a circle, an expanding disk of shadow. It emitted ominous sounds.

There was a wind, suddenly, slapping Armada's shanks and towers, strumming the city's rigging. Something was drifting down around Bellis, minuscule particles like mist, an arcane stink descending from the *Grand Easterly*'s funnels and spreading out, the effluent of whatever forces were tearing the clouds out of nothing. Bellis recognized the smell: rockmilk. Some aeromorphic engine was being boosted.

The sun was completely occluded. Bellis shivered in the newborn dark and cold. Beyond the city limits, the sea had become choppy, seesawing with foam. The sound from the sky increased: from low vibrations it became purring, and then a drawn-out shout, and finally a bark of thunder, and with that percussive noise the storm erupted out of the cloudmass.

The wind went berserk. The sea pitched. Thunder again, and with it the oily darkness over the city shattered a thousand ways, and through every crack lightning glared incandescent. Rain raced in screaming swells, dousing Bellis in moments.

Across all the ridings of the city, Armadans scrambled to get below. The decks emptied fast. Men and women struggled to uncouple the bridges as the vessels they linked began to buck. Here and there stood people transfixed like Bellis, in fear or fascination, staring into the storm.

"Godspit!" shouted Bellis. "Sweet Jabber protect us!" She could not hear her own voice.

The storm was muted for Tanner, cosseted deep as he was in the water of the deadeye. The surface above him lost its integrity in the rain. The city rose and fell as if the sea were trying to shuck it off. The huge chains moved below it.

Even through the tons of water, Tanner realized, the sound of thunder and the water's motions were increasing. He swam, agitated, waiting for the storm to reach its final pitch, growing more and more nervous as the violence did not dissipate, as it continued to increase.

'Stail, he thought in awe and fear. *They've done it this time, ain't they? What the fuck kind of storm is this? What the fuck have they done?*

Bellis held tight to the rail, terrified that the wind would pull her out and over, to be crushed between vessels.

The air was stained by shadows, a darkness burst by lightning like camera flashes.

Even with air rinsed by the torrent, the weird stink of rockmilk vapor was strong and increasing. Bellis could see ripples distorting the air. Lightning struck the city's masts again and again, lingering around the huge copper-shrouded column on the *Grand Easterly.*

Armada danced as the sky boiled. As the aeromorphic engine vented ever more power, the lightning patterns began to change. Bellis watched the clouds, mesmerized.

At first the streaks and jags were random, snapping and shivering like brilliant snakes in the darkness. But they began to synchronize. They grew closer in time, so that the light from one still scored Bellis' eyes while the next fired, and their movements grew more purposeful. The lightning bursts bolted toward the center of the cloud, vanishing at its core.

The thunder grew more intense. The rockmilk smell was nauseating. Bellis was hypnotized by what she saw through the deluge, capable only of thinking *come on come on!* without consciousness of what she was waiting for.

And then finally, with a single stunning report of thunder, the lightning reached phase.

They burst out of nothing at the same moment around the storm's edge, scored through the dark air together toward its heart as if they were spokes, meeting at the axis of the tempest in a single, painfully intense point of light that crackled and *did not dissipate.*

Energy burst up, invisible, amplified through the valves and transformers of occult engines, spurting out of the *Grand Easterly*'s smokestacks, racing skyward into the storm.

The invocation burst in the heart of the cloud.

The crackling star of lightning shone cold and intense and bluewhite, trembling, glowing brighter, taut as if pregnant as if full as if ready to explode and then it

burst

and a swarm of shrieking presences coalesced out of its shreds and were about the ship, crackling apparitions outlined in energy, in elyctricity, leaving trails of burned air as they raced with intent through the sky, informed and capricious and purposeful.

Fulmen. Lightning elementals.

They screamed and laughed as they zigzagged, their cries something between sound and current. The fulmen tore with astonishing speed over the skyline, metamorphosing in arcs of current, trailing a slew of ghost shapes formed in their discharge, mimicking the outlines of the city's buildings, mimicking fish and birds and faces.

A cluster swept down to the *Chromolith* deck, shrieking past Bellis and almost stopping her heart. They gusted around the funnel.

From somewhere in the *Grand Easterly* came a pulse of power, and all over the city the elementals snapped up from their games and eddied in agitation. Again the hidden machines gave out a jolt of energy, sending it coursing along the wires to the tip of the mast. The fulmen howled, and danced along chains and metal railings. They began to swarm. Bellis turned her head and watched them go, out over the body of her ship, through the channels of water between vessels, up and over reconstituted decks toward the huge steamer's mainmast.

Bellis did not notice the rain or the thunder. All she could see or hear were the living lightnings that outlined Armada with their blazing cold, squabbling and spasming in and out of existence by the city's tallest roofs. She peered through the storm, over the intervening vessels. Like bait, a flow of energy dangled at the tip of the *Grand Easterly*'s towering mast.

We fish for a storm to fish for the elementals to fish for the avanc, thought Bellis. She felt drunk.

The fulmen circled the mast, a sheet of bristling presences, spinning into a vortex. They spat in the storm's darkness, illuminating the city negatively, as if with black sunlight, until a last great gout of binding energy burst out of the wires.

The fulmen shrieked and gibbered and began to pour into the metal.

With hexes and machinery, the elementalists reeled them in.

The elementals screamed as they were taken, their forms conducted through the thick cabling, lights snuffed out in rapid succession. In half a second the sky was dark again.

The elyctric elementals coursed as supercharged particles along the network of copper, bleeding one into the other and becoming a stream of living power, racing down stairs and into the *Grand Easterly*'s guts, to the rockmilk engine, into the stump ends of the chain that stretched down into the rift below the sea.

Below millions of tons of brine, this condensed substance of a tribe of lightning elementals burst through the links of chain, through prongs the size of masts, out into the water in a bolt of massively potent energy that blazed white light and spasmed instantly into the deeps of the sinkhole, bleaching and destroying what rude life it passed, until it lanced the membrane between dimensions, many miles down.

In the bottom of the *Grand Easterly,* the rockmilk engine hummed, and sent potent pulses out along the chain.

Only now there was a rent beneath the sea, and now the enticing signals the machine sent out, inaudible to anything born in the seas of Bas-Lag, might be heard.

Tanner Sack heads down into the twilit water. The storm has dissipated, almost instantly, and the sea above him is bright. Tanner is testing himself, pushing on and down, as far as he can go, into the disphotic zone.

There are others around him: cray and menfish and Bastard

John, he supposes, curious to plumb as far as they are able, but he cannot see them. The water is cold, and silent, and dense.

He felt the jolts of energy pass him through the huge links of chain. He knows that astonishing events are unfolding directly below, and like a child he indulges himself, sinking toward the dark. He has never swum so deep before, but he follows the enormous chain links as far down as he can go, steeling himself, acclimatizing as the pressure wraps him tight. His tentacles reach out and seem to grasp, as if he can pull himself deeper, gripping the substance of the water.

His head hurts; his blood is constricted. He hangs still in the water when he can go no further. He does not know how far he has come down. He cannot see the great chain by his side. He can see nothing. He is suspended in the cold and the grey, and he is quite alone.

A long time passes while the signals from the rockmilk engine continue to reverberate enticingly into the deep water. Everything is still.

Until Tanner's eyes snap open (*he did not know they were closed*).

There has been a sound, a sudden feeling of slick grinding, like the snapping of bolts, things slotting into grooves. A long, rumbling report that travels through the water like whalesong, that he feels in his stomach more than he hears.

Tanner is still. He listens.

He knows what he has heard.

It was the restraints on the quarter-mile bridle—the jags and pegs and pins and rivets, the bolts as long as ships—sliding into place. Something has come snuffling up through layers of water and reality, he thinks, to investigate the delicious rockmilk pulses, and has slipped its neck or some part of itself into the collar until the harness is around it, and the spines and studs like tree trunks have jutted forward, piercing its flesh, and the cinctures have tightened, and the thing is trapped.

There is silence again, and stillness. Tanner knows that above him, the thaumaturges and engineers are sending carefully measured signals into what approximates the creature's cortex, soothing, suggesting, cajoling.

He feels minute shifts of tide and temperature—thaumaturgic washes rolling up at him.

Tanner feels vibrations against his skin and then, harder, inside him.

The thing is moving, way below the dying fringes of sunlight, in the midnight water miles down, past lantern fish and spider crabs, eclipsing their feeble phosphorescence. He feels it creeping nearer, displacing great gouts of cold water and sending them rolling up and out of the abyss in uncanny tides.

He is enthralled.

There is a lazy booming that makes the water shudder. Tanner imagines some monstrous appendage casually slapping the continental shelf, an unthinking apocalypse wiping out scores of crude bottom dwellers.

The water around him swirls. Thaumaturgic tides wash dissonant up from the hole. There is a sudden spasm of water pressure, and then a very faint sound of pounding reaches Tanner's ears. Uncertain, he strains to hear.

It is a faint, regular beat that he feels in his innards. A ponderous, smashing stroke. His stomach pitches.

He hears it only for an instant, a quirk of space and thaumaturgy, but he knows what it is, and the knowledge stuns him.

It is a heart the size of a cathedral, beating far below him in the dark.

On the rain-wet steps, below a fierce sun and cloudless skies, Bellis waited.

Armada was like a ghost town. All but the most enthralled of its inhabitants hid, still terrified.

Something had happened. Bellis had felt the shifting of the *Chromolith* and the knocking of the chains. There had been many minutes now of silence.

She started, once again hearing metal on metal: a slow, threatening percussion as the chains below the city shifted, moving up and stretching out, emerging from the sinkhole below the world, returning to their home dimension, immersing themselves fully in the waters of the Swollen Ocean.

They angled slowly away from vertical, extending until they were stretched taut out in front of the city. Miles below, the bridle was just above the ocean floor.

There was a sudden juddering noise, and Armada shifted violently against itself, its ships shifting into subtly new positions, pulled in new directions from below, altering its outlines.

The city began to move.

The spasm almost knocked Bellis down.

She was agog.

The city was *moving*.

Cruising southward at a leisurely pace that easily eclipsed anything that had ever been achieved by the scores of tugboats.

Bellis could see the waves against the flanks of the outside vessels. She could see the turmoil of the city's wake. They were traveling fast enough to leave a *wake*.

From the edge of Armada to the horizon, the city's fleet of untethered ships—merchant-pirates, factories, messengers and warships and tugs—were now frantically moving. They were turning to face the city, starting their motors, unfurling their sails to catch up with their mother port.

Oh dear gods, Bellis thought, stunned. *They must not be able to believe what they're seeing.* From the nearest of them, Bellis heard a chorus of delight. The sailors were standing on deck cheering.

The sound was taken up, slowly, all over Armada as people began to appear: opening windows and doors, emerging from bunkers, standing up at the railings behind which they had cowered. Everywhere Bellis looked, the citizens were shouting. They were toasting the Lovers. They were screaming with delight.

Bellis looked out to sea, watching the waves pass by as the city moved. As it was towed.

At the end of its four-mile reins, coddled by the rockmilk engine, held tight by hooks like recurved steeples, the avanc progressed steadily and curiously through what was, to it, an alien sea.

INTERLUDE VII
Basilisk Channel

For over four weeks, the *Tetneghi Dustheart* has been at sea.

The galleon has faced dreadful summer storms. It has been becalmed between Gnurr Kett and Porriok Nigh. In the dangerous channels of the Mandrake Islands it sailed too close to some nameless rock and was beset by marauding flying things that tore the sails and pulled several apes from the rigging to their deaths. In the cold waters by the Rohagi eastern coast, the ship was met and attacked—by nasty chance—by a Crobuzoner navy ship. With lucky winds, the *Tetneghi Dustheart* outran the ironclad, sustaining damage that slowed but did not destroy it.

Its cactacae crew whistle instructions to the exhausted simians above, and the gaudy vessel approaches port-peace, winds through the channel toward Iron Bay.

The day after his meeting with Tanner Sack, when Captain Nurjhitt Sengka announced his new orders to his crew, they reacted with the astonishment and bad feeling that he had expected. The relaxed discipline of Dreer Samher vessels had allowed them to express themselves more or less freely, and they had told Sengka they disapproved, they were pissed off, they did not understand, they were deserting their posts, that the anophelii needed more guards than the skeleton crew that would be left there.

He was implacable.

With every misfortune on the way, with every hold-up, every dragging minute of the month, the crew's grumbling grew louder. But Sengka, having decided to risk his career on the written promises Tanner had given him, did not deviate from his plan. And his standing with his crew is good enough that he has been able so far to contain their anger, to keep them waiting with hints and winks.

And now the *Tetneghi Dustheart* crawls toward the Gross Tar.

The galleon's ostentatious gold and sweeping curves are dulled by brutal spring weather that shocks the cactacae, their garish southern esthetic absurd beside the dark browns and blacks and muddy greens and faint blossom colors of the islands they pass.

They are weather-beaten, dilapidated. The crew are impatient. Sengka fingers the sealed pouch.

There is not long now. They are close to the bay and the river, the bricks and bridges. There are more and more rocks in the waters around them. The channel is shallowing. The coast is very close.

Captain Sengka looks closely at the New Crobuzon seal on the little cargo he is delivering. He hefts it in his big hands: the leather, the box bound in wax; the offer of a reward that New Crobuzon will honor; the letter of alarm, its melodramatic warning of war in obscure, absurd, quite meaningless code; the stubby, worthless little necklace that justifies the jewelry box; and beneath that box's velvet padding, sealed in its false bottom, cosseted in sawdust, a heavy disk the size of a large watch, and a long dispatch in tiny calligraphy.

Procurator Fennec's secret gift to New Crobuzon, and his real message.

INTERLUDE VIII

Elsewhere

There has been some stunning irruption into the world. The sea tastes of something new.

What is this?

None of the hunters knows.

What was that shattering that sudden shift the opening up the intrusion the trespass the arrival? What is it that has come?

None of the hunters knows. They can only tell that the sea has changed.

Signs are everywhere. The currents are tentative, shifting direction minutely, as if there is some new obstacle in their path that they do not know how to avoid. The salinae scream and gibber, desperate to communicate what they know.

Even such a massive new presence as this is a tiny change, on a world scale. Almost infinitely small. But the hunters are sensitive to water at a level smaller than atoms, and they know that something has happened.

The new thing has its own unique spoor, but it is a trail of particles and dung and taste that do not operate according to the physics of Bas-Lag. Gravity, random motion, physical existence do not work quite as they should around the intruder. The hunters can taste it, but not track it.

Yet they do not stop trying. Because it is obvious that this is the work of the floating city, and that if they can find the slow, huge thing, they find their quarry.

Time moves quickly.

There are bubbles of water, fresh and brine. They are breathed out by siblings many miles away, they rise, maintaining their integrity even surrounded by the stuff of their own substance, slip through little thaumaturgic vents and are displaced, continuing their upward motion without interruption, vast distances from where they started. They burst by the hunters' ears, bearing messages from home. Rumors and stories spoken as water. From the groac'h and magi in The Gengris, from the spies in Iron Bay.

We hear things, says one voice.

The hunters commune, and pour out their energy, tremulous and effortful, using their foci, the preserved relics of their dead. Their leaders whisper in response, and the hunters' own speech bubbles cross the distance back again, home.

Something new has entered the sea, they say.

And when the conversation is done, the magi, quiet in the darkness very far below the surface of the Swollen Ocean, three thousand miles from their home, blink and shake their heads, and the sound that has reached them from across the world dissipates with the water that carries it.

Boats are coming, they tell their hunters. *Many. Quickly. From Iron Bay. Hunting, too. Searching, like us. Crossing the sea. Our sisters and brothers are with them, clinging like remora, singing to us. We can find them easily.*

The boats. The boats seek the same thing we do. They know where they are going. They have machines to find it.

We track them, and they will track for us.

The hunters grin with their very long teeth and emit the barking gasps of water that are their laughter, folding their limbs away into streamlined shapes and setting out for the north, in the direction they have been given, aiming for where New Crobuzon's flotilla will be. So they will intercept it, and join their other troops, and at last find their quarry.

PART SIX

Morning Walker

Chapter Thirty-three

The avanc, and Armada behind it, maintained an unchanging, steady speed—always northward. Nothing like as quick as a ship, but faster by many times than the city had ever been able to travel before.

Armadan vessels were returning every day. Their secret mechanisms had shown them their home port's unprecedented pace, and they were racing across the sea in panic or jubilation to their city with booty of jewels and food and books and earth.

The returned sailors found the city an astounding sight. Surrounded by the fleet of tugs and steamboats that had always pulled it but that now followed it in a huge disparate mass like a second, disintegrating city, loyal and useless, Armada was powering slowly through the sea as if by its own will.

Some of those now-redundant ships were being integrated into the city's substance, hooked and welded into place, stripped and refitted, built up. Others were converted into pirate vessels, outfitted with armor and guns of a hundred different kinds. They were crossbred, bristling with found ordnance.

The city's bearing was north-northeast, but there were deviations this way and that, to avoid some storm or rocky island, or some irregularity in the ocean floor that the citizens of Armada could not see.

The pilots on the *Grand Easterly* were equipped with a rack of pyrotechnic flares in a variety of colors. When the avanc's course needed correcting, they would fire them in combinations, in prearranged signals. Engineers in the other ridings would respond, firing up the massive winches that would haul back on one or other of the submerged chains.

The avanc responded, uncomplaining and accommodating as a cow. It altered its course (*with a flickering of its fins or filaments or paws or gods knew what*) in response to the faint tugging. It allowed itself to be led.

In the bottom of the *Grand Easterly,* the work of the engine room quickly become routine. All day the juddering boilers were fed a thin stream of the rockmilk the *Sorghum* had drawn up, and they sent a steady pulse of coddling through the chain and the spines and into what approximated the avanc's cortex.

The huge creature was drugged, drowsy with contentment, mindless as a tadpole.

At first, after the avanc was called, when it became clear that the thaumaturgy, the hunting, had actually worked, that the fabled beast had entered Bas-Lag, Armada's citizenry were hysterical with excitement.

That first night had been a spontaneous party. The quarto's-end decorations were brought out again, and the boulevards and plazas across the city were filled with lines of dancing people, men and women, khepri and cactus and scabmettler and others, carrying aloft a variety of papier-mâché models of the avanc, as unlikely as they were inconsistent.

Bellis spent the evening in a pub with Carrianne, buoyed up by the revelry despite herself. The next day she was tired and downcast. It was the third Markindi of Flesh Quarto, and Bellis referred to the New Crobuzon calendar she had scribbled down and discovered that it was the fifteenth of Swiven—Badsprit Eve. This realization depressed her. It was not that she thought the baleful influence of the festival would extend this far, but the near coincidence of the avanc's arrival with that night was discomfiting.

As the days wore on, even with the excitement still fresh, even with the astonishment of waking each day to a sea slapping against a city in motion, Bellis sensed an anxiety growing in Armada. Central to that was the realization that the Lovers of Garwater, who controlled the avanc, were heading north and would not say why.

Discussions about where the avanc would take the city had so far been in general, nebulous terms. Garwater's representatives had stressed the creature's speed and power, the ability to escape storms and barren seas, to make for fair weather, where crops would thrive. Many citizens had assumed that the city would head for somewhere warm, where there were few naval powers, where goods and books and soil and other plunder could be taken from the shore with ease. The southern Kudrik, or perhaps the Codex Sea. Somewhere like that.

But as the days went on, the city continued north, without slowing or deviating. Armada was heading somewhere definite at the Lovers' behest, and nothing was being said.

"We'll find out soon enough," was what the loyalists said in the dockside pubs. "They've nothing to hide from us."

But when finally the news sheets and journals, the street speakers and polemicists composed themselves enough to ask the question on everyone's minds, there was still no answer. After a week, *The Flag*'s front page consisted of just four huge words: WHERE ARE WE GOING?

Still there was no answer.

There were those for whom this silence did not matter. What mattered was that Armada was a great power controlling something more astonishing than they could have imagined. The specifics of their journey were of no more concern to them than they ever had been before. "We've always left it to them who make the decisions," some said,

But there had never been really serious decisions before, only the vaguest agreement that the steamers would haul roughly in such-and-such a direction, in the hope that in a year or two—currents, tides, and Torque permitting—the city might reach congenial water. Now, with the avanc, came a new kind of power, and there were some who realized that everything had changed—that there were now real decisions to be made, and that the Lovers were making them.

In the absence of information, rumor flowered. Armada was heading for Gironella's Dead Sea, where the water was ossified in its wave forms, entombing all the life within. It was heading for the Malmstrom, for the edge of the world. It was heading for a cacotopic stain. It was heading for a land of ghosts, or talking wolves, or men and women whose eyes were jewels or who had teeth like polished coal, or a land of sentient coral, or an empire of fungus, or it was heading somewhere else, maybe.

On the third Bookdi of the quarto, Tintinnabulum and his crew left Armada.

For the best part of a decade, the *Castor* had been embedded near Garwater's foremost point, where it met Shaddler riding.

Lashed beside the *Tolpandy,* it had sat for a long time beside an
ironclad warship that had become a shopping district, its greys
mottled with commercial coloration, the byways between its
derelict guns surrounded by alleys of tin-shack shops.

People had forgotten that the *Castor* was not a permanent fix-
ture. Bridges had linked it to its surrounds, and chains and ropes
and buffers had tethered it. Those links were cut, one by one.

Under a hot sun, the hunters swung machetes and removed
themselves from the flesh of Armada, till they were free-floating,
a foreign body. Between the *Castor* and the open sea a pathway
was cleared between vessels. Bridges were uncoupled, tethers
were broken on a route leading by the barge *Badmark* into Shaddler, then alongside the *Darioch's Concern* with its cheap houses
and raucous industry. It continued past the *Dearly,* a submersible
long surface-bound, its interior a theater, and twisted starboard
between an ancient trading cog and a big chariot ship, its rein
stubs refitted to hold colored lights; then there was an open patch
of water and beyond it the Shaddler Sculpture Garden on the
Thaladin, the outer edge of Armada.

Beyond that was the sea.

The vessels that lined the pathway were crowded as people
leaned over to shout good-bye at the *Castor.* Yeomanry and
Shaddler guards kept the new channel free of traffic. The sea was
calm and the avanc's passage steady.

When the first of the city's clocks began to strike noon, the
Castor's motors started up, to a great squall of excitement from
the crowd. They cheered raucously as the vessel, a little over a
hundred feet long, topped by its absurdly tall bell tower, began to
putter forward.

The bridges, lines and chains and girders, were reconnected in
the vessel's wake. The *Castor* slipped like a splinter from the
city's flesh, which reknitted behind it.

In many places the route was only a little wider than the *Castor* itself, and it bumped against its neighbors, its swaddling of
rope and rubber absorbing the impact. It progressed sluggishly,
thumping its way toward the open sea. Beside it, the crowds
were shouting and waving, as triumphant as if they had freed the
hunters after years of imprisonment.

The ship finally slipped past the *Thaladin* into the ocean, traveling in the same direction as the avanc but outpacing it in order
to emerge from the city. In that wide water, the *Castor* kept its

speed up. It skirted around the front edge of Armada, turning to the south, letting the city drift past it as the avanc continued onward. Armada moved on, till the *Castor* was by the outskirts of The Clockhouse Spur; and then by the open entrance to the Basilio docks, thronging with free boats; and then it was past Jhour, and the *Castor*'s engine sounded again and it headed away, in among the free vessels that surrounded and followed the city. Tintinnabulum's boat passed through them, shedding its protective buffers as it went, dropping rubber and tar-soaked cloth overboard, before disappearing toward the southern horizon.

Many people watched the *Castor* from the Sculpture Garden until it disappeared around Armada's curve. Among them were Angevine and Shekel, holding hands.

"They did their job," said Angevine. She was still shocked to find herself out of a job, but she sounded only very slightly regretful. "They finished what they were brought here to do. Why would they have stayed?

"Do you know what he said to me?" she continued to Shekel impatiently, and he could tell that she had had this on her mind, "He said they might've been tempted to stay longer, but they didn't want to go where the Lovers are going."

Tanner watched the *Castor*'s progress from below.

He was not perturbed that the city was heading north, or that he did not know where it was going. He found a great pleasure in the realization that the summoning of the avanc was not the end of Garwater's project. He found it hard to understand those who saw in this some betrayal, who were angry, intimidated by their own ignorance.

But don't you think it's wonderful? he felt like saying to them. *It ain't over! There's more to be done! The Lovers've got more up their sleeves. There's more we can do; there's bigger things at stake. We can keep at it!*

He spent more and more hours under the surface, emerging to spend his time alone, or occasionally with Shekel, who was growing more closemouthed as the days passed.

Tanner grew closer to Hedrigall. Ironically, Hedrigall was a voice of opposition to the city's northerly trajectory, and to the Lovers' silence. But Tanner knew that Hedrigall's loyalty to Garwater was as strong as his own, that there was nothing snide in his disquiet. Hedrigall was an intelligent and careful critic who did not deride Tanner's loyalty as blind or unthinking, who understood the trust and commitment Tanner placed in the Lovers, and who treated Tanner's defense of them seriously.

"You know they're my bosses, Tanner," he had said, "and you know that I ain't got any soft feelings for my so-called home. Dreer fucking Samher means shit to me. But . . . this is too much, Tanner, man—this silence. Things were working, Tanner. We didn't have to do all this. They should tell us what's happening. Without that, they lose our trust; they lose their legitimacy. And godsdammit, mate, that's what they depend on. There's only two of them, Croom knows how many thousands of us. This ain't good for Garwater."

These sentiments made Tanner uneasy.

He was happiest below the water. The submerged life of the riding continued as before: the clouds of fish, Bastard John, the leather-and-metal-clad divers at the end of their guy ropes, the flickering menfish of Bask, the cray, the shadows of submersibles like stubby whales beyond the city. The sunken supports of the *Sorghum,* its girder-legs poking from them. Tanner Sack himself, swimming from job to job, mouthing instructions or advice to his colleagues, taking orders and giving them.

But nothing was the same; everything was utterly different. Because at the edges of all that banal activity, framing the mass of keels and undersides like the points of a pentacle, the five great chains angled in a steep slope down and forward into the pitch, tethering the avanc miles below.

Tanner's days were harder than before. He kept swimming all the time, simply to keep up with Armada. He often found himself grabbing hold of jutting pillars, barnacle-crusted timbers, to allow himself to be towed. At the end of the day, when he hauled himself out of the water and returned to his rooms, he was utterly exhausted.

Thoughts of New Crobuzon clouded his mind more and more. He wondered if the message he had delivered had got through. He hoped it had, very much. He could not think about his erstwhile home ruined by war.

The temperature did not waver. Each day was sweaty and bleached by light. When there were clouds they were fraught, stormy and elyctric.

The Lovers, the anophelius Aum, Uther Doul, and a cabal of others retreated into the *Grand Easterly* to work on their new secret project. The wider circle of scientists was cut loose, to wander disconsolate and aggrieved.

Bellis' job was over. During the working hours, for want of other friends, she began tentatively to speak again with Johannes. He too was cast-off, like her. The avanc was caught—his role was over.

Johannes was still wary of her. They would wander the swaying streets of Armada, stopping at pavement cafés and little gardens, while pirate children played around them. They both still received stipends and could live easily from day to day, but their hours were endless and purposeless now. There was nothing ahead of them except other days, and Johannes was angry. He felt deserted.

For the first time Bellis could remember, he began to mention New Crobuzon regularly.

"What month is it at home?" he asked.

"Swiven," Bellis replied, chastising herself silently for not appearing to have to work it out.

"Winter's over," he said, "back there. Back in New Crobuzon." He nodded toward the west. "Spring now," he said quietly.

Spring. *And here am I,* thought Bellis, *who had winter stolen from me.* She remembered the river journey to Iron Bay.

"Do you suppose they know by now that we never arrived?" he said quietly.

"Nova Esperium must do," said Bellis. "Or at least they assume we're very severely delayed. Then they'll wait for the next New Crobuzon boat, probably in another six months' time, to send them word. So they won't know for sure back home for a long time."

They sat and drank their thin city-grown coffee.

"I wonder what's been happening there," Johannes said eventually.

They did not say much to each other, but the air was pregnant with their quiet.

Things are speeding up, Bellis said to herself, not quite understanding her own thought. She did not think of New Crobuzon as Johannes seemed to: when she imagined it, it was preserved as if in glass, quite unmoving. She did not think of it *now.* Perhaps she was afraid to.

She was nearly alone in knowing what might have happened, what wars might be being fought on the banks of the Tar and the Canker. It was bewildering to think that if the city was saved it was down to her. Or that it might not, in fact, have been saved.

The uncertainty, she thought, *the silence, the potentiality of what might have happened, what might be happening . . . it should crush me.* But it did not. Instead, Bellis felt as if she were waiting.

She spent that evening with Uther Doul.

They would drink together perhaps one night in three. Or they might walk through the city, directionless, or they might return to his room, or sometimes to hers.

He never touched her. Bellis was exhausted by his reticence. He would spend minutes without speaking, only to embark on some mythic-sounding story or other in response to some vague statement or question. His wonderful voice would subdue her then, and she would forget her frustration until his story ended.

Uther Doul clearly drew something from his time with her, but still she could not be sure what. She was not intimidated by him anymore, even carrying her secrets. For all his deadly skills, his brilliance in branches of obscure theology and science, she thought she saw in him someone more lost and confused than she, someone removed from all societies, uncertain of norms and interaction, retreated behind cold control. It made her feel safe in his presence.

She was drawn to him, powerfully. She wanted him: his power and his grim self-control, his beautiful voice. His cool intelligence, the obvious fact that he liked her. The sense that she would be more in control than he, should anything happen between them, and not just because she was older. She would not coquette, but she engineered enough of a dynamic that he must know.

But he never touched her. Bellis was unsettled by that.

It made little sense. His behavior clearly spelled out battened-down, incompetent desire, but there was something else as well. His manner was like some chymical compound, most of the ingredients of which she could identify instantly. There was, though, some mysterious component she could not make sense of, that modified everything that made him. And when Bellis became flushed with lust or loneliness for Doul, when she would otherwise have set matters in motion between them, she held back, flustered by his secret. She was not certain her advances would be reciprocated. And she would not risk that rejection.

Bellis' desire for sex with him became almost petulant— added to her physical attraction she felt a desire to clarify matters. *What is he doing?* she thought, time and again.

She had heard nothing from Silas Fennec for many days.

His toes touching the cold foot-wide barrel jutting from an ancient gunboat, his head staring down from higher than the Grand Easterly's mainmast, the man stands still and gazes and the scud of waves beside the boats makes him feel as if he is falling.

He is stronger with every day that passes. More puissant, more controlled and controlling, more exact in his machinations.

His kisses grow more languorous.

The man holds the statue in his hand, and he caresses the flap of fin-tissue with his fingertips. His mouth is still bloody and salty from the last tonguing kiss.

He moves about the city in the impossible ways that the statue has granted him. Space and physical forces loosen their weft to him when his mouth and tongue tingle from the cold salt press of the stone. The man steps forward and straddles the water between vessels, unseen, and steps forward again and hides in the shadow of a yeoman's shoe.

Here and there and back again. He travels the city, tracing the rumors and information that he has set in motion. He watches his own influence spread like antibiotic in diseased flesh.

It is all true. Everything he says is true. The discord he leaves behind him in the trail of whisper and pamphlet and paper is a correct reaction.

The man slips under the water. The sea opens to him, and he drifts down past the huge links of chain, toward the unthinkable beast of burden that stretches its limbs in the deepest reaches. When he needs breath he pulls the statue to him, the little grotesquerie hunched and glowing in the night sea with faint biotic light, the toothed osculum a puncture-hole of dark, the open eye wide and mocking, tar-black, and he kisses it deeply and feels its flickering tongue-thing with the disgust that he can never banish.

And the statue breathes air into him.

Or it bends space again and lets him lift his chin—yards deep as he is—and break the water with his face and gasp a lungful.

The man moves through the water without his limbs shifting position, the statue's filigree of once-living fin moving, as if that is what propels him. He weaves in and around the five great chains, moving downward until he becomes frightened by the dark and cold and silence (even powerful and puissant as he is) and he rises again to walk in the secret compartments of the city.

All the ridings are open to him. He enters all the flagships with ease and without hesitation, except one. He visits the Grand Easterly *and the* Therianthropus *in Shaddler, and Thee-And-Thine's* Salt Godling *and all the others—except for the* Uroc.

He is afraid of the Brucolac. Even flushed with his statue's kiss as he is, he will not risk facing the vampir. The moonship is out of bounds to him—that is a promise he has made himself, and that he keeps.

The man practices the other things the statue has taught him while he licks at its mouth. It allows him more than travel and infiltration.

It is true what they say about the haunted quarter: it is inhabited. But those presences in the old ships see what he is doing, and they do not trouble him.

The statue protects him. He feels like its lover. It keeps him safe.

CHAPTER THIRTY-FOUR

Since it had been stolen, the *Sorghum* had drilled for many weeks, and there were now great stores of oil and rockmilk in Garwater's reserves. But Armada was hungry, almost as voracious for fuel as New Crobuzon.

Before Garwater had the *Sorghum,* Armada's boats had got by only with careful husbanding of what resources they stole. Now their demand increased with the available supply. Even the ships allied to Dry Fall and Bask took the oil that Garwater provided.

The rockmilk was more precious by far, and rarer. In guarded storerooms in the *Grand Easterly* the heavy liquid slopped in rows of jars. The rooms were secured and earthed by careful geo-thaumaturgic processes, to dispel any dangerous emanations. The engine that sent the lulling pulses into the avanc's brain was powered on the stuff, and the thaumaturges and technicians who ran it kept a careful eye on their reserves of fuel. They knew exactly how much they needed.

Tanner and Shekel and Angevine studied the air over the *Sorghum*'s cold derrick and saw there was no effluent.

They sat together in a beer tent on the *Dober,* under a sprawl of tarpaulin-covered poles. The *Dober* would not support more solid buildings. It was the body of a blue whale, disemboweled, its top half removed, its carcass preserved by some long-forgotten process. It was quite hard and inflexible, though its floor was disturbingly organic: the remnants of blood vessels and viscera varnished as solid as glass underfoot.

Tanner and Shekel were frequent visitors here. Its beer tent was good. They sat facing the whale's frozen flukes, which jutted from the water as if about to slap its surface and swim free. The *Sorghum* was directly in their line of sight, framed by the pointed edges of the whale's tale. The enormous, ugly presence lolled silently.

Angevine was quiet. Shekel was solicitous, making sure her glass was full, murmuring to her quietly. She was still somewhat shocked. Everything had changed for her since Tintinnabulum left, and she had not yet adapted.

(Tanner had no doubts that she would be alright. Gods knew he did not begrudge her a few days' befuddlement. Tanner just hoped Shekel himself was alright. He was glad the lad was spending a little time with him.)

What will I do? thought Angevine. She kept thinking that she would go along to see what Tinnabol had for her . . . and then of course she remembered that he was gone. It was not that she missed him. He had been courteous and pleasant to her, but there had been no closeness. He had been her boss, and he had given her orders that she had obeyed.

But even that was an overstatement. He had not really been her boss. Her boss was Garwater—the Lovers. It was Garwater money that paid her wages, Garwater that had commissioned her, in the first days after her arrival, to serve the strange, muscular, white-haired hunter. And having disembarked from a ship taking her away to slavery, from a city where her Remaking had stripped her of rights, made her work a duty, to be told that she would be paid as if she were any other citizen had stunned her. It was that which had bought her loyalty.

And now Tintinnabulum was gone, and she was not sure what she would do.

It was hard, having taken pride in work, to be reminded that it did not matter what she did, so long as she labored, for money. Eight years of her history had sailed with Tintinnabulum and his hunters.

It was just a job, she told herself. *Jobs change. Time to move on.*

"Where are we going?" Bellis asked Uther Doul.

She had finally given in and asked him.

As she had expected, he did not answer her. He looked up at her question, then down again without a word.

They were in Croom Park, in an evening darkness stained with the colors and the strong smell of flowers. Somewhere nearby, an inbred nightingale sounded its attenuated song.

I want to know, Doul, Bellis felt like saying. *There are ghosts clinging to me, and I want to know if the wind wherever we're going will blow them away. I want to know which way my life is likely to turn. Where are we going?*

She did not say any of that. Instead they walked.

A path was visible in the moonlight. It was rough, formed by footsteps rather than design. It wound up the steep slope of bushes and trees that rose above them, broken here and there by the remnants of architecture—railings and stairways, their shapes visible like optical illusions below the garden's surface.

They climbed the incline onto the raised, tree-shadowed plateau that had once been the poop deck. It looked down over the ships of Curhouse, lit up with their traditional green-and-white lanterns. Bellis and Uther Doul stood in the darkness below the trees. The park moved sedately beneath them.

"Where are we going?" said Bellis again, and again there was a long time when all they could hear were the boat sounds of the city.

"You told me once," she continued hesitantly, "about your life in High Cromlech. You told me about when you left. What happened then? Where did you go? What did you do?"

Doul shook his head, almost helplessly. After a time, Bellis gestured at his scabbard.

"Where did you get that sword? What does it mean, its name?" she said.

He drew his bone-white weapon. He held it flat in the air and stared at it, then looked up at Bellis and nodded once again. He seemed pleased.

"It's a large part of why they trust and fear me as they do: the Possible Sword." He moved it slowly in a precise, curving sweep. "How I got this sword? At the end of a long search . . . and a great, a phenomenal amount of research. Everything's there, in the Imperial Canon, you know. All the information you might need, if you know how to read it." He watched Bellis calmly. "The work I've done. The techniques I've learnt.

"The Ghosthead broke open the world, when they arrived. They made the Fractured Land with the force of their landing, and it was more than physical damage.

"They used the break. You've heard the refrain about the Ghosthead always 'digging for their chances'? It's normally taken to mean that they had an uncanny kind of luck, that they gripped every chance they had, no matter how tenuous." He smiled slowly.

"Do you really think that would be enough to keep control of a continent?" he said. "A world? To hold absolute power for five hundred years? You think they could do that by keeping a lookout for opportunities? It was much more than that. 'Digging for chance' is a clumsy rendition of what the Ghosthead really did. It was an altogether more exact science.

"Possibility mining."

Uther quoted something like a singer. " 'We have scarred this mild world with prospects, wounded it massively, broken it, made our mark on its most remote land and stretching for thousands of leagues across its sea. And what we break we may reshape, and that which fails might still succeed. We have found rich deposits of chance, and we will dig them out.'

"They meant all that literally," he said. "It wasn't an abstract crow of triumph. They had *scarred,* they had *broken* the world. And, in doing so, they set free forces that they were able to tap. Forces that allowed them to reshape things, to fail and succeed *simultaneously*—because they mined for possibilities. A cataclysm like that, shattering a world, the rupture left behind: it opens up a rich seam of potentialities.

"And they knew how to pick at the might-have-beens and pull out the best of them, use them to shape the world. For every action, there's an infinity of outcomes. Countless trillions are possible, many milliards are likely, millions might be considered probable, several occur as possibilities to us as observers—and one comes true.

"But the Ghosthead knew how to tap some of those that might have been. To give them a kind of life. To use them, to push them into the reality that in its very existence denied theirs, which is *defined* by what happened and by the denial of what did not. Tapped by possibility machines, outcomes that didn't quite make it to actuality were boosted, and made real.

"If I were to toss a coin, most certain it would land on one side or the other; it's just possible it might land on its edge. But if I were to make it part of a possibility circuit, I'd turn it into what the Ghosthead would have called a coin of possible falls—a Possible Coin. And if I toss *that,* things are different.

"One of either heads or tails or just maybe edge will come up as before, and lie there as strong as ever. That's the fact-coin. And surrounding it, in different degrees of solidity and permanence, depending on how likely they were, are a scattering of its *nighs*—close possibilities made real. Like ghosts. Some almost as strong as the factual, fading to those that are just barely there. Lying where they would have fallen, heads and tails and a fair few edges. Possibilities, mined and pulled through into the light. Fading as the possibility field shifts.

"This—" He indicated his sword again, seeing Bellis begin to understand. "—is a sword of possible strikes. A Possible Sword. It's a conductor for a very rare kind of energy. It's a node in a circuit, a possibility machine. This—" He patted the little pack strapped to his waist. "—is the power: a clockwork engine. These," the wires stitched into his armor, "draw the power up. And the sword completes the circuit. When I grip it, the engine's whole.

"If the clockwork is running, my arm and the sword mine possibilities. For every factual attack there are a thousand possibilities, nigh-sword ghosts, and all of them strike down together."

Doul sheathed the blade and stared up into the trees' pitch-black canopy.

"Some of the most likely are very nearly real. Some are fainter than mirages, and their power to cut . . . is faint. There are countless nigh-blades, of all probabilities, all striking together.

"There's no martial form I've not studied. I'm proficient with most of the weapons I've ever encountered, and I can fight without any weapons at all. But what most people don't know is that I've trained with this sword twice. I've mastered *two* kinds of technique.

"This engine . . . It's not tight. And it can't just be wound again, either—there's more to it than that.

"So I have to husband what seconds I have. When I fight, I rarely switch on the Possible Sword. For the most part, I fight with it as a dumb, purely factual weapon: a diamond-hard blade with edges finer than honed metal. And I wield it *precisely*. Every strike I make is exact, and lands where I wish it to land. It's what I trained for so many years to do."

Bellis could hear no pride in his voice.

"But when the situation's severe, when odds are very bad, when a display's needed, or I'm in danger . . . then I switch on the motor for a few seconds. And in that situation, precision is the one thing I cannot afford."

He was silent as a gust of warm wind shook the trees, making them sound as if they shivered at his words.

"A headsman knows where his blade must land. With every nuance of skill, he aims for the neck. He narrows the possibilities. If he were to use a Possible Sword, the vast bulk of the nighs would exist within an inch of the factual strike. The rub is this: the better the headsman, the more precise his strike, the more constrained potentiality, the more *wasted* the Possible Sword. But, obviously, put a weapon like this in the hands of an amateur, it's as lethal to him or her as to any quarry—the possibilities that'll manifest include self-harm, unbalancing, dropping the weapon, and so on. A middle way is needed.

"When I attack with a dumb weapon, I'm an executioner. My blade lands in the space I decide, and not to either side. That's how I learned to fight; it would be a stupid waste of power to use the Possible Sword so. So when I finally found it, after a very long time of searching, I had to learn swordsmanship again. A very different art: skill without precision.

"Fighting with a Possible Sword, you must never constrain possibilities. I must be an opportunist, not a planner—fighting from the heart, not the mind. Moving suddenly, surprising myself as well as the opponent. Sudden, labile, and formless. So that each strike could be a thousand others, and each of those nigh-swords is strong. That's how to fight with a Possible Sword.

"So I am two swordsmen."

When his lovely voice ebbed away, Bellis was aware again of the surrounds of the park, the warm darkness and the noise of roosting birds.

"What's known about possibility mining," he said, "I know. That's how I knew of the sword."

Uther Doul was stirring things in Bellis' mind. In New Crobuzon, during her time when the scientist Isaac was her lover, Bellis had observed his obsessions, and had learned certain things.

He had been of chaotic and heretical inclinations. Many of his projects came to nothing. She had watched him chase ideas. And during the months they had spent together, the one that she had seen him worry at with the greatest tenacity was the investigation of what he called crisis energy. It was theoretical physics and thaumaturgy of astonishing complexity. But what she had taken from Isaac's frantic, off-color explanations was his conviction that underlying the facticity of the world, in all its seeming fastness, was an instability, a crisis pushing things to change from the tensions within them.

She had always found it an idea that accorded with her own instincts. She drew obscure comfort from the sense that things, even while as they were, were always in crisis, always pulled to become their opposite.

In the possibility mining that Uther Doul had just described Bellis saw a radical undermining of crisis theory. Crisis, Isaac had once told her, was manifest in the tendency of the real to become what it was not. If what *was* and what was *not* were allowed to coexist, the very tension—the crisis at the center of existence—must dissipate. Where was that crisis energy in the real becoming what it was not, if what it was not was right there alongside what it was?

That was nothing but a vague, pluralist reality. Bellis disliked the notion, intensely. She even felt, bizarrely, some kind of weird residual loyalty to Isaac pushing her to disapprove of it.

* * *

"When I first came here," Doul went on, "I was very tired. Tired of making decisions. I wanted to be *loyal*. I wanted a wage. I'd learnt and sought and found whatever I'd wanted. I had my sword, I had knowledge, I'd seen places . . . I wanted to rest. To be a henchman, a paid soldier.

"But the Lovers, when they saw my sword, and the books I brought with me, they were . . . fascinated.

"Especially the Lover.

"They were fascinated by what I could tell them. By what I'd learnt.

"In a few places in Bas-Lag," he said, "possibility machines still remain. There are different kinds, to do different things. I've studied them all.

"You've seen one of them: the perhapsadian, the instrument in my room. It was used to play possibilities. In an aether rich in potentiality, a virtuoso could once play particular facts and nighs into existence—choose certain outcomes. Quite useless now, of course. It's old and broken—and anyway, we're not in a possibility seam.

"This sword . . . you only see an aspect of it. The warrior who once used it and the people it killed, millennia ago, wouldn't recognize the weapon I carry. When the Ghosthead ruled, they used possibility in architecture, in medicine, in politics and performance and all other spheres. Possible Sonatas, the ghost-notes winking out of existence in echoes above and around the fact-score, changing with every performance. I have been inside the ruins of a Possible Tower . . ." He shook his head slowly. "That is a sight you do not forget.

"They used the science in fighting, in sport and war. There are passages in the Covertiana describing a bout between Possible Wrestlers, a shifting multitude of limbs flickering in and out of existence with every moment, nigh grappling nigh grappling fact grappling nigh again.

"But all of this, the technique of the mining, was a product of the Ghosthead's arrival—the detonation of their landing. It was through the rent they left that the possibility seams were tapped. That wound," he said, his eyes flickering over to Bellis and away, and back again, "that scar, left by the Ghosthead . . . that's where the seam is. If the stories are true, it's on the far side of the world, at the end of the Empty Ocean.

"No ship's ever crossed that sea. The waters there . . . they militate against ships. And who'd want to go there? If it exists, it's thousands of miles away. And there are stories of what lives in the Fractured Land: terrible things, a dreadful ecology. Light-fungus. Dreadcurs. Butterflies with unholy appetites. Even if we *could*," he said with strong sincerity, "I'd not want to try to reach the Fractured Land."

He was staring at Bellis and, under the superb modulations of his voice she sensed a tremulous feeling. She swallowed, trying to concentrate. *This is important, now,* she told herself. *Listen, make sense of this. I don't know why, but he's telling me something, he's letting me know—*

And then—

oh good gods above, can that be what he I don't, is that possible, that he, surely, have I, have I misunderstood?

Is that what he means?

Her face was set, and she realized she was staring at him, and he her, both mute, staring through the gloom.

Certainly, she thought, giddy, *what boat could make it over the ocean to the Fractured Land? Who'd want to go to the Fractured Land? The Land's not worth it. It's too far, too dangerous, even for this. Even for* this. *But what was it he told me, what did they say, how did it go . . . ?*

"*We have scarred this world, wounded it, made our mark on its remote land . . . and stretching for thousands of leagues across its sea.*"

There's something in the sea. Nothing to hurt us there, not like the land. No monsters there, no lightfungus or butterflies to threaten the miner—the possibility miner. And what's in the sea is much closer—the Fractured Land would be at the very edge of the world, but the Ghosthead lays say the sea's scar stretches for countless miles. In toward the world's center. Toward us. Closer.

No ship has ever made it across the Empty Ocean . . . I believe that. I know the stories, the currents and wind that push incomers away. No ships could cross that ocean.

But what could stop an avanc?

Why is he telling me?

* * *

Is that where we're going, Uther? Across the sea? Across the Empty Ocean, to the remnants of that wound, that fracture? It's not just the land that was broken open—the sea, too. So is that where we're going? To mine the possibilities in what's left of that great . . . cosmic laceration, Uther?

That's what the Brucolac meant, isn't it, Uther? That's what he was talking about.

Why are you telling me? What have I done? What are you doing? Why do you want me to know?

The avanc can take us to see what happened to the wound in the sea. That's why it was summoned. That's why Tintinnabulum was employed; and why the Sorghum was stolen for fuel; and why we went to the island and brought back Aum; and why you, Doul, have been working on a secret project, because of your sword, because of your expertise in this science. This is what everything leads to. This is why the avanc was summoned. It can cross the water that Armada would never breach without it.

It can cross that ocean.

It can take us to the Scar.

CHAPTER THIRTY-FIVE

"How the fuck did you find me?" Silas Fennec was clearly troubled.

"You speak like I'm some ingenue," whispered Bellis. "What, you think you're invisible? You think I'm incapable?"

She was dissembling: tracking Fennec had been mostly luck. She had been listening out for word of Simon Fench for days. Since her conversation with Doul, she had redoubled her efforts.

Eventually it had not been she who had tracked him at all, but Carrianne. In response to Bellis' continuing requests for help, her friend had told her, with her usual sly cheerfulness, that she had heard that the mysterious Mr. Fench had been seen at The Pashakan. It was a pub built belowdecks in the *Yevgeny,* a hundred-foot sloop in Thee-And-Thine.

Bellis had not ventured much into King Friedrich's riding since her trip to the glad' circus. She made her way toward its raucous byways with concealed trepidation.

She had passed along the streets of the *Sudden Understanding,* the many-masted clipper that formed part of the edge of Urchinspine Docks and that linked Dry Fall and Thee-And-Thine ridings. The enormous vessel was one of the few in Armada that did not rest clearly in the control of one or the other ruler. The main bulk of its body was Dry Fall, but toward its forecastle, responsibility and control blurred with Thee-And-Thine. The streets became more boisterous and untidy.

Bellis had picked her way through rubbish where the feral monkeys bickered with cats and dogs, through the tumbling streets, and into what was indisputably Thee-And-Thine.

This was the most ill-kempt of Armada's ridings. Its buildings were mostly wood, and many were moldering or salt- and water-stained. It was not that the area was poor—there were plenty of riches, in the gold and silver and jet visible through the windows of some houses, in the vivid silks and satins that were worn by some of its inhabitants, in the quality of goods available. But in a place where everything was for sale, certain goods—such as the right to maintain the architecture and the streets—were not attractive buys.

Slums and factories and shabby opulence bobbed sedately side by side. Finally, Bellis had passed the *Salt Godling,* Friedrich's flagship, and had walked into the *Yevgeny*'s creaking, smelly innards, unclearly torchlit, to The Pashakan.

On her third visit, Silas was there. Bellis was angry at his surly surprise to see her.

"Will you listen to me?" she hissed at him. *"I know where we're going."*

He looked up, sharply, and caught her eye.

She laughed suddenly and unpleasantly. "Do you have déjà vu, Silas?" she said. "Jabber knows I do. Understand that I do not relish this relationship. I seem to find myself doing this with disturbing regularity: telling you that *I know a secret,* giving it to you to pass on, to make plans with, to *do* something with. I do *not* enjoy that. This is the last fucking time, you understand me?"

She meant it, absolutely. No matter what might happen, she would not deal with Silas Fennec like this again. There was nothing, less than nothing, between them anymore.

"But whether I like it or not," she went on, "I have little choice here. I need your help. The only way anything can be done about this is if . . . the word is spread, if more people know. And though no one listens to Bellis Coldwine, it seems that a growing minority are prepared to listen to the troublemaker Simon Fench."

"Where are we going, Bellis?" Fennec asked.

She told him.

"I wondered why you were fraternizing with that fucking lunatic Doul. Does he *know* you know?" Fennec seemed stunned.

"I think so," she said. "It's hard to tell. It was as if . . . He obviously wasn't supposed to tell me. But maybe he was so . . . caught up in it, he couldn't resist. So instead of coming out with it, which would be disloyal, he told me just enough.

"All the time I'd thought he was accompanying the Lovers and Aum and the scientists into those secret meetings because he's their bodyguard. But it wasn't that—he's an *expert* on this thing, on possibility mining. He knows everything about it, because of once researching that sword of his.

"This is what they've been working on. The Lovers want to get to the Scar; they want to tap possibilities, Silas." Her voice remained cool, though she did not feel it. "Like the Ghosthead Empire, do you understand?"

"That's why the avanc," he breathed, and Bellis nodded.

"That's why. It's just a means to an end. The Lovers must have been . . . entranced when they saw his sword, when he first came to the city. They heard his stories of the Fractured Land, and the Scar—all the secrets he knows—and it was nothing but a dream, then. But then they think of Tintinnabulum and his crew, who could be enticed. This is the ultimate big game, after all." She stared out of the little window at a sea that churned slowly by as the avanc progressed.

"And the Lovers already knew about the chains. Armada tried to capture an avanc before. That was a long time ago, and they don't give a cuss for tradition. But when Doul came, it was different. Before he came, calling the avanc would've been . . . a stupid, grandiose, pointless gesture. But now? Everyone knows no ship can cross the Empty Ocean. But what fucking force in

Bas-Lag could stop an *avanc*? All of a sudden, there's a way to get to this Scar that Doul's told them all about, the thing that the Ghosthead left behind."

The scale of the project was staggering. The realization that all the misery and money and terrible effort that the Lovers had gone to to secure the avanc, the realization that that was only the first part of their plan, was incredible.

"All this," breathed Silas, and Bellis nodded.

"All of it," she said. "The rig, the *Terpsichoria,* Johannes, the anophelii island, the chains, the fulmen, the fucking avanc . . . all of it. This is what it's about."

"Naked power." Silas mouthed it as if the words were dirty. "I assumed the avanc was to do with the piracy. That's what they implied: that it would make them more efficient thieves, for Jabber's sake! That at least would have made some kind of sense. But this . . ." He looked incredulous. "You can tell they're press-ganged, the Lovers; no fucking serious pirate would pursue this idiocy."

"They're dangerous," said Bellis simply. "They're fanatics. I've no idea if they can really cross the Empty Ocean, but godspit! I do not want to find out. I . . . I've heard them, Silas, when they're alone." He looked at her piercingly, but did not ask her how. "I know what they're like. I'm not letting people like that—visionaries, gods help us—command me to the other end of the world, to a place that may not even exist, and that if it does is the most deadly place in Bas-Lag. We'd be traveling further and farther from New Crobuzon. And I've still not given up on getting back there."

Bellis realized she was shaking at the thought of leaving her home so far behind. And if Uther and the others were right? If they survived the crossing?

A multitude of possibilities. The thought chilled her. She found it utterly threatening, existentially undermining. It made her feel so completely contingent that it offended and frightened her.

Like some waterhole in the veldt, she thought unclearly, *where the weak and the strong and predatory drink together in a truce: the gazelle, the wildebeest, the mafadet, and the lion. All the possibilities lined up together in fucking harmony, and the winner, the strongest, the* fact, *the real, letting the others that have failed live, letting them all live. Pacifist and pathetic.*

"That's why they're not telling," she said. "They know people won't stand for it."

"They're afraid," Silas murmured.

"The Lovers are strong," said Bellis, "but they couldn't face all the other ridings. And, more to the point, they couldn't face their own people."

"Revolt," breathed Silas, and Bellis smiled without humor.

"Mutiny," she said. "They're afraid of mutiny. And that's why we need Simon Fench."

Silas nodded slowly; then there was a long silence.

"He's got to spread the word," he said eventually. "Pamphlets, rumors, and all. That's what he does best; I can make sure he does that."

"I'm sorry, Bellis," Silas said when she stood to go. "I've not been a great friend. I've been so . . . Things have been busy, and difficult. I was rude when I saw you, and I'm sorry."

Observing him, Bellis felt dislike—as well, paradoxically, as the last faint stirrings of what had once been affection. Like a shred of memory.

"Silas," she said, smiling coldly, "we owe each other nothing. And we're not friends. But we have a shared interest in the Lovers' failing. And I can't stop it, and it's just possible that you might be able to. I expect you to try, and to tell me what's happening, and that's all. That's all the communication I expect from you. I don't want you to contact me as a *friend.*"

Silas Fennec remained in The Pashakan for a long time after Bellis left. He read through some inky pamphlets and newspapers, watching the sky darken. The days were noticeably longer now, and he thought about summer in New Crobuzon.

He waited there a long time: this was where people determined enough to find him were directed. But he drank and read alone. One woman, dressed in rags, looked up at his back curiously as he left the room—that was all the notice that was paid him.

Fennec wound home through the circuitous routes and byways of Thee-And-Thine to the oily iron ship *Drudgery.* It was in a quiet part of town. Beside it loomed a big old factory ship— Armada's asylum.

He waited at home in one of the nondescript concrete blocks built beside the *Drudgery's* funnel, directly in the asylum's shadow. At eleven o'clock there was a knock at his door: his contact had arrived. For the first time in many days, they had something serious and important to talk about. Fennec walked slowly to answer the door, and his gait, his expressions, his demeanor shifted fractionally.

By the time he opened the door, he had become Simon Fench.

Waiting on his doorstep was a big, aging cactus-man, looking nervously about him.

"Hedrigall," said Fennec quietly, in what was not quite his own voice. "I've been waiting for you. We must talk."

In the jagged and obscure architecture of the moonship *Uroc,* the vampir were gathering.

The Brucolac had called a conclave of his ab-dead lieutenants, his cadre. As the light shifted from drab dusk to night, they settled as lightly and soundlessly on the moonship as leafs.

All the citizens of Dry Fall knew that their vampir were always watching. They wore no uniform; their identities were not known.

The bacillus that induced photophobic haemophagy—the vampir strain—was capricious, and weak, carried solely in spit and quick to denature and collapse. Only if a vampir's victim did not die, and if the bite had been direct, mouth to skin so that some of the ab-dead's spittle entered their prey's bloodstream, was there a small chance that the survivor might be infected. And if they survived the fevers and the delirium, they would awaken one night, having died and been renewed, ab-dead, with a raging hunger, their bodies reconfigured, stronger and quicker by many times. Unaging, able to survive most injury. And unable to bear the sun.

Every one of the Dry Fall's cadre had been carefully chosen by the Brucolac. The goretax was decanted before drinking, to avoid inadvertent infection. Those from whom the Brucolac drank directly were his most trusted servants, his closest supporters, to whom he gave the honor of a chance at ab-death.

There had been occasional betrayals, of course, in the past. His chosen ones had turned against him, giddy with power. There had been unauthorized infection and attempts on his ab-life. The Brucolac had quashed them all, sadly and effortlessly.

His lieutenants surrounded him now, in the *Uroc*'s great hall. Scores of them, freed from the necessity of disguise, allowing their serpentine tongues to unroll luxuriously, tasting the air with relish. Men and women and androgynous youths.

At the front, almost beside the Brucolac, stood the ragged woman who had watched Fennec in The Pashakan. Every one of the vampir stared at their master with wide, light-enhancing eyes.

After a very long silence, the Brucolac spoke. His voice was quiet. Had those in the room been human, they would not have heard him.

"Kin," he said, "you know why we're here. I've told you all where we are heading, where the Lovers would have us go. Our opposition to their plans is well known. But we're in a minority; we're not trusted; we couldn't mobilize the city behind us. We can't usefully speak; our hands are tied.

"However, things may be changing. The Lovers are banking on momentum, so that by the time their aim becomes plain, it'll be too late to oppose it. And by that time, they hope, people will become willing abductees." The Brucolac sneered, and licked the air with his great tongue.

"*Now,* it appears, word may be about to get out. A fascinating conversation was overheard tonight. *Simon Fench* knows where we're going." He nodded at the woman in rags. "Doul's Crobuzoner dollymop, of all people, has worked out what's happening, and she's told Mr. Fench—or Fennec, or whatever he calls himself. We know where he lives, do we not?" The woman nodded.

"Fench is planning to put out one of his inflammatory pamphlets. We'd try to intervene if we could, to help him, but he's a solo operator, and if he discovered that we'd identified him, he'd shun us and disappear. We don't want to risk interfering with his efforts. We can hope," the Brucolac stressed, "that he's able to get this done soon, and that it'll cause a crisis for Garwater. After all, we've not yet reached the Empty Ocean.

"But." He made the word cold and hard, and his lieutenants were rapt.

"But we must make preparations, in case Fench fails. Kin . . ." He prodded at the air as he spoke in his guttural whisper. "Kin, this is not a fight we will lose. We hope that Fench succeeds. But in case he does not, we must be ready to put another plan in motion.

"I will take this fucking city by force, if I must."

And his ab-dead cadre hissed and muttered their agreement.

CHAPTER THIRTY-SIX

North, slow and inexorable. They were pulled on, days becoming weeks. The city waited. No one knew what would happen, but there was no way this steady gait could continue without incident. Armada became tense.

Bellis waited for word of Fench's pamphlet. She was patient, envisaging him in the belly of the city, deep in some ship, collating information, controlling his informants.

Some nights, drawn by queasy fascination and shocked at herself, Bellis made her own way into the *Grand Easterly*'s lower decks and huddled in the room below the Lovers'. In their spat and breathless love talk she heard a new tension.

"Soon," Bellis heard one Lover hiss, and "Fuck yes, soon," a whimpered response.

There were differences between their little cries, Bellis could now discern. The Lover seemed more intense, more committed. It was she who seemed impatient, hungry for resolution, it was she who whispered *soon* most often; she was the more engaged with the project. Her lover was engaged with her. He fawned and murmured in the wake of her words.

Time stretched out. Bellis became more and more frustrated with Uther Doul.

With the city's passage north, it had passed quickly out of the storms and the heat and into a more temperate zone, warm and breezy like New Crobuzon's summer.

Five days after Bellis and Silas met in The Pashakan, there was a commotion above Armada's skyline, in the dirigible *Arrogance*.

While Bellis stood with Uther Doul on the *Grand Easterly*, looking over to the fringe of Croom Park, Hedrigall was on deck duty, working with others near the great ropes that tethered the *Arrogance* to the aft of the ship.

"Mail drop," he yelled, and the crews quickly cleared the area around the rope. A weighted satchel plummeted its length, landing with a bang on the cushioning of rags.

Hedrigall's motions, when he pulled open the sack, were routine, and Bellis began to look away. But when the cactus-man unfurled the message within, his demeanor changed so violently that her eyes snapped back. Hedrigall ran toward Bellis and Doul with such astonishing speed that she thought for a second he was about to attack them. She stiffened as his great muscular body slammed down the boards of the deck.

Hedrigall held out the lookout's message in a rigid arm.

"Warships," he said to Doul. "Ironclads. A New Crobuzon flotilla. Thirty-five miles off, incoming. Be here within two hours." He paused, and his green lips moved without sound, until finally he spoke with a tone of absolute incredulity.

"We're under attack."

At first, people were bewildered, disbelieving of their orders. Great masses of men and women gathered in every riding, on every flagship, fingering weapons and pulling on pieces of armor, surly and confused.

"But it don't make any sense, Doul, sir," one woman on the *Grand Easterly* argued. "It's almost *four thousand miles* from New Crobuzon. Why'd they come so far? And how come the nauscopists didn't see anything? They would've noticed yesterday. And anyway, how're the Crobuzoners supposed to have found us—?"

Doul interrupted her, shouting loud enough to shock everyone in earshot into silence.

"We do not ask how," he bellowed. *"We do not ask why. Time enough after the killing. For now we have only time to fight, like fucking dogs, like sharks in frenzy. We fight or the city dies."*

Doul stilled all argument. People set their faces and prepared for war. And in every head the question *How have they done this?* was remembered, and put aside for later.

The city's five warships steered westward a handful of miles, presenting themselves like a curving wall between Armada and the approaching force.

Around and between them steamed Armada's smaller ironclads, squat vessels swathed in grey gunmetal, windowless, bristling with stubby cannons. They were joined by those of the city's pirate vessels that had been in dock. Their crews set their teeth and tried not to contemplate their suicidal bravery—they were armed and armored to defeat merchant vessels, not naval gunners. Few of them, they realized, would come home.

There was no division between the ridings. Crews loyal to every ruler tacked and stoked and armed themselves, side by side.

The lookouts in the *Arrogance* sent down more messages as they saw the Crobuzoner ships more clearly. Uther Doul read them out to the Lovers.

"They must be here for their fucking rig," he said quietly, so that only the two of them could hear. "Whatever it's about, they outgun us. We've got more vessels, but half of ours are just wooden freebooters. They've seven warships, and many more scouts than us. They must have sent nearly half their fleet."

Tanner Sack and the menfish of Bask; Bastard John; cray; the shadowy submersibles. Armada's underwater troops waited, suspended, the great chains moving slowly away from them. Armada was moving on, the avanc now slowed to a crawl so that the troops could regain the city, after the fight.

Nearby, a small group of cray huddled in tight communion on one of their submerged rafts. Witch-conveners, summoning their beasts.

When Tanner had faced the dinichthys, he had hurled himself unthinkingly into the water. He had not had time then to contemplate his fear. But it was almost another hour before the warships from his old home would arrive to destroy his new one. The purpose and intelligence that directed their propellers was much more terrifying than the imbecilic malice in the bonefish's eyes.

The minutes were very slow. Tanner thought about Shekel, at home where Tanner had ordered him to stay. Waiting with Angevine: both being armed, no doubt, by the yeomanry left behind. *But he ain't yet sixteen,* thought Tanner desperately. He wanted very much to be back there with them, with Shekel and his lady. Tanner hefted his huge harpoon and thought about the fighting that was coming, and he pissed suddenly in his fear. His urine warmed him briefly, then dissipated with the current.

Everywhere, throughout Armada and across all the free-floating ships preparing to defend it, there were weapons.

The city's armories and arsenals were unlocked, and the military technologies of thousands of years and hundreds of cultures were brought out and wiped clean: cannons, harpoons, and flintlocks; swords and crossbows and longbows and rivebows; and more esoteric weapons: stingboxes, baan, yarritusks.

Across the city, dirigibles of all sizes were rising slowly above the rooftops and rigging, like sections of architecture broken free. Over the horizon to the west, smoke could be seen from the Crobuzoner engines.

There was a huge scrum on the deck of the *Grand Easterly* as all the lieutenants, officers, captains, and rulers of all the ridings jostled to hear Uther Doul, the soldier, give them orders. Bellis stood motionless nearby, ignored by everyone around her, and listened.

"Their gunboats outnumber ours," he said tersely, "but look around." He pointed out at the morass of steamers and tugs that had until recently spent their days pulling Armada across the ocean, and that now circled it in aimless freedom. "Tell the crews manning those vessels to turn them by gods *into* gunboats.

"Word's been sent to the Brucolac and his cadre: they'll be informed as soon as they wake. Send some fast boats or airships to the edge of Dry Fall, to wait for them.

"We don't know the Crobuzoners' strength underwater," Doul continued. "Submariners, you'll have to judge when to attack. But they'll have no airships. The likes of that are our only real strength." He indicated the *Trident* bobbing from the *Grand Easterly*'s tail. It was being loaded with gunpowder and fat bombs. "Send them in first and fast. Don't hold back.

"And listen—concentrate on the warships. The ironclads and scouts will hurt us, but we can withstand their firepower. Those warships . . . they could sink the city." A rill of horror ran over the deck. "They're carrying the fuel reserves: the Crobuzoner fleet is depending on those warships to get home."

With a stunned jolt, Bellis realized what was happening. Her mind slipped like a broken gear, ignoring the rest of Doul's instructions and grinding over and over the same pattern of thought. *A ship from* home *a ship from* home . . .

With sudden, desperate eagerness, she gazed out at the faint shading of smoke in the west. *How do I reach them?* she thought, disbelieving, exultant, and giddy.

*   *   *

The Crobuzoner ships finally came close enough to be seen: a long line of smoke-spewing black metal.

"They're running up flags," said Hedrigall from the top of the superstructure at the *Grand Easterly*'s stern. He was staring through the ship's huge fixed telescope. "Sending us a message while they get good and close. Look: the name of their flagship and . . ." He hesitated. "They want to *parley*?"

Doul had dressed for war. His grey armor was studded with straps and with holstered flintlocks—on each hip, each shoulder, each thigh, in the center of his chest. About his body, the handles of daggers and throwing knives protruded from their scabbards. He looked, Bellis realized with a shiver, as he had when he came aboard the *Terpsichoria*.

She did not care; she was not interested anymore. She looked away and back toward the Crobuzoner ships, in agonies of excitement.

Doul took the telescope.

" 'Captain Princip Cecasan of the N.C.S. *Morning Walker*,' " he read slowly, and shook his head slowly as he scanned the pennants. " 'Parley requested regarding New Crobuzon hostage.' "

For one stunned instant, Bellis thought it was a reference to her. But even as her face spasmed with astonished joy, she realized how absurd that was (*and something deep in her mind waited to inform her of another explanation*). She turned and looked at the faces of Uther Doul, Hedrigall, the Lovers, and all the gathered captains.

She shivered to see them. Not a single one, she realized, had reacted to the *Morning Walker*'s offer to talk with anything but hard contempt.

In the face of that collective emotion, that absolute antagonism, the certainty of those before her that New Crobuzon was a power to be distrusted, fought against, destroyed, her own joy ebbed away. She remembered what she had read of the Pirate Wars, and New Crobuzon's attack on Suroch. She remembered, suddenly, her conversations with Johannes and with Tanner Sack. She remembered Tanner's rage at the thought of being found by Crobuzoner ships.

Bellis remembered her own terrified flight from New Crobuzon. *I crossed the sea because I was afraid for my life,* she thought. *Seeing the militia everywhere I looked. Afraid of the agents of the government. Agents like the sailors in those ships.*

It was not just the pirates—New Crobuzon's maritime rivals—and not just the Remade who had reason to fear the oncoming ships, Bellis realized. All her certainty left her. She, too, should be afraid.

"They're armed enough to level a city," Doul said to the assembled captains. "And they tell us they want to *bargain*?"

There was no one in the crowd who needed convincing. They listened silently.

"They'll destroy us, if they have any chance at all. And they can *find* us, gods know how, across half the world. If we don't take them now, they can come *back* again and again." He shook his head and slowly spoke a last sentence, to a cheer that was more tense than rousing. "Send them down."

The commanders were gone, carried to their vessels by aerocabs. Those rulers who would fight had been taken to their ships or dirigibles; those too frail or cowardly had been returned to their flagships in the city. Only Doul, Bellis, and the Lovers remained on the raised platform—and Bellis was ignored.

The Lovers were to fight in separate arenas: he from the warship *Cho Harbor*, she from the airship *Nanter*. They were taking their leave of each other. They kissed, tonguing deeply and murmuring the ecstatic sounds that Bellis recognized from her eavesdropping. They muttered to each other, telling each other they would be together again very soon, and Bellis realized that there was nothing touching about their parting, nothing tragic. They did not kiss as if it was their last chance, but hungrily and lasciviously, eager for more. They felt no fear; they seemed to feel no regret: they seemed to long to part, so that they might come together again.

She watched them with the disgusted fascination she always felt. Their scars twitched like little snakes as their faces moved against each other.

The Crobuzoner ships were less than ten miles away.

"Some of them will get through, Uther," said the Lover, turning to Doul. "We can afford to lose ships, aerostats, submersibles, citizens. We can't afford to lose the city, and we need you here to protect it. As our . . . last line.

"And Doul," she said finally, "we can't afford to lose you. We need you, Doul. You know what to do. When we get to the Scar."

Bellis did not know if the Lover had forgotten that she was present, to have spoken so openly, or if she no longer cared.

The last dirigible had gone, taking the Lovers to their stations. The avanc had been reined in, and the city had slowed. Doul and Bellis were alone. Below them, women and men armed themselves on the broad deck of the *Grand Easterly*.

Doul did not look at Bellis or speak to her. He stared out past the *Sorghum*. Less than five miles now separated the Armadan navy and the wedge of snub-nosed Crobuzon battleships. The distance was reducing.

Eventually Doul turned to Bellis. His jaw was clenched, his eyes open a little too wide. He handed Bellis a flintlock. She waited for him to tell her to get below, or to stay out of the way, but he did not. They stood together and watched the battleships closing.

The man kisses his statue, and strolls unseen behind Bellis and Uther Doul.

His heart is beating quickly. He is packed and ready. He is carrying everything he owns in his pockets and hands. The man is disappointed but not surprised that Armada did not agree to parley. This way will be slower—though perhaps, he acknowledges, ultimately no more bloody.

So close, so close. He can almost step onto the deck of the Morning Walker. *But not quite. It has a few miles yet to come. They'll send a boat for me,* he thinks, *and prepares to receive them.* I told them where I'd be.

Uther Doul is speaking to Bellis now, motioning to the frantic throng below. He is taking his leave of her; he is leaving her behind on the raised roof, descending to be with his troops, and she is watching him, hefting the gun, keeping her eyes on Doul as he descends.

The man knows that those who are coming, his compatriots, will have no trouble finding him. His descriptions were clear. There is no mistaking the Grand Easterly.

Separated by three miles of sea, the two navies faced each other. The Armadans in a mongrel mass of vessels in all colors and designs, sails and smoke billowing above countless decks. Opposite them, the *Morning Walker* and its sister-ships approached in formation, grey and darkwood blistered with large-bore guns.

A swarm of dirigibles approached the Crobuzoner ships: warflots and scouts and aerocabs weighed down with rifles and barrels of black powder. The air was still, and they made quick progress. At the front of the motley air force was the *Trident*, surrounded by smaller vessels, and aeronauts in single-pilot harnesses, swaying below their small balloons.

The Armadan captains knew that they had the weaker guns. Their ships were more than two miles from the enemy when the New Crobuzon ships began to fire.

Sound and heat burst over the sea. A fringe of explosions and boiling waves advanced way out in front of the *Morning Walker* like outriders. The Armadan guns were primed and stoked, but remained silent. There was nothing their crews could do but urge their vessels forward through the onslaught, to bring their enemies into their own shorter range. There were more than a thousand yards of fire to cross until they could retaliate, and they slipped into the one-sided battle with grim bravado, and time changed.

Metal and metal meet, and black powder ignites, and oil combusts and flesh bursts and burns.

Below the water Tanner rocks violently, stunned by ripples of pressure. He hemorrhages, blood gouting from his gills.

Above him, Armadan ships are shadows on illuminated water. Their formations are breaking down into chaos. Some of them are eddying in confusion, and (*Jabber*) breaking apart (*Jabber help us*), breaking in two or three, slipping closer, growing bigger as they descend toward him slow as nightfall, so slow he's imagining it, but then around him the menfish scatter and (*Godspitshitno*) broken slabs of metal are plummeting like comets with trails of grease oil dirt shrapnel blood.

The fall of broken ships howls past him spewing bubbles and bodies and disappears into the dark.

From the airships, the carnage is distant and muted: little puffs and booms, and the black-crusted glow of oil fires, and ships that are there and then are not. The Armadan fleet continues like a pack of stupid blind dogs through that merciless onslaught, diminishing as it goes, until at last its guns can reach the Crobu-zoner fleet.

Seen through hundreds of feet of air, the war is like a diorama. It seems a reconstruction. It does not look real.

The screaming cannot be heard over the explosions.

Blood sluices over the sides of Armadan ships. Metal bursts and tears, and the ships are suddenly serrated, murderous to their own sailors. The Armadan gunners fire, and their shells arc in fiery parabolas into their enemies. But those thousand yards have been merciless, and the Armadan fleet is already half broken.

The sea has become charnel. The water is littered with bodies. They move with the swells and currents, in a macabre dance. They emit clouds of blood like squid ink. They are transformed by the sea: entrails fan like coral; torn swathes of skin become fins. They are broken by jags of bone.

Tanner is very slow and cold. As he rises he passes a woman who still moves, too weak to swim up but not quite dead. He turns to her with soundless horror and hauls her skyward, but her movements become the juddering of dead nerves before they reach the air. And as Tanner lets her go he sees that there is more movement all around him, that there are men and women drown-ing as far as he can see, that he cannot help them, that they are too weak to live. He sees their ghastly desperate motions every-where he looks, and he feels suddenly removed, conscious not of men and women, khepri and cactacae and scabmettler and hotchi, but only of countless, mindlessly repetitive motions, wind-ing slowly down, as if he stares into a vat of rainwater at slowly dying insects.

He reaches the surface in a moment of calm, a chance stillness in the carnage, in the middle of what was the Armadan fleet. Around him vessels are breaking up with ugly noises. They are floundering, retching smoke and fire, hissing as they slip into the cool water, sucking their dying crews with them.

Tanner struggles. He is unable to think in words. The shells begin once again to pound the water around him, to make it into a bloody broth of metal and the dead.

* * *

The air sparks. Elyctro-thaumaturgic quarrels burst from the Crobuzoner vessels; arbalests hurl vats of strong acid. But now, even broken as they are, the remnants of the Armadan fleet fight back.

They fire shells the size of men, which smack into the Crobuzoner dreadnoughts and open in ragged metal flowers. Wooden warships sail into range, weaving between enemies, and their cannons sound, denting slabs of armor, breaking through smokestacks, and snapping the moorings of guns.

The *Trident* and its airborne flotilla have reached the sky over the Crobuzoner fleet. They begin a sporadic deluge of missiles: gunpowder bombs; oil skins that burst open as they fall, raining sticky fire; weighted darts and knives. Aeronauts snipe at Crobuzoner captains and gunners. The heat from the explosions rocks the dirigibles and knocks them off-course.

Still the Armadan ships approach. They fire and come closer and explode and capsize and burst into flames and still come closer, their crews doggedly driving them toward the dreadnoughts.

A mass of dark bodies rises.

Crobuzoner thaumaturges, channeling puissance from batteries and their own bodies, have animated flocks of golems: clumsy constructions of wire and leather and clay, inelegant and rough-hewn, with claws like umbrella's innards and clear glass eyes. Their ugly wings beat frantically to bring them skyward. They are strong as monkeys, mindless and tenacious.

They grip the ankles of the Armadan aeronauts and scrabble up their bodies, ripping open their flesh and tearing their balloons apart, sending them bleeding into the decks below.

Golems rise like smoke from the Crobuzoner fleet and slam themselves into the steering cabins and windows of the Armadan airships, blinding them, shattering their glass, slicing the fabric of their gasbags. Many fall, their bodies broken by gunfire and swords and gravity, collapsing into their lifeless inanimate components on their way down; but scores stay airborne, harrying the Armadan air fleet.

The air above the battle seems as thick as the sea. It is viscous and sluggish with the discharge from guns and fire-throwers and catapults; with sinking dirigibles bleeding dry of gas; with hunting golems and blood-mist and gouts of soot.

There is a terrible slowness, a solemn care behind every motion. Every cut, every crushing blow, every bullet boring into eye
and bone, every belch of fire and bursting vessel seems planned.

It is a sordid pretense.

Through the murk Tanner can see the undersides of the enemy's
boats, and surrounding them a hundred shapes: darting spiral
vessels, single-person subs in the shells of giant nautili. The Armadan submarines scatter the little craft, ram the iron flanks of
the dreadnoughts, rear up like whales.

Tanner is out, suddenly, in the open water, among the darting
Bask menfish who have let him into their ranks. He has reached
out with his long tentacles and gripped the chitinous shell of one
of the little nautilus subs. He faces the little glass porthole, and
he can see the man inside stare out aghast, thinking he has gone
mad to see this savagely wailing face, this New Crobuzon face,
in the water, mouthing curses at him in his own language, raising
a stubby weapon level to his face and firing.

The bolt bursts the glass and drives on into the New Crobuzon
sailor's face, its reinforced jag splintering his cheekbone and the
base of his skull and pinning his head to the back of his tiny
craft. Tanner Sack stares at the man he has killed, no, who is not
yet dead, whose mouth spasms with agony and terror as the sea
vomits into his ruptured sub and drowns him.

Tanner kicks backward, shaking violently, watching the man
die, watching the nautilus fill with water and begin to spin and
descend.

The dead and torn-apart are scattered across all the ships and
across the sea as if they are scraps of burned paper distributed
randomly by fire.

Tanner Sack hunts men.

Around him, vessels plummet. He is surrounded by dying men
from what was once his home. They bleed and scream bubbles.
They are too far down to reach the surface. None of them will
breathe again.

Tanner spews suddenly, the sick forcing his throat open and
billowing out from him. He feels nauseous, unstuck in time,
drunk or dreaming, as if this is not real but a memory, already,
even as it happens.

(*Below him pass dark curious things that he thinks are his allies the menfish, and then knows immediately are not.*

They are gone, and Tanner does not have the time, the luxury, to wonder what they were.)

The fighting progresses in spastic jerks. A clockwork ship from Booktown is torn open, and it sheds its gears and its massive coiled springs and the ruined bodies of khepri. The waters around Jhour vessels move oily with sap from slaughtered cactacae. Where scabmettlers are torn apart by bombs, the clouds of their blood harden as they burst, into a shrapnel of scabs. Hotchi are crushed between hulls.

The beasts summoned by the Armadan cray witches slam their fletches into Crobuzoner ships and tip the crews into the water, to snatch them up with sudden scissoring jaws. But there are too many to control, and they become a danger to their own witch-masters.

In the smog, Armadan shells find Armadan decks, and New Crobuzon javelins and bullets burst through the flesh of their own troops.

At different times, all across the battle, women and men look up and see the sky, the sun, through red clouds, through water, through films of their own and others' blood. Some lie where they have fallen, dying, knowing that the sun is the last light they will see.

The sun is low. Dusk is perhaps an hour away.

Two of Armada's great war steamers are destroyed. Another is badly damaged, its rear guns twisted like palsied limbs. Scores of its pirate ships and its smaller fighters are gone.

Of the New Crobuzon dreadnoughts, only the *Darioch's Kiss* is ruined. Others are torn, but they are fighting on.

The Crobuzoner fleet is winning. A wedge of their scouts, ironclads, and submersibles have broken through Armadan ranks and are bearing down on the city itself, a few miles beyond. Bellis watches them approach through the huge telescope on the *Grand Easterly*.

The *Grand Easterly* is the redoubt, the heart of the city.

"We stand," Uther Doul is shouting to those around him, to the snipers in the rigging.

No one has suggested anything else. No one has suggested that they goad the avanc and escape.

The Crobuzoner ships endure the barrage from the guns on the *Sorghum* (*and do not return fire, Bellis notices, do not risk damaging the rig itself*). They are close enough now that their structures can be seen: their bridges, their turrets and railings and their guns, and the crews who prepare, check weapons, gesticulate, and get into formations. Cordite billows over the deck, and Bellis' eyes water. The small-arms fire has begun.

This is an organized raid. The invaders do not land ragged across the aft edge of the city: they maintain formation, an arrowhead, and steam directly into the bay of boats around the *Sorghum.* The Crobuzoners are intently making their way toward the *Grand Easterly.*

Bellis backs away from the railing. The deck below her raised roof boils with Armadans ready to fight. She realizes that she is trapped on this platform by a flood of armed bodies, that it is too late to run.

Part of her wants to yell in greeting—in desperate welcome—when the Crobuzoners arrive. But she knows that they have no interest in taking her home, that it is irrelevant to them if she lives or dies. She is desperately uncertain, realizing that she does not know which side she wants to win this confrontation.

As she steps back, Bellis feels suddenly as if she has walked into somebody, that she has felt a disturbance in the air, heard someone retreat from her with a quick step. She twists quickly to see, panic punching her, but there is no one. She is alone above the fray.

She looks down into the seething, armed men and women and finds herself staring at Uther Doul. He is perfectly still.

Flintlocks firing, the Crobuzoner navy boards Armada. At the point where the two forces meet, there is the most savage bloodletting. The Armadan cactacae are at the front, and the Crobuzoners are faced by a line of their massive, thorned bodies. The cactacae split men with great strokes from their war cleavers.

But there are cactus-people on the New Crobuzon side, too; and men firing rivebows with weighted, spinning chakris that smash like axe blades into the vegetable-muscles and bones of the cactacae, severing limbs and cutting fibrous skulls; and there

are thaumaturges on the invading vessels who link hands and
send bolts of darkly glowing unlight into the Armadan mass.

The Crobuzoners are forcing the Armadans back.

Around the base of Bellis' squat platform, now, is the New
Crobuzon navy. She is paralyzed. Part of her wants to run to
them, but she waits. She does not know how this will turn. She
does not know what she will do.

Once again, someone is on the platform with her. That feeling
comes and goes.

With a drab and bloody inexorability, the New Crobuzon troops
encroach across the *Grand Easterly*'s deck.

Uniformed men approach Uther Doul from aft, port, and
star'd. He is waiting. Armadans are falling around him, pushed
back, felled by flintlock bullets and a cascade of blades.

Bellis is watching Uther Doul when finally, suddenly, surrounded now by fast-encroaching enemies, by pistols and rifles
and curving sabers, he moves.

He calls out: a long bark that is savage but musical, that takes
shape and becomes his own name.

"*Doul,*" he cries, repeating it, drawing it out like a huntsman's
call. "*Dooooouuuuul!*"

And he is answered. Armadans around the deck take up the
call as they fight, and his name echoes across the ship. And as the
Crobuzoners try to encircle him, try to pen him in with their
weapons, Uther Doul finally attacks.

*Suddenly he holds a pistol in each hand, drawn from his hip hol-
sters, and they are raised and firing in quite different directions,
each one bursting open the face of a man. Their bullets spent, he
hurls the guns away from him as he twists (the men around him
looking quite still), and they spin through the air at speed and
smash into one man's chest and another's throat, and Doul has
two more flintlocks in his hands, and is firing again simultaneously (and only now do his first two victims finish falling), sending two more men away in ugly cartwheels, one dead, one dying,
and he is turning and the guns are missiles again, clubbing a
man unconscious.*

*Every motion Doul makes is perfect: flawless and straight-
lined. There is no excess; there are no curves.*

The men around him are beginning to scream, but they are

pushed on by the force of their fellows behind. They move slug-gishly toward Doul, who is in the air, his legs bent under him, turning amid a pattering of bullets. He fires with new guns and hurls them away into the faces of more enemies, then lets his feet touch down again. He has a last pistol in his hand and is moving it from face to cringing face, firing, leaping, and throwing it aside, kicking out with bent legs, a stampfighting move, breaking a cactus-man's nose and pushing him back into the bodies of his Crobuzoner comrades.

Bellis watches, breathing hard, unmoving. Everywhere else the fighting is ugly: contingent and chaotic and stupid. She is aghast that Doul can make it beautiful.

He is still again for a moment as the Crobuzoner troops re-group and surround him. He is hemmed in. Then Doul's ceramic blade flashes like polished bone.

His first strike is precise, a thrust too fast to see that pushes into a throat and flicks out again in a spray of sap, drowning a cactus-man in his own life. And then Uther Doul is tightly encir-cled and he cries out his own name again, quite unafraid, and his stance changes, and he reaches across his body, releasing the pent-up motor on his belt, turning on the Possible Sword.

There is a crack like static, and a hum in the air. Bellis cannot see Doul's right arm clearly. It seems to shimmer, to vibrate. It is un-stuck in time.

Doul moves (*dancing*) and turns to face the mass of his at-tackers. His left arm flails backward with loose, simian grace, and with shocking speed he raises his weapon arm.

His sword blossoms.

It is fecund, it is brimming, it sheds echoes. Doul has a thou-sand right arms, slicing in a thousand directions. His body moves, and like a stunningly complex tree, his sword arms spread through the air, solid and ghostly.

Some of them can hardly be seen; some are quite opaque. All move with Doul's speed; all carry his blade. They overlap and move through each other—and bite where they land. He cuts left to right and right to left, and down and up, and he stabs and par-ries and slashes savagely, all at once. A hundred blades block every attack that his enemies make, and countless more retaliate brutally.

The men before him are carved and lacerated with a palimp-

sest of monstrous wounds. Doul strikes, and blood and screams
welter up from around him in unbelievable gouts. The New
Crobuzon sailors are frozen. For a second, they watch their comrades fall in bloody death. And Uther Doul moves again.

He calls his name, he turns, he leaps and coils above them,
kicking and spinning, always moving, and everywhere he faces
he lashes out with the Possible Sword. He is surrounded, shrouded,
hidden by nigh-swords, his grey armor half visible through a
translucent wall of his own attacks. He is like a spirit, a god of revenge, a murderous bladed wind. He moves past the men who
have boarded his ship and sends up a mist of their blood, leaving
them dying, limbs and body parts skittering over the deck. His
armor is red.

Bellis sees his face for one instant. It is ruined with a feral
snarl.

The Crobuzoner men die in great numbers and fire their
weapons like children.

With one stroke and countless wounds, Doul tears open a
thaumaturge who is trying to slow him, and the woman's puissance makes her blood boil as it dissipates; and he fells a huge
cactus-man who raises a shield that deflects many hundreds of
Doul's attacks but cannot protect him from them all; and he mur-
ders a fire-throwing sailor whose tank of pyrotic gas splits open
and bursts, igniting even as his face is cut apart. Countless cuts
with every stroke.

"Gods," Bellis whispers to herself, unhearing. "Jabber *protect*
us . . ." She is awed.

Uther Doul lets the Possible Sword run for less than half a
minute.

When he thumbs it off, and is suddenly absolutely still, and
turns to the remaining Crobuzoner sailors, his face is calm. The
cold, still solidity of his right arm is shocking. He looks like
some monster, some gore-ghost. He breathes deeply—wet, slick,
dripping with other men's blood.

Uther Doul calls his own name, breathless, savagely triumphant.

*Unseen in Bellis' shadow, the man moves the statue down from
his lips.*

He is horrified. He is utterly aghast. I didn't know, *he thinks,
frantic.* I didn't know it could be like that . . .

The man has watched his liberators board and has seen them slowly break through those who opposed them, winning the Grand Easterly, *taking charge of the vessel, of Armada's heart . . . And now he has seen them withered and bloodied and destroyed in seconds, at the hands of Uther Doul.*

He looks out frantically at the frigates wedged between the Sorghum *and the city, and he tongues the statue again and feels it spit power into him. He debates racing over the side of this superstructure, over the corpses below, and onto the New Crobuzon ships.*

"It's me!" he might call. "I'm here! I'm the reason you're here! Let's go, let's run, let's get out of here!"

He can't take all of them, *the man thinks, his courage returning as he stares at the red-drenched figure of Uther Doul below.* Even with that godsdamned sword, there are too many, and the Armadan ships are being wiped out. Eventually more Crobuzoner troops will get here, and then we can leave. *The man turns and looks out, to where the dreadnoughts are pounding the remnants of the Armadan fleet.*

But even as he readies himself again to leave, he sees something.

The legions of tugs and steamers that have surrounded Armada like a corona, hauling it for decades, and that have now been left redundant by the avanc, are beginning to pull away from the city's orbit and head for the Crobuzoner fleet.

They have been refitted by frantic crews over the last few hours: built up with guns; stuffed full of black powder and explosives, with harpoons and phlogistic cells and batteries and jags welded, bolted, soldered, and screwed into temporary place. None of them is a battleship: none is any match for an ironclad. But there are so many of them.

Even as they approach, a volley from the Morning Walker *destroys one with a contemptuous blast. But there are many, many more behind it.*

Unseen, the man's face falters, frozen. I didn't think . . . *he stutters to himself, silently.* I didn't think of them.

He has told his government everything—he warned them of the nauscopists, so that the Crobuzoner meteoromancers could hide their fleet's approach; of the airships, so that golems were prepared; and of how many ships they would have to face. The Crobuzoner forces have been calculated to defeat the Armadan navy, which this man has researched and communicated to them. But he did not think to count those useless, age-pocked

*tugs and steamers, trawlers and tramps. He did not imagine
them reckless and stuffed with explosives. He had not pictured
them driving across the sea, into the path of an ironclad or a
dreadnought, as they do now, firing their pathetic guns like pugnacious children. He did not imagine their crews abandoning
them when they were mere yards away, hurling themselves from
the sterns of the smoke-spewing ships and onto rafts and lifeboats and watching as their abandoned vessels ram the flanks of
the Crobuzoner ships, breaching their inches of iron and igniting, exploding.*

There is a smear of dirty colors to the west, and the sun is very
low. The crews of the two dirigibles waiting by Dry Fall's *Uroc*
are impatient.

The Brucolac and his vampir cadre will soon be awake and
ready to fight.

But something is changing in the sea aft of the city. The
Crobuzoner sailors who have boarded the city are staring in horrified astonishment, the Armadans watching with fierce hope.

The tugs and steamers continue to plow toward the oncoming
Crobuzoner fleet—driving on toward the battleships, their engines overheating, their wheels locked into position, their throt-
tles wedged full ahead—until, in ones and twos, they impact.
Several are blown from the water in fountains of metal and flesh
before they can reach any quarry. But there are so many.

When they reach the towering sides of a dreadnought, the
prows of the empty tugs and trawlers crumple, buckling backward. And as they compress, their red-hot engines burst, and the
oil or gunpowder or dynamite wedged beside the engines ignites. And with ugly, oily flames; with great gouts of smoke and
dragged-out explosions that dissipate some of the energy into
useless sound; with one-two-threes of smaller detonations in
place of one solid blast, the ships explode.

Even such imperfect torpedoes as these begin to hole the Crobuzoner dreadnoughts.

Way behind them, the broken Armada force starts to regroup.
The New Crobuzon vessels are being slowed, and slowly ruined,
by the onslaught of sacrificed vessels. The Armadan battleships
rally their fleet and begin to fire on their stalled enemies.

The sea is full of lifeboats: escapees from the abandoned vessels that shudder their way toward the dreadnoughts. The crews

row frantically, striving to avoid other oncoming Armadan ships. Some fail: some are crushed and sunk; some are swamped by the enormous bloody waves, or are caught in the heat of depth charges or are broken up by cannonballs. But many escape into the open sea, back toward Armada, watching their ugly little tugs smack into the invaders and explode.

These unexpected attackers—a ridiculous, wasteful line of defense—have stopped the Crobuzoners, ship after ship immolating itself, melting their target's iron sides.

The dreadnoughts are stopped.

The *Morning Walker* is sinking.

There is a cheer, a rising yell of astonished triumph, from the aft edge of Armada, where the citizens can see what is happening only a handful of miles out to sea.

The roar is picked up by those who hear the cry of triumph and mimic it; and then by those behind them, and behind them. It sweeps across the city. Within a minute, men and women in the far reaches of Dry Fall and Shaddler and the Clockhouse Spur, on the other side of Armada, are screaming their ecstatic approval, though they are not sure of what.

The Crobuzoner troops stare in total horror. A great crack spreads up the side of the *Morning Walker*. More of the little ships smash into it and explode, even as it begins to buckle, even as its magisterial outline begins to twist; and it starts to angle its massive length down, as if purposefully; and frantic little figures begin to hurl themselves from its sides; and the explosions continue until its stern rises suddenly from the sea and, with a terrible shattering explosion, breaks off, spewing men and metal and coal—tons and tons of coal—into the sea.

The New Crobuzon crews watch as their chance to return home disappears. The Armadans scream their approval again, as the huge shape rolls over in the sea, ponderous and regretful, resenting every movement, and burps up fire as it is dragged below.

The Crobuzoner flagship has gone.

Frantic, its fellow dreadnoughts begin to level volleys too soon at Armada itself, churning the sea and making the city pitch as if it were in a storm. But some of the smaller ironclads are now in range, and their heavy shells shatter masts and tear through the fabric of the city.

A bomb swamps Winterstraw Market, tearing apart a circle of stallholder's boats. Two shells arc chillingly overhead and break a hole in the side of the *Pinchermarn,* sending hundreds of library books flaming into the water. Ships are sunk, the bridges that tether them on all sides splintering.

Angevine and Shekel comfort each other, hiding from the remnants of the invading Crobuzoners. Shekel is bleeding profusely from his face.

But terrible though these attacks are, only the dreadnoughts could destroy the city, and they are not in range. They are being harried, contained, broken by the onslaught of gunpowder-stuffed tugs. The Armadan vessels keep coming. After a fifth explosion rocks its bows, the *Bane of Suroch* begins to buckle, to crack, to list, to collapse into the water.

Ironclads and scouts mill solicitous and useless around it, drones around a dying queen. Under renewed onslaught from the remnants of the Armadan fleet, but most of all under the unexpected and suicidal attacks of all those refitted steamers, the New Crobuzon dreadnoughts are, one by one, being destroyed.

From the raised deck above the Grand Easterly, *the man screams in unheard horror.*

The man tenses and kisses his statue with a fervent frenzy, then prepares to leap out and down, folding space a little, and land on that frigate below, which is rumbling and gearing up to leave. But he stops as a terrible realization shakes him.

He watches the last two dreadnoughts quiver under the attacks and fire their vicious guns at their tormentors. And even though those retaliations cost several Armadan vessels, the ugly explosions that rock the dreadnoughts' flanks continue until the Crobuzoner vessels go down.

The invaders' coal has been sunk. The man watches, quite numb. There is no point now in him jumping ship or swimming out for his home vessels. Even if the Armadans do not destroy every single ship, even if one or two fast-running ironclads escape, this is the middle of the Swollen Ocean, uncharted waters, almost two thousand miles from the nearest land and twice that far to home. Within a few hundred miles their boilers will grow cold, and the Crobuzoner vessels will be calmed.

They have no sails. They will rot and die.
There is no hope for them.
This rescue has failed. The man is still trapped.

He looks down and realizes with a dull shock that he has slipped back into phase with Bellis' space. If she turned now, she would see him. He mouths the statue again, numbly, and disappears.

Dusk fell, and finally the Dry Fall dirigibles lifted off, each containing its murderous crew. They sailed low and fast over the last dregs of battle, their vampir passengers ready. Long tongues flickered in the night air as the ab-dead prepared to hurl themselves into any fray.

They were too late. The fight was over.

The airships meandered pointlessly over water fouled with coaldust and twisted metal and acid and oil, and here and there the shimmering residue of rockmilk, and sap, and many gallons of blood.

Chapter Thirty-seven

At first the city welled up with exhausted delight, a kind of ragged, wounded euphoria.

It did not last long. In the days that followed, Bellis was acutely conscious of silence; Armada was endlessly quiet. It started after the battle, when the roars of triumph died out and the scale of devastation became clear.

Bellis had not slept in the night after the carnage. She stumbled out with the dawn, with thousands of other citizens, and walked, dumb, across the city. The skyline she knew was broken in strange new ways. Ships in which she had bought paper, or drunk tea, or walked across, unthinking, a hundred times, were gone.

Croom Park was quite untouched. The *Chromolith,* the *Tolpandy,* the *Grand Easterly* itself were quite whole.

Many times in the days that followed, Bellis would turn a corner in some backstreet maze—or cross a wooden bridge, or come into a well-lit plaza—and see people crying, mourning the dead. Some were staring at one piece or another of the damage to their city—a blank, wave-flecked hole where their home ship had been, a shattered mess of a marketplace, a church crushed by fallen masts.

It was quite unfair, Bellis thought nervously, that so few of her own haunts had been harmed. By what right was that? She, after all, did not even care.

A huge number of Armadans had died. Several members of the Curhouse Council and Queen Braginod of Jhour were among them. The Council voted in replacements, and the stewardship of Jhour passed quietly to Braginod's brother, Dynich. No one cared, particularly. Armada had left thousands of bodies in the sea.

People stared at the *Sorghum,* muttering that it was not worth it.

Bellis wandered through the brutalized cityscape as if she were dreaming. Even where no shells had fallen, the stresses caused by the bucking sea had ruined architecture. Arches were shattered, their keystones now resting on the ocean floor. There had been fires; narrow streets had crumbled, the rows of houses that seemed to lean into each other shifting, touching, their roofs cracking and collapsing. The city seemed to tremble with kinds of damage that would have been impossible on land.

As she wandered, Bellis heard hundreds of stories: exaggerated tales of heroism and ghoulish descriptions of injuries. She began to dig for specific information, tentatively. Moved by curiosity she did not understand (feeling in those hours like an automaton, moving without her own consent), Bellis asked what had happened to the other passengers from the *Terpsichoria.*

There were conflicting stories about the Cardomiums. Bellis heard about those crewmen still imprisoned, their commitment to Armada not yet trusted, having failed to make peace with their press-ganging. She heard that there had been an almighty ruckus from the prison ships in the fore of Garwater when the shelling began, and that the imprisoned men had screamed and screamed for their compatriots to come for them.

The boarders, of course, had never come close, and the shouts had gone unanswered.

Sister Meriope was dead. Bellis was shocked by that—in a

horrible, abstract way—as if at seeing an unexpected color. In the chaos, she heard, several prisoners had escaped from the asylum, Meriope among them. The massively pregnant nun had made her way to the city's aft edge, where she had run toward the New Crobuzon boarding party, shouting ecstatic greetings, and been shot down. It was impossible to tell whose guns had killed her.

That was the kind of story that Bellis heard again and again— the press-ganged who, faced with what seemed a sudden chance to go home, had tried desperately to switch sides in the battle, and had died. Several of those from the *Terpsichoria* had been killed in such a way, it seemed. And even if their numbers were exaggerated, even if the details were embellished as a moral caution about disloyalty, Bellis was sure that many must have died as described.

It was obvious to Bellis—no great revelation—that her safety would have been very, very far from secure had she sought refuge with the New Crobuzon troops. She had decided long ago that her return to her city would have to be her own doing. Bellis knew how little her government would care about her survival. She had fled them, after all, and for good reasons.

During the fighting, Bellis had felt paralyzed, had been numb to any kind of desire for one side or the other to win. She had watched like a chance spectator at a bloody prizefight. Now that Armada had triumphed, she felt no relief or happiness, nor any despair.

After the destruction of the dreadnoughts, the other Crobuzoner ships had sailed away to the northwest. They fled in a panic, too terrified to surrender, to beg quarter from the Armadans. They escaped, pretending that there was some hope for them, that they might make it to a port. Everyone knew that their crews would die.

Three Crobuzoner ironclads and a frigate were captured. Instantly, they became the most advanced ships in Armada, but still they were hardly recompense for the scores of vessels that Armada had lost. A good portion of its fleet, two submersibles, and half the hastily rebuilt steamers had been sacrificed to destroy the dreadnoughts. The *Trident* and tens of smaller airships were gone. The massive aeroflot had been weighed down by golems like attacking rats, brought into the rage of fire that had taken its hide and burst its skeleton.

Armadans had taken many hours to return to their city, paddling in their life rafts, swimming, clinging to debris. The thaumaturges and engineers in the base of the *Grand Easterly* kept the avanc slow for more than a day. It had made its dumb way on, untroubled by the murderous chaos above it.

Inevitably, some of those who reached the city were New Crobuzon troops. Perhaps an enterprising few stole the clothes off Armadan corpses and simply hauled themselves aboard into a new life—as sailors, all spoke at least passable Salt. But most were too traumatized to calculate like that, and in the hours after the battle, Crobuzoner sailors began to appear on the decks of Armada in sodden, ruined uniforms, miserable with fear. Their dread of drowning was stronger than that of Armadan revenge.

In those ruined days immediately after the war, under red- and black-smoked skies, those terrified Crobuzoner sailors caused a political crisis. Of course, in their rage of loss, the Armadans punished their bedraggled captives. The newcomers were beaten and whipped—some to death—while their tormentors howled the names of dead friends. But eventually weariness, disgust, and numbness set in, and the Crobuzoners were taken away and held on the *Grand Easterly.* After all, Armada's history was built on the assimilation of strangers and enemies—after any battle, any time a ship was taken.

This had been a more violent, a more terrible set of circumstances than any in the city's past, but still, there was no question as to what must be done with captured enemies. As with the *Terpsichoria,* those who could be won over were to be made Armadans.

Only this time, the Lovers said otherwise.

The Lovers had come back from the fighting enraged and elyctric, exhilarated, scarred all anew with random markings that did not match each other's (something they would fix over the nights to come). The whole riding, the whole city, was shocked when the news leaked that the Lovers intended to have the Crobuzoners cast out.

At a hastily convened mass meeting on the *Grand Easterly,* the Lover put her case. She declaimed violently against the Crobuzoners, reminding her citizens that their missing families had been slaughtered by such as these, their city blasted, half their Armadan ships destroyed. There were now many times more press-ganged aboard than Garwater or any other riding had

had to take in at one time before. With their resources stretched, with Armada vulnerable, with New Crobuzon having declared war, how could they possibly absorb so many enemies?

But many of those who were Armadans now had once been enemies. For as long as the city had existed, Armadans had held that once the fighting stopped, there was no quarrel with its enemies' foot soldiers. They were to be welcomed, and hopefully transformed, and made citizens. That, after all, was what Armada was—a colony of the lost, the renegade, the absent-without-leave, the defeated.

The New Crobuzon sailors shivered in their prisons, unaware of the controversy that surrounded them.

It would not be murder, the Lover claimed. The prisoners could be put aboard a ship, with provisions, and pointed in the direction of Bered Kai Nev. It was not impossible that they would make it.

That was a poor argument.

She changed her tack, arguing angrily that with the avanc, the city must go on, that it had the power to go to places Armadans had never dreamed of, to do unimagined things, and that to waste their resources wiping the noses of a thousand blubbering newcomers—murderers—was idiocy.

Even with their wounds still bleeding and fresh, even with the memory of war still painful, the mood of the crowd was turning against the Lover. She was not convincing them. The other rulers held their peace, watching.

Bellis understood. It was not that those gathered had any love, any particular pity or compassion, for their captives. It was not about those bloody, wounded troops holed up in agony and squalor below. The Armadans were not concerned for those captives, but for their own city. *This is Armada,* they were saying. *This is how it is what it is. Change that, and how do we know what we are? How do we know how to be?*

With one speech, the Lover could not defeat so many centuries of tradition—tradition thrown up for the city's survival. She was alone on the stage, and she was losing her argument. With a sudden, rocking uncertainty, Bellis wondered where the Lover was, whether he agreed.

Sensing the discontent, those among the crowd who agreed with the Lover's line began to shout, spontaneously offering support, crying revenge against the captured. But more voices rose in opposition, and quieted them.

Something shifted, decisively. It was obvious, suddenly, that this gathering would not allow the Crobuzoners to be murdered, even through the drawn-out pretense at mercy the Lover had suggested. It was obvious that the long, sometimes easy, sometimes cruel process of press-ganging would have to begin, and that many months of effort would be expended on the men and few women imprisoned below, and that eventually many of them would reconcile themselves to their new life, and some would not. The latter would remain imprisoned; and only eventually, after long efforts at persuasion, might they, perhaps, be executed.

"What's the fucking hurry?" someone shouted. "Where you fucking taking us, anyway?"

The Lover gave in then, swiftly, with charisma; shrugging in exaggerated humility, she acquiesced, announced her order rescinded. She won a ragged cheer from an audience still eager to forgive a bad suggestion made in anger. She did not answer the heckler's question.

Bellis remembered that moment later, and saw in it a fulcrum. *That was the moment,* she would tell herself in the weeks to come, *that everything changed.*

Vessels now too broken to sail hitched themselves to the city and were pulled on by the untiring avanc. It swam at a steady pace, without sudden darts or caprice, a little more than five miles an hour.

North.

The days were full of services for the dead: homages and homilies and prayers. Rebuilding began. Cranes twitched; the city bustled with subdued crews refitting the broken buildings, restoring what they could and changing what they could not. In the evenings, the pubs and drinking dens were full but quiet. Armada was not convivial, in those awful days. It was still bleeding, had not yet scarred.

People began to ask questions. Delicately, very carefully, they probed those wounds in their minds, tender places that the war had left. And when they did, terrible uncertainties arose.

Why did they come? people began to say to themselves and to each other (with shaking heads and lowered eyes). *And how, across half a world, did they ever find us?*

Can they do it again?

This slow, burgeoning spirit of anger and query raised wider issues than the war itself. Each question bore others.

What did we do to attract their notice?

What are we doing?

Where are we going?

With the days and insomniac nights, Bellis' numbness began to ebb. She had spoken properly to no one—she had spent time with no one—since the battle. Uther Doul had done without her; she had not found Carrianne or Johannes. Except to rake through the rumors that proliferated like weeds, Bellis had hardly spoken for days.

On the second day after the fighting, she began to think. Something in her woke, and she viewed the damaged city with the first emotion she had felt for some time—a cold horror. Bellis realized curiously that she was aghast.

As she lifted her eyes to the sun, she felt the stirrings of emotions and uncertainties and terrible certainties she had been storing.

"Oh gods," she said quietly. "Oh gods."

She knew so many things, she realized. So much was clear to her now—and so much that was terrible, that she balked at confronting, that she could not think about just yet. She had understanding and knowledge inside her, but she shied away from it as if from a bully.

That day, Bellis ate and drank and walked as if nothing had changed, her motions as jerky and fumbling as those of all the other traumatized around her. But at odd moments she would wince—she would blink and hiss and grit her teeth—as the knowledge inside her moved. She was pregnant with it—a fat, malign child that she was desperately ignoring.

Some part of her knew that she could not batten it down, but she played herself for time, never vocalizing, never thinking in words, always closing off the understanding she carried with an angry, frightened sense of *Not now, not now* . . .

She watched the sun set from her rough-cut windows and read and reread her letter, trying to steel herself to write something about the battle, not knowing what to do. At ten o'clock she heard a peremptory knocking, and opened the door onto Tanner Sack.

He stood on the little platform that jutted from the smokestack beyond her door, at the top of the stairs. He had been wounded in the fighting; his face was cut and septic, his left eye puffed closed. His chest was bandaged, the ugly tentacles springing from it wrapped close to him. Tanner was holding a pistol aimed at Bellis' face. His hand was unwavering.

Bellis stared into it, into the pit at its end. The fat, hateful understanding that she had nurtured came out of her, unstoppable. She knew the truth, and she knew why Tanner Sack was ready to kill her. And with exhaustion she knew that if he pulled the trigger, if she heard the blast, that in the sliver of a second before the bullet burst her brain, she would not blame him.

CHAPTER THIRTY-EIGHT

"You murderous fucking bitch."

Bellis gripped the back of her chair, gasping with pain, blinking to clear her eyes. Tanner Sack had hit her once, a hard backhanded slap that had sent her into the wall. The blow seemed to have taken the physical anger out of him and left him with only the strength to speak to her, hatefully. He kept his gun aimed at her head.

"I didn't know," said Bellis, "I swear to Jabber I didn't *know*." She felt little fear. Mostly, she felt a thick shame and a confusion that slurred her words.

"You fucking evil shit," said Tanner, not loud. "You fucking bloodsucker, you bitch, you bitch, fuck you . . ."

"I didn't know," she said again. The gun did not waver.

He swore at her again, a drawn-out drawl of invective, and she did not interrupt. She let him speak until he was tired. He cursed her for a long time, and then suddenly changed his tack, speaking to her in what was almost a normal tone.

"All them dead. All that blood. I was under the waves, you

know that? I was *swimming* in it." He whispered the words at her. "I was swimming in the fucking blood. Killing men like me. Stupid New Crobuzon boys that might've been my mates. And if I'd been took back, if they'd got their way, if they'd done what they wanted, if they'd taken this fucking city, then the killing wouldn't have stopped. I'd be on my way to the colonies now. A Remade slave.

"My boy," he said, suddenly hushed. "Shekel. You know Shekel, don't you?" He stared at her. "He helped you a few times. Him and his lady, Angevine, got caught up in the fighting. Ange can take care of herself, but Shekel? He got himself a rifle, stupid lad. A bullet hit the rail under him, and the splinters tore open his face. It's a mess. He'll always be marked—always. And there am I, thinking that if that Crobuzoner had moved his gun an inch—a fucking *inch*—then Shekel'd be gone. He'd be *gone.*"

Bellis could not insulate herself from his desolate tone.

"Like all the others who've gone." Tanner's voice was drab. "And who killed them, all the dead crews? Who killed 'em? Had to call for help, didn't you? Did you even think about what might happen? Did you? Did you care? Do you care now?" His words hammered her, and even as she shook her head—*that's not how it was*—she felt deep shame. "You killed them, you traitor fuck.

"You . . . and me."

He kept the gun steady, but his face distorted.

"Me," he said. "Why'd you bring *me* in?" His eyes were bloodshot. "You nearly killed my boy."

Bellis blinked away her own tears.

"Tanner," she said, and her voice was throaty. "Tanner," she said slowly, raising her hands in a helpless gesture. "I swear to you, I swear to you, I *swear* . . . I didn't know."

She supposed that he had always had some vestige of doubt, some uncertainty, or he would have simply blown her away. She spoke to him for a long time, stumbling over her words, trying to find ways to express what sounded impossible, utterly untrue, even to her.

All the time she spoke, his gun never left her face. As she told Tanner what she had realized, Bellis stopped speaking, from time to time, as the truth of it sank into her.

The window was visible over Tanner Sack's shoulder, and she

stared through it as she spoke. That was much easier than meeting his eyes. Whenever she glimpsed his face, she burned. The outrage of betrayal, and most of all the shame, scoured her.

"I believed what I told you," she told him, and remembering the carnage, she winced so hard it hurt. "He lied to me, too."

"I don't fucking know how they found Armada," she said, a little time later, still in the face of Tanner's scorn and livid disbelief. "I don't know how it works; I don't know what they did; I don't know what information or machinery he stole to let it happen. There was something . . . He must have hidden something; he must have given them something they needed, something to track us, in that message . . ."

"The one you gave *me*," Tanner said, and Bellis hesitated, then nodded.

"The one he gave me, and I gave you," she said.

"I was convinced," she said. "Jabber, Tanner, why do you think I was on the *Terpsichoria*? I was a fucking exile, Tanner." He kept quiet at that.

"I was running," Bellis went on. "I was *running*. And damn, I don't like it here, this isn't my place . . . But I was running. I wouldn't call those bastards; I wouldn't trust them. I was on the run because I was scared for my fucking neck." He looked at her curiously. "And anyway . . ." She hesitated to say more, fearing that she would sound ingratiating, though she wanted to tell him the truth.

"Anyway . . ." she continued, keeping her voice calm. "Anyway, I wouldn't have done that. I'd not do that to . . . to you, to any of you. I'm not a fucking magister, Tanner. I'd not wish their justice on any of you."

He gazed back at her, his face like stone.

What decided him, she realized later, what led him to believe her, was not her sadness or her shame. He did not trust those, and she did not blame him. What convinced him that she was telling the truth, that she had been as duped as him, was her rage.

For a long, wordless, miserable time, Bellis felt herself trembling, and her fists clenched bone-hard and white.

"You fucker," she heard herself say, and shook her head.

Tanner could tell she was not speaking to him. She was thinking of Silas Fennec.

"He told me lies," she spat suddenly to Tanner, surprising herself, "after lie after *lie* . . . so that he could use me."

He used me, she thought, *like he used everyone else. I watched him at work; I knew what he did, how he used people, but . . .*

But I didn't think he was doing it with me.

"He humiliated you," Tanner said. "Thought you were special, did you?" he sneered. "Thought you could see through him? Thought you was in it together?"

She stared at him, white-hot with rage and self-disgust at being gulled by Silas like some stupid naïve, like his puppets, like everyone else. *Me more than all the poor fools reading Simon Fench's pamphlets; me more than every poor stupid fuck acting as his contact.* She was sick at the contempt, the ease, with which he had lied to her.

"You piece of shit," she muttered. "I'll fucking destroy you."

Tanner sneered at her again, and she knew how pathetic she sounded.

"Do you think any of what he said was true?" Tanner Sack asked her.

They sat together, stiff and uncertain. Tanner still held the gun, but loosely. They had not become coconspirators. He looked at her with dislike and anger. Even if he believed that she had not set out to harm Armada, she was not his comrade. She was still the one who had persuaded him to be message-boy. It was she who had implicated him in the butchery.

Bellis shook her head in slow dudgeon.

"Do I think New Crobuzon is under attack?" she said disgustedly. "Do I think the most powerful city-state in the world is being threatened by malevolent fish? That two thousand years of history is about to end, and that only I can save my home? *No,* Tanner Sack, I don't. I think he wanted to get a message home, and that was all. I think that manipulative fuck played me like a fiddle. Like he plays everyone." *He's an assassin, a spy; he's an agent,* she thought. *He's exactly what I was running from. And still, lonely and credulous like some fucking lost fool, I believed him.*

Why would they come for him? she thought suddenly. *Why*

*would they cross four thousand miles just to rescue one man? It
wasn't for him, and I don't think it was for the* Sorghum.

"There's more to this . . ." she said slowly, and tried to form
thoughts. "There's more to this than we can see."

*They wouldn't come this far, risk this much, just for him, no
matter how good an agent he is. He* has *something,* she realized.
He has something they want.

"So what are we going to do?"

It was growing light. The city's birds were sounding. Bellis'
head ached; she was terribly tired.

She ignored Tanner's question for a moment. As she looked
out of the window, she could see the sky paling and the silhouettes of rigging and architecture etched in black. It was very still.
She could see the waves against the city's sides, could make out
Armada's faint northern passage. The air was cool.

Bellis wanted one more moment in this time, one more suspended second, when she could breathe, before she spoke, and
answered Tanner, and set in motion a clumsy, claustrophobic
endgame.

She knew the answer to his question, but she did not want to
give it. She did not look at him. She knew he would ask again.
Silas Fennec was still free in the city, having seen his attempted
rescue fail, and there was only one thing that could be done. She
knew that Tanner knew it, that he was testing her, that there was
only one possible answer to his question and that if she failed to
give it, he might still shoot her dead.

"What are we going to do?" he said again. She looked up at
him, weary. "You know that." She laughed unpleasantly. "We
have to tell the truth.

"We have to tell Uther Doul."

CHAPTER THIRTY-NINE

Here we drift, near the northern rim of the Swollen Ocean, and only—what?—a thousand, two thousand miles to the west, the northwest, is the Cunning Sea. And nestled in the crooks of its coast, on the shoreline of an unmapped continent, is the colony of Nova Esperium.

Is it the small, bright, glittering city of which I have seen pictures? I have seen heliotypes of its towers, and its grain silos, and the forests that surround it, and the unique animals of its environs: framed and posed, sepia, hand-colored. There's a new chance for everyone in Nova Esperium. Even the Remade, the indentured, the laborers, can earn freedom.

(Not that that is true.)

I have pictured myself looking down at the settlement from the slopes of the mountains I can see in those pictures (washed out by distance, out of focus). Learning the languages of the natives, picking over the bones of old books that we might find in the ruins.

It is ten miles from New Crobuzon to the estuary, to the edge of Iron Bay.

I keep finding myself in that place, in my memories, beyond the city, poised between the land and the sea.

I have lost my seasons. I left when autumn became winter, and that is the last strong sense I have of time. Since then the heat and cool and cold and heat again have been chaotic, ill-mannered, random, to me.

Perhaps it is autumn again in Nova Esperium.

In New Crobuzon, it is spring.

I have knowledge that I cannot use, on a journey I cannot control, the aims of which I do not share or understand, and I am longing for a home I fled, and for a place I have never seen.

* * *

There are birds beyond these walls, sounding to each other, vio-lent and stupid, wrestling with the wind, and with my eyes closed I can pretend to watch them; I can pretend to be on any ship, anywhere in the world.

But I open my eyes (I must), and I am still here, in this Senate chamber again, standing beside Tanner Sack, and my head is lowered, and I am in chains.

A few feet in front of Bellis and Tanner, Uther Doul was con-cluding his address to the city's rulers: the Lovers, Dynich, the new Curhouse Council, and all the others. It was after dark. The Brucolac was also attending. He was the only ruler not marked by the war—all the others bore scars or blasted expressions. The rulers listened to Uther Doul. Now and then they glanced at the prisoners.

Bellis watched them watching her and saw the anger in their eyes. Tanner Sack could not look up. He was wrapped very tight in misery and shame.

"We're agreed," said Uther Doul. "We must move quickly. We can assume that what we've been told is correct. We must bring Silas Fennec in, immediately. And we can also assume that if he hasn't yet worked out that we're hunting him, he will do so soon."

"But how did he fucking do it?" shouted King Friedrich. "I mean, I understand about this fucking *package,* this fucking message . . ." He glared at Bellis and Tanner. "But how did Fen-nec get hold of a fucking lodestone? The compass factory, for fuck's sake . . . it's guarded tighter than my fucking treasury. How did he get in?"

"That we don't yet know," said Uther Doul, "and it is one of the very first things we'll ask him. As far as possible, we have to keep this business quiet. As Simon Fench, Fennec . . . is . . . not without supporters," Doul went on. The Lovers did not look at each other. "We shouldn't risk . . . angering any citizens. We need to move now. Does anyone know how we might start?"

Dynich coughed and raised his hand. "I have heard rumors," he began hesitantly, "that Fench operates out of certain drinking holes—"

"King, let me speak," the Brucolac interrupted in his scraped-up voice. Everyone looked at him in surprise. The vampir seemed unusually hesitant. He sighed and unrolled his flickering tongue, then continued.

"It's no secret that Dry Fall riding has strong differences with the rulers of Garwater over the summoning of the avanc, and the city's trajectory—which is still undisclosed," he added with a brief flash of anger. "However—" His tan eyes took in the room like a challenge. "—I hope it would never be alleged that the Brucolac, or any of my cadre, are less than absolutely loyal to this city. It's a matter of deep regret to us that we weren't able to fight for Armada in the war that's just passed.

"I know," he went on quickly, "that my citizens fought. We have our share of the dead—but not me and mine. And we feel that. We owe you a debt.

"I know where Silas Fennec is."

There was a quick chorus of gasps.

"How do you know?" said the Lover. "How *long* have you known?"

"Not long," said the Brucolac. He met her eyes, but he did not look proud. "We found out where *Simon Fench* rested his head and printed his works. But you know . . ." he said with sudden fervor. "You *know* that we had no idea of his plans. We would never have allowed this."

The implication was obvious. He had allowed "Simon Fench" to spread his influence, to print his dissident literature and unleash damaging rumors, so long as he had thought the victim of that activity would be Garwater rather than the city as a whole. He had not known about the Crobuzoner fleet that Fennec had called. Like Tanner and Bellis, he found himself implicated in what had happened.

Bellis watched, sneering inwardly at the Lovers' ostentatious outrage. *As if you've never done the same or more,* she thought. *As if that's not how all of you bastards operate against each other.*

"I'm aware," hissed the Brucolac, "of how this stands. And I want this bastard brought down as much as any of you do. Which is why it will be a pleasure, as well as a duty, to take him."

"*You* don't take him," said Uther Doul. "I take him—my men and I."

The Brucolac turned his yellowing eyes to Doul. "I have certain advantages," he said slowly. "This mission is important to me."

"You do not get absolution this way, Deadman," Doul said coldly. "You chose to let him play his games unimpeded, and this is the result. Now, tell us where he is, and then your interference ends."

There was silence for several seconds.

"Where is he?" shouted the Lover suddenly. "Where's he been hiding?"

"That's another reason it makes sense for my cadre to hunt him," the Brucolac replied. "He's in a place many of your troops might refuse to go. Silas Fennec is in the haunted quarter."

Doul did not flinch. He stared at the vampir. "You do not take him," he said again. "I am *not* afraid."

Bellis listened with shame, and a slow-burning hatred for Fennec. *You fuck,* she thought with savage satisfaction. *Let's see you lie your way out of this.*

Even though he might still be her best hope to get out, she could never allow that fucking pig to lie to her, to use her. That could not go without payback, no matter the cost. She would rather take her chances in Armada, or at the Scar.

You should have fucking told me, Silas, she thought, breathing hard with fury. *I wanted—I want—to get away, too. If you'd told me the truth—if you'd been open, if you'd been honest, if you'd not used me—I might have helped you,* she thought. *We might have done it all together.*

But she knew that was not true.

Desperate as she was to get out of this place, she would not have helped him had she known his plans. She would not have been party to that.

With dreadful self-disgust, Bellis realized that Silas had judged her well. His job was to know what he could tell to whom, to know how far those around him would go, and to lie to them accordingly. He had to judge what to tell each of his pawns.

He had been right about her.

Bellis remembered Uther Doul's rage when she and Tanner had come to him.

He had stared at them as they explained, his face growing stiller and more cold, his eyes darker, as they spoke. Flustered, Bellis and Tanner in turn had tried to explain to him that they had known nothing, that they had both been used.

Tanner had gabbled, and Doul had been impassive, waiting for him to finish and punishing him with silence, saying nothing at all. But then he had turned to Bellis and waited for her explanations. He had unnerved her—he was quite unmoving when she told him that she knew Silas Fennec, *Simon Fench*. He had not seemed surprised at all by that. He had stood quietly, waiting for more information. But when she told him what she had done, what she had couriered for Fennec, then quite suddenly Doul had exploded with anger.

"No," he had shouted. "What did he *do*?"

And when she had murmured something to him—some shamefaced, stuttered assertion that she had had no idea, that she had never *dreamed,* that she could not have *known*—he had stared at her very hard, with an expression of cold dislike and cruelty that she had never seen him wear before and that had cut her to her innards.

"Are you sure?" he had said to her, appallingly. "Is that so? No idea? None at all?"

He had birthed a maggot of doubt in her head that grubbed pitilessly through her remorse and misery.

Did I never know? Did I never doubt?

The rulers were arguing about the geography of Armada's haunted quarter, about the ghuls and the tallow ghast, about how they should set their trap.

Bellis spoke loud enough to interrupt them all. "Senate," she said. They were silent.

Doul took her in, his eyes absolutely unforgiving. She did not flinch.

"There's something else that should be remembered," she said. "I don't believe that New Crobuzon would cross so many thousands of miles out of *love.* They wouldn't risk all those ships, and all that effort, not even for the *Sorghum,* and certainly not just to bring their man home.

"Silas Fennec has something they want. I don't know what it is, and I . . . I swear to you that I would tell you if I knew. I believe . . . One thing I believe is true, that he told me, is that he spent time in High Cromlech, and most recently in The Gengris. I saw his notebooks, and I believe that.

"He told me that the grindylow had hunted him. And maybe that was true, too. Perhaps because of something he'd taken:

something that New Crobuzon would risk crossing the world
for, when they found out he had it. Perhaps that's why they came.

"You've all agreed that he's done things he should never have
been able to do: stolen things, broken into impregnable places.
Well, perhaps whatever Silas Fennec has—whatever he stole,
whatever the Crobuzoners came to fetch—is behind all that. So I
suppose I'm saying . . . remember that, when you track him
down, that he might be using something . . . And be careful."

There was a long, unbending silence after she spoke.

"She's right," someone said.

"And what of her?" said a pugnacious youth from the Curhouse Council. "Do you—do *we*—believe them? That they knew
nothing? That they were just trying to save their own city?"

"*This* is my city," shouted Tanner Sack suddenly, to shocked
silence.

Uther Doul looked at Tanner, whose head slumped slowly
back down.

"We deal with them later," Doul said. "They'll be incarcerated
for now, until we bring in Silas Fennec. Then we can question
him, and we can judge."

It was Uther Doul himself who led Tanner and Bellis to their
cells.

He took them from the meeting room into the warren of tunnels that riddled the *Grand Easterly*. Through the darkwood paneled corridors, past ancient heliotypes of New Crobuzon sailors.
Down gaslit tunnels. Where they eventually stopped, there were
strange sounds of settling metal and laboring engines.

Doul pushed Tanner (*gently*) through a door, and Bellis
glimpsed a sparse berth within: a bunk, a desk and chair, a window. Doul turned away from Bellis and walked on. He judged
correctly that she would follow him: even like this, toward her
own imprisonment.

In the cell, the darkness beyond the window was not cloudy
night. They were lower than the waterline, and her porthole
opened onto the unlit sea. She turned and held onto the door,
stopping Doul from pushing it closed.

"Doul," she said, and looked for any sign of softness, or friendship or attraction or forgiveness, and saw none.

He waited.

"One thing," she said, meeting his eyes resolutely. "Tanner

Sack . . . he's a bigger victim here than anyone. He'd do nothing to endanger Armada. He's in hell; he's broken. If you're going to punish anyone . . ." She drew shaky breath. "I'm trying to say, if you're interested in justice, you'll . . . not punish *him,* at least. Whatever else you decide. He's the most loyal Armadan—the most loyal Garwater man—I know."

Uther Doul stared at her for a long time. He twisted his head slowly to one side, as if curious.

"Goodness, Miss Coldwine," he said eventually, his voice level: softer, more beautiful than ever. "By the gods. What a display of bravery, self-sacrifice. To take onto yourself the largest share of blame, to altruistically beg mercy for another. Had I suspected you of base motivations and manipulations—of deliberately and cynically or uncaringly bringing war to my city—had I been considering treating you severely for your actions, I believe I would have to rethink now, in the light of this, your obvious . . . selfless . . . nobility."

Bellis had looked up sharply as he began to speak, but her eyes widened as he continued. His level voice became sour as he mocked her.

She burned, utterly dismayed. Shamed, and alone again.

"Oh," she breathed. She could not speak.

Uther Doul turned the key and left Bellis alone to watch the fishes that swarmed stupidly to whatever light spilled from her window.

There was no such thing as silence in Armada. In the quietest part of the longest night, without a soul on any side, the city was full of noises.

The wind and water played it incessantly. Armada rode on swells, and compacted, and spread its substance wide and brought it tight again. The rigging whispered. Masts and smokestacks shifted uncomfortably. Vessels knocked together for hour upon hour, like bones, like someone infinitely stupid and patient at the door of an empty house.

The city came closest to true silence in its empty haunted quarter. The tapping and grating and slopping of water seemed more hollow there. But in that place there were other, more obscure sounds that frightened those who heard them, and kept intruders away.

A slow crackling, like a tower of kindling collapsing. The

rhythmic thudding of something mechanical piercing wood. A faint crooning like a mistuned flute.

The haunted quarter lolled among its odd noises, and moldered and swelled faintly with years of water, and continued its long, drawn-out collapse. No one knew what was hidden there in its age-blistered boats.

The *Wordhoard* was the largest vessel in the haunted quarter. An ancient ship more than four hundred feet long, carved in ocher wood, once deep-stained with intense colors, all blasted now by age and salt air. It was littered with the debris of five masts and a profusion of derricks and stays and yards. The staves and poles lay across the deck like crosshatching. They were losing their shapes, rotting and worm-eaten into nothing.

It was almost midnight. Sounds came from Dry Fall and Thee-And-Thine ridings: drinking and everything that went with it; mechanical noises of reconstruction from the building sites created by the war. There were still bridges linking the ridings to the haunted quarter, old and unused, put in place unknown numbers of years ago and tenaciously refusing to become dust.

From a rude little barge at the edge of Thee-And-Thine, a man crept across water to the derelict vessels beyond. He walked without fear through a shipscape of decay: mildew, and rust corrosive as frostbite. There was only starlight to see by, but he knew his way.

At the fore of an iron trawler, the great winches were split, and they splayed their mechanical innards as if they had been butchered. The man picked a way through the greased carnage and crossed onto the *Wordhoard*. Its long deck reared out before him, listing a little off true.

(It was held below by the vast chain, fitted long ago, that stretched down into the water and held the avanc in place.)

The man descended into the darkness at the haunted vessel's core. He was not quiet. He knew that if he was heard, he would be thought a phantom.

He moved through half-lit corridors, their contours outlined with thaumaturgy or phosphorescent mold.

The man slowed and looked around him, his face creasing in hard concern, his fingers tightening on the statue he held. When he reached age-slimed steps leading down, he stopped, resting

his free hand on the banister. He held his breath and turned his
head slowly around him, staring hard into every dark place,
listening.

Something was whispering.

That was a sound the man had never heard before, even on
these ghost-infested decks.

The man turned. He gazed into the pitch-black at the end of
the passageway as if it were a battle of wills, as if he tried to stare
down the darkness, until eventually he won, and it gave up what
it had been hiding.

"Silas."

A man stepped out of the shadow.

Instantly Silas Fennec brought up the statue in his hand and
slammed his tongue deep into its gorge. The figure was running
at him, covering the distance in the darkness, a sword extended.

And suddenly there were others. Hard-faced figures emerged
from boltholes in the wood, all around, and came at him with
shocking speed. They bore down on him with guns and weapons
outstretched.

"Keep him alive!" shouted Doul.

Silas Fennec felt a tremor from the lascivious tongue of his
stone icon, and puissance roared through him. He stepped up—
up onto spaces that he would not have seen or been capable of
treading a moment before. Fennec twisted as the first Garwater
man passed stupidly below him, then he opened his mouth and
gasped as his gut spasmed. With a retching growl he spewed up
a bolt of green-black glowing bile, a mouthful of thaumaturgi-
cally charged plasma that was not quite viscous liquid and not
quite energy. It burst from him and landed foursquare in his at-
tacker's face.

Silas Fennec stepped quickly through ways of seeing, leaving
the corridor, rising through the boat, the man on whom he had
spat shrieking weakly and clawing himself, and dying.

The yeomanry were everywhere, emerging from doors and
clutching at his clothes. They burst from closed spaces like rats
or dogs or worms or gods knew what, reaching out for him and
swinging their blades. They were quick, chosen for skill and courage: a plague, an infestation, an invasion, hemming him, pen-
ning him in, hunting him down.

Jabber and fuck they're all around me, Fennec thought, and hungrily pressed his mouth again to the statuette. Planes and angles folded around him, reconfiguring in his path and wake, and he twisted and bolted up stairs feeling like a drowning man, reaching for air. He was angry.

The Garwater crew grabbed for him, gripped hold of what they could. *You do not fuck with me,* he thought, and felt a swell of power. *I can do more than fucking run.* He turned, snarling, spat and spewed and puked at his attackers, venting the baleful coagulum that collected in him with the statue's kiss. He rolled his tongue and hawked snotty jets of the stuff at the faces around him.

Where the sputum hit, it corroded normal space like a dimensional acid, and the yeomen cried out in dreadful alien pain as their eyes and bones and flesh folded in on themselves and out of corporeality, dissolving, dissipating, torn away in impossible directions. They lay wounded and wetly screaming, and Silas looked at them without pity as he passed, seeing their faces flayed of reality, bleeding a viscous nothingness that spat and sizzled, their heads and chests punctured with holes into a void. They hemorrhaged into that unspace, a deadening vacuity spreading like gangrene from the edges of their wounds so that their flesh became hard to notice, vague and irrelevant, and then suddenly did not exist.

His attackers rolled and screamed as long as they still had mouths.

Fennec kept running, his heart hammering. He ran and kissed and bent space with his intricate steps, unfolding the planes around him.

Uther Doul followed him grimly, with such tenacity that even confined to conventional space, he stayed on Fennec's tail.

Doul was relentless.

Fennec burst from the dark confines of the *Wordhoard* and slammed into the air. He hung poised for a moment, tongue bloody from the statue's marble teeth.

Fuck you all, he thought fiercely, all his fear running out of him. He plunged his tongue deep into his statue, felt power coruscate him, felt aglow with it like a dark star. Whirling, he skittered through a fringe of torn rigging, moving up by the shadows of wires, bending reality around him, buckling it and sliding along the fold he had created—up, out over the decrepit ship.

A corps of grim yeomanry rose from the hatch below and

spread with expert speed across the deck. Uther Doul came with them, and he stared straight into Fennec's eyes.

"Fennec," he said, and raised his sword.

Silas Fennec looked down at him, grinned his rage, and answered in a voice that reverberated wrongly, sounding close up to the ear like a threatening whisper. "Uther Doul."

Fennec was poised fifteen feet above the deck, in a corona of warping aether. Reality rippled around him. He hung unclear, his outlines oscillating between states. He moved with a slow and predatory marine grace, blurring in and out of visibility. Blood drooled from his mouth and torn tongue. He turned like a pike in the air, held suspended by the power of his statue's kiss, staring at the men below him.

They raised their weapons. Fennec shimmered, and bullets passed through where he had been—through bristling air—and spat as they disappeared. He opened his mouth, and gobs of that corrosive spit-puke flew out of him like shrapnel from a shell.

They burst across the deck and into the faces of his attackers, and there was a percussion of shrieks. The men scattered in panic.

Fennec kept his eyes on Doul.

Doul leaped out of the path of the spittle with brutal economy, his face taut, still watching Fennec. Fennec flickered and was lower, was ghosting over the deck crooning his delight, leaving a slick of caustic drool. Any man came close to him and he spat, and they backed off, or died. He tracked Uther Doul.

"Take me, then," whispered Fennec with drunk bravado. His throat was raw with the uncanny spit, but he felt he could do anything, burn a hole in the universe. He felt uncontainable. Doul retreated before the puissant, bristling figure, leaping, moving with terse anger, gritting his teeth against Fennec's voice, which still muttered up close to his ear. *"Come on . . ."*

Then through the light and dark and the heaviness of wood, through the slap of water like little fists around him, the lights of Armada only a few yards away, Fennec heard a voice behind him.

"Siiiiiilgssssss."

Like the strike of a monstrous snake.

With his heart spasming Fennec turned, and through agitated space he saw the Brucolac—bestial, glowing, hate cast in bone.

Leaping up out of darkness, his vast tongue uncoiled. Hurtling for him.

Fennec screamed and tried to kiss his grotesque again, but the Brucolac reached him and punched out, straight-fingered, lancing his hand into Fennec's throat.

The strike sent Fennec caroming to the deck, supine, fighting to breathe. The Brucolac fell with him, his eyes burning. Still Fennec tried to bring the figurine toward his face, and with a kind of contemptuous ease, the Brucolac snatched Fennec's free hand and held it effortlessly. He raised his foot (*with humbling speed*) and brought it down on Fennec's right wrist, stamping savagely, pushing it into the deck and shattering it.

Fennec screamed in a high, silly vibrato as his ruined fingers spasmed. The statue spun across the wood.

He lay on the splinters and howled, blood leaking from his mouth and nose, and from a wrist torn apart. Fennec screamed in agony and terror and paddled his legs uselessly, trying to get away. He was fully corporeal again, broken and pathetically there. Uther Doul appeared, leaning into his field of vision.

As he floundered, Fennec's shirt tore and flapped open, baring his chest.

It was mottled, clammy, and discolored in great patches of dirt-green and white. It glowed unhealthily like dead flesh. Here and there were ragged flanges, extrusions like catfish whiskers, like fins.

Doul and the Brucolac took in his alterations.

"Look at you . . ." murmured Uther Doul.

"Is that what it was all about?" hissed the Brucolac, looking at the statue Doul held.

Fennec continued to scream, snottily. The stone doll stared inscrutably at Uther Doul, winking at him, its open eye limpid and cold. It hugged itself with its unclear limbs cut from freezing stone, green-grey or black by turns. It gurned at him with its horrible round mouth, showing its teeth. Doul fingered the flap of skin that was folded down the statue's back.

"That is a puissant thing," the Brucolac said to Fennec, who shivered as shock set in. "How many Armadans has it killed?"

"Bring him," said Doul to his unwounded men. They came forward, pausing nervously when the Brucolac did not move.

He had interfered despite Doul's orders, and perhaps had saved his life, but Doul denied him any rueful or apologetic thanks. He simply stared at the Brucolac coldly until, defeated, the vampir moved back.

"He's *ours*," whispered Doul to the Brucolac, hefting the figurine.

There were yeomen dying in incomprehensible agony across the deck. Their comrades hefted Fennec without any shade of pity, grabbing him roughly, ignoring his screams.

The citizens at the outer edges of Dry Fall and Thee-And-Thine shivered to hear the sounds from the haunted quarter, and made warding signs.

"That's like nothing I've heard before," they whispered, or similar words, as the screams rang out thinly in the night. "That's no ghast or ghul . . . That's something new, that's got no business in there."

They could tell it was a man.

CHAPTER FORTY

Uther Doul sat on the bed in Bellis' cell. The room was still sparse, though the surfaces were now piled with a few accoutrements he had had brought from her rooms: her notebooks, a few clothes.

He watched her as she turned the grindylow statue in her hands. She ran her fingers over it carefully, curiously, feeling the intricacies of its carving. She stared at its twisted face, and into its mouth.

"Be careful," Doul advised her as she touched her nail to one of its teeth. "It's dangerous."

"This is . . . the cause of it all?" said Bellis.

Doul nodded. "He carried it with him. He used it to kill several men. He folded space with it, performed thaumaturgy I'd never seen. That must be how he got into the compass factory."

Bellis nodded. She understood that Doul was talking about

the means by which Fennec had allowed New Crobuzon to find Armada. Some secret engine, some mechanism.

"It must be safe now," Doul went on. "The lodestone must have been on the *Morning Walker.*"

Probably, thought Bellis. A device that tracked Armada. *You'd better hope it's not languishing on one of those ironclads, drifting all sunbaked and pocked, stinking by now with its dead crew, where maybe it could be found one day.* She turned the statue over again and studied it closely.

"From what we can tell . . ." Doul continued slowly, "from what we've got out of Fennec, this statue is not the main thing. Just as the point of a gun isn't the gun but the bullet, so with this: it's not the statue itself that has the puissance. That's just a conduit. This," he said, "is the source of the power."

Doul tickled the tough, thin strip of flesh embedded in the statue's back.

"This is the fin of some ancestor, some assassin-priest, some thaumaturge, some *magus.* Housed in stone, in a shape that mimics its original form. This is a grindylow relic," said Doul, "the remnant of some . . . saint. That's what stinks of power.

"That's what Fennec told us," he said, and Bellis could imagine the techniques by which Fennec had been made to answer those questions.

"This is what's behind it all," said Bellis, and Doul nodded.

"It did amazing things. It allowed Fennec to do amazing things. But even so, I think he'd only just begun to understand it. I think New Crobuzon must have reason to believe that this . . . this charmed debris has far more power than Fennec had learnt to use." He looked Bellis in the eye. "I don't think New Crobuzon would come so far, try so hard, for anything less than the most powerful forces."

Bellis looked reverentially at the object in her hands.

"We have our hands," Doul said quietly, "on something extraordinary. We have found a very great thing. Gods know what it might allow us to do."

This is the cause of it all, she thought. *This is what Fennec stole. He even told me he'd stolen something from The Gengris. This is what he told New Crobuzon he had—didn't try to pass it on to them, of course. They'd never have come looking for him if he'd given it to them. This is what he dangled in front of them,*

*from across the world, said "Save me and this is yours," and
made them come.*

*This is what New Crobuzon crossed the world and waged war
for. It set everything in motion. For this (unknowingly) I led Armada to the mosquito island. To send some lying message to New
Crobuzon, I gave Armada the avanc instead of throwing Aum's
fucking book into the sea.*

This is what everyone's been chasing.

This magus fin.

Bellis did not know what had changed. Doul seemed to have for-
given her. His vicious demeanor had altered. He had come here
to show her what they had found, to talk to her as he had done before. She was nervous: she felt all uncertain of him.

"What will you do with it?" she said.

Uther Doul was rewrapping the figurine in a wet cloth. He
shook his head.

"We've no time to examine this properly, not yet. Not now.
There are too many other things to be done; too much is unfolding. We've been . . . distracted. This comes at a bad time." He
spoke without inflection, but she sensed that there was more
than that, as he hesitated.

"And anyway, it's done things to Fennec. It's changed him.

"Even he doesn't understand what, or if he does he's saying
nothing. No one knows what forces the grindylow can tap. We
can't reverse what's happened to Fennec, and we don't know
what the full effects are. No one's willing to become this statue's
new lover.

"So we'll store it, somewhere safe, till we finish our project,
till we reach our objective and have time and scholars to study
this thing. We'll keep all that's happened quiet, but in case anyone did discover what Fennec brought on board, I think we'll
keep it somewhere no one would think, or dare, to look for it.
Somewhere everyone knows there's already a charmed treasure
or two, and where they know the risks of trespass are just . . . too
severe."

As he said that, Doul stroked the grip of the Possible Sword
for an unthinking instant. Bellis noticed it and knew where the
magus fin would be hidden.

"And where," she said slowly, "is Fennec?"

Doul stared at her. "Taken care of," he said, and nodded briefly toward the corridor outside. "Held."

There was a silence that stretched out.

"What are you doing here?" said Bellis eventually, quietly. "How long have you believed me?" She studied him, her confusion exhausting her. *Since I stepped onto this fucking city,* she thought with sudden clarity, *I've been on the edge of my nerves, every moment. I'm tired.*

"I always believed you," he said, his voice expressionless. "I never thought you summoned New Crobuzon deliberately, though I know—I've always known—you have no love for this place. When you came to me before, I was expecting to hear something else.

"Listening to Fennec, hearing him talk, trying to stay silent, trying to implicate you, admitting the truth . . . He's saying different things with every minute. But the truth is obvious: you were stupid," Doul said without emotion. "You believed him. Thought you were . . . what? What did he tell you again? *Saving your city.* You weren't out to destroy us; you were trying to save your homeland so that one day you could return to it, still whole and saved. You weren't trying to destroy us; you were just stupid."

Bellis' face was set. She was burning.

Doul watched her. "You were caught up in it, weren't you?" he said. "In the idea of . . . connecting with your home. The fact of doing something. That was enough, wasn't it? You . . . saving your city."

Doul spoke in a soft monotone, and Bellis looked down at her hands.

"I bet," he continued, "that if you ever did think about what you'd been told . . . I bet you felt uneasy."

He said it almost kindly. The maggot of doubt was alive again, grubbing through Bellis' head.

"There was nothing of him," said Doul, "in the *Wordhoard.*

"His berth down in the hold, it was clean and dry. His walls were covered with notes, pinned everywhere. Diagrams telling him who's whose man or woman, and who runs what, and who owes whom. It was damned impressive. He'd learnt everything he needed. He had . . . spliced himself into the city's politics.

Always keeping himself hidden. Different rendezvous for different informants, and different names—Simon Fench and Silas Fennec were only two of many.

"But nothing of him. He's like an empty doll. Those notes everywhere, like posters, and a little hand printing press, and ink and grease. His clothes in a trunk, his notebook in his bag—that's all there was of him. It was pathetic." Doul met Bellis' eyes. "You could examine that room for hours, and you'd still have no idea what Silas Fennec was like.

"He's nothing but an empty skin stuffed with schemes."

But he's been quieted now, thought Bellis, *and we continue northward. The Lovers win. Their troubles are over, is that right, Uther?* She stared at him and tried to reestablish between them something she had lost.

"What were you writing?" said Doul, shocking her, "when I came in?" He indicated her pocket, where she had stuffed her letter.

She always kept it on her, its many thick pages growing heavier. It had not been taken away from her. It could not possibly help her escape.

It had been a while since she had added to it. There were times when she wrote it as regularly as a diary, and weeks when she did nothing. In that small, featureless prison room, with her window facing out into nothing but watery dark, she had turned to it again, as if it could settle her head. But she had found it almost impossible to write.

"Ever since I first saw you," said Doul. "You've always kept it. Even on the dirigible." Bellis' eyes widened. "What is it? What are you writing?"

What she said or did here, now, Bellis realized with a kind of cool panic, would reverberate for a long time. Things waited to fall into place. She felt as if she were holding her breath.

Bellis drew the paper from her pocket and read what she had written.

Dustday 9th Chet, 1780. Sixth Playdi of Flesh.
Hello again.

"It's a letter," she said.

"To whom?" said Doul. He did not lean over and peer at the paper. Instead he caught her eyes.

She sighed and leafed through the many pages of the letter,

finding its beginning and holding it up to him so that he could read the first word.

Dear, the letter said, and then there was a blank. A word-hole.

"I don't know," she said.

"It's not to no one," she said. "That would be sad, pathetic, to write a letter to no one. And it's not a letter to someone dead, or anything so . . . sad. It's the opposite of all that, the opposite. It's not closed down like that: it opens up; it's a door; it could be to anyone."

She heard herself, became aware of how she must sound, and was horrified.

"When I left," she said, more quietly, "I'd spent many weeks, many months, in fear. People I knew were disappearing. I knew that I was being hunted. You've never been in New Crobuzon, have you, Uther?" She looked at him. "For all your explorations and your skills, you've never been there. You've no idea—do you have any idea? There's a special kind of fear, a unique fear, when the militia are closing in on you.

"Who've they got to? Who've they taken, tortured, corrupted, frightened, threatened, bought? Who can you trust?

"It's damn hard to be on your own. When I started," she said hesitantly, "I thought I was probably writing to my sister. We're not close, but there are times when I crave talking to her. Still, there are things I'd never say to her. And I needed to tell them, so I thought that perhaps this letter was to one of my friends."

Bellis thought of Mariel, of Ignus and Téa. She thought of Thighs Growing, the cactacae cellist, the only one of Isaac's friends she had remained in touch with. She thought of others. *The letter could be to any of you,* she thought, and knew that was not true. She had pushed most of them away in those frightened months before she had fled. And even before then, she had not been close to many. *Could I have written to any of you?* she wondered suddenly.

"Whoever you speak to," she said, "whoever you write to, there are things you wouldn't say, things you'd censor. And the more I wrote—the more I *write*—the more I need to say, the more I need to be quite, quite open. So I'll write it all, and I'll not *have* to close it down. I can leave that to the end. I can wait and decide who it's to after I've said everything I have to say."

She did not mention the fact that she would never be able to deliver her letter, that she would be writing it on Armada until she died.

There's nothing strange about it, Bellis wanted to say. *It makes sense.* She felt fiercely protective. *Don't think about it as if there's an* emptiness *at the other end,* she thought at him fiercely. *That's not it at* all.

"You must write carefully," said Doul, "only about yourself. No shared jokes. It must be a cold kind of letter."

Yes, thought Bellis, looking at him. *I suppose it must.*

"You exiles," he said. "You exiles and your writing. Silas Fennec is the same. You look in there now, he's trying to scribble in his notebook, with his left hand."

"You let him keep it?" Bellis said, wondering what had happened to Fennec's right hand and suspecting that she knew. Uther Doul looked ostentatiously around her room: at the clothes, the notebooks, the letter.

"You see how we treat our prisoners," he said slowly, and Bellis remembered that she was a prisoner, just like Tanner Sack, just like Fennec.

"Why didn't you tell the Lovers," said Doul suddenly, "when Fennec told you that New Crobuzon was in danger? Why didn't you try to get a message back that way?"

"They wouldn't have cared," she said. "They might even have been glad: one less rival on the sea. And think of the bones to be picked over. They would've done nothing."

She was right, and she could sense that he knew it. Still, the maggot stirred in her again.

"Look in the letter," she said suddenly. "It proves I knew nothing."

For a long time, he did not respond.

"You've been judged," he said at last. She felt blood cold in her stomach. Her hands trembled, and she swallowed several times and clenched her lips closed.

"The Senate's met," he continued, "after we'd questioned Fennec. It's generally believed that Sack and you had no deliberate part in calling New Crobuzon here. Your story's been accepted. You don't need to show me your letter."

Bellis nodded and felt her heart beat quickly.

"You gave yourselves up," he said in a dead tone. "You told us

what you know. I know you. I've watched you—both of you. I've
watched you carefully."

She nodded again.

"So you're believed. So that's that. You'll be allowed to go
free, if you want." He paused then, for just a tiny second. And
later Bellis remembered that pause, and could not forgive him.
"You get to choose your sentence."

Bellis looked away and smoothed her letter and breathed
deeply for a while, then looked back at him.

"Sentence?" she said. "You said you believed me . . ."

"I do," he said. "I was the main reason you *were* believed." He
did not say this as if he expected gratitude. "Which is why your
prospective sentences are as they are. Why you're not dead, as
Silas Fennec will be dead, once we get what we need from him.

"But you knew you'd not go unpunished. Since when did intent determine judgment? Whatever you thought, or convinced
yourself you thought you were doing, you're responsible for unleashing a war that killed thousands of *my people*." His voice
hardened.

"You should consider yourself fortunate," he continued, "that
we want to keep the details of all this quiet. If the citizens ever
heard what you'd done, you'd definitely be dead. Secrecy allows
us a degree of leniency. You should be glad I've testified as to
your character. I fought hard to have you both freed." His beautiful voice was frightening her.

"Tell me," she heard herself ask, and Doul met her eyes as he
answered.

"I'm here representing the Senate, to see Tanner Sack and
Bellis Coldwine," he said clearly. "To sentence you both. Ten
years, here, alone. Or time already served, plus lashes.

"It's your choice."

Doul left soon after that, leaving Bellis very alone.

Fennec had betrayed her. There would be no pamphlets from
Simon Fench. No one would listen to her. The city would not
turn back.

Doul had not even asked to see her letter. He did not take it
from her; he did not peer over her shoulder as she held it; he did
not show any interest in it at all.

Don't you understand what I've told you? Bellis thought. *You
know what revelations are in this. This isn't any normal kind of*

communication, all personal secrets and details and nods and references meaningless to any but two people. This is unique— this is my clear communication; this is my own clear voice, everything I've done and seen here.

Don't you want to read it, Doul?

Doul had left once she had chosen her punishment, without glancing back at the thick sheaf of paper still in her hands. All its evidence went unread, languishing still. Uncommunicated.

Bellis turned the pages over, one by one, recounting what had happened to her in Armada. She tried to calm herself. There was something very important that she had to address. Her plans were collapsing. With Fennec caught, there was no one to put out the information she had, no one to stop the Lovers' crazy plan to cross the Hidden Ocean. And Bellis should turn her mind to that, should try to think of some way to disclose the truth.

But she could not concentrate on that, on anything but what Doul had just told her.

Her hands were shaking. She gritted her teeth, furious at that, and ran her hands over her swept-back hair and exhaled, but she could not stop herself from trembling. She had to press her pen quite hard upon the paper so that the trembling would not make her words illegible. She scrawled a single quick sentence, then stopped suddenly, and stared at it, and could not write any more. She read what she had written, again and again.

Tomorrow they flog me.

INTERLUDE IX
The Brucolac

Now in this deepest gutter of night where moments lie still like frightened things and we who are about are free of time I go walking.

My city moves. Its outlines shift.

Spires converge and part again and ropes coil like muscles and take the strain as Armada's skyline breaks, heals, breaks.

Wild animals alive in shadows keep their whimpers quiet, sniff my dead smell and move on (four-footed or two) quick and cowed through a randomly serrated shipscape, along trenches of brick and wood on reshaped decks. The cadavers of vessels incorporated. Backstay stools, coaming, pawls, davits, and cat-heads encased in salt-aged architecture.

Behind every wall a maritime atomy, a mummy, a sacrifice, like a servant murdered in the temple's foundations. This is a city of ghosts. Every quarter is haunted. We live like graveworms on our dead ships.

Withered flowers and weeds strain for what poor lamplight in the veins of walls, in ruts of concrete and wood. Life is tenacious, as we who have died know.

Trails of dust, parings of bone and brick, past ragged wounds of bomb-surgery: carbon and rubble, waste-ground punctuation in the city's dull monologue. Paint, age, all the rubbish of urban chance brands squat towerblocks (on foredecks) and tenements (in the shadows of bowsprits). Flowerpots and wheels like meager tattoos, deliberate defacements. Infinite markings, sculptures accidental and made (the drabness peppered with signs of life and preference, awnings left just so, ribbons on sleeping livestock).

Where glass is, it is burst and scored—intricate with shadows.

*Lit windows are edged with darkness. Austere and coldly
shining.*

*Moths and night-birds, things that move by the moon make
their little sounds. What footsteps there are dissolve and are
quickly formless. It is as if there is fog, though there is not. We
who walk tonight come out of nowhere and return to it quickly.*

*Past factories, music halls, churches; over bridges rattling
like vertebrae. Armada rides the waves dumb and buoyant like a
rust-flecked corpse.*

*Through the slats of scaffold is the sea. I see myself (shad-
owed and unclear) and through myself into black water. Into a
darkness so profound (random chymical lights like fireflies how-
beit) it is an alien communication. It has its own grammar. Un-
seeing I look to the farmed fish circling autistic in cages, the
menfish, the keels pipes crevices inked in, the spaces, the chains
splinted with molluscs and algae-slick and the great unseen
shape that bears us on, idiotic and futile.*

*History is formless and oppressive all around me, a night-
mare I will make into sense.*

*A rhythm becomes sensible (extruded from a covert place),
gives a shape to this night, gives it time again, and the clocks let
out their held breaths.*

*I make a rooftop way to my moonship. Over torn-up slates
and boards and their crossbreeds, through a low nightlit forest
of flues steeples watertowers, in ridings not my own. I do not rule
here, there is no goretax, it is a day since I have fed and it would
take very little to slip along this drainpipe groundward like the
drops of calcium that beard it. Very little to find a blood-filled
nightwalker and dispose of his her husk but those days are gone,
now I am bureaucrat not predator, and it is much better.*

*It is a long time till dawn but something has passed. We are
moving on toward morning. My time is over.*

*I am on trawlers and houseboats and gone again (fleeting
foot-strokes as if uncertain) through Shaddler and its cottages
and industry (on for my fat ship). Dry Fall where scored streets
are quieter and cushioned in dust.*

*Where does it come from? Swept hourly by neurotic sea-wind,
when does dust touch down?*

*In some lights (reveries no less than true for that) I see it thick
as snowfall and cobwebs clog my passage home. Alone I drown
in dust and choke in it, in time's desiccated exhaust.*

* * *

I know when things are stirring. I know all the city's rhythms. Something new is here.

There are tracks on the Uroc's *moon-white decks. Some hand unknown to me has held this rigging.*

   I watch for the newcomer.
   Let us see.
   What are you?
   In my corridors, toward my berth, you have left your spoor. One, two drops of brine. Smears of something mucal. Scuffed varnish and iron. What are you?
   You are hardly hiding from me. You are welcoming me home.
   And oh see, here on my threshold you have left me blood. Drizzled like sugar.
   I can hear you behind my door.

My room smells like an estuary. River coagulate and fishgut blood. You rattle for me stranger, like a summons you shake the bones you wear. I have not pulled open any sluices to let the moon illuminate my bedchamber, but light is for the living. These that look upon you are vampir eyes.
   And welcome to you.
   Three of you to wait for me in a grisly tableau: reclined upon my bed and in front of my window and by me now, closing my door, ushering me respectful into my home.
   Look at you.
   Look at you shimmering before me great salamander tails folded in layers on my floor, blunt streamlined skulls like viperfish, your teeth protruding like fistfuls of nails, eyes black and big as tarpits, wet skin stretched on muscled bone like sap on knotted wood. See you upright in my room.
   And you, recumbent on my covers like a painter's nude, grinning at me without intent on your piscine face, your neck wrapped all about with charms and bones, beckoning me politely, whose is the face you carry in your hand?
   Whose head is that you have taken, to bring blood for me? What woman was she? A guard who found you? Missing in the carnage of the New Crobuzon war, drowned or cut apart, was it you who split her neck to take that misshapen trophy? It is a frayed-enough edge, a bloody and fibrous laceration.

The tan-haired woman stares at me from your fist.

Look at you!

You drop her dead flesh and rise like something I have never seen.

—Seigneur Brucolac, you tell me in a voice colder than mine.—We must talk.

I don't mind. I will talk to you. I know who you are. I think I have expected you.

And as the hours unfold toward the morning oh what conspiracies oh what secrets we uncover.

You have come late, riverthing. Waterman. You have come late from the Cold Claw Sea, searching these salt currents for what was taken from you. Nothing you say to me with that spastically moving blood-flecked jaw is clear. Like the riverthing you are you flicker toward your meaning and disturb a silt of effluvial words that cloud your intent. But I have dealt with seers poets and Weavers and can track your insinuations.

You have hunted on currents. Cleaved parasitic to the undersides of our attackers and then fluttered free in the squalor of battle and you have plucked bodies from the dead and dying plenty.

And then, what am I to understand? Hiding away you have used them. You have kept some alive, fed them air and questioned them (questioned them after they have died, is that? have I that right?). Learning from them (terrified on the outskirts of death they have babbled everything to you, immobile in water, trapped under their homes).

Only days here and like the subtlest spies you have learnt most everything about this place.

That is why (what is that you say?) that is why you have come to me.

One took something from your towers a world away, something precious and unique that you would have back. One has escaped you for scores of miles, for the length of continents, onto this place, to my city. And it has taken you a long a very long time but that one was a benighted fool to think you would let him run.

You tracked him. You have found his home.

But there have been commotions through the floors above you as you lie and wait and prepare and ask questions of whomever you can snatch from Armada's decks. And cunning predatory

*and without fear as you may be there are too many above you,
there is no way you can scour the whole city. Step from the water
and you are unhidden, and hunted.*

*You cannot find your quarry. He has disappeared. And he will
not surrender what you have come for, not willingly, not without
terror. And if you were to ask for help of those who run the city
and they were not to take your side, you have played up all your
counters, and you could not oppose them if they turned on you.
You are not so many. You cannot wage war. You cannot search for
the one who has fled you.*

Not without help.

Why have you come to me?

Deepling why have you come to me?

*You come here kill my citizens and face me the Brucolac brazen
like a blackmailer. How do you know I will not destroy you?*

I understand.

*Oh you are fine, you are a prodigious spy. I am in awe of you
and of what you have learnt in only these few days and nights.
Let me—here—bow my head to you.*

Is there anything you have not learnt? Not understood?

You have come to me because you know that I am angry.

*You know what the Lovers have called up. Perhaps you even
know where we are going.*

*You know that I do not accept this. That I am the only force
that stands against them.*

Perhaps you know that I consider mutiny.

*Have you heard my name, again and again? I am sure that is
what has happened. You know that I am the most powerful person here who is hankering for something, who is angry, who
wishes things were not as they are.*

You know that I can be bought.

What is it you propose, hakenmann?

*There are actions none but you could perform that might tip a
balance. That might create new circumstances. Change forces,
force changes. Create facts.*

Perhaps this journey, this idiot pilgrimage, might be halted.

Oh yes, if you did that. If you could stop our progress.

Only you can help me, you tell me in your intricate ways. Only you can stop this mad journey. What then is up to me?

Even I, perhaps, could not fight my way through the gangs and gangs of guards who patrol their engines, their rockmilk spurs. I do not know what must be done. But there is another way—something else, some force—to bring us to a slow, and stop. You can halt the beast.

If you could do that.

And in return? (See? you tell me, strange pride flashing like scales, you know all about this barter by which we live.)

In return? I will help you find that hidden one who has run from you.

Perhaps you do not know what it is to laugh. Certainly you do not know why I laugh so hard so long.

You cannot know.

Whom I have held and bloodied. What I have seen him wield. You cannot know that loyal to Armada and without alternative I have put aside my anger at the Lovers and let them take him, shamed as I was, implicated in the carnage he brought us. He is no ordinary thief, this war criminal, and they hold him in limbo till we can sentence him right. When our lunatic journey ceases.

You have come just a little late.

Not too late, however. What's done is not too late to undo.

I know where they hold him.

You cannot know that what you offer me would any other time make me kill you. You cannot know that tonight is different, that I am tired of the dangerous idiocy into which my city is being led. That if mutiny is needed to turn us back, then I will do what I must to bring it about.

This is not an ordinary time, deepling. You come to me in a time of war.

You need a blind? A decoy while you search? Something to attract attention?

I have just the thing.

Hush. Let me tell you how it will be. What you will do, what I will do. I will help you find him, and this is what you will do for me. And I will tell you where your quarry is.

Now shall we plan?

* * *

Don't stop.

   We must finish this. See, there? We have the minutes we need to finish this.

   The sky is not yet light.

PART SEVEN

The Lookout

CHAPTER FORTY-ONE

While Armada moved north through dull air—temperate fronts so still that the weather seemed to be waiting for something—and while that expectancy communicated itself to the citizens, Bellis lay in sticky fever.

There were two days when she did not think at all. She burned up in temperatures severe enough to worry her nurses as she shied away from delirious visions, frightened into screaming fits she would never remember. The avanc pulled with its steady gait, not fast but faster by far than the city had ever traveled before. The shapes of waves changed with the currents.

(*Tanner Sack is hardier than Bellis. He is released into the care of Shekel, who is crying for worry of him, who grabs him and hugs him with a bawl of relieved misery to see Tanner's broken shuffle. Tanner shrieks as Shekel's hands grip his lacerated back, and their two voices mingle before Shekel leads Tanner on to where Angevine is waiting.*

"What they do to you?" Shekel moans repeatedly. "Why?" And Tanner shushes him and stutters that there were reasons, and that they'll not talk about it, that it's over now.

These are momentous days. There are great decisions taken. There are mass meetings to discuss the war and the city's history, and the avanc and the weather and the future.

Bellis knows nothing of any of this.)

Days later, Bellis Coldwine sat up, her fever almost gone. She ate and drank for herself, spilling a great deal from her violently shaking fingers. When she moved, she bit down against the pain. She did not know that all the guards in the corridor were very used to her screams.

She roused herself the day after that, moving as slow and

tentative as someone terribly aged. She half tied up her hair and draped a long, shapeless shirt over herself.

Her door was not locked. She was not a prisoner anymore. She had not been for a week.

There were guards in the corridor, in that deep prison wing of the *Grand Easterly,* and she called one over to her and tried to meet his eye.

"I will go home now," she said, and felt like crying when she heard her own voice.

To Bellis' shock, it was Uther Doul who helped her home.

The *Chromolith* was only two ships port of the *Grand Easterly,* but Doul took her by aircab. She sat away from him in the gondola, horrified to feel her fear of him—which had disappeared over the months, replaced by other emotions—returning. He studied her without visible pity.

He had not sentenced her, of course. But every time her mind returned to that extended, bloody, murderous, torturous hour a week previously, with cut-up images of pain, her own screaming, she saw Uther as what he was, an agent of Armada, the power that had done this to her. The man who wielded the whip had been irrelevant.

When she entered her rooms, Doul followed her, carrying her possessions. She ignored him. Moving carefully, she found a mirror.

It was as if the violence that had been done to her back had spread and ravaged her face. She looked drained of blood. The lines and crow's-feet that had been slowly marking her for more than ten years had become like gashes, like the wounds cut into the faces of the Lovers. Bellis fingered her cheeks and eyes in horror.

One of her teeth was cracked open, and pieces came away as she pulled at it. That was where she had bit down on the wooden gag they had given her.

She moved, and the cloth shifted against the scabs on her torn-up back, and she hissed in pain.

Doul stood behind her, his presence like an imperfection in the glass. She wanted him to leave, but she could not bear to address him. Bellis hobbled around her room on fever-weak legs. She could feel the gauze sticking to her back, where her injuries had wept.

The pain in her back was unpleasant and constant, but it did not vary much. Bellis treated it like white noise, ignoring it until it became a kind of aching nothing to her. She stood on her doorstep and looked all around her, at the airships and birds, the light wind mindlessly knocking Armada's walls. There was industry, men and women working furiously, as there had been on the first day, when she had drawn the curtains of *Chromolith* Smokestacks and seen her new city.

Something was new, she realized slowly. The air was different, the way the city rode the currents . . . the sea itself. The ships surrounding Armada no longer meandered on their own routes from horizon to horizon: the mass of vessels (still marked by war) were in tight formation behind the city, as if afraid of losing it.

There was something different about the sea.

She turned to stare at Doul.

"You're free," he said, not without gentleness, "and superfluous. Krüach Aum hasn't needed you for a long time. You'll need to heal. For the city's sake, any information about your accidental role in the war has been suppressed. I'm sure the library would take you back . . ."

"What's happened?" said Bellis in the plaintive croak her beating and sickness had left her. "Something's different about . . . everything. What's happened?"

"Two days ago," said Doul, "insofar as one can be exact, we passed through something. Everyone can feel it. The fleet . . ." He pointed at the vessels behind the city. "They're having a difficult time. There are strange currents. Their engines are untrustworthy.

"We've passed out of the Swollen Ocean," he said, and gazed at her impassively. "We're in the outskirts of a new sea. This . . ." The quick thrust of his arm took in the water, horizon to horizon. "This is the Empty, the Hidden Ocean."

So far from home, thought Bellis, surprising herself with fury. *Further and further they're taking us, me, further and further. They get their way.* She heard a ringing inside her like tinnitus. *Everything we've done—right and wrong—means nothing. They took us here so easily, to this fucked-up empty edge of sea no ship can cross. In we go, and my home is gone.*

Even the thought of the Lovers appalled her: their crooning

lovesounds; their sick, endless, sharp-edged betrothals. She was in their power. This was where they wanted to go. Bellis had tried to turn them, and failed.

"They got us here, then?" she said to Uther, cold and suddenly unafraid of him again. She jutted her chin. "And I know what happens now—on toward the Scar."

If he was surprised, he hid it well. He met her eyes, quite expressionless.

So Fennec was too slow with his pamphlets and rumors, she thought. *That doesn't mean it's over; that doesn't mean we have to accept this.*

When Shekel opened his door to Bellis, he stared at her for a long and silent moment, wildly confused.

He recognized her, but was suddenly convinced that he was wrong. It seemed that this blanched lady with her dark hair all dry and tumbling over her like old grass, her expression suggesting years of pain, could not be Coldwine, must be some ruined vagrant with a similar face.

"Shekel," she said in a voice that he could not believe was hers, "you have to let me in. I need to speak to Tanner Sack."

Mute and appalled, he moved aside for her, and she wheezed and entered the shadow.

Tanner Sack turned in his bed, muttering in thick tongues, his eyes rheumy, then bolted up, shedding sheets. He pointed at Bellis.

"Get her the fuck away, Shekel," he shouted. "Get her the fuck *out* of here . . ."

"Listen to me!" Bellis said, her voice urgent and guttural. "Please . . ."

"I got *fuck-all* to hear from you, bitch!" Tanner was shaking with fury. Behind Bellis was the puttering of a motor as Angevine trundled toward them.

"You have to hear me," Bellis growled, trying to shout. "You have friends, man; you can spread the word . . ." She broke off and twisted with pain as Angevine put a hand on her back. "Do you know where we're going?" she managed to say. "Do you know why we're in this sea, where nothing moves like it should?"

She saw Tanner look to Shekel and then to Angevine, and watched them share a look of blank bewilderment.

"Listen," Bellis shouted as Angevine pushed her out of the door to a final chorus of Tanner's cursing.

By the time she had walked slowly across the city's bridges to the library, blood had come through Bellis' bandages, and her shirt was spotted. She found the bombed quarter of the *Pinchermarn,* where the librarians were recovering what volumes they could from the wreckage.

"Bellis!" Carrianne was stunned by her.

Bellis was slightly delirious again. "Now you have to listen to me," she murmured.

And they were outside again, and Carrianne's arm was around her, protective. Bellis' back was dreadfully painful, and she was wincing as she said to Carrianne, "Johannes. Tearfly. Carrianne, you have to help me find *Johannes Tearfly . . .*"

Carrianne nodded. "I know, Bellis," she said. "You just told me."

They were in a room Bellis did not recognize, then another, so tired now that she felt faint. And Carrianne and Bellis were hanging over the city in the dark air, Armada's lights going out with complex timing. Bellis heard her own voice several times, though it sounded very strange to her.

She felt an ecstatic cold pain, and looked up and was on her own bed, in her chimneytop rooms, and it came to her—more like a leap of imagination than a memory—that Carrianne had lifted the bandage from her back and was smearing unguent on her. Bellis closed her eyes. She could hear something—some soft, repetitive sound.

"Gods. Gods. Gods. Gods."

It was Carrianne's voice. Bellis turned her head to one side and through blurred eyes saw her friend's face over her, staring down, wincing, biting her lip as she rubbed in the cream.

What's wrong? Bellis tried to say, for a second thinking her friend had been hurt; but then she realized, of course, what was wrong, and could not help whimpering a little for herself.

The next time she opened her eyes, Carrianne and Johannes were both there, drinking her tea, talking awkwardly as they sat by her bed.

It was night. Bellis' head had cleared.

Johannes started when he saw her move.

"Bellis, Bellis," said Carrianne gently. "Gods' sake, girl . . . what did you do?"

Carrianne was horrified. Bellis was deeply grateful for her ministrations, but she would not explain her wounds.

"She doesn't want to talk to us about it," Johannes said nervously. He seemed genuinely concerned, but uneasy. "I mean, you can see . . . she's been on the wrong side of . . . She's probably lucky to even be here."

"Gods*damm*it, Bellis," Carrianne said, furious. "Who gives a fuck about *them.*" The wave of her arm took in authority. "Tell us, what did they do you for?"

Bellis could not help smiling. *He's right, though,* she thought, lifting her bleary eyes to Johannes. *Pusillanimous coward that he is, and magnificent and brave and loyal to me (gods know why) as you are, Carrianne, he's right about this. You should stay out of this. Like it or not, I'll help you do that. I owe you.*

"You found him then?" she managed to say.

"Carrianne's been amazingly assiduous," Johannes said. "She got a message to me."

Bellis straightened a little in her bed and set her face against the movement of her broken skin.

"I need to talk to you," she said, her voice getting stronger. She shook her head slowly. "I've been . . . The last week . . . I've been alone. And, and everything's been changing around us. You must have seen it. But I know what it is; I know what's going on."

She closed her eyes and was silent for many seconds.

"You know where we are?" she said finally. "You know what waters we've entered?"

Carrianne and Johannes looked at each other, then back at her.

"The Hidden Ocean," said Carrianne, her voice guarded. Bellis managed to give a little smile.

"That's right," she said. *Damn you all,* she thought. *I don't need that treacherous fucker Fennec. I will make this happen myself.* "And do you know where we're heading?" She paused again, and in the silence, Johannes spoke.

"The Scar," he said, and Bellis' words withered in her throat. She stared at him, saw him watch her with concern and confusion and look to Carrianne, who nodded.

"The . . . Scar," Bellis heard herself say, all hesitant and stupid. Not a revelation but an absurd echo.

*   *   *

They had broken her. They had won. There was nothing left in her, nothing at all.

When Johannes left, Bellis and Carrianne sat up late, talking. Carrianne told her everything.

What a week, Bellis kept thinking with absurd understatement. *What a week to miss.*

The Lovers had announced it.

It could not be kept from the pilots and captains and nauscopists of Armada that the water and the air were changing. There was no disguising the sudden crosscurrents, the hidden streams that ran below the surface, counter to the waves. Compasses had begun to veer maniacally, losing north for minutes at a time. The winds were utterly unpredictable. The horizon's distance varied. Armada's fleet had begun to struggle.

The avanc, of course, was quite unconcerned by these forces. It plowed its undeviating course far below, with the city in its wake.

There had been a plethora of rumors, but there were enough experienced, well-read sailors in the city that the truth was impossible to hide. The avanc, directed by the Garwater pilots, was pulling Armada into the Hidden Ocean. About which, it seemed, all the stories were true.

And then, four days previously, on Flesh Quarto's sixth Khandi, the Lovers had held a series of mass meetings across Garwater and its allied ridings.

"He's a fucking fine speaker, the Lover," Carrianne said. "I heard him in Booktown. 'When I came here I was nothing,' he said, 'and I began to make me, and that was finished by my Lover, who made me and made herself and *made this city,*' his voice all trembling. 'And haven't we brought Armada *power?*' And people loved it. Because, you know, he has. These have been good years, great harvests and booty. And the *Sorghum*—you weren't here for that, were you? You weren't here when they took that." Carrianne smiled and shook her head appreciatively.

"He's made us a power, there's no denying it. And then the fucking avanc . . ."

"I thought you were loyal to Dry Fall," said Bellis, and Carrianne nodded hard.

"So I am, but I'm saying that here . . . I think the Brucolac may be . . . wrong about their plans. I mean . . . it does all fit into place."

* * *

There is a source of power, the Lover had told the crowds, on the edge of the world. An awesome place: a rip through which great waves of puissance pounded reality. One man in Armada has the proof, said the Lover, and knows how to tap that power. But for many years it could not be reached.

There is a beast, the Lover had told them: a stunning kind of thing, an animal that breaches into Bas-Lag and slips away again from time to time. And Armada had called to it certain famous men who could learn how to trap that animal.

The woman who made me, the Lover had thundered, pointing to the Lover, realized that the second fact meant the first could be acted on.

On the far side of the Hidden Ocean, the Lover had said, is the source of that power. But no ship has crossed the Hidden Ocean, they say. Friends—he had spread his arms with triumph, as Carrianne imitated to Bellis—the avanc is no ship.

And so, Bellis realized, the Lover had admitted the truth that he and his had kept from the city for years, the plans that they had already had in place when they employed Tintinnabulum, snatched the *Sorghum,* traveled to the anophelii island, raised the avanc. He had admitted the truth of those plans, and had done so in such a way that he was not stoned for his manipulation and lies, but was buoyed up by applause.

We can cross the Hidden Ocean, he had shouted to cheers. *We can tap the Scar.*

"That was when we learnt its name," Carrianne said.

"But it's so uncertain," said Bellis, and Carrianne nodded.

"Of course."

"The ships, the fleet . . ."

Carrianne nodded again. "Some are already tethered to the city. And when the others can't follow us, that's alright. Our ships have always sailed alone for months at a time, and they always find their way back to us. Those following us now know what's happening, and those that are away, well, this is nothing new. The city's always had its own movements. We're not going to disappear in the Hidden Ocean, Bellis. We're not here to stay . . . We're here to find the Scar, and then leave again."

"But what the fuck kind of place *is* this?" said Bellis thinly.

"We've no idea what's here, what kind of powers, what creatures, what enemies . . ."

Carrianne frowned and shook her head. "That's all true," she said. "I understand." She shrugged. "You're against the idea. Alright, you're not alone. There's a vessel leaving in two days, I think, heading back to the Swollen Ocean, crewed by naysayers, to wait for the city's return. Though . . ." Her voice petered away. They both realized that Bellis was not one of those who would ever be allowed off-city. "Most of us," continued Carrianne, "think this is worth doing."

"Not at all," Carrianne said quietly, a little later. "I trust the Brucolac, and I'm sure he has reasons for opposing the plans. But I think he's wrong. I'm excited, Bellis," she said. "Why shouldn't we try this? This could be . . . this could be the most exciting time, the finest hour in our history. We have to try."

Bellis felt something that at first she did not recognize. Not depression or misery or cynicism, but despair. The feeling of all plans, all options, dying.

I've lost, she thought, without melodrama or even anger.

Carrianne was not a brainwashed fool, someone unthinking and buffeted by rhetoric. She had heard the arguments—even partial and partisan as they had undoubtedly been. She must have realized that this venture had been a long time in the planning, and that therefore she and those around her had been deceived.

And still, considering all that, she had decided that the Lovers' plan was a good one. One that was worthwhile.

That was a sneaky trick, thought Bellis to the Lovers. *That was below the belt. I didn't foresee this.*

Lies, schemes, manipulations, bribery, violence, corruption— I expected all that, she thought. *But I never expected you simply to have the argument, and to win.*

The thought of Fench's stillborn pamphlet fleeted through her mind, and she moved her shoulders in a dead kind of laugh. THE TRUTH! she imagined. GARWATER DRAGS ARMADA TO THE SCAR!

The truth.

You win, she thought, and let go of hope. *I'll be here till I die. I'll grow old here, a crabby old lady imprisoned on a boat, and I'll scratch the scars on my back (dear gods they will be wicked) and mutter and complain. Or perhaps I'll die with the rest of you, and with you my rulers, in some stupid, terrible accident of the Hidden Ocean.*

Either way, I'm yours, if I like it or not. You've won.

You are taking me with you. You are taking me to the Scar.

CHAPTER FORTY-TWO

Where for the longest time there had been a shadow, the sky was clear.

The *Arrogance* was gone.

A rope stub lay on the deck where the airship had been tethered to the *Grand Easterly*. It had been severed, and the aerostat had flown free.

"Hedrigall," Bellis heard from all around her. She stood amid the crowd that had gathered, gaping at the hole in the skyscape. The yeomanry had made brief attempts to keep onlookers back, but had given up in the face of their numbers.

Bellis could move more freely now. She still recoiled at pressure on her back, but there was no more bleeding. Some of the smaller scabs were beginning to peel at the edges. She shifted slightly at the edge of the crowds.

"Hedrigall—and he was alone." Everyone was saying it.

As Armada slipped farther into the Hidden Ocean, its vessels had more and more difficulty keeping up with it. They trailed behind it like anxious ducklings, and several tethered to the edges of the city switched off their motors and were borne on by the avanc.

The second day after Bellis' shocking, revelatory discussion with Carrianne, the remaining ships and submersibles in Armada's orbit had turned back. They could no longer fight the Hidden Ocean. They gathered into a nervous convoy, tacking with the fractious winds, then steamed back to the south. They stayed together for protection, and to drag each other on, back to the Swollen Ocean, with its safer, comprehensible waters, where they would wait.

The city would return for them, within a month, or two at most.

And after that? If Armada had not returned? Well, they were to consider themselves free. That dispensation was given like an afterthought, and its implications were not discussed.

From her window, Bellis had watched the retreat of Armada's vessels. Others were left behind, now chained like limpets to the city's flank, or in the Basilio and Urchinspine harbors. They eddied apprehensively, surrounded by the vessels making up wharfs and quays, but they were trapped. They had waited too long to sail away, and they could only bob pointlessly, tied up as if loading or unloading, and wait.

Armadans had never seen their city without its nimbus of ships. They had crowded to the city's margins to gaze out at the sea. The emptiness had subdued them. But even those acres of vacant water were not so disturbing as the missing airship.

No one had seen anything; no one had heard a sound. The *Arrogance* had crept away in secret. To Garwater it was a stunning loss.

How was it possible? people asked. The dirigible itself was crippled, and Hedrigall was known to be absolutely loyal.

"He had doubts," Tanner told Shekel and Angevine. "He told me. He *was* loyal, ain't no doubt, but he never thought this avanc business was best for the city. I suppose the Scar thing was even worse, but he weren't winning any arguments."

Tanner was horrified by Hedrigall's flight. It wounded him. But he talked his thoughts out loud, trying hard to see things as his enigmatic friend had seen them. *Must've felt trapped,* Tanner thought. *All the years he lived here, to suddenly see the place doing things in a new way. He don't belong in Dreer Samher no more, and if he thought that he didn't belong here neither . . . what must that've done?*

He imagined Hedrigall fixing the *Arrogance*'s broken motors in some of the spare hours he spent aboard it on his own. Everyone knew that Hedrigall was a loner who spent a deal more time in the *Arrogance* than he needed to. Had he untwisted the girders in the *Arrogance*'s fins? Tested the pistons that had not moved for decades?

How long you been planning this, Hedrigall? thought Tanner Sack.

Couldn't he have had an argument? Did he feel so strongly? Did he feel that there was no point even fighting for his home? Did he doubt that that's what it was any longer?

Where you now, man?

Tanner imagined that big ungainly aerostat heading south, Hedrigall alone at its wheel.

I bet he's crying.

It was suicide of sorts. Hedrigall couldn't have amassed enough fuel to reach land, not anywhere. If he reached Armada's waiting fleet, they'd want to know what had happened and why he'd left the city, so he'd avoid them.

The winds would take him over the empty sea. The gasbags were very strong; they might keep him buoyant for years. *How much food did you store, man?* Tanner wondered.

An image came to his mind, of the *Arrogance* adrift for years, four or five hundred feet above the water, with Hedrigall's corpse rotting slowly in the captain's cabin. A windblown sepulchre.

Or maybe he could stay alive. Maybe he would unroll a great, absurdly long fishing line from the *Arrogance*'s bay doors. Tanner imagined it cascading through the air like a spring unwinding, till its baited hook reached the water. By choice the cactacae were vegetarians, but they could survive on fish or flesh if they had to.

There Hedrigall could sit, on the edge of the hatch, his legs swinging like a child's, reeling in fish. Rubbery bodies flapping on the journey up, air-drowned and long dead when they reached him. He could live for years, blown around the world. Slipping into the roundstream winds that circled the Swollen Ocean, growing old and obstreperous on his unchanging diet, his skin wrinkling and his thorns turning grey. Alone, going mad. Talking to the portraits and heliotypes on the *Arrogance*'s walls.

Till one day some chance might push him out of that great belt of wind, and his craft might eddy out into free air and be carried south or north or gods knew where, until one day, maybe, he might come into sight of land.

Drifting over mountains. Throwing down the anchor, snagging a tree and descending. Touching the ground again.

Is it such a bad fucking plan, Hedrigall, to search for the Scar?

Hedrigall was a traitor, Tanner supposed. He'd done a bunk;

he'd stolen Armada's crow's nest and lied to his rulers and friends. He'd been too cowardly to have the argument. He was a renegade, and Tanner knew that as a loyal Garwater man, he should condemn him. But he could not.

Good luck, mate, he thought after some moments, hesitantly raising his hand and nodding. *I can't not wish you luck.*

Garwater's champions felt Hedrigall's absence like a rebuke.

He was known to have been loyal, and he left in the wake of his passing more disturbed discussion, more uncertainty and condemnation of the Lovers' project than had so far existed.

Miles below the sea, the avanc continued its journey. It had slowed only a little on entering the new waters.

Tanner Sack swam and bathed his ravaged back in the sea. There were few divers below and few swimmers above, in these days. They had been scared away, terrified that they might be swept away on some unforeseeable current, borne off to some dead-pool in the Hidden Ocean.

Tanner found nothing wrong. He and the menfish and Bastard John flitted from place to place, around and between those enormous chains angling down. They swam quickly, careful not to let the city leave them behind, but there seemed to be no new hazards in the water. The chaos inhered at a larger scale—for the great intruders like ships and submersibles. Even the seawyrms had not been able to continue pulling their now misbehaving chariot ships, and they had swum back with the fleet, back out of the Empty Ocean.

It was peaceful now, with fewer people and fewer things to distract Tanner. Much of Armada's activity had ceased.

Of course the farmers still cared for their crops and flocks, above water and below, and harvested them when they could. There were still a thousand little jobs of repair and maintenance. The internal workings of the city continued, as they had to: bakers, moneylenders, cooks, and apothecaries put out their signs and took in money. But Armada was a city that had looked outward, to piracy and trade. The industries around the docks, the loading and unloading and counting and refitting and outfitting, were all in stasis now.

So Tanner did not dive daily to work on cracks or breaks or

faults or anything like that. He swam for himself, and for his back, and felt the salt bring his skin back to life.

"Come in, Shek," he said.

He was aware of the tension that was spreading through Armada, the uncertainty, as if Hedrigall had spilled a poison behind him as he left. Tanner wanted to offer Shekel a place where it could dissipate.

There were reasons for people's growing fears. Tanner had heard strange rumors. Three times now he had heard that some man or woman, some yeoman or Garwater engineer, had disappeared, their house and things left untouched (food half-eaten, in one story). Some said they, too, had fled, and others claimed that these were the depredations of spirits from the Hidden Ocean.

When he was in the water, Tanner's sense that things were wrong, dangerous, or uncertain dissipated with the currents. He offered Shekel the same respite. He persuaded the boy to swim with him. The pools between Armada's vessels were almost empty now. Shekel was excited to be one of those brave enough to go in. The great flitches of the ships moved above and around them sedately: they would not be left behind. Shekel struggled with his aggressive, ugly paddle, and Tanner tried to show him better strokes and realized that he did not know any suitable for those who had to breathe air.

Shekel slipped heavy goggles over his eyes and plunged his head below for as long as their imperfect seal kept out the water. He and Tanner would stare at the shoals of fishes, species they had never seen. Colored and finned intricately, as intense and bizarre as tropical species, here in these more temperate waters. Like scorpion and ratfish, their forms were broken with spindly appendages, and eyes that glowed with unlikely colors.

When Shekel and Tanner hauled themselves out again, Angevine would be waiting, with maybe a bottle of beer or liquor. And even if Tanner and Angevine still spoke to each other a little warily, and realized that they always would, what they shared in Shekel, and the way they had learned to share it, gave them a respectful connection.

It's kind of a family, Tanner thought.

It was not hard for Bellis to find Uther Doul again. She had only to wait on the deck of the *Grand Easterly,* knowing he would appear eventually. She was stiff with resentment and incensed by her own hurt. She could not believe how he had dropped her.

As she approached he stared at her, but not with the disgust that she feared. Not with hostility, or with interest, or any kind of connection or recognition. He simply stared.

She drew herself up. She had tied back her hair again, and she knew that the look of stunned pain was ebbing gradually from her face. She still moved stiffly, but nearly two weeks since her flogging she had regained much of herself.

Bellis did not greet Doul. "I want to see Fennec" was all she said.

Doul thought for a second, then inclined his head. "Alright," he said.

And although this was what she wanted, Bellis hated him for that, because she knew that he allowed it because there was nothing she could do or say to Fennec that could now come in Armada's way at all. Now that she was not any kind of threat, now that all her cards had been played.

Bellis was quite meaningless now, so she could be indulged.

His magus fin had been taken from him, but it was clear that Garwater was still afraid of Silas Fennec. The corridor along which he was imprisoned was thick with guards. All the doors could be sealed tight: it was below the waterline.

A man and woman sat outside Fennec's door, fussing over some arcane machine. Bellis felt the dry charge of thaumaturgy against her skin.

Inside, it was a large room, broken by a few portholes through which dark eddies could be seen. Half of the room was sectioned off by iron bars, and beyond them, in a little alcove, hunkered away from the windows and the entrance, Silas Fennec sat on a wooden bench, watching her.

Bellis took in the sight of him. She was caught in a quick kaleidoscope of images of him (their times together, friendly, cold, sexual, surreptitious). Her mouth twisted to see him, and she tasted something very sour.

He was thin, and his clothes were dirty. He met her eyes. She realized, with a sudden shock, that there was a bandage wrapped tight around his right wrist and that his right hand was gone. He saw her notice his injury, and his face twisted before he could control it.

Fennec sighed and stared straight at Bellis.

"What are you doing here?" he asked. He spoke with a drab
hostility.

Bellis did not answer. She examined his cell. She saw a heap
of unkempt clothes, paper, charcoal, his fat notebook. She studied the bars that kept him from her. They were wrapped around
with cables that coiled away and under the door into the room.
Fennec watched her trace them back to their source.

"Linked up to those machines out there," he said to her. He
sounded tired. "It's a dampener. Sniff the air. You can even hear
it. Kills the thaumaturgons. No one could do the slightest little
hex in here now." He sniffed and smiled without humor. "It's in
case I've got some secret plan. I've told them I can only do about
three little charms, and none of them would get me out of here
anyway but . . . Guess what? They don't believe me."

Bellis glimpsed weird flesh under his shirt. It looked necrotic,
speckled with amphibian markings. It pulsed, and Fennec pulled
his shirt closed.

Her eyes widening, Bellis turned her back on him and paced.

"Don't," Fennec said to her suddenly. He sounded almost kind.

"What the fuck do you mean?" she said, and was pleased to
hear her voice was cold.

He looked at her with an infuriating, knowing look.

"Don't do this," he said. "Don't come here; don't ask me;
don't do this. What are you here for, Bellis? You're not here to
rail at me—that's not your style. You're not going to crow. They
caught me; so what? They fucking caught you, too. How's the
back?"

That so stunned her that for a moment she could not breathe.
She blinked rapidly, bringing him back into focus. He watched
her without any particular cruelty or maliciousness in his face.

"You're not going to learn anything from me, Bellis," he said,
his voice unchanging. "You're not going to get anything out of
this. This won't be catharsis, and you won't feel better when you
leave. *Yes,* do you understand? Yes, I lied to you; I used you. And
a lot of other people. I did it without thinking twice. I'd do it
again. I wanted to go home. If you'd been there and it was
easy, I'd have taken you with me, but if you weren't, I wouldn't.
Bellis . . ." He leaned forward on his bench and rubbed his wrist
stump. "Bellis, you have nothing to confront me with." He shook
his head slowly, utterly unabashed by her.

She was shaking with hatred. He had been right not to tell her the truth about what he was doing. She would never have helped him then, even desperate as she was to get home.

"There's nothing special about you, Bellis: you were one of many. I treated you no differently from anyone else. I thought of you no more and no less. The only difference between you and any of the others is that you're *here* now. And you think there's some *point* to you being here. That you had to . . . what? *Have it out?*" Silas Fennec, procurator for New Crobuzon, shook his head, pitying.

"There is no *it*, Bellis," he said. "Go away." He lay down and gazed at the ceiling. "Go away. I wanted to get home, and you were useful. You know what I did, and you know why. There's no mystery, no resolution to be had.

"Go away."

Bellis stayed a few seconds longer, but managed to leave before speaking again. She had said only six words. She felt her stomach churn with a strong feeling to which she could not put a name.

They won't kill him, she thought bleakly. *They won't even punish him. He's not even been flogged. He's too valuable, too scary. They think he can teach them things, that they can get information out of him. Maybe they can.*

As she left, she could not help realizing that Fennec was right about at least one thing.

She felt no better at all.

Bellis was surprised to discover Johannes remaining in her life. There had been a time when he had seemed disgusted with her, not concerned ever to see her again.

She still found him spineless. Even when her own loyalty to New Crobuzon was such an odd, unsystematic thing, she could not help thinking of Johannes as a kind of turncoat. The speed of his accommodation with Armada disgusted her.

But now there was something plaintive in him. His rediscovered eagerness to be her friend was a little pathetic. And though Bellis spent what time she could with Carrianne, whose irreverence and affection were genuine pleasures, and though Carrianne did not much like Johannes, there were times when Bellis let him stay a while. She felt pity for him.

With the avanc caught, trapped, and tethered, and with Tintinnabulum's crew gone, Johannes' job was done. Now, after all

Johannes' work, Krüach Aum was working with the Lovers' thaumaturges and Uther Doul, ushered into the new inner circle to discover the secrets of possibility mining. Johannes had realized, Bellis supposed, that there were very many years ahead of him as a captive in the city.

Johannes still worked with a group overseeing the avanc: plotting its speed, estimating the biomass in the area, and the thaumaturgic flows. But it was make-work half the time. When drunk, he would whine about how he had been used up and dispensed with. Bellis and Carrianne would sneer at him behind his drink-fuddled back.

Johannes voiced cautious uncertainties about their trajectory, about their presence in the Hidden Ocean. To find any sign of dissonance, of opposition to the Lovers' journey, warmed Bellis with surprise. That was part of why she tolerated Johannes' presence.

He was too cowardly to admit it, but he wished they would turn back, as Bellis did. And as the days passed and Armada slipped further and further into uncharted waters, into the Hidden Ocean, Bellis discovered (with stabs of unexpected hope) that she and Johannes were not alone.

Hedrigall's desertion was a trauma that did not heal.

Armada moved on into seas that did not obey laws that any oceanologer understood. It could have seemed an adventure or some god-granted destiny to a citizenry still grimly fired up by triumph in war and by the rhetoric of Garwater's greatest-ever leaders. But then loyal, reliable Hedrigall had run, and that gave a terrible coloration to the city's journey.

The *Arrogance* had quickly been replaced. Now another airship hung over the *Grand Easterly,* watching the horizons. But it was not so large or quite so high. It did not have the *Arrogance*'s range of vision, and the metaphors thrown off from that fact troubled men and women otherwise loyal.

"What did he see coming?" they muttered. "Hedrigall, what did he see coming?"

The city's motion was its own dynamic. There were no strong voices arguing to turn back. Even those other rulers who disapproved of the Lovers' plans had given in, or only spoke their criticisms in camera. But Hedrigall's dissident ghost stalked the ridings, and the triumph, the excitement with which the journey had started, was gone.

* * *

Tanner and Shekel gave new names to the creatures they saw below the water: runrunners and dancing flies and yellowheads.

They watched Armada's naturalists drifting over the curious new animals, snatching a few in nets, keeping their distance from the big, snub-faced yellowheads, heliotyping them with unwieldy waterproof cameras and phosphoric flares.

Schools of the animals gusted through the pipes and hulls that jutted below like roots. They mixed with more recognizable fish—there were whiting and baitfish even in the Hidden Ocean—eating them or being eaten.

Tanner dived and teased a couple of hand-sized specimens with his tentacles. At the surface, Shekel looked down on Tanner's scars.

Further and further into that sea.

There were strange sounds at night: the rutting calls of unseen animals with voices like bulls. Some days there was no swimming at all, not by the hardiest or most inquisitive diver, and even the menfish hid themselves in their little city-bottom caverns. These were dangerous waters Armada passed through the unpredictable edges of boiltides, by the hunting grounds of piasa, living whirlpools that circled the city hungrily but kept their distance.

In moonless dark, lights pulsed below the waters, like the bioluminescence of benthic things magnified many hundreds of times. There were times when the clouds above the sea moved much faster than the wind. One day when the air was dry as elyctricity, shapes appeared off the city's star'd edge, like tiny islands. They were rafts of unknown weed, great clots of mutant bladderwrack that moved suddenly away from the city under some motive power of their own.

Across the whole of Armada, in every riding, in tumbledown slums and the most elegant townhouses, there was a tension, a neurotic expectancy. People did not sleep well. Bellis blenched when that began, remembering the misery of the nightmares that had racked New Crobuzon and that ultimately had led her here. *From one set of ruined nights to another,* she thought after several miserable, insomniac hours.

During some of those dark times, Bellis walked to the *Grand Easterly* to watch the city's journey through mysterious, faintly moving seas. She would stare out at the remorseless miles of water until, cowed by the scale of it, she fled into the corridors of the great ship, moved by a compulsion she did not understand.

She would wind through its warren of empty passages, into the forgotten zone of the steamer, to the little cubbyhole that Doul had shown her. And there she would perch, uncomfortable and disturbed, eavesdropping on the fucking and the bedroom talk of the Lovers.

It was a habit that revolted her, but she could not shake off the sly sense of power it gave her. *My little rebellion, my little escape—someone's listening, and you don't know,* she would think, and hear the Lovers mutter wetly to each other and grapple with an abandon that still appalled her.

They never gave her any revelations. They never spoke of anything important. They only rolled and lay together, and murmured their fetishistic connection. The Lover sounded more and more febrile with every night, her voice growing harder, and the Lover debased himself to her, eager to dissolve into her.

I do not want to be here, Bellis thought, fervently and repeatedly. She spoke it aloud, finally, to Carrianne one night, knowing that her friend would not agree.

"I do not want to be here." Bellis swilled the wine in her glass. "Now there's nightmares, and what comes next are fugues. I've seen it before. And we can't be heading anywhere that's any good—and what can happen then? Either we die . . . or the Lovers get control of the most . . . terrible, terrible power. Would you really trust them, Carrianne?" she demanded drunkenly. "That cut-up fuck and his psychopath woman? You'd trust them with power like that? I do not want to be here."

"I know, Bellis," Carrianne said, searching for words. "But I want to see what's out there. I think this is something amazing, you understand? Whether or not the Lovers get hold of . . . whatever's there. And no, I don't really trust them. I'm Dry Fall, remember? But I'll tell you what . . . Since Hedrigall did a runner, I think there's a lot of people who are starting to agree with you."

And Bellis nodded in sudden surprise, and raised her glass in a toast. Carrianne responded sardonically.

She's right, thought Bellis suddenly. *Godsdammit, she's fucking right. Something's changing.*

* * *

The avanc began to slow.

Perhaps ten days after Armada entered the Hidden Ocean, people began to notice.

At first it was Bastard John, the menfish and the cray, Tanner Sack and the other few upsiders who still swam. It was growing easier for them to keep up with the city. At the end of a few hours' immersion, skittering below the city's barnacle-scaled underside, their muscles burned less than they would have expected. They were not traveling so far, so fast.

It was not long before the air-breathing citizens noticed. Without land, in cryptic seas, it was not so easy to chart the distances the city was traveling. But there were methods.

Something was happening to the mile-long creature hidden in the deep. Something had changed. The avanc was slowing down.

At first it was hoped that it was a temporary change, that the avanc's pace would increase again. But the days went on, and still the beast slowed.

With delight and triumph, Johannes found himself suddenly back in favor. His old team was reassembled by the Lovers, to make sense of what was happening.

Bellis was surprised to discover that he still talked to her and Carrianne about his work, now that he had been brought back into the inner circle.

"There can't be anyone in the city who hasn't noticed," he told them one night, exhausted and mystified. "The Lovers are waiting for us to solve it." He shook his head. "Even Aum can't fathom it. The rockmilk engine's still controlling it; the avanc's still traveling . . . It's just slowing."

"Something in the Hidden Ocean?" suggested Bellis.

Johannes bit his lip. "Doesn't make sense," he said. "What in Bas-Lag can fuck with an *avanc*?"

"It must be sickening," said Carrianne, and Johannes nodded.

"I think it must be," he agreed slowly. "Krüach's confident that we can fix whatever's wrong. But I'm not sure we know enough to cure it."

The air above the Hidden Ocean was desiccated and suddenly hot. The city's crops became brittle.

All the ridings withdrew into themselves, and the ridiculous semblance of normality that Armada had recently affected began to break down. There was little work done. The pirate-citizens waited, motionless in their homes beneath a punitive sky. The city was bleached and vague. Marooned. Lolling like a lifeboat, almost immobile.

Its wake grew daily more faint as the avanc slowed.

A slow-burning panic began to spread. Meetings were called. For the first time, they were not organized by the rulers, but by popular committees operating across the ridings. And if at first they were made up almost totally of men and women from Curhouse and Dry Fall, the minorities from Jhour and Booktown and Garwater grew each day. They discussed what was happening, urgently, seeking answers no one was able to give them.

A nightmare image was recurring in people's heads: Armada, adrift, without motive power, in the barren waters of the Hidden Ocean. Or tethered by the motionless avanc, an anchor of unimaginable weight.

The city's speed was still decreasing.

(Much later, Bellis realized that the day when the avanc's condition became shockingly clear, the day that so many people died, was in Crobuzoner terms the first of Melluary—a Fishday. That fact made her cough with a desolate approximation of laughter, when she realized it later when the killing was over.)

It was midmorning when the impurities appeared in the sea.

At first, those who saw them thought they were more aggregates of the semisentient weed, but it became quickly obvious that they were something else. They were lighter, and lower in the water—sprawling patches of color, liquescent at the edges.

The blemishes appeared miles off, in the city's path. As they came gradually closer, word spread, and crowds gathered in Shaddler's Sculpture Garden, at Armada's fore, to watch whatever it was approach.

It was a mass of some viscous liquid, thick as dense mud. Where waves reached its outer edges they reduced to ugly ripples that crawled weakly across the surface of the substance and were swallowed up.

The stuff was the pallid yellow-white of a caveworm.

Bellis swallowed, feeling sick with anxiety, and then realized very suddenly as the wind shifted that it was not anxiety at all. It was the stench.

A rolling mass of smell oozed over them. The citizens blenched and puked. Bellis and Carrianne staggered and stared at each other, paling, managing not to spew even amid a chorus of retching. The wobbling white mass stank of the worst, most septic rot, air-starved flesh gone putrid.

"Jabber pre*serve* us!" gasped Bellis. Above her head Armada's carrion birds wheeled, coiling excitedly like some living cloud toward the rank stuff, then arcing suddenly away as they grew close, as if its degree of corruption defied even them.

The city reached the outer edges of the reeking substance. There were great swathes of it ahead, a bobbing purulent mass.

Most of those who had gathered to watch had run back to their houses to burn incense. Bellis and Carrianne remained, watching Johannes and his colleagues at the edge of the park. With perfume-soaked rags around their faces, Garwater's investigators leaned over the rail, trolling a bucket on a rope into the substance. They hauled it up and began to examine it.

Then recoiled from it, violently.

When Johannes saw Bellis and Carrianne, he ran over to them and tore off his mask. He was white and trembling, his skin reflective with sweat.

"It's pus," he said, and pointed to the sea with an unsteady finger. "It's a slick of pus."

CHAPTER FORTY-THREE

The avanc is sick.

Trying to continue its mindless motion at the rockmilk engine's command, it slows and slows. It is—what? Bleeding, wounded? Fevered? Chafed sore by the alien reality around it? Too mute or stupid or obedient to feel or show its pain, the avanc's lesions are not healing. They are shedding their dead matter in suppurating clots that eddy free and drift up like oil,

expanding as the crushing pressure lessens, enveloping and suf-
focating fish and weed, until what breaks the waves with a mucal
slurp is a noisome coagulate of infection and smothered sea-life.

Somewhere between two and three thousand miles into the
Hidden Ocean, the avanc is sick.

A few miles clear of the repulsive pus-flats, the avanc came to
a stop.

Desperately, signals from the rockmilk engine were increased,
sent down repeatedly, but there was no response. The avanc was
absolutely still.

It hovered, static, unable or unwilling to move, miles down.

And when everything that the avanc's protectors and doctors
knew how to do had been done, and nothing had happened;
when all the different wavelengths had been tried to entice the
great creature back into motion, and it had not responded; there
was only one option left. The city could not be allowed to molder
motionless.

The avanc was sick, and none of the scholars knew why. They
would have to examine it, from close quarters.

Garwater's bathyscaphos swung like an unwieldy pendulum
from a crane on the *Hoddling,* a factory ship at the *Grand Easterly*'s bow. The submersible was a stubby sphere, broken by
pipes and rivets, random extrusions in reinforced iron. Its engine
bulged at its rear like a bustle. Handspan-thick glass fronted its
four portholes and chymical lamp.

Engineers and work crews were hurriedly checking and refitting the deep-water vessel.

The crew of the bathyscaphos *Ctenophore* were preparing on
the *Hoddling*'s deck, pulling on overalls and checking the books
and treatises they had with them. A scabmettler pilot, Chion, her
face puckered by the remnants of ritual cuts; Krüach Aum (and
Bellis, watching, shook her head to see him, her erstwhile pupil,
his tight sphincter-mouth dilating with agitation); and at the
front, looking excited, proud, and terrified in equal parts, Johannes Tearfly.

He had no choice but to go—he more than anyone but Krüach
Aum understood the avanc, and it was imperative that the creature be tended as expertly as possible. Bellis knew that Johannes
would have gone even without the Lovers' coercion.

"We're going down," he had explained to Bellis earlier, staring at her with the same expression he wore now, while he kitted up on the *Hoddling*'s deck. "We're going to take a look. We have to cure it." And if he looked aghast, he looked no less excited.

As a scientist, he was fascinated. She saw fear in him, but no foreboding. Bellis remembered him describing the scar he carried, where he was once gored by a sardula. He could be utterly craven, but his cowardice was only social. She had never seen him flinch from the dangers his research entailed. He did not balk now at this appalling commission.

"Well," Bellis had said, carefully. "I'll see you in a few hours, I suppose." And Johannes was so excited that her measured voice, the careful neutrality of her tone, which undermined the meaning of her words and stressed the danger he was in, passed him by. He nodded naïvely and gripped her shoulder, an awkward gesture, then left.

The preparation took a long time. There was not much of a crowd around the city's aft edge to watch them and see them off. The strained air of the city kept people away—it was not that they did not care, but they felt without energy, as if they were sucked dry.

Johannes glanced up toward the few onlookers and waved. Then he climbed into the cabin of the *Ctenophore*.

Bellis watched the hatch being screwed down tight on the cramped vessel. She watched the bathyscaphos being tugged up above the water, lurching sickeningly, and she remembered that same motion from when she had been lowered into Salkrikaltor City. A huge wheel on the *Hoddling*, reeling out reinforced rubberized cable, began to revolve as the deepwater submersible descended.

It touched the waters of the Hidden Ocean with a muted splash and sank below without pause. It would take at least three hours for the bathyscaphos to reach the avanc. Bellis watched the ripples from the disappearing submersible till she felt someone behind her and turned to face Uther Doul.

She set her mouth and waited. He studied her calmly and did not speak for several seconds.

"You're worried for your friend," he said. "The *Grand Easterly* is out of bounds during this emergency, but if you'd like, you can wait there for him to return."

He took her to a small room at the rear of the *Grand Easterly,* whose porthole looked out over the *Hoddling,* which was suspending the submersible. Doul left her without a word, closing the door behind him. But he had taken her to a room more comfortable and better furnished than her own quarters and, five minutes after she arrived, one of the Garwater stewards brought her tea, unbidden.

Bellis sipped it as she watched the water. She was bewildered and untrusting. She did not understand why Doul was indulging her.

At first it was merely warm in the tiny spherical cabin of the *Ctenophore,* with three breathing bodies pushed together. They crushed each other uncomfortably, negotiating around each other's arms and legs to peer through the little portholes.

The light fell away with astonishing speed, and Johannes checked this waning visibility with nervous fascination. They descended by one of the great chains that tethered the avanc, slipping past one massive link after another, psoriatic with shellfish and generations of weed. Placid fish with eyes like cows' investigated their light, peering in at the intruders on their way down, spiraling the tubes that fed them air, shying away from the bubbles their vessel exhaled.

As the light in the sea declined, the chain became baleful. Its black shafts plumbed almost vertically, plaiting one into the other in patterns that seemed suddenly obscure and sinister, the links suggestive as hieroglyphs.

At the edge of absolute darkness, the sea seemed absolutely still, uncut by the Hidden Ocean's predatory currents. The crew did not speak. The cabin was now quite black. There were chymical lights and lanterns aboard, but they could not risk exhausting them during their descent—it was at the bottom that they must be able to see. So they sat, pressed together, in the most profound darkness any of them had ever experienced.

There was only the wheeze of breath and a faint percussion as they moved their cramped limbs and knocked them against metal or each other. The whisper of pumped air. The engine was not running—gravity took the vessel down.

Johannes listened to his own breath, and that of those around him, and realized that they were unconsciously synchronizing. Which meant that after every exhalation there was a pause, a moment when he could pretend for a fraction of a second that he was alone.

They were far beyond the sun's reach now. They warmed the sea. Heat leached through from the boilers into the cabin, through the vessel's metal skin into water that ate it hungrily.

Time could not survive this unbroken dark heat and monotonous susurrus of air and creaking leather and shifting skin. It was broken and bled. Its moments did not segue into each other, but were stillborn. *I am out of time,* Johannes thought.

For a shocking instant he felt claustrophobia like bile, but he held himself still and closed his eyes (uncomforted by the darkness he found there, no more or less profound than that he had shut out), swallowed, and defeated it. Stretching out his hand, Johannes found the glass of the porthole, and was shocked by its cold, condensation-wet surface—the water outside was like ice.

After uncountable minutes, the darkness outside was momentarily broken, and the crew gasped as time returned to them like an elyctric shock. Some living lamp was passing them by, some tentacular thing that inverted its body with a peristaltic wave, enveloping itself in its luminescent innards and shooting away, its austere glimmer snuffed out.

Chión ignited the lamp at the bathyscaphos's front. It stuttered on, its phosphorous glow casting a cone of light. They could see its edges as clearly as if they were marble. There was nothing visible in the lamp's field except a soup of minute detritus, particles that seemed to eddy upward as the *Ctenophore* plunged. There was nothing to see: no ocean floor, no life, nothing. That crushing emptiness they had illuminated depressed them more profoundly than the darkness. They descended unlit.

The iron carapace began to creak under the pressure. Every ten or twelve seconds there would be another sudden shuddering creak, as if the pressure increased in sudden, discrete zones.

The percussive stroke became stronger the lower they went, until suddenly Johannes realized that it was not just their own craft, not just the metal around them that shook, but the sea—the whole sea, the tons of water to all sides—vibrating, spasming with sympathetic shock, in echoes of the thunderous strokes rising from below.

The avanc's heart.

* * *

When miles of wire had been played out by the huge wheel on the *Hoddling,* a safety catch snapped into place and halted their plunge. The *Ctenophore* jerked, buffeted by the arterial booming around them. The avanc's heart felt solid through the metal.

Chion lit a lantern. The three bathynauts stared at each other's sweat-moist, sepia faces. They looked grotesque, drowned in shadows. With every heartbeat that made the bathyscaphos tremble, a tic of fear and awe passed over every one of them. Darkness flickered around the close cabin, over its gauges and dials.

Chion began to work at the levers, pushing cards into the analytical engine by her side. There was a heart-stopping moment when nothing happened, and then the sphere began to shudder with the sound of its engines.

"It should be a couple of hundred yards below us," said Chion. "We'll take it slowly."

With a puttering groan, the *Ctenophore* curved down, pulling toward the avanc.

The lamp flared into life again. The cold beam speared into the unceasing marine night. Johannes studied the water, its suspension of particles, and saw it judder with the avanc's heart. His mouth was thick with saliva at the thought of the millions of tons of water eager to crush them.

Something became sensible below them, like a ghost. Johannes was chilled. They descended toward a great flat zone of lighter darkness—a ruptured, pebbled field that insinuated itself into visibility. At first utterly faint, it grew in solidity, its random, rugged contours sliding into sight in the phosphor beam. Slimed and rocky, it stretched out on all sides, broken by stains, lichen growths of the deepest sea. It harbored deepwater animal life. Johannes saw the faint flickerings of blind, eel-like hagfish; squat echurians; thick, blanched trilobites.

"We're in the wrong place," said Chion thickly. "We're coming down above the ocean floor." But as she spoke the last word her voice broke and became a trembled whisper as she realized her mistake. Johannes nodded with a kind of triumph and awe, like a man in the presence of his god.

The avanc's heart beat again, and a huge ridge cracked the vista, reconfiguring it suddenly, rising twenty feet high, sending dust and muck particles spinning. The thick crest burst up across the surface of the gnarled plain, scoring as far as *Ctenophore*'s lamp could pierce, and branching, splitting into two or three, tracing pathways across the plateau.

It was a vein.

Filling with blood, pulsing, protruding, and sinking slowly back again.

The submersible was perfectly positioned. They were above the avanc's back.

Even Krüach Aum, emotionless as he was, seemed stunned. They hunkered together and muttered for comfort.

The landscape below them was all beast.

The *Ctenophore* cruised slowly, twenty-five feet above the avanc's surface, over a valley between two veins. Johannes gazed down through the dense water. He was mesmerized by the creature's colors. He would have expected an anemic white, but the thing's mottled hide contained striations in hundreds of shades, coiled in whorls as distinct as fingerprints: pebbled grey, reds, ocher.

In places the avanc's skin was broken by jags that looked like rock or horn—whiskers reaching up around the *Ctenophore* like ossified trees. Chion steered the submersible carefully between them.

They passed over orifices. Puckered impurities in the avanc's flesh that would suddenly and randomly dilate, open gaping pits, smooth-edged, pulsing tunnels into the interior of the carcass, lined with alveoli bigger than men.

The *Ctenophore* drifted like dust over the skin.

"What in the gods' names are we doing?" Johannes whispered.

Krüach Aum was sketching rapidly, making notes, as Johannes stared at what he had helped conjure.

"We don't have more than a couple of hours' light," said Chion anxiously.

The submersible edged up, over a little copse of those steeple-sized hairs, and descended again between two extrusions—maybe the ends of gills, or scars, or fins. The skinscape heaved and rippled with subcutaneous motion. Its contours were slowly changing, the plain sloping away and down.

"We're coming to its flank," said Johannes.

Quite suddenly the corium below them was precipitous, a callused dermal cliff into dense darkness. Johannes heard his breath come shaky as the avanc fell away and the *Ctenophore* descended by its side. Light played over strata of cells and parasitic life that were suddenly sheer beside them, an organic precipice.

The geography of their patient humbled them.

Wrinkles began to appear, scores of great rucks like the edges of tectonic plates, where the avanc's skin rode over itself in slab-like folds, curving to what might be a haunch, a paddle, or a tail.

"I think . . ." said Johannes, pointing for the others. "I think we're coming to a limb."

The water spasmed and was still, again and again. The corrugations of skin grew tighter. Here, with every beat of the avanc's heart, great networks of the huge veins appeared, as intricate as shattered glass, tracing muscles like mountains. Crabs scuttled out of the light, into their burrows in the avanc's skin.

There were impurities in the water. The lamp caught on a billow of opaque liquid like ink.

"What's that?" whispered Johannes, and Krüach Aum wrote something down for him.

Blood.

The heart beat again, and the water was full of the dark stuff. It dissipated quickly, folding in all directions. The lamplight broke through the blood's tentacles and glinted on something beyond: a hard, regular surface.

The bathynauts gasped. It was the massive iron edge of Armada's harness. Crusted with the remains of limpets long-killed by pressure, and the rude life native to these deeps. One corner, one clasp, folding around the avanc's body.

"Gods," whispered Chion, "maybe it's us. Maybe it's just the buckles, the bridles—maybe they've been rasping it sore."

The *Ctenophore* bobbed through currents of displaced blood, back over the avanc's body. The blood welled up from behind hills in its hide.

"Look there!" shouted Johannes suddenly. "There!"

Twenty feet below them, the avanc's skin was raw and seeping. It was like an excavation: a wide, ragged trench at least thirty feet deep and many yards long, curling into the darkness. Its inner walls were a crumbling mess of shattered cells fouled with the residue of that oily pus. Even as they watched, clots of the semiliquid broke away and began to rise, strings of matter stretching and snapping behind them.

In the deepest part of the gash, at its base, the phosphor illuminated a wet flesh-red.

"Jabber and *fuck*," hissed Johannes. "No wonder it's been slowed."

Krüach Aum was scribbling madly, and he held up his paper to the lantern light. *Is nothing,* Johannes read. *Think of avanc size. Must be more.*

"Look," hissed Chion. "The edges of that cut . . . they don't meet the bridle. It's not the metal that's caused this." There was a silence at that. "We're missing something."

The avanc's lacerated epidermis rose to either side of them as they descended into the trench.

Like explorers in some lost river, they traced the wound toward its source.

The V of split flesh disappeared in sharp perspective before them, but was swallowed by darkness long before any vanishing point. With every heartbeat, a wash of blood welled up around them, blinding them for seconds till it evanesced.

There were small motions below them, and on either side, as scavengers ate at the exposed meat.

The submersible moved slowly in the shadows of this meat ravine. And everyone in the little bubble of metal and air thought and did not say, *What did this?*

They turned as the split turned, as hard corners of ruined skin reared before them. The *Ctenophore* swiveled in the water.

"Did you see something move?"

Chion's face was white.

"There! There! Did you? Did you see it?"

Silence. The stroke of blood. Silence.

Johannes tried to see what Chion saw.

The gulch is widening. They are at the edge of a deep pit. Its base is blood and pus. It stretches out, a hollow scores of yards across. This is the avanc's wound.

Something moves. Johannes sees it and cries out, and the others answer him.

There is motion in the blood below them.

"Oh dear gods," he whispers, and his voice dies and becomes

a thought. *Oh gods*. Something inevitable and very bad is unfolding.

The *Ctenophore* rocks, to more screams. Something buffets it.

A part of Johannes' mind is frozen, and he thinks, *We must find it and cure it, find what's wrong and cure it, cut out what's bad, cure it*, but on top of that, and smothering it, a shock of fear descends as they enter the pit, the heart of the malady.

(*It's been in me since the waves closed over my head.*)

The rotten blood below them is pulsing with strange tides. The submersible shudders again as something heavy hits it, unseen. Chion begins to keen.

Moving his head slowly, through time suddenly congealed, Johannes watches the scabmettler's hands, as sluggish and clumsy as stumps, grappling with the controls, hauling backward, tugging to pull the vessel away; but it is hit again, and it eddies unsteadily.

Johannes hears himself shrieking with Chion to *get out get out.*

Something outside is knocking at the *Ctenophore*'s hatch.

Johannes cries out, staring aghast at the blood-plain below.

A dark harvest, a thicket of black flowers, has burst from it in the oscillating glare of the lamp, blossoms that thrust upward toward that cold false sun on thick stems, muscled and veined, that are not stems but arms, those are not flowers but hands; claws, crooked, and arms spread wide and predatory, and now chests and heads and bodies rise, shoved up from below the slick of blood where they have been gnawing and spitting venom.

Like spirits rising from graveyard earth, bodies are ascending, dissipating the blood with their tails, staring up at the newcomers with colossal eyes into which Johannes gazes with awe and horror. Their faces are fixed in unwitting grins that mock him, flesh scraps fluttering free from teeth bigger than his fingers.

They swim with the grace of eels toward the vessel, which rolls under their weight, which is borne down by their outstretched hands, whose portholes sway and face suddenly up, tipping the three within into each other, where they lie screaming, staring up and screaming in the dying lantern light at the faces at their windows, the scrabbling hands.

Johannes feels his mouth stretched wide, but he can hear

nothing. His arms smash against the bodies of his crew, and they beat him in terrified turn, and he feels nothing.

The light pours up from the *Ctenophore* and is eaten by the abyss. Johannes watches the creatures press down on the portholes, and a rage of thoughts arc through him. *These are the sickness,* he keeps thinking hysterically. *These are the sickness.*

The sickness crowd around the submersible. They burst the phosphor lamp, which douses in a rush of bubbles, and now all that illuminates their distended faces is the faint yellow from the lantern within.

Johannes is staring up through the cabin into a pair of eyes outside, four miles below the sea. For a tiny fraction of a second he sees, absolutely vividly and clearly, how he must appear to those eyes, his own face bloodied from the tumbling and stark with lines and lantern light, his frozen, stricken expression.

He watches as the battered portholes vein. He watches the cracks crawl like busy things over and around each other, tracing pathways, riddling the glass until it creaks and the submersible shakes. He crawls backward from the ruined window, as if another handful of inches might save him

As the *Ctenophore* stutters in its last moments, as the blood-smeared creatures and the sea outside eddy with hungry expectation, the lantern winks out, and in the middle of the heat and chaos and the three voices, three bodies fumbling together, Johannes is absolutely alone.

CHAPTER FORTY-FOUR

The sun was gone, but the water was still warm. It was very still. Below its surface the constellation of cray lightglobes picked out Armada's underside.

Tanner and Shekel swam between the *Hoddling* and the *Dober,* the ossified whale, in a runnel of water forty feet wide. They were cosseted from the city's sounds, only the debris of which floated down to their heads, bobbing on the surface like seals'.

"We'll not go too close," warned Tanner. "It could be dangerous. We're staying on this side of the ship."

Shekel wanted to dive the few feet he dared, and see through his goggles the line running down to the bathyscaphos. Tanner's descriptions of the avanc's chains had always held him transfixed, but they were invisible to him except as faint dark shapes even if he held his courage and swam below the lowest ships in the city. He wanted to see such a cord stretching from the air into the darkness. He wanted to be faced by the scale of it.

"I doubt you'll see it," warned Tanner, watching the boy's enthusiastic, inefficient strokes. "But we'll see how close we can get, alright?"

The sea lapped at Tanner. He unstretched in it, unrolled his extra limbs. He dived below into the rapidly darkening water and felt himself framed by the cool cray lights.

Tanner breathed water and swam a few feet below Shekel, watching his progress. He thought he could feel something vibrating in the water. He had grown sensitive to the sea's little shudders. *Must be the cable,* he thought, *still letting the sub down. That's what it must be.*

Three hundred feet from them, the bulky girdered legs of the *Sorghum* rose from the water. The sun had set behind the rig, and the plaited metal of its struts and derricks were dark stitches in the sky.

"We'll not get too close," warned Tanner again, but Shekel was not listening.

"Look!" he crowed, and pointed for Tanner, losing his momentum and sinking momentarily, coming up laughing, pointing again toward the far end of the *Hoddling*. They could see the thick wire, taut and rigid, descending into the water.

"Keep away, Shek," warned Tanner. "No closer now."

The cable penetrated the water like a needle.

"Shekel." Tanner spoke decisively, and the boy turned, spluttering. "That's enough. Let's see what we can see while there's still a bit of light."

Tanner reached Shekel and sank below him, staring up as the boy pulled the goggles over his eyes, took a lungful of air, and kicked down, holding Tanner's hand.

The outlines of the city rose, ominous like storm clouds. Tanner was counting down in his head, allowing Shekel twenty seconds of stored air. Tanner peered through the Hidden Ocean's dusk, still watching for the shaft of the cable.

When he veered up and hauled the boy into the air, Shekel was smiling.

"It's fucking *brilliant,* Tanner," he said, and coughed, swallowing seawater. "Do it again!"

Tanner took him deeper. Seconds moved slowly, and Shekel showed no discomfort.

They were ten feet below, by the crusted slope of the *Hoddling.* Some shank of moonlight splashed down, and Shekel pointed. Forty, fifty feet away, the submersible's cable was momentarily clear.

Tanner nodded, but turned his head to the blackness congealed below the factory ship. He had heard a sound.

Time to rise, he thought, and turned back to Shekel. He touched Shekel and pointed up, reaching out with his hands. Shekel grinned, parting his lips and showing his teeth, even as air slipped from his mouth.

There was a sudden spurting rush of water, and something sinuate and very quick punched in and out of Tanner's vision. It was gone and there and gone like a fish flashing in to feed. Tanner blinked, stunned. Shekel still stared at him, his face collapsing into perturbation. The boy frowned and opened his mouth as if to speak, and in a great belching roar released all his air.

Tanner spasmed with shock and reached out, and saw that something followed the racing bubbles from Shekel's mouth, billowing up darkly. For a moment Tanner thought it was vomit, but it was blood.

Still staring with an expression of confusion, Shekel began to sink. Tanner grappled with him, hauling him up with his tentacles, kicking out for the surface, his mind filled up with a shattering sound. And blood smoked up ferociously not only from Shekel's mouth but from the massive wound on his back.

It seemed so far to the surface.

There was only one word in Tanner's mind. *No no no* no no *no* no *no* no *no no no.*

He shrieked it without sound, his suckered polyp arms gripping Shekel's skin, pulling him fitfully toward the air, and indistinct shapes gusted around Tanner, in and out of shadows, baleful and predatory as barracuda, jackknifing and twisting away, there and gone, moving with an effortless piscine ease that made him feel clumsy and heavy, fumbling with his boy, fleeing the sea. He was an intruder, disturbed and making an escape, cowed by real sea-things. His reconfigured body was suddenly a terrible joke, and he cried and floundered with his burden, struggling in water suddenly quite alien to him.

When he broke the surface he was screaming. Shekel's face came up in front of him, twitching, leaking brine and gore from his mouth, emitting little sounds.

"Help me!" screamed Tanner Sack, *"Help me!"* But no one could hear, and he clamped his ridiculous suckered limbs to the side of the *Hoddling* and tried to drag himself from the water.

"Help me!"

"Something's wrong! *Something's wrong!*"

For hours, the laborers on the *Hoddling*'s deck had tended the great steam pumps that sent air to the *Ctenophore,* and prepared themselves to haul it back. One by one they had slipped into a kind of torpor. They had noticed nothing at all until the cactus-woman greasing the safety wire began to bellow.

"Something's fucking wrong!" she yelled, and they came running, panicked by her voice.

They watched the wire, their hearts slamming. The great wheel—almost empty now, its harness almost all played out—was shaking violently, juddering against the deck, trembling the screws that held it down. The cable began to shriek, tearing its way past the guard-piece.

"Bring them *up,*" someone shouted, and the crews ran to the massive winch. There was a snap and the noise of slipping gears. The pistons punched into each other like boxers. The engine's cogs bit down and tried to turn, but the cable fought them. It was taut as a treble string.

"Get them *out,* get them *out,*" someone screamed uselessly, and then with a hideous cracking sound the huge winch rocked backward violently on its stand. The engine smoked and steamed and whined childishly as its guts began to spin freely. Its complex of ratchets and flywheels blurred, revolving so fast they were as dim as apparitions.

"It's free!" the cactus-woman reported to a hysterical cheer. "It's coming up."

But the bathyscaphos was never designed to rise that fast.

The wheel accelerated in ridiculous haste, hauling up the cable at dizzying speed. The gears gave off the dry stink of burning metal and grew red-hot as they whirred.

It had taken three hours to send the *Ctenophore* to the bottom. The disk of rewound cable increased so quickly they could watch it grow, and they knew it would be no more than minutes before it was all pulled back.

"It's coming up too fast! Get away!"

A mist of brine boiled where the thigh-thick cable was torn from the sea. It scored through the water. Where it met the *Hoddling*'s side, it wore a deep groove in the metal, howling in a monsoon of sparks.

Engineers and stevedores scrambled to get away from the machinery, which struggled with its remaining bolts like a terrified man.

Tanner Sack hauled himself onto the *Hoddling*'s deck, dragging Shekel's wet, cooling shape behind him.

"Help me!" he screamed again, but still no one heard a word.

(At the edge of Dry Fall, the Brucolac was leaning over the edge of the *Uroc,* watching the water intently. A domed, toothed head rose before him, framed by ripples, nodded once, and disappeared. The Brucolac turned to his cadre, on the deck behind him.

"It's time," he said.)

With a vaulting plume of water, the end of the cable burst from the sea and arced over the spinning winch, heavy metal cordage whipping toward the deck, its end splayed jagged where the submersible had been pulled free.

The *Hoddling*'s workers watched, aghast.

The frayed end of the wire slammed into the deck with a cataclysmic sound, leaving a long stripe of shattered wood and metal shavings, and the winch kept turning. The end of wire lashed around and under it and flogged the ship again and again.

"Turn it off!" the foreman screamed, but no one could hear him over the punishment, and no one could get close. The motor kept the great wheel spinning, flagellating the *Hoddling,* until the boiler exploded.

When it did, and showered the factory ship with molten detritus, there was a moment of still and shock. And then the *Hoddling* lurched again, from more fire and explosions within.

* * *

Alarms were sounding across the city.

Yeomanry and armed cactacae from Garwater and Jhour were taking up positions on the vessels around the *Hoddling,* which glowed and boomed as the great bonfire on its deck spread. Its crews raced, frantic, away from it, over the rope bridges and into the city. The *Hoddling* was a huge ship, and there was a steady stream of men and women surging up out of its guts, through the smoke and away from its ruins.

Etched in black against the flames, a figure could be seen shambling slowly in a vague path toward a bridge, bent under a burden that lolled and dripped. His mouth was open wide, but what he said could not be heard.

"Do you all know what to do?" whispered the Brucolac, tersely. "Then go."

Moving too fast for the eye easily to follow, a swarm of figures spread out from the *Uroc.*

They raced like apes, swinging with easy speed over roofs and rigging, their passage soundless. The unclear garrison fractured into smaller forces.

"Bask and Curhouse won't help, but they won't hinder, either," the Brucolac had told them. "Dynich is young and nervous—he'll wait and go where the wind blows. Shaddler's the only other riding with which we have to concern ourselves. And there's a quick way of taking them out of the equation."

A small group of the vampir made their uncanny way toward Shaddler, toward the *Therianthropus* and Barrow Hall, toward the general's court. The main force loped and leaped aft, stretching their limbs, febrile and excited, heading for Garwater.

Behind them, walking briskly but without any attempt to rush or hide, came the Brucolac.

There was something on the *Hoddling.* The men and women who escaped and collapsed on the surrounding vessels gasped for breath and shrieked warnings.

Something had burst through the ship's hull, somewhere in its lowest quarters, and scored a tunnel up through the metal. As the engine had spun and lashed the deck with the stub of the *Ctenophore*'s cable, things had emerged from the hidden decks, attacking those on the bridge and in the boilers and engine rooms, tearing the ship apart.

Things that were hard to describe—there were reports of chattering teeth like razored slabs, vast corpsy eyes.

The deck of the *Grand Easterly* was almost empty, only crossed occasionally by some running servant or bureaucrat. The yeomanry guarded its entrance points, where the bridges rose to it from below—they could not allow such chaos to spread to the flagship. The crowds gathered as close as they could get to the violence, on roofs and balconies, towerblocks, thronging the vessels that surrounded the *Hoddling*. They surged forward like waves. Aerostats came near the gusting updraft from the fire.

Forgotten in her room at the *Grand Easterly*'s rear, Bellis watched in horror as the crisis took shape.

Johannes is gone, she thought, staring at the shattered ruins of the winch engine.

He was gone—and she had no words for the weird, muted shock and loss she felt.

She looked down on the trawlers that abutted the *Hoddling*. Their decks thronged with injured, terrified men and women being dragged to safety from the flames.

On one of them, Bellis saw Uther Doul. He shouted, moving sparely, his eyes darting ceaselessly.

The fire on the *Hoddling* was abating, though the Armadans had not put it out.

Bellis gripped the windowsill. She could see shadows moving through the windows of the factory ship. She could see things within.

Armed pirates were arriving from all over the city. They took up positions, checking their weaponry and massing by the bridges leading to the *Hoddling*.

Something streaked from the factory ship's smoke-fouled bridge: a jet of disturbance that buckled the air as it lanced out. It struck the wooden mast of a schooner just beyond the *Hoddling*.

Agitated particles coiled around the mast and soaked into it, and then Bellis let out an astonished sound. The mast was *melting* as if it were wax, the great pillar of wood bending like a snake, its substance oozing over itself as it spat and drooled downward, spitting in and out of existence, leaving an effervescence in the air—a blistered reality through which Bellis caught glimpses of a void. Folds of denaturing wood slid like toxic sludge over the crowded deck.

Uther Doul was pointing with his sword, directing a group of cactacae to bring their rivebows to bear on the *Hoddling*'s windows, when a chorus of cries rose *away* from the factory ship, out of Bellis' sight. She saw the men and women below shift their attention, watched an expression of horror and astonishment pass through them like a virus.

Something was approaching from the city's fore, bearing down on the assembled pirates—something Bellis could not yet see. She saw the armed groups splinter, some turning to face the new threat with terror scrawled all over them. Bellis ran from the room, heading up to the deck to see.

The *Grand Easterly* was all confusion. The bridges were still guarded by nervous patrols, unclear on their orders, desperately watching the storm of arrows and cannonfire that assaulted the *Hoddling*. Pirates were leaving the *Grand Easterly,* running to join their comrades.

Bellis ran to the edge of the deck, past the bridge, hiding in the darkness beside its raised quarters. She was at the level of Armada's roofs. She tried to make out what was happening in the city.

Firepower was beating down on the *Hoddling,* and on whatever it contained. The hidden enemy sent out more of their bizarre and murderous thaumaturgic strikes, like fireworks, dissolving the substance of the surrounding vessels and the attacking Armadans. But beyond the nearby vessels, Bellis could see an indistinct second front spreading into the city. She could see undisciplined, chaotic attacks, could hear the irregular staccato of gunfire.

The new attackers grew closer to the tight tangle of boats below her, where most of Garwater's yeomanry had been waiting to retake the *Hoddling.* She could see, suddenly, who had launched the second assault, from within the city. The Garwater forces were suddenly hemmed in and stormed by Dry Fall's vampir.

Bellis peered around, her hand held tight to her mouth, breathing hard. She did not understand what she was seeing—some collapse of trust, some revenge? Mutiny, at the Brucolac's hand.

She could not keep the vampir in her eyes. They moved like

nightmares. Congregating and atomizing and re-forming, moving with feral speed.

They would swing down with terrifying grace in some cul-de-sac where only five or six or seven armed fighters at a time could attack them, and would dispatch the defenders with appalling ferocity, punching horn-hard nails through throats, savaging with their predatory teeth until their chins were sopped with blood, salivating and growling with bloodlust. And then they were gone, bounding over the collapsing bodies and onto some other concrete block or bridge or gun tower or ruin. Rustling like lizards they would disappear from sight.

Bellis could not tell how many there were. Wherever she looked, there seemed to be fighting, but she could only ever see Garwater's troops clearly.

Uther Doul, she realized, had turned his attention to the vampir. She saw him shoving people out of his way and sprinting back onto the *Grand Easterly*'s deck, to stare down onto the zones of battle. He spun and screamed orders, directed reinforcements toward the various combats. Then he hurled himself toward the rear of an ancient war trimaran by the *Grand Easterly*'s side, lumpen with brick housing, where through a thicket of ragged washing Bellis glimpsed a brutal melee.

It was only two hundred feet from her, and she could still see Doul. She could watch him sliding down the steeply angled bridge, thumbing on the Possible Sword, which shimmered and became a thousand ghost-swords as he ran. She watched him disappear behind a billowing sheet, as if it had swallowed him up. The sheet gusted and cracked with the wind, and beyond it there were a series of sudden noises.

The stark white linen was streaked from behind with red.

It fluttered twice, as if wounded, and then was torn down as a staggering body collapsed into it and gripped it in death, staining it bloodier and twisting it into a makeshift shroud, revealing the scene behind. Doul stood among a mass of wounded, who were cheering and kicking the swaddled vampir corpse.

Their triumph was brief. Thaumaturgic energy spat like hot fat across from the *Hoddling,* and the wood and metal around the men and women began to buckle and ooze. Uther Doul pointed with his red-dripping sword, sending the exhausted fighters running from the boat.

The vampir they left behind was not the only one to fall. Bellis could not see much of the fighting—her view was interrupted by cobbled streets and building sites and cranes and avenues of stumpy trees. But she thought she could see, here and there, other vampir succumbing. They were terrifyingly fast and strong, and they left a trail of punctured bodies, bleeding and dead, but they were vastly outnumbered.

They used the architecture and the shadows as their allies, but they could not avoid every one of the deluge of bullets and sword strokes that followed them. And though those wounds might not kill them as they would an ordinary woman or man, they hurt and slowed them down. And inevitably there were places where a gang of terrified pirates closed in on one of the buckling, snarling figures and hacked the head from its shoulders, or savaged it so remorselessly that they destroyed its bones and innards beyond even the preternatural vampir capacity for self-repair.

Alone, the vampir might eventually have been contained, but too many of Garwater's fighters were engaged with the unseen enemy on the *Hoddling*.

Small, low boats had been launched, forty-footers with cannons and fire-throwers on their decks. They raced across the little bay toward the factory ship, to cover it from its open sides, to surround it.

But in the water around the *Hoddling*, shapes were rising.

The sea was illuminated by the glow from the fires and the firepower, and through a few feet of brine Bellis could make out the outlines of the things below: bloated bodies wobbling like sacks of rotten meat; malignant little pig eyes; degenerate fin stubs. Splitting them wide open, mouths mounted with irregular footlong teeth of translucent cartilage.

They breached fleetingly. *What in Jabber's name are they?* thought Bellis, dizzily. *How can the Brucolac control those? What's he done?* The men who approached them fired volleys of missiles at them, and the things disappeared again.

But when the little boats came close and the men within leaned out to take aim again, there was a quick organic twitching and they were in the sea, in stunned shock, and with an inrush of water and a quick glare of teeth, they were taken down.

Armada was tearing itself apart. Bellis heard gunshots and saw a flickering of flames where Dry Fall met Garwater. A human mob was approaching, and there were running fights between them and the Garwater sailors. It was not now the city against the vampir alone—as news of the rebellion spread, those who opposed the Lovers' plans had come out to fight. Hotchi slammed their spines against men; cactacae hurled their great bulks against each other in ugly combat.

There was no structure to the fighting. The city was burning. Dirigibles moved overhead in ungainly panic. Above it all towered the *Grand Easterly*. Its dark iron was still silent and empty, still deserted.

Bellis became sluggishly aware that this was bizarre. She stared at the trireme below her. The rope bridge that had linked it to the *Grand Easterly* had been severed, and so, she realized, had the one beyond it.

Bellis flattened herself carefully against the wall, inched forward, and peered out of the darkest shadows onto the main deck. She saw three dim figures moving with vampir speed, hacking at the chains and knots that attached the bridges to the ship. They split one and sent it swinging into the sea, its far end slapping the flank of the vessel to which it was attached, and then they flitted to the next and began again.

Bellis's stomach lurched. The vampir were cutting her off, confining her on the ship with them. She pressed against the wall and could not move, as if a film of ice held her.

On an old trawler, below mildewing eaves, Uther Doul put his blade through a man's face. He turned away from the split, screaming thing he had made and raised his voice over the sounds of violence.

"Where," he bellowed, "is the fucking Brucolac?"

And as he spoke, he was facing the *Grand Easterly*. He paused for a second at his own words and looked up at the steamer's rail, toward its invisible deck and its miles of corridors, where he had left the Lovers in emergency session with their scientific advisors, and his eyes widened.

"Gods*dammi*t!" he shouted, and began to run.

Bellis could hear a voice.

It came from very close to her, just around the corner from where she stood frozen, by the doors to the raised section. She held her breath, her heart quite cold with fear.

"Do you understand?" she heard. The voice spoke tersely, hoarse and guttural. The Brucolac. "He'll be somewhere in *that* section—I don't know exactly where, but I've no doubt that you can find him."

"We understand." Bellis closed her eyes at that awful second voice. It sounded as if the whispered words were chance echoes in parting slime. *"We will find him,"* it continued, *"and take back what was stolen, and then we will leave, and the avanc will move freely again."*

"Well, I'll be quick then," the Brucolac said. "There's two people I still have to kill."

Footsteps receded. Bellis risked opening her eyes and moving her head a tiny way, and she saw the Brucolac stalking calmly and at speed toward the raised section of superstructure below which were the *Grand Easterly*'s meeting rooms.

Bellis heard the door open, and quick wet sounds brushing the threshold as the intruders entered.

Understanding and amazement hit her so hard she reeled. She knew in a sudden gust of insight what those newcomers were, and what—and whom—they were seeking.

So far . . . ? she thought, giddy. *So far?* But she had no doubt.

Holding her breath so that her terrified hyperventilation would not betray her, Bellis looked around the corner. There was no one in sight.

She tried desperately to think of what to do. She heard a rushing sound and a series of terrible screams from the ships below. She could not help but give a quiet cry when she saw what the intruders' thaumaturgy had done, what was now happening to the men and women of Armada. She shook her head and moaned, stupefied by the blood and disfigured corpses she saw.

Another burst of energy crossed the air from the *Hoddling*, and a vivid anger settled very suddenly in Bellis' guts, making her tremble. Her fear remained, but this new rage was much stronger.

It was directed at Silas Fennec.

You fucking bastard! she thought. *You fucking stupid selfish swine! Look what you've done! Look what you've brought here!* She watched the carnage, her own hands bloodless.

I have to stop this.

And then she knew how.

She knew what had been stolen, and she knew where it was.

* * *

As the vampir sawed at the age-fused rope of the last of the *Grand Easterly*'s bridges, a sword-wielding figure hurled himself up the slats. The vampir stepped back in surprise and fumbled for their weapons.

Uther Doul reached the deck. The vampir closest to him brought out her flintlock and turned it on him, flickering her tongue and snarling, her fangs extending like a snake's. Doul beheaded her with a kind of contempt.

Her two fellows watched the tattoo of her heels on the wood. Doul walked toward them without hesitation, and they ran.

"Where," Uther Doul bellowed after them, "is the *Brucolac?"*

Crying out with every stroke, Bellis battered at the handle and lock with the candlestick she had grabbed, swinging it with all her strength. She wedged it into the crack and levered. The wood splintered and dented, but the door was thick and well made, and it was several loud minutes before the lock gave way. Bellis bayed in triumph as the door swung open, bleeding wood chips.

She threw open Doul's cupboards and rummaged under his bed, kicking at floorboards, searching for the statue. It was not in the weapons rack, or by the weird instrument he had said was a Ghosthead artifact. Minutes passed and kept her in agonies as she imagined the bloodshed that must be continuing outside.

Bellis found the statue suddenly, wrapped in its cloth at the bottom of a cylinder in which Doul stored arrows and javelins. With a sudden reverential fear, she cradled the heavy thing as she ran through the *Grand Easterly*'s empty corridors, finding her bearings, remembering where she herself had been held in jail, searching for the secure wing of the old ship, looking very much as if she held a baby.

The Lovers were gathered in a meeting room with those few of their advisors they could find. The fighting was not yet an hour old.

The Lover was yelling uselessly at the frightened scientists, telling them that Aum and Tearfly were *dead,* and that there was something *tearing their city apart,* and that they had to know what it *was,* to *fight it,* when the door flew open, its bolt disintegrating.

In the shocked silence, everyone in the room turned to face the Brucolac.

He stood in the doorway, breathing heavily, his jaw stretched wide and his teeth wicked. He tasted the air with his serpent's tongue and cast his yellow eyes over the assembled. Then he swept his arm quickly, encompassing everyone in the room except the Lovers.

"Leave," he whispered.

The exodus took only a few seconds, and the Lovers and the Brucolac were left alone.

They watched the vampir, not fearful but wary, as he stalked toward them.

"This ends," he whispered, "now."

Without speaking, the Lovers moved slowly apart, making themselves two targets. Each had drawn their pistols; neither spoke. The Brucolac made sure neither could get past him to the door.

"I don't want to rule," he said, and there seemed to be a quite genuine note of despair in his voice, "but this ends. This isn't a plan; it's fucking lunacy. I won't let you destroy this city." He drew back his lips, and he hunkered down to leap. The Lovers hefted their weapons, knowing that it was pointless. They stole a glance at each other but looked quickly back at the Brucolac, who was ready to take them.

"Stand down."

It was Uther Doul. He stood in the doorway, his sword glinting bone-white in his hand.

The Brucolac did not turn around. His eyes did not leave the Lovers.

"I know one thing about you, Uther," he said, "one thing at least. Armada's your home, and you need it. And I know that for all your stiff-faced shit about *loyalty*"—his voice became very hard for a second—"the city's the one thing you won't betray. And you know that *they* will destroy it."

He waited, as if for a response.

"Stand down," was all Doul said.

"If the fucking Scar *exists,*" whispered the Brucolac, still without turning, "and if they get us there and by some gods-fucked miracle we survive, then they'll still destroy us. We are not an expeditionary force; we are not on some fucking *quest*. This is a city, Uther. We live; we buy; we sell; we steal; we trade. We are a *port*. This is *not* about *adventures*." He turned and faced Uther Doul with his eyes caustic. "You know that. That's why you came here, dammit, Uther. Because you were sick of *adventures.*

"Let's have some rationality . . . We don't need the fucking beast. We don't need to haul arse across the world—we never have. The point's not that some fucker centuries ago built those chains; the point is that they were left *empty.* And if we survive this lunacy, as long as we're tethered to the bastard avanc these two will take us on another fucking voyage, and another, until we all die.

"That's not our logic, Doul; that's not how Armada works. That's not why we came here. I will not let them end this."

"Brucolac," Doul said, "you do not make this choice."

Slowly, the vampir's eyes widened, and hard lines broke his face.

"Gods . . . You know I'm right, Uther, don't you? I can fucking see it on you. So what are you doing?" he hissed. "What do you have planned?"

"Deadman," Doul spoke softly. "You *will* stand down."

"You think so, Liveman Doul?" the Brucolac whispered. His voice was coarse with swallowed rage. Long strings of slaver stretched down from his extended teeth. The bones in his hands cracked as he closed his fists. "You think so? You're a fine soldier, Liveman Doul. I've seen you fight. I've *fought beside you* . . . But I'm more than three centuries old, Doul. You take on a couple of my cadre, and you think you can face *me*? I killed my way to this city before you were born. I won my riding in war and fire. I've butchered things no liveman has even seen.

"I am the Brucolac, and your sword won't save you. You think you can face *me*?"

The corridors of the *Grand Easterly* were absolutely empty. Bellis wound through the passageways, down stairways toward the jailhouse, her footsteps coming back to her in echo.

Even the hallway where Fennec was imprisoned was deserted, its guards summoned to defend Garwater like all the others. That was the bargain, Bellis understood suddenly. That was the deal. These empty corridors were what the Brucolac had delivered to the intruders.

Only the two thaumaturges outside Fennec's cell had been left, and they were dead. Blood was still slicking across the floor as Bellis approached the corpses. The man had been attempting some hex, and little arcs of energy spat and dissipated like static from his fingers, which spasmed as his nerves died. The woman was next to him, splayed and opened.

Bellis was clumsy with fear, which welled up like vomit in her. She hovered outside the cell, standing in the blood, her hand poised to open the door, held back by terror. She battled with herself, utterly unsure of what to do.

Just throw it in there, a part of her said. *Just leave it by the door, just run, just get out.* And at that second there was a scream from inside the room, a dreadful panicked noise all full of terror. Bellis echoed it, crying out in horror, and she threw open the door and stepped in.

"It's here!" she screamed, ripping the cloth from the hideous statue and holding it like an offering. *"Stop! I've got it here. Stop! Take it; you can take it and go!"*

At the far side of the room, separated from her by the bars, Silas Fennec was crawling backward, screaming again, driving himself into a corner of his cell. He did not even look at her. He was scrabbling like a child, gazing in a stupefaction of terror at what had come for him.

With a horrible slowness, turning her head through thick air, Bellis followed his line of vision, and with a spasm of cold shock that made her stumble, she saw the grindylow.

There were three. They were staring at her.

They jutted prognathous jaws, their bulging teeth frozen in meaningless grimaces, massive eyes absolutely dark and un-blinking. Their arms and chests were humanoid, tightly ridged with muscles and stretched skin, grey-green and black, shiny as if with mucus. And narrowing at the waist, the grindylow bodies extended like enormous eels into flat tails several times longer than their torsos.

The grindylow swam in the air. They flickered, sending quick S-curves down the lengths of their extended tails, rippling them liquidly. They moved their arms in a random dance, like sub-merged swimmers controlling their buoyancy, clenching and un-clenching their webbed claws.

They were absolutely quiet. Even with their hideous faces turned to her, Bellis was wooed by their languid, constant, silent motion. Their bodies were level with hers as their tails eddied in the air, suspending them above the floor.

One of them was adorned with a mass of necklaces in stone and bone. It was streaked with human blood.

Oh gods and Jabber look at you, thought Bellis in a kind of frantic croon. *Look at you. You've come so fucking far . . .*

The grindylow waited.

"Here . . ." Bellis' voice was spastic with fear. She held out the statuette to them, gripping it carefully, scared that it would slip from her violently shaking hands. "I have it for you here," she whispered. "I brought it. So you can leave now. You can go."

Cold and quiet as abyssal fish, the grindylow merely watched her, flicking their tails.

"Please take it," she said. "Please, I brought what was stolen from you. Take it, and . . . you can leave. Back to The Gengris." *Leave us alone,* she prayed. *Leave us be.* The statue was heavy in her outstretched hands.

With a swift flash of his tail, the necklaced grindylow swam closer to her through the air, close enough to touch.

Bellis flinched violently as Silas Fennec screamed at her, *"Bellis get out!"*

The grindylow twisted its head toward her, quizzical, the blood that fouled it running in all directions across its skin, against gravity. With a languid yawn it opened its jaws.

Bellis flinched, let out a cry.

But from within its throat came a deep, breathy cough. Beadlets of blood from its teeth spattered the statue that Bellis held. Then another cough, and another, in careful rhythm: *uh . . . uh . . . uh.*

The grindylow was laughing.

A horrible, incompetent parody of human laughter.

The grindylow stared at her, unblinking, as she lowered her quivering hands. It clenched its teeth with a stone sound, then opened them again, and with its mouth held open and still, its throat flexing with the precision of human lips, it spoke.

"You think this?" the voice whispered, without nuance or intonation. *"You woman think this is what was taken? For this you woman think we cross a world?*

"We siblings cross from the dark cold of the lake, from pabulum towers and the vats, the algae palace, from The Gengris. We track this place across two four eight many thousands miles, many thousands. Tired *and hungry and very angry. Many months. We siblings sit and wait under your place, and hunt, and*

at last find word, always looking for this man. This robberman, thief. For this?"

The grindylow began to ebb back and forth in front of Bellis, watching her, still pointing at the figurine.

"For this you think we came? This stone thing? Our magus fin? Like primitives you think we abase before gods carved in rock? For hocus-pocus in trinkets?"

The grindylow snatched out, and Bellis gasped and pulled back her hand, letting go of the statue as if it were hot, and the grindylow caught it before it had begun to fall. It hefted the rock figure, holding it up to its face. It stroked its cheek with the filigree of skin.

"There is essence here, but still, for this?" The throat gasped. *"You think we are children, we siblings, to cross the world for a puissant toy?"*

With a long, exaggerated, slowed-down motion, the grindylow swung its arm in a great arc, curling the figurine through the air with a dramatic, petulant movement, releasing it. It must have been traveling very fast, but Bellis could see it clearly as it spun toward the bars, its arms tucked tight around a coiled-up tail, exquisitely and unpleasantly rendered, its gross mouth puckered and ready, its one eye glinting at her with cold humor.

The figurine hit the iron with a massive sound and broke apart.

Shards scattered, and cold drops of something like oil.

Bellis was stunned. She watched the particles settle and felt something in the aether resonate and go out.

In the middle of the floor, surrounded by stone dust and gelatinous residue, was a sliver of flesh. The magus fin, looking like some rotten wrinkled fillet.

The grindylow ignored it, and fluttered their tails, and approached Silas Fennec behind his bars.

"We have found what was stolen from us," the grindylow whispered. And then it moved with a strange violence, wriggling through air as if the air fought back, and reaching up, it parted the bars as if they were waterweed, pulling them apart so that it seemed they might tear into stringy fronds. But they held; they oozed back and were solid and upright once more, and the grindylow had passed through them to the other side.

It hovered quite still over Silas Fennec, and he flailed in its shadow.

Bellis could not watch Fennec's degradation, see him so stripped. She could not have imagined that he could be so afraid.

"We have what was taken," the grindylow murmured, and it pulled back knife-sharp fingers and stabbed them down, and when she did not hear a cry or some wet sound Bellis opened her eyes again and saw that the grindylow had rummaged in the rags that lay on the floor like castoff skins, and from them had pulled Silas Fennec's notebook.

Bellis remembered it well: black-bound and thick, distended with inserted papers. She recalled its reams of nebulous jottings, heliotypes and inexpert sketches, notes, questions, and mementos.

The grindylow turned slowly through the pages. Periodically it would turn and hold up a page to the bars, showing Bellis something that told her nothing.

"The salp vats. The weapon farms. The castle. Our anatomy. A gazetteer of the second city. And see here," it said with opaque triumph, *"coastline maps. The mountains between the ocean and the Cold Claw Sea. Where our placements are. Where there are fissures, where the rock is weakest."* And something moved in Bellis' mind: the first stirrings of comprehension.

"Would you tell your masters where is best for their excavations, robberman?" it asked. Cradling the stump of his arm, Fennec tried to move further away.

Bellis could see the page the grindylow had opened. She had seen it before, in her room, and in Croom Park, months before. Rough scribbles suggesting engines, red lines of force and striae of rock types crosshatched in ink. The hidden positions of The Gengris on the Cold Claw side; the paradoses and defenses; the traps.

Understanding was uncoiling in Bellis like cold water. She remembered the conversations she had had with Fennec, when they had first grown close. She remembered his stories, the extraordinary tales of his travels. She remembered what he had said.

If you can get across the Cold Claws, if you can reach the islands and the far shores, if you can trek across those miles and miles of punitive geography, to the Shatterjack Mines and Hinter, to those hungry trade partners and those untouched miles of resources, then you are made. But most can't make it, because the route is so terrible; because you can't come at it from the

south, because The Gengris are in charge of the southern tip of
the Cold Claw Sea and won't let outsiders pass.

But what if you could *reach it from the south, directly,* Bellis
thought, *coming straight? Not into some tumbling fucked-up
overland caravan shedding its goods and machines and crews
like spoor across the mountains and the grasslands, but by ship.
What if you could sail from New Crobuzon, safely past The Gengris in safety, and straight up to the north?*

"My good gods," she murmured, and stared at Fennec. "A
canal. They're planning a canal."

It made such sense. The rock ridge between the freshwater of the
Cold Claw Sea and the Swollen Ocean's brine was only thirty,
forty miles wide in places, its ridges wrinkled with valleys. Bellis could picture the work. A prodigious project, true, but what a
prize.

Ships sail north from Iron Bay, skirting the harsh coastline of
Lubbock Scrub and the Bezheks, then out to sea to avoid the ruins and residuum of Torque by Suroch, skirting the straits between the Pirate Islands and the mainland; and then a week's
sailing north of New Crobuzon, the flint spines that shield the
Cold Claw Sea would rise to port, to the west.

But no longer impenetrable. Breached.

A wide runnel scored at the bottom of a strath. Tall ships
and steamers passing sedately between overhangs and scree
landscapes.

And there would be locks. Huge locks segmenting the canal,
raising the brackish water in stages, massive wooden doors and
careful engineering, bringing the ships closer to the Cold Claws,
step by ponderous step. They would ascend the strata of the
canal while the ocean barnacles clinging to their hull grew weak
and died as the water lost its salt.

Until—what?

Out.

The rock monoliths part before the ships, and the canal bleeds
into the deep waters of the freshwater sea: the Cold Claw Sea.

Perhaps Fennec's papers, his researches, planned for a passage that emerged north of The Gengris and its wider borders.
Perhaps the traders and industrialists and soldiers of New Crobuzon could ignore the grindylow, sail blithely past them to the

pickings beyond, leaving them raging, pathetic and ignored, in their little corner to the south.

But surely that was not enough. Fennec's book contained too many details, assiduously and covertly collected, of grindylow strategies, weapons, and plans. Perhaps any such incursion by New Crobuzon would necessitate war, and Fennec had gathered the information to ensure that his paymasters would win it.

A constellation of places that were so far little more than myth would open to New Crobuzon. With trade, colonies, and all that they entailed. Bellis remembered the stories she had heard about Nova Esperium, the riches and the brutality.

Whatever happened, the grindylow monopoly on terror in the Cold Claw Sea would be broken. New Crobuzon's canal would open up a free market in power—control of which only New Crobuzon could possibly win.

Bellis shook her head, astonished. This hadn't been some dramatic, romantic escapade. Fennec's theft had been planned carefully, an analysis of costs and difficulties carried out by an expert. And how much more sense this made of the grindylow. They were not like the vengeful bugaboos of the stories she had read to Shekel, chasing a symbol. Their motivations were clear. They were protecting the source of all their power, their interests, and existence.

"The statue was just a trinket, wasn't it?" Bellis said, and even in his fear Fennec met her eyes, for a second. "A bonus just for you? That wasn't why New Crobuzon sent you there, or why the grindylow came.

"You were doing a *feasibility study* . . ."

He could have sent it home. He could have hidden his papers in the message he had given Bellis, to courier for him like a fool, but then, of course, his masters would not have come to rescue him. So he had held on to his research, knowing what it was worth, knowing that for those scrawls New Crobuzon would send its navy across the world.

But they had failed to recover him, or his precious notes. There would be no canal, thought Bellis, watching the grindylow. Not now.

Fennec was jabbering. For a moment Bellis thought he was having a fit and venting random sounds, but she realized that he was speaking in some attenuated, human version of the grindy-low tongue. He leaned back against the wall for strength and held forth with controlled panic. Pleading, Bellis supposed, for his life.

But the grindylow had what they wanted, and he had nothing to offer them.

The figure eddying before him in the cell raised its claws. It spoke, slowly and loudly, in its own language, and Silas Fennec let out a shriek.

Bellis felt the air beside her twitch, disturbed, as the other two grindylow wriggled their bodies, sending a ripple from their shoulders through their taut bellies and down their elongated tails. They moved with that same marine suddenness to the bars. Their leader moved his hands in brute arcana till the iron became flaccid again, and they squeezed through.

Fennec began to shriek louder as the three grindylow sur-rounded him.

With a horrible sense of nausea, Bellis was certain that she was about to see him butchered, and she heard herself protest weakly. *No more,* she thought.

But the grindylow reached out and gripped him, and he screamed and battered at them, but they plucked at him easily with their intricate cruel fingers and, linking together in an un-settling, ill-defined morass, the three deepwater creatures locked him into a tangle of limbs, and began to rise.

They were suspended above the floor. Fennec's shrieks were muting. His feet did not touch the ground. He was being borne up, across the little cell, swaddled in limbs and thick eel tails.

The grindylow magus gripped the notebook hard in one hand, and with the other he reached out, for a moment releasing his grip on his companions and his captive, and gesticulated at the largest porthole that broke the wall of the little prison. She heard the bones around his neck rattle balefully.

As if it were liquid, as if it were a still pool into which some-one had slipped a stone, the glass in the porthole rippled, and Bellis realized what the grindylow was doing as the glass began to vein. She pulled herself from her daze—a torpor of disgust and shock and fear—and slipped in blood as she scrambled for the door.

She heard Fennec cry out once, and then a moist exhalation and the sound of wetness as the magus clamped his massive mouth over Fennec's, lacerating his face with sharp teeth but breathing air into him as the hexed glass burst like a boil and the sea blasted into the room.

In seconds the room was inches deep, and the cannoning water did not slow. Bellis' fingers were numb as she pulled at the door handle, the water pushing against the hatch. She hauled it open and turned for half a second at the threshold, her skirt wrapping her wetly, cold water bleeding torrentially past her feet into the corridor and chilling her.

The grindylow floated, poised, in this gush of ocean. Fennec's hands extruded from their tight-cloyed mass, clenching and unclenching. As the water level grew higher beneath them, with stunning speed the grindylow triumvirate moved together in the air, congealing tightly, impossibly tightly, until with a perfectly timed spasm of their tails they jetted for the porthole, passing through it without pause, and on, and out, taking Fennec away, carrying what was stolen from them—information, secrets—into the sea.

As Bellis spun the lock on the door, sealing off that ruptured room, the corridor around her swilled with water. It swept in a thin layer back and forth, illustrating all the *Grand Easterly*'s movements.

She leaned back, sat back, her thighs and arse splashing down, feeling nothing as a wave of trembling took her over. She did not weep, but as the adrenaline dissipated through her body, she let out the most bestial croaking cries, absolutely without control, retching as all the pent-up fear in her spewed out.

She sat like that for a long time.

Somewhere out in the night, in the cold and the dark of deep water, was Silas Fennec. Borne away. For interrogation or unthinkable punishment. Alive.

It took Bellis a long time to retrace her steps, up out of the *Grand Easterly*'s jailhouse cellars. She moved doggedly, her long salt-wet skirt abrading her skin. Assiduously, she thought of nothing. She had never been so tired, or cold.

When finally she emerged into the night air, below the gently swinging old rigging and the enormous iron masts, she felt a drab surprise that everything was still as it had been, that everything was still there.

She was alone. The sound of shouts and fire could still be heard, but were very distant to her now.

Breathing hard and walking slowly, Bellis made her way to the boat's edge and leaned her head against the rail, pushing it against her cheek, closing her eyes. When she looked up, she realized that she was watching the *Hoddling*. The outlines of the fat ship came into slow focus. Its fires had gone out.

There were no jets of weird energy emitted from behind its walls. There were no deep-sea monstrosities guarding it like a moat. There were men and women on its decks, moving without urgency, but with exhaustion and despondency.

She saw the waves nodding against the sides of the city, and with a sensitivity that had grown inside her without her knowing it, Bellis became aware that Armada was moving again.

Very slowly, as yet no faster than it had when the masses of tugs had hauled it. But it was being borne forward again. The avanc was moving, the pain of its wound receding.

The grindylow had gone.

(*And Silas is alive.*)

Walking forward, clutching the rail, Bellis headed toward the *Grand Easterly*'s great prow, and as she rounded a low set of cabins, she heard sounds. There were people ahead of her.

She gazed out over Garwater and Dry Fall and Jhour and Booktown. The sounds of the fighting were subdued. She could no longer hear the great massed movement of crowds, the constant drum of gunshots. Only a few ragged shouts and isolated attacks.

The war was dying. The mutiny was over.

She heard no declamations of revolt or stability; there was nothing around her that might hint at which side had won. And yet somehow when she rounded the last wall and witnessed the scene on the *Grand Easterly*'s foredeck, she felt no surprise.

Around the edges of the deck stood grim-faced men and women of all races, carved and bloodied. They carried their weapons drawn.

Before them lay a mass of corpses. Many were shattered, their chests torn open and burned dry or emptied out. Most had been decapitated; heads littered the charnel ground randomly, all gaping, fanged, and snake-tongued.

The vampir. Tens of them. Beaten. Executed and dispatched.

Overpowered when the tide turned, when their mysterious allies had disappeared and the spontaneous small riots supporting them had petered out in confusion. It was a doomed adventure without the people of their own riding behind them, without a movement of revolt. Eventually the Garwater fighters had lost their fear, and terrorism could not win once the real terror went.

There was a weak movement above her. Looking up at the foremost of the *Grand Easterly*'s masts, Bellis widened her eyes in shock. And she thought, *Oh . . . so that was when it was over.*

That was when the Dry Fall cadre lost. After that, they couldn't win. With that macabre pennant swinging there, the fear they spread must have faded like an echo.

Ten feet up, lashed cruciform to a crossbar, his heels and hands tied tightly with great thick skeins of rope, his snarls pathetic, tongue lolling like a dead animal's, the blood that discolored his teeth and lips his own, was the Brucolac.

CHAPTER FORTY-FIVE

When day broke, the Brucolac found the strength to scream.

The sun bleached him. He closed his eyes and shook his head pointlessly, trying to get his eyes out of the light. His skin began to welt, as if some punishing chymical had been poured on him. His grave-pale face reddened, blistering, suppurating in the daylight.

He flopped with ugly motion, like a sea-thing beached. His strength leached from him, and he emitted little gasps of pain.

The sun might not kill him for some time, strong as he was: but it disabled him, and more than anything it hurt mercilessly. Two hours after dawn he was too groggy to make a sound. His spittle and venom drooled from him, denaturing.

The sunlight scalded the flesh of his slaughtered cadre, too. As the day crawled on, the tens of frozen bodies became blebbed and misshapen. At dusk, they were swept together and tipped into the sea.

Darkness came like unguent to the Brucolac. The pain began very slowly to bleed from him, and he cracked open his rheum- and pus-locked eyes. His body began to repair, but the sun's depredations were severe, and it was not till nearly midnight that he found the strength to speak.

His ruined croaking was ignored. He was not tended; he was not fed. Cramp and pain ossified his limbs. Throughout the night he bayed for help or mercy; he tried to issue threats. But his words broke down into a despairing animal wail as the hours sluggishly passed and he saw the darkness diluting in the east.

He had only started to heal. His wounds were still raw when the sun reached out and probed them with its sadistic fingers as, like a cog in some remorseless engine, the day came round again.

The clean-up began quietly. Crews entered the cooling *Hoddling* and gauged the damage, trying to see how much could be salvaged.

Whole rooms and corridors had been reshaped by the heat, their edges made fluid. There were many bodies: some pristine, some variously disturbed.

Across Garwater, and in the fringes of its neighboring ridings, the conflict was manifest in broken glass and bullet holes, and bloodstains in the city's gutters. What rubble there was was swept up and taken to foundries and factories, to be broken down or resmelted.

Garwater loyalists patrolled the streets. Bask and Curhouse ridings were quiet. Their rulers had known nothing of the revolt, and they had waited, paralyzed, watching it, carefully gauging the forces, ready to join against a defeated Garwater. But the vampir had been defeated. Their rulers kept themselves low, cowed by the Lovers. Quiescent.

The general of Shaddler was dead, killed by the vampir who had held him hostage, acting in their panic when they heard their ruler was captured. They had been killed in turn, at great cost to the scabmettlers. The walls of Barrow Hall were disfigured with great streaking sculptures in dark red, where scabmettler blood had spattered.

No one knew exactly how many vampir had made up the Bru- colac's cadre, and no one was exactly sure how many had been killed. Without question, some had survived. Defeated, they must have gone underground, become nondescript new citizens. Squatting in ruins, lodging in flophouses. Invisible.

They would have to be careful when they fed. They would have to be selective, and restrained, and quite brutal—they could leave no prey alive. Because when they were found—and they would be found, the Garwater crews swore implacably—they would be killed.

The fear of them was gone.

And meanwhile the arch traitor, the Brucolac himself, was stretched out on his metal cross, slowly scorching and starving to death.

The avanc had picked up its stupid, ponderous progress. But it remained slow, and its pace was not so steady. It swam, and dragged the city, and sped up and slowed, and never achieved the speed it had previously reached.

As the hours and days passed, the navigators became convinced that its wounds, sustained in mysterious circumstances known only to a small clutch of Armadans, were not healing. It was bleeding, weakening, still.

No revenge was taken against the citizens of Dry Fall, whom the Lovers announced curtly to be innocent of their ruler's guilt. There was even amnesty for those who had rioted. It was a chaotic time, the Lovers ruled, and no one had known what was happening; there was confusion. This was a time to bring the city together, they said, and blame was not appropriate.

Still, the patrols of Garwater's yeomanry and armed citizens were kept largest and best-armed in Dry Fall. The Dry Fallen watched them resentfully, staring from doorways, hiding bruises and wounds sustained that night, not trusting the Lovers' mercy.

Like smoke from the riots' fires, something had spread over the city that night, and it remained: a traumatizing uncertainty, a rancor. And even many of those who had fought hard to repulse the Brucolac were touched by it.

Blood, violence, and fear—they seemed the legacy of the Lovers' projects. After centuries of peace, Armada had been twice to war in less than thirty days—once with itself. Armada's intricacies of diplomacy had collapsed under the Lovers' fervor, the networks of obligations and interests splitting, tearing the city apart.

The Lovers were subordinating everything to their search for the abstract power of the Scar. This was a break with Armada's mercantile venality: that kind of intrepidity, that kind of voyage, was governed by an other, older logic. The citizens of Armada were pirates, and as their understanding of the Lovers' project grew, so did their alienation. The Lovers were not proposing thievery or usury, nor even a tactic for survival. This was something very different.

While Armada was riding high, while its power was growing and feat after incredible feat was performed, the Lovers had buoyed up the citizens with their rhetoric and zeal.

When the *Sorghum* had been stolen, it was the greatest military feat of Armada's recent history, and everyone could see that it gave the city power, that their ships and engines were better fueled. When the avanc had been raised, the Lovers had spoken of the ancient chains; of fulfilling Armada's secret, historic mission; of the swift sailing from port to port that was now a possibility; of the quick, worldwide search for booty.

But now all that was shown to be deceit. The purpose instead was this opaque quest. And though there were still thousands of Armadans excited by what they undertook, there were thousands more who no longer cared, and a growing number who felt duped.

And with the avanc so weak—everyone could tell—even the real purpose of all this, the search for the Scar, might come to nothing. If the avanc kept slowing, who knew what might happen?

In the aftermath of the Brucolac's mutiny, and the deaths and broken trust that came out of it, morale in Armada was low and worsening. The loyal Garwater patrols felt the growing hostility, the shapeless anger—even in Garwater.

Hundreds of Armadans were dead. Torn open, caught in crossfires, bitten and paralyzed and drained by the vampir, crushed by collapsing architecture, burned in fires, beaten to death. It was far fewer than had been killed in the battle against New Crobuzon, but the trauma of these deaths was vastly larger. This had been a civil war; these people had been killed by their own. People were numbed and blasted by it.

There were those who had seen glimpses of the grindylow and

who realized that there was no way the Brucolac could ever have stopped the avanc moving, and no way he could have warped reality with those thaumaturgic blasts. But in the whole of Armada, only a handful knew the truth of the deal that had been struck. For the most part people made vague, curt references to weird vampir magic and did not press discussion further.

The grindylow had come and gone, and of those few who had seen them, almost no one knew what they had been. Their presence remained inexplicable and overshadowed by the civil war.

Hundreds of Armadans were dead, killed by their own.

Krüach Aum was dead. Bellis did not mourn him—he had unsettled her with his sociopathic calm and his brain like a difference engine—but she felt a sense of pathos at his murder.

Escapee from a prison island locked down by its own history. Stepping out into the strangest city of Bas-Lag, used as ruthlessly as he had previously been used by the Kettai authorities, killed investigating the creature he had helped conjure. What a weird, etiolated life.

Johannes Tearfly was dead. It was a surprise to Bellis how that affected her. She was truly sad, truly sorry that he was gone. She remembered him with a catch in her throat. The manner of his death was unthinkable—so fearful it must have been, so dark and cold, so claustrophobic, so far below the world. She remembered him preparing to descend, all excitement and fascination. It had been impressive, for a coward.

Shekel was dead.

That shattered her.

In the day after the mutiny, when her legs had strengthened enough to walk, she had wandered random and dumb through the battle sites.

There was nothing to stop her shuffling through scenes of war, past the cadavers, trailing blood on her shoes.

On one of the trawlers by the ruined *Hoddling,* in the shadow of a wooden warehouse that belled over gory cobblestones, Bellis found Tanner Sack. She saw him bent double, by a wall. Beside him was Angevine, the Remade woman, tears cutting the filth on her face.

Bellis realized then, but she could not stop herself running forward with her hands over her mouth, wincing at Tanner

Sack's grief. As she had known it would be, the thing on his lap was Shekel's corpse. Eviscerated. He looked dumbstruck, astonished at his own state.

She had to walk through her memories of him. She hated it. She hated the sadness. She hated the misery, the *astonishment* she felt when she thought of him dead. Bellis had liked the boy a great deal.

More than anything she hated the guilt. She was awash in it. She had used him. Without ill-feeling, of course, but still she had used him. She was aware in a hateful, inchoate way that had it not been for things she had done, Shekel would be alive. Had she not taken the book from him and used it; had she only thrown the fucking thing away.

Aum was dead, Johannes was dead, Shekel was dead.

(*Silas Fennec is alive.*)

Much later, Bellis found Carrianne wandering stunned through the streets around her house. She had hidden throughout the night, with her door locked, and had emerged to discover herself a citizen of a non-riding.

She could not believe the Brucolac had tried to take control, and she could not believe that he had been captured. She was as confused as a child, watching events she did not understand.

Bellis could not tell Carrianne anything about what she herself had done and seen in the bottom of the *Grand Easterly*. All she told her was that Shekel had died.

They went together to see the Lovers speak.

It was two days since the mutiny, and Garwater's rulers called a public rally on the *Grand Easterly*'s deck. At first Carrianne said she would not go. She had heard what had been done to the Brucolac, and she said she would not see him like that. It was a violence he did not deserve. Whatever he had done, she insisted, he did not deserve that.

But finally it was not hard for Bellis to persuade her. Carrianne had to come—she had to hear. The Lovers knew what was at stake; the Lovers knew what was happening in their city. This was their attempt to regain control.

The foredeck was very full: men and women massed in ranks, bruised and wounded, every one haggard and unsmiling, waiting.

Above them all, the Brucolac gibbered and whined thinly in the sun. His skin was burn-scarred and stained as a map.

When Carrianne saw him she cried out in disgust and unhappiness, and she turned her head away and told Bellis tersely that she would leave. But after a minute she glanced back at him. She could not take seriously the notion that the emaciated, festering figure drooling and champing slack jaws was the Brucolac. She could look up at the jabbering husk with nothing but pity.

The Lovers stood on a platform and addressed the crowd, with Uther Doul beside them. They looked careworn and terribly tired, and the assembled citizens stared up at them with a weird spirit of respect and challenge.

So, they said in their stares. *Tell us. Convince us all over again. Tell us that this is worth it.*

And they did an impressive job. Bellis listened and watched the mood soften.

The Lovers were clever. They did not start with bombast, or claims of power and prowess that they had repelled the threat from traitors.

"Many of those who are dead," the Lover began, "many who *our fighters killed* . . . were loyal. They were good people doing what they were sure was right for our city." And in that way, respectfully and mindful of the tragedy, he continued.

They spoke in turns, imploring those who were gathered not to lose heart now. "We are very close," the Lover said, and an edge of excitement crept into her voice. Very close to powers that could never have been imagined before. Very close to making Armada truly great, a dynamo powered by potentiality, able to do anything—able to do contradictory things at once.

"Mutiny is not the way," said the Lover. "If this project is not all of ours, it cannot go ahead." *You brought us here,* she told the crowd. *This is your doing, and it is great work.*

This was not any time for division, the Lovers said, and unity meant unity in purpose, and the purpose of the moment was to find the Scar.

There would be rewards. It would be so fantastically, incredibly worthwhile.

The rhetoric grew stronger as their overlapping speech progressed. From the eulogies to the dead, the crowd's children were invoked—skillfully, with promises about what their young lives, their city could be like, after it had mined possibilities from the Scar.

It was a good speech, sensitive and sincere. The Lovers' fascination with the Scar was affecting. And when the speech was done the crowd's respect, though subdued, was distinct and meant. The mood had lifted, a very little. The Lovers had won a reprieve—the argument was not finished.

All they have to do is keep the naysayers talking, thought Bellis. *We can't be so far from the Scar now. If they're right, if it exists, we must be going to get there soon.*

Standing a little behind the Lovers, Uther Doul met her eye. She realized for the first time what she had done the night of the mutiny, what she had risked. She had broken into his room and stolen an alien artifact, then delivered it to the marauders. But she was simply too tired of fear to feel it now.

When the talk was done, and as the crowd dissipated, Doul crossed the deck and stood still before Bellis, without sign of rancor or friendship.

"What happened?" he said softly. "It was you, in my room. You took it. I found the shards, at the bottom of the jail. The magus fin was there, rotting. I burned it. So that wasn't what they wanted, after all?"

Bellis shook her head.

"They came," she said, "but not for that. I thought it was, which is why . . . I'm sorry about your door. I was trying to get rid of them. They said they'd leave when they had what was taken from them. But that wasn't what they wanted. It was they who . . . Fennec . . ."

Doul nodded.

"He's alive," Bellis whispered, wondering whether that was still true.

Doul's eyes flashed wide for a moment.

Bellis waited. She wondered with tired nervousness what he would do. There were many things he could punish her for. She had lost Armada the grindylow figurine, for nothing at all. Needlessly. Or was there a trace of the old closeness in him?

But there seemed nothing but a flatness, a resignation in his manner, and Bellis was not surprised when finally he nodded and turned from her, walked back across the deck. She felt deflated, watching him. *What do the Lovers think of that?* she wondered. She could not imagine the Lovers giving up the magus fin without some rage. *Don't they care?*

Do they even know? she thought suddenly. *And if they know it's gone, do they know it was me?*

That night, Tanner Sack came to her door. She was astonished.

He stood on her doorstep, staring at her with eyes so bloodshot, in skin so grey, he looked like a junkie. He stared at her with dislike for several silent seconds, then pushed a sheaf of papers at her.

"Take these," he said. They were used and reused scraps on which she recognized Shekel's enthusiastic script. Lists of words he had found, that he had seen and wanted to remember, to cross-reference, to look for in the storybooks he pillaged.

"You taught the boy to read," Tanner said, "and he loved that." He kept his eyes on hers and his face expressionless. "You might want to keep some of these, to remember him by."

Bellis was shocked and embarrassed. She was not constructed that way. It was absolutely against her instincts to accumulate mawkish, morbid remembrances of the dead. Not even when her mother or father had died, and certainly not at the death of this child she had barely known, no matter how she felt his loss.

She almost refused the papers. She almost framed some cant about not deserving them—*as if one could deserve these ragged scraps!*—but two things stopped her.

One was guilt. *Don't run from it, you coward,* she thought. She would not allow herself to escape it. Her personal taste in death, she told herself, was not the issue—how convenient it would be for that to let her reject these evidences. And besides her guilt was her respect for Tanner Sack.

He stood there, holding out these things that must be precious to him, offering them to someone who had caused him so much pain. And not because they shared some spurious community of grief. He offered the papers to her because he was a good man, and he imagined that she had lost Shekel, too.

Shamed, she took them, and nodded thanks to him.

"One more thing," Tanner said. "We bury him tomorrow." His voice skipped only a moment on the word *bury.* "In Croom Park."

"How . . . ?" Bellis began, surprised. Armadans gave their dead sea burials. Tanner gesticulated the question away.

"Shek weren't a . . . a sea animal at heart," he said carefully. "He was a *city* boy more than anything, and I suppose there are traditions I thought I'd left . . . I want to know where he is. When they told me I couldn't do it, I told them to try and stop me."

"Tanner Sack," she said as he turned to go, "why Croom Park?"

"You told him about it one time," he said. "And he went to see for himself and he loved it. I think it reminded him of Rudewood."

Bellis cried when he had gone, could not stop herself. She told herself furiously that it was for the last time.

It was a brief service, clumsy and poignant. A mongrel of theology, gods of New Crobuzon and Armada asked humbly to look after Shekel's soul.

No one was sure what gods, if any, Shekel had respected.

Bellis brought flowers, stolen from the colorful beds elsewhere in the park.

The city was dragged on, east-northeast, decelerating very gradually as the avanc slowed. No one knew how badly it was wounded. They would not risk sending another crew down.

In the days after the war, and especially after Shekel's funeral, Bellis felt unable to focus. She spent much of her time with Carrianne, who was as subdued as she, and who refused even to discuss where the city was going. It was hard to concentrate on the journey, and impossible to imagine what would happen when they arrived.

If the Garwater scholars were correct, the city was drawing close. Perhaps two weeks, perhaps one; that was what was whispered. A few days more until Armada reached the wound in this empty sea; and then the hidden engines and arcane science would be let loose, and all the possibilities that swarmed around the Scar would be mined.

The air was tense with expectancy, with fear.

When Bellis opened her eyes in the morning, sometimes she felt that the aether bristled, as if forces she did not understand coursed around her. Strange rumors began to spread.

First it was the gamblers, the cardsharps in the late-night games at Thee-And-Thine. There were stories of hands changing in the instant they were raised, the colored costumes of the suits shimmering like kaleidoscopes, dimly glimpsed for the tiniest moment, freezing into a configuration *after* they had been dealt.

There were stories of intrusive spirits, browners or kelkin, fleeting invisibly through the city, moving things. Objects put down were discovered again inches from their place—in places where they might have been left, but had not been. Things that were dropped broke and then were not broken, and perhaps had not been dropped but waited on the side.

The Scar, Bellis thought with dull wonder. *It's bleeding.*

The sea and sky became very suddenly dangerous. Rain clouds appeared and raged and very suddenly went again, not quite hitting the city, skirting it. The avanc dragged Armada through violent patches, where the waves were suddenly choppy and high, in a tightly circumscribed area, with gentle waters clearly visible to either side.

Tanner no longer swam, but only dipped himself daily. He was afraid to immerse himself for long. The sounds and lights from beneath the water were strong enough now that even those on the city above could hear and see them—ejections from unseen things.

Sometimes clots of the sentient weed passed by Armada, and sometimes there were other shapes on the waves—they moved and could not easily be identified, that looked at once organic, random, and made.

Still the Brucolac floundered and did not die. The deck below him was stained with his emissions.

Walking the decks and corridors of the *Grand Easterly,* over the quiet city noise Bellis heard faint and cryptic music. It was hard to trace, evanescing across frequencies, audible at random moments and places. She strained and made it out in snatches. It was ugly and uncanny: a web of halftones and minor chords, mutating rhythms. A dirge overlaid with plucked strings. On the second night she heard it, she was sure that it came from Uther Doul's room.

The flotsam, the strange currents in the sea, and odd events in Armada grew more frequent and powerful as the avanc plowed on. When, on the fifth morning after the mutiny, something was seen bobbing within two miles of the city, no one was surprised.

But when telescopes were turned to it, a great screaming cacophony of excitement began. The lookouts on the *Grand Easterly* barked for people's attention and ran madly from room to room, looking for the Lovers.

Word swept the city with startling rapidity through every riding, and a great rush of citizens congregated in Jhour's aft edge. A small aerostat set out overhead, over the treacherous currents, toward the speck that eddied closer and closer to the city. Those in the crowd were gazing out at it, sharing their telescopes and jabbering in incredulity as its outlines became clear.

Clinging to a ragged raft of wood and ocher canvas, staring up exhaustedly at his home, was Hedrigall the cactus-man, the renegade.

"Bring him here!" "What the fuck happened?" "Where'd you *go*, Hed? Where've you *been*?" "Bring him the hell *here*!"

As soon as it was obvious that the airship that had gone to fetch him was returning to the *Grand Easterly,* there were angry cries. Wedges of people tried to run from whatever vessel they were on, through the obstructed streets, to intercept the dirigible. Crowds collided chaotically.

Bellis had been watching from her window, her heart hammering with foreboding. She joined the rush toward the flagship, impelled by motivations she did not fully understand. Bellis reached the foredeck of the steamer before the airship had come low enough for anyone within to disembark. A crowd of loyalists were waiting, surrounding Uther Doul and the Lovers.

Bellis joined the growing crowd, who jostled and pushed at the yeomanry, trying to see the returned man.

"Hedrigall!" they shouted. "What the fuck happened?"

There was a roar as he stepped down, gaunt and exhausted, but he was quickly enveloped in armed men. The little group began to approach the doorways to the lower decks, with Doul and the Lovers at its head.

"Tell us!" The shouts were insistent and turning ugly. "He's one of us; bring him back." The guards were nervous, drawing their flintlocks as the Armadans pressed in on them. Bellis saw Angevine and Tanner Sack at the front of the crowd.

Hedrigall's head was visible, bowed and sun-bleached, his spines withered and snapped. He looked around him at the con-

gregated citizens, staring and reaching out for him, calling
solicitous, and he drew back his head and began to howl.

"How are you all here?" he bellowed. *"You're dead. I saw
every one of you die . . ."*

There was a shocked silence, and then a cacophony. The
throng began to push in again. The yeomanry shoved them back.
The masses grew hushed and menacing.

Bellis watched Uther Doul draw the Lovers aside and whisper
to them sharply, then indicate the door. The Lover nodded, then
stepped forward with his hands outstretched.

"Armadans," he shouted, "for gods' sakes *wait*." He sounded
sincerely angry. Behind him, Hedrigall began to shout again, as
if in a fever, *You're dead, you're all dead,* and he was bundled
back toward the door, the yeomen hissing as his thorns pierced
their skins. "None of us know what's happened here," the Lover
said. "But *look* at him, by Croom. He's a wreck; he's ill. We're
taking him below, to our own berth, away from everything, for
him to rest, to recover."

Blazing with displeasure, he moved back, toward where
Hedrigall lolled in yeomen's arms and Uther Doul swept his eyes
quick and hard over the crowd.

"It ain't right," someone suddenly shouted, forcing his way
forward. It was Tanner Sack. "Hed!" he called. "He's my mate,
and Jabber knows what you're going to do to him."

There were shouts of agreement around him, but the crowd's
momentum was draining away, and though there were some
curses, no one tried to follow and intercept Hedrigall or the
Lovers. There was too much uncertainty.

Bellis realized that Uther Doul had found her in the crowd,
and was watching her carefully.

"It ain't *right*," yelled Tanner, veins protruding with rage as
the party entered the doors and the guards moved in behind
them. Uther Doul still did not move his eyes. Bellis could not
help but meet them, uncomfortable in his gaze. "He's my *mate*,"
said Tanner. "It's my *right*. It's my *right to hear what he has to
say . . .*"

And as he spoke, at that moment, something extraordinary
happened.

Bellis still met Doul's unshaking stare, and as Tanner claimed
his right to hear Hedrigall, Doul's eyes spasmed and opened
wide with an almost sexual intensity. Bellis watched, stunned, as

his head inclined a fraction of an inch, as if in invitation, or agreement.

He gazed at her even as his party entered the corridors, walking backward to join them, holding her attention, raising his eyebrows a tiny bit, suggestive, as he disappeared.

Oh my gods.

Bellis felt as if she had been punched hard in her solar plexus.

A great revelatory wave washed over her: a stunned appreciation, an insinuation of the layers and layers and *layers* of manipulation in which she was caught, frozen, maneuvered and exploited, used and supported and betrayed.

She still understood virtually nothing of what was happening around her, what was being done, what had been planned, and what was contingent.

But some things she knew, humbly and suddenly.

Her own place. So much, so many plans, so much effort had been expended to bring her to this place at this instant, to hear the words that she had heard. Everything came together here and now; everything coalesced and became clear.

And in her astonishment and awe, and in her humiliation, and despite her anger, feeling herself danced undignified as a marionette to her allotted mark, Bellis bowed her head and readied herself, knowing she had one more job to do, to effect a change she wanted, and knowing she would not spite herself for revenge, and that she would do it.

"Tanner," she said to him as he raged and cursed, arguing furiously, shouting against the majority, at those who told him he was overreacting, that the Lovers knew what they were doing.

He paused and stared at her in angry bemusement. She beckoned him.

"Tanner," she said, unheard by any but him. "I agree with you, Tanner," she whispered. "I think you have every right to hear what Hedrigall might say, down there in the Lovers' berth.

"Come with me."

It was not hard to find a way through empty hallways in the *Grand Easterly*. The loyal guards were stationed at points by which someone might make their way to the Lovers' quarters, down in the boat's low reaches. But only those corridors, and that was not where Bellis and Tanner were heading.

She took him down other passageways she had learned very well over the weeks of indulging what she could only think of as her perversion.

They passed storerooms and engines and armories. Walking quickly but openly, not like trespassers, Bellis led Tanner lower and lower, into a dimly lit zone.

She did not know it, but Bellis took Tanner close by the way to the rockmilk engines that were churning and whirring and sparking, driving the avanc on.

And eventually, in a dark and narrow passage where the walls were free of aging wallpaper and heliotypes and etchings, were lined instead with knotted pipework as intricate as veins, Bellis turned to Tanner Sack and gestured him to enter. She stood in the cramped and cosseted environs, turned her head to him, and kept him silent with a raised finger.

They stood without movement for some time, Tanner looking around him, at the ceiling at which Bellis stared, at Bellis herself.

When finally they heard the sound of a door opening and closing, it was so loud and flawless to the ear that Tanner stiffened violently. Bellis had never seen the room above, but she knew its echoes well. She knew where above her were chairs, and tables, and a bed. She followed the four sets of footsteps above with her stare—light, heavier, heavier, and massive and slow—as if she could see through the ceiling-floor the Lover, the Lover, Doul, and Hedrigall.

Tanner followed her example, his eyes widening. He and Bellis could trace the bodies above them. One was by the door; two ranged near the bed, sinking now into chairs; and the fourth, the big one, shuffled back and forth toward the far wall, locking his legs as the cactacae did in sleep or exhaustion, his weight driving down through the wood.

"So," said Uther Doul, his voice astonishingly clear. "Tell us, Hedrigall." He was hard. "Tell us why you ran. And how you ended back here again."

"Oh, *gods*." Hedrigall sounded drained and shattered. It was just barely his voice. Tanner shook his head in amazement.

"Gods, dear gods please don't start that again." Hedrigall

sounded as if he would cry. "I don't understand you. I've never run from Armada in my life. I never would. Who *are* you?" he screamed suddenly. "*What* are you? Am I in *hell*? *I saw you die* . . ."

"What's happened to him?" whispered Tanner, appalled.

"You're talking fucking dung, Hedrigall, you treacherous shit," the Lover exclaimed. "Look at me, you dog. You were scared, weren't you? Too frightened, so you patched up the *Arrogance* in secret and cut loose. Now, where did you go, and how did you get back here?"

"I've never betrayed Armada," Hedrigall shouted, "and I never would. Croom, look at me . . . disputing with a dead man! How can you be here? Who are you? I saw all of you die." He sounded quite mad with grief or shock.

"When, Hedrigall?" It was Doul's voice, clipped and dangerous. "And where? Where did we die?"

Hedrigall whispered his answer, and something in his voice made Bellis shiver, though she had expected it. She nodded as she heard it.

"The Scar."

When they had calmed him, Uther Doul and the Lovers conferred quietly, moving away from him.

". . . mad . . ." said the Lover, not quite audible. "Either mad . . . strange . . ."

"We have to know." Doul's voice. "If he's not mad he's a dangerous liar."

"It makes no sense," said the Lover furiously. "Who is he lying to? Why?"

"Either he is a liar, or . . ." said the Lover.

Tanner and Bellis could not tell if she said more, quietly, or if her words petered out.

"How has this happened?"

"We'd been a month, more than a month in the Hidden Ocean."

Many minutes had passed. Hedrigall had been silent for a long time while the Lovers debated what to do, whispering so low that Bellis and Tanner could not hear them. When suddenly he spoke, it was unbidden, and his voice was low and unchanging, as artless as if he were drugged.

The Lovers and Uther Doul waited.

Hedrigall spoke as if he knew it was expected of him.

He spoke for a long time, and he was not interrupted. He spoke with unnatural grace, with a trained fabler's eloquence; but there was in his careful monotone a hesitance, and underlying that a trauma that was frightening to sense.

Hedrigall stumbled on his words, and paused suddenly, sporadically, and drew shaking breaths; but he spoke for a long time. His audience—those in the room with him and those below—were absolutely silent and attentive.

"We'd been more than a month in the Hidden Ocean."

CHAPTER FORTY-SIX

"We'd been more than a month in the Hidden Ocean, and the sea was in chaos. We couldn't plot a course, we couldn't keep north at the top of our compasses, we couldn't navigate. Every day I'd stare out from the *Arrogance,* looking for sign of the Scar, the Fractured Land, anything at all. And there was nothing.

"You kept us moving.

"You insisted; you fired us up. You told us what we'd do when we reached the Scar. What powers it would give you, give us. You told us that we would all have power.

"I'll not pretend there was no dissent. As we went on, people were more and more . . . fearful. And they began to whisper that maybe the Brucolac had been right to mutiny. That maybe there wasn't so much wrong with the way the city was before.

"They came to you . . . we came to you and asked you to turn back. Said we were happy with how things had been. That we didn't need this, that too much had gone wrong already, and that we were fearful there was worse to come. Some of us had been having terrible dreams. The city was . . . so tense. Like a cat, fur all sparking and jagged.

"We asked you to turn us back. Before it was too late. We were afraid.

"I don't know how you did it, but you kept . . . for just enough time, you kept us . . . I'll not say happy; I'll not say willing. You kept us obedient; and we waited, and let you take us further in, fearful as we were."

"If it had been another week, I don't think we would have put up with any more. I think we would have turned back, and then you all wouldn't have *died*.

"But it wasn't like that, was it? It was too late.

"At six in the morning, on the ninth Playdi of Flesh, from the cabin of the *Arrogance* I saw something, forty miles ahead, at the edge of the horizon. A disturbance in the air, very faint, very frightening. And there was something else.

"The horizon was too close.

"An hour, five miles later, I knew we were definitely approaching something. And the horizon was still too close, and getting closer.

"I sent messages down below. And I could see them all preparing. I could look down and see the mass of ships all pushed together—all colors, all different shapes. I could see the crews setting up the cranes on the city's edge, and firing up engines and gods knew what else. Getting ready with all the sciences they'd been preparing. Little aerostats belting from one end of the city to another. Way below me.

"I was watching where the sea and sky met. I didn't believe it for the longest time; I kept thinking I must have it wrong and that any moment I'd see it right, make sense of it, but I didn't. And finally I couldn't deny what I saw.

"The horizon was only twenty miles away. I could see it clear, jagging across the face of the sea. The Scar.

"It was like seeing a god.

"You'd told us almost nothing, when you described it.

"It was a big wound in reality, broken open by the Ghosthead, you told us, thick with seams of what might be, all the possible ways. A big wound in reality, you said, and I thought you were speaking . . . like poetry.

"When the Ghosthead touched down in that continent, the force of it split the world right open, broke a fissure right through Bas-Lag. A split. Jagging in from the world's rim for more than two thousand miles, splintering the continent.

"That's the Scar. That crack. Teeming with the ways things weren't and aren't but could be.

"We were only a few miles away.

"It was a crevice in the sea.

"It was uneven, listing across us as we approached it, so the horizon seemed tilted. And because it was irregular, not guillotined but *cracked,* jutting a bit this way and the other, serrating back on itself here and there, there were places I could see over the edges. I could see the sides of the split. They were sheer.

"The ocean was choppy, a strong current heading north even though the wind went south. All the waves washed up past the city, carrying it along, and where they reached the edge of the Scar it was a wall, a clear wall. The water right-angled sharp and plunged down, vertical and split-smooth perfect as glass. Dark, moving water, pressing up against nothing and holding fast. And then . . .

"Empty air.

"A precipice.

"And way, way beyond it, scores of miles, a hundred miles away, only just visible on the other side of that empty gulf, there was a matching face. Hazy with distance. The other side of the crack.

"In between, that emptiness that I could still feel kicking out all manner of puissance. Welling out of the fucking lesion. The Scar."

"I can't hardly imagine what it must have been like on the city. They must have been able to see it. Was there panic? Were you excited?"

Of course the Lovers did not answer.

"I knew what the plan was. In sight of the Scar we'd stop at five miles' distance. And from there a dirigible would set out, and see if it could cross just that short distance to the Scar. And I was the lookout. Any sign of danger, I was to fire my flares, hang out my flags, call the airship back in.

"I don't know what danger you thought we might face. You had no idea. I don't think you knew what the Scar was. What did you think might happen? Did you think it might be crawling with Possible Beasts? Things that might have evolved but didn't, patrolling?

"It was nothing like that.

"The scale of it. The scale of that fucking thing. It was humbling.

"The city didn't slow," he said.

He was silent then, for several seconds. He had spoken his last sentence in the same hypnotic monotone he had been using for a long time, and it took Bellis a few heartbeats to realize what it meant.

Her heart spasmed and began to hammer.

"It didn't slow," Hedrigall said. "The avanc wasn't slowing down at all. The avanc was speeding up.

"We were ten miles away, then we were five miles away, and then four, and the city didn't stop, and didn't slow down.

"The world was foreshortened . . . The horizon was only a few thousand yards away, and it was growing closer, and Armada was accelerating.

"I began to panic then." There was no emotion in Hedrigall's voice, as if he had bled dry of it in the sea. "I began to fire off my flares, trying to warn you of what you must have known.

"Probably . . . probably there was panic then," he said. "I wouldn't know; I couldn't see. Maybe you were all mesmerized, glass-eyed and stupid. But I bet not. I bet there was panic, as the end of the world crept up. With my flares bursting over you, ignored.

"Three miles, two.

"I was unmoving for a long time. Frozen.

"The southerly wind was strong, so the *Arrogance* was lowering, stretching back away from the Scar as if it was afraid, as afraid as me. That woke me.

"Who knows what happened? Maybe you knew, before you died. I wasn't there.

"Maybe it was the avanc. Maybe after weeks of obedience it broke free of the impulses being fed into it. Maybe some spine that was supposed to plug into its brain snapped off, and the beast woke, confused and snared, and it tugged to try to free itself, careering on.

"Maybe the rockmilk engines failed. Maybe some possibility spilt out from the Scar, a *possibility* that the engines didn't work. Gods know what happened.

"When I looked down I saw flotillas of little boats being dropped over the sides of the city, and tiny frantic crews hauling at oars and throwing up sails to get away. But the sea fought them, and I saw their sails bellying in all directions. The lifeboats, the yachts, the little skiffs began to eddy in those waters and curl around the city, overtaking it northward, even as they fought to go the other way. But the currents and the waves pulled them on like they were hungry.

"It was only minutes before the first of them reached the Scar. I watched that little dinghy spinning toward the edge, and saw specks that must have been the people inside it jumping out into the sea, and then the stern of the boat tipped suddenly and went over and was gone. Into that airy emptiness.

"There was a trail of them, little boats peppering the sea between the city and the Scar, sliding north toward it. And dirigibles, too. A flock of them, trying to get airborne. Men and women were weighing them down, trying to get aboard, clinging to ropes to drag themselves in. All overloaded, they hauled themselves over the city's edge and flopped into the sea, where the current took them and they spun like dead whales, shedding their crews, heading for the Scar.

"Armada began to spin, slowly. The horizon lurched and angled as the city coiled clockwise in the water.

"We were half a mile away now and my mind went all cold and I suddenly knew what I had to do. I ran to the *Arrogance*'s bay and looked down through the hatches. I took up my rivebow and steadied myself on the edge of the bay doors and fired at the rope that held me tethered.

"It was thick as a thigh, attached to the aerostat thirty feet from me, swinging like a python. I had six chakris. Three of them I sent wide, way wide. The fourth connected, but not cleanly—cut half the rope's width. The fifth went wide, and I only had one more chance.

"But even though my aim felt good, and I'd steadied my hands, I missed.

"And I knew that I was dead. I dropped my rivebow, my fingers all thick and stupid, and I clung to the bars at the edge of the hatchway. I could only watch. I could feel the wind buffeting me, up through the doors, and I watched the rope fray too slowly to save me.

* * *

"The roofs, the slates, the towers, the aircabs, the flags, the monkeys all frantic with fear they didn't understand, the citizens running stupid from one place to the next as if anywhere would be spared.

"I watched them all through my telescope. I wonder what it was like, under the sea. I wonder how the cray and the menfish and Bastard John were acting. Maybe they're still alive, who knows? Maybe they could swim free. Maybe they quit the city as it went on toward its end.

"The *Sorghum* rig and Croom Park and the *Grand Easterly* and me were first to reach the edge.

"The wind changed for a moment, and the *Arrogance* drifted out over the cliff of water, and looked down into the chasm.

"Time was very slow as the *Arrogance* passed above the Scar. Just handfuls of seconds, but they lasted a long time.

"I crossed past the rim of the sea and looked down, over my knees dangling from the hatch, at the edges of the water. They were vertiginous.

"The sun angled down through the surface of the sea, filtered and refracted by the waves, and passed out again through the vertical face. I could see fishes bigger than me nosing up to the edge where it met the air, a hundred feet below the surface. Light bathed into it. There must be a whole ecology around the edges of the Scar. Even two, three miles down, where the pressure's merciless, the water there's sunlit.

"That sheer face of water, colors and eddies moving in strata, extended down *miles*. Perspective defeated me.

"And then mud. I could see it: a thick, sandwiched band of mud, black, at the bottom of the sea. And then rock. Rock extending down for so many miles that it dwarfed the layer of water. Red and black and grey rock, split wide, clean-edged. And many miles down a glow that moved and burned, showing dimly through the air. Magma. Rivers of molten stone, geothermal tides.

"And then? Below that?

"Then the void."

Hedrigall's voice was hollow and appalled.

* * *

"It must have been seconds I saw it," he said, "but I remember every layer, like colors of sand drooled into a bottle. It defeated the eye. It was too big to see.

"Armada paused, poised for seconds on the edge of that abyss, and the avanc gave a final push forward.

"I saw it first through the water. I saw it four miles down, a little way above the dark sea bottom. I saw a shape appear in the deeps, unclear through the sea, suddenly nearer, its outline visible, as it powered itself forward. Until with a sound like a cataclysm it began to breach. To push itself through the brine cliff.

"A mile of flesh.

"Its head was through, water splintering, shattering around it, cataracts thousands of yards long booming and splitting, drops of water the size of houses spinning and disintegrating, falling voidward, into the Scar.

"I could see the first of its chains, colossal, bursting through the water in a four-mile straight tear, splitting the sea between the avanc and the city above. Other chains came through after it, so that the sea wall was scored with parallel vertical rips, like a claw wound.

"The avanc's body continued through, indescribable, fins and spines, cilia, and as it came through into the air gravity took it, and it began to pitch forward. The chains tightened on the city, and the edges of Armada reached the edge and were pulled on, over.

"The avanc gave out a sound that burst all the glass around me.

"I saw the submarine hulks on which the *Sorghum* rested welling up toward the flat cliff face of water and then burst through, and all around them, hundreds of feet away on either side, the aft of Garwater and Bask and Curhouse reached the end of the sea, and jutted out, and trembled, and fell.

"There are so many ships in Armada.

"Steamers reached the edge flat-on, and rolled terribly and ponderously over, houses and towers spilling from them like crumbs, a rain of masonry and bodies, hundreds of bodies, pitched kicking and convulsing into the air and down, down many miles. Past all the inner layers of the world.

"I wasn't even praying. I had no will. I could only watch.

"Bridges and tethers snapped. Trawlers came apart as they

fell. Barges and lifeboats, and tugs and wooden warships. Splintering. Bursting, exploding, on fire as boilers spun and red-hot coals spewed through them. Ships six hundred feet long and centuries old cartwheeled as they went down.

"The *Grand Easterly*'s aft was over the Scar now, jutting out into the air.

"Armada spilt over the lip of the ocean and broke down into a random, plummeting constellation of parts, the live and the dead falling through an avalanche of bricks and masts. I could hear nothing except the splintering water and the avanc's cry.

"Three hundred feet of the *Grand Easterly* was jutting over the void now, and all around it much smaller ships spewed into the ravine. And suddenly its weight told, and I heard a cracking like some god's bone breaking, and the rear third of the ship, to which I was tethered, split and hinged down, hauling me with it, clinging with my arms locked around a girder, down, into the Scar.

"You wonder how you're going to die, don't you? Bravely, screaming, unaware, or what? Well, I met my death in a stupor, my mouth hanging like a fucking fool, as a steamer's arse pulled me down.

"The edge of water rose up past me as I plummeted past the Scar's lip, below the surface level of the sea.

"For a second I could see through water to the keels of ships that were *above* me, watch them plow on to their destruction. I was rushing down, and the rest of the *Grand Easterly* and every ship of the city was collapsing toward me.

"Once or twice, for moments, I saw dirigibles. Little cabs, men in harnesses, who'd managed to leap from the decks of their vessels as they went over, and were caught in the slipstream fighting to haul their balloons skyward. They were crushed and killed, again and again. A falling hull or shards of towerblocks would smash them out of the air.

"The *Arrogance* was accelerating down. I closed my eyes and tried to die.

"And then, four miles below me, the avanc moved.

"It must have been in agony, its body bursting and hemorrhaging in the air, folding over and bending double as it came out of the water wall. Half a mile of its back was through into the Scar, now. Maybe it was spasming in pain. It pushed itself very suddenly out, bursting right out of the sea, into the Scar, and down.

"It cried out again as the whole of its fucking bulk emerged, and its thrust shoved it down faster than gravity would have taken it. The avanc lurched; its chains went suddenly taut and tugged the rest of the city over the edge. The aft of the *Grand Easterly* was wrenched down, too, and the *Arrogance* was snatched so suddenly that the tattering rope that held it snapped.

"It snapped.

"My eyes flew open as the aerostat hurtled skyward, up past the falling city, up and out of the shadow of that wall of ocean, pelted by metal and sharp-split wood, out of the Scar, into the sky.

"I roared out of that crevice and careered into the sky. My arms were locked tight, holding me into place. I was going to live.

"Below me, the last of Armada slipped into the Scar. Winterstraw Market in a rain of little vessels. The *Uroc*, the *Therianthropus*, the asylum, the old sawdust boats of the haunted quarter—all become nothing. Tipping up, in sheets of spray, and going over, till the surface of the Hidden Ocean was left undisturbed.

"As I rose, I looked down directly into the Scar and saw an interference, a haze like dust, as Armada fell, and far below that the avanc, spinning as it went, wrapping itself in twenty miles of chain, moving pathetically, trying to swim out of that endless fall. Even it looked small and dwindling.

"Eventually I fell back, exhausted and stunned to be alive, and when I looked down again I could see nothing at all."

Hedrigall's voice ebbed away. He spoke again after several seconds of quiet.

"I went higher than I've ever been before. High enough to look down and see the Scar as it really is. A crack, that's all. A crack in the world.

"I don't know if any other aeronauts got free. But I was more than a mile up, and I saw nothing.

"The wind that high was strong, gusted me south for hours. It took me away from there. Out of that murderous place in the

water, where all the currents lead to the Scar. The *Arrogance* was
leaking. Split and burnt by debris. I was coming down.

"I sawed myself some hide from the dirigible, lashed it to
wood from the cabin. Made myself a raft, knowing what was
coming. I waited by the bay doors till we were scudding low and
fast, and I threw out the raft and leapt after it.

"And *then* finally, only then, curled in my little raft, I let myself remember what I'd seen.

"I was all alone with those memories for two days. I thought
I'd die.

"I thought for a moment that maybe if I could stay alive for
long enough, the currents might take me and shove me out into
the Swollen Ocean, where our other ships are waiting. But I'm
not a fool. I knew there was no chance of that.

"And then . . . this."

For the first time in his extraordinary story, Hedrigall sounded
as if he would break down again.

"What is this? What *is* this?" The hysteria in his voice grew
louder. "I thought I was dying. I thought you were a dying man's
dream. *I saw you die* . . ." He whispered it. "I saw you die. What
are you? What city is this? What's happening to me?"

Hedrigall became dangerous then, shouting, feverish, and terrified. The Lovers tried to soothe him, but it was some time before
his rantings became subdued and he fell into a stupefied sleep.

A long silence followed—a long, stretched-out quiet—and
Bellis felt herself back in her own skin again as the spell of
Hedrigall's story slowly faded. Her skin was elyctric; she bris-
tled with tension. She felt all drunk on awe from his telling.

"What," hissed the Lover coldly, his voice fraught, "has
happened?"

"It's the Scar," Tanner whispered to Bellis. "I know what it is.
This close to the Scar, it's *leaking*. And that Hed up there . . ." He
paused and shook his head, his face haggard and bleached with
wonder. Bellis knew what he would say.

"That ain't the real Hedrigall," said Tanner, "not the *factual*
one, not the one from . . . from here. Our Hedrigall ran away.
That Hedrigall's leaked out . . . from another possibility. He's
from one where he stayed on, and where we traveled that bit

faster, got to the Scar earlier. He's what happened . . . what *will* happen.

"Oh my Jabber, oh dear Jabber and shit."

Above them, the Lovers and Uther Doul were arguing. Someone—Bellis had not heard who—had said the same thing as Tanner. The Lover was reacting violently.

"Dung!" she spat. "Fucking *dung*! It doesn't work that way; that's not what happens. Out of the whole sea, you think we'd *happen to* find him, even if he *had* leaked through? This is a fucking setup. That's Hedrigall, alright. It's *our* Hedrigall, and he *never left*. This is a setup to turn us back. He is *not* effluvium from the Scar."

She was furious. She let no one else speak. She raged at Uther Doul, and even at the Lover, to Bellis' amazement; he was asking her to calm down, to just *think* . . . So close to what she sought, the Lover felt it threatened, and she was thundering.

"I'll tell you what," she said. "This is shit, and we will keep this lying bastard locked up until we get the truth from him. We say he's recovering; we wait; we find out what really happened. We don't accept this *crap* he's spouted to us."

"Is she *mad*?" hissed Tanner Sack to Bellis. "What's she talking about?"

"This is obviously designed to create panic," the Lover continued. "This is a plan to ruin everything. He's in fucking league with gods knows who, and we can't let them win. Uther, take him away. Brief the guards and pick them well; pick those you're certain of. Brief the guards about the lies he might shout to them.

"We will stop this, right here," she said, hard. "We'll not let this seditious shit succeed. This goes no further. We bury this story, right now, right here, and we go on. Agreed?"

Perhaps the Lover and Uther Doul nodded to her. Bellis heard nothing.

She had turned her face to Tanner at those last words. She watched him listen to his ruler—to whom he had committed himself absolutely, declared himself utterly loyal—announce her plans to deceive everyone in the city. To keep secret everything she had heard. And to drive on to the Scar.

Bellis watched a cold, a dead and frightening cast come over

Tanner's face as he listened. The muscles of his jaw clenched, and Bellis knew that he was thinking of Shekel.

Was he remembering how he'd said and thought that this—what had happened to them, being found—was a blessing? Bellis did not know. But something had set in Tanner's face, and he looked at her with murderous eyes.

"She," he hissed to her, "will bury *nothing*."

CHAPTER FORTY-SEVEN

Tanner Sack was known. He was the one who had fought a bonefish to save a dying man. He had Remade himself into a kind of manfish, the better for life in Armada. He had lost his boy.

Tanner was known, and he was respected.

You listened to Tanner, and you believed him.

Bellis could tell no one anything. Her mouth was hard and cold as a stone.

She had to turn to others to spread words.

Everyone knew Tanner Sack.

If Bellis had tried to tell what she had heard in that unpleasant little cubbyhole, if she tried to tell the secrets she had listened to, she would not be believed. She would not be heard. But she had introduced someone else to her room, so that he could speak for her and tell the story.

She could not help nodding. Smiling without warmth. *Gods, it's well done,* she thought, bowing her head, acknowledging consummate work. She felt skeins of cause, effect, effort, and interaction tying around her. She felt things all coming together, pushing her into this place, at this time, having done this thing.

Oh, it's well done.

It started almost as soon as she and Tanner came up out of the lower decks.

She blinked, and looked around her at the flags and the washing and the bridges and the towers, still all strong and knotted together with mortar. She was haunted by the images from Hedrigall's story. She saw the city shattering and falling so clearly that it was a true relief to emerge and see it all solid.

Tanner began. The Lovers were still below, still organizing, trying to hide Hedrigall. While they secreted themselves below the air and schemed, Tanner began.

He looked first for the people he knew well. He spoke quickly and fiercely. One of the first he found was Angevine, and he involved her carefully with the group of dockers to whom he was speaking, who did not know her.

His passion was genuine, utterly guileless. He did not orate.

Bellis watched him move through the crowd still milling on the *Grand Easterly*'s decks, arguing in angry tones about what it was they had heard, about what Hedrigall had seen—how and why he had come back. There were still a good number of pirates on the huge old ship, and Tanner spoke to them all.

He trembled with rage. Bellis followed him by an irregular and discrete course. She watched him, and was impressed by his fervor. She watched the stunned reactions move like a disease through the masses. She watched the disbelief quickly become belief and frightened anger, and then resolve.

Tanner insisted—she heard him—that they had the right to know the truth, and something uncertain moved inside Bellis.

She did not know what the truth was; she was not sure what she believed. She was not sure what lay behind Hedrigall's extraordinary story. There were several possibilities. But it did not matter. She refused to think about that now. She had been brought to this place, and she would do what was required, and bring this to an end.

Bellis watched as those whom Tanner had told then told others, and they told more, until it was quickly impossible to track the story. It moved under its own momentum. Very soon, most of those who told a garbled story of Hedrigall's escape from the Scar could not have said how they knew it.

The Lovers had told a great deal of the truth about the Scar, as they understood it, in a popular form. There were few people in Armada who did not know that possibilities spilled from it, that that was the source of its power. Several had seen Uther Doul's sword switched on: they knew what probability mining did. And here, so deep in the Hidden Ocean, so close to the Scar itself, with its seepage, with probabilities welling up from it like plasma, it was not hard to believe that Hedrigall—*this* Hedrigall, raving in the lower decks of the steamer—was telling the truth.

And while their own Hedrigall might be thousands of miles away, fled weeks ago, adrift above the ocean or crashed or surviving as a hermit on some foreign land or drowned in the sea, the Armadans accepted that the one they had picked up was a nigh-man. A refugee from a terrible Bas-Lag in which Armada had been lost.

"Two days ago," Bellis heard one woman say with a dreadful awe. "All of us, we've been dead for two days."

It was a warning. No one could possibly miss that.

While the sun crossed toward the lowest quarter of the sky, the story spread its fingers, passing into all the ridings. Its presence clogged up the atmosphere.

Hedrigall was hidden, and the Lovers made a stupid mistake by staying below, trying to work out plans. Over their heads, Tanner vented and ran from ship to ship, spreading word.

On the *Grand Easterly,* Bellis waited, remembering Hedrigall's story—remembering it so that it filled her head, and she saw all the dreadful collapse again. She did not try to evaluate what he had said. It was a story, an awesome story, awesomely told. That was all that was important.

She watched the Armadans come and go around her, debating and conferring darkly. There were plans, she could see that; there was movement. Something was coming to a close.

Time moved quickly. The sun was low. All over Garwater, workshops were closing, their workers amassing, converging on the *Grand Easterly.*

At six o'clock the Lovers emerged. Some sense of what was happening had filtered down to them, some inchoate awareness that their riding and their city were in crisis.

They came out into the light, followed by Uther Doul, wearing hard and nervous expressions. Bellis saw them blink with shock at the ranks of their citizens who faced them. Scores lined up like a ragged army: hotchi and cactacae among the humans, even the Garwater llorgiss.

Above them, twitching as his nerves died in the light, was the Brucolac. And at their head, standing a little forward, his chin pushed out, facing the Lovers, was Tanner Sack.

The Lovers looked out at their men and women, and Bellis was certain that she saw them flinch. She glanced at them and then ignored them, staring past them at their mercenary. Uther Doul did not meet her eyes.

"We have spoken to Hedrigall," the Lover began, her voice not showing any anxiety.

Shockingly, Tanner Sack interrupted her.

"Spare us," he said. All around him, people glanced at each other, held by the force of his voice.

The Lovers stared at him, their eyes widening very slightly, their faces inscrutable.

"Enough lies," Tanner said. "We know the truth. We know where Hedrigall—this maybe-Hedrigall, the one you've locked away, hiding him from us—we know where he's been. Where he's *from.*"

He moved forward, and the mass moved up behind him, shuffling, determined.

"Jaddock," Tanner shouted, "Corscall, Guddrunn, you lot, go find Hedrigall. He's down there somewhere. Bring him out here." A group of cactacae stepped forward nervously toward the Lovers and Uther Doul, and the door behind them.

"Stop!" shouted the Lover. The cactacae halted and looked to Tanner. He moved forward, and the crowd came with him. Emboldened, the cactus-people moved on.

"Doul . . ." said the Lover, her voice dangerous. Everyone stopped, instantly.

Uther Doul stepped forward, between the Lovers and the advancing Armadans.

And after a second, Tanner came to meet him.

"All of us, Uther Doul?" he said, loud enough for everyone around him to hear. "You want to take every one? You think you can do that? Because we are fetching Hedrigall up here, and if you threaten them—" He indicated the cactacae. "—then the rest of us are coming with them, and you threaten all of us. Think you can take us all? Shit, maybe you can, maybe you can. But if you fucking do . . . what then? Who are your bosses going to rule?"

There were hundreds of Armadans behind him, and they nod-ded as he spoke, and some of them shouted their agreement.

Uther Doul looked from Tanner to the masses behind him, back to Tanner again. And then he showed weakness, his com-mand broke, he hesitated and turned his head. Uncertain, he turned, to look to his bosses, to seek clarification. His shoulders moved in a minuscule shrug; he tilted his head in a question: *He's right, what do you want me to do, do you want me to kill them* all . . . ?

When he turned like that, when he showed doubt, Tanner won. He moved his hand again, and the cactacae moved past Doul and the Lovers and into the corridor, setting out to find Hedrigall, un-easy but not afraid, knowing that they would be safe.

The Lovers did not even look at them. They stared instead at Tanner Sack.

"What more could you ask?" said Tanner, his voice hard. "You've been shown what'll happen to us. But you're so fucking insane with this, so fucking caught up in it, that you'd ignore *this*? You still want to go on.

"And you'd keep this quiet from us. You'd *lie* to us, let us drive ourselves, mute and stupid as the fucking avanc, over the edge. That's *enough*. This stops here. You take us no further. We are turning back."

"Dammit!" The Lover jabbed her hand at Tanner, meeting his eye. She spat on the deck before him. "You fucking coward! You *fool*! Do you really think that story he told is the truth? *Think* about it, godsdammit. You think that's how the Scar really is? And you think that out of all the ocean, out of the *entire fucking Hidden Ocean,* we found him by sheer chance? You think it's a fucking *coincidence* that our own Hedrigall runs and then we meet *another,* from some other place, with stories to scare us stupid?

"*It's the same man!* This was always his plan. Can't you fuck-ing see? We thought he'd left us, but he didn't. Where would he go? He cut loose the *Arrogance,* and he hid somewhere. And now, when we get so close, so fucking close to the most amazing place in our world, he comes out to frighten us away. Why? Be-cause he's a coward, like you, like all of you.

"That was his plan. He didn't even have the courage to run away in shame. He waited to take all of you with him."

There were those who wavered at that. Even in her blistering rage, her points scored home.

But Tanner gave her nothing.

"You were going to keep it from us," he said. "You were going to lie. We've come so far with you, and you were going to lie to us about this. Because you're so blinded by some greed you couldn't risk us facing you down. You know nothing about the Scar," he shouted. "*Nothing*. Don't tell me coincidence; don't tell me unbelievable—maybe this is how it *works*. You don't even know.

"All we know is that one of the best fucking Garwater men I ever knew is down there in your jail, warning us that if we go to the Scar we'll die. And I believe him. This ends here. *We* say what happens now. We're taking control. We're turning around; we're heading home. Your orders to proceed . . . are *in-fucking-validated*. You can't jail or kill us all."

There was a roar at that, a mass exhalation of excitement, and people began sporadically to chant *Sack Sack Sack*.

Bellis paid no attention. Something extraordinary was happening, something almost inaudible under the noisy approval around her.

Behind Uther Doul, the Lover had been watching and listening with a terrible uncertainty in his eyes. He had reached forward, touched the Lover, and turned her around, then had said something low and urgent to her, something inaudible that had made her react with incredulity and rage.

The Lovers were arguing.

Quiet came down over the crowd as they realized what was happening. Bellis held her breath. It shocked her deeply. That they could whisper to each other, their faces growing red, their scars white-scored with anger, their voices hissed, muttered curt, growing slowly louder until they shouted, ignoring those around them, who stared at them in stupid amazement.

". . . *he's right,*" Bellis heard the Lover shout. "He's right. We don't know."

"Don't know *what*?" the Lover shouted back. Her face was outraged and terrible. "Don't know *what*?"

Overhead, a little flock of cowed city birds cut across the sky, touching quickly down, somewhere out of sight. Armada creaked. The silence went on and on. Tanner Sack and his mutineers were frozen. They watched the argument between the Lovers unfold with an awe more fitting to a geological event.

As Bellis watched the last of the birds, her eyes came to the Brucolac's blasted figure and stayed there, though the vampir disgusted her. His convulsions were dying down, his body calming. He opened eyes seared milk-white and blind by the daylight, and turned his head slowly.

He was listening. Bellis was sure of it.

The Lovers ignored everything outside them. Uther Doul moved silently aside, as if to give those assembled a better view.

There was no other sound at all.

"We don't know," said the Lover again. Bellis felt as if an arc of heat or electricity spat between the Lovers' eyes. "We don't know what's ahead. He might be right. Can we be sure? Can we risk it?"

"Oh . . ." the Lover responded, her voice coming out of her in a querulous sigh. She stared at her lover with a terrible disappointment and loss. "Oh, godsdammit," she breathed quietly. "Gods rot and fuck you dead."

Again there was quiet, and palpable shock. The Lovers stared at each other.

"We cannot force them," the Lover said finally. His voice shook violently. "We can't rule without concord. This isn't a war. You can't send Doul to fight *them*."

"Don't turn away from this now," the Lover said, her voice unstable. "You're turning from me. After what we've done. After I made you. After we made ourselves together. Don't deny me . . ."

The Lover glanced up around him, at the encircling faces. A visible panic came over him. He held out his hands. "Let's go inside."

The Lover was rigid, her scars glowing. She was tense with self-control. She shook her head at him, tightly raging. "Who the fuck are we to care who hears? What is this? What's happened to you? Are you as stupid as these fools? You think the lying cant that returned bastard told us rings true? Do you? You believe him?"

"Am I still *you*," the Lover screamed back at her, "and are you *me*? Or not? That's the only question here!"

He was losing something. Something was slipping from him. Bellis watched a connection as vital as an umbilicum attenuate and wither in him, and dry up and snap. Flailing, raging, terror-

ized very suddenly, alone for the first time in many years, he
tried to say more.

"We can't do this; we can't. You'll lose us *everything* . . ."

The Lover watched him, and her face set dead cold.

"I thought more of you," she said slowly. "I thought I'd made
my soul whole."

"And you have, you have, you did," said the Lover frantically,
so pathetic that Bellis turned her face away in shame.

They brought Hedrigall up from belowdecks, draped over the
shoulders of the cactacae who had gone after him, and he was
greeted with a wave of welcoming joy.

Everyone shouted questions at him that he shied away from
and could not answer. People danced and shouted and called his
name while he stared at them, drunk with what seemed disoriented terror. Cactacae, untroubled by his thorns, grabbed him
and rode him on their shoulders, where he bobbed unsteadily
and stared bewildered about.

"Turn!" shouted Tanner Sack. "We *turn* the city! Get the Lover!
Get someone who knows how. Get crews to the rein-winches.
We're sending a signal to the fucking avanc; we're *turning.*"
Buoyed up, the throng looked around for the Lovers, demanding
that they tell how it was done, but the Lovers were gone.

In the crush surrounding Hedrigall, in that carnival, the Lover
had turned fiercely and run back toward her room, the Lover behind her.

And watching them carefully, following a little behind them,
getting ready to take a different route, for one final time to try to
understand what she had done and what had been done to her,
was Bellis Coldwine.

As she stepped into the passageway, she heard another
exchange.

"I rule here," she heard the Lover say, his voice thick and careful. "I rule this place; *we* rule it. That's what we do; that's what
we fucking *are* . . . Don't do this. You'll lose it all for us."

The Lover turned to him, and Bellis was suddenly in plain
view. But the Lover took her in for only a second, then turned her
scarred face away, uncaring. Not giving a damn who heard.

"You . . ." she said, touching the Lover's face. She shook her
head, and when she spoke again it was with great sadness and

resolve. "You're right. We don't rule here anymore. That was never why I was here.

"I won't ask you to come with me." For a second, her voice almost broke. "You've stolen yourself from me."

She turned, and with the Lover pleading with her, begging her to listen to him, to hear reason, to understand, she walked away.

Bellis had heard enough. She stood alone for a long time in between old heliotypes stripped of meaning before turning back to the celebrations outside, where Tanner was trying to give orders, trying to have the city turned.

Raucous gangs, reeling at what they did, turned the winches that tugged at the avanc's reins. And slowly, over miles, the avanc turned its nose in dumb obedience, and the city's massive wake began to arc, and Armada turned.

It was a long, very shallow curve that took the rest of the day's light to complete. And while the city turned tail on the featureless sea, the pirate-bureaucrats of Garwater ran frantic through their riding, trying to discover who was now in control.

The truth terrified them: in those anarchic hours there was no one giving orders. There was no chain of command, no order, no hierarchy, nothing but a rugged, contingent democracy thrown together by the Armadans as they needed it. The bureaucrats could not accept this, and they saw leaders in Tanner Sack and Hedrigall. But those two were participants, nothing more: one enthusiastic, the other looking bewildered, dragged about on shoulders like a mascot.

Is this how it ends?

Bellis is lost with excitement. She is weak with it. It is night now, and she is running with a crowd of smiling citizens along the edge of Jhour, to watch the crews come in from the winchboats. She realizes that she is smiling, too. She does not know when that began.

Is it finished?

Is this how it ends?

The authority that kept Garwater in control, and which spread beyond that to assert its will on all Armada, is gone. It was so strong, so powerful, for so long, and now it has melted with a speed and a quiet that leave Bellis stunned. *Where have they all gone?* she wonders. The rulers have disappeared, and their integument of law and control, their yeomanry and their authority, have gone with them.

The rulers of the other ridings have wisely remained silent and hidden. It would not work for them to try to take control of this, this popular rage and exhilaration. They are not so stupid as to try. They are waiting.

All the fears and resentments and uncertainties, everything that has welled up in the citizens for weeks and months, the residue from every time they had doubts and said nothing: that is what powers this movement. This mutiny. Hedrigall's extraordinary, improbable story has set them free, given them the certainty they needed.

They pull the city around.

There is no looting that Bellis can see, no violence, no fires or gunshots. This is about a single issue. This is about not dying, about escaping this dreadful sea alive. The avanc is still injured, but it is progressing, and Bellis can see the stars, and she knows that the beast is heading back toward the Swollen Ocean.

This is what she has wanted. Every mile that took her away from New Crobuzon was a defeat. She had tried everything to get the fucking city to turn, to take her back toward her home; and now, suddenly and utterly unexpectedly, she has succeeded.

How did this happen? she thinks, feeling as if she should be triumphant or proud, not like a bewildered, happy bystander.

She knows why she is troubled. She has questions and resentments. She remembers what she saw in Doul's eyes. *Used again,* she thinks, aghast and wondering. *Used again.*

It is a complex chain of manipulation, what has been done to her. She cannot untangle it now. Now is not the time.

Flares, the pilots' signals to the winch-boats, were set off in a big vulgar display. It was a celebration and a defiance—we do not need these anymore, the mutineers were saying.

There were men and women still out, in frenetic celebration, when the sky first lightened in the east.

Bellis stood on the *Grand Easterly,* near the entrance to the corridors where the Lovers' quarters were. She had been waiting for some time. She remembered what the Lover had said: *I will not ask you to come.* Something was ending, and Bellis wanted to witness it.

There were others on the deck, mostly tired and drunk, singing and watching the sea, but they quieted when the Lover appeared on deck with Uther Doul beside her. There was a moment, an ugly moment, when the bystanders remembered their anger and something might have happened, but it went quickly.

The Lover carried packs that bulged oddly. She did not look at anyone but Doul. Bellis saw that one of the packs contained the perhapsadian, Doul's weird instrument.

"This is all of it?" the Lover said, and Doul nodded.

"Everything I collected," he said, "except my sword." The Lover's face was set. Calm and hard.

"Is the boat all ready?" she said, and Doul nodded.

They walked together, unmolested, watched by all the pirates, toward the *Grand Easterly*'s port side, and the streets that wound over a tight crush of vessels, and Basilio Harbor beyond.

Bellis kept looking back to the doorway. She expected the Lover to appear, to call his lover back or to run to her and tell her he would go, too, that nothing would part them, but he did not.

They had never been each other. They had never been doing the same thing. Perhaps it was only chance that they had traveled together so far.

At the edge of the *Grand Easterly,* the Lover stopped Uther Doul and turned for a last look at the ship. The sun was not yet up, but the sky was light, and Bellis could see the Lover's face clear.

Cutting across it, scored over her right cheek from the hairline to her jaw, was a new wound. It glistened with a faint coating of salve like varnish. It was deep, and dark red, and it sliced straight through several of her other, older scars, as if it were brushing them aside.

Bellis never heard any stories about that last journey, which astonished her. In all the days and weeks that followed, when everyone was talking about the night of the mutiny, she never once heard about the Lover and Uther Doul moving sedately through a city tired and drunk on its rebellion.

She could imagine it, though. She saw them progressing sedately, the Lover sad and pensive, looking around her, memorizing the details of the city she had helped rule for so long. Hefting her pack, feeling the weight of all the books of arcane science, the tracts on possibility mining, the ancient machines that Doul had given her.

Doul beside her, his hand ready by his sword, to protect her in her last minutes in Armada. Was it necessary? Did he need to step in? Bellis heard no stories of him cutting Armadans down.

And was the Lover really alone?

It seemed hard to believe that after the years of her presence she would have no one ready to follow her. Her narrative logic was not the brutal mercantilism that drove Armada, but could it be alien to all its citizens? She could not have controlled a ship, even a small one, on her own. Bellis found it easier to imagine that as she walked through the city, she drew certain men and women out of their hiding places, that they sensed her passing and came to her. Alienated from their neighbors, impelled by other motivations, a gathering come out to drift in behind the Lover and Uther Doul, walking at her pace, themselves packed and ready to leave their city.

Romantics, storytellers, misfits, the suicidal and the mad. Bellis imagined them behind the Lover.

She could not help thinking that there was a small crew of them by the time the Lover emerged from below the eaves and crossed the deserted warehouses of the docks. She imagined that they must have joined the Lover on the deck of the prepared ship, helping her to stoke the engines, casting off, saying good-bye.

But Bellis did not know. The Lover might have gone alone.

All Bellis knew was that after almost an hour, with the sun very low and its light thick, a sail passed unmolested through the narrow entrance to Basilio Harbor and out into the sea. It was not large. Its deck was equipped with little cranes and winches and all manner of engines and boilers, the purposes of which Bellis had no idea of. It seemed well equipped and clean.

Bellis could not see it clearly. She was watching over the irregular contours of Armada's roofs, all those flats and slopes in grey and red, slate, concrete, iron. She could just make out the vessel's progress through oily morning sunlight, past the other vessels tied up carefully in the harbor, out through the gap in the city's ship matter. She could see the woodsmoke it vented as the strong, strange currents of the Hidden Ocean took it away.

A little way from Bellis, the Lover was watching.

His eyes were so raw with tears it looked as though they had been rubbed with dust. And of course, his cheek had only its old scars.

The boat powered on. It moved with an undeviating speed that Bellis had never witnessed on the Hidden Ocean. Without fuss, without a fusillade of shots or fireworks, it headed north, directly away from the city, slipping into Armada's wake and heading for the horizon, toward the Scar.

A long time after that, after it had disappeared from sight, Uther Doul came back to the *Grand Easterly,* alone.

Doul stood below the mast on which the Brucolac was crucified, the vampir's early-morning shrieks beginning weakly with the sun.

"Cut him down," said Uther Doul with authority to a nearby group of men and women. They looked up, startled, but did not question him. "Cut him down and take him home."

And on that extraordinary morning, while the city felt its way toward new rules and nobody knew what was permissible or normal or acceptable or right, Uther Doul's merciful order was obeyed.

Not the Lover anymore, thought Bellis suddenly. She stared out toward the horizon's rim, where the little vessel had disappeared. She thought of the Lovers' argument, and of the new wound—a newborn scar that tore across the Lover's face, re-creating and separating her. *You're not the Lover anymore.*

Bellis tried to reconceive of the Lover, out there at the helm of her ship, heading toward the most extraordinary place in the world. Bellis tried to rethink her, to be clear, to give credit or blame where it was due and think about the woman piloting that lost vessel toward the edge of the world according to no one's plans or desires but her own.

But Bellis kept thinking of her as *Lover Lover Lover,* even as she tried not to.

She did not know the woman's name.

Coda

Tanner Sack

It's been bloody mad here. You'd never believe what I've been doing.

We ain't heading for the Scar no more. We're heading back for waters way back the way we came. We're going back to how things were.

Strange. I put it like that, but I never knew this place when it wasn't hankering for the Hidden Ocean. Neither did you. Everything that happened, it was all geared up to getting us out there. I've never lived here when it was just a pirate port.

Neither have you.

I've been spending time with your Angevine. I'll be lying if I tell you we're best friends. We're a bit shy, you might say. But we see each other, and talk about you, mostly.

We were lied to, and we had had enough, and they were risking our necks, dammit, so we made them turn back.

It doesn't go away, that you're gone.

I don't live here anymore. I live nowhere. This place killed you.

I don't know what it was, the things in that water. I know that what we fought in the water that night was no vampir. No one talks about them. No one knows what they were. Only that they helped to try to turn us.

Bastard John saw them. I see it in his little piggy eyes. But he says nothing.

It was me who turned the city. Those things, the things that took you, the vampir man who fought beside them, they failed.

I did the job for them. Turned us round.

I don't know if that's funny. I only know I don't want to live here anymore, and I can't go.

I'm a sea-thing now. It's a bad joke. We both know what real sea-things are, how they move, how fast. Not like me, heavy clumsily stolen fins flapping, slimy sweating, Remade.

And I'm scared, now. I put myself in the sea I sweat. Now every little blenny looks like one of the things that took you.

But I can't live in the air now. I ain't got that option no more.

What'll I do? I can't go back to New Crobuzon, and if I could I'd rot, without brine.

I'll make myself swim. It'll get easier again. I'll get it done.

They can't hold me. I can leave. Maybe we'll go near some coast one day, and there I'll slip away. There I'll go and live alone in the shallows so I can see rock under me, where trees and scree meet in the water. I can live there alone. I've had enough of it, I tell you.

I ain't got nothing. I've got nothing.

In time, in time they tell me, I'll not feel so bad. I don't want time to heal me. There's a reason I'm like this.

I want time to set me ugly and knotted with loss of you, marking me. I won't smooth you away.

I can't say good-bye.

Dustday 2nd Tathis, 1780. Armada.

The avanc is slowing again, one final time.

It is still wounded from the grindylow's abuse. Whatever they did to it has not healed, not scarred, but remains raw and unpleasant. We pass from time to time by messes of its pus again.

Its heart, I think, is winding down.

We all know that the avanc is dying.

Perhaps it is looking for its home. Perhaps it is trying to find its way back to the universe of lightless brine from where we fished it. And all the time it grows ill, and weak, its blood thickening, decaying and clotting, its great flukes moving more slowly.

Never mind. We are very close to the edge of the Hidden Ocean. We will emerge soon—any day, perhaps within hours—and there the Armadan fleet will be waiting. The avanc will live till then.

The day is close, though, when the city will come to a final stop.

We will be stranded, attached to an organic anchor, millions of tons of corpse rotting on the floor of the abyss.

Five chains, five links to sever. For each link, two cuts. Each link many feet thick, and thaumaturgically tempered. It will take some time, but eventually, one by one, the miles of metal will fall free.

What a catastrophe that will be, to the bottom dwellers—like divine anger. Tons of metal falling, accelerating, through four, five miles, eventually to slam into the ooze at the sea's bottom, cutting through to the rock below. Landing across the poor avanc's corpse, perhaps, bursting it open, its miles of intestines littering the dark mud.

Perhaps in time whole ecosystems will evolve around that unprecedented richness.

We will be gone.

We will have reached the fleet, and they will reattach themselves, and Armada will be as it was. There will be fewer vessels to drag it, of course, after the carnage of the Crobuzoner War, but the city will have shed countless thousands of tons of chain. It will balance.

Armada will be as it was.

Back across the Swollen Ocean, back toward the richest shipping lanes, back toward the ports and traders. The Armadan pirates who have waited for months, tracking the city with strange devices, will find it again. We will go back toward the Gentleman's Sea, the Hebdomad, Gnurr Kett, the Basilisk Channel.

Back toward New Crobuzon.

It has been a month since the woman left, whose name I did not know. Things have changed.

It did not take long for the mutineers to relinquish control. They had no program, no party. They were only ever a disparate group who found out they had been lied to, who did not want to die. They snatched power in an anarchic and momentary coup, and gave it up easily.

Within days, the Lover reemerged. He came out of the *Grand Easterly* and issued orders. People were glad to carry them out. No one has a quarrel with him.

He is lost, though. Everyone knows it. His eyes do not focus, and his orders are vague. Uther Doul whispers to him carefully, and the Lover will nod and issue some meaningful command, Doul's words through the Lover's mouth.

Doul will not allow that to continue. He is a mercenary: he works for money; he sells his loyalty. If he must have control, I do not believe he wants it to be so unsubtle. If he rules, he hides it, for the freedom of paid subordinance. I have learnt that, if nothing else.

I do not know what happened to him, to make him flinch from naked power so much.

I have never met a more complicated man, or, I suspect, a more tragic one. His own history planted the ideas that brought us all here, so far from what he himself sought in Armada. It is hard to tell what in him has been intent, and what reaction. I cannot believe that this is satisfactory for him: that he looks at his position, and that of the Lover, and he nods, and says, "This is what I wanted."

Either he spends his life in control of everything, or in panicked fear. Either he has planned everything to a dizzying degree, or he moves us all desperately from crisis to crisis, not knowing what he wants, showing nothing on his face.

The Lover keeps his dead gaze on the horizon. Although at the end, the woman was despised and feared as a liar, she was never pathetic, and her erstwhile lover has become so. I suspect that he will not survive this. Perhaps one day he will discover that Doul is no longer at his side. Especially now that the Brucolac controls Dry Fall again.

Few actually saw the grindylow, and fewer talk about it. It is only I who cannot forget them.

I have seen the Brucolac at night. He walks free.

He is sun-scarred, and will always be. He is subdued. Carrianne talks of him with an austere kind of affection. His citizens have rallied to him, and most others were fast to forgive him—even those who lost lovers on the night he rebelled. After all, he led his cadre against Garwater because he said we must turn the city around. And he was right, and that has now been done.

There is no war between Dry Fall and Garwater. Doul visits the Brucolac, at night, on the *Uroc,* Carrianne tells me.

I spend many of my days with Carrianne. She is quiet about her one-time support for the Lovers' project. For almost a fortnight she did not speak much at all. Perhaps she was ashamed, to have found herself on the side of that woman who was so ready to lie, to lead us to our deaths.

That is the accepted story, apparently. We believe what the returned Hedrigall said. That is what people believe; that is why the city was turned.

Tanner Sack and I—we see each other, from time to time. He has begun to work again, under the city. He never mentions the time I took him to the little room and spurred a rebellion.

Did I do that?

Was this mutiny my doing? This city heading southward again, toward the waters we have passed through before, to the places that mean something to me—was this my doing?

And does that mean that I have won?

Perhaps she made it safely, the woman, and moored herself at the water's rim, and lowered her equipment into the chasm and extracted all the energies she needed, and is now as powerful as a god.

Perhaps she fell in.

Perhaps there was nothing to fall into.

Hedrigall is ill, delirious from his ordeal, we are told, somewhere in the innards of the *Grand Easterly.* When I hear that I think: we were not told the truth.

The woman was right. What kind of stupid, idiot coincidence would we have to believe—what chain of unlikeliness— to think that *our* Hedrigall leaves, and in a nigh-world *another* stays, and is lost—and found again, in the whole of the sea, by us. We have not been told the truth.

I remember the look Doul gave me.

He looked for me and found me, on the *Grand Easterly,* and told me with his eyes to come, listen, and finish this. He told me so much with that glance, and left so much unexplained. So much was clear: What he had done. His games, his manipulations.

I picture him, meeting with Hedrigall, the loyal cactus-man frightened and appalled by the Lovers' plan. Doul, making his suggestions. Hiding Hedrigall somewhere secret and quiet. Slipping out silently as only he could move, cutting the *Arrogance* free; bringing Hedrigall out again, later, to terrify the populace with his stories of canyons in the sea. So that Doul would have to say nothing. Safe in his loyalty.

Or perhaps it was Fennec who suggested that Hedrigall hide: a plan in case the Crobuzoner rescue failed to turn us back to home waters.

But I saw Doul's look. If all this was Fennec's doing, then Doul knew of it, and helped it run.

I think of all the times that Doul told me things, and hinted to me, letting me know where we would go, what we would do. Knowing that I knew Silas Fennec, Simon Fench, knowing that I would spread the word to him. Angry only when I spread the *wrong* sedition.

Spending time with me, and bringing me close. I came close. Using me as a conduit.

I am agog with how much he knew, and watched. I wish I could know when it started— whether I have been used for many, many months, or only in the final days. I do not know how much of what Doul does is strategy, and how much is recoil. Certainly he has known far, far more than I had thought.

I am left uncertain of how much I was used.

There is another possibility. It disturbs me.

I have heard again and again, from many people, many times, that this Hedrigall is not quite the same as ours. His manner is different, his voice more hesitant. His face, they say, is more—or perhaps less—scarred. He is a refugee from another world. People believe that.

It is possible. It is possible that he told us the truth.

But even so, it could not be luck alone. I saw Doul: he was waiting for this Hedrigall, and for me. So it cannot be chance that this Hedrigall came. There is another explanation.

Maybe it was Doul's doing. I heard music. Maybe this was Doul, playing possibilities, making a concerto of likelihood and unlikelihood.

Did he play his perhapsadian at night, as we approached the Scar, as the possible worlds around us grew more intrusive? Finding the one where Hedrigall survived, pulling him out of it, pulling him here to be found?

Such a tenuous chain: that I would be there with someone who would be believed, that Doul could find me with his eyes. So many chances: Doul must be the luckiest man in Bas-Lag. Or he planned the unplannable. Preparing me for that moment.

Could he play possibilities like a virtuoso, making sure the one that occurred was the one that had me there, beside Tanner, watching and listening as Hedrigall arrived, ready?

And what if fact-Bellis would not be there at that time? Did he bring out another? Bring out me? The one who would be in the right place at the right time, for his plans?

Am I a nigh-Bellis?

And if I am, what happened to the other? The fact?

Did he kill her? Is her body floating somewhere, rotting and eaten? Am I a replacement? Pulled through into existence to replace a dead woman—to be where Doul needed her to be?

All that so that he could turn the city around, and never come forward. Was this the only way? He would do all this to have his way, and to seem to have no will at all.

I will never be certain of what happened, of exactly how and how much, amid all the chaos and the blood and fighting, I was used.

That I was used, I have no doubt.

Doul has no interest in me now.

All the time we were together, he was playing me, making me his agent to turn the city around, so that it was not him that did it. A loyal mercenary, making the city merely pirate again.

Now that I have done what I was required to do, I am less than nothing to him.

It is strange to find yourself a game piece. I am humbled by him, but I am too old to be wounded by betrayal.

Still, twice now I have tried to see him, to understand what it was he did. Twice I have knocked and had him open the door to me, and stare at me unspeaking as if I am a stranger. And both times my words have gone sour in my mouth.

There is no "it," I remember Silas Fennec scolding me.

It is probably the best advice.

Right now, there are a small handful of possibilities that can explain what happened. Any of them might be true. And if Doul were to claim innocence of all of them, I would have less to make sense with, less than I have now. I would have to contemplate the possibility that there was no plan—that there is nothing to be explained.

Why would I risk that? Why in the world would I relinquish what understandings I have?

Tanner Sack came to my rooms. Angevine waited for him below on the *Chromolith*'s deck. Her treads could not take my stairs.

I am sure that they are a comfort to each other. But what I heard between them was uncertain and careful, and I think they will move apart. Sharing loss, I suspect, will not be enough.

Tanner brought me a heliotype he had found: of Shekel, holding two books, grinning outside the library. Tanner has decided that everything to do with Shekel and books is mine. I am embarrassed. I don't know how to tell him to stop.

After he left, I looked at the sepia scrap he had left me. It was not a good print. Vague suggestions of architecture and biology burnt onto the paper, scarring it. Wounding it and healing it in a new configuration. Scars are memory.

I carry my memories of Armada on my back.

I took the dressings off some weeks ago, and with angled mirrors I have seen what Garwater has written on me. It is a breathtakingly ugly message, in a brutal script.

Contours ridge my back, lines stretched horizontal across it, roughly parallel, where the whip landed. They seem to emerge from one side of my back, break my skin, and descend on the other.

Like sutures. They stitch the past to me.

I look at them with wonder. It is as if they are nothing to do with me. Armada is sewn fast onto my back, and I know that I will carry it with me everywhere.

So many truths have been kept from me. This violent, pointless voyage has been sopping with blood. I feel thick and sick with it. And that is all: contingent and brutal without meaning. There is nothing to be learnt here. No ecstatic forgetting. There is no redemption in the sea.

Carrying it on my back, I will take Armada home with me.

Home.

The second time Doul found me at his door, he must have seen something in my face. He nodded once and then spoke.

He said: "Enough is enough. We will take you back."

Back again.

I was stunned. I bowed my head, nodded, and thanked him.

He gave me that. And not for any residue of what he once pretended was between us.

He is rewarding me. He is paying me.

For the jobs I have done. Since he has used me.

Doul passed messages to Fennec through me, for Fennec to give the city. But Fennec did the wrong thing, and the Lovers outmaneuvered us all by telling the truth. So Doul found other uses for me.

And now he will take me home. Not for warmth or out of justice. He is offering me a wage.

I will accept.

He is not stupid. He knows that nothing I could do in New Crobuzon could undermine or threaten Armada in any way. I would not be listened to if I tried to tell Parliament, and why would I do that, renegade that I am?

Eventually there will be a ship charged to rob the Basilisk Channel. And I will be on it. I will be taken on some tiny boat, perhaps, dropped in that ugly port Qé Banssa that I saw from the *Terpsichoria*'s deck. And I will wait there until a New Crobuzon ship appears, heading home for Iron Bay and the Gross Tar, and the city.

Uther Doul will not deny me that. It costs him nothing.

It is many months since we left Iron Bay. By the time we are dragged back again, it will be much more than a year. I will take another name.

The *Terpsichoria* is lost. There is no reason for the city to chase Bellis Coldwine anymore. And even if some interfering swine back in New Crobuzon were to remember, were to recognize me and pass information on to some uniformed bastard, I have had enough of running. And I cannot find it in me to believe they will. That part of my life is over. This is a new time.

After all that has happened—after all my frantic, fruitless efforts to escape—I find that quite unwittingly I have done what was necessary for me to go home, carrying the memories of Armada stitched to my flesh.

I am surprised to find myself writing this letter to you again. Once I told Uther Doul the truth about it, I felt that it was closed to me.

Hearing myself admit it, I felt like a lonely child. Was there anything more pathetic than these scraps of paper that I was so eager to post, not even having decided yet to whom they would go?

I put them away, then.

But this is a new chapter. The city is going back in time, readying itself to start again with its simple piracy in the rich shores near my home. Everything has changed, and I find myself trembling, excited, biding my time, eager to finish this letter.

It does not embarrass me. I am opened up by it.

This is a Possible Letter. Until the last second, when I write your name beside that word "Dear," all those sheets and months ago, this is a Possible Letter, pregnant with potentiality. I am very powerful right now. I am all ready to mine the possibilities, make one of them fact.

I have not been the best friend to you, and I need you to forgive me that. I think back to my friends in New Crobuzon, and I wonder which of them you are to be.

And if I want this letter to be a remembrance, to be something with which to say *good-bye* instead of *hello again,* then you will be Carrianne. You are my dear friend, if that is so, and the fact that I did not know you when I started to write you this letter means nothing. This is a Possible Letter, after all.

Whoever you are, I have not been the best friend to you, and I am sorry.

Now we approach the fleet that is ranged just beyond the waters of the Hidden Ocean, like a phalanx of anxious guards, and I write this letter to you, to tell you everything that has happened to me. And as I tell you, I come to understand that I have been manipulated, used at every step of the way, that even when I was not a translator, I passed on others' messages. I find myself detached from such knowledge.

It is not that I do not care. Not that I am not angry at being used, or, gods and Jabber help me, for the awful, brute times I was used to bring about.

But even when I spoke for others (wittingly or not), I was doing things for myself. I have been present throughout all this, my own fact. And besides, as I sit here, ten thousand miles from New Crobuzon, on the other side of foreign seas, I know that we are heading slowly home. And though sadness and the guilt are stitched indelibly to me with my scars, two things are clear.

The first is that everything has changed. I cannot be used anymore. Those days are over. I know too much. What I do now, I do for me. And I feel, for all that has happened, as if it is *now,* only now in *these* days, that *my* journey is beginning. I feel as if this—even all this—has been a prologue.

The other is that all my anxiety to send this letter off, to get it to someone—to you—to cut a little mark upon New Crobuzon, all that neurotic eagerness has blown away. The desperation I had, in Tarmuth, in Salkrikaltor, to post this, to decide at the last minute who you were and send it, so that I might be noted, all that frantic fear is gone.

It has become nothing. It is not necessary anymore.

I am coming home. I will amass much more to tell you on the return journey, which will be long, but *will end.* I do not need this letter delivered. Whoever I decide you are, dear friend, I will give it to you myself.

I will deliver it by hand.

China Miéville's third Bas-Lag novel takes readers back to the teeming city of New Crobuzon. Set twenty-five years after the events of *Perdido Street Station* and *The Scar*, war between New Crobuzon and the shadowy city-state of Tesh has reached unseen heights. In desperation, a small group of renegades escapes from the city and crosses the strange and alien continent in search of a lost hope, a legend that must return.

Chapter One of *Iron Council* follows.

A man runs. Pushes through thin bark-and-leaf walls, through the purposeless rooms of Rudewood. The trees crowd him.

This far in the forest there are aboriginal noises. The canopy rocks. The man is heavy-burdened, and sweated by the unseen sun. He is trying to follow a trail.

Just before dark he found his place. Dim hotchi paths led him to a basin ringed by roots and stone-packed soil. Trees gave out. The earth was tramped down and stained with scorching and blood. The man spread out his pack and blanket, a few books and clothes. He laid down something well-wrapped and heavy among loam and centipedes.

Rudewood was cold. The man built a fire, and with it so close the darkness shut him quite out, but he stared into it as if he might see something emergent. Things came close. There were constant bits of sound like the bronchial call of a night bird or the breath and shucking of some unseen predator. The man was wary. He had pistol and rifle, and one at least was always in his hand.

By flamelight he saw hours pass. Sleep took him and let him away again in little gusts. Each time he woke he breathed as if coming out of water. He was stricken. Sadness and anger went across his face.

"I'll come find you," he said.

He did not notice the moment of dawn, only that time skidded again and he could see the edges of the clearing. He moved like he was made of twigs, as if he had stored up the night's damp cold. Chewing on dry meat, he listened to the forest's shuffling and paced the dirt depression.

When finally he heard voices he flattened against the bank and looked out between the trunks. Three people approached on the paths of leaf-mould and forest debris. The man watched them, his rifle steadied. When they trudged into thicker shanks of light, he saw them clearly and let his rifle fall.

"Here," he shouted. They dropped foolishly and looked for him. He raised his hand above the earth rise.

They were a woman and two men, dressed in clothes more ill-suited to Rudewood than his own. They stood before him in the arena and smiled. "Cutter." They gripped arms and slapped his back.

"I heard you for yards. What if you was followed? Who else is coming?"

They did not know. "We got your message," the smaller man said. He spoke fast and looked about him. "I went and seen. We were arguing. The others were saying, you know, we should stay. You know what they said."

"Yeah, Drey. Said I'm mad."

"Not *you*."

They did not look at him. The woman sat, her skirt filling with air. She was breathing fast with anxiety. She bit her nails.

"Thank you. For coming." They nodded or shook Cutter's gratitude off: it sounded strange to him and, he was sure, to them too. He tried not to make it sound like his sardonic norm. "It means a lot."

They waited in the sunken ground, scratched motifs in the earth or carved figures from deadwood. There was too much to say.

"So they told you not to come?"

The woman, Elsie, told him no, not so much, not in those words, but the Caucus had been dismissive of Cutter's call. She looked up at him and down quickly as she spoke. He nodded, and did not criticise.

"Are you sure about this?" he said, and would not accept their desultory nods. "Godsdammit are you sure? Turn your back on the Caucus? You ready to do that? For him? It's a long way we've got to go."

"We already come miles in Rudewood," said Pomeroy.

"There's hundreds more. *Hundreds*. It'll be bastard hard. A long time. I can't swear we'll come back."

I can't swear we'll come back.

Pomeroy said, "Only tell me again your message was true.

Tell me again he's gone, and where he's gone and what for. Tell me that's true." The big man glowered and waited, and at Cutter's brief nod and closed eyes, he said, "Well then."

Others arrived then. First another woman, Ihona; and then as they welcomed her they heard stick-litter being destroyed in heavy leaps, and a vodyanoi came through the brush. He squatted in the froggish way of his race and raised webbed hands. When he jumped from the bank, his body—head and trunk all one fat sac—rippled with impact. Fejhechrillen was besmirched and tired, his motion ill-suited to woodland.

They were anxious, not knowing how long they should wait, if any others would come. Cutter kept asking how they had heard his message. He made them unhappy. They did not want to consider their decision to join him: they knew there were many who would think it a betrayal.

"He'll be grateful," Cutter said. "He's a funny bugger and might be he'll not show it, but this'll mean a lot, to me and to him."

After silence Elsie said: "You don't know that. He didn't ask us, Cutter. He just got some message, you said. He might be angry that we've come."

Cutter could not tell her she was wrong. Instead he said: "I don't see you leaving, though. We're here for us, maybe, as well as for him."

He began to tell them what might be ahead, emphasising dangers. It seemed as if he wanted to dissuade them though they knew he did not. Drey argued with him in a rapid and nervy voice. He assured Cutter they understood. Cutter saw him persuading himself, and was silent. Drey said repeatedly that his mind was made up.

"We best move," said Elsie, when noon went. "We can't wait forever. Anyone else is coming, they've obviously got lost. They'll have to go back to the Caucus, do what's needed in the city." Someone gave a little cry and the company turned.

At the hollow's edge a hotchi rider was watching them, astride his gallus. The big war-cockerel plumped its breast-feathers and raised one spurred claw-foot in curious pose. The hotchi, squat and tough hedgehog man, stroked his mount's red comb.

"Militia coming." His accent was strong and snarling. "Two

men militia coming, a minute, two." He sat forward in the ornate saddle and turned his bird around. With very little sound,
with no metal to jangle on wood-and-leather straps and stir-
rups, it picked away high-clawed and belligerent, and was hidden by the forest.

"Was that—?" "What—?" "Did you fucking—?"

But Cutter and his companions were shushed by the sound
of approach. They looked in unsaid panic, too late to hide.

Two men came stepping over fungused stumps into view.
They were masked and uniformed in the militia's dark grey.
Each had a mirrored shield and ungainly pepperpot revolver
slack at his side. As they came into the clearing they faltered
and were still, taking in the men and women waiting for them.

There was a dragged-out second when no one moved, when
befuddled and silent conference was held—*are you, are they,
what, should we, should we*—till someone shot. Then there
were a spate of sounds, screams and the percussion of shots.
People fell. Cutter could not follow who was where and was
gut-terrified that he had been hit and not yet felt it. When the
guns' heinous syncopation stopped, he unclenched his jaw.

Someone was calling *Oh gods oh fucking gods*. It was a militiaman, sitting bleeding from a belly-wound beside his dead
friend and trying to hold his heavy pistol up. Cutter heard the
curt torn-cloth sound of archery and the militia man lay back
with an arrow in him and stopped his noise.

Again a beat of silence then "Jabber—" "Are you, is
everyone—?" "Drey? Pomeroy?"

First Cutter thought none of his own were hit. Then he saw
how Drey was white and held his shoulder, and that blood dyed
his palsying hands.

"Sweet Jabber, man." Cutter made Drey sit (*Is it all right?*
the little man kept saying). Bullet had taken muscle. Cutter tore
strips from Drey's shirt, and wound those cleanest around the
hole. The pain made Drey fight, and Pomeroy and Fejh had to
hold him. They gave him a thumb-thick branch to bite while
they bandaged him.

"They must've fucking *followed you,* you halfwit bastards."
Cutter was raging while he worked. "I told you to be fucking
careful—"

"We *were*," Pomeroy shouted, jabbing his finger at Cutter.

"Didn't follow them." The hotchi reappeared, its rooster

picking. "Them patrol the pits. You been here long time, a day nearly." It dismounted and walked the rim of the arena. "You been too long."

It showed the teeth in its snout in some opaque expression. Lower than Cutter's chest but rotundly muscular, it strutted like a bigger man. By the militia it stopped and sniffed. It sat up the one killed by its arrow and began to push the missile through the body.

"When them don't come back, them send more," it said. "Them come after you. Maybe now." It steered the arrow past bones through the dead chest. It gripped the shaft when it came out the corpse's back, and pulled the fletch through with wet sound. The hotchi tucked it bloody into his belt, picked the revolving pistol from the militiaman's stiffening fingers and fired it against the hole.

Birds rose up again at the shot. The hotchi snarled with the unfamiliar recoil and shook its hand. The arrow's fingerthick burrow had become a cavity.

Pomeroy said: "Godspit . . . who in hell are you?"

"Hotchi man. Cock-fighting man. Alectryomach. Help you."

"Your tribe . . ." said Cutter. "They're with us? On our side? Some of the hotchi are with the Caucus," he said to the others. "That's why this place's all right. Or was supposed to be. This lad's clan got no time for the militia. Give us passage. But . . . can't risk a real fight with the city, so they've to make it look like it was us killed the officers, not their arrows." He understood as he said it.

Pomeroy and the hotchi rifled the killed men together. Pomeroy threw one of the pepperpot revolvers to Elsie, one to Cutter. It was modernistic and expensive and Cutter had never held one before. It was heavy, with its six barrels arranged in a fat rotating cylinder.

"They ain't reliable," said Pomeroy, harvesting bullets. "Fast, though."

"Jabber . . . we better fucking go." Drey's voice went up and down with pain. "Fucking *guns* going off going to call them for miles . . ."

"Not so many nearby," said the hotchi. "Maybe none to hear. But you should gone, yes. What you for? Why leave city? You looking for him come by on the clay man?"

* * *

Cutter looked to the others and they watched him carefully, letting him speak.

He said: "You seen him?" He stepped toward the busy hotchi. "You seen him?"

"I not seen him, but I know them as has. Some days, week or more gone. Man come through the wood on a grey giant. Running through. The militia come after."

The light of afternoon came down to them all and the forest animals began to make their noises again. Cutter was locked in by miles of trees. He opened his mouth more than once before he spoke.

Cutter said: "Militia followed him?"

"On Remade horses. I heard."

On Remade horses with hammered metal hoofs, or with tiger's claws or with a tail prehensile and coated in poison glands. With steam-pistons giving their legs ridiculous strength or with stamina from a boiler-excrescence behind the saddle. Made carnivorous and long-tusked. Wolf-horses or boar-horses, construct-horses.

"I didn't see," said the hotchi. He mounted his cockerel. "Them went after the clay-man rider, south in Rudewood. You best go. Fast now." He turned his fight-bird and pointed a smoke-brown finger. "Stay careful. This is Rudewood. Go now."

He spurred his gallus into the undergrowth and dense trunks. "Go," he shouted, already invisible.

"Damn," said Cutter. "Come on." They gathered their little camp. Pomeroy took Drey's pack as well as his own, and the six of them went up out of the cock-fighting pit and into the forest.

They went southwest by Cutter's compass, along the path the hotchi had taken. "He showed us the way," Cutter said. His comrades waited for him to guide them. They drove between root masses and blockages of flora, changing whatever they passed. Quickly Cutter's tiredness was so profound it was an astonishing, alien sensation.

When they noticed darkness they fell where they were, in a pause between trees. They spoke in puny voices, affected by the undertones of the wood. It was too late to hunt: they could only pull biltong and bread from their packs and make weak jokes about what good food it was.

By their little fire Cutter could see that Fejh was drying.

They did not know where there was any freshwater, and Fejh poured only a little of what they had on himself though his big tongue rolled for it. He was panting. "I'll be all right, Cutter," he said, and the man patted his cheek.

Drey was paper-white and whispering to himself. Seeing how blood had stiffened his sling, Cutter could not imagine how he had kept going. Cutter murmured his fears to Pomeroy, but they could not turn back and Drey could not make the return on his own. He stained the ground below him.

While Drey slept, the others pulled around the fire and told quiet stories of the man they were following. Each of them had reasons for answering Cutter's call.

For Ihona the man they sought had been the first person in the Caucus who had seemed distracted, who reminded her of herself. His unworldliness, the quality that some mistrusted, made her feel there was room for imperfection in the movement: that she could be part of it. She smiled beautifully to remember it. Fejh, in turn, had taught him as part of some investigation of vodyanoi shamanism, and had been moved by his fascination. Cutter knew they loved the man they followed. Of the hundreds of the Caucus, it was no surprise that six loved him.

Pomeroy said it aloud: "I love him. It ain't why I'm here, though." He spoke in terse little bursts. "Times are too big for that. I'm here because of where he's going, Cutter, because of what he's after. And what's coming after that. That's why I'm here. Because of what was in your message. Not because he's gone—because of where he's gone, and why. That's worth everything."

No one asked Cutter why he was there. When it came to his turn, they looked down and said nothing while he studied the fire.

A war-bird woke them, wattle rippling, blaring a cock's crow. They were stunned by their uncivil wakening. A hotchi on his mount watched them, threw them a dead forest fowl as they rose. He pointed eastward through trees and disappeared in the green light.

They stumbled in the direction indicated through underbrush and the morning forest. Sunlight flecked them. It was warm spring, and Rudewood became dank and heated. Cutter's clothes were sweat-heavy. He watched Fejh and Drey.

Fejh was stolid as he moved by kicks of his hind legs, by lurches. Drey kept pace, though it seemed impossible. He leaked through his leather and did not scatter the flies that came to taste him. Blooded and white, Drey looked like an old meat-cut. Cutter waited for him to show pain or fear, but Drey only murmured to himself, and Cutter was humbled.

The simplicity of the forest stupefied them. "Where we going?" someone said to Cutter. *Don't ask me that.*

In the evening they followed a lovely sound and found a burn overhung by ivy. They hallooed and drank from it like happy animals.

Fejh sat in it and it rilled where it hit him. When he swam, his lubberly motion became suddenly graceful. He brought up handfuls and moulded with vodyanoi watercræft: like dough the water kept the shapes he gave it, coarse figurines shaped like dogs. He put them on the grass, where over an hour they sagged like candles and ran into the earth.

The next morning Drey's hurt was going bad. They waited when his fever made him pause, but they had to move. The treelife changed, was mongrel. They went by darkwood and oak, under banyan hirsute with ropy plaits that dangled and became roots.

Rudewood teemed. Birds and ape-things in the canopy spent the morning screaming. In a zone of dead, bleached trees, an ursine thing, unclear and engorged with changing shapes and colours, reeled out of the brush toward them. They screamed, except Pomeroy who fired into the creature's chest. With a soft explosion it burst into scores of birds and hundreds of bottle-glass flies, which circled them in the air and recongealed beyond them as the beast. It shuffled from them. Now they could see the feathers and wing cases that made up its pelt.

"I been in these woods before," said Pomeroy. "I know what a throng-bear looks like."

"We must be far enough now," said Cutter, and they bore westward while twilight came and left them behind. They walked behind a hooded lantern hammered by moths. The barkscape swallowed the light.

After midnight, they passed through low shinnery and out of the forest.

And for three days they were in the Mendican Foothills, rock tors and drumlins flecked with trees. They walked the routes of long-gone glaciers. The city was only tens of miles away. Its canals almost reached them. Sometimes through saddles in the landscape they saw real mountains far west and north, of which these hills were only dregs.

They drank and cleaned in tarns. They were slowing, pulling Drey. He could not move his arm and he looked bled out. He would not complain. It was the first time Cutter had ever seen him brave.

There were insinuations of paths, and they followed them south through grass and flowers. Pomeroy and Elsie shot rock rabbits and roasted them, stuffed with herb-weeds.

"How we going to find him?" Fejh said. "Whole continent to search."

"I know his route."

"But Cutter, it's a whole *continent* . . ."

"He'll leave signs. Wherever he goes. He'll leave a trail. You can't not."

No one spoke a while.

"How'd he know to leave?"

"He got a message. Some old contact is all I know."

Cutter saw fences reclaimed by weather, where farms had once been. The foundations of homesteads in angles of stone. Rudewood was east, weald broken with outcrops of dolomite. Once, protruding from the leaves, there were the remnants of ancient industry, smokestacks or pistons.

On the sixth day, Fishday, the 17th of Chet 1805, they reached a village.

In Rudewood there was a muttering of displaced air below the owl and monkey calls. It was not loud but the animals in its path looked up with the panic of prey. The empty way between trees, by overhangs of clay, was laced by the moon. The tree-limbs did not move.

Through the night shadows came a man. He wore a black-blue suit. His hands were in his pockets. Stems of moonlight touched his polished shoes, which moved at head-height above the roots. The man passed, his body poised, standing upright in the air. As he came hanging by arcane suspension between the canopy and the dark forest floor the sound came with him, as if space were moaning at his violation.

He was expressionless. Something scuttled across him, in and out of the shadow, in the folds of his clothes. A monkey, clinging to him as if he were its mother. It was disfigured by something on its chest, a growth that twitched and tensed.

In the weak shine the man and his passenger entered the bowl where the hotchi came to fight. They hung over the arena. They looked at the militiamen dead, mottled with rot.

The little ape dangled from the man's shoes, dropped to the corpses. Its adroit little fingers examined. It leapt back to the dangling legs and chittered.

They were as silent for a while as the rest of the night, the man knuckling his lips thoughtfully, turning in a sedate pirouette, the monkey on his shoulder looking into the dead-black forest. Then they were in motion again, between the trees with the fraught sound of their passing, through bracken torn days before. After they had gone, the animals of Rudewood came out again. But they were anxious, and remained so the rest of that night.

PERDIDO STREET STATION

A Hugo and Nebula Award Finalist

by China Miéville

Beneath the towering bleached ribs of a dead, ancient beast lies the city of New Crobuzon, where the unsavory deal is stranger to no one—not even to Isaac, a gifted and eccentric scientist who has spent a lifetime quietly carrying out his unique research. But when a half-bird, half-human creature known as the Garuda comes to him from afar, Isaac is faced with challenges he has never before encountered. Though the Garuda's request is scientifically daunting, Isaac is sparked by his own curiosity and an uncanny reverence for this curious stranger. Soon an eerie metamorphosis will occur that will permeate every fiber of New Crobuzon—and not even the Ambassador of Hell will challenge the malignant terror it evokes.

Published by Del Rey
Available wherever books are sold

**Visit www.delreybooks.com—
the portal to all the
information and resources
available from Del Rey Online.**

• Read sample chapters of every new book,
special features on selected authors and
books, news and announcements, readers'
reviews, browse Del Rey's complete
online catalog, and more.

• Sign up for the Del Rey Internet Newsletter
(DRIN), a free monthly publication e-mailed to
subscribers, featuring descriptions of new
and upcoming books, essays and interviews
with authors and editors, announcements
and news, special promotional offers,
signing/convention calendar for our authors
and editors, and much more.

To subscribe to the DRIN: send a blank e-mail to
sub_Drin-dist@info.randomhouse.com or
sign up at www.delreybooks.com

 www.delreybooks.com